# Profile: Maggie O'Dell

THREE THRILLING NOVELS

# ALEX KAVA

SPLIT SECOND

THE SOUL CATCHER

AT THE STROKE OF MADNESS

Also available by ***Alex Kava***

A PERFECT EVIL
A NECESSARY EVIL
ONE FALSE MOVE

*Coming soon*

WHITEWASH

# ALEX KAVA

## Profile: Maggie O'Dell

THREE THRILLING NOVELS

SPLIT SECOND
THE SOUL CATCHER
AT THE STROKE OF MADNESS

MIRA

*All the characters in this book have no existence outside the imagination of the author, and have no relation whatsoever to anyone bearing the same name or names. They are not even distantly inspired by any individual known or unknown to the author, and all the incidents are pure invention.*



*First published in Great Britain 2007*
*MIRA Books, Eton House, 18-24 Paradise Road, Richmond, Surrey, TW9 1SR*

PROFILE: MAGGIE O'DELL



*ISBN: : 978 0 7783 0160 8*

*60-0707*

*Printed and bound in Great Britain by Creative Print and Design (Wales), Elbow Vale*

CONTENTS

# SPLIT SECOND

For Amy Moore-Benson, Dianne Moggy and Philip Spitzer,
an incredible team that makes dreams come true.
One book was a privilege; two, an honour.

# PROLOGUE

*North Dade County Detention Center*
*Miami, Florida*
*Halloween—Friday, October 31*

Del Macomb wiped the sweat from his forehead with the sleeve of his shirt. The stiff cotton of his uniform stuck to his back, and it was only nine in the morning. How could it be this hot and humid in October?

He had grown up just north of Hope, Minnesota. Back home, ice would be forming at the edges of Silver Lake. His daddy would be writing his sermons while watching the last of the snow geese pass overhead. Del pushed wet strands off his brow. Thinking about his daddy reminded him that he needed a haircut. Crazy stuff to be thinking about. Even crazier that it was stuff that could still make him homesick.

"So who's the fucking asshole we're chaperoning today?"

Del's partner startled him. He winced at Benny Zeeks's language, then glanced over at the barrel-chested ex-marine to see if he had noticed. He certainly didn't need another lecture—not that he didn't have a lot to learn from Benny.

"Guys said his name is Stucky." He wondered if Benny had heard him. He seemed preoccupied.

At North Dade County Detention Center Benny Zeeks was somewhat of a legend, not only because he was a twenty-five-year veteran, but because he had spent most of that time working up in Starke on death row and even on X Wing. Del had seen his partner's scars from scuffles he'd won over X Wingers trying to avoid the coffinlike solitary confinement.

He watched Benny shove his shirtsleeves up over his veiny

forearms, not bothering to fold or roll them, revealing one of those legendary scars. It intersected a tattoo, a Polynesian dancer who now had a jagged red line across her abdomen as if she had been sliced in half. Benny could still make the dancer dance, flexing his arm and sending the lower half of her into a slow, sexy sway while the other half—the top half—froze in place, disconnected. The tattoo fascinated Del, intriguing and repulsing him at the same time.

Now his partner climbed into the armored truck's passenger seat, concentrating on negotiating the narrow steps up into the cab. The man moved slower than usual this morning, and Del immediately knew his partner had another hangover. He swung up into the driver's seat, buckling himself in and pretending, once again, not to notice.

"Who'd you say this asshole is?" Benny asked, while he twisted his thermos lid, the short stubby fingers desperate to get at the coffee. Del wanted to tell him the caffeine would only compound his problem, but after four short weeks on the job, he knew better than to try to tell Benny Zeeks anything.

"We're taking Brice and Webber's run today."

"What the hell for?"

"Webber's got the flu and Brice broke his hand last night."

"How the fuck do you break a hand?"

"All I heard was that he broke it. I don't know how. Look, I thought you hated the monotony of our regular route. Plus, all the traffic just to get to the courthouse."

"Yeah, well, there better not be more paperwork," Benny shifted restlessly as if anticipating the dreaded change in his routine. "And if this is Brice and Webber's run, that means this asshole's headed up to Glades, right? Puttin' him in close custody until his fucking hearing. Means he's some big-time fuckup they don't want down here in our wussy detention lockup."

"Hector said the guy's name is Albert Stucky. Said he's not such a bad guy, pretty intelligent and friendly. Hector says he's even accepted Jesus Christ as his savior."

Del could feel Benny scowling at him. He turned the key in the ignition and let the truck vibrate, then rumble to a slow start while he braced himself for Benny's sarcasm. He turned the air-conditioning on, blasting them with hot air. Benny reached over and punched it off.

"Give the engine some time, first. We don't need that goddamn hot air in our faces."

Del felt his face grow red. He wondered if there would ever be anything he could do to win the respect of his partner. He ignored his simmering anger and rolled down the window. He pulled out the travel log and jotted down the truck's odometer and gas tank readings, letting the routine calm him.

"Wait a minute," Benny said. "Albert Stucky? I've been reading about this guy in the *Miami Herald.* Feebies nicknamed him The Collector."

"Feebies?"

"Yeah, FBI. Jesus, kid, don't you know anything?"

This time Del could feel the prickle of red at his ears. He turned his head and pretended to be checking the side mirror.

"This Stucky guy," Benny continued, "he carved up and slaughtered three or four women, and not just here in Florida. If he's the guy I'm thinking of, he's one badass motherfucker. And if he's claiming he's found Jesus Christ, you can bet it's because he wants to save his sorry ass from being fried by Old Sparky."

"People can change. Don't you believe people can change?" Del glanced at Benny. The older man's brow was beaded with sweat and the bloodshot eyes glared at him.

"Jesus, kid. I bet you still believe in Santa Claus, too." Benny shook his head. "They don't send guys to wait for their trial in close custody because they think he's found Jesus-fucking-Christ."

Benny turned to stare out the window and sip his coffee. In doing so, he missed Del wince again. He couldn't help it. Twenty-two years with a daddy for a preacher made it an instant reaction, like scratching an itch. Sometimes he did it without even knowing.

Del slipped the travel log into the side pocket and shifted the truck into gear. He watched the concrete prison in his side-view mirror. The sun beat down on the yard where several prisoners milled around, bumming cigarettes off each other and enduring the morning heat. How could they enjoy being outside if there was no shade? He added it to his mental list of unfair treatment. Back in Minnesota, he had been quite the activist for prison reform. Lately he'd been too busy with the move and starting his new job, but he kept a running list for when he had more time. Little by little he'd work his way up to battling causes like eliminating Starke's X Wing.

As they approached the final checkpoint he glanced at the rearview mirror. He almost jumped, startled to find their prisoner staring back at him. All Del could see through the thick slit of glass were the piercing black eyes, and they were looking directly at him in the mirror.

Del recognized something in the prisoner's eyes, and a knot tightened in his stomach. He had seen that look years ago as a boy, on one of his trips accompanying his father. They had visited a condemned prisoner, who Del's father had met at one of his prison fellowship meetings. During that visit, the prisoner had confessed all the horrible, unimaginable things he had done to his own family before he murdered them—a wife, five children and even the family dog.

As a boy, the details Del heard that day had been traumatizing, but even worse was the evil pleasure the prisoner seemed to get from retelling each detail and watching the impact on a ten-year-old boy. Now Del saw that same look in the eyes of the man in the back of the armored truck. For the first time in twelve years, he felt as if he was looking straight into the eyes of pure evil.

He made himself look away and avoided the temptation to glance back. He pulled out from the last checkpoint and onto the highway. Once they got on the open road, he could relax. He enjoyed driving. It gave him time to think. But when he took a quick left, Benny, who had appeared to be lost in his thoughts, suddenly became agitated.

"Where the hell you going? I-95's the other direction."

"I thought we'd take a shortcut. Highway 45 has less traffic, and it's a much nicer drive."

"You think I fucking care about nice?"

"It's shorter by about thirty minutes. We get the prisoner delivered, and then we'll have an extra half hour for lunch."

He knew his partner wouldn't argue with an extended lunch hour. In fact, he had hoped Benny would be impressed. Del was right. Benny leaned back in his seat and poured another cup of coffee. He reached over and punched the AC. This time, cool air began filling the cab, and Benny rewarded Del with a rare smile. Finally, he had done something right. Del sat back and relaxed.

They had left Miami's traffic and had been on the road only thirty minutes when a thump rattled the back of the truck. At first Del thought they had dropped a muffler, but the thumping continued. It came from the back of the truck but inside, not underneath.

Benny slammed his fist against the steel partition behind them. "Shut the fuck up."

He twisted around to look through the small rectangle of glass that separated the cab from the back. "Can't see a damned thing."

The noise grew louder, sending vibrations under the seat. It felt to Del as though a baseball bat were being swung against the truck's metal sides. Ridiculous, really. No chance the prisoner would have anything remotely like a baseball bat. Each blast sent Benny reeling, grabbing at his temples. Del glanced over and saw the Polynesian dancer swinging her hips with each slam of Benny's fist against the partition.

"Hey, cut it out," Del yelled, adding his voice to the noisy din that was beginning to make his head pound.

Obviously, the prisoner had not been completely restrained and was ramming himself against the walls of the truck. Even if it didn't drive them crazy during the rest of the trip, it could cause some serious damage to the prisoner. He certainly didn't want to be responsible for delivering a battered prisoner. He slowed down, pulled the truck to the side of the two-lane highway and stopped.

"What the hell you doing?" Benny demanded.

"We can't have this going on for the rest of the trip. The guys obviously didn't completely restrain him."

"Why would they? He's found Jesus Christ."

Del only shook his head. As he climbed out of the truck it occurred to him that he had no idea what to do with a prisoner who had gotten an arm or leg loose from one of the leather restraints.

"Now hold on, kid," Benny yelled after him, scrambling out from the passenger side. "I'll take care of this bastard."

It took Benny too long to come around the truck. When he did, Del noticed a stagger in his walk.

"You're still drunk!"

"The hell I am."

Del reached into the cab and pulled out the thermos, jerking it away when Benny grabbed for it. He twisted off the top and in one whiff could smell the alcohol-laced coffee.

"You son of a bitch." Del's words surprised him as much as they did Benny. Instead of apologizing, he threw the thermos and watched it explode against a nearby fence post.

"Shit! That was my only thermos, kid." Benny looked as though he might head into the overgrown ditch to retrieve the pieces. But he turned and stomped toward the back of the truck. "Let's make this fucker shut up."

The banging continued, louder, now rocking the truck.

"You think you're up for this?" Del asked, feeling angry and betrayed enough to allow the sarcasm.

"Hell, yes. I was shutting up assholes like this when you were still suckin' at your momma's tit." Benny grabbed at his service revolver, fumbling with the holster's snap before pulling the gun free.

Del wondered how much alcohol Benny Zeeks had in his system. Could he still aim his gun? Was the gun even loaded? Up until today, Brice and Webber transported the hard-core criminals, making the trips up to Glade and Charlotte, while he and Benny were assigned petty thieves and white-collar criminals, escorting them in the other direction to the county courthouse in Miami. Del unbuckled the strap on his holster, his hand shaking, the butt of his gun feeling awkward and unfamiliar.

The noise stopped as soon as Del started sliding the locks open on the heavy rear door. He looked to Benny who stood beside him with his revolver drawn. Immediately, Del noticed the slight tremor in Benny's hand. It sent a wave of nausea loose in Del's stomach. His back was soaked, his forehead dripping. Wet pools under his armpits soiled his once-crisp uniform. His heart pounded against his rib cage, and now in the silence, he wondered if Benny could hear it.

He took a deep breath and tightened his hold on the handle. Then he flung the door open, jumping aside and letting Benny have a full view of the dark inside. Benny stood, legs apart, arms extended in front of him, both hands gripping the gun as he tilted his head, ready to take aim.

Nothing happened. The door slammed back and forth, hitting against the side of the truck. The sound of metal clanking against metal was amplified by the peaceful surroundings and the deserted highway. Del and Benny stared into the darkness, squinting to see the corner bench where the prisoner usually sat, restrained by thick straps that snaked out of the wall and floor.

"What on earth?" Del could see the leather straps, cut and hanging from the wall of the truck.

"What the fuck?" Benny mumbled as he slowly approached the open truck.

Without warning, a tall, dark figure flew out at Benny, knocking him and the gun to the ground. Albert Stucky clamped his teeth onto Benny's ear like a rabid dog. Benny's scream dismantled Del. He stood paralyzed. His limbs refused to react. His heart knocked against his chest. He couldn't breathe. He couldn't think. By the time he pulled out his service revolver, the prisoner was on his feet. He ran straight at Del, colliding with him and shoving something sharp and smooth and hard into Del's stomach.

Pain exploded throughout his body. His hands were useless, and the gun slid from his fingers like water. He forced himself to look into Albert Stucky's eyes, and instantly he saw the evil staring back at him, cold and black, an entity of its own. Del felt the demon's hot breath on his face. When he glanced down, he saw the large hand still gripping the dagger. He looked up just in time to see Stucky's smile as he shoved the dagger deeper.

Del slipped to his knees. His eyes blurred as he watched the tall stranger split into several images. He could see the truck and a sprawling Benny. Everything began to spin and blur. Then he slammed hard against the pavement. The steaming concrete sizzled up through his wet back, but it wasn't as hot as his insides. A wildfire spread through his stomach, catching each of his organs on fire. Now, on his back, he saw nothing but the clouds swirling above him, brilliant white against solid blue. The morning sun blinded him. Yet, it was all so beautiful. Why hadn't he noticed before how beautiful the sky was?

Behind him a single gun shot blasted the silence. Del managed a weak smile. Finally. He couldn't see him but good ole' Benny, the legend, had come through, after all. The alcohol had just slowed him down a bit.

Del pulled himself up, just enough to look at the damage to his stomach. He was startled to find himself staring down at the bloody carved image of Jesus. The dagger causing his insides to spill onto the deserted highway was actually a mahogany crucifix. Suddenly, he couldn't feel the pain anymore. That had to be a good sign, didn't it? Maybe he'd be okay.

"Hey, Benny," he called out, laying his head on the pavement. He still wasn't able to see his partner behind him. "My daddy's gonna make a sermon out of this when I tell him I was stabbed with a crucifix."

A long, black shadow blocked the sky.

Once again Del found himself looking into those empty, dark eyes. Albert Stucky loomed above him, tall and straight, a lean, muscular man with sharp features. He reminded Del of a vulture, perched with black wings pressed patiently against its sides, cocking its head, staring, waiting for its prey to stop struggling, to give in to the inevitable. Then, Stucky smiled as though pleased with what he saw. He raised and pointed Benny's service revolver at Del's head.

"You won't be telling your daddy anything," Albert Stucky promised in a deep, calm voice. "Tell it to Saint Peter, instead."

The metal slammed into Del's skull. A blast of brilliant light swirled together with oceans of blue and yellow and white and then finally...black.

# CHAPTER 1

*Northeast Virginia*
*(just outside Washington, D.C.)*
*Five months later—Friday, March 27*

Maggie O'Dell jerked and twisted, trying to make herself more comfortable, only now realizing she had fallen asleep in the recliner again. Her skin felt damp with perspiration and her ribs ached. The air in the room was stale and warm, making it difficult to breathe. She fumbled in the dark, reaching for the brass floor lamp, clicking the switch but getting no light. Damn! She hated waking to complete darkness. Usually she took precautions to prevent it.

Her eyes adjusted slowly, squinting and searching behind and around the stacks of boxes she had spent the day packing. Evidently Greg had not bothered to come home. She couldn't have slept through one of his noisy entrances. It was just as well he didn't come home. His temper tantrums would only annoy the movers.

She tried to get out of the recliner but stopped when a sharp pain raced along her abdomen. She grabbed at it, as if she could catch the pain and keep it from spreading. Her fingers felt something warm and sticky soaking through her T-shirt. Jesus! What the hell was going on? Carefully, she pulled up the hem and even in the dark she could see it. A chill slipped down her back and the nausea washed over her. A slit in her skin ran from below her left breast across her abdomen. It was bleeding, soaking into her T-shirt and dripping down into the fabric of the recliner.

Maggie bolted from the chair. She covered the wound and pressed her shirt against it, hoping to stop the bleeding. She needed to call 911. Where the hell was the phone? How could this have happened? The scar was over eight months old, and yet it was bleeding as profusely as the day Albert Stucky had cut her.

She knocked over boxes, searching. Lids popped open as cartons fell, scattering crime scene photos, toiletries, newspaper clippings, underwear and socks and sending pieces of her life bouncing off the floor and walls. Everything she had taken such care to pack suddenly flew, rolled, skidded and crashed around her.

Then, she heard a whimpering sound.

She stopped and listened, trying to hold her breath. Already her pulse beat too rapidly. Steady. She needed to stay calm. She turned slowly, cocking her head and straining to hear. She checked the desktop, the surface of the coffee table, the bookshelf. Oh dear God! Where the hell had she left her gun?

Finally, she saw the holster lying at the foot of the recliner. Of course, she would have kept it close by as she slept.

The whimpering grew louder, a high-pitched whine like a wounded animal's. Or was it a trick?

Maggie edged her way back to the recliner, eyes darting, watching all around her. The sound came from the kitchen. And now she could smell a foul odor seeping in from that direction, too. She picked up the holster and tiptoed toward the kitchen. The closer she got, the easier it was to recognize the smell. It was blood. The acrid scent stung her nostrils and burned her lungs. It was the kind of stench that came only from massive amounts of blood.

She crouched low and eased through the doorway. Despite the warning smell, Maggie gasped at the sight of it. In the moonlit kitchen, blood had sprayed the white walls and pooled on the ceramic tile. It was everywhere, splattered across the countertops and dripping down the appliances. In the far corner of the room stood Albert Stucky. His tall, sleek shadow hovered over a whimpering woman who was down on her knees.

Maggie felt the prickling start at the back of her neck. Dear God, how had he been able to get inside her house? And yet, she wasn't surprised to see him. Hadn't she expected him to come? Hadn't she been waiting for this?

Stucky yanked the woman's hair in one hand and in the other he held a butcher knife to the woman's throat. Maggie prevented another gasp. He hadn't seen her yet, and she pressed herself against the wall, into the shadows.

Steady. Calm. She repeated the mantra in her head. She had prepared herself for this very moment. Had dreaded and dreamed and anticipated it for months. Now was not a time to let fear and panic unravel her nerve. She leaned against the wall, strengthening her position, though her back ached and her squatting knees trembled. From this angle, she could get a clean shot. But she knew she'd be allowed only one. One was all she needed.

Maggie gripped the holster, reaching for her gun. The holster was empty. How could it be empty? She spun around, searching the floor. Had the gun dropped out? Why hadn't she noticed?

Then suddenly, she realized her startled reaction had just blown her cover. When she looked up, the woman was reaching out to her, pleading with her. But Maggie looked past the woman, her eyes meeting Albert Stucky's. He smiled. Then, in one swift motion, he slit the woman's throat.

"No!"

Maggie woke up with a violent jolt, nearly falling out of the recliner. Her fingers groped along the floor. Her heart pounded. She was drenched in sweat. She found her holster and this time ripped the gun out, jumping to her feet and swinging her outstretched arms back and forth, ready to spray the stacked cartons with bullets. Sunlight had only begun to seep into the room, but it was enough to show that she was alone.

She slumped down into the chair. The gun still clenched in her hand, she wiped the perspiration from her forehead and dug the sleep from her eyes with trembling fingers. Still not convinced it was a dream, she clawed at the hem of her T-shirt, pulling it up and twisting to see the bloody cut across her abdomen. Yes, the scar was there, a slight pucker of skin. But no, it was not bleeding.

She leaned back in the chair and raked her fingers through her tangled, short hair. Dear God! How much longer could she put up with the nightmares? It had been over eight months since Albert Stucky had trapped her in an abandoned Miami warehouse. She had chased him for almost two years, learning his patterns, studying his depraved habits, performing autopsies on the corpses he left behind and deciphering the bizarre messages for the game he, alone, had decided the two of them would play. But that hot, August evening, he had won, trapping her and making her watch. He had no intention of killing her. He simply wanted her to watch.

Maggie shook her head, willing the images to stay away. She knew she'd be successful as long as she remained awake. They had captured Albert Stucky that bloody night in August, only to have him escape from prison on Halloween. Her boss, FBI Assistant Director Kyle Cunningham, had immediately taken her out of the field. She was one of the Bureau's top criminal profilers, and yet Cunningham had stuck her behind a desk. He had exiled her to teaching at law enforcement conferences, as if complete boredom would be some sort of protection from the madman. Instead it felt like punishment. And she didn't deserve to be punished.

Maggie stood, immediately annoyed at her wobbly knees. She weaved through the maze of cartons to the cabinet in the corner. She checked the clock on the desktop and saw that she had almost two hours before the movers arrived. She laid her gun close by, sorted through the cabinet and brought out a bottle of Scotch. She poured herself a glass, noticing that already her hands were more steady, her heartbeat almost back to normal.

Just then she heard a high-pitched whine coming from the kitchen. Jesus! She dug her fingernails into her arm, feeling the sting and finding no comfort in the fact that she was, indeed, awake this time. She grabbed for her gun and tried to steady her pulse, already racing out of control. She slid against the wall, making her way to the kitchen, trying to listen and sniffing the air. The whining stopped as she got to the doorway.

She prepared herself, arms secure and close to her chest. Her finger pressed against the trigger. This time she was ready. She took a deep breath and swung into the kitchen, her gun pointed directly at Greg's back. He spun around, dropping the freshly opened can of coffee, jumping backward as it crashed to the floor.

"Damn it, Maggie!" He wore only silk boxers. His normally styled blond hair stuck up, and he looked as if he had just gotten out of bed.

"Sorry," Maggie said, desperately trying to keep the panic from her voice. "I didn't hear you come in last night." She tucked the Smith & Wesson .38 into the back waistband of her jeans in an easy, casual motion, as if this was a part of her regular morning routine.

"I didn't want to wake you," he snapped through gritted teeth. Already he had a broom and dustpan and was sweeping up the mess. Gently, he lifted the tipped can, rescuing as much of his precious gourmet coffee as possible. "One of these days, Maggie, you're gonna shoot me by mistake." Then he stopped and looked up at her. "Or maybe it wouldn't be a mistake."

She ignored his sarcasm and walked past him. At the sink, she splashed cold water on her face and the back of her neck, hoping he didn't notice that her hands were still shaking. Though she needn't worry. Greg saw only what he wanted to see.

"I'm sorry," she said again, keeping her back to him. "This would never happen if we had gotten a security system."

"And we would never need a security system if you'd quit your job."

She was so tired of this old argument. She found a dishcloth and wiped the coffee grounds from the counter. "I'd never ask you to quit being a lawyer, Greg."

"It's not the same thing."

"Being a lawyer means just as much to you as being an FBI agent means to me."

"But being a lawyer doesn't get me cut up and almost killed. It doesn't have me stalking around my own house with a loaded gun and almost shooting my spouse." He returned the broom, slamming it into the utility closet.

"Well, after today I guess it won't be an issue," she said quietly.

He stopped. His gray eyes met hers and for a brief moment he looked sad, almost apologetic. Then he looked away, snatching the dishcloth Maggie had set aside. He wiped the counter again in careful, deliberate swipes as though she had disappointed him even in this small task.

"So when are the guys from United getting here?" he wanted to know, as if it were a move they had planned together.

She glanced at the wall clock. "They'll be here at eight. But I didn't hire United."

"Maggie, you have to be careful about movers. They'll rip you off. You should know..." He stopped, as if reminding himself it was no longer any of his business. "Suit yourself." He started filling the coffeemaker with level, precise scoops, pursing his lips to confine the scolding he normally would have unleashed on her.

Maggie watched him, predicting his movements, knowing he'd fill the pot to the three-cup line and that he'd squat to eye level to make certain it was exact. She recognized the familiar routine and wondered when they had become strangers. After almost ten years of marriage, they couldn't even afford each other the courtesies of friendship. Instead, every conversation seemed to be through clenched teeth.

Maggie turned and went back to the spare room, waiting, but hoping he wouldn't follow her. Not this time. She wouldn't get through this day if he continued to scold and pout or worse, if he resorted to telling her he still loved her. Those words should have been a comfort; instead, they had come to feel like a sharp knife, especially when he followed them with, "And if you loved me you would quit your job."

She returned to the liquor cabinet where she had left the glass of Scotch. The sun had barely risen and already she needed her daily dose of liquid bravery to get her through the day. Her mother would be proud. The two of them finally had something in common.

She glanced around the room while she sipped. How could this stack of cartons be the sum of her life? She rubbed a hand over her face, feeling the exhaustion as though it had taken up permanent residence in her bones. How long had it been since she had slept through an entire night? When was the last time she had felt safe? She was so tired of feeling as though she was trapped on a ledge, coming closer and closer to falling.

Assistant Director Cunningham was fooling himself if he believed he could protect her. There was nothing he could do to stop her nightmares, and there was no place he could send her that would be out of Albert Stucky's reach. Eventually, she knew Stucky would come for her. Although it had been five months since Stucky's escape, she knew it with certainty. It could be another month or it could be another five months. It didn't matter how long it took. He would come.

# CHAPTER 2

Tess McGowan wished she had worn different shoes. These pinched and the heels were too tall. Every nerve ending in her body concentrated on not tripping as she walked up the winding sidewalk, all the while pretending not to notice the eyes that followed her. The movers had stopped unloading the truck as soon as her black Miata pulled into the drive. Sofa ends stayed in midair. Hand-trucks remained tipped. Boxes were ignored while the men in sweaty, blue uniforms stopped to watch her.

She hated the attention and cringed at the possibility of a wolf whistle. Especially in this well-manicured neighborhood where the sanctuary-like silence would make the whistles even more obscene.

This was ridiculous; her silk blouse stuck to her, and her skin crawled. She wasn't close to being stunning or beautiful. At best, she had a decent figure, one for which she sweated hours at the gym, and she still needed to monitor her cravings for cheeseburgers. She was far from being *Playboy*-centerfold material, so why did she suddenly feel naked though dressed in a conservative suit?

It wasn't the men's fault. It wasn't even their primal instinct to watch that bothered her as much as what seemed to be her involuntary reflex to put on a show for them. The annoying habit clung to her from her past, like the scent of cigarette smoke and whiskey. Too easily she found herself reminded of Elvis tunes coming from a corner jukebox, always followed by cheap hotel rooms.

But that had been a lifetime ago, certainly too many years ago to trip her up now. After all, she was on her way to becoming a successful businesswoman. So why the hell did the past have such a hold on her? And how could something as harmless as a few indiscreet stares, from men she didn't know, dismantle her poise and make her question her hard-earned respectability?

They made her feel like a fraud. As if, once again, she was masquerading as something she was not. By the time she reached the front entrance, she wanted to turn and run. Instead, she took a deep breath and knocked on the heavy oak door that had been left half-open.

"Come on in," a woman's voice called from behind the door.

Tess found Maggie O'Dell at the panel of buttons and blinking lights that made up the house's newly installed security system.

"Oh, hi, Ms. McGowan. Did we forget to sign some papers?" Maggie only glanced at Tess while she punched the small keyboard and continued to program the device.

"Please, you really must call me Tess." She hesitated in case Maggie wanted to say the same, but wasn't surprised when there was no such invitation. Tess knew it wasn't that Maggie was rude, just that she liked to keep her distance. It was something Tess could relate to, something she understood and respected. "No, there aren't any more papers. I promise. I knew today was the big move. Just wanted to see how things were going.

"Take a look around, I'm almost finished with this."

Tess walked from the foyer into the living room. The afternoon sunlight filled the room, but thankfully all the windows were open, a cool south breeze replacing the stale warm air. Tess wiped at her forehead, disappointed to find it damp. She examined her client out of the corner of her eyes.

Now, this was a woman who deserved to be ogled by men. Tess knew Maggie was close to her own age, somewhere in her early thirties. But without the usual power suit, Maggie could easily pass for a college student. Dressed in a ratty University of Virginia T-shirt and threadbare jeans, she failed to hide her shapely athletic figure. She had a natural beauty no one could manufacture. Her skin was smooth and creamy. Her short dark hair shone even though it was mussed and tangled. She possessed rich brown eyes and high cheekbones that Tess would kill for. Yet, Tess knew that the men who had stopped in their tracks just moments before to stare at her would not dare do the same to Maggie O'Dell, though they would definitely want to and it would take tremendous effort not to.

Yes, there was something about this woman. Something Tess

had noticed the very first day they had met. She couldn't quite describe it. It was the way Maggie carried herself, the way she appeared, at times, to be oblivious to the outside world. The way she seemed totally unaware of her effect on people. It was something that invoked—no, demanded, respect. Despite her designer suits and expensive car, Tess would never capture that ability, that power. Yet for all their differences, Tess had felt an immediate kinship with Maggie O'Dell. They both seemed so alone.

"Sorry," Maggie said, finally joining Tess who had moved to the windows overlooking the backyard. "I'm staying here tonight," she explained, "and I want to make certain the alarm system is up and running."

"Of course," Tess nodded and smiled.

Maggie had been more concerned about the security system than the square footage or the seller's price of any of the houses Tess had shown her. In the beginning, Tess chalked it up to the nature of her client's profession. Of course FBI agents would be more sensitive to security matters than the average home buyer. But Tess had witnessed a look in Maggie's eyes, a glimpse of something that Tess recognized as vulnerability. She couldn't help wondering what the confident, independent agent hoped to lock herself away from. Even as they stood side by side, Maggie O'Dell seemed far away, her eyes examining her new backyard like a woman looking for and expecting an intruder, rather than a new home owner admiring the foliage.

Tess glanced around the room. There were plenty of stacked boxes, but very little furniture. Perhaps the movers had only begun to bring in the heavy stuff. She wondered how much Maggie was able to take from the condo she and her husband owned. Tess knew the divorce proceedings were growing messy. Not that her client had shared any of this with her.

Everything Tess knew of Maggie O'Dell, she had learned from a mutual friend, Maggie's attorney, who had recommended Tess. It was this mutual friend, Teresa Ramairez, who had told Tess about Maggie O'Dell's bitter lawyer husband, and how Maggie needed to invest in a substantial piece of real estate or risk sharing—maybe even losing—a large trust left in her name. In fact, Maggie O'Dell had confided nothing in Tess, other than those necessities required for the business transaction. She wondered if Maggie's secrecy and her aloof manner were an occupational hazard that carried over into her personal life.

It didn't matter—Tess was used to just the opposite. Usually clients confided in her as if she was Dear Abby. Being a real estate agent had proven to be a little like being a bartender. Perhaps part of her colorful past had been good preparation, after all. That Maggie O'Dell didn't wish to bare her soul was perfectly fine with Tess. She certainly didn't take it personally. Instead, she could relate. It was exactly the way she handled her own life, her own secrets. Yes, the less people knew, the better.

"So, have you met any of your new neighbors?"

"Not yet." Maggie answered while she stared out at the huge pine trees lining her property like a fortress. "Only the one you and I met last week."

"Oh sure, Rachel...um...I can't remember her last name. I'm usually very good with names."

"Endicott," Maggie supplied without effort.

"She seemed very nice," Tess added, though what little she had gleaned from the brief introduction made her wonder how Special Agent O'Dell would fit into this neighborhood of doctors, congressmen, Ph.D.'s and their stay-at-home society-conscious wives. She remembered seeing Rachel Endicott out for a jog with her pure white Labrador, while dressed in a designer jogging suit, expensive running shoes and not a blond hair out of place nor a single bead of sweat on her brow. And in contrast, here was Agent O'Dell in a stretched-out T-shirt, worn jeans and a pair of gray Nikes that should have been thrown out ages ago.

Two men grunted their way through the front entrance with a huge rolltop desk. Immediately, Maggie's attention transferred to the desk, which looked incredibly heavy and was quite possibly an antique.

"Where ya want this, ma'am?"

"Over against that wall."

"Sorta centered?"

"Yes, please."

Maggie O'Dell's eyes never left them until the piece was carefully set down.

"Dat good?"

"Perfect."

Both men seemed pleased. The older one smiled. The tall, thin one avoided looking at the women, slouching not from pain but as though he wasn't comfortable being tall. They unwrapped the tape and unlatched the plastic fasteners from the desk's many nooks. The tall man tested the drawers, then stopped suddenly, snapping his hand back as though he had been stung.

"Um...ma'am. Did you know you had this in here?"

Maggie crossed the room to look inside the drawer. She reached in and pulled out a black pistol encased in some kind of holster.

"Sorry. I forgot about this one."

This one? Tess wondered how many the agent had stashed. Maybe the obsession with security was a bit over the top, even for an FBI agent.

"We should be done in a bit," the older man told her, and he followed his partner out as though there was nothing unusual about hauling loaded guns.

"Do you have anyone coming to help you unpack?" Tess tried to disguise her mistrust, her distaste for guns. No, why kid herself? It was more than a simple distaste, it was a genuine fear.

"I really don't have much."

Tess glanced around the room, and when she looked back, Maggie was watching her. Tess's cheeks grew hot. She felt as though she had been caught, because that was exactly what she had been thinking—that Maggie O'Dell really didn't have much. How could she possibly fill the huge rooms that made up this two-story Tudor?

"It's just that...well, I remember you mentioning that your mother lives in Richmond," Tess tried to explain.

"Yes, she does," she said in a way that told Tess there would be no further conversation on the topic.

"Well, I'll let you get back to work." Tess suddenly felt awkward and anxious to leave. "I need to finish up the paperwork."

She extended her hand, and Maggie politely shook it with a strong, firm grip that again took Tess off guard. The woman exuded strength and confidence, but unless Tess was imagining things, Maggie's obsession with security sprung from some vulnerability, some deep-seated fear. Having dealt with her own vulnerabilities and fears for so many years, Tess could sense them in others.

"If you need anything, anything at all, please don't hesitate to call me, okay?"

"Thanks, Tess, I will."

But Tess knew she would not.

As Tess backed her car down the driveway, she wondered whether Special Agent Maggie O'Dell was simply cautious or paranoid, careful or obsessive. At the corner of the intersection, she noticed a van parked along the curb, an oddity in this neighborhood where the houses were set far back from the street and the long driveways afforded plenty of parking space for several cars or utility vehicles.

The man in dark glasses and a uniform sat behind the wheel, absorbed in a newspaper. Tess's first thought was how odd to be reading a newspaper with sunglasses on, especially with the sun setting behind him. As she drove by, she recognized the logo on the side of the van: Northeastern Bell Telephone. Immediately, she found herself suspicious. Why was the guy so far out of his territory? Then suddenly, she shrugged and laughed out loud. Perhaps her client's paranoia was contagious.

She shook her head, pulled out onto the highway and left the secluded neighborhood to return to her office. As she glanced back at the stately houses tucked away between huge oaks, dogwoods and armies of pine trees, Tess hoped Maggie O'Dell would finally feel safe.

# CHAPTER 3

Maggie juggled the boxes that filled her arms. As usual she had taken on more than she should have. Her fingers searched the door, grasping for a knob she couldn't see, yet she refused to put anything down. Why in the world did she own so many CDs and books when she had no time to listen to music or read?

The movers had finally left, after a thorough search for one lost carton, or as they insisted—one misplaced carton. She hated to think of it still at the condo, and hated even more the thought of asking Greg to check. He would remind her that she should have listened to him and hired United Movers. And knowing Greg, if the carton was still at the condo, his anger and curiosity would not leave it alone. She imagined him ripping off the packing tape as though he had discovered some hidden treasure, which to him it would be. Because, of course, it would be the one container with items she'd rather have no one thumb through, items like her personal journal, appointment calendar and memorabilia from her childhood.

She had torn her car's trunk apart, looking through the few boxes she had loaded on her own. But these were the last. Perhaps the movers had honestly misplaced the carton. She hoped that was the case. She tried not to worry about it, tried not to think how exhausting it was to be on alert twenty-four hours a day, to be constantly looking over her shoulder.

She set the boxes on the handrail, balancing one with her hip, while she freed a hand to grab at the tightening knot in the back of her neck. At the same time, her eyes darted around her. Dear God, why couldn't she just relax and enjoy her first night in her new home? Why couldn't she concentrate on simple things, stupid everyday things, like her sudden and unfamiliar hunger?

As if on cue, her mouth began to water for pizza, and immediately she promised herself one as a reward. Her appetite had long been gone, making this craving a novelty, one she needed to relish. Yes, she would stuff herself with pizza garnished with spicy Italian sausage, green peppers and extra Romano cheese. That is, after she drank several gallons of water.

Maggie's T-shirt stuck to her skin. Before she ordered the pizza, she'd take a quick, cool shower. Ms. McGowan—Tess—had promised to call all the utility companies. Now Maggie wished she had double-checked with her to make certain she had done so. She hated depending on other people, having recently found herself with a full cast of them in her life, from movers and real estate agents, to lawyers and bankers. Hopefully the water would, indeed, be on. Tess's word had been good so far. In all fairness, there was no need to question it now. The woman had gone out of her way to make this accelerated sale go as smoothly as possible.

Maggie repositioned the boxes to her other hip. Her fingers found the knob. She pushed the door open, carefully maneuvering her way in, but still sending several loose CDs and books crashing onto the doorstep. She bent just enough to look down at Frank Sinatra smiling up at her through his cracked plastic window. Greg had given her the CD several birthdays ago, although he knew she hated Sinatra. Why did that gift suddenly feel like some prophetic microcosm of their entire marriage?

She shook her head and the thought out of her mind. The memory of their brief morning exchange stayed annoyingly fresh in her mind. Thankfully, he had left for work early, mumbling about all the construction on the interstate. But tonight he would be having his last laugh, sifting through her personal things. He would see it as his right. Legally she was still his wife, and she had given up long ago arguing with him when he shifted into lawyer mode.

Inside her new home, the wood floors' recent varnish glowed in the late-afternoon sunshine. Maggie had made certain there wasn't a stitch of carpet in the entire house. Footsteps were too easily muffled by floor coverings. Yet, the wall of windows had cinched the deal for Maggie, despite them being a security nightmare. Okay, so even FBI agents weren't always practical. But each individual window was set in a narrow frame that not even Houdini could squeeze through. The bedroom windows were another story, but reaching the second floor from outside would require a tall ladder. Besides, she had made certain that both security systems, inside and outside, rivaled those at Fort Knox.

The living room opened into a sunroom with more windows. These stretched from the ceiling almost to the floor, and though they were also thin and narrow, they made up three walls in the room. The sunroom extended into and looked out over the lush green backyard. It was a colorful, wooded fairyland with cherry and apple blossoms, sturdy dogwoods, a blanket of tulips, daffodils and crocus. It was a backyard she had fantasized about since she was twelve.

Back then, when she and her mother had moved to Richmond, they could afford only a tiny, suffocating third-floor apartment that reeked of stale air, cigarette smoke and the body odor of the strange men her mother invited overnight. This house was more like the one Maggie remembered of her real childhood, their house in Wisconsin, where they had lived before her father was killed, before Maggie was forced to grow up quickly and become her mother's caretaker. For years, she had longed for someplace like this with lots of fresh air and open spaces, but most importantly—plenty of seclusion.

The backyard sloped down only to be met by a dense wooded area that lined a steep ridge. Below, a shallow stream trickled over rocks. Though she couldn't see the stream from the house, Maggie had checked it out at great length. It made her feel safe, as if it were her own personal moat. It provided a natural boundary, a perfect barrier that was reinforced by a line of huge pine trees standing guard like sentries, tall and straight, shoulder to shoulder.

That same stream had been a nightmare for the previous owners who had two small children. Fences of any kind were against the development's covenant. Tess McGowan had told Maggie that the owners simply realized they couldn't keep two curious kids from being enticed or lured by such a dangerous adventure. Their problem became Maggie's safeguard, her potential trap. And their impulsive purchase became Maggie's bargain. Otherwise, she would never have been able to afford this neighborhood where her little red Toyota Corolla looked out of place next to BMWs and Mercedeses.

Of course, she still would never have been able to afford the house had she not used the money from her father's trust. Having received scholarships, grants, fellowships and then working her way through college and graduate school, Maggie had been able to leave most of the trust alone. When she and Greg got married, he was adamant about not touching the money. In the beginning, she had wanted to use it to buy them a modest home. But Greg insisted he would never touch what he called her father's blood money.

The trust had been set up by fellow firefighters and the city of Green Bay to show appreciation for her father's heroism, and probably to assuage their guilt as well. Maybe that was part of the reason she had never been able to bring herself to use the money. In fact, she had almost forgotten about the trust until the divorce proceedings began and until her lawyer highly recommended she invest the money in something not so easily divided.

Maggie remembered laughing at Teresa Ramairez's suggestion. It was ridiculous, after all, knowing the way Greg had always felt about the money. Only it wasn't ridiculous when the trust showed up on an assets sheet, which Greg had shoved at her several weeks ago. What for years Greg had called "her father's blood money," he was now calling community property. The following day she asked Teresa Ramairez to recommend a real estate agent.

Maggie added the boxes to those already arranged and stacked in the corner. She glanced over the labels one last time, hoping the missing one would miraculously show itself. Then, with hands on her hips, she turned slowly around, admiring the spacious rooms decorated for the time being in Early American corrugated brown. She had brought very few pieces of furniture with her, but more than she had expected to extract from Greg's lawyerly clutches. She wondered if it was financial suicide for anyone to ask for a divorce from a lawyer spouse. Greg had handled all of their joint financial and legal affairs for almost ten years. When Teresa Ramairez had started showing Maggie documents and spreadsheets, Maggie hadn't even recognized some of the accounts.

She and Greg had married as college seniors. Every appliance, every piece of linen, everything they owned had been a joint purchase. When they moved from their small Richmond apartment to the expensive condominium in the Crest Ridge area, they had bought new furniture, and all of it went together. It seemed wrong to split up sets. Maggie smiled at that and wondered why she couldn't bring herself to split up furniture but could do so with their ten-year marriage?

She did manage to take with her the pieces of furniture which mattered most. Her father's antique rolltop desk had made the trip without a scratch. She patted the back of her comfortable La-Z-Boy recliner. It and the brass reading lamp had been exiled long ago to the condo's den, because Greg said it didn't match the leather sofa and chairs in the living room. Maggie couldn't recall much living having ever occurred on them.

She remembered when they had first bought the set. She had tried to break it in with some passionate memories. Instead of letting his body respond to her flirtatious suggestions, Greg had been horrified and angered by the idea.

"Do you know how easily leather stains?" He had scolded her as though she was a child spilling Kool-Aid instead of a grown woman initiating sex with her husband.

No, it was easy to leave those pieces behind. As long as the memory of their crumbling marriage stayed with them. She pulled out a small duffel bag from the pile in the corner and set it on the desk next to her laptop. Earlier she had opened all the windows to remove the stale, warm air. As the sun set behind the line of trees, a moist but cool breeze swirled into the room.

She unzipped the duffel bag and carefully removed her holstered Smith & Wesson .38 revolver. She liked the way the pistol fit in her hands. There was a familiarity and ease, like the touch of an old friend. While other agents had upgraded to more powerful and automatic weapons, Maggie drew comfort from the gun she knew best. The same gun with which she had learned.

She had depended on it numerous times, and though it had only six rounds compared to an automatic's sixteen, she knew she could count on all six without any jamming. As a newbie—as FBI recruits were called—she had watched an agent go down, helpless with a Sig-Sauer 9 mm and a magazine half-full, but jammed and useless.

She pulled out of the bag her FBI badge in its leather holder. She laid both it and the Smith & Wesson on the desk, almost reverently, alongside the Glock 40 caliber found earlier in the desk drawer. Also in the duffel bag was her forensic kit, a small black pouch that included an odd assortment of things she had learned over the years never to be without.

She left the forensic kit safely tucked in place, zipped the duffel bag and slid it under the desk. For some reason, having these things close by—her guns and badge—made her feel secure, complete. They had become symbols of who she was. They made this feel more like home than any of the possessions she and Greg had spent their adult lives collecting. Ironically, these things that meant so much to her were also the reasons she could no longer be married to her husband. Greg had made it quite clear that Maggie needed to choose either him or the FBI. How could he not realize that what he was asking her to do was like asking her to cut off her right arm?

She traced a finger over the leather case of her badge, waiting for some sign of regret. But when none came, it didn't necessarily make her feel any better. The impending divorce brought sadness, but no regret. She and Greg had become strangers. Why hadn't she seen that a year ago when she lost her wedding ring and hadn't felt compelled to replace it?

Maggie swiped at strands of hair that stuck to her forehead and the back of her neck. Its dampness reminded her that she needed a shower. The front of her T-shirt was dirty and stained. Her arms were marred with black and purple scuffs. She rubbed at one to discover a bruise instead of dirt. Just as she began to search for her newly installed phone, she noticed a police cruiser whiz by.

She found the phone under a stack of papers. She dialed from memory and waited patiently, knowing it would take more than five or six rings.

"Dr. Patterson."

"Gwen, it's Maggie."

"Hey, how the hell are you? Did you get moved in?"

"Let's just say my stuff is moved." She noticed the Stafford County Coroner's van drive past. She went to the window and watched the van curve to the left until it was out of sight. The street had no outlet. "I know you're swamped, Gwen, but I was wondering if you had a chance to check on what we talked about last week?"

"Maggie, I really wish you'd leave the Stucky case alone."

"Look, Gwen, if you don't have time, all you need to say is that you don't have time," she snapped, and immediately wished she could take her words back. But she was tired of everyone trying to protect her.

"You know that's not what I meant, Maggie. Why do you always make it so goddamn hard for people to care about you?"

She let the silence hang between them. She knew her friend was right. Suddenly in the distance, Maggie heard a fire engine's siren, and her stomach turned to knots. What was happening just around the corner? Her knees threatened to buckle at the thought of a possible fire. She sniffed the breeze coming in through the window. She couldn't smell or see smoke. Thank God. If it was a fire, she would be incredibly useless. The thought alone scared the hell out of her, reviving memories of her father's death.

"How about I stop over tonight?"

Gwen's voice startled Maggie. She had forgotten she was still on the phone.

"The place is a mess. I haven't even started to unpack."

"It doesn't bother me if it doesn't bother you. Why don't I pick up a pizza and some beer? We can picnic on the floor. Come on, it'll be fun. Sort of a housewarming party. A prelude to your new independence."

The fire engine's siren began to grow distant, and Maggie realized it was not on its way to her neighborhood. Her shoulders relaxed, and she sighed in relief.

"You can pick up some beer, but don't worry about the pizza. I'll have it delivered."

"Just remember, no Italian sausage on my side. Some of us need to watch our weight. I'll see you around seven."

"Fine. Sure. That'll work." But Maggie was already distracted as another police cruiser sped by. Without a second thought, she put down the phone and grabbed her badge. She quickly reset the security system. Then she tucked her revolver in her back waistband and headed out the front door. So much for seclusion.

# CHAPTER 4

Maggie hurried past three of her new neighbors who politely stayed in the street, a safe distance from the house flanked with police cruisers. The coroner's van sat in the driveway, already empty. She ignored a police officer on his hands and knees who had gotten a roll of crime scene tape tangled in a rosebush. Instead of tearing it and starting over, he took on the thorns and kept snapping his hand back with each prick.

"Hey," he finally yelled when he realized Maggie was headed for the door. "You can't go in there."

When his voice didn't slow her down, he scrambled to his feet, dropping the roll of tape and sending it unraveling down the slope of the lawn. For a minute he looked as though he'd go for the tape instead of Maggie. She almost laughed, but kept her face serious as she held up her badge.

"I'm with the FBI."

"Yeah, right. And this is what the FBI is wearing these days." He snatched the leather case from her, but his eyes took their time making their way down her body.

Instinctively, Maggie stood up straight and crossed her arms over her sweat-drenched chest. Ordinarily, she paid close attention to her presentation and attire. She had always been self-conscious and aware that her hundred-and-fifteen-pounds, five-foot-five stature did not live up to the FBI's authoritarian image. In a navy blazer and trousers, her aloof, cold attitude could pull it off. In a T-shirt and faded jeans, she realized she might not be able to.

Finally, the officer took a closer look at her credentials. The smirk slid off his narrow face as he realized she was not a reporter or a curious neighbor playing around with him.

"Son of a bitch. You're on the level."

She held out her hand for the badge. Now a bit embarrassed, he quickly handed it back.

"I didn't realize this was something the FBI would be in on."

It probably was not. She failed to mention that she was just in the neighborhood. Instead, she asked, "Who's the lead detective?"

"Excuse me?"

She pointed to the house.

"Who's leading the investigation?"

"Oh, that would be Detective Manx."

She headed for the entrance, feeling his eyes follow her. Before she closed the door behind her, he hurried after the tangled ribbon of tape that now trailed over much of the front lawn.

No one greeted Maggie at the door. In fact, no one was in sight. The house's foyer was almost as large as Maggie's new living room. She took her time, peeking into each room, stepping carefully and touching nothing. The house looked impeccable, not a speck of dust, until she got to the kitchen. Scattered across the butcher-block island were all the makings for a sandwich, now dried up, wilted and crusty. A head of lettuce sat on a cutting board amongst the remnants of tomato seeds and bits and pieces of green pepper. Several candy bar wrappers, containers left on their sides and an open mayonnaise jar waited to be cleaned up and put away. In the middle of the table sat the sandwich, thick with its contents spilling over the wheat bread. Only one bite taken from it.

Maggie's eyes examined the rest of the kitchen, shiny countertops, sparkling appliances and a spotless ceramic floor, marred only by three more candy bar wrappers. Whoever made this mess didn't live here.

She could hear voices now, muffled and coming from above. She climbed the stairs while avoiding contact with the oak handrail. She wondered if the detectives had been as careful. On one of the steps she noticed a clump of mud, left perhaps by one of the officers. There was something unusual in it that glittered. She resisted the urge to pick it up. It wasn't as though she carried evidence bags in her back pocket. Though at one time it wouldn't have been odd to find a stray in one of her jacket pockets. These days the only evidence she came across was in books.

She followed the voices down the long, carpeted hall. There was no longer a need to scrounge for evidence. At the doorway to the master bedroom a puddle of blood greeted her, the imprint of a shoe stamped at one edge, while the other edge soaked into an expensive Persian rug. With little effort, Maggie could see a spatter pattern on the oak door. Oddly, the spatter reached only to about knee level.

Maggie was lost in thought and hadn't entered the room when the detective in a bright blue sports jacket and wrinkled chinos yelled at her.

"Hey, lady. How the hell did you get in here?"

The two other men stopped their work in opposite corners of the room and stared at her. Maggie's first impression of the detective was that he looked like a wrinkled advertisement for the Gap.

"My name's Maggie O'Dell. I'm with the FBI." She opened her badge to him, but her eyes were examining the rest of the room.

"The FBI?"

The men exchanged looks while Maggie took a careful step around the puddle and into the room. More blood speckled the white down comforter on the four-poster bed. Despite the spatter of blood, the bedcovers remained neatly spread with no indentations. Whatever struggle took place did not make it to the bed.

"What's the FBI's interest in this?" the man in the bright sports jacket demanded.

He scraped a hand over his head, and Maggie wondered if the buzz cut was recent. His dark eyes slid down her body, and again she was reminded of her inappropriate attire. She glanced at the other two men. One was in uniform. The other, an older gentleman—who Maggie guessed was the medical examiner—was dressed in a well-pressed suit and a silk tie held down by an expensive gold collar bar.

"Are you Detective Manx?" she asked the buzz cut.

His eyes shot up to hers, the look not only registering surprise but alarm that she knew his name. Was he worried that his superiors were checking up on him? He looked young, and Maggie guessed he was close to her age—somewhere in his early thirties. Perhaps this was his first lead in a homicide.

"Yeah, I'm Manx. Who the hell called you?"

It was time to confess.

"I live down the street. I thought I might be able to help."

"Christ!" The same hand swiped over his face as he glanced at the other two men. They quietly watched as though observing a standoff. "Just because you've got a fucking badge, you think you can barge in here?"

"I'm a forensic psychologist and a profiler. I'm used to examining scenes like this. I thought I could—"

"Well, we don't need any help. I've got everything under control."

"Hey, Detective." The yellow-tape officer from outside walked into the room and immediately all eyes watched him step into the puddle. He jerked his foot up and awkwardly stepped back into the hall, holding up the dripping toe of his shoe.

"Hell, I can't believe I did that again," he muttered.

Just then Maggie realized the intruder had been more careful. The toe print she had seen was worthless. When she looked back at Manx, his eyes darted away. He shook his head, disguising the embarrassment as disdain for the young officer.

"What is it, Officer Kramer?"

Kramer looked desperately for somewhere to place his foot. He glanced up apologetically as he rubbed the sole on the hall carpet. This time Manx avoided looking at Maggie. Instead, he shoved his large hands into his jacket pockets as if needing to restrain them from strangling the young rookie.

"What the hell do you need, Kramer?"

"It's just...there are a few neighbors out front asking questions. I wondered if maybe I should start questioning them. You know, see if anybody saw something."

"Get names and addresses. We'll talk to them later."

"Yes, sir." The officer seemed relieved to escape the new stain he had created.

Maggie waited. The other two men stared at Manx.

"So tell me, O'Donnell. What's your take of this mess?"

"O'Dell."

"Excuse me?"

"The name's O'Dell," she said, but she wouldn't wait for another invitation. "Is the body in the bathroom?"

"There's a whirlpool bath with more blood, but no body. In fact, we seem to be missing that small detail."

"The blood seems to be confined to this room," the medical examiner told her.

Maggie noticed he was the only one wearing latex gloves.

"If someone ran out, but was injured, you'd think there'd be some drips, some scuffs, something. But the house is fucking clean enough to eat off the floors." Manx swiped at his new hairdo again.

"The kitchen's not so clean," Maggie contradicted him.

He scowled at her. "How goddamn long have you been sneaking around here?"

She ignored him and kneeled down to get a closer look at the blood on the floor. Most of it was congealed, some dried. She guessed it had been here since morning.

"Maybe she didn't have time to clean up after lunch," Manx continued instead of waiting for her to answer his question.

"How do you know the victim is a woman?"

"A neighbor called us when she couldn't get her on the phone. Said they were supposed to go shopping. She saw the car in the garage, but no one answered the door. See, I'm thinking the guy—whoever he was—must have interrupted her lunch."

"What makes you think the sandwich was hers?"

The three of them stopped simultaneously. Again, they exchanged looks, then stared at Maggie, like foreign diplomats relying on each other for interpretation.

"What the hell are you saying, O'Donnell?"

"The name is O'Dell, Detective Manx." She let him hear her irritation this time. His blatant disregard was a small but familiar and annoying way to discredit her. "The victim's house is impeccable. She wouldn't have left a mess like that, let alone sit down to eat before she cleaned it up."

"Maybe she was interrupted."

"Perhaps. But there's no sign of a struggle in the kitchen. And the alarm system was off, right?"

Manx looked annoyed that she had guessed correctly. "Yeah, it was off, so maybe it was someone she knew."

"That's possible." Maggie stood and let her eyes take in the rest of the room. "If he did interrupt or surprise her, that didn't happen until they were up here. She may have been waiting for him, or perhaps she invited him up. That's probably why there's no signs of a struggle until we get into the bedroom. She may have changed her mind. Didn't want to go through with whatever they had agreed to. This spatter pattern here on the door is strange." She pointed to it, careful not to touch. "It's so far down, one of them would need to be on the floor when this wound was inflicted."

She walked to the window, feeling the men's eyes follow her. Suddenly she had their attention. Through the sheer curtains she could see the backyard, similar to her own, spacious and secluded by flowering dogwoods and huge pines. None of the neighbors' houses were even visible, all hidden by the foliage and trees. No one would see an intruder come or go back here. But how would he maneuver the steep ridge and the stream? Had she overestimated the strength of that natural barrier?

"There really is not much blood," she continued. "Unless there's a lot more in the bathroom. Perhaps there's not a body simply because the victim left on her own."

She heard Manx snort. "You think they had a nice little lunch, he beat the shit out of her because she decided not to fuck him, but then she left willingly with this guy? And in the meantime, the whole goddamn neighborhood didn't notice?" Manx laughed.

Maggie ignored his sarcasm. "I didn't say she left willingly. Also, this blood is much too congealed and dry to have happened a few hours ago during lunch. I'm guessing it happened early this morning. She glanced at the medical examiner for confirmation.

"She's right about that." He nodded in agreement.

"I don't think they had lunch together. He probably fixed the sandwich for himself. You should bag the sandwich. If you can't get a dental imprint, there may be some saliva for a DNA test."

When she finally turned to face him, Manx stared at her. Only now his frustration had turned to wonder and the crinkles at his eyes became more pronounced. Maggie realized he was older than her initial assessment. Which meant the clothes and the hair might be part of a midlife crisis rather than a youthful indiscretion. She recognized Manx's stunned look. It was the same look that often followed her on-the-spot, blunt profiles. At times, that look made her feel like a cheap fortune-teller or a psychic. But always beneath their skepticism lay just enough amazement and respect to vindicate that initial reaction.

"Mind if I check out the bathroom?" she asked.

"Be my guest." Manx shook his head and waved her through.

Before Maggie got to the bathroom door, she stopped. On the bureau was a photograph. She recognized the beautiful blond-haired woman who smiled out at her, one arm wrapped around a dark-haired man and the other around a panting white Labrador retriever. It was the same woman she and Tess McGowan had met the first day Maggie looked at her new house.

"What is it?" Manx asked, now standing directly behind her.

"I've met this woman before. Last week. Her name's Rachel Endicott. She was out jogging."

Just then, in the bureau mirror, she saw more blood. Only this was smeared on the bottom of the bed ruffle. She stopped and turned, hesitating. Was it possible that whoever had been bleeding was still under the bed?

# CHAPTER 5

Maggie stared at the bloodied ruffle then slowly walked to the bed.

"Actually she was walking," she said, keeping the excitement from her voice. "She had a dog with her, a white Lab."

"We haven't found any fucking dog," Manx said. "Unless he's out in the backyard or the garage."

Carefully, Maggie got down on one knee. There was blood in the grooves of the hardwood floor, too. Here the intruder must have taken the time to mop it up. Why would he do that, unless some of it was his own?

The room grew silent as the men finally noticed the blood on the hem of the bed ruffle. Maggie felt them standing over her, waiting. Even Manx stood quietly, though out of the corner of her eye she could see the toe of his loafer tapping impatiently.

She lifted the ruffled material, avoiding the bloodied area. Before she could get a closer look underneath, a deep-throated growl caused her to jerk her hand away.

"Shit!" Manx spat, jumping back with such force he sent a nightstand scraping into the wall.

Maggie saw the glint of metal in his hand and realized he had drawn his service revolver.

"Move out of the way." He was next to her, shoving her shoulder and almost knocking her over.

She grabbed his arm as he recklessly took aim, ready to fire at anything that moved underneath the bed even though he couldn't see it.

"What the hell are you doing?" she yelled at him.

"What the fuck do you think I'm doing?"

"Calm down, Detective." The medical examiner took hold of Manx's other arm and gently pulled him back.

"This dog might be your only witness," Maggie said, getting down on her knees again but staying back a safe distance.

"Oh right. Like a dog's gonna tell us what happened."

"She's right," the M.E.'s voice was amazingly calm. "Dogs can tell us a lot. Let's see if we can get this one under control."

Then he looked to Maggie as if waiting for her instructions.

"Most likely, he's wounded," she said.

"And in shock," the M.E. added.

She stood and looked around the room. What the hell did she know about dogs, let alone how to subdue one?

"Check the closet and grab a couple of jackets," she told him. "Preferably thick, something like wool and something that's been worn and not laundered. Maybe there are some clothes on the floor."

She found a tennis racket leaning against the wall. She rummaged through the bureau's drawers then noticed a tie rack on the back of the closet door. She snatched a silk pinstripe and knotted one end of the tie to the handle of the racket. She made a slipknot at the other end.

The medical examiner came back with several jackets.

"Officer Hillguard," he instructed. "See if you can find some blankets. Detective Manx, get at the end of the bed. We'll have you lift up the bedspread when we're ready.

Maggie noticed Manx's impatience did not extend to the doctor. In fact, he seemed to regard the older man as an authority figure and willingly took his post at the end of the bed.

The medical examiner handed Maggie one of the jackets, an expensive wool tweed. She sniffed the sleeve. Excellent. There was still the faint scent of perfume. She pulled the jacket on backward, pushing the sleeves over her bare arms but keeping enough at the end to ball up in her fists. Then she grabbed the tennis racket and kneeled about two feet from the bed. The doctor kneeled next to her as Officer Hillguard set a quilt and two blankets on the floor beside them.

"Are we ready?" The medical examiner glanced at all of them. "Okay, Detective Manx. Lift the bedspread up, but slowly."

This time the dog was prepared, his eyes glazed, teeth bared, the growl deep and low. But he didn't lunge at them. He couldn't.

Underneath the bloody mess of fur that was once white, Maggie spotted the main wound, a gash just above the shoulder and barely missing the throat. The matted fur must have temporarily stopped the bleeding.

"It's okay, boy," Maggie told the dog in a quiet, calm voice. "We're going to help you. Just relax."

She scooted closer, extending a part of the sleeve and letting it hang beyond her hand. He snapped at it, and Maggie jerked backward, almost losing her balance.

"Jesus!" she muttered. Had she completely lost her mind? She tried not to think of her aversion to needles, yet found herself wondering if the treatment for rabies was still six shots.

Maggie steadied herself. She needed to stay focused. She tried again, more slowly this time. The dog sniffed at the dangling sleeve, possibly recognizing the scent of his owner. His growl turned into a whine and then a whimper.

"It's okay," Maggie promised in a hushed tone, uncertain whether she was trying to convince the dog or herself. She inched closer with the tennis racket in her other hand, the tie's loop hanging down, moving in while the dog watched and continued to whimper. She let the dog sniff the tie. He didn't resist when she slipped it over his snout. Gently, she tightened the knot.

"How're we gonna get him out from under there?" Officer Hillguard was now on his knees on the other side of Maggie.

"Let's unfold one of those blankets and get it next to him."

But as soon as Officer Hillguard's hands got close, the dog snapped and snarled, growling and struggling against the makeshift muzzle. He jumped toward the officer, and Maggie used the opportunity to grab the dog's collar from behind. She yanked him forward onto the blanket, all the while holding the tennis racket and keeping the muzzle tight. The dog yipped, and immediately Maggie worried that she had opened one of the wounds.

"Holy shit," she heard Detective Manx say, but this time he kept his revolver in its holster.

"We got him." The medical examiner stood and waved Officer Hillguard over to his side. The two men tugged on the blanket corners and pulled the dog out from under the bed. "We can use my van to transport him to Riley's Clinic."

Maggie sat back on her feet, only now noticing that she was soaked with perspiration.

"Shit." Manx was back to his belligerent mood. "That means all the blood by the door and in the bathtub is probably the fucking dog's blood, and we don't have a damn thing."

"I wouldn't count on that," Maggie said. "Something violent happened here, and the dog's owner may have suffered the brunt of it." She watched the doctor and officer cover the trembling dog and secure their blanket stretcher, grateful they were too busy to notice how much effort it took for her to stand.

"I'm guessing this guy—" she pointed to the Lab "—tried to stop whatever happened. He may have gotten in a couple of good bites. There's a chance some of the blood, especially here by the bed, may be the intruder's. Your forensics people should be able to get a sampling even though it's been wiped up."

"You think you can allow me to do my own investigation?" Manx shot her a look of contempt.

Maggie wiped strands of hair off her forehead. Jesus! Couldn't this guy give her a break? Just then she realized she had blood on her hands and now had blood on her forehead and in her hair. When she glanced at the medical examiner, he was shaking his head at Manx and giving him a warning look as though he, too, was fed up with Manx's arrogance.

"Yes, of course, the investigation is all yours," Maggie finally said, and grabbed a corner of the blanket to help the men move the swaddled dog. "I'm sure the whole neighborhood will sleep soundly tonight, knowing you're on the case."

Manx seemed surprised by her sarcasm, then turned red when he noticed the two men would not be coming to his defense. Maggie caught the medical examiner smiling. She didn't turn to see if Manx had caught it, too.

"Just keep your big FBI badge and your pretty little butt out of my investigation," he said to her back, determined to get in the last word. "You got that, O'Donnell?"

She didn't bother to look at him or answer, the ungrateful son of a bitch. He wouldn't have even found the dog if it wasn't for her. Now she wondered if he would bother to take blood samples, simply because it had been her suggestion.

She held her corner of the blanket tight and followed Officer Hillguard and the medical examiner. As they reached the landing, Maggie turned to look at Manx, who had stayed in the bedroom's doorway.

"Oh, Detective Manx," she called to him. "One more thing. You might want to check out this mud here on the steps. Unless, of course, you're the one who tracked it in and contaminated your own crime scene."

Instinctively, Manx lifted his right foot, taking a look at the sole before he realized his defensive reaction. The M.E. laughed out loud. Officer Hillguard knew better and confined himself to a smile. Manx's face went red again. Maggie simply turned, concentrating on keeping their patient steady and calm while they hauled him down the stairs.

# CHAPTER 6

Tess McGowan stuffed a copy of the closing papers into her leather briefcase, ignoring its worn sheen and cracked handle. A couple more sales and just maybe she could afford a new briefcase instead of the hand-me-down she had bought at the thrift store.

She jotted a note on her desk blotter, "Joyce and Bill Saunders: a dozen long-stemmed chocolate chip cookies." The Saunderses kids would get a kick out of them, and Joyce was a chocoholic. Then, she wrote, "Maggie O'Dell: a garden bouquet." Quickly, she scratched out the notation. No, it was too simple, and Tess liked to customize her thank-yous to her customers. They had become one of her trademarks and paid off big-time in referrals. But what would O'Dell like? Hey, even FBI agents liked flowers, and O'Dell seemed nuts about her huge backyard, but a bouquet didn't seem right. No, what seemed right for Agent O'Dell was a killer Doberman. Tess smiled and jotted down "a potted azalea" instead.

Pleased with herself, Tess switched off her computer and slipped on her jacket. The other offices had gone silent hours ago. She was the only one nuts enough to be working this late. Though it didn't matter. Daniel would be at his office until eight or nine and not ready to think about her for several more hours. But she wouldn't dwell on his inattentiveness. After all, she'd be running in the other direction if Daniel was constantly calling her, infringing on her independence or pushing for a commitment. No, she liked things just the way they were—safe and uncomplicated with very little emotional investment. It was the perfect relationship for a woman who couldn't handle any real commitments.

She passed by the copier room but stopped when she heard shuffling. Her eyes darted to the front door at the end of the hall, making certain nothing obstructed her path in case she needed to run. She leaned against the wall and peeked around the door to the room where a copy machine buzzed into action.

"Girl, I thought you went home hours ago." Delores Heston's voice startled Tess as the woman stood up from behind the machine and shoved a tray of paper into the mouth of the copier. Finally, she looked at Tess and her face registered concern. "Good Lord! I'm sorry, Tess. I didn't mean to scare you. You okay?"

Tess's heart pounded in her ears. Immediately she was embarrassed at being so jumpy. The paranoia was a leftover from her old life. She smiled at Delores while she leaned against the doorjamb and waited for her pulse to return to normal.

"I'm fine. I thought everyone else was gone. What are you still doing here? Aren't you supposed to be taking the Greeleys to dinner?"

Delores punched some buttons, and the machine whizzed to life with a soft, almost comforting, hum. Then she looked at Tess, hands on her ample hips.

"They had to reschedule, so I'm catching up on some paperwork. And please don't tell Verna. She'll scream at me for messing with her precious baby." The machine beeped as if on cue.

"Holy Toledo! What did I do now?" Delores turned and began punching buttons again.

Tess laughed. The truth was, Delores owned the machine just like she owned every last chair and paper clip. Delores Heston started Heston Realty nearly ten years ago and had made quite a name for herself in Newburgh Heights and the surrounding area. Quite an accomplishment for a black woman who had grown up poor. Tess admired her mentor who, at six o'clock in the evening after a full day of work, still looked impeccable in her deep purple custom-made suit. Delores's silky, black hair was swept up into a compact bun, not a strand out of place. The only indication that she was finished for the day were her stocking feet.

In contrast, Tess's suit was wrinkled from too many hours of sitting. Her thick, wavy hair frizzled from the humidity, strands breaking free from the clasp she used to tie it back. She was probably the only woman alive who dyed her naturally blond hair a nondescript brown in order to buy herself more credibility and to avoid sexual advances. Even the eyeglasses, which dangled from a designer cord around her neck, were a prop. Tess wore contact lenses, but didn't young, attractive women always look more intelligent when they wore glasses?

Finally, the machine stopped beeping and started spitting out copies. Delores turned to Tess and rolled her eyes.

"Verna's smart not to let me touch this thing."

"Looks like you've got it under control."

"So, girl, what are you doing here so late? Don't you have a handsome man you should be home snuggling with on a Friday evening?"

"Just wanted to finish all the paperwork on the Saunders' house."

"That's right. I forgot you closed this week. Excellent job, by the way. I know the Saunderses were in a hell of a hurry to sell. How much of a beating did we take?"

"Actually, it turned out quite well for everyone involved. Plus, we beat their two-week deadline, so on top of our commission we'll also be receiving the selling bonus they tacked on."

"Ooooh, I do so love to hear that. There's no better advertising than surpassing a customer's expectations. But that selling bonus is all yours, dearie."

Tess wasn't sure she heard her boss correctly.

"Excuse me?"

"You heard me. You're keeping that selling bonus for yourself. You deserve it."

For a minute Tess didn't know what to say. The bonus was almost ten thousand dollars. That was almost six months' pay back when she had been bartending. Her look of surprise sent Delores into gales of laughter.

"Girl, I wish you could see the look on your face."

Tess waited quietly. She managed a weak smile. She was embarrassed to ask if her boss was joking. It would be a cruel joke. But then, it wouldn't be the first time Tess had experienced such cruelty. In fact, she expected it, accepted it, almost more readily than kindness.

Delores was staring at her again, with a look of concern.

"Tess, I am serious. I want you to have the selling bonus. You worked your ass off to move that property in two weeks. I know it's a beautiful house and the asking price was a steal, but with all the paperwork and hedging and negotiating—selling anything right now that quickly, and especially in that price range, is nothing less than a miracle."

"It's...well, it's just an awful lot of money. Are you sure you want to—"

"Absolutely. I know what I'm doing, girlfriend. I'm investing in you, Tess. I want you to stick around. Don't need you going out on your own and becoming my competition. Besides, I'm making a nice piece of change off that property, as it is. Now go home and celebrate with that handsome man of yours."

On the way home Tess wondered if it was possible, the part about celebrating with her "handsome man." Daniel had been so angry with her last week when she'd refused to move in with him. She wasn't sure she blamed him. Why was it that every time a man wanted to get close to her, she pushed him away?

Jesus, she wasn't a kid anymore. In a couple of weeks she'd be thirty-five. She was becoming a successful and respected businesswoman. So why couldn't she get her personal life right? Was she destined to fail at every damn relationship she attempted? No matter what she did, the past seemed to follow her around, sucking her back into its old, comfortable, but destructive, cocoon.

The last five years had been a constant battle, but finally she was making progress. And this last sale had proven that she was actually good at this. She could make a living without conning anyone. Even Daniel had become a sort of trophy, with his refined handsome features, his educated and cultured background. He was sophisticated and ambitious and so completely unlike any man she had ever been with. So what if he was a little arrogant, or that they had so few things in common. He was good for her. She winced at the thought. It made Daniel sound like cod liver oil.

Tess found herself pulling her leased Miata into the back-alley parking lot of Louie's Bar and Grill. She decided to pick up a bottle of wine. Then she'd call Daniel, apologize for last week and invite him over for a late dinner to help her celebrate. Surely he would be excited for her. He had said he liked her independence and determination, and Daniel was stingy with compliments, even the halfhearted ones.

She sat back in the leather seat and tried to remember why she felt she needed to apologize to him again. Oh well. It didn't matter, as long as they put it behind them and moved forward. She was getting good at putting things in the past. Yet, if that were true, what was she doing back here at Louie's? Shep's Liquor Mart was only three blocks down the street and on her way home. What in the world did she need to prove to anyone? Or rather, what was it she still needed to prove to herself?

She reached for the key in the ignition and was just about to start the car and leave when the back door swung open, startling her. A stocky, middle-aged man came out, his hands filled with trash bags, his apron grimy and his balding head glistening with sweat. A cigarette hung from his lips. Without removing it, he heaved the bags into the Dumpster and wiped the sweat from his forehead with the sleeve of his shirt. As he turned to go back in, he saw her, and then it was too late.

He grabbed the cigarette—one last puff—and tossed it to the ground without stomping it out. He strolled up to the car, carrying his bulk with a swagger Tess knew he imitated from the professional wrestlers he idolized. He thought he looked cool. When, in fact, he simply looked like a pathetic, overweight, balding, middle-aged man. Despite all that, she found him endearing, the closest thing she had to an old friend.

"Tessy," he said, then waited as the window hummed opened. "What the hell you doin' here?"

She noticed the beginning of a smile before he wiped at it, pretending instead to scratch the five o'clock shadow.

"Hi, Louie." She got out of the car.

"Fuckin' nice ride ya got here, Tessy," he said, checking out the shiny black Miata.

She let him examine and admire it, neglecting to tell him it was a company car and not her own. One of Delores's mottoes was that to be successful you must first look successful.

Finally, Louie turned his sights on Tess. She felt his eyes slide down her designer suit and his whistle made her blush. She should have felt proud. Instead, his attention made her feel like a fraud for a second time in the same day.

"So whatcha doin' here? Slummin'?"

Immediately, her face grew hot.

"Of course not," she snapped.

"Hey, I'm just jokin' with ya, Tessy."

"I know that." She smiled, hoping she sounded convincing and not defensive. She turned to the car and pretended to lock the door, though the remote could do it from ten feet away. "I need to pick up a bottle of wine. Just thought I'd give you the business rather than Shep's."

"Oh really?" He stared at her, his eyebrow raised, but quickly gave in to a smile. "Well, I appreciate it. And you never need no excuse to come see us, Tessy. You know you're always welcome."

"Thanks, Louie."

Suddenly she felt like that restless, going-nowhere bartender she had left here five years ago. Would she ever be rid of her past?

"Come on," Louie said as he swung a muscular arm up around her shoulder.

Wearing heels, Tess was a couple inches taller, making the dragon tattooed on his arm stretch its neck. The smell of body odor and French fries made her stomach turn, only she was surprised to find it was homesickness she was feeling instead of nausea. Then she thought of Daniel. Later, he would smell the cigarette smoke and the greasy burgers. She realized that would be enough to ruin the celebration.

"You know what, Louie. I just remembered something I forgot back at the office." She turned and slipped out from under his arm.

"What? It can't wait a few minutes?"

"No, sorry. My boss will have my ass in a sling if I don't take care of it right now." She bleeped her car door open and climbed inside before Louie had a chance to do any more objecting. "I'll stop in later," she said through the half-opened window, knowing full well she would not. The window was already on its way up again when she said, "I promise."

She shifted the car into gear and carefully maneuvered the

narrow alley, watching Louie in the rearview mirror. He looked more confused than pissed. That was good. She didn't want Louie pissed at her. Then immediately wondered why it mattered. She didn't want it to matter.

She turned the car onto the street, and when she knew she was safely out of sight, she gunned the engine. But it took several miles before she felt like she could breathe and before she could hear the car radio instead of the pounding of her heart. Then she remembered that she had passed Shep's Liquor Mart. She didn't care. She no longer felt as if she deserved a celebration, yet she tried to concentrate on her recent successes and not the past. In fact, she remained so focused, she hardly noticed the dark sedan following her.

# CHAPTER 7

Before the pizza or Gwen arrived, Maggie poured a second Scotch. She had forgotten about the bottle until she discovered it staring up at her, safely stored in the box—a necessary antidote accompanying the contents of horror. The box was labeled #34666, the number that had been assigned to Albert Stucky. Perhaps it was no accident that his file number would end in 666.

Assistant Director Cunningham would be furious if he knew she had copied every last piece of paper from Stucky's official file. She would have felt guilty if each report, each document, each note had been recorded by someone other than herself. For almost two years Maggie had tracked Stucky. She had viewed every one of his scenes of torture and dissection, scanning his handiwork for fibers, hairs, missing organs, anything that would tell her how to catch him. She had a right to his file, considering it some strange documentation of a portion of her own life.

She had taken a quick shower after her unexpected trip to the vet. Her UVA T-shirt soaked in the bathroom sink. She might never be able to remove the bloodstains. The T-shirt was old, stretched and faded, but she had an odd attachment to it. Some people kept scrapbooks, Maggie kept T-shirts.

Her years at the University of Virginia had been good ones. It was there she discovered a life of her own outside of being her mother's caretaker. It was where she had met Greg. She glanced at her watch, then checked her cellular phone to make certain it was on. He still hadn't returned her call about the missing carton. He'd make her wait, but she wouldn't let herself get angry. Not tonight. She was simply too exhausted to take on one more emotion.

The doorbell chimed. Maggie glanced at her watch again. As usual, Gwen was ten minutes late. She tugged at her shirttail, making certain it hid the bulging Smith & Wesson tucked into her waistband. Lately, the gun had become as common an accessory as her wristwatch.

"I know I'm late," Gwen said before the door was fully open. "Traffic was a bitch. Friday night and everyone's trying to get the hell out of D.C. for the weekend."

"Good to see you, too."

She smiled and pulled Maggie in for a one-armed hug. For a brief moment Maggie was surprised by how soft and fragile the older woman felt. Despite Gwen's petite and feminine stature, Maggie thought of her as her own personal Rock of Gibraltor. She had leaned on Gwen and depended on her strength and character and words of wisdom many times during their friendship.

When Gwen pulled away, she cupped Maggie's cheek in the palm of her hand, attempting to get a good look at her.

"You look like hell," was her gentle assessment.

"Gee, thanks!"

She smiled again and handed Maggie the carton of longnecked Bud Light she carried in her other hand. The bottles were cold and dripping with condensation. Maggie took them and used the action as an excuse to keep her eyes away from Gwen's. It had been almost a month since the two women had seen each other, though they talked on the phone regularly. On the phone, however, Maggie could keep Gwen from seeing the panic and vulnerability that seemed to lie so close to the surface during these past several weeks.

"Pizza should be here any minute," Maggie told her as she reset the security system.

"No Italian sausage on my half."

"Extra mushrooms, instead."

"Oh, bless you." Gwen didn't wait for an invitation to come in. She took off to roam through the rooms.

"My God, Maggie, this house is wonderful."

"You like my designer?"

"Hmm...I'd say brown cardboard is you, simple and unpretentious. May I check out the second floor?" Gwen asked, already making her way up the stairs.

"Can I stop you?" Maggie laughed. How was it possible for this woman to sweep into a place and bring a trail of energy as well as such warmth and delight?

She and Gwen had met when Maggie had first arrived at Quantico for her forensic fellowship. Maggie had been a young, naive newbie who hadn't yet seen blood except in a test tube, and had never fired a gun except during training on the firing range.

Gwen had been one of the local psychologists brought in by Assistant Director Cunningham to act as a private consultant and to help profile several important cases. Even back then she had a successful practice in D.C. Many of her patients were some of the elite of Washington—bored wives of congressmen, suicidal generals and even one manic-depressed White House cabinet member.

However it was Gwen's research, the many articles she had written and her remarkable insight into the criminal mind that had attracted Assistant Director Cunningham when he first asked her to be an independent consultant for the FBI's Investigative Support Unit. Though Maggie learned quickly that the assistant director had been attracted to Dr. Gwen Patterson in other ways as well. A person would have to be blind not to see the ongoing chemistry between the two, though Maggie knew firsthand that neither had acted upon it, nor ever intended to.

"We respect our professional relationship," Gwen explained to Maggie once, making it clear she didn't want the subject brought up again, though this was long after Gwen's stint as a consultant had ended. Maggie knew that Assistant Director Cunningham's estranged marriage probably had more to do with their hands-off policy than any attempt to remain professional.

From the first time Maggie met Gwen, she had admired the woman's vibrancy, her keen intellect and her dry sense of humor. Gwen refused to think inside the box and didn't hesitate to break any of the rules while still appearing to be respectful of authority. Maggie had seen her win over diplomats as well as criminals with her sophisticated but charming manner. Gwen was fifteen years older than Maggie, but the woman had instantly become a best friend as well as a mentor.

The doorbell chimed again, and Maggie's hand reached back and grabbed her revolver before she could stop herself. She glanced up the stairs to see if Gwen had witnessed her knee-jerk reaction. She smoothed her shirttail over her jeans and checked the portico from the side window before she disarmed the alarm system. She stopped and looked out the peephole, examining the fish-eye view of the street, then she opened the door.

"Large pizza for O'Dell." The young girl handed Maggie the warm box. Already she could smell the Romano cheese and Italian sausage.

"It smells wonderful."

The girl grinned as though she had prepared it herself.

"It comes to $18.59, please."

Maggie handed her a twenty and a five. "Keep the change."

"Gee, thanks."

The girl bounced down the circular drive, her blond ponytail waving out the back of her blue baseball cap.

Maggie set the pizza down in the middle of the living room. She returned to the door to reset the security system just as Gwen came rushing down the steps.

"Maggie, what the hell happened?" she asked, holding up the dripping T-shirt, splattered with blood.

"What is this? Did you hurt yourself?" Gwen demanded.

"Oh, that."

"Yes, oh that. What the hell happened?"

Maggie quickly cupped a hand under the dripping T-shirt and grabbed it away, racing up the stairs to drop it back into the sink. She drained the red, murky water, tossed in more detergent and ran fresh water over the fabric. When she looked up in the mirror, Gwen was standing behind her, watching.

"If you're hurt, please don't try to take care of it yourself," Gwen said in a soft but stern voice.

Maggie met her friend's eyes in the mirror and knew that she was referring to the cut Albert Stucky had sliced into her abdomen. Maggie had slipped away into the night, after all the commotion had ended, and tried to discreetly dress her own wound. But an infection had landed her in the emergency room a few days later.

"It's nothing, Gwen. My neighbor's dog was injured. I helped take it to the vet. This is the dog's blood. Not mine."

"You're kidding." It took a minute for relief to wash over Gwen's face. "Jesus, Maggie, you just can't keep your nose out of anything that involves blood, can you?"

Maggie smiled. "I'll tell you about it later. We need to eat, because I am starving."

"That's new and different."

Maggie grabbed a towel, wiped her hands and led the way back downstairs.

"You know," Gwen said from behind her, "you need to put on some weight. Do you ever eat regular meals anymore?"

"I hope this isn't going to be a lecture on nutrition."

She heard Gwen sigh, but knew she wouldn't push it. They went into the kitchen, and Maggie pulled out paper plates and napkins from a carton on the counter. Each grabbed a cold bottle of beer and returned to the living-room floor. Already Gwen had kicked out of her expensive black pumps and thrown her suit jacket over the arm of the recliner. Maggie scooped up pizza as she noticed Gwen examining the open carton next to the rolltop desk.

"This is Stucky's, isn't it?"

"Are you going to rat me out to Cunningham?"

"Of course not. You know me better than that. But I am concerned about you obsessing over him."

"I'm not obsessing."

"Really? Then what would you call it?"

Maggie took a bite of pizza. She didn't want to think about Stucky, or her appetite would be ruined again. Yet that was one of the reasons Gwen was here.

"I simply want him caught," Maggie finally said. She could feel Gwen's eyes examining her, looking for signs, watching for underlying tones. Maggie hated it when her friend tried psychoanalyzing her, but she knew it was a simple instinct with Gwen.

"And only you can catch him? Is that it?"

"I know him best."

Gwen stared at her a few more moments then picked up her bottle by its neck and twisted off the cap. She took a sip and put the drink aside.

"I did some checking." She reached for a slice of pizza, and Maggie tried not to show her eagerness. She had asked Gwen to use her connections to find out where the Stucky case was stalled. When Assistant Director Cunningham exiled Maggie to the teaching circuit, he had also made it impossible for her to find out any information about the investigation.

Gwen took her time chewing. Another sip while Maggie waited. She wondered if Gwen had called Cunningham directly. No, that would have been too obvious. He knew the two of them were close friends.

"And?" She couldn't stand it any longer.

"Cunningham has brought in a new profiler, but the task force has been dismantled."

"Why the hell would he do that?"

"Because he has nothing, Maggie. It's been, what? Over five months? There's no sign of Albert Stucky. It's like he's fallen off the face of the earth."

"I know. I've been checking VICAP almost weekly." Initiated by the FBI, the Violent Criminal Apprehension Program recorded violent crimes across the country, categorizing them by distinguishing features. Nothing close to Stucky's M.O. had shown up. "What about in Europe? Stucky has enough money stashed. He could go anywhere."

"I checked my sources at Interpol." Gwen paused for another sip. "There's been nothing that looks like Stucky."

"Maybe he's changed his M.O."

"Maybe he's stopped, Maggie. Sometimes serial killers do that. They just stop. No one can explain it, but you know it happens."

"Not Stucky."

"Don't you think he'd be in touch with you? Try to start his sick game all over again? After all, you're the one who got him thrown in jail. If nothing else, he'd be mad as hell."

Maggie had been the one who had finally identified the madman the FBI had nicknamed The Collector. Her profile, and a lucky discovery of an almost indistinguishable set of fingerprints—arrogantly and recklessly left behind at a crime scene—

were what led to the unveiling of The Collector as a man named Albert Stucky, a self-made millionaire from Massachusetts.

Like most serial killers, Stucky seemed pleased by the exposure, enjoying the attention and wanting to take the credit. When his obsession turned to Maggie, no one was really surprised. But the game that followed was anything but ordinary. A game that included clues to catch him, only the clues came as personal notes with a token finger, a dissected birthmark, and once, a severed nipple slipped into an envelope.

That was about eight or nine months ago. Almost a year had passed and Maggie still struggled to remember what her life had been like before the game. She couldn't remember sleep without nightmares. She couldn't remember not feeling the constant need to look over her shoulder. She had nearly lost her life capturing Albert Stucky, and he had escaped before she could remember what feeling safe felt like.

Gwen reached over and pulled a stack of crime scene photos from the box. She laid them out while she continued eating her pizza. She was one of the few people Maggie knew who wasn't a member of the FBI and who was able to eat and look at crime scene photos at the same time. Without looking up, she said, "You need to let this go, Maggie. He's chopping away pieces of you, and he isn't even around."

The images from the scattered photos stared out at Maggie, just as horrific in black and white as they had been in color. There were close-ups of slashed throats, chewed-off nipples, mutilated vaginas and an assortment of extracted organs. Earlier, with only a glance, she had discovered how many of the reports she still knew by heart. God, that was annoying.

Greg had recently accused her of remembering more details about entry wounds and killers' signatures than she remembered about the events and anniversaries in their life together. There had been no point in arguing with him. She knew he was right. Perhaps she didn't deserve a husband or a family or a life. How could any female FBI agent expect a man to understand her job, let alone something like this...this obsession? Was it an obsession? Was Gwen right?

She set the pizza aside and realized that her hands had a slight tremble. When she looked up, she saw that Gwen noticed the tremor, too.

"When was the last time you slept through the night?" Her friend's brow crinkled with concern.

She chose to ignore the question and avoided Gwen's green Irish eyes as well. "Just because there hasn't been a murder doesn't mean he hasn't started his collection again."

"And if he has, Kyle will be watching." Gwen rarely slipped, using Assistant Director Cunningham's first name, except times like now, when she seemed genuinely concerned and worried. "Let it go, Maggie. Let it go before it destroys you."

"It's not going to destroy me. I'm pretty damn tough, remember?" But she couldn't meet her friend's eyes for fear that Gwen would see the lie.

"Ah, tough," Gwen said, sitting back. "So that's why you're walking around your own home with a gun stashed in the back of your pants."

Maggie winced. Gwen caught it and smiled.

"Now, see, instead of tough," she told Maggie, "I think I would have called it stubborn."

# CHAPTER 8

He couldn't remember pizza delivery girls being so cute back in his younger days when he had worked at the local pizza place. Hell, he couldn't remember there being delivery girls back then.

He watched her hurry up the sidewalk, strands of long blond hair trailing behind her. She had her hair in a cute ponytail—sticking out the back of her blue baseball cap, a Chicago Cubs cap. He wondered if she was a fan. Or maybe her boyfriend was. Surely she had a boyfriend somewhere.

It was too dark now to depend on the streetlights. His eyes were already stinging and a bit blurred. He slipped on the night goggles and adjusted the magnification. Yes, this was good.

He saw her check her watch as she waited on the front porch. This time another man answered the door. Of course, the guy would give her that dumb-ass look of astonishment. The man fished bills out of the pockets of his blue jeans, jeans that sagged at his bulging waist. He was a slob, grimy with sweat stains under the armpits of his T-shirt and a tuft of hair sticking up out the neckline. And yet...yep, there it was, another wiseass remark about how cute she was or what he wouldn't mind tipping her with. But again, she smiled politely, despite the color rising in her cheeks.

Just once he'd like to see her kick one of these idiots in the groin. Maybe that was a lesson he could teach her. If things worked out as he planned, he'd have plenty of time with her.

She hurried away along the winding sidewalk, and the cheap bastard who had tipped her only a dollar, watched her ass the whole trip back to her shiny little Dodge Dart. That sight alone was worth much more than a dollar. The cheap son of a bitch. How the hell was she supposed to put herself through college on dollar tips?

He decided that women were better tippers when it came to delivery services. Maybe they felt some odd sense of guilt for not having prepared the meal themselves. Who knew. Women were complicated, fascinating creatures, and he wouldn't change that if he could.

He replaced the goggles with dark sunglasses, simply out of habit now, and because the oncoming headlights burned his eyes. He waited for the Dodge Dart to reach the intersection before he turned around and followed. She was finished with this batch. He recognized the route back to the pizza place, Mama Mia's on Fifty-ninth and Archer Drive. The cozy joint took up the corner of a neighborhood strip mall. A Pump-N-Go occupied the other entrance. In between were a half-dozen smaller shops, including Mr. Magoo's Videos and Shep's Liquor Mart.

Newburgh Heights was such a friendly little suburb it gagged him. Not much of a challenge. Nor much challenge in the cute pizza delivery girl either. But this wasn't about challenge, it was simply for show.

The girl parked behind the building, near the door, and gathered up the stack of red insulators. She'd be back in a few minutes with another load ready to deliver.

The neon sign for Mama Mia's included a delivery number. He flipped open the cellular phone and dialed the number while he unfolded a real estate flyer. The description promised a four-bedroom colonial with a whirlpool bath and skylight in the master bedroom. How romantic, he mused, just as a woman barked in his ear.

"Mama Mia's."

"I'd like two large pepperoni pizzas delivered."

"Phone number."

"555-4545," he read off the flyer.

"Name and address."

"Heston," he continued reading, "at 5349 Archer Drive."

"Would you like some breadsticks and soda with that?"

"No, just the pizza."

"It'll be about twenty minutes, Mr. Heston."

"Fine." He snapped the phone shut. Twenty minutes would be plenty of time. He pulled on his black leather driving gloves, and then he wiped the phone with a corner of his shirt. As he drove by the Dumpster, he tossed the phone.

He headed south on Archer Drive, thinking about pizza, a moonlit bath and that cute delivery girl with the polite smile and the tight ass.

# CHAPTER 9

Maggie's eyes begged to close. Her shoulders slouched from exhaustion. It was almost midnight by the time Gwen left. Maggie knew she'd never be able to sleep. She had already checked every window latch twice, leaving only a choice few open to keep the wonderful chilly breeze flowing through the main floor. Likewise, she had double-checked the security system several times after Gwen's departure. Now she paced, dreading the night hours, hating the dark and vowing to put up drapes and blinds tomorrow.

Finally she sat back down cross-legged in the middle of the pile created from the contents of Stucky's personal box of horror. She pulled out the folder with newspaper clippings and articles she had downloaded. Ever since Stucky's escape five months ago, she had watched newspaper headlines across the country by using the Internet.

She still couldn't believe how easily Albert Stucky had escaped. On his way to a maximum-security facility—a simple trip that should have taken a couple of hours—Stucky killed two transport guards. Then he disappeared into the Florida Everglades, never to be seen again.

Anyone else may not have been able to survive, having become a nifty snack for some alligator. But knowing Stucky, Maggie imagined him emerging from the Everglades in a three-piece suit and a briefcase made of alligator skin. Yes, Albert Stucky was intelligent and crafty and savvy enough to charm an alligator out of its own skin, and then reward it by slicing it up and feeding it to the other alligators.

She sorted through the most recent articles. Last week, the *Philadelphia Journal* had an article about a woman's torso found in the river, her head and feet found in a Dumpster. It was the closest thing she had seen in months to Stucky's M.O., yet it still didn't feel like him. It was too much. It was overkill. Stucky's handiwork, though inconceivably horrible, had never included chopping away a victim's identity. No, Stucky enjoyed doing that with subtle psychological and mental tricks. Even his extraction of an organ from the victim was not a statement about the victim but rather his attempt to continue the game. Maggie imagined him watching and laughing as some unsuspecting diner found Stucky's appalling surprise, often tucked into an ordinary take-out container and abandoned on an outside café table. It was all a game to Stucky, a morbid, twisted game.

The articles that frightened Maggie more than the ones with missing body parts were the ones of women who had disappeared. Women like her missing neighbor, Rachel Endicott. Intelligent, successful women, some with families, all attractive, and all described as women who would not suddenly leave their lives without telling a soul. Maggie couldn't help wondering if any of them had become part of Stucky's collection. By now he had surely found somewhere isolated, somewhere to start all over again. He had the money and the means. All he needed was time.

She knew Cunningham and his defunct task force, and now his new profiler, were waiting for a body. But if, and when, the bodies did start showing up, they were the ones Stucky killed only for fun. No, the ones they should be looking for were the women he collected. These were the women he tortured—who ended up in remote graves deep in the woods, only after he was completely finished playing his sick games with them. Games that would drag on for days, maybe weeks. The women Stucky chose were never young or naive. No, Stucky enjoyed a challenge. He carefully chose intelligent, mature women. Women who would fight back, not those easily broken. Women he could torture psychologically as well as physically.

Maggie rubbed her eyes. She wanted another Scotch. The two earlier, added to the beer, were already making her head buzz and her vision blur. Though she had brewed a pot of coffee earlier for Gwen, she hated the stuff and stayed away from it. Now she wished she had something to help her stay alert. Something like the Scotch, which she knew was becoming a dangerous anesthetic.

She lifted another file folder and a page fell out. Seeing his handwriting still sent chills down her spine. She picked it up by its corner as though its evil would contaminate her. It had been the first of many notes in the sick game Albert Stucky had played with her. He had written in careful script:

> What challenge is there in breaking a horse without spirit? The challenge is to replace that spirit with fear, raw animal fear that makes one feel alive. Are you ready to feel alive, Margaret O'Dell?

It had been their first insight into the intellect of Albert Stucky, a man whose father had been a prominent doctor. A man who had been afforded all the best schools, all the privileges money could buy. Yet he was thrown out of Yale for almost burning down a women's dormitory. There were other offenses: attempted rape, assault, petty theft. All charges had been either dropped or were never pressed, due to lack of evidence. Stucky had been questioned in the accidental death of his father, a freak boating accident though the man had supposedly been an expert yachtsman.

Then, about six or seven years ago, Albert Stucky took up a business partner, and the two of them succeeded in creating one of the Internet's first stock-market trading sites. Stucky became a respectable businessman, and a multimillionaire.

Despite all of Maggie's research, she never felt certain about what had set Stucky off in the first place. What had been the event, the precursor? Usually with serial killers, their crimes were precipitated by some stressor. An event, a death, a rejection, an abuse that one day made them decide to kill. She didn't know what that had been for Stucky. Perhaps evil simply couldn't be harnessed. And Stucky's evil was especially terrifying.

Most serial killers murdered because it gave them pleasure, some form of gratification. It was a choice, not necessarily a sickness of the mind. But for Albert Stucky, the kill was not enough. His pleasure came from psychologically breaking down his victims, turning them into sniveling, pleading wretches—owning them body, mind and soul. He enjoyed breaking their spirit, turning it into fear. Then he rewarded his victims with a slow, torturous death. Ironically, those he killed immediately, those whose throats he slashed and whose bodies he discarded in Dumpsters—only after extracting a token organ—those were the lucky ones.

The phone startled her. She grabbed the Smith & Wesson .38 that sat by her side. Again, it was a simple reflex. It was late, and few people had her new number. She had refused to give it to the pizza place. She had even insisted Greg use her cell phone number. Maybe Gwen had forgotten something. From the floor, she reached up to the desktop and pulled the phone down.

"Yes?" she said, her muscles tense. She wondered when she had stopped answering hello.

"Agent O'Dell?"

She recognized Assistant Director Cunningham's matter-of-fact tone, but the tension did not leave her.

"Yes, sir."

"I couldn't remember if you were already using the new number."

"I just moved in today."

She glanced at her wristwatch. It was now after midnight. They spoke infrequently these days, ever since he had taken her out of the field and assigned her to training duty. Was it possible he had some information on Stucky? She sat up with an unexpected flutter of hope.

"Is there something wrong?"

"I'm sorry, Agent O'Dell. I just realized how late it is."

She imagined him still at this desk at Quantico, never mind that it was Friday night.

"That's quite all right, sir. You didn't wake me."

"I thought you might be leaving for Kansas City tomorrow, and I didn't want to miss you."

"I leave on Sunday." She kept the question, the anticipation from her voice as best she could. If he needed her to stay, she knew Stewart was able to fill in for her at the law enforcement conference. "Does there need to be a change to my schedule?"

"No, not at all. I just wanted to make sure. I did, however, receive a phone call earlier this evening that gave me great concern."

Maggie imagined a body, sliced and left for some unsuspecting person to find beneath the trash. She waited for him to give her the details.

"A Detective Manx from the Newburgh Heights Police Department called me."

Maggie's anticipation quickly dissipated.

"He told me that you interfered with a crime scene investigation this afternoon. Is that true?"

Maggie reached to rub her eyes again, only now realizing she still gripped the revolver. She put it aside and sat back, feeling defeated. Damn that prick, Manx.

"Agent O'Dell? Is that true?"

"I just moved into the neighborhood this afternoon. I noticed police cruisers at the end of the block. I thought perhaps I could help."

"So you did barge in uninvited on a crime scene."

"I did not barge in. I offered my help."

"That's not the way Detective Manx described it."

"No, I don't imagine it is."

"I want you to stay out of the field, Agent O'Dell."

"But I was able to—"

"Out of the field means you don't go using your credentials to walk onto crime scenes. Even if they are in your own neighborhood. Is that understood?"

She ran her fingers through her tangled hair. How dare Manx. He wouldn't have discovered the dog, had it not been for her.

"Agent O'Dell, is that clear?"

"Yes. Yes, it's perfectly clear," she said, almost expecting an additional reprimand for the sarcasm in her voice.

"Have a safe trip," he said in his usual abrupt manner and then hung up.

She threw the phone onto the desktop and began rifling through the files. The tension tightened in her back, her neck and shoulders. She stood up and stretched, noticing the anger still slamming in her chest. Damn Manx! Damn Cunningham! How long did he think he could keep her out of the field? How long did he intend to punish her for being vulnerable? And how could he ever expect to catch Stucky without her help?

Maggie reset the security system a third time, double-checking the red On light, even though the mechanical voice told her each time, "Alarm system has been activated." The hell with the buzz in her head. She poured another Scotch and convinced herself that one more would surely relieve the tension.

The mess stayed scattered on the living-room floor. It seemed appropriate that her new home be initiated with a pile of blood and horror. She retreated to the sunroom, grabbing her revolver and snatching an afghan from a box in the corner, wrapping it around her shoulders. She shut off all the lights, except the one on the desk. Then she curled into the recliner that now faced the wall of windows.

She cradled and sipped the Scotch as she watched the moon slip in and out of the clouds, making shadows dance in her new backyard. In her other hand she gripped the revolver resting in her lap, tucked under the cover. Despite the progressive blur behind her eyes, she would be ready. Perhaps Assistant Director Cunningham couldn't stop Albert Stucky from coming for her, but she sure as hell would. And this time, it would be Stucky's turn for a surprise.

# CHAPTER 10

*Reston, Virginia*
*Saturday evening*
*March 28*

R. J. Tully peeled off another ten-dollar bill and slid it under the ticket window. When had movie tickets started costing $8.50 each? He tried to remember the last time he had been to a movie theater on a Saturday night. He tried to remember when he had last been to a movie theater, period. Surely he and Caroline had gone some time during their thirteen-year marriage. Though it would have been early on—before she began preferring her co-workers to him.

He glanced around to find Emma dawdling far behind him, off to the side and at least three moviegoers back. Sometimes he wondered who the hell this person was. This beautiful, tall fourteen-year-old with silky blond hair and the beginnings of a shapely body she blatantly emphasized with tight jeans and a tight knit sweater. She looked more and more like her mother every day. God, he missed the days when this same girl held his hand and jumped into his arms, anxious to go anywhere with him. But just like her mother, that too had changed.

He waited for her at the ticket taker and wondered how she'd be able to sit next to him for two hours. He saw her eyes dart around the crowded lobby. Immediately, his heart sank. She didn't want any of her new friends to see her on a Saturday night, going to a movie with her dad. Was she really that embarrassed by him? He couldn't remember ever feeling that way about either of his parents. No wonder he spent so many hours at work. At the moment, understanding serial killers seemed much easier than understanding fourteen-year-old girls.

"How 'bout some popcorn?" he offered.

"Popcorn has, like, tons of fat."

"I don't think you have a thing to worry about, Sweet Pea."

"Oh my God, Dad!"

He stopped abruptly, checking to see if he had stepped on her toes. She sounded so pained.

"Don't call me that," she whispered.

He smiled down at her, which seemed to embarrass her more.

"Okay, so no popcorn for you. How about a Pepsi?"

"Diet Pepsi," she corrected him.

Surprisingly, she waited next to him in line at the concession stand, but her eyes still roamed the crowded lobby. It had been almost two months since Emma had come to live with him full-time. The truth was, he saw even less of her than when they were all back in Cleveland, and he was only a weekend dad. At least then they did things together, trying to make up for lost time.

When they first moved to Virginia he had tried to make sure they had dinner together every night, but he was the first to break that routine. His new job at Quantico had swallowed up much more of his time than he realized. So in addition to he and Emma settling into a new home, a new job, a new school and a new city, she also had to get used to not having her mother.

He still couldn't believe that Caroline had agreed to the arrangement. Maybe when she got tired of playing CEO by day, and the dating game by night, she would want her daughter back in her life full-time.

He watched Emma's quick, nervous swipes at the misbehaving strands of her long hair. Her eyes were still casing the theater. He wondered if fighting for full custody had been a mistake. He knew she missed her mother, even if her mother had been less available to her than he was. Damn it! Why did this parenting thing have to be so damn hard?

He almost ordered buttered popcorn, but stopped himself and ordered plain, hoping Emma might change her mind and snitch some.

"And two medium Diet Pepsis."

He looked to see if she was impressed by her influence on

him. Instead, her light complexion paled, as discomfort converted to panic.

"Oh my God! It's Josh Reynolds."

Now she stood so close, Tully had to take a step back to collect their sodas and popcorn.

"Oh God! I hope he didn't see me."

"Who's Josh Reynolds?"

"Just one of the coolest kids in the junior class."

"Let's say hi."

"Dad! Oh God, maybe he didn't see me."

She stood facing Tully, her back to the young, dark-haired boy who was making his way toward them, his destination definitely Emma. And why shouldn't it be? His daughter was a knockout. Tully wondered if Emma was really panicked or if this was part of the game. He honestly had no clue. He didn't understand women, so how could he possibly expect to understand their predecessors?

"Emma? Emma Tully?"

The boy was closing in. Tully watched in amazement as his daughter manufactured a nervous but glowing smile from the twisted panic that had existed just seconds before. She turned just as Josh Reynolds squeezed through the concession line.

"Hi, Josh."

Tully glanced down to check if some impostor had replaced his obstinate daughter. Because this girl's voice was much too cheerful.

"What movie you seeing?"

"*Ace of Hearts,*" she admitted reluctantly though it had been her choice.

"Me too. My mom wants to see it," he added much too quickly.

Tully found himself sympathizing with the boy, who shoved his hands into his pockets. What Emma called cool visibly took effort. Or was Tully the only one who could see the boy nervously tapping his foot and fidgeting? After an awkward silence and them ignoring his presence, Tully said, "Hi, Josh, I'm R. J. Tully, Emma's father."

"Hi, Mr. Tully."

"I'd offer you a hand, but they're both filled."

Out of the corner of his eye he could see Emma roll her eyes. How could that possibly embarrass her? He was being polite. Just then his pager began shrieking. Josh offered to take the sodas before it even occurred to Emma. Tully snapped the noise off, but not before getting several irritated stares. Emma turned a lovely shade of red. At a glance, he recognized the phone number. Of all nights, why tonight?

"I need to make a phone call."

"Are you a doctor or something, Mr. Tully?"

"No, Josh. I'm an FBI agent."

"You're kidding? That is so cool."

The boy's face brightened, and Tully saw that Emma noticed. Instead of heading directly for the phone bank, Tully stalled.

"I work at Quantico, in the Investigative Support Unit. I'm what you'd call a criminal profiler."

"Wow! That is so cool," Josh repeated.

Without looking at her, Tully saw Emma's face change as she watched Josh's reaction.

"So do you track serial killers just like in the movies?"

"I'm afraid the movies make it look more glamorous than it is."

"Geez! I bet you've seen some pretty weird stuff, though, huh?"

"Unfortunately, yes, I have. I really need to make a phone call. Josh, would you mind keeping Emma company for a few minutes?"

"Oh sure. No, problem, Mr. Tully."

He didn't look at Emma again until he was safely at the pay phone. Suddenly, his belligerent daughter was full of smiles, genuine this time. He watched the two teenagers talk and laugh while he dialed the number. For the first time in a long time, he felt happy and glad that Emma was with him. For a few minutes, he had almost forgotten that the world could be cruel and violent, then he heard Assistant Director Cunningham's voice.

"It's Tully, sir. You paged me?"

"Looks like we may have one of Stucky's."

Tully felt instant nausea. He had been anticipating and dreading this call for the last couple of months.

"Where at, sir?"

"Right under our noses. About thirty to forty-five minutes from here. Can you pick me up in about an hour? We can go to the site together."

Without asking, Tully knew Cunningham meant picking him up at Quantico. He wondered if the man ever went home.

"Sure. I'll be there."

"I'll see you in an hour."

This was it. After years of sitting behind a desk in Cleveland and profiling killers from afar, this was his chance to prove himself and join the real hunters. So why did he feel sick to his stomach?

Tully made his way back to his daughter and her friend, anticipating her disappointment.

"I'm sorry, Emma, I've got to leave."

Immediately, her eyes grew dark, her smile slid off her face.

"Josh, did you say you were here with your mom?"

"Yeah, she's getting us popcorn." He pointed to an attractive redhead in the line. When she noticed Josh pointing, she smiled at him and shrugged at the stagnant line in front of her.

"Josh, Emma, would you mind if I ask Josh's mom if Emma could join you for the movie?" Tully steeled himself for his daughter's panic and horror.

"No, that would be cool," Josh said without hesitating, and Emma immediately seemed pleased.

"Sure, Dad," she said.

Tully wondered if she knew how cool she was pretending to be right now.

When he introduced himself to Jennifer Reynolds, she also seemed pleased to help him out. He offered to repay her another night by treating all of them to another movie. Then he kicked himself when he noticed her wedding band. But Jennifer Reynolds accepted his offer without hesitation, and with a flirtatious look that even an out-of-practice, newly single guy didn't need to decipher. Despite his curiosity, he couldn't help feeling a bit excited.

He smiled all the way to his car, greeting people in the parking lot and jingling his car keys. The evening was still warm and the moon promised to be brilliant despite wisps of clouds. He slid behind the steering wheel and checked his reflection in the rearview mirror, as though he had forgotten the configuration of his face when it was happy. What an unusual feeling, happiness and excitement, and all in the same evening. Two things he hadn't felt in years, though he knew both would be short-lived. He drove out of the theater's parking lot feeling he could take on anything and anyone. Maybe even Albert Stucky.

# CHAPTER 11

Tully followed Cunningham's directions and turned at the intersection. Immediately, he saw spotlights in the back alley of a small strip mall. Police cruisers blocked the street, and Tully pulled up beside one, flashed his badge and drove through the maze. He tried to take a lesson from his daughter's new friend Josh by pretending to be cool. Fact was, his stomach felt hollow and perspiration slid down his back.

Tully had seen plenty of crime scenes, severed limbs, bloodied walls, mutilated bodies and sick, disgusting killer signatures that ranged from a single long-stemmed rose to a decapitated corpse. But all those scenes, up until now, had been only in photographs, digital scans and illustrations sent to him at the FBI Cleveland Field Office. He had become one of the Midwest's experts in developing precise criminal profiles from the bits and pieces law enforcement officers sent him. It was his accuracy that had prompted Assistant Director Kyle Cunningham to offer Tully a position at Quantico in the Investigative Support Unit. In one phone call and without ever having met him, Cunningham had offered Tully a chance to work out in the field, starting with the hunt for one of the FBI's most infamous fugitives—Albert Stucky.

Tully knew Cunningham had been forced to dismantle the task force after months of nothing to show for their time and expense. He also knew he owed his good fortune to the agent he had replaced, an agent who had been temporarily assigned to teaching at law enforcement conferences. Without much digging, he discovered the agent was Margaret O'Dell, whom he had never met but knew by reputation. She was one of the youngest and one of the best profilers in the country.

The unofficial word was that O'Dell had burned out and

needed a break. Rumors suggested that she had lost her edge, that she was combative and reckless, that she had become paranoid and obsessed with recapturing Albert Stucky. Of course, there were also rumors that Assistant Director Cunningham had sidelined Margaret O'Dell to protect her from Stucky. The two had played a dangerous game of cat and mouse about eight months ago that had eventually led to Stucky's capture, but only after he had tortured and almost killed O'Dell. Now after months of studying, searching and waiting, Tully would finally meet the man nicknamed The Collector, if only through his handiwork.

Tully pulled the car as close to the barricades as he could. Cunningham jumped out before Tully had it in park. He almost forgot to turn off the lights. He noticed his palms were sweaty when he pulled the key from the ignition. His legs seemed stiff, his knee suddenly reminding him of an old injury as he hurried to catch up with his boss. Tully stood four inches taller than the assistant director, and his strides were long, yet it took an effort to keep up. He guessed Cunningham to be at least ten years his senior, but the man had a lean, athletic body, and Tully had witnessed him bench-pressing twice the weight the academy recruits started at.

"Where is she?" Cunningham wasted no time asking a police detective who looked to be in charge.

"She's still in the Dumpster. We haven't moved a thing, except the pizza box."

The detective had a neck as thick as a linebacker's and the seams of his sports jacket bulged. He was treating this like an everyday traffic check. Tully wondered which big city the detective had come from, because he definitely had developed his no-nonsense manner somewhere other than Newburgh Heights. He and the assistant director seemed to know one another and took no time for introductions.

"Where is the pizza box?" Cunningham wanted to know.

"Officer McClusky gave it to the doc. The kid who found it sorta dropped it, and the stuff got all jostled."

Suddenly the smell of stale pizza and the sounds of police radios made Tully's head hurt. During the drive, the adrenaline had pumped him into action. Now the reality was a bit overwhelming. He ran unsteady fingers through his hair. Okay, this couldn't be that much different than looking at photos. He could do this, and he ignored the recurring nausea as he followed his boss to the Dumpster where three uniformed officers stood guard. Even the officers stood a good ten feet away to avoid the stench.

The first thing Tully noticed was the young woman's long blond hair. Immediately, he thought of Emma. He could see over the Dumpster's edge easily, but waited as Cunningham pulled up a crate. His boss's face remained emotionless.

Though covered in garbage, Tully could tell the woman had been young, not much older than Emma. And she had been beautiful. Discarded lettuce and spoiled tomatoes clung to her naked breasts. The rest of her was buried in garbage, but Tully saw glimpses of thigh, and then realized she wore only a blue baseball cap. He could also see that her throat had been slashed from ear to ear, and there was an open wound in her side, almost at her lower back. But that was all. There were no severed limbs, no bloody mutilation. He wasn't sure what he had expected.

"She looks like she's in one piece," Cunningham said as though reading Tully's thoughts. He stepped off the crate and then addressed the detective again. "What was in the box?"

"Not sure. Looked like a bloody glob to me. Doc can probably tell you. He's over in the van."

He pointed to a dusty silver van marked with the Stafford County emblem on the side. The doors were open and a distinguished gray-haired man in a well-pressed suit sat in the back with a clipboard.

"Doc, these gentlemen from the FBI need to see that special delivery."

The detective turned and started to leave just as a media van pulled into an adjacent parking lot.

"Excuse me, gentlemen. Looks like the zoo visitors have arrived."

Cunningham stepped up into the van, and Tully followed, though it seemed crowded with the three of them. Or was Tully the only one having problems breathing? Already he could smell the contents of the box, which sat in the middle of the floor. He sat on one of the benches before his stomach started to churn.

"Hello, Frank." Assistant Director Cunningham knew the medical examiner, too. "This is Special Agent R. J. Tully. Agent Tully, Dr. Frank Holmes, deputy chief medical examiner for Stafford County."

"I don't know if this is your man, Kyle, but when Detective Rosen called me, he seemed to think you might be interested."

"Rosen worked in Boston when Stucky kidnapped Councilwoman Brenda Carson."

"I remember that. What was that two, three years ago?"

"Not quite two."

"Thankfully, I was on vacation. Fishing up in Canada." The doctor cocked his head as though trying to remember some sporting event. Tully found everyone's ease, all the casualness, a bit unnerving. He sat still, hoping no one could hear his heart pounding. The doctor continued. "But now if I remember right, Carson's body was buried in a shallow grave in some woods. Outside Richmond, wasn't it? Certainly not in some Dumpster."

"This guy's complicated, Frank. The ones he collects are the ones we rarely find. These women...these are his rejects. They're simply for sport—for show-and-tell." Cunningham sat forward, leaning his elbows on his knees, the balls of his feet rocking as though ready to jump into action at any moment. Everything about Cunningham telescoped his constant energy, his immediacy. Yet, his face, his voice remained calm, almost soothing.

Tully stared at the pizza box on the floor of the van. Despite the scent of pizza dough and pepperoni, he recognized the acrid scent as blood. So much for eating pizza ever again.

"Nothing happens in this quiet little suburb," Dr. Holmes said while continuing to jot details on the forms he had clipped to his board. "Then two homicides in one day."

"Two?" Cunningham's patience seemed to wear thin with the doctor's slow, deliberate manner. He stared at the pizza box, and Tully knew his boss wouldn't touch it without first being invited to do so by Dr. Holmes. Tully had discovered early on that despite the director's authority, he showed great respect for those he worked with, as well as for rules, policy and protocol.

"I'm not aware of another homicide, Frank," he said when the doctor took too long to offer an explanation.

"Well, I'm not sure the other one is a homicide, yet. We never did find a body." Dr. Holmes finally put the clipboard aside. "We had an agent on the scene. Maybe one of yours?"

"Excuse me?"

"Yesterday afternoon. Not far from here in the nice quiet neighborhood of Newburgh Heights. Said she was a forensic psychologist. Just moved into the victim's neighborhood. Very impressive young woman."

Tully watched Cunningham's face and saw the transformation from calm to agitated.

"Yes, I did hear about that. I had forgotten her new neighborhood was in Newburgh Heights. I apologize if she got in the way."

"Oh, no apology necessary, Kyle. On the contrary, she proved very helpful. I think the arrogant bastard who was supposed to be investigating the scene may have even learned a thing or two."

Tully caught the assistant director with a smile at the corner of his lips, before he realized he was being watched. He turned to Tully and explained, "Agent O'Dell, your predecessor, just bought a new home in this area."

"Agent Margaret O'Dell?" Tully held his boss's eyes until he saw that Cunningham had now made the same connection Tully had just made. Both of them stared at Dr. Holmes as he slid the pizza box closer. Suddenly, Tully knew it didn't matter what they found in the box. Whatever had been discarded, neither of them needed to see the bloody mess to confirm that this was most likely the work of Albert Stucky. And Tully knew it was no coincidence that he had chosen to start again, close to Agent Margaret O'Dell's new home.

# CHAPTER 12

Exhaustion seeped into his bones and threatened to incapacitate him by the time he returned to the safety of his room. He shed his clothes with minimal movement, letting the fabric slide off his lean body, though what he really wanted to do was rip and tear. His body disgusted him. It had taken almost twice as long for him to come this time. Of all the fucking things he had to deal with, that one was the most annoying.

His fingers fumbled through his duffel bag, searching frantically, tossing items haphazardly to the floor. Suddenly, he stopped when he felt the smooth cylinder. Relief washed over him, chilling his sweat-drenched body.

The fatigue had moved to his fingers. It took three attempts to snap off the plastic cap and poke the needle into the orange rubber top of the vial. He hated not having complete control. The anger and the irritability only added to his nausea. He steadied his hands as best he could and watched the syringe suck the liquid from the vial.

He sat on the edge of the bed, his knees weak and perspiration sliding down his naked back. In one quick motion he stuck the needle into his thigh, forcing the colorless liquid into his bloodstream. Then he lay back and waited, closing his eyes against the red lines that jetted across his field of vision. In his mind he could hear the blood vessels popping—pop, pop, pop! The thought might drive him completely mad before it drove him completely blind.

Through closed eyelids he was aware of the flickers of lightning that invaded his dimly lit room. A rumble of thunder vibrated the window. Then the rain began again, soft and gentle, tapping out a lullaby.

Yes, his body disgusted him. He had pushed it to be strong and lean, using weights, steel machines and gut-wrenching wind sprints. He ate nutritious meals high in protein and vitamins. He had freed himself of all toxins including caffeine, alcohol and nicotine. Yet, his body still failed him, screaming out its limitations and reminding him of its imperfections.

It had only been three short months since he had noticed any of the symptoms. The first ones were simply annoying, the eternal thirst and the constant urge to piss. Who knew how long this damn thing had been lying dormant inside him, ready to strike at just the right moment.

Of course, it would be this one abnormality that would eventually do him in, a gift from his greedy mother whom he had never even known. The bitch would have to give him something that could destroy him.

He sat up, ignoring the slight dizziness in his head, his vision still blurred. The lapses came more often and were getting harder and harder to predict. Whatever the limitations, he refused to let them interfere with the game.

The rain tapped more persistently now. The lightning came in constant flickers. It made the room crawl with movement. Dusty objects sprang to life, jerky miniature robots. The whole frickin' room jumped and jerked.

He grabbed the lamp on the bedstand and twisted it on, making the movement halt in the yellow glow. In the light, he could see the heap from his spilled duffel bag. Socks, shaving kit, T-shirts, several knives, a scalpel and a Glock 9 mm lay scattered on the plush carpet. He ignored the familiar buzz that had begun to invade his head, and rifled through the mess, stopping when he found the pink panties. He rubbed the soft silk against his bristled jaw, then breathed in their scent, a lovely combination of talcum powder, come and pizza.

He noticed the real estate flyer crumpled under the pile and pulled it out, unfolding it and smoothing its wrinkles. The eight-and-half-by-eleven sheet of paper included a color photo of the beautiful colonial house, a detailed description of its amenities and the shiny blue logo of Heston Realty. The house had definitely lived up to its promises, and he was sure it would continue to do so.

At the bottom corner of the flyer was a small photo of an attractive woman, trying to look professional despite something...what was it in her eyes? There was an insecurity, something that made her look uncomfortable in her cute conservative white blouse and navy blue suit. His thumb rubbed over her face, smudging the ink and dragging a trail of black and blue over her skin. That looked better. Yes, already he could feel her vulnerability. Perhaps he could see and feel it only because he had spent so much time watching her, had taken time to study and examine her. He wondered what it was that Tess McGowan was trying so hard to hide.

He walked across the room, taking slow, deliberate steps deciding not to get angry because his knees were still weak. He tacked the flyer to the bulletin board. Then, as if the memory of Tess and those shapely legs of hers had reminded him, he slid a box out from under the table. Unfortunately, movers were so negligent these days. Going off and taking breaks without tending to the precious possessions left in their care. He smiled as he broke the packaging tape and then flipped off the lid that was marked "M. O'Dell."

He took out the yellowed newspaper clippings: Firefighter Sacrifices Life, Trust Fund Established for Hero. What a horrible way for her to lose her father, in a hellish fire.

"Do you dream about him, Maggie O'Dell?" he whispered. "Do you imagine the flames licking off his skin?"

He wondered if he had finally found an Achilles' heel to the brave, unflinching Special Agent O'Dell.

He set the articles aside. Underneath, he discovered a bigger treasure—a leather appointment book. He flipped to the upcoming week, immediately disappointed. The anger returned as he double-checked the penciled notation. She would be in Kansas City at a law enforcement conference. Then he calmed himself and smiled again. Maybe it was better this way. Still, what a shame Agent O'Dell would miss his debut in Newburgh Heights.

# CHAPTER 13

*Sunday, March 29*

Maggie unpacked the last of the boxes labeled Kitchen, carefully washing, drying and placing the crystal goblets on the top cupboard shelf. It still surprised her that Greg had allowed her the set of eight. He claimed they had been a wedding gift from one of her relatives, though Maggie didn't know anyone remotely related to her who could afford such an expensive gift or have such elegant taste. Her own mother had given them a toaster oven, a practical gift void of sentiment, which more likely reflected the characteristics of the O'Dells she knew.

The goblets reminded her that she needed to call her mother and give her the new phone number. Immediately, she felt the familiar tightness in her chest. Of course, there would be no need for the new address. Her mother rarely left Richmond and wouldn't be visiting any time soon. Maggie cringed at the mere thought of her mother invading this new sanctuary. Even the obligatory phone call felt obtrusive to her quiet Sunday. But she should call before leaving for the airport. After years, flying still unhinged her, so why not take her mind off being out of control at thirty thousand feet with a conversation that was sure to clench her teeth?

Her fingers moved reluctantly over the numbers. How could this woman still make her feel like a twelve-year-old caretaker, vulnerable and anxious? Yet, Maggie had been more mature and competent at twelve than her mother ever was.

The phone rang six, seven times, and Maggie was ready to hang up when a low, raspy voice muttered something incomprehensible.

"Mom? It's Maggie," she said in place of a greeting.

"Mag-pie, I was just going to call you."

Maggie grimaced, hearing her mother use the nickname her father had given her. The only time her mother called her Magpie was when she was drunk. Now Maggie wished she could just hang up. Her mother couldn't call her without the new number. Maybe she wouldn't even remember this call.

"You wouldn't have gotten me, Mom. I just moved."

"Mag-pie, I want you to tell your father to stop calling me."

Maggie's knees buckled. She leaned against the counter.

"What are you talking about, Mom?"

"Your father keeps calling me, saying stuff and then just hanging up."

The counter wasn't good enough. Maggie made it to the step stool and sat down. The sudden nausea and chill surprised and annoyed her. She placed her palm against her stomach as if that would calm it.

"Mom, Dad's gone. He's been dead for over twenty years." She gripped a kitchen towel, the nearest thing she could lay her hands on. My God, could this be some new dementia brought on by the drinking?

"Oh, I know that, sweetie." Her mother giggled.

Maggie couldn't ever remember her mother giggling. Was this a sick joke? She closed her eyes and waited, not sure there would be an explanation, but certain she had no idea how to continue this conversation.

"Reverend Everett says it's because your father still has something he needs to tell me. But hell, he keeps hanging up. Oh, I shouldn't swear," and she giggled, again.

"Mom, who's Reverend Everett?"

"Reverend Joseph Everett. I told you about him, Mag-pie."

"No, you haven't told me anything about him."

"I'm sure I have. Oh, Emily and Steven are here. I've got to go."

"Mom, wait. Mom..." But it was too late. Her mother had already hung up.

Maggie dragged her fingers through her short hair, resisting the urge to yank. It had only been a week...okay, maybe two weeks, since she had talked to her last. How could she be making so little sense? She thought about calling her back. She hadn't even given her the new phone number. But then her mother wasn't in any condition to remember it. Maybe Emily and Steven or Reverend Everett—whoever the hell these people were—maybe they could take care of her. Maggie had been taking care of her mother for far too long. Maybe it was finally someone else's turn.

The fact her mother was drinking again didn't surprise Maggie. Years ago, she had accepted the compromise. At least when her mother was drinking she wasn't attempting suicide. But that her mother thought she was talking to her dead husband disturbed Maggie. Plus, she hated the reminder that the one person who had truly loved her, loved her unconditionally, had been dead for more than twenty years.

Maggie tugged the chain around her neck and brought out the medallion from under her shirt collar. Her father had given her the silver cross for her First Holy Communion, claiming it would protect her from evil. Yet, Maggie couldn't help remembering that his own identical cross had not saved him when he ran into that burning building. She often wondered if he had honestly believed it would protect him.

Since then Maggie had witnessed enough evil to know that a body armor of silver crosses would never be enough to protect her. Instead, she wore the medallion out of remembrance for her brave father. The medal against her chest dangled between her breasts and often felt as cool and hard as a knife blade. She let it remind her that there was a fine line between good and evil.

In the last nine years she had learned plenty about evil, its power to destroy completely, to leave behind empty shells that once were warm, breathing individuals. All those lessons were meant to train her to fight it, to control it, to eventually annihilate it. But in doing so, it was necessary to follow evil, to live as evil lives, to think as evil thinks. Was it possible that somewhere along the way evil had invaded her without her realizing it? Was that why she felt so much hatred, so much need for vengeance? Was that why she felt so hollow?

The doorbell rang, and again Maggie had her Smith & Wesson in her hand before she realized it. She tucked the revolver into what was becoming its regular spot, the back waistband of her jeans. Absentmindedly, she pulled down her T-shirt to conceal it.

She didn't recognize the petite brunette standing on her front portico. Maggie's eyes searched the street, the expanse between houses, the shadows created by trees and bushes before she moved to disarm the security system. She wasn't sure what she expected. Did she honestly believe Albert Stucky would have followed her to her new house?

"Yes?" she asked, opening the door only wide enough to place her body in the space.

"Hi!" the woman said with a false cheerfulness.

Dressed in a black-and-white knit cardigan and matching skirt, she looked ready for an evening out. Her dark shoulder-length hair didn't dare move in the breeze. Her makeup enhanced thin lips and concealed laugh lines. The diamond necklace, earrings and wedding ring were modest and tasteful, but Maggie recognized how expensive they were. Okay, so at least the woman wasn't trying to sell anything. Still, Maggie waited while the woman's eyes darted around her, hoping for a glimpse beyond the front door.

"I'm Susan Lyndell. I live next door." She pointed to the split-timber house, only a corner of its front roof visible from Maggie's portico.

"Hello, Ms. Lyndell."

"Oh, please call me Susan."

"I'm Maggie O'Dell."

Maggie opened the door a few inches more and offered her hand, but stayed solidly in the doorway. Surely the woman didn't expect an invitation inside. Then she caught her new neighbor glance toward her own house and back at the street. It was a nervous, anxious look, as though she was afraid of being seen.

"I saw you on Friday." She sounded uncomfortable, and it was obvious she wasn't here to welcome Maggie to the neighborhood. There was something else on her mind.

"Yes, I moved in on Friday."

"Actually I didn't see you move in," she said, quick to make the distinction. "I mean at Rachel's. I saw you at Rachel Endicott's house." The woman stepped closer and kept her voice soft and calm even though her hands were now gripping the hem of her cardigan.

"Oh."

"I'm a friend of Rachel's. I know that the police..." She stopped and glanced this time in both directions. "I know they're saying Rachel may have just left on her own, but I don't think she would do that."

"Did you tell Detective Manx that?"

"Detective Manx?"

"He's in charge of the investigation, Ms. Lyndell. I was simply there trying to lend a hand as a concerned neighbor."

"But you're with the FBI, right? I thought I heard someone say that."

"Yes, but I wasn't there in an official capacity. If you have any information, I suggest you talk to Detective Manx."

All Maggie needed was to step on Manx's toes again. Cunningham had already questioned her competency, her judgment. She wouldn't let some prick like Manx make matters worse. However, Susan Lyndell didn't seem pleased with Maggie's advice. Instead, she stalled, fidgeting, her eyes darting around while she seemed to become more and more agitated.

"I know this is an awkward introduction, and I certainly apologize, but if I could just talk to you for a few minutes. May I come in?"

Her gut told her to send Susan Lyndell home, to insist she call the police and talk to Manx. Yet, for some reason she found herself letting the woman into her foyer, but no farther.

"I have a flight to catch later this afternoon," Maggie allowed impatience to show in her voice. "As you can see I haven't had time to unpack, let alone pack for a business trip."

"Yes, I understand. It's quite possible I'm simply being paranoid."

"You don't believe Ms. Endicott just left town for a couple of days? Maybe to get away?

Susan Lyndell's eyes met Maggie's and held her.

"I know there was something...something in the house that suggests Rachel didn't do that."

"Ms. Lyndell, I don't know what you've heard—"

"It's okay." She stopped Maggie with a wave of a small hand, long slender fingers that reminded Maggie of a bird's wing. "I know you can't divulge anything you may have seen." She fidgeted again, shifting her weight from one foot to another as though her high-heeled pumps were the cause of her discomfort. "Look, I don't have to be a rocket scientist to know that it's not routine for three police cruisers and the county medical examiner to come rescue an injured dog. Even if it belongs to the wife of Sidney Endicott."

Maggie didn't recognize the man's name nor did she care. The less she knew about the Endicotts, the easier it would be to keep out of this case. She crossed her arms over her chest and waited. Susan Lyndell seemed to interpret it as having Maggie's full attention.

"I think Rachel was meeting someone. I think this someone may have taken her against her will."

"Why do you say that?"

"Rachel met a man last week."

"What do you mean she met a man?"

"I don't want you to get the wrong impression. It's not something she's in the habit of doing." She said this quickly, as if needing to justify her friend's actions. "It just sort of happened. You know how that is." She waited for some sign of agreement from Maggie. When there was none, she hurried on. "Rachel said there was this...well, she described the guy as wild and exciting. It was strictly a physical attraction. I'm sure she had no intention of ever leaving Sidney," she added as though needing to convince herself.

"Ms. Endicott was having an affair?"

"Oh God, no, but I think she was tempted. As far as I know, it was just some heavy-duty flirting."

"How do you know all this?"

Susan avoided Maggie's eyes, pretending to watch outside the window.

"Rachel and I were friends."

Maggie didn't point out that Susan had suddenly switched to past tense. "How did she meet him?" she asked, instead.

"He's been working in the area for the last week or so. On the phone lines. Something to do with new cable that's going to be laid. I haven't heard much about it. It seems like they're constantly putting in something new and different in this area."

"Why do think this man may have taken Rachel against her will?"

"It sounded like he was getting serious, trying to escalate their flirting. You know how guys like that can be. They really just want one thing. And for some reason they always seem to think us lonely, rich wives are more than ready to let them—" She stopped herself, realizing she may have revealed more than she intended. Immediately, she looked away, her face a bit flushed, and Maggie knew Susan Lyndell was no longer talking about her friend, but speaking from experience. "Well, let's just say," she continued, "that I have a hunch this guy wanted more from Rachel than she meant to give him."

The image of the bedroom came to Maggie. Had Rachel Endicott invited a telephone repairman to her bedroom and then changed her mind?

"So you think she may have invited him in and that things got carried away?"

"Isn't there something in the house that makes it look that way?"

Maggie hesitated. Were Susan Lyndell and Rachel Endicott really friends, or was Susan simply looking for some juicy gossip to share with the other neighbors?

Finally Maggie said, "Yes, there is something that makes it look like Rachel was taken from the house. That's all I can tell you."

Susan paled beneath the carefully applied makeup and leaned against the wall as though needing the support. This time, her response seemed genuine.

"I think you need to tell the police," Maggie told her again.

"No," she said quickly, and immediately her face grew scarlet. "I mean, I...I'm not even sure she met him. I wouldn't want Rachel to get in trouble with Sid."

"Then you need to at least tell them about the telephone repairman so they can question him. Have you seen him in the area?"

"Actually, I've never seen him. Just his van once—Northeastern Bell Telephone Company. I'd hate to have him lose his job because of my hunch."

Maggie studied the woman who clutched and wrung the hem of her cardigan. Susan Lyndell didn't care about some nameless repairman's job.

"Then why are you telling me all this, Ms. Lyndell? What do you expect me to do?"

"I just thought...well..." She leaned against the wall again, and seemed flustered that she had no clue what she expected. Yet, she made a weak effort to continue. "You're with the FBI. I thought maybe you could find out or do a check...you know, discreetly without...well, I guess I don't know."

Maggie let the silence hang between them as she examined the woman's discomfort, her embarrassment.

"Rachel's not the only one who's flirted with a repairman, is she, Ms. Lyndell? Are you afraid of your husband finding out? Is that it?"

She didn't need to answer. The anguished look in Susan Lyndell's eyes told Maggie she was right. And she wondered if Ms. Lyndell would even call Detective Manx, though she promised to as she turned and left, hurrying away, her head pivoting with worried glances.

# CHAPTER 14

Tess McGowan smiled at the wine steward who waited patiently. Daniel had rambled on into the cellular phone the whole time the tall young man had uncorked the bottle and poured the obligatory amount for the taste test. At first, when he noticed Daniel on the phone, he had offered the glass to Tess. She quickly shook her head. Without a word, she directed the steward to Daniel with her eyes, so as not to embarrass the inexperienced man, whose smooth, boyish face still blushed.

Now they both waited. She hated all the interruptions. It was bad enough they were having an unusually late Sunday dinner because of Daniel's business dealings. Why couldn't he, at least, take Sundays off? She fingered the long-stemmed rose he had brought her, and found herself wishing that just once he could be more creative. Why not some violets or a clump of daisies?

Finally, Daniel firmly, but calmly, called the person on the other end of the line "an incompetent asshole." Fortunately for Tess and the wine steward, that was his closing.

He snapped the cellular phone in half and slipped it into his breast pocket. Without looking up, he grabbed the glass, sipped then spit the wine back without giving it a swirl in his mouth.

"This is sewer water. I asked for a 1984 Bordeaux. What the hell is this crap?"

Tess felt her nerves tense in anticipation. Not again. Why couldn't they ever go out without Daniel making a scene. She watched the poor wine steward twist the bottle around, desperate to read the label.

"It *is* a 1984 Bordeaux, sir."

Daniel snatched the bottle from the young man's hands and

took a look. Immediately, he snorted under his breath and handed it back.

"I don't want a goddamn California wine."

"But you said domestic, sir."

"Yes, and as far as I remember, New York is still in the United States."

"Yes, of course, sir. I'll bring another bottle."

"So," Daniel said, letting her know he was ready to talk to her though his hands rearranged his silverware and folded the napkin in his lap. "You said we had something to celebrate?"

She pushed up her dress strap, wondering why she had spent two hundred and fifty dollars on a dress that wouldn't stay up on her. A sexy, black dress that Daniel hadn't noticed. Even when he looked up at her, he raised an eyebrow at her fumbling instead of at the dress, and instantly he frowned at her. Dear God, she didn't need another lecture about fidgeting in public. The man spent more time rearranging his dinnerware than he did eating, and yet, he felt he could lecture her about fidgeting. She pretended not to notice his frown and launched into her good news. If she kept enthusiastic, he couldn't possibly ruin this night for her. Could he?

"I sold the Saunders' house last week."

His brow furrowed, reminding her that he didn't have time to remember where the hell each of her clients lived.

"It's the huge Tudor on the north side. But the best part is that Delores is letting me keep the entire selling bonus."

"Well, that *is* good news, Tess. We should be having champagne and not wine." He turned in his chair, going into what looked like a search-and-destroy mode. "Where the hell is that incompetent imbecile?"

"No, Daniel, don't."

He scowled at her for squelching his noble gesture, and she hurried to correct it.

"You know I enjoy wine much more than champagne. Please, let's have wine."

He raised his hands in mock defeat. "Whatever pleases you. Tonight is your night."

He began to sip from his water glass but stopped, grabbed his napkin and wiped at the water spots. Tess braced herself for another scene, but Daniel managed to get the glass in satisfactory condition on his own. He replaced his napkin and the glass without taking a sip.

"So, how much is this selling bonus? I hope you didn't spend it all on that overpriced frock that won't stay on your shoulders."

She felt the heat crawl up her neck before she had a chance to contain it.

"Of course not." She kept her voice strong and managed a quick smile, pretending to enjoy his savage attempt at what he called dry humor.

"So? How much?" he wanted to know.

"Almost ten thousand dollars," she said, holding up her chin proudly.

"Well, that is a nice little chunk of change for you, isn't it?"

This time he sipped his water without cleaning the glass. Already his eyes darted around the room, looking for familiar faces. She knew it was a sort of professional habit and not meant to be rude, but each time, she felt as though he was hoping to be rescued from a mundane conversation with her.

"Do you think I should invest it?" she asked, hoping to bring his attention back to her with the one topic he loved to discuss.

"What's that, sweetie?" His eyes only glanced at her. He had spotted a couple he seemed to know at the reservation stand, waiting for their table.

"The bonus. Do you think I should invest it in the stock market?"

This time he looked back at her with that smile she immediately recognized as the beginning of another lesson.

"Tess, ten thousand dollars really isn't enough for you to be getting into the market. Maybe a nice little CD or less risky mutual fund. You really don't want to mess with something you don't understand."

Before she could protest, his cellular phone started ringing. Daniel quickly flipped it out of his pocket as though it were the most important thing in the room. Tess pushed up her strap. Why kid herself. The damn phone *was* the most important thing in the room.

The wine steward returned, glanced at Daniel on the phone again, and Tess wanted to laugh at the young man's pained expression.

"Why the hell is it so hard to fucking get this right?" Daniel barked into the phone loud enough for other diners to look over. "No, no, forget it. I'll do it myself."

He slapped the phone shut and was on his feet before he had it tucked back into his pocket.

"Tess, sweetie, I need to go take care of something. These idiots can't seem to get one fucking thing right." He pulled out a credit card and slipped out two hundred-dollar bills from his money clip. "Please have a shamefully expensive dinner to celebrate your bonus. And you don't mind taking a cab home, do you?"

He handed her the credit card and the folded bills. He pecked her on the cheek and then left before she could object. But she noticed he had enough time to stop at the door and talk to the couple he had seen earlier.

Suddenly, she realized the wine steward was still at the table and now staring at her, stunned and waiting for her instructions.

"I think I'd like the bill, please.

He continued to stare, then held up the uncorked bottle. "I didn't even pour one glass."

"Enjoy it later with the other waiters."

"Are you serious?"

"I'm serious. On me. Really. Oh, and before you bring the bill, would you add two of the most expensive entrées you have on the menu."

"You want them as takeout?"

"Oh no. I don't want them at all. I just want to pay for them." She smiled and held up the credit card. Finally, he seemed to get the message, smiled back and hurried off to take care of it.

If Daniel insisted on treating her like a hooker, she could certainly accommodate him. Maybe her silly little mind couldn't possibly comprehend something as complex as the stock market, but there were plenty of other things she knew about that Daniel didn't have a clue about.

She signed the bill for the wine steward, making sure to add a hefty tip for him. Then she took her two hundred dollars and hailed a cab, hoping the anger would burn off by the time she got home. How could he ruin this for her? She had been looking forward to a celebration. Maybe ten thousand dollars was a drop in the bucket for Daniel, but for her it was a tremendous accomplishment in a long journey uphill. She deserved a pat on the back. She deserved a celebration. Instead, she had a long, lonely cab ride home from D.C.

"Excuse me," she said, leaning forward in the stale-smelling cab. "When we get to Newburgh Heights, forget the address I gave you. Take me to Louie's Bar and Grill on Fifty-fifth and Laurel."

# CHAPTER 15

*Kansas City, Missouri*
*Sunday evening*

It was almost midnight when Agents Preston Turner and Richard Delaney knocked on Maggie's hotel-room door.

"How 'bout a nightcap, O'Dell?"

Turner wore blue jeans and a purple golf shirt that enhanced the rich brown of his skin. Delaney, on the other hand, still wore a suit, his lopsided tie and open collar the only indications that he was no longer on duty.

"I don't know, guys. It's late." Not that sleep mattered. She knew she wouldn't be going to bed for hours.

"It's not even midnight." Turner grinned at her. "Party's just gettin' started. Besides, I'm starved." He glanced back at Delaney for reassurance. Delaney only shrugged. Five years older than both Turner and Maggie, Delaney had a wife and two kids. Maggie imagined Delaney had been a conservative Southern gentleman even when he was ten years old, but somehow Turner managed to bring out a reckless competitive side.

Both men noticed that Maggie had answered the door with her Smith & Wesson gripped firmly in her right hand, dropped at her side. However, neither mentioned it. Suddenly it felt extra heavy. She wondered why they put up with her, though she knew Cunningham purposely assigned the three of them to the same conferences. They had been her shadows since Stucky had escaped last October. When she complained to Cunningham, he had been insulted by her accusation that he was providing watchdogs to make certain she didn't go after Stucky on her own. Only later did it occur to her that her boss might do so in an attempt to protect her. Which was ridiculous. If Albert Stucky wanted to hurt her, no show of force would stop him.

"You know you guys don't need to baby-sit me."

Turner pretended to be wounded and said, "Come on, Maggie, you know us better than that."

Yes, she did. Despite their mission, Turner and Delaney had never singled her out as some damsel in distress. Maggie had spent years working to be treated like one of the guys. Perhaps that's why Cunningham's motive, however honorable or well intentioned, still angered her.

"Ah, come on, Maggie," Delaney finally joined in. "Knowing you, your presentation is all ready for tomorrow."

Delaney politely stayed in the hallway while Turner leaned against the door frame as though taking up permanent residence until she agreed.

"Let me get my jacket."

She closed the door enough to make Turner retreat into the hall and give her some privacy. She strapped on her holster, looping the leather contraption over her shoulder and buckling it tight against her side. Then she slid her revolver in and put on a navy blazer to hide the bulge.

Turner was right. The nearby bar and grill in what was called Westport buzzed with late-night conventioneers. Turner explained that the midtown Bohemian district, which still showed quaint signs of its early days as a trading post, was "KC's nightlife hub." How Turner always knew these details Maggie had never bothered to find out. It did seem as if Turner quickly became the expert at finding the hot spots in every city they visited.

Delaney led the way, squeezing through the crowd along the bar and finding a table in a dark corner. Only when he and Maggie sat down did they realize they had lost Turner, who had stopped to talk to a couple of young women perched on bar stools. From their tight knit dresses and shiny dangling earrings, Maggie took a wild guess that they weren't law enforcement officers, but rather a couple of single women looking to meet a man with a badge.

"How does he do that so easily?" Delaney asked, watching and admiring.

Maggie glanced around while she scooted her chair against the wall so she could see the entire room. She hated having her back to a crowd. Actually, she hated crowds. Clouds of cigarette smoke hung over the room like fog settled in for the evening. The din of voices and laughter blended together, making it necessary to speak louder than comfortable. And though she would be with Turner and Delaney, she hated the looks thrown her way, some of which reminded her of vultures waiting for their prey to be left alone and vulnerable.

"You know, even when I was single, I hated dating," Delaney confessed, still watching his buddy. "But Turner makes it all look so easy." He twisted his chair closer to the table and leaned in as though ready to give Maggie his full attention. "So what about you? Are you thinking about getting back into the game?"

"The game?" She had no idea what he was talking about.

"The dating game. What's it been? Three, four months?"

"The divorce isn't final yet. I just moved out of the condo on Friday."

"I didn't realize the two of you were still living together. I thought you broke up months ago."

"We did. It was more practical for both of us to live there until things were settled. Neither one of us is hardly ever there."

"Shoot! For a minute there I thought maybe the two of you were thinking about giving it another shot." He looked hopeful. She knew Delaney was a firm believer in marriage. Despite admiring his partner's finesse at dating, Delaney seemed to love being married.

"I don't think reconciliation is possible."

"You sure?"

"What would you do if Karen made you choose between her and being in the FBI?"

He shook his head, and before he answered she was sorry she'd asked. He pulled his chair closer and his face got serious. "Part of the reason I became an instructor was because I know Karen gets nervous about me being in the middle of hostage negotiations. That last one in Philly, she had to watch most of it on TV. Some sacrifices are worth making."

She didn't want to have this conversation. Discussing her

failed marriage accomplished nothing these days except to remind her of the hollowness in her gut.

"So I'm the bad guy because I'm not willing to sacrifice my career to make my husband feel better?" The anger in her voice surprised her. "I would never ask Greg to stop being a lawyer."

"Relax, Maggie. You're not the bad guy." Delaney remained calm and sympathetic. "There's a big difference between asking and expecting. Karen would never have asked. *I* made the decision. Besides, Greg's got some major screws loose if he would let you get away, period."

Her eyes met his, and he smiled, then quickly looked back around to see that Turner was still with his new friends. Though Delaney, Turner and Maggie spent hours together, week after week, there were usually no emotional revelations or personal discussions.

"Do you miss it?"

He glanced back at her and laughed. "What's to miss? Standing in freezing-cold or stinking-hot weather for hours, trying to talk some asshole out of blowing away innocent people?" He rested his elbows on the table and scratched his jaw, his eyes serious again. "Yeah, I do miss it. But I get called in on a case every now and then."

"What can I get you two?" a waitress asked as she squeezed between two diners to get to their table.

Immediately, Maggie felt a wave of relief, welcoming the interruption. She saw Delaney's face relax, too.

"Just Diet Coke for me." He smiled up at the pretty redhead.

Maggie was impressed with his unconscious flirting. Had it simply become a habit from hanging around Turner so long?

"Scotch, neat," she said when the waitress looked her way.

"Oh, and that guy over at the end of the bar—" Delaney pointed "—it doesn't look like it now, but he will eventually be joining us. Is your grill still on?"

The waitress checked her watch. A small beauty mark above her upper lip twitched as she scrunched her eyes to make out the time. In the dim light, Maggie could see the lines of exhaustion in the woman's attractive face.

"They're supposed to close down at midnight." She kept her voice friendly though Maggie could tell it was an effort. "There are still a few minutes if I get it in now." Her offer was genuine. "Any idea what he wants?"

"A burger and fries," Delaney said without hesitation.

"Medium rare," Maggie added.

"With pickles and onion."

"And a bottle of A.1 sauce, if you have it."

"Oh, and cheddar cheese on the burger, too."

The waitress smiled at them. Maggie glanced at Delaney, and they burst out laughing.

"God, I wonder if Turner realizes how predictable he is?" Maggie said while wondering if there was anyone who paid as much attention to her habits and quirks.

"It sounds like the three of you are very good friends." The waitress had relaxed, looking a little less fatigued. "I don't suppose you know what he'll be drinking?"

"Do you have Boulevard Wheat?" Delaney asked.

"Of course. Actually, it's a Kansas City brew."

"Okay. Well, that's what he'll want."

"I'll get his order in and bring back your drinks. Sure I can't get either of you something to eat?"

"Maggie?" Delaney waited for her to shake her head. "Maybe some fries for me."

"You got it."

"Thanks, Rita," Delaney added as though they were old friends.

As soon as she left their table, Maggie gave Delaney's shoulder a shove. "I thought you said you weren't good at this stuff?"

"What stuff?"

"This flirting stuff. Usually Turner's doing it, so I don't get to see the real master at work."

"I don't have any idea what you're talking about." But it was obvious from his grin that he was enjoying the attention.

"'Thanks, Rita'?"

"That's her name, Maggie. That's why they wear those name tags, so we can all share a friendly meal."

"Oh, right, only she never gets to know our names or sit down and eat with us. How friendly is that?"

"Hey, guys." Turner slid into the last chair. "Lots of attorneys here this time."

"Those two women are attorneys?" Delaney craned his neck to get a better look.

"You betcha." He waved a piece of paper with their phone numbers before tucking it into his pocket. "And I never know when I might need an attorney."

"Yeah, right. Like the three of you were talking legal matters."

Maggie ignored their banter and simply asked, "What conference is this anyway?"

Both men stopped and stared at her as if waiting for the punch line.

"You're serious?" Turner finally asked.

"Hey, I make the same presentation every time, whether I'm in Kansas City or Chicago or L.A."

"You really don't get into these things, do you?"

"It's definitely not why I joined the FBI." Suddenly she felt uncomfortable with both of them studying her as if she had slipped and said something wrong. "Besides, Cunningham keeps my name off the program roster, so it's not like anyone is coming specifically to hear me and my words of wisdom."

She had interrupted their jovial moods, reminding them why she was really here. Not because she longed to teach profiling to a bunch of cops, but to keep her out of the field, away from Albert Stucky. Rita returned, relieving Maggie once again, this time with a tray of drinks. Turner immediately raised his eyebrows at her when she placed the bottle of beer and a glass in front of him.

"Rita, you're a mind reader." He wasted no time using her name just as Delaney had, as if they, too, were old friends.

The pretty waitress blushed, and Maggie watched Delaney, searching for signs of rivalry. Instead, he seemed pleased to leave the flirting to his single friend.

"Your burger and fries should be ready in about ten minutes."

"Oh my God! Rita, will you marry me?"

"Actually, you should thank your friends. They got the order in just before Carl closed the grill." She smiled at Maggie and Delaney this time. "I'll bring out the rest of the order as soon as it's ready." Then she hurried away.

Maggie couldn't help thinking that Rita was a seasoned

waitress who already knew which of her customers were the big tippers. Turner rewarded his waiters and waitresses with attention and familiarity, but it was Maggie or Delaney who remembered to leave a substantial tip.

"So, Turner," Delaney said. "Why are there attorneys at this conference?"

"Mostly prosecutors. Sounds like they're all here for that computer workshop. You know, the database thing the Bureau's been setting up. Lots of D.A. offices are finally getting connected. At least in the bigger cities. And since they're all *sooooo* very busy, and can never spare an experienced attorney, it looks like they've sent their fresh young things." He sat back and surveyed the room.

Maggie and Delaney shook their heads at each other. Just as Maggie tipped back her glass, she saw a familiar figure in the long mirror that stretched behind the bar. She slammed her glass down and stood, sending the table rocking and her chair screeching. She looked over in the direction from where she thought the mirror had reflected the image.

"Maggie, what is it?"

Turner and Delaney stared at her as she stretched to see over the bar patrons. Was it her imagination?

"Maggie?"

She checked the mirror again. The figure in the black leather jacket was gone.

"What's going on, Maggie?"

"Nothing," she said quickly. "I'm fine." Of course she was fine. Yet her eyes searched for and found the door. There was no man in a long, black leather jacket coming or going.

She sat down, pulling her chair in and avoiding her friends' eyes. They were getting used to her jumpy, erratic behavior. Soon, she'd be like the little boy who cried wolf, and no one would pay any attention. Maybe that was exactly what he wanted.

She grabbed her glass and watched the amber liquid swirl. Had it only been her imagination? Had she really seen Albert Stucky or was she simply losing her mind?

# CHAPTER 16

He waited for her at the rear exit, knowing this was the door she would use when she was finally ready to leave. The alley was dark. The brick buildings stood tall enough to block out any moonlight. A few bare lightbulbs glowed above some of the back doors. The bulbs were dull, covered with bug shit and swarmed by moths, but still his eyes stung when he looked at them directly. He tucked his sunglasses into his jacket pocket and checked his watch.

Only three cars remained in the small parking lot. One was his, and he knew neither of the other two belonged to her. He knew she wouldn't be driving this night. He had decided to offer her a ride, but would she accept?

He knew how to be charming. That was simply a part of the game, a part of his disguise. If he was to take on this new identity, he would need to play the role that came with it. And out of the two of them, women always preferred him to Albert.

Yes, he knew what women liked to hear, and he didn't mind telling them. In fact, he enjoyed it. It was part of the manipulation, an integral piece of the puzzle to gaining complete control. He had discovered that even strong, independent women didn't mind giving up control to a man they found charming. What silly, wonderful creatures. Maybe he would give her his sad story about his failing eyesight. Women loved being caretakers. They loved to play roles of their own.

The challenge excited him, and he could feel his erection swelling. He would have no trouble tonight. Now, if he could just wait. He must be patient—patient and charming. Could he be charming enough to get her to invite him home with her? Already, he tried to imagine what her bedroom looked like.

A door screeched open halfway down the alley, and he

stepped into the shadows. A short, burly guy in a stained apron came out to toss several trash bags into the Dumpster. He lingered, lighting a cigarette and sucking in several quick drags before stomping it out and going back in.

Most of the other places had closed. He didn't worry about being seen. If anyone noticed him, he could tell them almost anything, and they would believe it. People heard what they wanted to hear. Sometimes it was too easy. Though if he had guessed right, she would be a bit of a challenge. She was much older, much more street savvy than the cute little pizza girl. He would need to do some serious talking to get her to trust him. He would need to pour on the charm, compliment her and make her laugh. Again, he could feel his erection as he thought of winning her over, wondering how far he could go.

Perhaps he would start with a gentle touch, a simple caress of her face. He'd pretend he was getting a strand of her lovely hair out of her eyes or tell her she had an eyelash on her cheek. She would think him concerned, attentive and sensitive to her needs. Women loved that crap.

Suddenly the door opened, and there she was. She hesitated, looking around first. She checked the sky. A light mist had begun about fifteen minutes ago. She popped open a bright red umbrella and started walking quickly toward the street. Red was definitely her color.

He waited, giving her a head start, while he reached down and checked the scalpel, safe in its custom-made, leather sheath, and tucked inside his boot. He caressed its handle, his fingers lingering, but he left it there. Then he followed her down the alley.

# CHAPTER 17

*Monday, March 30*

Tess McGowan awoke with a splitting headache. Sunlight streamed through her bedroom blinds like lasers. Damn it! She had gone to bed again without removing her contact lenses. She threw her arm over her eyes. Why hadn't she gotten the type she could leave in forever? She hated this recent reminder of her age. Thirty-five was not old. Okay, so she had squandered her twenties. She wasn't doing the same with her thirties.

Suddenly she realized she was naked beneath the covers. And then she felt the sticky mess beside her. Alarmed, she pushed herself up, keeping the bedsheets to her breasts, searching the room through blurred vision for clues.

Why couldn't she remember Daniel being here? He never stayed over at her house. He said it was too quaint. She noticed her clothes in a tangled mess on the chair across the room. Heaped on the floor next to the chair were what looked like men's trousers, the tips of shoes peeking out from underneath. A black leather bomber jacket hung from the doorknob. She didn't recognize it as anything Daniel would wear. That's when she heard the shower, aware of its sound only as the water stopped. Her pulse quickened as she tried to remember something, anything, from last night.

She checked the bedside stand. It was eight forty-five. Somehow she remembered it was Monday morning. She knew she didn't have any appointments on Mondays, but Daniel would. Why couldn't she remember him coming over? Why couldn't she remember herself coming home?

Think, Tess! She rubbed her temples.

Daniel had left the restaurant and she had taken a cab home, but of course she hadn't gone straight home. The last thing she did remember was doing tequila shooters at Louie's. Had she called Daniel to pick her up? Why couldn't she remember? And would he be furious if she asked him to fill in the blanks? Obviously he hadn't been angry with her last night, and she shifted away from the damp spot.

She laid her head back on the pillows, squeezing her eyes shut and wishing the throbbing would stop threatening to split her head open.

"Good morning, Tess," a rich, deep voice came into the room.

Before she could open her eyes, she knew the voice didn't belong to Daniel. In a panic she sat up again and pushed her back against the headboard. The tall, lean stranger with only a blue towel wrapped around his waist looked startled and concerned.

"Tess?" he said softly. "You okay?"

Then she remembered, as if a dam broke loose in her brain, releasing the memories in a flood. He had been at Louie's, watching her from the corner table, handsome and quiet, so very unlike anyone who frequented Louie's. How could she have brought him into her home?

"Tess, you're starting to scare me."

His concern seemed genuine. At least she hadn't brought home a mass murderer. But then, how in the world did she think she'd know the difference? With his hair still wet, he looked harmless, wrapped in only a towel. Immediately she noticed his hard, firm body and realized he would be strong enough to overpower her without much effort. How could she have been so foolish?

"I'm sorry. I...you startled me." She tried to keep the alarm from her voice.

He grabbed his trousers from the floor but stopped suddenly before putting them on as if something had just occurred to him.

"Oh Christ! You don't remember, do you?"

Beneath the morning bristles, his boyish face looked embarrassed. He fumbled into his trousers, stumbling once and accidentally dropping the towel before the trousers were all the way up. Tess watched, flustered and annoyed that his muscular body was turning her on, despite her confusion. She should be worried he could hurt her, instead she found herself wondering how young he was. And dear God, why couldn't she remember his name?

"I should have known you had too much to drink," he apologized as he frantically searched for his shirt, going through her things and carefully folding them as he put them back on the chair. He stopped at her bra, and his embarrassment only grew. His distraught politeness made her smile. When he glanced over at her, he did a double take, startled by her expression. He sank into the chair, now ignoring her clothes and absently wringing his hands and her bra without realizing it.

"I'm a complete idiot, aren't I?"

"No, not at all." She smiled again, and his obvious discomfort relaxed her. She sat up, keeping the sheet carefully pressed against her as she drew her knees up to her chest and placed her arms on top to rest her chin.

"It's just that I don't do this sort of thing," she tried to explain. "At least, not anymore."

"I don't usually do this sort of thing at all." He noticed her bra in his hands, folded it and set it on the nearby bookcase. "So you really don't remember any of last night?"

"I remember you watching me. I remember being very attracted to you." Her revelation surprised her almost as much as it surprised him.

"That's it?" He looked wounded.

"Sorry."

Finally, he grinned and shrugged. She couldn't believe how comfortable she felt with him. There was no more panic, no more alarm. The only tension seemed to be the obvious sexual attraction, which she tried to ignore. He didn't look as if he was even thirty. And he was a stranger, for heaven's sake. She wanted to kick herself. Dear God! How could she have been so reckless? Had she not changed at all after all this time?

"If I ever find my shirt, could I maybe take you to lunch?"

Then she remembered Daniel. How would she explain any of this to Daniel? She felt the sapphire ring he had given her stabbing into the soft underside of her chin, like some painful reminder. What was wrong with her? Daniel was a mature, respectable businessman. Sure, he was arrogant and self-absorbed sometimes, but at least he wasn't some kid she had picked up in a bar.

Still, she watched the handsome young stranger put on socks and shoes while he waited for her answer. He glanced around the room in search of the missing shirt. Her toes felt a wad at the end of the bed. She reached beneath the covers, unearthing a pale blue, wrinkled oxford shirt. She held it up to him and instantly remembered having worn the shirt. The memory of him taking it off her made her cheeks flush.

"Is it salvageable?" he asked, stretching to take it from her while keeping a safe distance.

He was being a gentleman, pretending he hadn't had access to every inch of her body only hours ago. The thought should have repulsed or terrified her. It didn't. Instead, she continued to watch him, enjoying his nervous but fluid motions, yet at the same time annoyed with herself. She should not be noticing that the color in his shirt brought out the blue flecks in his otherwise green eyes. How had she been so certain he wouldn't hurt her? One of these days a stranger's eyes might not be a safe way to judge his character.

"So what about lunch?" he asked, looking as though he was steeling himself for further rejection. He had trouble buttoning the shirt, had it almost finished when he realized he was off a button and started all over again.

"I don't even remember your name," Tess finally admitted.

"It's Will. William Finley." There was a glance and a hesitant smile. "I'm twenty-six, never been married. I'm a lawyer. Just moved to Boston, but I'm visiting a friend here in Newburgh Heights. His name's Bennet Cartland. His father has a law practice here. Pretty high-profile one, actually. You can check it out if you want." He hesitated. "Probably more than you wanted to know, right?" When she rewarded him with a smile, he continued. "What else? I have no diseases, except I did have the mumps when I was, like, eleven, but then so did my buddy, Billy Watts, and he has three kids. Oh, but don't worry, I used protection last night."

"Um...there's a damp spot," she said quietly.

When he met her eyes, the embarrassment seemed to be replaced by a flicker of desire that his memory must have triggered.

"I had only two condoms, but the third time I...well, I pulled out before, well, you know."

Suddenly she remembered the intensity, could feel it fill her body. The unfamiliar rush surprised her, frightened her. She couldn't allow herself to slip back into her old habits. She wouldn't. Not now when she had worked so hard.

"I think maybe you better leave, Will."

He opened his mouth to say something, maybe to try to change her mind. He hesitated, staring at his feet. She wondered if he wanted to touch her. Did he have the urge to kiss her goodbye or to convince her to let him stay? Maybe she even wanted him to. Instead, Will Finley found his jacket on the doorknob and left.

She lay back into the pillows, now noticing remnants of his aftershave, a subtle scent, not like Daniel's overpowering musk. Dear God, twenty-six fucking years old! Almost ten years her junior. How could she be such an idiot? Yet, this time when she closed her eyes, their night together started coming back to her in clear, crisp sights and sounds and sensations. She could feel his body rubbing against hers, his tongue and hands playing her like some delicate instrument, knowing just where and when to touch her and how to send her to places she hadn't been in a long time.

The memories that embarrassed her more were those of her own urgency, her own hunger, her own fingers and mouth devouring him. They had taken turns ravishing each other as if they had been starving. The passion, the urgency, the desires were nothing new. She had experienced plenty in her sordid past. What was new, what was different had been Will's gentle caresses, what seemed to be a genuine concern that she feel the same pleasure, the same sensations he was experiencing. What was new and different was that she and Will Finley hadn't just had sex last night, but that Will Finley had actually made love to her. Perhaps she should have taken some comfort in that realization. Instead, it stirred up an unsettling restlessness within her.

Tess rolled onto her side, twisting her pillow and hugging it to her. She couldn't let someone like Will Finley sidetrack her. Not now. Not when she had worked so hard for what she had. She needed to remain focused. She needed to think of Daniel. Despite their differences, Daniel gave her credibility in a community where credibility was everything. He was good for her in all the ways that were necessary for her to become a respected, successful businesswoman. So why did she feel as though she had let something valuable slip from her fingers when she asked Will Finley to leave?

# CHAPTER 18

Will slammed the front door, rattling its beveled glass. For a brief moment, his anger gave way to concern while he checked to make sure he hadn't cracked or broken anything. The door looked old but solid. The glass looked custom-made, maybe antique. Not that he would know such things. But he had noticed that Tess McGowan had a taste for antiques. Her small cottage was decorated with an eclectic mix, creating a soothing, comfortable environment. He had felt incredibly warm and cozy waking up and being surrounded by lavender sheets and wallpaper with tiny little violets.

Last night when she invited him in, he had initially been surprised. He would never have guessed that the wild, passionate woman who had shamelessly hustled him at pool while throwing back tequila shooters would surround herself with old lace, hand-carved mahogany and what looked like original watercolors. But after only one night, he knew Tess McGowan's home was a reflection of a woman who was as passionate and independent as she was sensitive and vulnerable.

It was that unexpected vulnerability that had made it difficult to leave. It had surprised him last night—or was it already early this morning—when he held her in his arms. She had curled into his body as though finding some long-sought-after shelter.

He scraped a sleeve over his face in an attempt to wake up to reality. Christ! Where did he come up with this crap? Vulnerability and finding shelter. He sounded like something out of a fucking chick flick.

He got into his car and immediately glanced up at what he knew to be the bedroom window. Hell, maybe he expected her to be standing there, watching him. But it was easy to see no one was standing behind the sheer curtain.

He felt angry again, used. It was ridiculous. He was the one who had picked her up. His friends had dared him, goaded him into one last fling before his impending wedding. A wedding that at one time seemed far into the future was now suddenly less than a month away.

At first he did it simply to shock his friends. They'd never expect good ole' Will, the eternal choirboy, to flirt with any woman, let alone a woman like Tess. Geez, maybe he needed some new friends, ones whose maturity levels weren't stuck back in college. But he couldn't blame them for his stupidity last night, nor for his going as far as he had. Nor could he say he'd had too much to drink, because unlike Tess, he had known exactly what he was doing from start to finish.

He had never met anyone like Tess McGowan. Even before she shed her conservative black shawl and started shooting pool with the bar's owner, Will thought she was the sexiest woman he had seen. It wasn't like she was a knockout or centerfold-sexy. She was definitely attractive, with thick, wavy hair she wore loose and down to her shoulders. And she had a good body, not like some bulimic model, but with plenty of curves and amazing shapely legs. God, he got hot just thinking about her. Just thinking about running his hands over the curve of her hips and the swell of her breasts.

Back at Louie's, long before he had up-close-and-personal access, it wasn't those curves so much as it was the way she moved—it was the way she carried herself that had gotten his attention. His and everyone else's. And it was like she enjoyed the attention, enjoyed putting on a show, hiking her dress's skirt up to her thighs to take a shot while straddling the corner of the table. Every time she leaned over her pool cue, the strap of her dress slipped off her shoulder, the silky fabric allowing just a peek at her voluptuous breasts captured behind black lace.

Will shook his head and jammed the key into the ignition. It had been a hell of a night, one of the most passionate, erotic, exciting nights of his life. Instead of being angry, he should be patting himself on the back that Tess McGowan was letting him off with no strings attached. He was a lucky bastard. Hell, he hadn't been with another woman since he and Melissa had started seeing each other. And four years of sex with Melissa couldn't come close to one night with Tess.

He glanced up at the bedroom window again, and caught himself hoping Tess would be there. What was it about this woman that made him not want to leave? Was he simply imagining that there had been some connection, some special bond? Or had it just been sex?

He checked his wristwatch. He had a long trip back to Boston. He'd be pushing it to get there in time for dinner with Melissa and her visiting parents. It had been the only reason he had taken off a precious Monday from his brand-new job. And here he was, miles away from Boston and miles away from even thinking about Melissa.

Christ! How would Melissa not see the betrayal in his eyes? How fucking stupid was he to risk throwing away the last four years for one night of passion? So if it was such a mistake, why hadn't he left already? Why couldn't he get Tess's fragrance, the taste of her skin, the sounds of her passion...why couldn't he erase it all? Why did he want to go back up and do it all over again? That certainly didn't sound like a remorseful guy. What the hell was wrong with him?

He shifted the car into gear and peeled out of her driveway, letting his frustration squeal the tires. He swerved into the street and almost sideswiped a car parked at the opposite curb. Briefly the man behind the wheel glanced up at him. He wore sunglasses and had a map spread over the dash as though he was looking for directions. Tess's neighborhood was blocks away from any major thoroughfare. Immediately, Will wondered if the guy had been watching the house. Was it possible this was the owner of the expensive sapphire ring Tess wore on the wrong hand?

Will checked the rearview mirror and took one last look at the car. Then he noticed it had District of Columbia license plates instead of Virginia. Maybe because it was a little odd, maybe because he was a new assistant D.A.—hell, maybe it was just out of curiosity about the type of man who thought he owned Tess McGowan. Whatever the reason, Will committed the license number to memory, then headed back to Boston.

# CHAPTER 19

The conference room went silent as soon as Maggie walked through the door. Without hesitating she continued to the front, disappointed to find the room arranged for a lecture. Chairs were set side by side, all facing the front of the room instead of at long, narrow tables as she had requested. She preferred more of a business setting where she could scatter crime scene photos in front of the participants. Where they felt more comfortable discussing rather than simply listening. However, the only table in the room was filled with coffee, juice, soft drinks and an assortment of pastries.

She felt her audience's stares as she pulled up a chair for her briefcase. Then, she began digging through the contents, pretending to search for something she had to have before she could start. Instead, she was waiting for her stomach to settle. She had eaten breakfast hours ago, and never got nauseated anymore before presentations. But her lack of sleep and several additional Scotches in her room last night, long after Turner and Delaney had left her, now punished her with a fuzzy head and a dry mouth. It was definitely not a good way to start a Monday.

"Good morning," she finally said, buttoning her double-breasted jacket. "I'm Special Agent Margaret O'Dell with the FBI. I'm a criminal profiler with the Investigative Support Unit at Quantico, which some of you may still refer to as the Behavioral Science Unit. This workshop focuses—"

"Wait a minute, ma'am," a man in the second row interrupted, shuffling uncomfortably in a chair that was too small to accommodate his considerable size. He wore tight trousers, a crisp, short-sleeved button-down shirt that stretched across his swollen belly, and scuffed shoes that refused to look new despite a fresh polish.

"Yes?"

"No disrespect intended, but what happened to the guy who was supposed to give this workshop?"

"Excuse me?"

"The program..." He looked around the room until he seemed to find encouragement from some of his comrades. "It said the guy wasn't just an FBI profiler, but an expert in tracking serial killers, a forensic psychologist with, like, nine or ten years' experience."

"Did the program actually say this person was a man?"

Now he looked puzzled. Someone beside him handed over a copy of the conference's program.

"Sorry to disappoint you," Maggie said, "but I'm him."

Most of the men simply stared at her. One woman in the group rolled her eyes in empathy when Maggie looked her way. Maggie recognized two men in the back. She had briefly met the Kansas City detectives Ford and Milhaven last night at the Westport bar and grill. Both men smiled as though they were in on her secret.

"Maybe they should say that in the program," the man persisted, trying to justify his objection. "They don't even use your name."

"Would it matter?"

"Yeah, to me it would've. I came here to learn some serious stuff, not listen to some desk jockey."

Her evening dosage of Scotch must have desensitized her emotions. Instead of feeling angry, his chauvinism simply made her feel more exhausted.

"Look, Officer—"

"Wait a minute. What makes you think I'm an officer? Maybe I'm a detective." He shot a smug grin to his buddies, giving himself away and reinforcing Maggie's initial assessment.

"Let me take a shot here," she said, walking to the center of the room, standing in front of him and crossing her arms. "You're a street cop in a metropolitan area, but not here in Kansas City. You're used to wearing a uniform and not business attire, not even business casual. Your wife packed your bag and picked out what you're wearing now, but you've gained some weight since she last bought anything for you. Except the shoes. You insisted on wearing your beat shoes."

Everyone including the officer shuffled in their chairs to get a look at his shoes. She failed to point out the subtle but permanent indentations in his close-cropped hair from too many hours spent wearing a hat.

"You're not able to carry your weapon at the conference, but you feel lost without your badge. It's inside your jacket pocket." She motioned to the tan jacket hidden by his hefty bulk and draped over the back of the chair. "Your wife also insisted on the jacket, but again you're not used to wearing one. Not like perhaps a detective might be used to wearing a jacket and tie."

Everyone waited as if watching a magic act, so the officer reluctantly twisted around, tugged at the jacket and brought out his badge to show them.

"All lucky guesses," he said to Maggie. "Whatcha expect from a roomful of cops?"

"You're right. You're absolutely right." Maggie nodded as eyes came back to her face, still waiting, still testing. "Most of what I said might be seen as obvious. There's a certain profile that goes along with being a cop. Just like there's a certain profile that goes along with being a serial killer. If you can pinpoint what those characteristics are and which ones apply—though some of them may seem obvious—you can use that information, that knowledge, as the beginning foundation for a profile."

Finally she had their attention, and with their minds diverted from what she looked like to what she was saying, her entire body began to relax, to access some auxiliary energy and override her initial fatigue.

"However, the tricky part is looking beyond the obvious, picking apart and examining small tidbits that might seem insignificant. Like, for instance, in this case—I'm sorry, Officer, would you mind telling me your name?"

"What? You mean you can't guess that?" He smirked, proud of what he considered a quick comeback and drawing a few laughs from the others.

Maggie smiled.

"No, I'm afraid my crystal ball leaves out names."

"It's Danzig, Norm Danzig."

"If I were to examine your profile, Officer Danzig, I'd try to break down everything I did know."

"Hey, you can examine me all you like." He continued to play with her, enjoying the attention, while looking at his buddies instead of Maggie.

"I'd wonder," she continued, ignoring his comment, "why your wife had bought clothes for you that were the wrong size."

Suddenly Officer Danzig sat still and quiet.

"I'd ask myself if there was a reason." From the rising color in his face, Maggie knew the reason was one he didn't care to expose. Her guess was that he and his wife had not shared a bed for some time. Perhaps there had even been a temporary separation, one that included Officer Danzig eating a few more fast-food meals. That could account for the extra pounds his wife hadn't expected when she purchased his clothes for the conference. Instead of embarrassing him with her theory, she simply said, "I'd guess your wife finally got fed up with you wearing the same outdated navy blue suit that you keep in the back of your closet."

The others laughed, and Officer Danzig looked around at them, smiling with relief. But when his eyes met Maggie's, she saw a hint of humbled awareness. His subtle show of appreciation was the slightest shift in his chair, crossing his arms, facing the front of the room as if finally ready to give her his full attention.

"It's also important not to get bogged down by the stereotypes." She began her ritual pacing. "There are a handful of stereotypes that seem to be perpetuated with serial killers. We should start by laying some of those to rest. Anyone care to guess what some of those stereotypes are?"

She waited out their silence. They were still summing her up. Finally, a young Hispanic man decided to take a shot.

"How about the idea that they're all crazy. They're total mental cases. That's not necessarily true, right?"

"Right. In fact, many serial killers are intelligent, well educated and as sane as you and I."

"Excuse me," a graying detective from the back of the room interrupted. "Son of Sam claiming a Rottweiler made him do it, that's not mental?"

"Actually it was a black Labrador named Harvey. But even Berkowitz later owned up to the hoax when profiler John Douglas interviewed him.

"I'm not saying some of these killers are not crazy, what I am saying is that it's a mistake to believe they have to be insane to do the things they do. When, in fact, killing for them is a conscious choice. They are masters of manipulation. Their crimes are all about dominating and controlling their victims. It's not usually because they hear orders to kill from a three-thousand-year-old demon living inside a black Lab.

"If they were simply nuts, it wouldn't be possible for them to carry out their elaborate murders over and over again—to perfect their methods and still avoid getting caught for months, sometimes years. It's important to recognize them not as deranged crazies, but for what they are. What they are is evil."

She needed to change the subject before she got carried away with a sermon on the effects of evil. How there was a shadow side to everyone's human nature; a shadow side that was capable of evil. But to discuss it always led to the question of what made some step over the line, while others dared not. After years of examining evil, Maggie hadn't a clue what that answer was.

"What about motive?" she asked instead. "What are some of the stereotypical motives?"

"Sex," a young man in the back said loudly, enjoying the sudden attention and laughs that the single word drew. "Don't most serial killers get some sexual gratification from killing, just like rapists?"

"Hold on," the one woman challenged. "Rape isn't about sex."

"Actually, that's not a true statement," Maggie said. "Rape is very much about sex."

Immediately there were a few sighs, some disgruntled shakes of heads as though they expected this from a woman.

"Rape is very much about sex," she repeated, ignoring their skepticism. "It's the one variable that distinguishes rape from any other violent crime. No, that's not to say that rapists rape simply for sexual gratification, but yes, they do use sex as one of their weapons to achieve their goals. So it's wrong to say rape isn't about sex when sex is definitely one of the weapons they use.

"In fact, rapists and serial killers use sex and violence in much the same way. Both are powerful weapons used to degrade the victim and gain control. Some serial killers even start out as serial rapists. But somewhere along the line they decide to take it a step further to achieve their gratification. They might begin by experimenting to reach different levels, starting with torture, working up to strangulation or stabbing. Sometimes that's not enough, so they begin different rituals with the dead body. That's when you see cases like the Pied Piper who sliced up his victims, made stew and fed it to his other captives.

She caught several of them grimacing. Skepticism seemed to be replaced by morbid curiosity.

"Or in Albert Stucky's case," she continued, "he began to experiment with different rituals of torture, slicing off victims' clitorises or nipples, just to hear them scream and plead with him."

She said these things calmly and casually, yet she could feel the tension in her muscles, an involuntary reflex as her body seemed to prepare for flight or fight anytime she thought of Stucky.

"Or you find more solemn rituals," she said, trying to expel Stucky from her mind. "Last fall in Nebraska, we tracked a killer who gave his young victims their last rites after he strangled and stabbed them to death."

"Hold on," Detective Ford interrupted. "Nebraska? You're the profiler who worked on that case with the dead little boys?"

Maggie cringed at the simplicity of his description.

"Yes, that was me."

"Morrelli was just telling us about that case last night."

"Sheriff Nick Morrelli?" An unexpected but pleasant flutter invaded her already tense body.

"Yeah, we all went out for ribs last night. But he's not Sheriff Morrelli anymore. Turned in his badge for a suit and tie. He's with the D.A.'s office in Boston."

Maggie retreated to the front of the room, hoping the distance would shield her and prevent them from witnessing her sudden discomfort. Five months ago, the cocky, small-town sheriff had been a thorn in her side from the day she arrived in Platte City, Nebraska. They had spent exactly one week chasing a killer and sharing an intimacy so palpable, just the thought of it was able to generate heat. Her class was staring at her, waiting. How was it possible for Nick Morrelli to dismantle her entire thought process by simply being in the same city?

# CHAPTER 20

Tully reached under his glasses and tried to rub out the exhaustion. As though blaming them for lack of relief, he pulled the glasses off, tossing them onto one of the many piles on his desk. The glasses used to be for reading only. Now he found himself wearing them more often.

Ever since he'd hit forty three years ago, his body parts seemed to be failing him, one by one. Last year it was surgery on his knee, just a torn ligament, but it had put him out of commission for two weeks. Of course, it didn't help matters having a fourteen-year-old daughter telling him how "out of sync" he was. It seemed as if he couldn't do anything right as far as Emma was concerned.

Earlier she had been furious with him for having to spend another evening next door with Mrs. Lopez. Maybe that was part of the reason he was still here working, stalling, avoiding going home to his own daughter and the silence she wielded as punishment. Ironically, this was the same daughter he had fought so hard to keep near him.

Though it wasn't much of a fight once Caroline realized what kind of freedom she might have without the responsibility of a teenage daughter. This was the same woman who couldn't bear to be separated from her daughter and husband six or seven short years ago, when she took an account executive job at a national advertising firm. But as the high-profile clients rolled in and the promotions took her all the way to the top, somehow those expensive trips to New York City and London and Tokyo seemed to get a lot easier. By the final years of their marriage, she had become a stranger to him. A beautiful, sophisticated, ambitious woman, but a complete stranger.

Tully stretched back in his chair, lacing his fingers together behind his head. God, how he hated change! He glanced around the small fluorescent-lit room. He missed having an office with windows. In fact, if he even thought about being sixty feet under ground, he knew his claustrophobia would easily kick in. He had seriously considered turning down the position at Quantico, knowing the Investigative Support Unit was still located in what he considered the bowels of the training facility.

He was rubbing his eyes again when he heard the tap on his open door.

"Agent Tully, you're here late."

Assistant Director Cunningham wore shirtsleeves, but still carefully buttoned at the wrists and collar, whereas Tully's sleeves were rolled up in uneven folds and shoved above his elbows. Cunningham's tie was cinched tight at his neck, making Tully self-conscious about his own, now wrinkled and tossed aside somewhere on a file cabinet, leaving his collar unbuttoned and open.

"I was waiting for a phone call from the medical examiner," Tully explained. "From Dr. Holmes."

"And?"

The assistant director leaned against the door, and Tully wondered if he should clear off one of the chairs. Unlike his boss's immaculately neat office, Tully's looked like a storage closet, with piles of papers, scattered files and overflowing bookcases. He sorted through the stack of notes from his phone call, not wanting to depend on his memory, which at this time of night had shut down like a computer hard drive.

"The girl...the young woman had an incision in her left side that extended to the small of her back about four inches long. Dr. Holmes said it was very precise, almost as if he had performed surgery on her."

"Sounds like our boy."

"He removed her spleen."

"A spleen isn't very big, is it? It looked like there was much more in that pizza box."

Tully reached for the copy of *Gray's Anatomy* that he had borrowed from the library. He quickly thumbed to the place where he had used a gum wrapper as a bookmark. He grabbed his glasses.

"The spleen is about five inches in length, three inches in breadth and an inch or an inch and a half in thickness," he read out loud, then closed the book and set it aside. "The book says the spleen weighs about seven ounces, but that depends on what stage of digestion it's in. It can get much bigger. Our victim hadn't eaten much that day, so her spleen was fairly small. Dr. Holmes said that some of the pancreas was also attached."

"Were there fingerprints found anywhere at the scene?"

"Yes, we got two pretty good ones—a thumb and an index finger. But they're not matching Stucky's. It's possible they may have been made accidentally by someone on the scene, but it sure seems as though they were left behind on purpose. The entire rim of the Dumpster was wiped down, and then there are these two fingerprints right smack in the middle."

Cunningham frowned, his weathered brow creasing as if he remembered something. "Double-check Stucky's early file. Make sure the prints haven't been switched or altered or that there were any computer mistakes. If I remember correctly, Agent O'Dell was finally able to identify him because of a fingerprint Stucky left behind. He blatantly left it behind, too. But it took us a while to identify it at the time. Someone hacked into the county computer system and switched the prints on file."

"I'll double-check, sir, but we're not dealing with a county sheriff department's computer system here. We're checking these against the ones AFIS has on Stucky, prints they've taken directly off Stucky. And with all due respect, I don't think anyone can easily hack into the Bureau's system." AFIS (Automated Fingerprint Identification System) was the FBI's master database. Though it networked with local, state and federal agencies, dozens of precautions were in place against computer hackers.

Cunningham sighed and scratched his jaw. "You're probably right," he conceded with a fatigue Tully hadn't witnessed before.

"It may end up being a rookie cop's," he told his boss, as if hoping to relieve some of Cunningham's exhaustion. "If it is, we'll know in the next twenty-four hours. If they don't make a match to any law enforcement officers, then I'll have someone do a cold search."

Tully kept his glasses in place, feeling more alert with them on and needing to appear in control. "Sir, I haven't found anything that would suggest Stucky is trying to send some sort of message by which organ he extracts. I wonder if I'm missing something."

"No, you're not missing anything. Stucky does this for shock value and simply because he can," Cunningham said as he came farther into Tully's office, but remained standing.

"Did he study to be a surgeon at some point in his life?" Tully flipped through a file Agent O'Dell had put together on Stucky's past. In many ways it read like a résumé for a Fortune 500 executive.

"His father was a doctor." Cunningham wiped a hand over his jaw. Tully recognized the gesture as something his boss did when exhausted and trying to retrieve information from his vast memory bank. He took the opportunity to study his boss's face, which seemed thinner, the hollows in his cheeks and eyes darker in the fluorescent light. Even exhausted, his posture remained straight, no hunched shoulders as he now leaned against the bookcase. Everything about the man spoke of a quiet dignity.

Finally he continued, "If I remember correctly, Stucky and his partner started one of the first Internet, online stock-trading companies. Made millions and has it stashed in foreign banks."

"If we could track some of those accounts, maybe we could track him."

"The problem is we've never been able to find out how many different accounts he has or what names he uses. Stucky's sharp, Agent Tully. He's cunning, very intelligent and almost always in control. He's not quite like any of the others. He doesn't kill because he needs to, or because it's a mission or some urgency. Or even because he hears some inner voices. He kills for one major reason—because he enjoys it. It's a game for him to manipulate, to break down the human spirit, to shock people with what he's capable of doing, and also to thumb his nose at those of us who are trying to catch him."

"Certainly even Albert Stucky makes mistakes."

"Let's hope so. Have you found anything on where the victim may have been taken?"

Again, Tully dug out his notes from a variety of stacks, not wanting to depend on his fatigued memory. Immediately he found himself self-conscious and a bit embarrassed. His notes were scrawled on everything from a deli napkin to a brown paper towel from the men's rest room.

"We know she was taken before she finished her route. There were some customers who called complaining they hadn't received their pizzas. The manager is working on getting me a list of the addresses she was to deliver to."

"Why is that taking so long?"

"They write down the addresses in one place as the orders are phoned in. The delivery person takes the only copy."

"You're kidding," Cunningham sighed, and for the first time Tully thought he saw that it was an effort for him to confine his frustration. "Doesn't seem very efficient."

"It's probably never been a problem until now. The lab is trying to raise the addresses from the indentations on the notepad page underneath. Of course, our best bet is if we find the victim's car. Maybe the lists will have been left behind."

"Any luck finding the car?"

"Not yet. I got the make, model and plate number from DMV. Detective Rosen put out an APB. Nothing's shown up so far."

"Have Reagan National and Dulles airport security check their long-term parking lots."

"Good idea." Tully jotted another note to himself, this time using the cash-register receipt from his lunch. Why the hell didn't he have notepads like the rest of the world?

"He had to take her someplace," Cunningham said, staring over Tully's head, lost in thought. "Somewhere he could have plenty of uninterrupted time with her. I'm guessing he didn't go far from where he apprehended her. If we could get that list, we might be able to narrow down some possible locations."

"The thing is, sir, I've driven around within a ten-mile radius of where the body was found. The whole area is this picture-book community. We're not going to find any abandoned warehouses or condemned buildings."

"It's also easy to miss the most obvious place, Agent Tully. You can bet Stucky will be gambling on us doing just that. What else do you have?" he asked more brusquely now as he stood away from the bookcase, suddenly in a rush.

"There was a cellular phone recovered from the Dumpster. It was reported stolen a few days ago from a local shopping mall. I'm hoping once I get the phone record, maybe it'll lead us someplace, depending on what calls were placed."

"Good. Sounds like you've got everything under control." Cunningham started to leave. "Let me know what help you need. Unfortunately, I can't promise a whole task force again, but maybe I can pull a few people from other cases. Now, you need to go home, Agent Tully. Spend some time with your daughter."

He pointed to the photo Tully kept on the edge of his desk. It was the only one he had. It included the three of them, arms wrapped around each other and smiling for the camera. It couldn't have been taken that long ago, and yet he couldn't remember them being that happy. It was the first time Cunningham had referred to Tully's personal life. He was surprised his aloof boss remembered that his wife hadn't made the move with him.

"Sir?"

Cunningham stopped halfway into the hall.

Tully wasn't sure how to ask. "Should I give Agent O'Dell a call?"

"No." The answer was brisk and firm.

"You want to wait until we're sure it's Stucky?"

"I'm ninety-nine percent certain it is Stucky."

"Then shouldn't we at least tell Agent O'Dell?"

"No."

"But, sir, she might—"

"What part of my answer did you not understand, Agent Tully?" Again, his manner was firm without raising his voice. Then he turned and left.

# CHAPTER 21

Once again, Turner and Delaney dragged Maggie from her hotel room to join them for dinner. This time their new Kansas City friends, Detectives Ford and Milhaven, treated them to what they claimed was the best barbecue place in the city, located not far from the bar and grill they had visited the night before.

Maggie had never seen two men put away more ribs than her FBI buddies. Their compulsion to compete with each other was ridiculous and getting old. Although Maggie recognized it was no longer for her benefit, but was now extended to their new friends. Ford and Milhaven encouraged Turner and Delaney's heartburn fest like spectators at a major sporting event. Ford had even placed a five-dollar bill on the table for the first man who would clean the current stack of ribs off his plate.

Maggie sat back, sipped her Scotch and tried to find something more interesting to watch through the dimly lit, smoke-filled restaurant. She found her eyes wandering to the entrance. She half expected to see Nick Morrelli walk in, and then realized she had no idea what she would do if he were to show up. Ford had told Maggie after class that he and Nick had gone to college together at the University of Nebraska. He said he had left a message at the hotel's front desk for Nick to join them at dinner. Now hours later, Nick obviously hadn't gotten the message or had other plans for the evening. Yet, Maggie found herself watching for him. It was ridiculous, but just knowing that he was at the conference had stirred up all those feelings she thought she had safely tucked away since the last time she had seen him.

That was over five months ago. To be more precise, it had been the Sunday after Halloween when she left Platte City, Nebraska, to go home to Virginia. She and Nick, who had been the county sheriff at the time, had spent exactly one week together, hunting a religious psychopath who had murdered four little boys. Two men had been captured and were awaiting trial, neither of whom Maggie was convinced was the real killer. Despite all the circumstantial evidence, Maggie still believed the real killer was a charismatic Catholic priest named Father Michael Keller. Only, Keller had disappeared somewhere in South America, and no one, not even the Catholic Church, seemed to know what had happened to him.

For the last five months, all Maggie had come up with were rumors of a handsome young priest who traveled from one small farming community to another, serving as their parish priest, though no assignment had officially been made. By the time Maggie tracked down the location, the elusive priest was gone, disappearing into the night with no explanation. Months later, the rumors would find him at another small parish, miles away. But again, by the time the location was narrowed down, Keller was gone. It was as though the communities protected him, keeping him safe like some fugitive unjustly accused. Or perhaps like some martyr.

The thought made Maggie sick to her stomach. That was what Maggie believed to be Keller's motive for murdering boys he thought were abused. He had hoped to make martyrs of them, as though he could administer a perfectly evil salvation. It seemed unfair that Keller would now be protected like a martyr, instead of executed for the evil monster he was. She wondered how long it would take before these poor farmers would start to find their little boys dead along some riverbank, strangled and stabbed to death but washed clean and given their last rites.

Would they be willing to see Keller punished then? There seemed to be a problem with punishing evil these days, an evil that gained strength by conspiring with other evil. Maggie knew Keller had been the one who had visited Albert Stucky in a Florida prison. Several guards had later identified Keller from a photograph. And though she had no proof, she also knew it had been Keller who had given Stucky the wooden crucifix. It was that dagger-like crucifix Stucky had used to cut himself free of his restraints and stab a transport guard.

She shook the thought from her mind and gulped the remainder of her Scotch. Turner and Delaney looked as though they were finally at a standstill. Delaney looked miserable. Turner's brown face had a greasy sheen to it, despite his efforts at wiping it clean. She was about to order another Scotch when Ford waved down the waitress for the check. Neither detective had allowed any of the FBI agents to pay. Maggie insisted on at least leaving the tip, which Ford did allow. Maybe he realized his detective's salary would never be able to keep up with Turner and Delaney's appetites.

Milhaven had driven them, but Maggie wished she could walk rather than be squashed once again into the Grand Am's back seat between her two bodyguards. The night was clear but crisp enough to provoke a shiver. Before they got to the parking lot, they noticed a gathering in the alley. One uniformed cop stood in front of a metal Dumpster and attempted to keep a small crowd of well-dressed onlookers at a distance.

Without a word, the detectives and FBI agents made their way to the scene.

"What's the problem here, Cooper?" Ford knew the frustrated officer.

"Let's move out of the way," Milhaven said to the onlookers as he and Delaney pushed them back into the parking lot that ran parallel to the alley.

The officer glanced at Maggie and Turner.

"It's okay," Ford reassured him. "They're FBI. Here for the conference. So what's going on?"

Officer Cooper pointed to the Dumpster behind him with a tilt of his head.

"Dishwasher at the Bistro took out the trash about a half hour ago. Noticed a hand sticking up out of the pile. Freaked. Called it in, but not before he announced it to the whole goddamn world."

Maggie felt the familiar knot in her stomach. Turner was already at the Dumpster, his six-foot-three frame allowing him to look over the edge without assistance. Maggie dragged an empty milk crate and joined him. Now she wished she hadn't drunk so much. She paused and waited for the brief spell of light-headedness to pass.

The first thing Maggie noticed was a red umbrella, its handle looped over the edge of the Dumpster as if the owner hadn't meant for it to be mistaken for trash. Or had it purposely been left as evidence?

"Officer Cooper." She waited for his attention. "You might mention to the detectives when they arrive that there's an umbrella here. It probably should be bagged and taken in for fingerprints."

"Will do."

Without disturbing anything, Maggie could see the woman was naked and lying on her back. The patch of red pubic hair was a stark contrast to the white skin. Immediately, Maggie knew the scene had been tampered with. Officer Cooper said the dishwasher had noticed only a hand sticking up out of the pile, yet the woman's entire torso was exposed. What looked like vegetable peels had been tossed onto her face. Her head was turned to the side, her brilliant red hair littered with pieces of leftovers.

Maggie could see the woman's mouth, partially opened as though something may have been shoved inside. Then she noticed a dot, a beauty mark above the upper lip. The knot in her stomach tightened. She leaned forward, stretched on tiptoe, sending the crate wobbling while she reached in.

"O'Dell, what the hell are you doing?" Turner scolded her as he watched.

Gently, she swiped at a potato peel and a clump of angel-hair pasta that was stuck to the side of the woman's face.

"It's Rita," she said, wishing she had been wrong.

"Rita? Rita who?"

Maggie waited, glanced at Turner and watched the recognition register on his face.

"Shit! You're right."

"You guys know her?" Ford asked as he looked over the top.

"She's a waitress from the bar and grill down the street," Maggie explained as her eyes continued to examine what she could of Rita's body.

Her throat had been slashed, so deep it had nearly decapitated her. The rest of her body had few bruises and no punctures except for her wrists, which showed ligature marks. Whatever the method of capture, the struggle had been minimal, suggesting that hopefully death had come quickly. Maggie found herself relieved and at the same time disparaged to be relieved by such a thing.

Then she saw the bloody incision in Rita's side underneath a mass of spaghetti. She shoved herself away from the Dumpster, half jumping, half falling off the crate. The light-headedness was quickly replaced by a dizzy buzz. She rushed a safe distance away before she wrapped her arms around herself to stop the wave of panic. Damn it! She never got sick at crime scenes anymore. But this was different. This was a mixture of dread and fear, not nausea.

"O'Dell, you okay?"

Turner was at her side. His large hand touched her shoulder, startling her. She avoided his eyes.

"Stucky did this," she said, keeping her voice steady and free of the quiver invading her lower lip.

"O'Dell, come on now."

"I thought I saw him when we were in the bar and grill last night."

"As I remember, we all had plenty to drink."

"No, Turner, you don't understand. Stucky must have seen her. He must have noticed us talking, joking with her. He chose her because of me."

"O'Dell, we're in Kansas City. You're not even on the conference roster. Stucky couldn't possibly know you're here."

"I know you and Delaney think I'm losing it. But this is exactly Stucky's M.O. We should start looking for a container, a take-out container, before someone else finds it."

"Look, O'Dell. You're just on edge."

"It's him, Turner. I know it. And whatever he sliced out of her is going to show up at some outdoor café table. Maybe even in front of this restaurant. We need to—"

"O'Dell, slow down," he whispered, looking around as if to make sure he was the only one witnessing her hysteria. "I know you're feeling like you need to be checking over your shoulder, thinking—"

"Damn it, Turner. This isn't my imagination."

He went to touch her shoulder again, and this time she jerked back just as she noticed a dark figure across the alley.

"O'Dell, relax."

The man stood at the edge of the crowd, a crowd that had doubled in only a few minutes. He was too far away, and it was too dark for her to be certain, but he wore a black leather jacket, like the man she had seen last night.

"I think he's here," she whispered, and positioned herself behind Turner so she could look without being obvious. Her pulse quickened.

"O'Dell." By the tone of his voice, she knew Turner was growing impatient.

"There's a man in the crowd," she explained, keeping her voice low, "tall, thin, dark, sharp features. From what I can see of his profile, it could be Stucky. My God, he's even carrying what looks like a take-out container."

"As are a whole bunch of others. Come on, O'Dell, this is a restaurant district."

"It could be Stucky, Turner."

"And it could be the mayor of Kansas City."

"Fine—" she let him hear her anger "—I'll just go talk to him myself."

She started around him, but Turner grabbed her arm.

"Stay put and stay cool," he said with an exaggerated sigh.

"What are you going to do?"

"I'm gonna talk to the man. Ask a few questions."

"If it's Stucky—"

"If it's Stucky, I'll recognize the bastard. If it's not, you're picking up the dinner tab tomorrow night. I'm thinking you better get your credit card ready for prime rib."

She watched Turner while trying not to be obvious about it. She positioned herself behind Delaney and Milhaven, who were deep in discussion about baseball. Neither man seemed to notice her. Through the space between them, Maggie could see Turner walk with his casual yet authoritarian gait toward the crowd. She knew he wasn't taking her seriously, and he wouldn't be prepared if it was, indeed, Stucky.

She reached inside her jacket and unsnapped the restraint on her holster, then kept her hand on the butt of the gun. Already her heart was pounding against her rib cage. All other motion, all other conversation stood still as she concentrated on the man in the black leather jacket. Could it really be Stucky? Could the bastard be so arrogant to kill in a city crawling with law enforcement officers from across the country, then stand back and watch? Yes, Stucky would love the challenge. He'd love to be able to thumb his nose at them all. A shiver slid down her back as a night breeze swirled around her, wet and cold.

Turner didn't reach the crowd before the man turned to leave.

"Hey, wait a minute." Turner yelled at the man loud enough for even Delaney and Milhaven to look. "I want to talk to you."

The man bolted and so did Turner. Delaney started to ask Maggie something, but she didn't wait to hear. She raced across the parking lot, gun drawn, its nose to the ground. The crowd scattered out of her way with gasps and one scream.

All Maggie could think was this time Albert Stucky would not escape.

# CHAPTER 22

Maggie's heart slammed against her chest. Turner had disappeared around a corner and into another alley. She followed without slowing down and without hesitation. Halfway down, she made herself stop. The alley was unusually narrow, barely wide enough to accommodate a small vehicle. The tall brick buildings blocked out any streetlights. The moon was only a sliver, leaving dim bulbs to light the way, some cracked but most bare, hanging above rickety back doors.

She squinted, examining the shadows and trying to listen over the pounding in her ears. By now she was breathing much too hard from such a short run. Her skin felt clammy. Every nerve ending in her body seemed to be on alert. Her muscles tensed. Where the hell had they gone? She had been minutes, no, seconds, behind them.

Something rattled behind her. She spun around, her Smith & Wesson kept close to her body, but aimed and ready to blow to pieces the empty Burger King cup. She watched the breeze lift and push it down the alley as she tried to steady her nerves. Calm. She needed to stay calm, keep focused.

She turned, keeping her grip firm on the revolver. Again she strained to hear over the thunder in her ears. The cool night air sent a shiver down her back. She needed to breathe, to control the gasps. They were gasps caused by fear, not exhaustion. Damn it! She wouldn't let him do this to her. She needed to slow down. She needed to concentrate.

She took careful steps as she proceeded. The cobblestone street was old, with uneven and chipped bricks, some oddly spaced. It would be easy to twist an ankle, to stumble or trip, to become vulnerable. Still, she didn't look down. She kept her eyes moving, watching though it was difficult to see beyond fifty to a hundred feet. Was it getting darker, or was it simply her imagination? Her eyes darted over everything, checking stacks of boxes, black doorways, rusty fire escapes, anyplace Albert Stucky could hide behind or sneak into. He wouldn't trick her this time.

Where the hell was Turner? She wanted to call out, but couldn't risk it. Was it possible they had run another way? No, she was certain they had disappeared around this corner and into this alley.

Ahead she could see an open space where two cars were parked. A Dumpster blocked her view of the entire area. Behind her in the distance footsteps ran past, missing this narrow alley. From the open space she heard muffled voices. She pushed her body against the grimy brick wall and inched her way along. Her chest ached. Her knees felt mushy. Her palms were sweaty, but she gripped the gun's handle, keeping her finger on the trigger and the gun's nose down.

She came to the edge of the building and had nowhere else to go. She crouched and snuck behind the Dumpster. Where the hell were Delaney and Milhaven? By now they should have backtracked. Her eyes strained to see beyond the darkness to the end of the alley. Nothing. Now the voices ahead of her were more clear.

"Hold on a minute." She recognized Turner's voice. "What the hell do you have there?"

She waited, but there was no answer to his question. If Stucky had a knife, she'd never hear the damage until it was too late. She peeked out just enough to see the back of the leather jacket. Good. He was facing the opposite direction. He wouldn't see her. But how close was he to Turner?

She heard footsteps behind her, making their way noisily toward her over the cobblestone. From her hiding spot, she couldn't see them, couldn't wave them off, couldn't warn them. Damn it! In seconds Stucky would hear them, too, if he hadn't already. She needed to move now, take her chances.

In one quick motion, she jumped out from behind the Dumpster, scrambling to take a firm stance, legs apart, arms in front, aim focused on the back of the bastard's head. It wasn't until she cocked the gun's hammer that she saw Stucky flinch.

"Don't move an inch, or I'll blow your goddamn head off."

"O'Dell," she heard Turner say.

She could finally see him. He was standing close to the building, a shadow covering most of his face. With Stucky between them, Maggie couldn't see if Turner had his gun drawn. Instead, she concentrated on her target, not ten feet in front of her.

"O'Dell, it's okay," Turner told her, yet he still didn't move. Did Stucky have a gun pointed at him?

"Drop whatever you're holding and put your hands up behind your head. Do it. Now!" she yelled, surprised at her own voice, amplified and bouncing off of the brick buildings.

The footsteps behind her had slowed, their echo making what Maggie knew to be only several men sound instead like a whole troop. She didn't turn. Her eyes never left the back of Stucky's head. He hadn't moved, but hadn't obeyed her command either.

"I said hands up. Now, goddamn it!"

"O'Dell, it's okay," Turner said again.

But there was still no movement, not from Stucky, not from Turner, not from the men keeping their distance behind her. Maggie inched closer. Perspiration trickled down her back. A breeze swept strands of damp hair off her forehead but whipped others into her face. Still, she didn't move, didn't flinch. Her finger remained firmly on the trigger, pressing, ready to squeeze. Her entire body had gone rigid, freezing much too stiffly, threatening to lock her muscles into position.

"Last time. Drop what you're holding and put your hands up behind your head, or I'll blow your skull wide open." This time the ultimatum came through clenched teeth. Maggie's head throbbed. Her hand began to ache from the effort it took not to squeeze the trigger.

Finally, his hands went up while something slapped and crunched against the cobblestone. She could feel it splatter her feet, and knew it was the plastic take-out container he had been carrying. But she refused to look down. She didn't want to see what part of Rita had been spread all over the ground. Instead, she kept her sights on where the nose of her gun pointed, in the middle of the tuft of black hair at the base of his skull. At this close range and at this angle, the bullet would drive through the skull and into the brain, shredding the cerebellum and ripping through the frontal lobe before it exited the top of his forehead. He'd be dead by the time his body hit the ground.

"Ease up, Maggie," she heard Delaney say, and suddenly he was beside her.

The others stayed behind them. Turner stepped out so she could see that he hadn't been injured. Silence filled the alley so completely, she wondered if they were all holding their breaths. Yet, she hadn't dropped her stance or lowered her weapon.

"Turn around," she ordered the back of Stucky's head.

"O'Dell, you can put away your gun," Turner said, but she didn't look at him. She wouldn't slip this time. She wouldn't let her guard down.

"I said turn around, damn it." Her stomach twisted into a series of knots. Would she be able to look him in the eyes?

He turned slowly. Her finger pressed tighter. All it would take was a minor adjustment, a split second for her to refocus between his eyes. Then one more second to squeeze the trigger. But she wanted him to see it coming. She wanted him to look at her. She wanted him to know what it felt like to know another person had total control over his life. She wanted him to feel fear, and yes, she wanted to see that fear in his eyes.

The man stared down at her with wide, frightened eyes, a thin, drawn face and shaking bony hands. He looked as if he'd faint from fear. It was the exact reaction Maggie had dreamed about. It was the exact revenge she had hoped for. Only the man was not Albert Stucky.

# CHAPTER 23

*Early Tuesday morning*
*March 31*

Maggie opened her hotel-room door to Delaney. Without a word or an invitation, she turned and walked back into the room, leaving him there while she continued the pacing he had interrupted. Out of the corner of her eyes, she saw him hesitate. Even after coming in, he held on to the doorknob, looking as though he wished he could escape. She wondered how he and Turner had decided which of them would talk to her. Had Delaney lost the coin toss?

She ignored him as he walked across the room, careful to stay out of her path. He sat down at a small table that wobbled when he leaned his elbows on it. He picked up her empty plastic glass and fingered the miniature bottle of Scotch, giving both a sniff before replacing them. His shirtsleeves were rolled up. His collar button opened. His tie removed. He looked wrinkled and tired. During one of her turns, she saw him rub his hands over his bristled face and up through his thinning hair. She'd make him speak first. She was in no mood to talk. And certainly in no mood for a lecture. Why couldn't they just leave her alone?

"We're worried about you, Maggie."

So there it was. He'd have to start with a low blow, all that worrying-and-caring stuff. Plus, he was using her first name. This was serious stuff. She almost wished Turner had come instead. At least he would yell a little.

"There's no need to worry," she said calmly.

"Look at you. You're wound so tight you can't even sit still."

She shoved her hands into the pockets of her trousers, briefly alarmed, noticing for the first time how baggy the pants felt. When had she lost weight? She continued to pace, keeping her hands hidden in her pockets. No sense in showing Delaney how badly her hands had been shaking since she'd returned to her room.

"It was an honest mistake," she defended herself before he had a chance to make the obvious accusation.

"Of course it was."

"From the back he looked exactly like Stucky. And why the hell did he ignore my instructions three times?"

"Because he doesn't understand English."

She stopped and stared at him. The thought had never occurred to her. Of course it hadn't. She had been convinced it was Stucky. There had been no doubt in her mind.

"Then why did he run from Turner?"

"Who knows." Delaney dug his fingers into his eyes. "Maybe he's an illegal alien. Point is, Maggie, you not only made him splatter his veal capellini all over the pavement, you almost blew his frickin' head off."

"I did not almost blow his head off. I followed protocol. I couldn't see Turner. I couldn't see what this fucking idiot had in his hands, and he wasn't responding. What the hell would you have done, Delaney?"

His eyes met hers for the first time, and she held him there, despite his discomfort.

"I probably would have done the same thing." But his admission made him look away.

Maggie thought she saw a hint of embarrassment. There was more to this little visit than concern or a lecture. She braced herself and leaned against the chest of drawers, the only solid piece of furniture in the room.

"What's going on, Delaney?"

"I called Assistant Director Cunningham," he said, glancing up at her but avoiding her eyes. "I had to tell him what happened."

"Goddamn you, Delaney," she said under her breath, and began pacing once more to steady the brewing anger.

"We're worried about you, Maggie."

"Right."

"I saw the look in your eyes, Maggie, and it scared the hell out of me. I saw how much you wanted to pull the trigger."

"But I didn't, did I? Doesn't that count for anything? I didn't pull the goddamn trigger."

"No, not this time."

She stopped at the window and stared down at the lights of the plaza below. She bit her lower lip. The lights were beginning to blur. She would not cry. She closed her eyes tight against the urge. Behind her, Delaney remained still and quiet. She refused to give him anything other than her back.

"Cunningham wants you to return to Quantico," he said in a low, apologetic voice. "He's sending Stewart to finish your workshop. He'll be here in a couple of hours, so you don't need to worry about the morning session."

She watched several cars below as they glided through intersections. At this height, they reminded her of a slow-motion video game. Streetlights flickered, confused whether to stay on or shut off as the sky lightened in anticipation of sunrise. In less than an hour, Kansas City would be waking up, and she hadn't even been to bed yet.

"Did you, at least, tell Cunningham about Rita?"

"Yes."

When he offered nothing more, she turned to him, suddenly hopeful. She watched his face when she asked, "Does he believe it was Stucky?"

"I don't know. He didn't say, and I didn't ask."

"So maybe he wants me to return to finally help on the case?"

Again, Delaney looked away, staring at the tabletop. She knew without any response that she was wrong.

"Jesus! Cunningham thinks I'm losing it, too," she said quietly, and turned back to the window. She leaned her forehead against the cool glass, hoping it would steady her nerves. Why couldn't she just feel numb, instead of all this anger and now this sudden feeling of defeat?

After a long silence, she heard Delaney get up and start for the door.

"I already made arrangements for you. Your flight leaves a little before one this afternoon. I don't have any sessions today, so I can drive you to the airport."

"Don't bother. I'll take a cab," she said without moving.

She heard him waiting, fidgeting. She refused to give him her eyes. And she certainly would not give him the absolution she knew Delaney would feel guilty without. Down below, cars began to fill the video-game slots, black and red and white, stopping and going.

"Maggie, we're all just worried about you," he said again, as if it should be enough.

"Right." She didn't bother to disguise the hurt and anger.

She waited for the soft slap of the door to close behind him. Then she crossed the room and turned the dead bolt. She stood with her back leaning against the door, listening to her heart pound, waiting for the anger and disappointment to leave. Why couldn't she replace it with acceptance or, at least, complacency? She needed to go home to her new, huge Tudor house with her belongings stacked in cardboard boxes and her shiny new state-of-the-art security system. She needed to let this go, before she did slip so far over the edge there would be no return.

She waited, pressed against the door, staring at the ceiling and listening, if not for her heart to stop banging then at least for her common sense to return. Then making up her mind, she stomped to the middle of the room. She began stripping out of the clothes she had worn since yesterday morning. In minutes she was dressed in blue jeans, a sweatshirt and an old pair of Nikes. She slipped on her shoulder holster, shoved her badge into the back pocket of her jeans and wrestled into a navy FBI windbreaker.

Her forensic kit hadn't been used in months, but she still didn't leave home without it. She pulled out several pairs of latex gloves, some evidence bags and a surgical face mask, transferring the items to the pockets of her jacket.

It was almost 6:00 a.m. She had only six hours, but she wasn't leaving this city until she connected Albert Stucky to Rita's murder. And she didn't care if that meant checking every last Dumpster and every last discarded take-out container in Westport's market district. Suddenly feeling energized, she grabbed her room's key card and left.

# CHAPTER 24

"Hey lady. What the hell you looking for?"

Maggie looked over her shoulder but didn't stop digging through the rubble. She was up to her knees in garbage. Her Nikes were stained with barbecue sauce, her gloved hands sticky. Her eyes stung from a smelly concoction of garlic, mothballs, spoiled food and general human crap.

"FBI," she finally shouted through the paper face mask, and turned just enough for him to see the yellow letters on the jacket's back.

"Shit! No kidding? Maybe I can help"

She glanced at him again, resisting the urge to swipe at the strands of hair in her face, instead waving at the flies who regarded her as an invader of their territory. The man was young, probably in his early twenties. A scar, still pink and swollen, ran along his jaw and a purple bend in his nose indicated a recent break. Maggie's eyes darted around the alley, wondering if the rest of his gang was close by.

"Actually, I have more help than I need. The KC cops are a couple of Dumpsters down" she lied, pleased when the kid immediately began a nervous dance. His head jerked in both directions. He shifted his weight from one foot to the other as if preparing to run.

"Yeah, well. Good luck then." Rather than decide which direction to risk, he found an unlocked door and disappeared into the back of a warehouse.

She tossed a bulging garbage bag to the side without opening it. Stucky would never leave it hidden inside a bag. In the past, his surprises had been left in plain sight, where they were easily discovered, often by unsuspecting citizens. Maybe she was wasting her time going through Dumpsters.

Just then she saw the corner of a white cardboard take-out container. Slowly, she stepped closer, lifting each leg high as if wading through water, ignoring the squish-squash sounds beneath her feet. The last two containers had yielded one green meatball sandwich and some moldy ribs. Yet, each time she spotted a new one her pulse quickened. She felt a surge of adrenaline as she swatted at flies and brushed off wilted lettuce, cigarette butts and wadded pieces of tinfoil.

She lifted the container carefully, keeping it level and setting it on the edge of the Dumpster. The box was about the size of a small cake or pie. It'd provide ample room for a kidney or a lung. Neither organ required much space. She had once found a lung from one of Stucky's victims stuffed inside a container no bigger than a sandwich.

Sweat trickled down her back, despite the morning being damp and chilly. By now, she imagined she reeked as bad as the garbage she stood in. She steadied her fingers and sucked in her breath. The surgical mask clung to her mouth and nose. She slipped off the container's tab and pulled open the lid. The smell made her turn her head and hold her breath. After a few seconds, she was able to look again. Who'd ever guess spoiled fettuccine Alfredo would curdle and stink like rotten eggs? At least that's what Maggie thought the contents had once been. It was difficult to tell without lifting the thin film of fuzzy green and gray scum off the top. She closed and secured the lid.

"Find anything interesting?"

The deep voice startled her. Had the young gangster changed his mind? She grasped the Dumpster's edge so she wouldn't slip and fall backward into the trash. When she turned, she found Detective Ford staring up at her. Only this morning she hardly recognized him. Like her, he was dressed in street clothes, blue jeans, a gray hooded sweatshirt and a blue Kansas City Royals baseball cap. He looked much younger without the suit and tie and without his older partner.

She tugged off the surgical mask and let it dangle at her neck.

"I'm finding that we waste entirely too much food in this country," she said, dropping the container and wading to the opposite side of the Dumpster where she had left a milk crate on the cobblestone to aid in her climb.

"I didn't realize the FBI was trying to police that sort of thing."

She checked to see if there would be a lecture. He smiled.

"So are you undercover or off duty?" she asked, pointing to the baseball cap as she peeled off the latex gloves.

"I should ask you the same thing."

"I had some free time this morning," she said, as if that should be explanation enough for her to be knee-deep, sifting through garbage.

"Hey, Ford, where the hell did you disappear?" a familiar voice called from around the corner.

"Over here," Detective Ford answered.

Even before he came into view, Maggie felt the annoying flutter in her stomach. Nick Morrelli looked just as handsome as she had remembered, tall and lean with a confident stride. He, too, wore blue jeans with a red Nebraska Cornhuskers sweatshirt. He was at Ford's side before he recognized her, and when he did, his smile revealed dimples in an otherwise strong, square jaw.

"Maggie?"

She tossed the sticky gloves and yanked off the surgical mask from around her neck, adding it to the garbage.

"Hi, Nick." She pretended to sound casual while wading the rest of the way out, suddenly acutely aware of flies now attracted and interested in her. She swatted at them and tucked wild strands of hair behind her ears and away from her face.

"That's right. I keep forgetting you two know each other." Ford was smiling, too. "Maggie had some free time this morning," he said to Nick.

"Jesus, it's good to see you, Maggie."

Immediately, she felt her face flush.

"It might not be so good to smell me," she said, needing to stop any sentimental reunion.

She gripped the edge of the Dumpster and swung a leg over the side. Her foot dangled, searching for the milk crate. Before she could find it, Nick's hands were on her waist to help. Her hip brushed against his chest on the way down. Despite being bombarded with smells all morning, she recognized the subtle scent of his cologne.

Once both her feet were on the ground, his hands lingered, but she avoided looking up at him. She avoided looking at either of them, needing the extra time to compose herself while waiting for the unexpected flutter to leave. Damn it! She wasn't some schoolgirl. Why the hell did her body respond like this?

She occupied herself wiping the sticking garbage from her pant legs and shoes. Unfortunately, when she did look up, both men were watching her. She continued to avoid Nick's eyes, remembering how they could look deep inside her and uncover vulnerabilities she had hidden even from herself.

"So," Ford finally said, glancing back into the Dumpster, "did you find anything interesting?"

She wondered how much Turner and Delaney had shared with Ford about her obsession with Stucky. Had Detective Ford seen how close to the edge she had come last night? And what had he discussed with Nick? She didn't think for a minute he had forgotten they knew each other. After all, Ford had invited Nick to have dinner with them last night, though there had never been an explanation as to why Nick hadn't joined them. Suddenly she was curious if Nick had simply wanted to avoid seeing her again. After all, if he was now living in Boston, why hadn't he called? She could feel his eyes taking her in, watching her, smiling at her, but thankfully not making a big deal of their reunion.

"No, I didn't find anything," she finally answered. She needed to change the subject before Detective Ford discovered it was body parts she had been rummaging for and not simply overlooked evidence. "Is this your case now?"

"Not officially. More than likely Milhaven and I will be putting in some hours on it. Today's supposed to be my day off. Nick and I were just about to get an early lunch."

"And you always take the alleys?"

Ford grinned and glanced at Nick.

"She doesn't let anybody get away with anything, does she?"

"No, she certainly doesn't." Nick's eyes caught hers, and she knew his simple statement had much deeper meaning, reminding her of the intimacies they had shared and those they had almost shared.

"So come on, Detective Ford." She needed to keep things light, capitalize on their jovial mood. She needed to keep Ford from realizing she had no business snooping around in his jurisdiction. She was already in enough trouble with Cunningham. "You're down here taking another look, too, right?"

"Okay, you caught me." He held up both hands as if in surrender. "I was telling Nick about last night."

Maggie cringed, and again she wondered what exactly had been discussed. Nick knew the whole story, all the gory details about her and Stucky. He had experienced firsthand her nightmares. Still, she kept her face impassive, pretending last night had been just another routine chase for her. Truth was, she didn't care if Ford thought she was losing it. But maybe she did care if Nick thought it. She waited and Ford continued.

"You sorta got my curiosity up last night, O'Dell."

Oh God, she thought, but instead said, "How is that?"

"All that talk about Albert Stucky sorta spooked me."

She glanced from Detective Ford to Nick, looking for some indication of whether or not they were taking her seriously. If this was Ford's way of patting her on the head and reassuring her how mistaken she was, she didn't need to waste her breath responding.

"You think I'm being paranoid?" She couldn't help it. The beginning anger slipped out. Nick noticed immediately and looked concerned. Ford looked genuinely confused.

"No, that's not at all what I meant.... Well, that's not exactly true. I guess I was thinking that last night."

"Albert Stucky has the financial wherewithal and the intelligence to go anywhere he wants, anytime he chooses. Don't think for a second Kansas City is safe, simply because he hasn't struck in the Midwest before." There it was. She hadn't meant to let the anger out. She hated how Stucky had such power over her emotions, triggering them with the mere mention of his name. Again she avoided Nick's eyes, and again she could feel them.

Ford stared at her, but there was no accusation on his face. Instead, he looked as though he was only waiting for her to finish her tirade.

"Can I talk now?"

"Be my guest." Maggie crossed her arms over her chest, bracing herself and yet doing her best to look defiant. It was a newly acquired talent.

"That was my way of thinking last night. Like, why in the world would this Stucky guy just happen to pick Kansas City instead of the East Coast? I know enough about serial killers to know they keep to familiar territory. But before I met Nick this morning, I sat in on the autopsy of your friend, Rita."

Detective Ford glanced at Nick, and it was obvious this was what the two of them had already discussed. He looked back at Maggie, waited until he had her full attention then said, "Seems our victim is missing her right kidney."

# CHAPTER 25

Tully checked his watch. It wasn't like Assistant Director Cunningham to be late for a meeting. He sat back and waited. Maybe his watch was running fast again. According to Emma, it was ancient and uncool.

Tully stared at the huge map spread on the wall behind his boss's desk. It was Cunningham's personal log for his twenty years as head of the Investigative Support Unit. Each pushpin indicated a spot where a serial killer had struck. Each pushpin color designated a particular serial killer. Tully wondered how soon the assistant director would run out of colors. Already there were repeats: purple, light purple and translucent purple.

Tully knew his boss had worked on some of the most shocking cases, including John Wayne Gacy and the Green River Killer. By comparison, Tully was a rookie, with only six years' experience in profiling and most of that on paper, not in the field. He wondered how anyone lived day in, day out for decades examining such brutality without becoming jaded or cynical.

He glanced around the office again. Everything on the desk—a leather appointment book, two Bic pens with the caps intact (a talent Tully had not yet perfected), a plain memo pad with no doodles in the corners and a brass nameplate—all of it was organized in straight lines, perpendicular to one another, almost as if Cunningham used a T square every morning. It occurred to Tully that the tidy but stark office contained not one single personal item. There were no sweatshirts wadded in the corner, no miniature basketballs, not a single photo. In fact, Tully knew very little of who his boss was outside the office.

He had noticed a wedding band, yet Assistant Director Cunningham seemed to live at Quantico. There was never any rearranging of appointments for Little League games or school plays or visits to kids in college. Before this morning, he had never even been late for an appointment. No, Tully knew absolutely nothing about the quiet, soft-spoken man who had become one of the most respected men in the FBI. But at what cost? Tully wondered.

"Sorry to keep you waiting," Cunningham said as he breezed in, shedding his suit jacket and swinging it carefully over the back of his chair before sitting down. "What have you found out?"

In the beginning, that brisk, straight-to-the-point attitude had flustered Tully, who was accustomed to the courtesies of the Midwest. Now he appreciated getting down to business with no obligatory exchanges of chitchat or greetings. Though it also prevented the two men from knowing a single thing about each other's personal lives.

"I just received the files faxed over from the Kansas City police."

He pulled out the summary sheet from a group of folders he had brought along. He made certain it was the correct one and handed it across the desk. Cunningham pushed up his glasses.

Tully continued, "Early autopsy reports indicate a slashed throat as cause of death. No other defense wounds or injuries. There was one incision in the victim's right side through which the right kidney was extracted."

"Any sign of the organ?"

"No, not yet. But then the Kansas City cops weren't looking for it right away. It's quite possible someone found it, had no clue what it was and tossed it."

Tully waited patiently, watching his boss as he finished reading. He laid the report on the desk, sat back and rubbed a hand over his jaw.

"What's your perspective on this, Agent Tully?"

"The timing is off. It's much too soon after the delivery girl. And it's much too far away, entirely out of his territory. There was another latent fingerprint, a thumb. Again, it looks like it was deliberately left behind on an umbrella that belonged to the victim. Didn't even have the victim's fingerprints on it. It was definitely wiped down with the print left later. And again, it doesn't match Albert Stucky."

Cunningham frowned, squinting at the report and tapping his index finger to his lip. Tully thought the lines in his face seemed more pronounced this morning, his short hair peppered with more gray.

"So is it Stucky, or isn't it?"

"The M.O. definitely matches Stucky's," Tully said. "And there hasn't been enough in the news or even enough time for a copycat to get motivated. The print may belong to someone who came across the scene. A waiter found her. There's some speculation the scene had been contaminated. KC's faxing a copy of the print to the guys at CJIS in Clarksburg. We'll see if it matches the unidentified one left in Newburgh Heights. There's a good chance these belong to civilians coming across the scene after everything's been wiped clean."

"Okay, let's say that's the case. So what if it is Stucky?"

Tully knew exactly what Cunningham was thinking, but he evidently wanted or needed to hear it, to confirm what seemed to be the obvious.

"If it is Stucky, it's more than likely he followed O'Dell to Kansas City. He may be looking for a way to drag her into this again."

Cunningham glanced at his wristwatch. "She should be headed back right now."

"Actually, I checked, sir. I thought I'd meet her at the airport. She changed to a flight later tonight."

Cunningham shook his head and let out a sigh of frustration as he grabbed his phone and punched several buttons.

"Anita, do you have Special Agent Margaret O'Dell's hotel phone number in Kansas City?" He sat back while he waited.

Tully imagined the methodical Anita quickly accessing her records. Assistant Director Cunningham had kept the same secretary, inheriting her from his predecessor and yielding to her experience and expertise on important matters he couldn't saddle himself with. If such a thing was possible, Anita was even more meticulous than her boss.

"Good," Cunningham said into the phone. "Would you please get in touch with her even if it's through a message. Track her down if she's already checked out. I want to see her in my office tomorrow morning at eight."

He hesitated and listened as he rubbed the bridge of his nose under his glasses. "Oh yes, I forgot about that. Tell O'Dell nine o'clock then. Thanks, Anita."

He replaced the receiver and looked up at Tully, waiting.

"How long do you intend to keep her off this case?" Tully finally asked what he thought was the obvious question.

"For as long as is necessary."

Tully studied his boss's face, but had no clue how to read the composed and reserved expression. He respected the man tremendously, but he didn't know him well enough to know how far he could push him. He decided to take a chance anyway.

"You realize she's checking this one out on her own? That's more than likely why she's taking a later flight."

"All the more reason to get her back here." Cunningham held Tully's eyes, warning him to step carefully. "What else is happening in Newburgh Heights?"

"We found the pizza delivery girl's car. It was left in long-term parking at the airport, right next to a telephone company van that was reported stolen a couple of weeks ago."

"I knew it," Cunningham sat back and began drumming his fingers on the desk. "Stucky's done it before. He'll steal a vehicle, or sometimes only the license plates, from the airport's long-term parking. Chances are he has the plates or even the vehicle returned before the owner is back home. Has forensics impounded the van?"

Tully nodded, sorting through the information he had on both vehicles. "Not likely they'll find anything. It's pretty clean. However, we did find two delivery slips in the girl's car.

He dug in the folder, pulling out one torn piece of paper and another creased with fold lines. Both had been recovered from the floor of the girl's car. A red stain on one corner had tested as pizza sauce, not blood. Tully handed both over the desk. "The torn one is from her first route. Number four on the list is Agent O'Dell's new home address."

Cunningham sat forward, resting elbows on his desk. For the first time in Tully's three months of working at Quantico, he saw anger on his boss's face. The assistant director's dark eyes narrowed and his hands clenched the paper.

"So the damn bastard not only knows where she lives, but he's watching her."

"It looks that way. When I talked to Agent Delaney, he said the waitress in Kansas City had joked and talked with the three of them Sunday evening while she served them. He may be choosing women O'Dell comes in contact with in hopes of making her feel responsible."

"It's another of his goddamn games. He's still obsessed with O'Dell. I knew it. I knew he wouldn't let it go."

"It appears that way. May I say one more thing, sir?"

"Of course."

"You've offered me another agent to help on this case. You've also offered a forensic psychologist, which O'Dell is. You even suggested we have someone on hand to answer medical-related questions. If I'm not mistaken, Agent O'Dell has a premed background."

Tully hesitated, giving Cunningham a chance to cut him off. Instead, he only stared at Tully, his face back to its stoic expression as he simply waited.

"Rather than three or four people," Tully continued, "I'm officially requesting Agent O'Dell. If Stucky is targeting her, she may be the only one who can help us catch him."

Tully expected a flicker of anger or at least impatience. But Cunningham's face remained unchanged.

"I'll give your request careful consideration," he said. "Let me know what else you find out from Kansas City."

"Yes, sir," Tully said as he stood to leave, recognizing the signs of dismissal. Before he reached the door, Cunningham was on the phone again, and Tully couldn't help wondering if his request had also been dismissed.

# CHAPTER 26

Maggie couldn't wait to peel off her damp, smelly clothes. Everyone in the hotel lobby had confirmed her suspicions—she reeked. Two people insisted on getting off the elevator, and the brave souls who continued the ride up with her looked as though they had held their breath for all twenty-three floors.

Detective Ford had dropped her and Nick at the front door then drove home to explain to his wife why he smelled like garbage on his day off. Nick's room was in the south tower of the huge hotel complex, explaining why they hadn't run into each other before. Which meant both banks of elevators would need disinfecting.

The three of them had spent several hours digging through Dumpsters, sifting through trash cans and looking for discarded containers on outdoor tables, window ledges, fire escapes and flower boxes. Maggie hadn't even noticed the thick, gray thunderheads that had rolled in until the rain came in sheets, forcing them to end their search and take shelter. She would have continued if she had been alone. The rain had felt good, slashing at her and perhaps peeling away the tension along with the rancid smells from her skin. But the cracks of thunder and flashes of lightning only made her more anxious and jumpy.

Detective Ford had assured her that Albert Stucky would, indeed, be considered a suspect in Rita's murder, despite their not finding the missing kidney. Maggie couldn't understand why Stucky would deviate from his game, or had some unsuspecting customer taken the container home? Was it possible someone could have placed it in his refrigerator without looking, without knowing what was inside? That seemed ridiculous, and Maggie didn't even want to think about it. The fact was, there wasn't anything more she could do.

As soon as she came into her room, she noticed the phone's red message light flashing. She grabbed the receiver and punched in the necessary numbers to retrieve her voice messages. She was used to getting emergency messages about her mother who attempted suicide as often as other women her age treated themselves to a manicure. But weren't her mother's new friends supposed to be taking care of her? Who could be calling? There was only one message, and it was, indeed, marked urgent.

"Agent O'Dell. This is Anita Glasco calling for Assistant Director Cunningham. He needs to see you in his office tomorrow morning at nine. Please call me back if you won't be able to make it. Thank you and have a safe trip home, Maggie."

Maggie smiled at Anita's soothing voice, though the message itself set her on edge. She listened to her options, punched the number to erase and hung up. She began pacing, trying to contain the anger before it grabbed hold of her. It was Cunningham's way of seeing to it that she returned immediately. He knew she would never blow off a request to meet with him. She wondered what he already knew about Rita's murder, or if he had even considered looking into it. After all, Delaney had probably made it sound as though she was losing her mind, simply imagining things.

She checked her wristwatch and scraped something dry and crusty from its face. She still had about six hours before her rescheduled evening flight. It was the last one to D.C. tonight. If she was to make the appointment with Cunningham in the morning, she couldn't afford another delay. But how the hell could she leave Kansas City knowing Albert Stucky was here, lurking somewhere in the city? Maybe looking for his next victim right this very minute.

She double-checked the door, making sure it was locked. She added the chain and rammed the back of the wooden desk chair up under the knob, kicking the legs until she was satisfied it was secure. Then she stripped down to her underwear and bra and tossed her smelly clothes and shoes into one of the plastic dry-cleaning bags in the closet. Still smelling them, she triple-bagged them, until the scent seemed to be contained.

She brought her Smith & Wesson with her to the bathroom, leaving it close by on the counter. She left the bathroom door open, slipped out of her bra and panties, then crawled into the shower.

The water beat and massaged her skin. She turned the temperature as hot as she could stand it. She wanted to be rid not only of the smells, but of that crawly feeling just under her skin. That infestation of maggots that invaded her system every time she knew Albert Stucky was nearby. She scrubbed at her skin until it was red and raw. She wanted her mind to be swept clean, and her body to forget the scars.

When she stepped out of the shower, she wiped at the foggy mirror. The brown eyes stared back at her with that damn vulnerability so close to the surface. And the scars were still there, too. Her body was becoming a scrapbook.

The scar began just beneath her breast. With the tip of her index finger, she forced herself to touch it. To trace its puckered line down across her abdomen.

"I could gut you in seconds," she remembered him telling her—no, promising, not telling. By then, she had resigned herself to death. He had already trapped her. He had already forced her to watch while he bludgeoned and gutted two women to death. He had threatened that if Maggie closed her eyes he would simply bring out another woman and start all over. And he had been true to his word.

There was still no escaping those images and sounds: bloodied breasts, the crack of bones, the hollow thud of a baseball bat against a skull. There had been so much blood from severed arteries and from knives sinking into flesh, into abdomens and vaginas—places where knives should never be allowed. No place was out of limits for Stucky. Nothing on a woman's body was sacred. He carved and sliced, pleased and encouraged by the screams.

After feeling the splatters of blood, the pieces of bone and brain, after hearing the mind-shattering cries for help and smacks of bloodied flesh, what more could he have done to her? Death would have been a relief. So instead, he left her with a constant reminder of himself, a scar.

Maggie snatched a T-shirt and wrestled into it, anxious to cover herself despite her skin being damp. She marched to the dresser and pulled out clean underwear and khakis. Her hair was still dripping as she rummaged through the service butler, relieved to find two new miniature bottles of Scotch. Thank God for the hotel staff's efficiency.

A soft tap on the door startled her. She stopped at the bathroom, retrieving her revolver. Before pulling the chair away, she checked the peephole. Nick's hair was damp and tousled. He wore clean blue jeans and a crisp oxford shirt with the sleeves rolled up.

She returned the chair to the desk and slipped the revolver into the back of her waistband. It wasn't until she opened the door and his eyes slid down her body that she realized she had nothing on underneath the thin T-shirt that now clung to her damp body.

"That was fast," she said, ignoring the flutter this man seemed to activate on sight.

"I was anxious to crawl out of those clothes." He returned to her face, a hint of embarrassment coloring his own. "I think I might need to throw out my shoes. There's gunk on them that I don't even want to know about."

They stared at each other. His presence, his scent seemed to dismantle her thought process. She felt hot and damp. She told herself it was from her shower and the extra-hot water she had used.

"I thought maybe we could get something to eat or drink," he finally said. "You do still have time before your flight?"

"I should...um...put something else on."

His eyes wouldn't let her go. Suddenly it unnerved her how much she wanted to touch him. She needed to close the door, get control of her senses, pull herself together. Instead, she heard herself saying, "Why don't you come in."

He hesitated, enough so that she could have taken back the invitation. Instead, she moved away from the door. She retreated to the dresser again, pulling things out at random, pretending to be searching while giving herself any excuse not to look up at him.

He came in and closed the door behind him.

"We seem to spend a lot of time in hotel rooms."

She glanced at him, immediately annoyed that the reminder brought a flush to her cheeks. In a small hotel room in Platte City, Nebraska, they had come dangerously close to making love. Five months later, she could still feel the same rush of heat. With all the emotions assaulting her over the past few days, how was it possible for Nick Morrelli to walk in and assault her with a whole new set?

She pulled out a white crew-neck sweater, the cotton knit cool but bulky and comfortable. She snatched a bra from the drawer as well.

"I'll just be a minute," she said as she disappeared into the steamy bathroom.

She changed quickly, avoiding any extra touches. She toweled the wetness out of her hair and brushed it back, grabbing the blow dryer, then deciding against it. She reached to remove her Smith & Wesson, hesitated, and left it in her waistband, pulling the loose sweater down and checking in the mirror to make sure it couldn't be seen. She knew she'd have to grab her badge on the way out.

Nick was at the window and watched as she tugged on socks and slipped on shoes. She noticed he had both miniature bottles of Scotch in his hand.

"Still having nightmares?" His eyes searched hers as he returned the bottles to the small table.

"Yes," she said quite simply, and gave him her back as she found her badge and some cash. She didn't need Nick Morrelli barging into her life and thinking he had any right to share or expose her vulnerabilities.

"Ready?" she asked as she headed for the door and opened it before looking back at him. She almost tripped over the room-service tray that sat on the floor outside her door. She stared down at the single dinner plate covered by a silver insulator. The two empty glasses and accompanying silverware sparkled on a crisp, white linen napkin.

"Did you order something from room service?" she turned to ask, but Nick was already by her side.

"No. And I didn't hear a knock, either."

He stepped over the tray and out into the hallway to look in both directions. Maggie listened. There were no slamming doors, no footsteps, no wisping elevators.

"Probably just a mistake," Nick said, but she could hear his tension.

Maggie kneeled next to the tray. Her pulse quickened. Carefully, she slipped the linen napkin out from under the silverware, using thumb and index finger. She unfolded it, then used it to grab the handle of the metal insulator. She lifted it slowly and immediately the smell filled the hall.

"Jesus," Nick said, jerking back a step.

In the middle of the shiny dinner plate lay a bloody glob Maggie knew was Rita's missing kidney.

# CHAPTER 27

Within minutes, the hotel's lobby was filled with law enforcement officers from across the Midwest. All entrances and exits were guarded. Elevators were checked and watched. Stairwells were examined at all twenty-five levels. The hotel's room-service kitchen had been invaded and the staff questioned. Despite the overwhelming brigade of manpower, Maggie knew they would never find him.

Most criminals would consider it suicide to show up in a hotel where hundreds of cops, sheriffs, detectives and FBI agents were staying. For Albert Stucky it would simply be another challenge to his game. Maggie imagined him sitting somewhere, watching and amused by the commotion, the blunders, the unsuccessful attempts at catching him. That's why she was checking the most obvious places.

The second floor included an atrium overlooking the lobby. She stayed at the brass railing while her eyes searched down below—the line at the reservations counter, the man at the grand piano, the few diners at bistro tables in the glass-encased café the man behind the concierge desk, the cabdriver hauling out luggage. Stucky would blend in. He'd look as though he belonged. Even the room-service staff would not have noticed him had he walked into their kitchen in a white jacket and black tie.

"Any luck?"

Maggie jumped but managed to restrain herself from automatically reaching for her gun.

"Sorry." Nick looked genuinely concerned. "He'd be nuts to stick around. I'm guessing he's long gone."

"Stucky likes to watch. It isn't much fun if he doesn't get to see people's reactions. Half of these officers don't know what he looks like. If he plays it cool, they might never spot him. He has the uncanny ability to blend in."

Maggie continued searching, standing quietly and still. She could feel Nick examining her. She was tired of everyone watching for signs of some kind of mental meltdown, though she knew Nick was sincere.

"I'm fine," she said without looking at him, answering his unspoken question.

"I know you are. I still get to be concerned." He leaned over the railing, conducting his own search. His shoulder brushed against hers.

"Assistant Director Cunningham thinks he's protecting me by keeping me off the investigation."

"I wondered why you were teaching. John said there were rumors that you were burned out, losing your touch."

She had guessed as much, yet it felt like a slap in the face to hear it out loud. She avoided looking at him. She pushed strands of damp hair out of her eyes, tucking them behind her ears. She probably looked the part of the crazed FBI agent, with her tangled hair and baggy clothes.

"Is that what you think?" she asked, not certain she wanted to hear his answer.

They stood side by side, leaning against the railing, shoulders brushing while their eyes stayed safely ahead and away from each other. His silence lasted too long.

"I told John that the Maggie O'Dell I know is tough as nails. I saw you take a knife to the gut and still not give up."

Another of her scars. The mad child killer she and Nick had chased in Nebraska had stabbed her and left her for dead in a graveyard tunnel.

"Getting stabbed seems so much easier than what Stucky's doing to me."

"I know this isn't what you want to hear, Maggie, but I think Cunningham may be smart in keeping you out of this."

This time she turned to stare at him.

"How can you say that? It's obvious Stucky is playing with me again."

"Exactly. He wants to drag you into his little games. Why give him exactly what he wants?"

"But you don't understand, Nick." The anger bubbled too close to the surface. She tried to keep her voice calm and level. Talking about Stucky could bring her to the edge of sounding hysterical. "Stucky will continue to goad me whether I'm on the case or not. Cunningham can't protect me. Instead, he's keeping me from the one way I have to fight back."

"I'm guessing he must have told you he wants you on that flight back to D.C. tonight?"

"Agent Turner is escorting me." Why bother hiding her anger. "It's ridiculous, Nick. Albert Stucky is right here in Kansas City. I should stay here."

More silence. They were back to searching the crowd below, standing side by side, again leaning their elbows on the railing and again keeping their hands and eyes carefully away from each other. Nick moved closer as though purposely bringing their bodies in to contact. His shoulder no longer accidentally brushed hers. Now it stayed against her. She found a weird sense of comfort in this subtle touch, this slight contact, feeling perhaps that she wasn't in this alone.

"I still care about you, Maggie," he said quietly, without moving and still not looking at her. "I thought I didn't care anymore. I tried to stop. But when I saw you this morning, I realized I hadn't stopped caring at all."

"I don't want to have this conversation, Nick. I really can't. Not now." Her stomach churned with anticipation, with panic, with fear. She didn't need to feel anything more.

"I called you when I first moved to Boston," he continued as if he hadn't heard her.

She glanced at him. Was this some line? That boyish charm, that flirtatious reputation of his surely couldn't have disappeared so easily.

"I didn't get any message," she said, now curious and anxious to call him on his bluff if, in fact, that was what it turned out to be.

"Quantico wouldn't give me any information as to where you were, or when you'd be back. I even told them I was with the Suffolk County D.A.'s office." He glanced at her and smiled. "They weren't impressed."

It was a safe story. She wouldn't be able to confirm it or deny it. She concentrated on the lobby. Below, three men toted luggage behind a well-dressed woman with silver hair and a London Fog raincoat that didn't have a raindrop on it.

"I ended up calling Greg's law firm."

"You did what?"

She pushed herself away from the railing and waited until he did the same, giving her his attention and his eyes.

"Neither of you are listed in the Virginia telephone directory," he defended himself. "I figured the law office of Brackman, Harvey and Lowe might be more understanding. They might actually care about someone from a D.A.'s office getting in touch with one of their attorneys. Even if it was after hours."

"You talked to Greg?"

"I didn't mean to. I was hoping to catch you at home. I thought if Greg answered, I could tell him I needed to talk to you about unfinished business in Nebraska. After all, I knew you were still looking for Father Keller."

"But Greg didn't buy it."

"No." Nick looked embarrassed. He continued anyway. "He told me the two of you were working on your marriage. He asked me as a gentleman to respect that and stay away."

"Greg said that? About being a gentleman? As if he knew." She shook her head and returned to her perch, pretending to be distracted by the activity below. Greg had become so good at lying, Maggie wondered if he actually believed his own bullshit. "How long ago was this?"

"Couple months ago." He joined her again, but this time kept some distance.

"Months ago?" She couldn't believe Greg hadn't mentioned it, or that he hadn't let it slip out during one of their arguments.

"It was right after I moved, so it had to be around the last week of January. I got the impression the two of you were still living together."

"Greg and I both decided to stay at the condo, since neither of us were there that often. But I asked Greg for a divorce on New Year's Eve. That probably sounds heartless—I meant to wait." She watched as a maintenance crew pushed huge floor waxers into the lobby. "We were at his law firm's holiday party. He wanted us to masquerade as the happy couple."

The supervisor of the maintenance crew had a clipboard and wore shiny leather dress shoes. Maggie craned over the railing to get a glimpse of his face. Too young and too tall to be Stucky.

"People at the party kept congratulating me and welcoming me to the firm. They spoiled Greg's surprise. He had managed to get me a job as the head of their investigations department without even talking to me about it. Then he couldn't understand why I wouldn't jump at the chance to be digging through corporate files, looking for misappropriation of funds instead of digging through Dumpsters, looking for body parts."

"Right. Jesus, how silly of him."

She turned and rewarded his sarcasm with a smile.

"I am a pain in the ass, aren't I?" she said.

"An awfully beautiful pain in the ass."

She felt a blush and looked away, annoyed that he could make her feel sensual and alive while the world was going nuts around them.

"I finally moved into a house of my own last week. In a few weeks the divorce should be final."

"Maybe it would have been safer to stay at the condo. I mean as far as this thing with Stucky is concerned."

"Newburgh Heights is just outside D.C. It's probably one of the safest neighborhoods in Virginia."

"Yeah, but I hate thinking about you being all alone."

"I'd rather be alone when he comes for me. That way no one else gets hurt. Not this time."

"Jesus, Maggie! You *want* him to come after you?"

She avoided looking at him. She didn't need to see his concern. She couldn't take on the weight of it, the responsibility of it. So instead, she concentrated on the men in blue overalls wrestling with cords and mops. When she didn't answer, Nick reached for her hand, gently taking it. He intertwined her arm with his, bringing her hand to his chest and keeping it there, warm and tight against the pounding of his heart. Then they stood there while they watched the hotel lobby get its floors waxed.

# CHAPTER 28

*Washington, D.C.*
*Wednesday, April 1*

He could feel Dr. Gwen Patterson staring at him while he stabbed at her furniture with his white cane, fumbling for a place to sit down. Nice stuff. The office even smelled expensive, fine leather and polished wood. But why would he expect anything less? She was a classy woman; sophisticated, cultured, wise and talented. Finally, a challenge to up the ante, so to speak.

He swiped his hand across her desktop, but there wasn't much to disturb—a phone, a Roledex, several legal pads and a daily calendar, flipped open to Wednesday, April 1. Only now did it occur to him that it was April Fools' Day. How ironically appropriate. He resisted the urge to smile, instead turning again and bumping into a credenza, barely missing an antique vase. The window above the credenza looked out over the Potomac River. In its reflection, he watched her grimace at his bold and reckless fumblings.

"The sofa is just to your left," she finally instructed, but stayed seated behind her desk. Though her voice sounded tight, restraining her impatience, she wouldn't embarrass him by coming to his rescue. Excellent. She had passed his first test.

He put his hand out and patted down the soft leather, feeling for the arm, and carefully sitting himself down.

"Would you like something to drink before we get started?"

"No," he snapped, being unnecessarily rude. Invalids could get away with shit like that. It was one of the few advantages he could look forward to. Then, to let her know he wasn't such a bad guy, he politely added, "I'd rather we just get started."

He set the cane by his side where he could find it easily. He bunched up his leather jacket and laid it in his lap. The room was dark, the blinds half-closed, and he wondered why she had bothered. He adjusted his sunglasses on the bridge of his nose. The lenses were extra dark so that no one could see his eyes. So that no one could catch him watching. It was a lovely twist to voyeurism. Everyone thought they were being the voyeurs, safe in staring at him, watching him, pitying him. No one seemed to question whether or not a blind guy could actually see. After all, why in the world would someone fake something like that?

Except that, ironically, the lie might be coming true. The drugs weren't working, and he couldn't deny that his eyesight was getting worse. He had lucked out so many times before, was his number finally up? No, he didn't believe in such a stupid thing as fate. So what if he needed a little extra help these days, a prop or two, or some assistance from an old friend to bring a little excitement into his life. Wasn't that what friends were for?

He cocked his head to one side, waiting, pretending to need to hear her before he could turn in her direction. In the meantime, he watched her. Through the dark lenses in the dark room, he found himself squinting. She was still staring at him, sitting back in her chair, looking comfortable and in control.

She stood and reached for her suit jacket on the back of her chair, but stopped, glanced over at him and left the jacket there. Then she came around to the front of the desk, leaning against the pristine top and standing directly in front of him. She looked soft and fragile, curves in all the right places, tight skin and few wrinkles for a woman in her late forties. She wore her strawberry-blond hair loose, letting it brush her jawline in delicate wisps. He wondered if it was her natural color, and he caught himself smiling. Maybe he would need to find out for himself.

He leaned back into the sofa, waiting, sniffing in her fragrance. God, she smelled good, though he couldn't name the fragrance. Usually he could narrow it down, but this scent was new. Her red silk blouse was thin enough to reveal small, round breasts and the slight pucker of nipples. He was glad she thought she didn't need the jacket. He tucked his hands into his lap, making sure his folded jacket covered the swelling bulge, pleased that his new diet of porn movies seemed to be helping his temporary lapses.

"As with all my patients, Mr. Harding," she said finally, "I'd like to know what your goals are. What you hope to accomplish in our sessions?"

He held back a smile. She was already accomplishing one of his goals. He tilted his head toward her and continued to stare at her breasts. Even if she could see his eyes, people accepted, they expected his eyes to be looking anywhere but in their own eyes.

"I'm not sure I understand the question." He had learned it was good to make women explain. It allowed them to feel in control, and he wanted her to believe she was in control.

"You told me on the phone," she began carefully as though measuring her words, "that you had some sexual issues you wanted to work on." She neither emphasized nor hesitated over the phrase "sexual issues." That was good, very good. "In order for me to help you, I need to know, more specifically, what you expect from me. What you'd like to see come out of these sessions."

It was time to see how easily she could be shocked.

"It really is quite simple. I want to be able to enjoy fucking a woman again."

She blinked and her light complexion flushed slightly, but she didn't move. It was a bit of a letdown. Maybe he should go ahead and add that he wanted to enjoy fucking a woman without wanting to fuck her to death. His new habit really wasn't much different than many of those in the animal and insect world. Perhaps he should compare his sexual habits to those of the female praying mantis who bites off her mate's head just as he is beginning to copulate.

Would she understand that the orgasm, the erotic surge was incredibly powerful when it included pain? Should he confess that seeing his women smeared in blood and screaming for mercy made him come in an orgasmic explosion like none he could achieve otherwise? Could she understand that this hideous thing inside threatened to take away the foundation of his being, his last primal instinct?

But no, he wouldn't share any of this with her—that would probably be a bit much. That was something Albert Stucky would do or say, and he needed to resist the urge to stoop to his old friend's level.

"Can you do that, Doc?" he asked, sticking his chin out and up as though he was listening for her movement, for her reaction.

"I can certainly try."

He looked over her shoulder, his body slightly turned to the side, despite her standing in front of him.

"You're blushing," he said, and allowed a curt smile.

The color in her cheeks deepened. Her hand went to her neck in the useless attempt to stop the blush.

"What makes you say that?"

Would she deny it? Would she disappoint him this soon and lie?

"I'm guessing," he said, letting his voice be soft and soothing, encouraging her to confide in him, hoping to gain access to her own vulnerabilities. If he was to accomplish his ultimate goal, he would need Dr. Gwen Patterson not to feel threatened. The good doctor had a reputation for delving into some of the most famous and devious of criminal minds. He wondered what she would think if she knew she was to be the guinea pig this time.

"Let me just say, I've been a psychologist quite a while." She tried to explain her reaction away casually, but he noticed the color remained in her cheeks. "I've heard many shocking things, much more so than your problem. You needn't worry about embarrassing me, Mr. Harding."

Okay, so she chose to play it safe and cool, refusing him access to her inner self. The idea of this excited him nevertheless. He did so enjoy a challenge.

"Perhaps," she continued, "we should start by you telling me why you no longer enjoy sex."

"Isn't that obvious?" He used the tone he had perfected. The one that sounded angry, offended, yet sad enough to invoke the right amount of pity. It usually worked.

"Of course it's not obvious."

He let one of his hands stray under the pile of leather. She was making this so easy. Playing right into his hands, so to speak. He cupped a palm over his erection.

"If you're thinking your—" she hesitated "—your handicap—"

"It's okay. You can call it what it is. I'm blind. I don't mind anyone saying the word."

"Okay, but your blindness certainly should not mean a loss of libido."

He liked the way she said "libido." Though her lips were thin and her mouth small, he liked the shape. He enjoyed watching the upper lip curl a bit at the corner. He detected a slight accent, but he couldn't place it—maybe upper New York? It made him anxious to hear her say "penis" and "fellatio," and he wondered how her lips would curl around those words.

"Is that what you're saying, Mr. Harding?" she interrupted his thoughts.

"That somehow your loss of sight has rendered you incapable of performing?"

"Men are highly visual creatures, especially when it comes to being sexually aroused."

"Very true," she said as she reached behind her and grabbed a file folder, his folder, his case history. "When did you begin losing your eyesight?"

"About four years ago. Do we have to talk about that?"

She looked up at him over the open file. She had shifted to the other end of the desk, but he kept his gaze on the spot where she had been.

"If it will help us deal with your current problem, then yes, I do think we should talk about it."

He liked her decisive manner, her direct tone. She wouldn't be pussyfooting around him. What a wonderful word—pussyfooting. He rubbed his hidden hand against his bulge.

"Do you have an objection to that, Mr. Harding? You certainly don't appear to be a man who runs away from a challenge."

He hesitated only because he didn't want to interrupt the sensation. It was okay. She'd think he simply needed a moment to think about it.

"I have no objection," he said, having some difficulty containing a smile. No, anyone who knew Walker Harding would never accuse him of running away from anything. But if he was to accept his new challenge, he'd need to depend on the master criminal mind that Dr. Patterson yet had the pleasure of examining. Yes, despite playing this new role, he would still need to depend on the genius of his old friend, Albert Stucky.

# CHAPTER 29

Tully ripped off the latest fax that had just come in from the Kansas City Police Department. He scanned its contents while he gathered folders and notes and crime scene photos. In ten minutes he was meeting with Assistant Director Cunningham, and yet his mind was still preoccupied with the argument he'd had with his daughter less than an hour ago. Emma had waited until he was dropping her off at school to drop her bomb. Damn she was good. But then what did he expect? She had been schooled in the fine art of surprise attack by none other than the master, her own mother.

"Oh, by the way," she had announced in a matter-of-fact voice. "Josh Reynolds asked me to the junior/senior prom. It's a week from Friday, so I'll need to buy a new dress. Probably new shoes, too."

Immediately he had gotten angry. She was only a freshman. When had they decided she could date?

"Did I miss that conversation?" he had asked with enough sarcasm that he was now embarrassed in retrospect.

She had given him her best insulted, wounded look. How could he not trust her? She was "almost fifteen." Practically an old maid compared to her friends who, she assured him, had been dating for two or three years already. He passed on the opportunity to counter with the old argument that just because your friends jump off a bridge... Besides, the real problem was not that he didn't trust her. At forty-three, he could still remember how horny fifteen- and sixteen-year-old boys could get. He wished he could discuss it with Caroline, but he knew she'd side with Emma. Was he really just being an overprotective father?

He jammed the fax sheets into a file folder, adding it to the pile in his arms and headed down the hall. After talking to

Kansas City Detective John Ford late last night, Tully was prepared for Cunningham to be in a foul mood. The waitress's murder looked more and more like the work of Albert Stucky. No one else would deliver the woman's kidney to Agent O'Dell's hotel room. Actually, Tully couldn't figure out why he wasn't on a plane to Kansas City to join O'Dell.

"Good morning, Anita," he greeted the gray-haired secretary who looked alert and impeccable at any hour of the day.

"Coffee, Agent Tully?"

"Yes, please. Cream but—"

"No sugar. I remember. I'll bring it in to you." She waved him by. Everyone knew not to set foot into the assistant director's office until Anita gave the signal.

Cunningham was on the phone, but nodded to Tully and pointed to one of the chairs in front of his desk.

"Yes, I understand," Cunningham said into the phone. "Of course I will." He hung up, as was his usual manner, without a goodbye. He adjusted his glasses, sipped coffee, then looked at Tully. Despite the crisp white shirt and perfectly knotted tie, his eyes betrayed him. Swollen from too little sleep, the red lines were magnified by the bifocal half of his glasses.

"Before we get started," he said, glancing at his watch, "do you have any information on Walker Harding?"

"Harding?" Tully had to think past horny high-school boys and pink prom dresses. "I'm sorry, sir, I don't recognize the name Walker Harding."

"He was Albert Stucky's business partner," a woman's voice answered from the open doorway.

Tully twisted in his chair to look at the young, dark-haired woman. She was attractive and wore a navy blue suit jacket with matching trousers.

"Agent O'Dell, please come in." Cunningham stood and pointed to the chair next to Tully.

Tully stared up at her, shuffling his files, awkwardly shoving them aside.

"Special Agent Margaret O'Dell, this is Special Agent R. J. Tully."

The chair wobbled as Tully stood and shook Agent O'Dell's outstretched hand. Immediately he was impressed with her firm grip and the way she looked directly into his eyes.

"I'm pleased to meet you, Agent Tully."

She was genuine. She was professional. There was no trace of what she must have gone through last night. This certainly didn't look like an agent who was on the verge of mental collapse.

"The pleasure is mine, Agent O'Dell. I've heard a great deal about you."

Tully could see Cunningham already growing impatient with all these pleasantries.

"Why were you asking about Walker Harding?" O'Dell asked as she sat down.

Tully picked up his files again. Okay, so she was used to the assistant director's style of getting right down to business. Now Tully wished he had spent some time preparing instead of agonizing over Emma's virginity. He honestly hadn't thought O'Dell would show up.

"For Agent Tully's benefit," Cunningham began explaining, "Walker Harding and Albert Stucky started an Internet stock-trading business, one of the first of its kind, in the early 1990s. They ended up making millions."

"I'm sorry, but I don't think I have any information on him," Tully said as he riffled through his files, double-checking.

"You probably don't." Cunningham sounded apologetic. "Harding was out of the picture long before Stucky took up his new hobby. He and Stucky sold their company, split their millions and went their separate ways. There was no reason for any of us to know about Walker Harding."

"I'm not sure I follow," Tully said, glancing at Agent O'Dell to see if he was the only one missing something. "Is there some reason why we should now?"

Anita interrupted, floating into the room and handing Tully a steaming mug.

"Thanks, Anita."

"Anything for you, Agent O'Dell? Coffee? Or perhaps your usual early-morning Diet Pepsi?"

Tully watched Agent O'Dell smile in a way that said the two women were quite familiar with each other.

"Thank you, Anita, but no, I'm fine."

The secretary squeezed the agent's shoulder in a gesture that looked more motherly than professional, and then she left, closing the door behind her.

Cunningham sat back and made a tent with his fingertips, picking up the conversation exactly where they had left off, as if there had been no interruption. "Walker Harding became a recluse after he and Stucky sold their business. Practically disappeared off the face of the earth. There seems to be virtually no records, no transactions, no sign of the man."

"Then what does this have to do with Albert Stucky?" Tully was puzzled.

"I checked the airline schedules within the last week for flights going from Dulles or Reagan National to Kansas City. Not that I expected to find Albert Stucky's name on any of the manifests." He looked from Tully to O'Dell. "I was looking for any of the aliases Stucky has used in the past. That's when I noticed that there was a ticket sold for a KC flight, Sunday afternoon out of Dulles, to a Walker Harding."

Cunningham waited, looking for some reaction. Tully watched, tapping his foot nervously but not impressed with the information.

"Excuse me, sir, for saying so, but that may not mean much. It may not even be the same man."

"Perhaps not. However, Agent Tully, I suggest you find out whatever you can about Walker Harding."

"Assistant Director Cunningham, why am I here?" Agent O'Dell asked politely but with enough candor to indicate she wasn't willing to continue without an answer.

Tully wanted to smile. Instead, he kept his eyes and his attention on Cunningham. It was hard not to like O'Dell. Out of the corner of his eye, he could see her shift in her chair, uncomfortable and restless but holding her tongue. She had been kept off this investigation since the beginning. Tully wondered if she was angry with having to sit and listen to these details if she couldn't be involved. Or had Cunningham changed his mind? Tully studied his face, but saw no clue as to what his boss was thinking.

When he didn't answer immediately, O'Dell must have seen it as an opportunity to proceed.

"I mean no disrespect, but the three of us are sitting here talking about a ticket that may or may not have been issued to a man who Albert Stucky may or may not have talked to for years. Yet, there is one thing that we can be certain of—Albert Stucky murdered a woman in Kansas City, and most likely he is still there."

Tully crossed his arms and waited, all the while wanting to applaud this woman he had heard was burned out and slipping over the edge. She certainly soared at the top of her game this morning.

Cunningham caved in his finger tent and sat forward, leaning elbows on his desk and looking as though he had been ambushed in a chess match. But now he was ready for his move, his turn.

"Saturday night about twenty miles from here, a young woman was found murdered, her body tossed into a Dumpster, her spleen surgically removed and placed inside a discarded pizza box."

"Saturday?" Agent O'Dell fidgeted while she calculated the unusually short time line. "Kansas City is not a copycat. He left the goddamn kidney at my door."

Tully winced. Forget chess. This would be more like a showdown at the OK Corral. Cunningham, however, didn't blink.

"The young woman was a pizza delivery person. She was taken while delivering her route."

Agent O'Dell became agitated, crossing her legs, then uncrossing them as if restraining her words. Tully knew she had to be exhausted.

Cunningham continued, "She had to have been taken somewhere close by. Perhaps in the neighborhood. He raped and sodomized her, slit her throat and removed her spleen."

"By sodomized are you saying he raped her himself from behind or with another item?"

Tully couldn't see a difference. Wasn't either hideous enough? Cunningham looked to him for the answer. This, unfortunately, he could answer without digging through a single file. The young girl had looked too much like Emma for him not to remember every detail. Whether he wanted them to be or not, they were stamped in his memory.

"There was no semen left behind, but the medical examiner seemed convinced it was penile stimulation. There were no traces or remnants that a foreign object might leave behind."

"Stucky's never done that before." O'Dell sat at the edge of her chair, suddenly animated. "He wouldn't do that. There would be no point. He likes to watch their faces. He enjoys seeing their fear. He wouldn't be able to see that from behind."

Cunningham tapped his fingertips on the desktop as if waiting for O'Dell to finish.

"The young woman delivered a pizza to your new home the night she was murdered."

The silence seemed amplified when the drumming of the fingertips stopped. Cunningham and Tully watched O'Dell. She sat back, looking from one to the other. Tully saw the realization in her eyes. He expected to see fear, maybe anger. It surprised him to find what looked like resignation. She rubbed a hand over her face and tucked strands of hair behind her ears. Otherwise, she sat quietly.

"That's why, Agent O'Dell, I'm guessing it didn't matter that you stayed in Kansas City. He'll follow you." Cunningham loosened his tie and rolled up his sleeves as though he was suddenly too warm. Both gestures seemed foreign. "Albert Stucky is pulling you into this, no matter what I do to keep you out of it."

"And by keeping me out of it, sir, you're taking away my only defense." O'Dell's voice had an undeniable quiver to it. Tully saw her bite down on her lower lip. Was it to restrain her words or control the quiver?

Cunningham glanced over at Tully, sat back and released his own sigh of resignation. "Agent Tully has requested that you assist him on the case."

O'Dell stared at Tully with surprise. He found himself a bit embarrassed and not sure why. It wasn't as if he had made the request to do her any favors. It could be putting her in even more danger. But the fact was, he needed her.

"I've decided to grant Agent Tully's request on two conditions, neither of which I'm willing to negotiate or compromise." Cunningham leaned forward again, elbows on his desktop, hands fisted together. "Number one, Agent Tully is to remain the lead on this investigation. I expect you to share all information and knowledge as soon as it becomes available to you. You will not—and I repeat, Agent O'Dell—you will not go off on a wild-goose chase or check on hunches without Agent Tully accompanying you. Is that understood?"

"Of course," she answered, her voice now strong and firm again.

"Number two. I want you to see the Bureau's psychologist."

"Sir, I really don't think—"

"Agent O'Dell, I said there will be no negotiating, no compromise. I'll leave it up to Dr. Kernan as to how many times he wants to see you each week."

"Dr. James Kernan?" O'Dell seemed appalled.

"That's right. I had Anita set up your first appointment. Check with her on your way out for the time. She's also setting up an office for you. Agent Tully occupies your old one. I saw no reason in moving both of you. Now, if the two of you will excuse me." He sat back, dismissing them. "I have another appointment."

Tully gathered his mess and waited for O'Dell at the door. For a woman who had just been given what she had wanted for the last five months, she looked more agitated than relieved.

# CHAPTER 30

Tess looked forward to her morning appointment, although while she drove down the empty streets, the guilt crept over her for tiptoeing out of Daniel's house without waking him to say goodbye. She simply didn't have the energy for another battle. He would grumble about her leaving so early to run home and shower and change clothes, when she could do all that just as easily at his house. What he really wanted was for her to stay, because he was more easily aroused in the mornings, and he wanted to have sex.

Yet he would say ridiculous things like, "We have so little time for each other, we need those few extra minutes in the morning."

Each time she stayed over, it was the same thing, the same old argument—"How will we ever know if we're compatible, Tess, if we don't read the *New York Times* together or share breakfast in bed?"

He had actually given those examples. How could he believe any of that when he barely spoke to her over their dinners together? The mornings when he wanted her to stay for a quick fuck seemed to be the only time he was concerned about their compatibility. Ninety-nine percent of the time, he could care less what was good for their relationship. Not that Tess had any clues about what made a successful relationship. Maybe it did include sharing the *New York Times* and breakfasts in bed. How would she know? She had never been in a relationship she could call a success, and she had never been in one with someone like Daniel Kassenbaum.

Daniel was sophisticated, intelligent, refined and cultured. My God, the man completed the *New York Times* crossword puzzle in ink. But unlike Daniel, she didn't kid herself about their relationship. She knew they had little in common. He certainly didn't consider her his equal, and often pointed out her deficiencies as if she were his Eliza Doolittle. Even the other night when she had asked him about investing her bonus money, she had felt as if he had patted her on the head with his "don't get into something you don't understand" comment.

However, the one area where Tess excelled, above and beyond Daniel, was sex. What Daniel lacked, Tess made up for. He had told her many times—though only in the heat of passion—that she was "phenomenally the best fuck" he had ever had. For some twisted reason, it pleased her to have this power over him, though it left her cold and hollow inside. Having sex with Daniel, despite being phenomenal for him, was neither enjoyable nor satisfying for Tess.

In fact, she had begun to wonder whether she was capable of feeling genuinely aroused—if she would ever feel the sort of passion she continuously faked with Daniel. Having Will Finley, a complete stranger, resurrect those feelings proved more unsettling and annoying than reassuring. And having those memories, still so fresh in her mind, of Will's hands and mouth knowing exactly how to touch her, made Daniel's inadequacies more pronounced. She almost wished that she had never been able to remember her night with Will, that the tequila could have erased her memory. Instead, she seemed able to think of nothing else. And those memories reeled over and over in her mind.

At one time she had been so good at blocking out memories. That was usually the purpose of the tequila. In the past, she used to drink too much. She danced and flirted and had sex with as many men as she wanted. She played and hustled pool, putting on wild, sexy shows for anyone interested in encouraging her. She used to believe that if her life ran constantly in fast-forward, she could forget the horrors of her childhood. After all, nothing she could do would be more shocking, more destructive, more frightening than what she had lived through as a child, right?

But in the process, all Tess had managed to do was create a life empty and hollow. Ironically, it had taken a fifth of vodka and a bottle of sleeping pills to wake her up. That was almost seven years ago. The last five years she had worked her ass off to re-create herself and leave not only her childhood behind, but those dark years spent covering it up and running away from it.

In order to do that, she had left the mad rush of D.C. and all its temptations of drugs, all-night clubs and congressmen's beds. Louie's had been a sort of halfway house for Tess. She took a job tending bar and found a tiny apartment by the river. When she finally felt ready, she went back to Blackwood, Virginia, and sold the family farm—the living hell—where she had lived with her aunt and uncle. They had died years before, her only notice coming by way of certified letter from an attorney. Somehow she had expected to automatically know when they died, as if the earth would sigh a relief. There had been no sigh, no relief.

Tess glanced up at herself in the rearview mirror, annoyed that the memories could still wrinkle her brow and clench her teeth. After her aunt's and uncle's deaths, she had let the farm sit empty, refusing to set foot on the property. Finally she had the courage to sell the place, but first destroying the house and all the dilapidated buildings. She had made certain that the storm cellar—her personal punishment chamber—had been bulldozed and filled in. Then, and only then, was she able to sell the place.

It had brought a decent price, supplying her with enough money to start a new life, which only seemed fair since it had taken away half her life in the first place. It was enough money for Tess to go back to school and get her real estate license, and to buy and furnish her brick cottage, in a nice neighborhood, in a quiet city, where no one knew her.

After getting the job at Heston Realty, she joined several business associations. Delores signed her on as a member at the Skyview Country Club. She had insisted it would be essential, allowing Tess to meet potential clients. Although Tess still had a problem seeing herself as a member of a country club. It was there she had met Daniel Kassenbaum. It had been a tremendous victory, proof of her successful new lifestyle. She would be able to do anything, go anywhere, if she was able to win someone as sophisticated, arrogant, well-bred and cultured as Daniel.

She reminded herself that Daniel was good for her. He was stable, ambitious, practical and most importantly, he was taken seriously. All things she wanted—no, needed in her life. That he didn't know or care how to touch her mattered very little in the larger scope of things. Besides, it wasn't as if she was in love with him. She preferred having no emotional investment. Love and emotions had never been key ingredients to a successful relationship. If anything, they had been ingredients for disaster.

Tess pulled the Miata in front of 5349 Archer Drive. Her eyes checked up and down the cul-de-sac, confirming that she had arrived too early. There was no sign of her 10:00 a.m. appointment. Actually, there were no signs of life. The neighborhood's residents had already left for their long commute, and those who were able to stay behind were probably still in bed. She decided to use the extra time to make certain the two-story colonial was in show condition.

She checked her reflection one more time. When had the lines around her mouth and eyes become so pronounced? For the first time in her life she was actually beginning to look her age. It had taken her years to get to where she was. Daniel was an important piece of the puzzle for her new professional persona. He lent credibility to her. She couldn't ruin it now. So why did she keep remembering Will Finley in that blue towel, looking so lean and handsome, and arousing senses she had buried long ago?

She shook her head and grabbed her briefcase, slamming her car door too hard and sending the echo throughout the quiet neighborhood. To make up for the noise, she walked slowly up the sidewalk, preventing her heels from clacking.

The house had been on the market for over eight months with little activity in the last three months. However, the sellers continued to stand firm on their selling price. Like so many of the houses on the outskirts of Newburgh Heights, money seemed to be no problem for the owners, which certainly made negotiations a problem.

Tess went to unlock the steel security door, but the key turned too easily. The dead bolt didn't click. The door wasn't locked, and now standing in the foyer, she could see the security system had also been disarmed.

# CHAPTER 31

"Damn it!" Tess muttered, and flipped the light switch. Yes, the electricity was on, so there was no excuse for the alarm system not to be working.

She made a mental note to check on the last agent who had shown the house. Without even looking, she could guess it had been one of the imbeciles from Peterson Brothers. They were constantly forgetting things like this, and they had the professional ethics of pimps. There had been recent rumors about one of the Peterson brothers using empty client houses for sleazy sex parties.

Suddenly Tess remembered that this house had an extra-large master bedroom and bath with a skylight.

"There better not be a mess."

She checked her wristwatch. Only fifteen minutes left. She tossed her briefcase into a corner of the living room, pushed up the sleeves of her suit jacket, and started up the stairs, stopping to kick off her heels. She didn't need this crap, not this morning. Not when her patience and nerves had already been frayed and tested by her disappearing act from Daniel's bed. He'd be getting to his office right about now. Thankfully, she had left her cellular phone in the car, because knowing Daniel, he'd be calling to scold her.

She stomped up the stairs when halfway up she heard the front door open. He was early. Why did he have to be early? She shoved her sleeves back in place and searched for her leather pumps, slipping them on one by one as she found them. By the time she reached the bottom of the staircase, a tall, dark-haired man was wandering through the spacious living room. Without window treatments, sunlight cascaded in sheets of blinding light, surrounding him.

"Hello?"

"I know I'm a bit early."

"That's fine." Tess kept the annoyance from her voice, wishing she had been able to check the damn master bedroom first.

He turned, and only then did she notice the white cane. Immediately, she wondered how he had gotten here. She glanced out the window but saw no signs of another vehicle in the winding circular driveway.

She guessed he was around her age, middle to late thirties, though she found it hard to determine anyone's age when she couldn't see his eyes. His Ray-Ban sunglasses contained particularly dark lenses. She took notice of his designer silk shirt with the open collar, his expensive leather jacket and well-pressed chinos. She caught herself checking to see if everything matched. His features were handsome but sharp, with a chiseled jaw that was much too taut, thin but nicely curved lips and pronounced cheekbones. He had a bit of a widow's peak, but his dark hair was thick and close cropped.

"I'm Walker Harding," he said. "Are you the agent I spoke to on the phone?"

"Yes, I'm Tess McGowan." She offered her hand, then snatched it back quickly, embarrassed, when she realized he couldn't see it.

He hesitated and slowly removed his hand from his pocket. She noticed how strong and muscular it was as he held it out to her. He was a little off target, his fingers pointed to the side of her. She stepped in closer and shook it. Immediately she felt his large hand swallow hers. The long fingers wrapped all the way around her wrist, surprising her in what felt more like a caress than a handshake. She dismissed the thought and ignored her unexpected discomfort.

"I just arrived," she said, extracting her hand. "I didn't get a chance to make a quick run-through," she explained, wondering how in the world he would know the difference. How was she supposed to show him a house when he couldn't see a damn thing?

He left her and wandered without a word across the living room, tapping his cane in front of him and walking confidently. He stopped at the bay window that looked out over the backyard. He fumbled for the latch and opened it. Then he stood quietly, staring out as if transfixed by something in the yard.

"The sun feels wonderful," he finally said, tilting his head back and letting his face be warmed by the brilliant light. "I know it might seem silly, but I like lots of windows."

"No, it's not silly at all." She caught herself talking louder and immediately chastised herself. He was blind not deaf.

Tess studied his profile. The straight nose had a slight bend, and from this angle she could see a scar just below his jawline. She couldn't help wondering if his blindness had been caused by an accident of some kind. Despite his disability, he seemed to possess confidence. There was a self-assurance in his manner, the way he walked, the way he handled himself. However, his gestures seemed stiff, his hands constantly retreated to his pockets. Was he nervous, anxious?

"How big are the evergreens?" he asked, his voice startling her as though she had forgotten what they were here for.

"Excuse me?"

"I can smell evergreens. Are there a lot and are they big or small?"

She walked up beside him, keeping a safe distance without seeming rude and still being able to look out the window. The property lots here were huge, and the evergreens, mostly cedar and pine, created a natural border at the far edge. She couldn't smell them. But of course his other senses had probably become more refined.

"They're very large. Some cedar, some pine. There's a line of them that separates the properties."

"Good. I do like my privacy." He turned to her and smiled. "I hope you're not uncomfortable having to describe things to me."

"No, of course not," Tess said, hoping that she sounded convincing. "Where would you like to start your tour?"

"I was told there is a fabulous master bedroom. Could we start there?"

"Good choice," she told him. Damn it! She wished she had come earlier. That Peterson asshole better not have left a mess.

"Do you prefer walking alone or would you like me to take your arm?"

"You smell quite lovely."

She stared at him, taken off guard.

"It's Chanel No. 5, right?"

"Yes, it is." Was he flirting with her?

"I'll follow your lovely scent. Just lead the way."

"Oh, yes. Okay."

She walked slowly, almost too slowly, causing his outstretched hand to bump into her once on the landing. He let it linger on her hip as though needing to get his bearings. Or at least that was what Tess told herself. She had experienced more outrageous come-ons and intentional gropes than this.

The master bedroom smelled of cleaning formula, and Tess's eyes darted around. Whoever had been here last had indeed cleaned up. Thankfully, the room looked in order. In fact, it smelled and looked freshly scrubbed. Tess found it odd that Mr. Harding, whose senses had been so keen downstairs, made no comment about these new overpowering scents.

"This room is about thirty by twenty," she proceeded casually. "There's another bay window on the south wall that looks out over the backyard. The floor is an oak parquet. There's a—"

"Excuse me, Ms. McGowan."

"Please, call me Tess."

"Tess, of course." He stopped and smiled. "I hope you won't find this offensive, but I like to have an idea of what the person I'm talking to looks like. May I touch your face?"

At first she thought she must have heard him wrong. She didn't know what to say. She remembered his touching her on the landing and now wondered if indeed it had been a grope and not a harmless miscalculation.

"I'm sorry. You're offended," he said apologetically, his voice low and soothing.

"No, of course not," she answered quickly. If she wasn't careful, her paranoia could lose her the sale. "I'm afraid I'm just not as prepared as I should be to help you."

"It's really quite painless," he told her as though he were explaining a surgical procedure. "I use only my fingertips. I assure you, I won't be pawing you." His lips curved into another smile, and Tess felt ridiculous making a fuss.

"Please, go ahead." She stepped closer, despite her apprehension.

He set the cane aside and started slowly, gently at her hair, using both hands, but only the tips of his fingers. She avoided looking up at him, staring off over his shoulder. His hands smelled faintly of ammonia, or was it simply the overpowering scent of the freshly scrubbed wooden floor? His fingers stroked her forehead and moved over her eyelids.

She tried to ignore their dampness, but glanced at his face for any indication that he was as uncomfortable as she was. No, he seemed calm and composed and his fingers began their descent on either side of her face, sliding down her cheeks. She dismissed what felt like a caress. But then his fingertips moved to her lips. His index finger lingered too long, rubbing back and forth. For a second it felt as though he might press it into her mouth. Startled by the sensation and the thought, Tess looked at his eyes. She tried to see beyond the dark lenses, and when she was successful, getting a glimpse of his black eyes, she saw that he was staring directly at her. Was that possible? No, of course not. She was simply being paranoid, an annoying tendency left over from her past life.

By now his fingers had wandered to her chin, tracing their way down to her neck. They briefly wisped beneath the neckline of her blouse, brushing her collarbone, hesitating as if he was testing her, as if asking how far she would let him go. She began to step back just when he wrapped his fingers around her throat.

"What are you doing?" Tess gasped and grabbed at his large hands.

Now he squeezed, choking her, his eyes definitely staring into hers, a twisted smile at his lips. She clawed at the fingers, steel vise grips clamped like the jaws of a pit bull. She struggled and twisted, but he shoved her back. Her head knocked into the wall with such a force she closed her eyes against the pain. She couldn't breathe. She couldn't think. God, he was so strong.

When she opened her eyes, she saw that he had released one of his hands. She was able to suck in air, her lungs aching and greedy. Before she could gather her strength, he shoved his arm up against her to hold her in place, stabbing his elbow into her throat and cutting off her air once again. That's when she saw the syringe in his free hand.

The terror spread through her quickly, her arms and legs flaying in defense. It was useless. He was much too strong. The needle poked through her jacket and sunk deep into the skin of her arm. She felt her entire body jerk. In seconds the room began to spin. Her hands, her knees, her muscles became limp, and then the room went black.

# CHAPTER 32

The minute Maggie walked into Dr. James Kernan's office she felt like a nineteen-year-old college student again. The feelings of confusion, wonder and intimidation all came back to her in a rush of sights and smells. His office, set in the Wilmington Towers in Washington, D.C., and no longer on the University of Virginia's campus, still looked and smelled the same.

Immediately, her nostrils were accosted by stale cigar smoke, old leather and Ben-Gay rubbing ointment. The tiny space was littered with the same strange paraphernalia. A human brain's dissected frontal lobe bulged in a mason jar filled with formaldehyde. The jar acted as a makeshift bookend, ironically holding up such texts as *Explaining Hitler: The Search for the Origins of Evil,* Freud's *Interpretation of Dreams* and what Maggie knew to be a rare first edition of *Alice In Wonderland.* Of the three, the last seemed most appropriate for the professor of psychology who easily conjured up images of the Mad Hatter.

On the mahogany credenza across the room were antique instruments, their shapes and points intriguing until they were recognized as surgical instruments once used to perform lobotomies. On the wall behind the matching mahogany desk were black-and-white photographs of the procedure. Another equally disturbing photograph included a young woman undergoing shock treatment. The woman's empty eyes and resigned posture beneath the ominous iron equipment had always reminded Maggie more of an execution than a medical treatment. Sometimes she questioned how she could be involved in a profession that, at one time, could be so brutal while pretending to cure the ailments of the psyche.

Kernan, however, embraced the eccentricities of their profession. His office was simply an extension of the strange little man.

A man as notorious for his crude jokes about "nutcases" as he was for his own version of shock treatment, which he had perfected on his students.

The man loved mind games and could lure and trick a person into them without warning. One moment he would drill an unprepared freshman with rapid-fire questions, not allowing the poor student to even answer. The next minute he'd be in a corner of the classroom, standing silently with his face to the wall. Then still later, he'd climb atop a desk and lecture while teetering from one desk to another, his small, stocky but aging body threatening to send him falling while he lectured and did a balancing act at the same time. Even the seniors in his classes had no idea what to expect of their odd professor. And this was the man the FBI trusted to determine her sanity?

Maggie heard the familiar clomp-squeak of his footsteps outside the office. Instinctively, she sat up straight and stopped her browsing. Even the man's footsteps transformed her into an incompetent college kid.

Dr. Kernan entered his office unceremoniously and shuffled to his desk without recognizing or acknowledging Maggie. He plopped down into the leather chair, sending it into a series of creaks. Maggie couldn't be sure that all the creaks came from the chair and not the old man's joints.

He began rummaging through stacks of papers. She watched quietly, her hands folded in her lap. Kernan looked as though he had shrunk since the last time she had seen him, over ten years ago. Back then he had seemed ancient, but now his shoulders were hunched, his hands trembled and were speckled with brown spots. His hair, just as white as she remembered, was thin and feathery, revealing more brown spots on his forehead and the top of his head. Tufts of white hair protruded from his ears.

Finally he appeared to find what he had been so desperately in search of. He struggled to open the tin box of breath mints, took two without offering any to Maggie and snapped the container shut.

"O'Dell, Margaret," he said to himself, still not acknowledging her presence.

He sorted through the rubble again. "Class of 1990." He

stopped and thumbed through a folder. Maggie glanced at the cover to see if he was reading her file, only to discover a label that read, Twenty-five Best Internet Porn Sites.

"I remember a Margaret O'Dell," he said without looking up at her, and in a voice that sounded like a senile old man talking to himself. "O'Dell, O'Dell, the farmer and the dell."

Maggie shifted in her chair, forcing herself to be patient, to be polite. Nothing had changed. Why was she surprised to find him treating patients the same way he had treated his students, playing silly word games, reducing names and identities to nursery rhymes? It was all part of his intimidation.

"Premed," he continued while riffling through the list of porn sites. Several times he stopped, smacking his lips together or hissing out a "tis, tis." "Sat in the back left corner of my classroom, taking very few notes. B student. Asked questions only about criminal behavior and hereditary traits."

Maggie hid her surprise. These could easily be odd little facts he may have noted and kept in a student file. And of course, he would have reviewed her file before she arrived, so as to have an advantage. Not that he needed an advantage. She waited, forcing her hands to keep still when they wanted to grip the arms of her chair. She wanted to dig her fingernails into the leather to steady herself and prevent her from storming out of this ridiculous inquisition.

"Got a master's in behavioral psychology," he went on in his droll tone. "Managed to land a forensic fellowship at Quantico." Finally he looked up at her, his pale blue eyes magnified and swimming behind the thick square glasses. Bushy white eyebrows stuck out in every direction. He rubbed his jaw and said, "Wonder what the hell you would have done if you'd been an A student." Then he stared at her, waiting.

As usual, he caught her off guard. She didn't know what to say. He had a talent for disarming people by making them feel invisible. Then suddenly he expected a response to what was never a question. Maggie remained silent and returned his steady gaze, vowing not to flinch. She hated that he could reduce her to an unsure, speechless teenager with only a few words and that goddamn look of his. This was certainly not her idea of therapy. Assistant Director Cunningham was way off base on this one. Sending her to see anyone was a waste of time. Sending her to see Kernan would only challenge her sanity further and would certainly not be a remedy.

"So, Margaret O'Dell, the quiet little bird in the corner, the B student who was so interested in criminals but didn't think she belonged in my classroom, is now Special Agent Margaret O'Dell, who wears a gun and a shiny badge and now doesn't think she belongs in my office."

He stared at her again, waiting for a response, still not asking a question. His elbows leaned on the wobbly stacks of paper as he laced his fingers together.

"That's true, isn't it? You don't think you should be here?"

"No, I don't," she answered, her voice strong and defiant despite the man's ability to intimidate the hell out of her.

"So your superiors are wrong? All those years of training. All that experience, and they're flat out wrong. Is that right?"

"I didn't say that."

"Really? That wasn't what you said?"

Word games, mind games, confusion—Kernan was a master. Maggie needed to concentrate. She couldn't let him twist her words. She wouldn't let him trap her.

"You asked me if I thought I should be here," she explained calmly. "I simply said no, I don't think that I should be here."

"Awwww," he said, drawing it out into a sigh as he sank back in his chair. He rested his hands on his thick chest, letting his wrinkled jacket fall open. "I'm so glad you clarified that for me, Margaret O'Dell."

She remembered that her one-on-one encounters with the man had always felt like an interrogation. It was disconcerting that this befuddled, little old man who looked as if he slept in his clothes, still possessed that same power. She refused to let him unnerve her. Instead, she stared at him and waited.

"So, tell me, Margaret O'Dell, who doesn't think she belongs in my office, do you enjoy this obsession you have with Albert Stucky?"

Suddenly she felt a knot in her stomach. Damn it! Leave it to Kernan to cut to the chase, to strike without warning.

"Of course I don't enjoy it." She kept her voice steady, her eyes level with his. She mustn't blink too many times. He would be counting the blinks. Despite those Coke-bottle glasses, Kernan wouldn't miss a twitch or a grimace.

"Then why do you continue to obsess?"

"Because I want him caught."

"And you're the only one who can catch him?"

"I know him better than anyone else."

"Oh yes, of course. Because he shared his little hobby with you. That's right. He left you with a little tattoo, a sort of brand to remember him by."

She had forgotten how cruel Kernan could be. Yet she forced herself to stay calm. She couldn't let him see the anger. That was exactly what he wanted.

"I spent two years tracking him. That's why I know him better than anyone else."

"I see," he said, tilting his head as if necessary to do so. "Then your obsession will end after you catch him?"

"Yes."

"And after he's punished?"

"Yes."

"Because he must be punished, right?"

"There is no punishment great enough for someone like Albert Stucky."

"Really? Putting him to death won't be punishment enough?"

She hesitated, well aware of his biting sarcasm and anticipating his trap. She proceeded anyway.

"No matter how many victims, no matter how many women Stucky kills, he can die only once."

"Ah yes, I see. And that wouldn't be a fitting punishment. What would be?"

She didn't answer. She wouldn't take his bait.

"You'd like to see him suffer, wouldn't you, Margaret O'Dell?"

She held his gaze. Don't flinch, she told herself. He was waiting for her to slip. He was setting her up, pushing her, forcing her to expose her anger.

"How would you choose to make him suffer? Pain? Excruciating, drawn-out pain?" He stared at her, waiting. She stared back, refusing to give him what he wanted.

"No, not pain," he said finally, as if her eyes had answered for her. "No. You prefer fear, don't you? You want him to suffer by feeling fear," he continued in a casual voice with neither accusation nor confrontation, inviting her to confide in him.

Her hands stayed in her lap. She continued to sit up straight, eyes never leaving his while the anger began churning in her stomach.

"You want him to experience the same fear, that same sense of helplessness that each of his victims felt." He sat forward in his chair, the creak amplified in the silence. "The same fear that you felt when he had you trapped. When he was cutting you. When his knife was slicing into your skin."

He paused, and she felt him examining her. The room had become hot, with very little air. Yet she kept her hands from wiping the strands of hair that had become damp on her forehead. She resisted the urge to bite down on her lower lip. Instead, she simply returned his stare.

"Is that it, Margaret O'Dell? You want to see Mr. Albert Stucky squirm, just like he made you squirm."

She hated that he referred to Stucky with the respect of using mister. How dare he?

"Seeing him squirm in the electric chair isn't enough for you, is it?" he continued to push.

Maggie's fingers started wringing in her lap. Her palms were sweaty. Why was it so damn hot in the room? Her cheeks were flushed. Her head began to throb.

"No, the electric chair isn't a punishment appropriate for his crimes, is it? You have a better punishment in mind, don't you? And how do you propose to administer this punishment, Margaret O'Dell?"

"By making him look directly at me when I shoot the goddamn bastard between his eyes," she blasted, no longer caring that she had just allowed herself to be swallowed whole into Dr. James Kernan's psychological trap.

# CHAPTER 33

Tess McGowan tried to open her eyes, but her eyelids were too heavy. She managed a flutter, seeing a flash of light, then darkness. She was sitting up, but the earth was moving beneath her in a low rumble and steady vibration. Somewhere a soft, deep voice with a country twang was singing about hurting the ones you love.

Why couldn't she move? Her arms were limp, her legs like concrete. But the only restraint was across her shoulder, across her lap. A car. Yes, she was buckled into a car. That explained the movement, the vibration, the muffled sounds. It didn't explain why she couldn't open her eyes.

She tried again. Another flutter. Headlights flickered before her heavy eyelids fell closed. It was night. How could it be night? It had just been morning. Hadn't it?

She leaned against the headrest. She smelled jasmine, just a hint, soft and subtle. Yes, she remembered a few days ago she had bought a new sachet and stuck it under the passenger seat. So she was in her own car. The scent, the notion calmed her until she realized that if she wasn't driving, someone else was here with her. Was it Daniel? Why couldn't she remember? Why did her mind feel as though it was filled with cobwebs? Had she gone out drinking again? Oh dear God! Had she picked up another stranger?

She turned her head slightly to the side without removing it from the headrest. It took such effort to move, each inch as if in slow motion. One more time she attempted to open her eyes. Too dark, but there was movement. The eyelids dropped shut again.

She listened. She could hear someone breathing. She opened her mouth to speak. She would ask where they were going. It was a simple question, but nothing came out. There was a slight groan but even that hadn't come from her. Then the car began to slow, followed by a faint electric buzz. Tess felt a draft, smelled fresh tar and knew the window had opened. The car stopped, but the engine continued to hum. Gas fumes told her they were stalled in traffic. She tried once again to open her eyes.

"Good evening, Officer," a deep voice said from the seat next to her.

Was it Daniel? The voice sounded familiar.

"Good evening," another voice bellowed. "Oh, sorry," came a whisper. "Didn't see your wife sleeping."

"What seems to be the problem?"

Yes, Tess wanted to know, too. What was the problem? Why couldn't she move? Why couldn't she open her eyes? What wife was sleeping? Did the officer mean her?

"We've got an accident we're cleaning up on the other side of the toll bridge. A leftover from the rush-hour traffic. Be just a minute or two. Then we'll let you through."

"No hurry." the voice said much too calmly.

No. It wasn't Daniel. Daniel was always in a hurry. He'd be making the officer understand how important he was. He'd be causing a scene. Oh, how she hated when he did that. But it if wasn't Daniel beside her, then who?

A flutter of panic crawled over her. "No hurry?" Yes, the voice was familiar.

She began to remember.

"You smell quite lovely," that same voice had told her. It came to her in pieces. The house on Archer Drive. He wanted to see the master bedroom. "I hope you're not offended."

He wanted to see her face. "It's really quite painless." No, he wanted to feel her face. His hands, his fingers on her hair, her cheeks, her neck. Then wrapping those hands around her throat, tight and hard, the muscles squeezing. She couldn't breathe. She couldn't move. Dark eyes. And a smile. Yes, he had smiled while his fingers squeezed and wrung her neck. It hurt. Stop it. It hurt so bad. Her head hurt, and she could hear the smack of it hitting against the wall. She fought with fists and fingernails. God, he was strong.

Then she had felt it. A prick of the needle as it sunk deep into her arm. She remembered the rush of heat that flowed through her veins. She remembered the room spinning.

Now she tried to raise that same arm. It wouldn't move, but it ached. What had he given her? Who the hell was he? Where was he taking her? Even the fear felt trapped, a lump caught deep inside her throat, straining to be set free. She couldn't wave or swing her arms. She couldn't kick or run. My God, she couldn't even scream.

# CHAPTER 34

Maggie had passed the exit for Quantico without a glance and had gone straight home after her meeting with Kernan. Meeting? That was a joke. She shook her head and now continued to pace in her living room. The hour-long drive from D.C. hadn't even begun to cool off her anger. What kind of psychologist left his patients wanting to slam fists through walls?

She noticed her bags at the bottom of the staircase, still packed from her Kansas City trip. Boxes remained stacked in the corners. Her nerves felt as if they had been rubbed raw. A knot tightened at the base of her neck and her head throbbed. She couldn't remember when she had last eaten. It had probably been on the flight last night.

She considered changing and going for a run. It was getting dark but that had never stopped her before. No, what did stop her was knowing Stucky could be watching. Had he returned from Kansas City? Was he out there somewhere hiding, waiting, watching? She paced from window to window, examining the street and then the woods behind her house, squinting to study the twilight shadows dancing behind the trees. She searched for anything out of the ordinary, anything that moved, but in the light breeze every rustle of a bush, every sway of a branch made her uneasy. She could already feel her muscles tightening, her nerves unraveling.

Earlier she had noticed a construction worker at the end of her street inspecting sewage grates and setting up pylons. His coveralls had been too clean, his shoes too polished. Maggie knew immediately that he had to be one of Cunningham's surveillance crew. How the hell did Cunningham expect to catch Stucky with such amateurish strategies? If Maggie had been able to see through the impostor, certainly Stucky, a professional chameleon, would find it laughable. Stucky took on identities and roles with such ease that surely he would spot someone doing the same thing, only doing it poorly.

She hated feeling like a caged animal in her own home. To make matters worse, the house was deathly quiet. Other than the clicking of her heels on the polished wood floor, Maggie heard nothing. No lawn mowers, no car engines, no children playing. But wasn't the peace and quiet, a piece of seclusion, exactly what she longed for when she bought this house? Hadn't that been her intention? What was that old saying—be careful what you wish for?

She unearthed her CD player, an inexpensive oversize boom box. She dug through the overflowing box of CDs. Some were in sealed wrappers, gifts from friends she hadn't taken time to open, let alone enjoy. Finally she decided on an early Jim Brickman, hoping the piano solos would soothe her agitated insides. The music barely began when Maggie noticed Susan Lyndell making her way up the circular drive. It looked as though there would be no stress relief.

She opened the door before Susan made it up the steps to the portico. Her eyes darted everywhere but at Susan, checking, double-checking.

"How was your trip?" Susan asked as though they were old friends.

"It was fine." Maggie grabbed the woman's elbow gently and quickly urged her into the foyer.

Susan stared at her, surprised. On her first visit Maggie had barely let the woman through the door, and now she was pulling her in.

"I got back late last night," Maggie continued, closing the door. All she could think about was Stucky watching. Stucky choosing his next victim.

"I tried to call but you're not listed yet."

"No, I'm not," she said with finality in case Susan expected she might tell her. "Did you speak with Detective Manx?"

"Actually, that's what I wanted to tell you. I think I was mistaken about what we discussed the other day."

"Why do think you were mistaken?" Maggie waited while her

neighbor glanced around at her stacked cartons, taking in Maggie's living room and probably wondering how Maggie could ever afford such a house.

"I spoke with Sid," Susan told her, finally looking at Maggie, though she still seemed distracted by Maggie's things, or rather her lack of things.

"Mr. Endicott? What exactly did you speak to him about?"

"Sid's a good man. I hate to see him going through this all alone. I felt he had a right to know. Well, you know...about Rachel and that man."

"The telephone repairman?"

"Yes." Now Susan wouldn't meet Maggie's eyes, but it had nothing to do with the surroundings.

"What did you tell him?"

"Just that quite possibly she may have left with him."

"I see." She wondered why Susan Lyndell could so easily betray her friend. And why was it suddenly so easy to believe Rachel had left with some stranger who, only days ago, Susan thought might hurt her friend? "And what did Mr. Endicott say?"

"Oh, maybe you haven't heard. Rachel's car was not in the garage. The police initially saw Sid's Mercedes and didn't realize that Rachel's was gone. See, she usually drives Sid to the airport when he goes out of town so he won't need to leave the car in airport parking. Sid's always worried about his car. Anyway, I think Rachel must have taken off with this guy. She was certainly infatuated by him."

"What about the dog?"

"The dog?"

"We found her dog stabbed...injured under the bed."

Susan shrugged. "I have no idea about that," she said as if she couldn't be expected to figure out everything.

Maggie's cellular phone started ringing from inside her jacket pocket. She hesitated. Susan waved a birdlike hand at her to go ahead and get it as she backed away. "I won't keep you. Just wanted to fill you in." Before Maggie could protest, her neighbor was out the door and walking down the driveway in what Maggie thought looked almost like a skip. She definitely didn't seem like the same nervous, anxious woman she had met a few days ago.

Maggie quickly closed the door and took time to activate the alarm system while the phone continued to ring. Finished, she twisted the contraption out of her pocket.

"Maggie O'Dell."

"Jesus, finally. You need a better cell phone, Maggie. I think your battery must be low again."

Immediately, Maggie felt the tension return to her neck and shoulders. Greg's greetings always sounded like scoldings.

"My phone's been off. I've been out of town. You got my message." She went directly to the point, not wanting to encourage his attempt to chastise her for being unreachable.

"You should have some sort of messaging service," he persisted. "Your mother called me a couple of days ago. She didn't even know you moved. For Christ's sake, Maggie, you could at least call your mother and give her your new number."

"I did call her. Is she okay?"

"She sounded great. Said she was in Las Vegas."

"Las Vegas?" Her mother never left Richmond. And what a choice. Yes, Las Vegas was the perfect place for a suicidal alcoholic.

"She said she was with a Reverend Everett. You need to keep better tabs on her, Maggie. She is your mother."

Maggie leaned against the wall and took a deep breath. Greg had never understood the dynamics between Maggie and her mother. How could he? He came from a family that looked as if it had been special-ordered from a 1950s family catalog.

"Greg, did I leave a carton at the condo?"

"No, there's nothing here. You do realize that none of this would have happened if you had used United?"

Maggie ignored his I-told-you-so. "Are you sure? Look, I don't care if you've opened it or if you've gone through it."

"Listen to you. You don't trust or believe anybody anymore. Can't you see what this goddamn job is doing to you?"

She rubbed her neck and squeezed at the knot. Why did he have to make this so difficult?

"Did you check in the basement?" she asked, knowing there was no way it had ended up there, but giving him one last chance for a way out if he had, indeed, opened the box.

"No, there's nothing. What was in it? One of your precious

guns? Are you not able to sleep at night without all three or four or however many of those things you have?"

"I have two, Greg. It's not unusual for an agent to have a backup."

"Right. Well, that's one too many for me."

"Would you just call me if the carton shows up?"

"It's not here."

"Okay, fine. Goodbye."

"Call your mom sometime soon," he said in place of a closing and hung up.

She leaned her head against the wall and shut her eyes. She tried to calm the throbbing in her head and neck and shoulders. The doorbell chimed, and she was grabbing for her revolver before she even realized it. Jesus! Maybe Greg was right. She did live in a crazy paranoid world.

Beside a lamppost in her driveway, she could see a van with Riley's Veterinary Clinic imprinted on the side. A man in white overalls and a baseball cap stood on the portico. Sitting patiently beside him with a blue collar and leash was a white Labrador retriever. Despite there being no massive bandage around the dog's chest and shoulder, Maggie recognized it as the dog she had helped rescue from the Endicotts' house. Nevertheless, she examined the man, making certain this wasn't a disguise. Finally she decided he was too short to be Stucky.

"The Endicotts live farther down the street," she said as soon as she opened the door.

"I know that," the man snapped. His jaw was taut, his face red, his forehead glistening with sweat as though he had run here instead of driving. "Mr. Endicott refuses to take the dog."

"He what?"

"He won't take the dog."

"Is that what he said?" Maggie thought the idea incredible after what the dog had been through.

"Well, his exact words were, it's his wife's frickin' dog—excuse my language, I'm just repeating what he said, but let me tell you, he didn't use 'frickin',' okay? Anyway, he said it's his wife's frickin' dog and if she took off and left the stupid dog, then he doesn't want him either."

Maggie glanced at the dog who cowered close to the ground, either from the man's raised voice or because he knew they were talking about him.

"I'm not sure what you expect me to do. I don't think my talking to Mr. Endicott will change his mind. I don't even know the man."

"Your name and address is on the release form you signed when you brought in the dog. Detective Manx told us to leave the dog with you."

"He did, did he?" Of all the nerve. It was Manx's one last dig. "And what if I refuse to take him? What will you do with him?"

"I have orders from Mr. Endicott to take him to the pound."

Maggie looked at the dog again, and as if on cue he stared up at her with sad, pathetic brown eyes. Damn it! What did she know about taking care of a dog? She wasn't home enough to take care of a dog. She couldn't have a dog. Her mother had never allowed her to have one while she was growing up. Greg was allergic to dogs and cats, or so he had said once when she had brought home a stray she had found while out running. Allergic or not, she knew he would never have been able to tolerate anything with four paws climbing on his precious leather furniture. Suddenly Maggie realized that seemed like a good enough reason.

"What's his name," she asked as she took the dog's leash from the man's hand.

"It's Harvey."

# CHAPTER 35

*Boston, Massachusetts*
*Thursday, April 2*

Will Finley couldn't sit still. He had been jumpy all morning. Now he roamed the halls of the county courthouse. He swiped a jerky hand over his face. Too much caffeine. That was his problem. That and very little sleep. It also didn't help matters that Tess McGowan hadn't returned any of his phone calls. Today was already Thursday. Since Monday, he had left messages on her answering machine and at her office. Or, at least, what he thought was her office. He had taken one of her business cards from the antique desk in her bedroom. Otherwise, he wouldn't have had her home phone number or known her last name. Hell, he had even tried leaving her messages at Louie's until the burly owner told him to "leave Tess alone and fuck off."

So why couldn't he leave her alone? Why did she consume his thoughts? He had never been obsessed with a woman before. Why this one? Even Melissa had noticed his preoccupation, but she had accepted his explanation of being overloaded at his new job and stressed out about all the last-minute wedding preparations.

It didn't help matters that he had avoided having sex with her since his night with Tess. Hell, it had only been three nights and yet he'd been afraid Melissa would notice, especially last night when she had hinted about spending the night at his place. He had practically shoved her out the door, using the lame excuse that he had to get some sleep for a big trial in the morning. What was his problem? Was he really afraid that Melissa would discover his betrayal somehow if he touched her differently? Or did he simply not want to erase the memories of having sex with Tess? Because he had played back that night over and over in his head so many times he could conjure it up at will.

Shit, he was fucked up!

As he turned the corner, heading to Records he ran into Nick Morrelli. The contents of Will's folder spilled across the floor, and he was on his knees before Nick had a chance to know what hit him.

"Hey, what's the hurry?" Nick said, joining Will on the floor.

Others stepped around them, not paying any attention as their heels smashed and crumpled the scattered papers.

Nick handed him the papers he had gathered while they stood up. But Will's eyes darted across the floor, making sure he had everything. That was all he needed—to lose some piece of paper that would give the defense an edge in whatever this trial was.

"So what's the rush?" Nick asked again, hands in his pockets, waiting.

"No rush." Will straightened the stack and raked his fingers through his hair. He wondered if Nick could see the slight tremor in his hand. Although the two men were new to the D.A.'s office, Nick had been one of Will's professors in law school back at the University of Nebraska. He still looked up to Nick as a mentor instead of a colleague. And he knew Nick had sort of taken him under his wing, helping a fellow Midwesterner adjust to the rush of big-city life in Boston.

"You look like shit." Nick looked concerned. "You feeling okay?"

"Yeah. Sure. I'm fine."

Nick didn't look convinced. He glanced at his watch. "It's almost lunchtime. How 'bout we get burgers down the street? I'm buying."

"Okay. Yeah, sure. If you're buying." Geez! Even his speech was jerky. "Let me drop this stuff at Records."

It was warm enough for shirtsleeves, but both men wore their jackets. Will realized he'd need to wear his jacket for the rest of the day if the pools under his arms were as obvious as they felt. Maybe all these physical reactions were simply cold feet. After all, the wedding was, what, three or four weeks away? Holy crap! How could it be that close?

Will filled the conversation with boring stuff about the trials Nick had missed while in Kansas City. It was the only way to ignore the concerned look in his ex-professor's eyes. Nick politely listened, then seemed to wait until Will's mouth was full of fries before he asked.

"So you ready to tell me what the hell's bugging you?"

Will wiped away the ketchup on the corner of his mouth and swallowed. He grabbed his Pepsi and washed down what threatened to stick in his throat.

"What makes you think something's wrong?"

"I didn't say wrong. I said what's bugging you?"

"Oh." He wiped his mouth again, buying time. Leave it to a lawyer to fuss over the wording.

"So what's wrong?"

Will shoved his plate aside. He had managed to wolf down half his burger and almost all his fries before Nick had taken a second bite of his burger. He could feel the heartburn tightening into a fist and settling in the middle of his chest. As if he needed one more physical discomfort.

"I think I fucked up big time."

Nick continued eating, waiting, examining him over the burger that he held with both hands. Finally he said, "It wasn't the Prucello case, was it?"

"No. No, it wasn't anything to do with work."

Nick looked relieved. Then his brow furrowed again. "You getting cold feet about the wedding?"

Will gulped his Pepsi. He waved at the waiter and pointed to his glass for another, wishing he could trade it for something stronger.

"Maybe. I don't know." Then he pulled in his chair and leaned across the table so he could keep his voice down despite the noisy lunch-hour crowd. Two of the tables next to them were filled with people he knew from the courthouse.

"Sunday night I met this woman. Christ, Nick! She was...incredible. I haven't been able to stop thinking about her."

Nick chewed and watched him as if contemplating what to say. If anyone would understand, surely it would be Nick

Morrelli. Will knew that years ago, all the talk around campus about Nick and some of his own students, as well as several female professors, had not been idle rumor. Nick Morrelli had had his share of one-night stands. Even after he had left the university to take the position as sheriff of Platte City, the reputation and the activity had followed him.

"This woman," Nick said slowly, carefully, "was she a hooker?"

Will almost choked.

"No, hell no," he said, glancing around the small diner to make certain no one noticed he was agitated. "The guys—Mickey, Rob, Bennet—they sort of dared me into picking up this woman who was at the bar. She was incredible, sexy and so...I don't know, uninhibited. But no, she's no goddamn hooker." He stopped and lowered his voice, noticing two women at the next table staring at him. "She's older, probably about your age. Very attractive with this amazing...sensuality. But in a sophisticated sort of way, not, you know, cheap or anything like that. In fact, I think she's a real estate agent or something."

The waiter brought Will's refill. He slid back in his chair, grabbed the glass and gulped half of it. Nick continued eating, as if it was no big deal. Will started feeling anxious and a bit angry. Hell, he had just spilled his guts, and Nick seemed more interested in finishing his goddamn burger.

"So what you're really saying is that she's a pretty incredible fuck?"

"Jesus Christ, Nick!"

"Well? Isn't that what this is all about?"

"You know, man, I thought you of all people would understand this. But forget it. Forget I mentioned it." Will pulled his plate closer and started shoving French fries into his mouth, avoiding looking at Nick. One of the women at the next table smiled at him. Evidently she didn't know that he was an idiot.

"Come on, Will. Be sensible for one minute." Nick waited until he had Will's attention. "Are you willing to piss away three or four years with Melissa for one incredible fuck?"

"No. Of course not." Will slumped in his chair and wrestled

with the knot in his tie. He looked up and met Nick's eyes. "I don't know what to think."

"Look, Will. I've been with a lot of women, incredible women. But you can't let one incredible fuck rule your life's decisions."

They sat in silence as Nick finished eating. Will sat up, leaned across the table again, only now noticing the sleeve of his jacket dripping with ketchup. Shit! These days he seemed to spend more money on dry cleaning than he did on food.

"It wasn't just the sex, Nick." He felt he needed to explain, but wasn't sure he understood it himself. "There was something else. I don't know what. Something about her. I can't get her out of my mind. I mean, here's this strong, passionate, sexy, independent woman, who could also be...oh, hell I don't know...vulnerable and sweet and funny and...and real. I know we both had too much to drink, and we know very little about each other, but...I can't stop thinking about her."

He watched Nick take out crisp bills and lay them on the plastic tray with the tab. Had it been a mistake to say any of this out loud? Should he have kept it to himself?

"Okay, so what do you want to do about it?"

"I don't know," Will said, giving in and fidgeting with the ketchup on his sleeve. "I guess maybe I want to see her again, just to talk, to see...hell, I don't know, Nick."

"So call her. What's stopping you?"

"I tried. She won't return my messages."

"Then stop by and see her, buy her lunch. Women like a guy taking action, not just talking."

"It's not that easy. It's a five-hour drive. She lives in this little town outside D.C.—Newton, Newberry, Newburgh. Yeah, Newburgh, I think."

"Wait a minute. Outside D.C.? Newburgh Heights? In Virginia?"

"Yeah. You know it?"

"I think a friend of mine bought a house there."

"Small world." Will watched Nick, whose mind suddenly seemed preoccupied. "You think they know each other?"

"I doubt it. Maggie's an FBI profiler."

"Hold on. Is this the same FBI Maggie who helped you on that case last fall?"

Nick nodded, but he didn't need to answer at all. Will could see it was the same woman. Will had noticed months ago that this woman couldn't be mentioned in general conversation without Nick getting all weirded out. Maybe this woman was Nick's obsession.

"So how come you've never called this Maggie or stopped by to see her?"

"Well, for one thing I didn't realize until a few days ago that she was getting a divorce."

"A few days ago? Wait a minute. Was she at the Kansas City thing?"

"Yes, she was at the Kansas City thing. She was one of the presenters."

"And?"

"And nothing."

Will noticed Nick's demeanor had changed to frustration with a hint of irritation. Yep, he was all weirded out again.

"But you saw her, right? You talked to her?"

"Yeah. We spent an afternoon digging through garbage together."

"Excuse me? Is that some new code for foreplay?"

"No, it isn't," Nick snapped, suddenly not in the mood for Will's attempt at humor. "Come on. Let's get back to work."

Nick stood, straightening his lopsided tie and buttoning his jacket, indicating that was the end of this conversation. Will decided to ignore it and press on.

"It sounds like this Maggie is your Tess."

"Jesus, kid. What the hell is that supposed to mean?" Nick shot him a look, and Will knew he was right.

"This Maggie drives you as crazy as Tess drives me. Maybe we both need to make a trip down to Newburgh Heights."

# CHAPTER 36

Maggie was surprised to find that Agent Tully had managed to make her old office look smaller than it was. Books that didn't fit in the narrow floor-to-ceiling bookcase formed leaning towers in the corner. A chair intended for visitors was hidden under stacks of newspapers. On his desk, the in-tray was crushed under a pile of lopsided documents and file folders. Strings of paper clips were left in odd places, a nervous habit of a man who needed to keep his fingers occupied. One lone mug teetered on a stack of legal pads and computer manuals. Peeking from behind the door, Maggie glimpsed gray running gear where normal people hung a trench coat or rain slicker.

The only thing in the office that held some prominence was a photo in a cheap wooden frame that sat on the right-hand corner of the desk. The entire corner had been cleared for its place of honor. Maggie immediately recognized Agent Tully, though the photo appeared to be several years old. The little blond girl had his dark eyes, but otherwise looked exactly like a younger version of her mother. The three of them looked so genuinely happy.

Maggie resisted the urge to take a closer look, as if doing so might expose their secret. What was it like to feel that completely happy? Had she ever felt that way, even for a brief period? Something about Agent Tully told her that happiness no longer existed for him. Not that she wanted to know. It had been years since she had worked with a partner, and the fact that Cunningham had made it one of the conditions of her return to the Stucky investigation was annoying. She felt as if he was still punishing her for the one stupid mistake of her career—going to that Miami warehouse alone. The warehouse where Stucky had been waiting for her. Where he had trapped her and made her watch.

Okay, so partly she knew Cunningham was doing it to protect her. Agents usually worked together to protect each other's backs, but profilers often worked alone and Maggie had grown accustomed to the solitude. Having Turner and Delaney hanging around had been stifling enough. Of course, she would abide by Cunningham's rules, but sometimes the best agents, the closest partners forgot to share every detail.

Agent Tully came in carrying two cartons, stacked so that he peered around the sides of them. Maggie helped him find a clear spot and unload his arms.

"I think these are the last of the old case files."

She wanted to tell him that every last copy she had made for herself had fit nicely into one box. But instead of pointing out what a little organization could do, she was anxious to see what had been added to the case in the last five months. She stood back and allowed Agent Tully to sort through the mess.

"May I see the most recent file?"

"I have the delivery girl on my desk." He jumped up from his squatting position next to the cartons and quickly riffled through several piles on his desk. "The Kansas City case is here, too. They've been faxing us stuff."

Maggie resisted the urge to help. She wanted to grab all his piles and make order of them. How the hell did this guy get anything done?

"Here's the file on the delivery girl."

He handed her a bulging folder with corners of papers and photos sticking out at odd angles. Immediately, Maggie opened it and started straightening and rearranging its contents before examining any of them.

"Is it okay if we use her name?"

"Excuse me?" Agent Tully continued to rummage over his messy desktop. Finally he found his wire-rimmed glasses, put them on and looked at her.

"The pizza delivery girl. Is it okay if we use her name when we refer to her?"

"Of course," he said, grabbing another file folder and shuffling through it.

Now he was a bit flustered, and Maggie knew he didn't know

the girl's name without looking. It wasn't a matter of disrespect. It helped to disconnect. Profilers often referred to a body simply as "the victim" or "Jane Doe." Their first introduction to the victims came when they were bloody, tangled messes, often sharing little or no resemblance to their former selves. Maggie used to be the same, using general terms to disassociate, to disconnect. But then several months ago she met a little boy named Timmy Hamilton who took time to show her his bedroom and his baseball card collection just before he was abducted. Now it suddenly seemed important to Maggie to know this girl's name. This beautiful, young, blond woman who she remembered being so cheerful when she had delivered Maggie's pizza less than a week ago. And who was now dead simply because she had done so.

"Jessica," Agent Tully finally blurted out. "Her name was Jessica Beckwith."

Maggie realized she could have found the girl's name just as easily. The top document was the medical examiner's autopsy report, and the girl had already been identified at that point. She tried not to think of the parents. Some disconnection was necessary.

"Any trace recovered at the scene that could be used for DNA testing?"

"Nothing substantial. Some fingerprints, but they aren't matching Stucky's. Weird thing is, everything looked wiped clean except for this set of fingerprints—one index, one thumb. Chances are they belong to a rookie cop who touched stuff he wasn't supposed to touch and now he's afraid to admit it. AFIS hasn't come up with anything yet."

He sat on the edge of the desk, laying his folder open on a pile, leaving his fingers free to string more paper clips together.

"The weapon was not retrieved. Is that right?"

"Correct. Looks to be very thin, razor sharp and single edged. I'm thinking maybe even a scalpel, from the way he's able to slice and dice so easily."

Maggie winced at his choice of description, and he caught her.

"Sorry," he said. "That's the first thing that came to mind."

"Any saliva on the body? Any semen in the mouth?"

"No, which I know is different from Stucky's usual M.O."

"If it is Stucky."

She felt him staring at her but avoided his eyes and examined the autopsy report. Why would Stucky hold back or pull out early now? He certainly wouldn't go through the trouble of using a condom. After they had revealed his identity as being Albert Stucky, he had blatantly gone on to do whatever he wanted. And that usually meant showing off his sexual prowess by raping his victims several times, and often forcing them to perform oral sex on him. She wished she could take a second look at the girl's body. By now she knew what kinds of things to look for, otherwise insignificant physical evidence that telegraphed Stucky's patterns. Unfortunately, she saw at the bottom of the form that Jessica's body had already been released to her family. Even if she stopped the transfer, all the PE would be gone, washed away by a well-intentioned funeral director.

"We did find a stolen cellular phone in the Dumpster," Agent Tully said.

"But it was wiped clean?"

"Right. But the phone records show a call to the pizza place earlier that evening."

Maggie stopped and looked up at Agent Tully. My God, could it have been that easy? "That's how he abducted her? He simply ordered a pizza?"

"Initially that's what we were thinking," he explained. "We just found the delivery lists in her abandoned car. We've been running down the list, checking addresses and phone numbers. When Cunningham recognized Newburgh Heights as your new neighborhood, we checked for your address. Found it right away. Likewise, all the addresses are residential. But most of the people I've talked to so far were actually home and did receive their pizza. I have only a few left that I can't reach by phone, but I plan to drive to Newburgh Heights and check them out."

He handed her two photocopies of what looked like pieces of paper torn from a spiral notebook. The copier had even picked up the frayed edges. There were almost a dozen addresses on both lists. Hers was close to the top of the list labeled "#1." She leaned against the wall. The exhaustion from the night before was catching up with her. Of course, she had spent most of last night pacing from window to window, watching and waiting. The only sleep she had gotten had been on the flight back from Kansas City, and how could anyone get any rest while bobbing thirty-eight thousand feet above control? Now she couldn't even remember how long ago that was.

"Where did you find her car?"

"The airport's long-term parking lot. Also found a telephone company van parked alongside it that was reported stolen a couple of weeks ago."

"Any trace inside Jessica's car?" she asked as she glanced over the list of addresses.

"There was some mud on the accelerator. Not much else. Her blood and some blond hair—also hers—were recovered from the trunk. He must have used her own car to dump her body. No signs of a struggle inside the car, though, if that's what you're thinking. He had to have taken her someplace where he could take his time with her. Problem is, there aren't many abandoned warehouses or condemned properties in Newburgh Heights. I was thinking he might have given a business address, knowing the offices would be empty at night. But nothing commercial shows up on either list."

Suddenly Maggie recognized an address on one of the lists. She stood up straight and away from the wall. No, it couldn't be this easy. She reread the address.

"Actually, he may have had someplace much more luxurious in mind."

"Did you find something?" Agent Tully was at her side, staring at the list that he must have examined over and over himself. But of course, he wouldn't have seen it. How could he?

"This address," Maggie pointed halfway down the page. "The house is for sale. It's empty."

"You're kidding? Are you sure? If I remember correctly, the phone is still connected to a voice messaging service."

"The owners may be forwarding their phone calls. Yes, I'm sure it's for sale. My real estate agent showed it to me about two weeks ago."

She no longer cared about the rest of the file, which she had tucked under her arm. She was almost out the door before Agent Tully stopped her.

"Hold on," he said, grabbing his wrinkled jacket from the chair behind his desk. As he did so, he stumbled over a worn pair of sneakers Maggie hadn't noticed. Agent Tully reached for the corner of his desk to catch his balance and one of the piles gave way, scattering papers and photos across the floor. When he waved off her help, Maggie leaned against the doorjamb and waited. It was bad enough Cunningham was making her see Dr. James Kernan, but saddling her with her Dudley DoRight seemed almost laughable.

# CHAPTER 37

Maggie tried to wait patiently while Delores Heston of Heston Realty attempted to find the right key. The sun was sinking behind the ridge of trees. She couldn't believe how much time they had wasted trying to track down Tess McGowan. And although Ms. Heston had been more than accommodating, Maggie felt agitated, on edge and overly anxious. She knew this was where Albert Stucky had killed Jessica Beckwith. She could feel it. She could sense it. It was so easy, so simple, so very much like Stucky.

Ms. Heston dug out another bundle of keys and Maggie fidgeted, shifting her weight from one foot to the other. Ms. Heston noticed.

"I don't know where Tess is. I'm sure she probably just decided to take a couple of days off."

It was the same explanation the woman had given Maggie over the phone, but again Maggie could hear the concern.

"One of these has to work."

"I would think you'd have them labeled." Maggie tried to contain her irritation. She knew Ms. Heston was doing them a favor by letting them take a look after their bogus explanation about investigating possible break-ins. Since when did the FBI get involved in local burglaries? Luckily, Ms. Heston didn't question them.

"Actually, these are the spare keys. We do keep a labeled set, but Tess must have forgotten to return it after she showed the house yesterday."

"Yesterday? She showed the house to someone yesterday?"

Ms. Heston stopped and gave Maggie a nervous glance over her shoulder. Maggie realized her voice must have sounded too shrill, too alarmed.

"Yes, I'm sure it was yesterday. I checked the show schedule before I left the office tonight—Wednesday, April 1. Is there a problem? Do you think the house may have been broken into before that?"

"I really can't say," Maggie said, trying to sound indifferent when she wanted to kick in the door. "Do you know who she showed the house to?"

"No, we keep the names off the schedule for confidentiality reasons."

"You don't have the name of the person written down anywhere?"

Ms. Heston shot her another concerned look over her shoulder. The woman's flawless deep brown skin now had worry lines in her forehead and around her mouth. "Tess would have it written down somewhere. I trust my agents. No need for them to have me standing over their shoulder." Concern was quickly turning to frustration.

Maggie hadn't meant to make the woman defensive. She simply wanted the goddamn door opened.

She glanced around and saw Agent Tully finally emerge from the house across the street. He had been inside a long time, and Maggie wondered if the blonde in spandex who had answered the door simply found him charming, or if she really had some information to share. Judging by the woman's smile and wave, Maggie guessed it to be the former. She watched the tall, lanky agent hurry across the street. Out here, he moved with a confident, long-legged gait. In his dark suit, sunglasses and closely cropped hair, he looked like standard government-issue FBI, except that Agent Tully was too polite, too friendly and much too accommodating. If he hadn't told her he was from Cleveland, she would have guessed the Midwest. Maybe it was something in Ohio's water.

"This house has a security system." Ms. Heston was still trying to find the right key. "Oh, here we go. Finally."

The lock clicked as Agent Tully bounded up the steps. Ms. Heston turned, startled by his sudden appearance.

Ms. Heston, this is Special Agent R. J. Tully.

"Oh my. This must be important."

"Just routine, ma'am. We tend to travel in pairs these days," Tully said with a smile that relaxed the woman and immediately reminded Maggie of Sergeant Joe Friday.

She wanted to ask him if he had learned anything from the neighbor, but knew she'd have to wait for a more appropriate time. She hated waiting.

As soon as they entered the foyer, Maggie noticed the security system had been disarmed. None of the regular lights flashed or blinked.

"Are you certain the service has been continued?" Maggie asked as she pointed out the silent box. By now it should have been buzzing incessantly, screeching for the correct code to be entered.

"Yes, I'm quite certain. It's in our contract with the owners." Heston punched several buttons and the box came alive. "I don't understand this. Surely Tess wouldn't have forgotten to set it."

Maggie remembered Tess McGowan being very careful about deactivating and reactivating the alarm systems of the houses she had shown Maggie, this one included. Security systems had been one of Maggie's priorities, and she knew this one had not been anything out of the ordinary. She remembered it as being sufficient for the regular home owner. Most people didn't need to barricade themselves in at night away from serial killers.

"Mind if we look around?" Agent Tully asked, but Maggie was already halfway up the open staircase. She reached the first landing when she heard Ms. Heston's panicked voice.

"Oh, good Lord!"

Maggie leaned over the oak railing to see Ms. Heston pointing to a briefcase she had discovered in the corner of the living room.

"This belongs to Tess." Up until now, the woman had been incredibly professional. Now her sudden panic was unnerving.

By the time Maggie came down the steps, Agent Tully had taken the briefcase and started carefully extracting its contents with a white handkerchief.

"No way that girl's gonna leave this and not come back for it." The panic rushed her words, reducing her previous crisp dialect to a slang version she obviously found more comfortable.

"There's her appointment book, her pocketbook...good Lord, something's just not right here."

Maggie watched as Agent Tully brought out the last item—a labeled set of keys. Without getting a closer look, Maggie knew they were the keys for this house. Suddenly she felt nauseated. Tess McGowan may have shown this house yesterday, but she certainly didn't leave of her own free will.

# CHAPTER 38

"We don't know that Stucky had anything to do with this." Tully tried to sound convincing, but he wasn't sure he believed his own words.

It was obvious he needed to be the objective one. Ever since Ms. Heston left them, Agent O'Dell seemed to be coming apart at the seams. The calm, controlled professional now paced, quick long steps, back and forth. She ran her fingers through her short dark hair too many times, tucking strands behind her ears, tousling it with her fingers and tucking it in again. Her voice was clipped, and possessed an edge that hadn't existed before. Tully thought he heard it quiver several times.

He felt as if he was watching from the sidelines as she passed by him. She didn't seem to know what to do with her hands. They ducked into her trouser pockets, then a quick swipe through her hair again. Several times they slipped into her jacket, and he knew she was checking her revolver. Tully wasn't sure what to do with her. This was so unlike the woman he had spent most of the day with.

It had gotten dark, and Agent O'Dell had gone through the entire two-story house, turning on lights and pulling closed what few draperies there were, but only after staring out into the night at each window. Was she expecting him to be there?

She was doing a second check downstairs now. Tully decided they needed to leave. The house was spotless. Though the master bedroom smelled strongly of a recent dousing of ammonia, there was no trace that anything had occurred in the house. Least of all, a brutal murder and a violent kidnapping.

"There's no evidence that anything suspicious happened here," he tried again. "I think it's time we leave." He glanced at his watch and cringed when he saw that it was after nine. Emma would be furious with him for having to spend the entire evening with Mrs. Lopez.

"Tess McGowan was the real estate agent who sold me my house," O'Dell repeated. It was the most she had said to him in the last several hours. "Don't you see? Don't you get it?"

He knew exactly what she was thinking. It was the same thing he was thinking. Albert Stucky would have known too, especially since he must be spending a good deal of time watching Agent O'Dell. He would have seen the two of them together, just the way he saw the pizza girl and the Kansas City waitress. But the truth was, they had absolutely no evidence that McGowan was even missing, other than a forgotten briefcase, and that was hardly proof. He refused to fuel O'Dell's panic.

"Right now there's nothing substantial to prove Ms. McGowan was abducted. And there's nothing more we can do here. We need to call it a night. Maybe we can track down Ms. McGowan tomorrow."

"We won't track her down. He's taken her." The quiver was there though she did her best to hide it. "He's added her to his collection. She may be dead already." Her hands reached for her holster then disappeared into her pockets. "Or if she's not dead, she may be wishing she was," she added in almost a whisper.

Tully rubbed his eyes. He had removed his glasses hours ago. O'Dell was starting to spook him. He didn't want to think about the fact that Albert Stucky may have added to his collection. Back on his desk, buried under manuals and documents, he had a bulging file of missing women from across the country. Women who had disappeared without a trace in the last five months since Stucky's escape.

The volume wasn't that unusual. It happened all the time. Some of the women left and didn't want to be found. Others had been abused by husbands and lovers and chose to disappear. But too many were gone without any explanation, and Tully knew enough about Stucky's games to pray that none of them in his file folder were actually in Stucky's new collection.

"Look, there's nothing more we can do tonight."

"We need to do a luminol test. We can have Keith Ganza bring it and the Lumi-Light, so we can go over the master bedroom."

"There's nothing here. There's absolutely no reason to believe anything happened in this house, Agent O'Dell."

"The Lumi-Light might show any latent prints. And the luminol will show any blood left in the cracks, any stains we can't see. He obviously tried to clean things up, but you can't clean enough to get rid of blood." It was almost as if she didn't hear him. As though he wasn't there and she was talking to herself.

"We can't do anything more tonight. I'm exhausted. You must be exhausted." When she started for the stairs again, he gently grabbed her arm. "Agent O'Dell."

She wrenched her arm away, turning on him with eyes flashing anger. She stood solidly, firmly in place, staring at him as though challenging him to a dual. Then without warning she turned on her heel and marched to the door, snapping off lights in her path.

Tully followed her cue before she changed her mind. He ran upstairs and shut off those lights, and when he returned, O'Dell was in the foyer, activating the security system. It wasn't until he locked the front door and walked alongside her to his car that he saw her revolver in her hand, dropped at her side but in a tight grip.

Suddenly Tully realized that the hysteria, the frustration, the anger he had witnessed was actually fear. How stupid of him not to have seen it before now. Special Agent Maggie O'Dell was scared to death, not just for Tess McGowan, but for herself, too.

# CHAPTER 39

Tess jerked awake. Her throat felt like sandpaper, so dry it hurt to swallow. Her eyelids felt like lead shutters. Her chest ached as though some massive weight had pressed against her. There was nothing on top of her now. She lay on what appeared to be a narrow, lumpy cot. The room was dimly lit, forcing her to squint. The smell of mildew surrounded her. A draft made her pull the scratchy blanket up under her chin.

She remembered feeling paralyzed. In a mad panic, she lifted both her arms, grateful to find no restraints but quickly disappointed to find her limbs heavy, movement awkward. They felt detached and unresponsive. But at least she could move and at least she was not tied down.

She started to sit up, and immediately her muscles protested. The room began to spin. Her head throbbed and nausea washed over her so sudden and so strong, she lay back. She was used to hangovers, but this was much worse. Something had been injected into her bloodstream. Then she remembered the dark-haired man and the needle. Dear God, where the hell had he taken her? And where was he?

Her eyes darted around the small space. The nausea forced her to keep her head on the pillow as she twisted and turned her neck to examine her accommodations. She was inside some sort of wooden shack. Rotted wood allowed faint light to seep in between the slats. That was the only light. From what Tess could tell, it was cloudy or else too early or late for sunshine. Either way, she'd only be able to guess. There were no windows, or at least not anymore. One wall had boards nailed over a small area that may have been a window at one time. Other than the cot, there was nothing else except a tall plastic bucket in the corner.

Tess's eyes searched and found what looked like a door. It was difficult to tell. The wood blended in with the rest of the shack. Only a couple of rusted hinges and a keyhole gave it away. Of course, it would be locked, maybe even bolted from the outside, but she needed to make an attempt.

She sat up slowly and waited. Again, the nausea sent her head to the pillow.

"Damn it!" she shouted, and immediately regretted it. What if he was watching, listening?

She needed to concentrate. She could do this. After all, how many hangovers had she survived? But her surroundings only added to her vulnerability. Why was he doing this? What did he want from her? Had he mistaken her for someone else? A fresh panic began to crawl in her stomach. She couldn't think about his intentions now or about him. She couldn't think about how she got here. She wouldn't think about any of it or it would immobilize her exactly like the contents of that syringe.

She rolled onto her side to assuage the nausea. A sharp pain pierced her side, and for a brief moment she thought she had rolled onto a spike. But there was nothing there, only the hard, lumpy mattress. She moved her fingers up under her blouse, noticing the hem had already been pulled out from her trouser's waistband. A button was missing and the rest were off a buttonhole.

"No, stop it," she scolded herself in a whispered rush.

She had to focus. She couldn't think about what he may have done while she had been unconscious. She needed to check and see if she was okay.

Her fingers found no open wound, no sticky blood, but she was almost certain one of her ribs had been broken or badly bruised. Unfortunately, her past afforded her the knowledge of what broken ribs felt like. Carefully, her fingers probed the area under her breasts while she bit down on her lower lip. Despite the stabbing pain, she guessed bruised, not broken. That was good. She could function just fine with bruised ribs. Broken could sometimes puncture a lung. Another piece of trivia she wished she didn't know firsthand.

She slipped a foot out from under the covers and dangled it

close to the floor. She was barefoot. What had he done with her shoes and stockings? Again, she glanced around the room. Her eyes had adjusted to the dim light, though her vision remained a bit off focus and her contact lenses felt gritty. It didn't matter. There was nothing more to see in the shack.

She let her toes and the ball of her foot touch the floor. It was colder than she expected, but she kept the foot there, forcing her body to grow accustomed to the change in temperature before she tried to stand up. The air in the shack felt damp and chilly.

Then she heard the beginning tap-tap-tap, soft against the roof. The sound of rain had usually been a comfort to her. Now she frantically wondered how badly the rotted roof leaked and felt a new chill. She knew the bucket in the corner hadn't been placed there for leaks. Instead, it was meant to accommodate her. He obviously intended to keep her here for a while. The thought reawakened the fear.

She pushed herself out of the cot and stood with both feet flat on the cold floorboards while she bent at the waist and held on to the bed. Again, she bit her lip, ignoring the taste of blood, fighting the urge to vomit and waiting for the room to stop spinning.

Her pulse quickened. The sound inside her head hummed like wind in a tunnel. She tried to concentrate on the tap-tap-tapping of the rain. Maybe she could find some level of comfort, some level of sanity, in the rain's natural and familiar rhythm. A sudden rumble of thunder startled her like a gunshot, and she spun around to the door as though expecting to see him there. When her heart settled back in her chest, she almost burst out laughing. It was only thunder. A little bit of thunder. That's all.

Slowly she tested her feet, coaxing her stomach to behave, trying to ignore the pain in her side and the panic from strangling her. Only now did she realize that her breathing came in gasps. A lump obstructed her throat, and it threatened to come out screaming. It took a conscious effort to prevent it from doing so.

Her body began shivering. She grabbed the wool blanket, wrapped it around her shoulders and tied two ends together in a knot at her neck, keeping her hands free. She checked under the cot, hoping to find something, anything to aid in her escape, or at least her shoes. There was nothing, not even furballs or dust. Which meant he had prepared this place for her, and recently. If only he hadn't taken her shoes and stockings. Then she remembered she had worn panty hose under her trousers.

Oh God! He had undressed her, after all. She mustn't think about it. She had to concentrate on other things. Stop remembering. Stop feeling aches and bruises in places that might remind her of what he had done. No, she couldn't, she wouldn't remember. Not now. She needed to focus all her energies on getting out of here.

Again she listened to the rain. Again she waited for its rhythm to calm her, to regulate her raspy breathing.

When she could walk without the threat of nausea crippling her, she carefully made her way to the door. The handle was nothing more than a rusted latch. One more time, she looked around to see if she had missed anything that could be used to help pry open the door. Even the corners had been swept clean. Then she saw a rusted nail swept into a groove in the floor. She pried it out with her fingernails and began examining the keyhole. The door was indeed locked, but was it bolted as well?

She steadied her fingers and inserted the nail into the keyhole, slipping it in and out, jingling and twisting it expertly. Another talent acquired in her not so illustrious past. But it had been years, and she was out of practice. The lock groaned in rusted protest. Oh, dear God, if only—something gave way with a metallic click.

Tess grabbed the latch and gave it a yank. The door swung open freely, almost knocking her over in her surprise. No force had been necessary. It hadn't been bolted. She waited, staring at the open doorway. This was too easy. Was it a blessing or another trap?

# CHAPTER 40

*Friday, April 3*

Tully drove with one hand on the steering wheel and the other fumbling with the plastic lid of his coffee container. Why did fast-food places have to make the contraptions like child-protective caps? His finger punched at the uncooperative triangular perforation, cracking the plastic and splashing hot coffee onto his lap.

"Damn it!" he yelled as he swerved to the side of the road and screeched on the brakes, splattering more coffee onto the fabric of his car seat. He grabbed napkins to sop it up, but already the brown stain spread deep into the cream color. As an afterthought, he checked the rearview mirror, relieved no one was behind him.

He shoved the car's gearshift into park and released his foot from the brake pedal, only now realizing how tense and rigid his body had become in response to the stress. He sat back and rubbed a hand over his jaw, immediately feeling the nicks he had inflicted earlier with his razor. It had been one day and already Agent O'Dell had him feeling as if he was on the rim of her personal cliff, and he was straddling the ledge while pieces of rock crumbled at his feet.

Maybe it had been a mistake asking Assistant Director Cunningham to let O'Dell help on the Stucky case. Last night may have been proof that she simply couldn't handle the pressure. But then her phone message this morning telling him to meet her back at the Archer Drive house made Tully realize that he was in for an even more difficult task.

They had found nothing at the house to warrant a further search. Yet O'Dell had told him she had written permission from Ms. Heston and the owners to do so. Now he wondered if she had gotten them out of bed. How else had she been able to obtain written permission between last night and early this morning? And how the hell would he make her see that she was being irrational and paranoid and possibly wasting precious time?

After last night, Tully knew O'Dell was wound so tight, that controlling her could be impossible, and trying to restrain her could make matters worse. But he wouldn't talk to Cunningham. He couldn't. Not yet. He needed to handle this. He needed to settle O'Dell down so they could move forward.

He sipped what coffee was left and glanced at his watch. Today the damn thing was slow, according to the car's digital clock. It wasn't even seven o'clock. O'Dell had left the message on his machine at about six while he was in the shower. He wondered if she had gone to bed at all last night.

He put the coffee container safely into a cup holder, massaged the tension in his neck and then shifted into drive. He had only three blocks to go. When he turned onto the street, his tension turned to anger. Parked in the driveway were O'Dell's red Toyota and a navy blue panel van, the kind the forensic lab used. She hadn't wasted any time nor bothered to wait for his okay. What was the use of being lead in an investigation if no one paid any goddamn attention? He needed to put a stop to this now.

As he walked toward the front door, lampposts along the driveway blinked, trying to decide whether to stay on or shut off. They needed rain. Each time it looked like spring showers, the rains dumped on the shoreline or just offshore before rolling inland. But this morning thick clouds smudged out the sunrise. A low rumble could be heard in the distance. It suited Tully's mood, and he caught himself making fists as he got closer to the door. He hated confrontation. If he couldn't get his own daughter to obey him, then how the hell did he expect to get Agent O'Dell to?

The front door was unlocked, the security system silent. He followed the voices upstairs to the master bedroom. Keith Ganza wore a short white lab coat, and Tully wondered if the man even owned an ordinary sports jacket.

"Agent Tully," O'Dell said, coming from the master bathroom, wearing latex gloves and carrying jugs of liquid. "We're almost ready. We just finished mixing the luminol."

She set the jugs on the floor in the corner where Ganza had set up shop.

"You two know each other, right?" O'Dell asked as though she thought that was the reason for Tully's frown.

"Yes," he answered, trying to restrain his anger and maintain his professionalism.

Ganza simply nodded at Tully and continued loading and preparing a video camera. A Will comm camera on a tripod stood in the center of the room, already assembled. Several duffel bags, more jugs and four or five spray bottles were carefully set on the floor. A black case leaned against the wall. Tully recognized it as the Lumi-Light. Each of the windows were covered with some kind of black film taped to the frames so that light couldn't filter in from the outside. Even now the room required the ceiling light. The bathroom lights were on too, and Tully wondered what, if anything, they had used to block out the skylight. This was ridiculous.

Agent O'Dell began filling spray bottles with the luminol, using a funnel and steady hands. There seemed to be no sign of the jumpy, nervous, frazzled woman he had seen last night.

"Agent O'Dell. We need to talk."

"Of course, go ahead." Except she didn't look up at him and continued to pour.

Ganza appeared oblivious to Tully's anger, and he wanted to keep it that way.

"We need to talk in private."

Both O'Dell and Ganza looked up at him. Yet neither stopped what they were doing. O'Dell screwed the spray top onto the bottle she had filled. Tully expected her to see his anger. He expected her to be concerned or at least somewhat apologetic.

"Once we have the luminol mixed, we need to use it immediately," she explained, and began filling another spray bottle.

"I realize that," Tully said through clenched teeth.

"I have written permission," she continued without interrupting her pouring. "The luminol is odorless, and it leaves little residue. Nothing more than a sprinkle of white power when it dries. Hardly noticeable."

"I know that, too," Tully snapped at her, though her tone was not at all condescending. This time O'Dell and Ganza stopped and stared at him. How had he suddenly become the hysterical one, the irrational one?

"Then what seems to be the problem, Agent Tully?" She stood to face him, but again there was nothing challenging in her manner, which only made it worse.

Even the expression on Ganza's lined and haggard face was one of impatience. They continued to stare at him, waiting as though he was holding up the process unreasonably.

"I thought we decided last night that there was nothing here."

"No, we decided there was nothing more we could do last night. Although it would have been much better to do this last night. Hopefully, it'll be dark enough. We lucked out with it being so cloudy."

Ganza nodded. They both waited. Suddenly all of Tully's objections—which seemed completely logical minutes ago—now sounded immature and arrogant. There was nothing here. It was a ridiculous waste of time and effort. But rather than telling O'Dell that, perhaps it was better for her to see for herself. Maybe only then would she be satisfied.

"Let's get this over with," he finally said. "What do you want me to do?"

"Close the door and stay there next to the light switch." Ganza motioned to him while he picked up the video camera. "I'll let you know when to flip it off and on again. Maggie, grab a couple of spray bottles. You spritz. I'll be right beside you filming."

Tully got into position, no longer bothering to hide his reluctance or his impatience. However, he could see that anything he did would be wasted on O'Dell and Ganza. They were so involved in the task at hand, they barely noticed him except as a utility.

He watched O'Dell load both her hands with spray bottles, holding them like revolvers, her index fingers ready on the triggers.

"Let's start at the wall closest to the door and move toward the bathroom," Ganza instructed in his monotone. He reminded Tully of Icabod Crane. The man's voice never showed emotion—

a perfect match for his tall, slumped appearance and deliberate and precise movements.

"Maggie, you remember the drill. Start on the walls, top to bottom. Then the floor, wall to center," Ganza went on. "Let's keep a steady spray going all the way to the bathroom. We'll stop at the bathroom door. You'll probably need to reload with luminol by then."

"Gotcha."

Tully just then realized that O'Dell and Ganza had done this as a team before. They seemed comfortable with each other, knowing each other's roles. And O'Dell had managed to get Ganza here at the break of dawn, despite the man's overloaded schedule.

Tully manned his post, waiting with arms crossed over his chest and his shoulder leaning against the closed door. He caught himself tapping his foot, an unconscious nervous habit that Emma accused him of when he was being "close-minded." Where the hell did she come up with stuff like that? Nevertheless, he stopped his foot from tapping.

"We're ready, Agent Tully. Go ahead and hit the lights," Ganza told him.

Tully flipped the switch and immediately felt swallowed by the pitch black. Not a hint of light squeezed in past the film on the windows. In fact, Tully could no longer tell where the windows were.

"This is excellent," he heard Ganza say.

Then Tully heard a faint electronic whine and a tiny red dot appeared where he imagined the video camera was in Ganza's hands.

"Ready when you are, Maggie," Ganza said as the red dot bobbed up.

Tully heard the spritz of liquid, steady and insistent. It sounded as if she was dousing the entire wall. Tully wondered how many bottles, how many jugs of luminol it would take for her to realize that there was nothing here. Suddenly the wall began to glow. Tully stood up straight, and so did the hairs on the back of his neck and arms.

"Jesus Christ," he gasped, staring in disbelief at the streaks, the smudges and handprints that smeared the entire wall and now glowed like fluorescent paint.

# CHAPTER 41

Maggie stepped back, giving Keith room. It was worse than she expected. The smears stretched, reached, clawed and swiped with the undeniable motion of someone desperate and terrified. The handprints were small, almost child-size. She remembered Jessica Beckwith's delicate hands holding out the pizza box for her.

"Jesus, I can't believe this."

She heard Tully's voice again come out of the black. She knew he had believed they wouldn't find a thing, that nothing had taken place here. There was no victory in proving him wrong. Instead, she found herself light-headed and nauseated. Suddenly it was too hot in the room. What the hell was the matter with her? She hadn't been sick at crime scenes since the early days, those first years of initiation. Now for a second time in less than a week, her stomach attempted to revolt against her.

"Keith, what are the chances of this being a cleaning solution? The house is for sale. It still smells like someone has given it a recent scrubbing."

"Oh, it's been scrubbed all right. Someone was trying to get rid of this."

"But luminol can be sensitive to bleach," she continued. "Maybe a residential-cleaning company scrubbed down everything including the walls." After a fitful, sleepless night of anticipating, of knowing what they'd discover, why did she not want to believe it? Why did she find herself wanting to believe the streaks and swipes in front of her were simply an overzealous maid?

"In the linen closet there's a bunch of cleaning supplies. Mop, bucket, sponges and liquid cleaners. Smells like the same stuff that was used. None of it contains bleach," Ganza countered. "I checked. Besides, no one cleans and leaves handprints like that."

She forced herself to stare at the prints before they faded. The small fingers were elongated as they had grabbed and clawed and slid. She closed her eyes against the images her mind was trained to concoct. With little coaxing, she knew she could see it all in slow motion as if visualizing a scene from a movie, a horror movie.

"Ready, Maggie?" Keith's voice made her jump. He was right beside her again as the room started to return to darkness. "Let's get the floor from here to the bathroom."

She felt her fingers shaking as she repositioned them on the spray bottles. Gratefully, neither Keith nor Tully could see them. She steadied herself and tried to remember exactly what direction and how far it was to the bathroom. Once she felt back in control, she began spritzing, keeping the mist away from her feet as she slowly walked sideways. Maggie hadn't reached the bathroom door when the floor began lighting up like a runway, long skid marks following her.

"Oh my God!" She heard Tully mutter from his dark perch, and she wanted to tell him to shut up. His shock unnerved her and worse, reminded her of her own.

Ganza pointed the red dot to the floor, following the trail that had once been bloody feet dragged across the parquet floor. Maggie pushed back strands of hair and swiped at the perspiration on her forehead. Was Jessica unconscious by the time he got her to the bathroom? The girl would have lost a lot of blood putting up a fight like the one smeared on the wall. Maggie wondered if she was conscious when Stucky lifted her into the whirlpool bath. When he told her all the horrible things he would do to her. Was she dead or alive when he started cutting?

"Let's take a break here," Keith said. "Agent Tully, go ahead and switch the lights back on."

Maggie blinked against the burst of light, relieved at the interruption of her mind's descent into the depths of hell. If she tried, she would be able to hear Jessica's screams, her pleas for help. Maggie's memory bank seemed filled with audio clips of what sheer terror sounded like. It was something she'd never forget, no matter how many years went by.

"Agent O'Dell?"

Tully startled her, suddenly standing in front of her. She

looked around to see Keith busy in the corner, and only now did she notice that he had taken the spray bottles from her hands and was filling them.

"Agent O'Dell, I owe you an apology," Agent Tully was saying. At some point he had removed his jacket and rolled up his shirtsleeves in haphazard and uneven folds. He unbuttoned his collar and twisted the knot of his tie loose. "I really thought there was nothing here. I feel like such an asshole."

Maggie stared at him and tried to remember the last time anyone, especially in law enforcement, had apologized to her, let alone admitted to making a mistake. Was this guy for real? Instead of looking embarrassed, he genuinely looked sorry.

"I have to admit, Agent Tully, I was simply acting on gut instinct."

"Maggie, we should remember to pull the drain from the whirlpool bath," Ganza interrupted without looking up. "I'm betting that's where he cut her open. We may find some left-overs."

Agent Tully's face grew paler, and she saw him wince.

"One thing we didn't check last night, Agent Tully, was the garbage cans outside," she told him, offering to save him. "Since the house is for sale and empty, the garbage collectors may have skipped it."

He seemed grateful for the chance to escape. "I'll go check."

As he left, Maggie realized he could possibly find something equally shocking in the garbage. Perhaps she wasn't saving him at all. She pulled out a fresh pair of latex gloves from her forensic kit and tossed out the ones she had contaminated with luminol. Keith unpacked a wrench, screwdriver and several evidence bags.

"You're being awfully nice to the new guy," he said.

She glanced at him. Though he kept his eyes on the items he was unearthing from his bag, she could see the corner of his mouth caught in a smile.

"I can be nice. It's not like it's an impossibility."

"Didn't say that it was." He dug out Q-Tips, several brushes, forceps and small brown bottles, lining everything up as if taking inventory. "Don't worry, Maggie, I won't tell anyone. Wouldn't want to ruin your reputation." This time he gave her his eyes, light blue behind hooded, heavy lids that Maggie knew in the last thirty years had seen more horror and evil than any one person should ever be allowed to see. Yet now they were smiling at her.

"Keith, what do you know about Agent Tully?"

"I've heard nothing but good things."

"Of course there are nothing but good things. He looks like a cross between Mr. Rogers and Fox Mulder."

"Fox Mulder?" He raised his eyebrows at her.

"You know, from the TV show *The X-Files?*"

"Oh, I know who he is. I'm just surprised you know who he is."

She found herself blushing as though he'd discovered some secret.

"I've caught a couple of episodes. What things have you heard? About Tully?" She quickly returned to the subject.

"He's here from Cleveland at Cunningham's request, so the guy has to be good, right? Someone said he's able to look at crime scene photos alone and come up with a profile that nine times out of ten is on target."

"Crime scene photos. That explains why he's so squeamish with the real thing."

"I don't think he's been with the Bureau long—five, six years. Probably slipped in right at the age limit."

"What did he do before? Please don't tell me he's a lawyer."

"Something wrong with lawyers?" Agent Tully interrupted from the doorway.

Maggie checked his eyes to see if he was angry with them. Keith went back to his task, leaving Maggie feeling as though she was the one who needed to explain.

"I was just curious," she said without apology.

"You could just ask me."

Yes, he was angry, but she saw him pretending not to be. Did he always make certain his emotions were so carefully kept in check?

"Okay. So what did you do before you joined the Bureau?"

He held up a black garbage bag in one hand.

"I was an insurance fraud investigator." In his other latex-gloved hand he held up a wad of what looked like candy bar wrappers. "And I'd say our boy has a serious sweet tooth."

# CHAPTER 42

Maggie gripped the revolver and aimed at the dark figure in front of her. Her right hand shook. She could feel her jaw clench and her muscles tense.

"Goddamn it!" she yelled though no one could hear her in the empty firearms target alley. She had come in just as Agent Ballato, the firearms instructor, had ended his class. This late on a Friday, she would have the place to herself.

She relaxed her stance once again, dropping her arms and rolling her shoulders, flexing her neck. Why the hell couldn't she relax? Why did she feel wound so tight? Like something would explode inside her at any minute?

She pushed her goggles up on top of her head and leaned against the half wall of her galley. After she and Agent Tully had left the house on Archer Drive she had called Detective Ford in Kansas City. She had listened to him describe the details of Rita's murder, of her blood-soaked apartment, the semen-stained sheets and the remnants of skin and tissue the KC forensic team had found in Rita's bathtub. It wasn't that different from what they had found in the whirlpool bath at Archer Drive. Only, Stucky didn't bother to clean up after himself in Rita's apartment. Why did he clean up at Archer Drive after killing Jessica? Was it because he needed to use the house again? Did he lure Tess McGowan there and take her for later? And if he did take her, where the hell was he keeping her?

Maggie closed her eyes and wished the tightness in her chest would let up. She needed to focus. She needed to relax. It was too easy to conjure up the images. It was what she had been trained to do, but this time she wished she could shove them away. Her mind wouldn't listen. Despite her effort to stop the images, they came anyway. She could see Jessica Beckwith's small hands passing her the pizza box. Then she could see those same hands clawing and grabbing at the walls of the empty bedroom. Why hadn't anyone heard her screams when they seemed so loud and vivid in Maggie's head?

She set the gun aside and rubbed her eyes with both hands. It didn't help. She could remember Rita's face, the waitress's fatigued but friendly smile as she had served the three of them Sunday evening in the smoke-filled bar and grill. And then, without effort or warning, came the images of Rita's garbage-riddled body, her slashed throat and the glob that once was her kidney lying on a shiny dinner plate. Both women were dead only because they had had the misfortune of meeting her. And now Maggie was certain that two more women had been taken for the same reason; they had met her.

She wanted to yell and scream. She wanted the throbbing to go away. She wanted her goddamn hand to stop shaking. Ever since Tully found that handful of candy bar wrappers, Maggie kept wondering about Rachel Endicott. Was it possible she was simply jumping to conclusions, trying too hard to connect Rachel's disappearance with Tess's?

There had been mud on the steps in Rachel's house. Mud with some odd metallic substance. Tully had said that a sparkling dirt had been found on Jessica's car accelerator. Could it be the same? There was something else that Tully had told her. She couldn't remember what it was. It nagged at Maggie, but she couldn't remember. Maybe something in the police report?

"Goddamn it!" Why couldn't she remember?

Lately she felt as if her mind was unraveling, pieces shredding and peeling away. Her nerves felt raw, her muscles exhausted from constantly being on alert. And the worst part, the most infuriating part, was that she seemed to have absolutely no control over any of it.

Albert Stucky had her right where he wanted her, clinging to some imaginary mental ledge. He had made her an accomplice to his evil. He had made her his partner by letting her choose who his next victim would be. He wanted her to share the responsibility. He wanted her to understand the power of evil. By doing so, did he also expect to unleash some evil beast from inside her?

She picked up the Smith & Wesson, letting her hands stroke the cool metal, wrapping her fingers around the handle with care, almost reverence. She ignored the earplugs dangling around her neck and left the goggles perched on top of her head. She raised her right arm, keeping the elbow bent, just a little. Her left hand crisscrossed her right, adding strength and reinforcement. She stared down the front sight, willing it, commanding it not to move, not to quiver. Then without further hesitation, she squeezed the trigger, firing in rapid succession until all six bullets were spent and the scent of the discharge filled her nostrils.

Her ears were ringing when she allowed her arm to relax and drop to her side. Her heart pounded as she punched the button on the wall, flinching at the screech of the pulley as it wheeled the target toward her. The dark figure, the silhouette of her pretend assailant stopped in front of her with a rustle of paper and a clank of metal. Maggie saw that her aim had been right on target. She took a deep breath and sighed. She should have been relieved at her precision. Instead, she felt that ledge getting closer and crumbling beneath her. Because the six bullets she had just fired had expertly and intentionally been placed right between the eyes of her target.

# CHAPTER 43

Tess skidded to a stop. Her bare feet were caked with mud. She could smell it and looked to find mud stuck to her hands, her trousers, her skinned elbows. She didn't remember ripping her blouse, yet both elbows showed through, the flesh scraped and bloody, and now dirty with rancid mud. The rain had stopped without her noticing, but she knew it would be temporary because the clouds had darkened and the fog became a thicker gray, wisping around her like unsettled spirits rising from the ground. Dear God, she couldn't think of such things. She shouldn't think at all, just run.

Instead, she leaned against a tree, trying to catch her breath. She had followed the only path she could find in the dense woods, hoping it would lead to freedom. Her nerves were frayed. The terror raced inside her, completely beyond her control. She expected him to step out and grab her at any second.

Dry burrs and broken twigs poked through her blanket cape. It had been caught many times, yanking her backward like hands gripping her neck. It was a constant reminder of the painful bruises his fingers had left. Yet she refused to let it go, as if it was a flimsy shield, a makeshift security blanket. She was soaked from the rain and her own perspiration, wet strands of hair plastered against her face. Her silk blouse clung to her like a second skin.

The thick fog added to the dampness. In less than an hour darkness would enshroud these endless woods. The thought brought fresh panic. She could hardly see through the damp haze. Twice she had slid down a ridge, almost tumbling into the body of water that had seemed like a gray mist when seen from above. The dark would make further movement impossible.

He had taken her wristwatch, for obvious reasons, though he

had left the sapphire ring and earrings. She'd gladly trade the three-thousand-dollar ring for her Timex. She hated not knowing the time. Did she know what day it was? Could it still be Wednesday? No. She remembered it being dark when she was in the car. Yes, there had been oncoming headlights. Which meant she had slept most of Thursday. Suddenly it occurred to her that she really had no idea how long she had been unconscious. It may have been days.

Her breathing became labored again as the fear crawled through her insides. Calm. She needed to stay calm. She needed to figure out what to do for the night. She would take this moment by moment. Despite the instinct to continue running, it was more important that she find someplace to wait out the night. Now she wondered if she should have stayed in the shack. Had she really accomplished anything by leaving it? At least it had been dry, and that lumpy cot now sounded wonderful. Instead, she had no idea where she was. It certainly didn't feel as if she had gotten any closer to escaping this endless wooded prison, though she must have covered several miles.

She crouched down, her back pressed against the rough bark. Her legs begged to sit, but she needed to stay alert and ready to run. Black crows screeched down at her. They startled her, but she remained still and quiet, too tired, too weak to move out of their way. The crows were settling in the treetops for the night. Hundreds of them flapped overhead, coming from all directions, their rude caws a warning as they claimed their evening roost.

Suddenly it occurred to Tess that these birds wouldn't settle here if they didn't perceive it to be somewhat safe. And if there was danger sometime during the night, they would probably react better than an alarm system.

Her eyes began searching the area for a safe resting place. There were plenty of fallen leaves and pine needles, bits and pieces left over from last fall. However, everything was damp from the rain and fog. She shivered just thinking about lying on the cold ground.

The crows' squawks continued. She looked up and began examining branches. She hadn't climbed a tree since she was a kid.

Back then it had been a survival tactic, one more way to hide from her aunt and uncle. Her aching muscles reminded her how foolish the thought of climbing anything was right now. Foolish or not, it would be the safest place to be. He'd never look for her up above, not to mention other nightly predators. Dear God, she hadn't even thought of other animals.

The tree beside her had a perfect Y to accommodate her. Immediately, she pushed herself into action and began dragging logs and branches. She stacked them, crisscrossing the larger ones to construct a crude stepladder. If she could reach the lower branches, she might be able to swing her feet up into the Y.

She tried to ignore her fatigue, tried to pretend her feet weren't already cut and stinging. With every load of branches or lift of a log, her muscles screamed out for her to stop. But she could feel a new surge of energy. Her heart pounded in her ears, only this time with excitement.

Overhead the crows had gone silent, as if watching and interested in her frantic work. Or did they hear something else? She stopped. Her arms were full. Her breathing rasped. She couldn't hear over the pounding of her heart. She held her breath as best she could and listened. It was as if the entire woods had gone silent, as if the impending dark had swallowed every sound, every movement.

Then she heard it.

At first it sounded like a wounded animal, a muffled cry, a high-pitched hum. Tess turned slowly, her eyes squinting against the fog and into the dark. A sudden breeze created night shadows. Swaying branches became waving arms. Rustling leaves sounded like footsteps.

Tess unloaded her arms while her eyes continued to dart around her. Could she get into the tree without building her makeshift ladder? Her fingers clawed into the bark. Her feet tested the pile's strength and structure. She pulled herself up and grabbed onto the closest branch. It creaked under her weight, but didn't break. Her fingers clung to the branch despite loose bark falling into her eyes. She was ready to swing her feet up into the Y when the muffled cry transformed into words.

"Help me. Please, help me."

The words, drifting with the breeze, were crisp and clear. Tess froze. She hung from the branch, her toes barely reaching the pile. Maybe she was hearing things. Maybe it was simply exhaustion playing tricks on her.

Her arms ached. Her fingers felt numb. If she was going to make it up into the tree, she needed to use this last surge of energy.

The words came again, floating over her as if a part of the fog.

"Please, someone help me."

It was a woman's voice, and it was close by.

Tess dropped to the ground. By now she could see only a foot or two into the thickening darkness. She walked slowly, following the path, silently counting her steps with arms stretched out in front of her. Twigs grabbed at her hair and unseen branches reached for her. She moved in the direction of the voice, still afraid to call, afraid to give away her presence. She stepped carefully, continuing her count so she could turn around and hopefully find her tree sanctuary.

Twenty-two, twenty-three. Then suddenly the ground opened beneath her. Tess fell and the earth swallowed her.

# CHAPTER 44

Tess lay at the bottom of the pit. Her head roared. Her side burned as if on fire. Her breathing came in gasps and quick bursts as the terror swept through her veins. Mud oozed up around her, sucking at her arms and legs like quicksand. Her right ankle twisted under her. Even without attempting to move it, she knew she would have trouble doing so.

The smell of mud and decay gagged her. The black dark squeezed around her. She couldn't see in any direction. Above her she could barely make out a few shadows of branches, but the fog and the night had already begun devouring the twilight. What shadows she could see were only enough to reveal how deep her earthly tomb was. It had to be at least fifteen feet to the top. Dear God, she'd never be able to climb out.

She struggled to stand, falling when the ankle refused to hold her up. A fresh wave of panic sent her to her feet again. This time she clawed and scratched at the dirt to hold herself up. She ripped at the wall with fingers digging and searching for a ledge that didn't exist. Chunks of damp earth came off in her hands. She could feel the worms slithering through her fingers. She flung them off. They reminded her of snakes. And dear God, how she hated snakes. The thought alone unleashed a new terror.

Suddenly her bare feet and hands slashed and pounded, climbed and slid. The wind tunnel in her head continued to roar. Her heart slammed against her rib cage. She couldn't breathe. That's when she realized she was screaming. It wasn't the sound that alarmed her as much as her raw throat and her aching lungs. When she stopped, the screaming continued. Surely she was losing her mind. The scream transformed into a whine, then a low moan that emanated from the black corner of the hole.

A shiver slid down Tess's mud and sweat-drenched back. She

remembered the voice. The voice that had led her to this hellhole. Had it all been a trap?

"Who are you?" she whispered into the dark.

The moans became muffled sobs.

Tess waited. She slid along the wall, ignoring her throbbing ankle and refusing to sit back down. She needed to be alert. She needed to be ready. She glanced up, expecting her captor to be smiling down at her. Instead, there was a flicker of light she recognized as lightning. A low rumble in the distance confirmed it.

"Who are you?" she shouted this time, giving in to the raw emotion that squeezed her chest and made it difficult to breathe. "And what the hell are you doing here?" She wasn't sure she wanted or needed an answer to her second question.

"He...did this." The voice came with effort, high-pitched and quaking. "Awful things..." she continued. "He did...this. I tried to stop him. I couldn't. I wasn't strong enough." She started moaning again.

The woman's fear was palpable. It grabbed Tess by the throat and crawled under her skin. She couldn't afford to take on this woman's terror, too.

"He had a knife," the woman said between sobs. "He...he cut me."

"Are you hurt? Are you bleeding?" But Tess stayed against the wall, unable to move. Her eyes tried to adjust to the dark, but she could see nothing but a huddled shadow only six or seven feet away from her.

"He said...he told me he'd kill me."

"When did he put you down here? Do you remember?"

"He tied my wrists."

"I can help you untie—"

"He tied my ankles. I couldn't move."

"I can—"

"He ripped my clothes, then he took off my blindfold. He said...he told me he wanted me to watch. He...wanted me to see. Then he...then he raped me."

Tess wiped at her face, replacing tears with mud. She remembered her own clothes, the misbuttoned blouse, the missing panty hose. She felt nauseated. She couldn't think about it. She didn't want to remember. Not now.

"He cut me when I screamed." The woman was still confessing, her voice rambling now out of control. "He wanted me to scream. I couldn't fight him. He was so strong. He got on top of me. So heavy. My chest...he crushed my chest, sitting there on top of me. He was so heavy. My arms were pinned under his legs. He sat on top of me so he could stick...so that he could...he shoved himself down my throat. I gagged. He shoved farther. I couldn't breathe. I couldn't move. He kept—"

"Shut up!" Tess yelled, surprising herself. She didn't recognize her own voice, frightened by the shrillness of it. "Please just shut up!"

Immediately there was silence. No moans. No sobs. Tess listened over the pounding of her heart. Her body shook beyond her control. A liquid cold invaded her veins. Air continued to leak out, replaced by more of the rancid smell of death.

Thunder grew closer, vibrating the earth against her back. The flashes of lightning lit up the world above, but didn't make it down into the black pit. Tess leaned her head against the dirt wall and stared up at the branches, eerie skeletal arms waving down at her in the flickering light. Her entire body hurt from trying to control the convulsions threatening to take over.

She wrapped her arms around herself, determined to ward off those childhood memories, those childhood fears she had worked so hard to destroy. She could feel them crashing through her carefully constructed barriers. She could feel them seeping into her veins, a poison infecting her entire body. She couldn't...she wouldn't allow them to return and render her helpless. Oh dear God! It had taken years to lock them away. And several more years to erase them. No, she couldn't let them back in. Please, dear Lord, not now. Not when she was already feeling so vulnerable, so completely helpless.

The rain began, and Tess let her body slide down against the wall until she felt the mud sucking at her again. Her body began rocking back and forth. She hugged herself tight against the cold and against the memories, but both broke through anyway. As though it had been only yesterday, she remembered what it felt like. She remembered being six years old and being buried alive.

# CHAPTER 45

"I think Stucky may have taken my neighbor, too."

"Come on, Maggie. Now you're just sounding paranoid." Gwen sat in Maggie's recliner, sipping wine and petting Harvey's huge head, which filled her lap. The two had become instant pals. "By the way, this wine is very nice. You're getting good at this. See, there are things other than Scotch."

However, Maggie's glass of wine remained full to the rim. She rummaged through the files Tully had given her on Jessica's and Rita's murders. Besides, she hadn't waited for Gwen to arrive before she drank just enough Scotch to settle the restlessness that seemed to have taken up permanent residence inside her. She had hoped target practice would have helped dislodge it. But even the Scotch had not done its usual job of anesthetizing it. Still she was having trouble reading her own handwriting through the blur. She was pleased, though, that she had finally been able to choose a wine that Gwen liked.

A gourmet cook, Gwen enjoyed fine food and wine. When she had called earlier, offering to bring over dinner, Maggie had rushed out to Shep's Liquor Mart to search the aisles. The clerk, an attractive but overly enthusiastic brunette named Hannah, had told Maggie that the Bolla Sauve was "a delicious semi-dry white wine with touches of floral spiciness and apricot." Hannah assured her that it would complement the chicken and asparagus en papillote that Gwen had promised.

Wine was much too complex. With Scotch she didn't need to choose from merlot, chardonnay, chablis, blush, red or white. All she needed to remember was Scotch, neat. Simple. And it certainly did the job. Though not this evening. The tension strangled her muscles and tightened her rib cage, squeezing and causing her chest to ache.

"What do the police say about Rachel's disappearance?"

"I'm not sure." Maggie flipped through a file folder with newspaper clippings, but still couldn't find what she was looking for. "The lead detective called Cunningham and complained about me barging in on his territory, so it's not like I can just call him up and say, 'Hey, I think I know what happened with that case you want me to keep my nose out of.' But my other neighbor gave me the impression everyone, including the husband, is treating it as though Rachel just decided to leave."

"That seems odd. Has she done this sort of thing before?"

"I have no clue. But doesn't it seem odder that the husband wouldn't want the dog?"

"Not if he thinks she ran off with someone. It's one of the few ways he has left to punish her."

"It doesn't explain why we found the dog in the condition we did. There was a lot of blood, and I'm still not convinced it was all Harvey's." Maggie noticed Gwen stroking Harvey's head as though administering therapy. "Who names a dog Harvey?"

He looked up at Maggie's mention of his name, but didn't budge.

"It's a perfectly good name," Gwen declared as she continued her generous strokes.

"It was the name of the black Lab that David Berkowitz believed was possessed."

Gwen rolled her eyes. "Now, why is it that you think of that immediately? Maybe Rachel is a Jimmy Stewart fan or a classic-movie buff, and named him after Harvey the six-foot invisible rabbit."

"Oh, right. Why didn't I think of that?" It was Maggie's turn for sarcasm. The truth was, she didn't want to think of Harvey's owner and what she believed may have happened to her, or was still happening to her. She returned her attention to the folders. She wished she could remember exactly what it was that Agent Tully had said. There was something nagging at her. Something that connected Rachel's disappearance to Jessica's murder. Not just the mud. Yet she couldn't remember what it was that made her think that. She was hoping one of the police reports would trigger her memory.

"Why the hell isn't the husband the prime suspect?" Gwen suddenly sounded irritated. "That would be a logical explanation to me."

"You'd need to meet Detective Manx to understand. He doesn't seem to be approaching any of this logically."

"I'm not so sure he's the only one. The husband does seem to be the logical suspect, and yet here you are jumping to the conclusion that Stucky kidnapped her because...let me get this straight. You think Stucky kidnapped Rachel Endicott because you're sure he killed this pizza delivery girl and you found candy bar wrappers at both scenes."

"And mud. Don't forget the mud." Maggie checked the lab's report on Jessica's car. The mud recovered from the accelerator contained some sort of metallic residue that Keith was now going to break down. Again she remembered the mud with sparkling flecks on Rachel Endicott's stairs. But what if Manx hadn't bothered to collect it? And even if he had, how would she be able to compare the two? It wasn't like Manx would easily hand over a sample.

"Okay," Gwen said. "The mud I can understand, if you can make a match. But finding candy bar wrappers at both houses? I'm sorry, Maggie, that's a bit of a stretch."

"Stucky leaves body parts in take-out containers just for fun, to toy with people. Why wouldn't he leave candy bar wrappers, sort of his way of thumbing his nose at us? Like he was able to commit this inconceivably horrible murder and then have a snack afterward."

"So the wrappers are part of the game?"

"Yes." She glanced up. Gwen didn't buy it. "Why is that so hard to believe?"

"Did you ever consider they could be a necessity? Maybe the killer or even the victims have an insulin deficiency. Sometimes people with diabetes keep candy bars to prevent fluctuations in their insulin intake. Fluctuations possibly caused by stress or an injection of too much insulin."

"Stucky's not diabetic."

"You know that for sure?"

"Yes," Maggie said, quite certain, then realized their lab

analysis of Stucky's blood and DNA had never been tested for the disease.

"How can you be so certain?" Gwen persisted. "About a third of people with Type 2 diabetes don't even know they have it. It's not something that's routinely checked unless there are symptoms or some family history. And I have to tell you, the symptoms, especially the early ones, are very subtle."

She knew Gwen was right. But she would know if Stucky had diabetes. They had his blood and DNA on file. Unless this was some recent development. No, she couldn't imagine Albert Stucky being susceptible to anything other than silver bullets or maybe a wooden stake through his heart.

"How about the victims?" Gwen suggested. "Maybe the candy bars belonged to the victims. Any chance they're diabetic?"

"Too much of a coincidence. I don't believe in coincidences."

"No, you'd much rather believe that Albert Stucky has kidnapped your neighbor, who by the way wasn't your neighbor yet, *and* took a real estate agent simply because you bought a house from her. I have to tell you, Maggie, it all sounds a bit ridiculous. You have absolutely no proof that either of these women are even missing, let alone that Stucky has them."

"Gwen, it's no coincidence that the waitress in Kansas City and the pizza delivery girl had both come in contact with me only hours before they were murdered in the same manner. I'm the only link. Don't you think I want to believe that neither Rachel nor Tess were taken by Stucky? Don't you think I'd rather believe they are both on some secluded beach sipping piña coladas with their lovers?"

She hated that her voice could get so shrill, that her hands could shake and her heart pound in her ears. She went back to the pile, shuffling through the folders and trying to make sense of Tully's attempt at order, or rather his disorder. She could feel Gwen's eyes examining her. Maybe Gwen was right. Perhaps the paranoia skewed her rationality. What if she was blowing all this out of proportion? What if she was slipping over some mental edge? It certainly felt like that.

"If that's true, then it would mean Stucky is watching you, following you."

"Yes," Maggie said, trying to sound as matter-of-fact as possible.

"If he's choosing women he sees you with, then why hasn't he chosen me?"

Maggie looked up at her friend, startled by the flicker of fear she thought she saw in the otherwise strong and confident eyes. "He only targets women I come in contact with, not women I know. It makes his next move less predictable. He wants me to feel like an accomplice. I don't think he wants to destroy me. And hurting you would destroy me."

She went back to her search, wanting to close the subject and dismiss the possibility. Fact was, she had thought about Stucky moving on to those who were close to her. Nothing would stop him from doing so if he wanted to up the ante.

"Have you talked to Agent Tully about any of this?"

"You're my friend, and you think I'm nuts. Why in the world would I share any of it with him?"

"Because he's your partner, and the two of you should be working through this mess together, no matter how crazy every tidbit appears to be. Promise me you won't be checking out stuff on your own."

Maggie found a new set of documents and began flipping through the pages. Was it possible she was only imagining that there was something else that linked Rachel Endicott to Stucky?

"Maggie, did you hear me?"

She glanced up to find Gwen's normally smooth forehead wrinkled with concern, her warm green eyes filled with worry.

"Promise me you won't go off on your own again," Gwen demanded.

"I won't go off on my own again." She dug out a brown manila envelope and started extracting its contents.

"Maggie, I mean it."

She stopped and looked up at her friend. Even Harvey stared at her with sad, brown eyes. This from the same dog who had spent the last two nights going back and forth, checking the front door and each of the windows, looking for and waiting for his master to pick him up as though he couldn't stand to spend one more moment with Maggie.

"Please, don't worry, Gwen. I promise I won't do anything stupid." She unfolded several copies and immediately found what she had been searching for. It was the report from the airport authority and a police impound notice for a white Ford van. "Here it is. This is it. This is what's been nagging at me."

"What is it?"

Maggie stood and began pacing.

"Susan Lyndell told me that the man Rachel Endicott may have run off with was a telephone repairman."

"So what's your proof? Her phone bill?" Gwen sounded impatient.

"This is an impound notice. When the police found Jessica Beckwith's car at the airport, they found a van parked alongside it. The van had been stolen about two weeks ago."

"I'm sorry, Maggie, but I'm lost. So Stucky stole a van and abandoned it when he was finished with it. What does that have to do with your missing neighbor?"

"The van that was recovered belonged to Northeastern Bell Telephone Company." Maggie waited for Gwen's reaction, and when it was less than satisfactory, she continued, "Okay, it's a long shot, but you have to admit, it's too much of a coincidence and—"

"I know, I know." Gwen raised her hand to stop her. "And you don't believe in coincidences."

# CHAPTER 46

Tess couldn't remember a night so long and dark and brutal, despite having a repertoire of many in her childhood. She sat curled in a corner, hugging her knees and trying not to think about her bare, swollen feet buried in the rancid mud. The rain had finally stopped although she heard thunder in the distance, a low rumble like a boulder rolling overhead. Was it the clouds that were preventing the sun from rising or had the madman made a deal with the devil?

At times she could hear the woman moaning quietly to herself. Her breaths, her gasps were so close. Thankfully, the sobs and the high-pitched whine had stopped. As the sky lightened, the huddled form began to take shape.

Tess closed her eyes against the gritty, burning sensation. Why had she been so stubborn and refused the ever-wear contact lenses? She wanted to rub and dig at her eyes. Soon she'd need to make a choice about taking the contacts out or leaving them in. When she opened her eyes again, she blinked several times. She couldn't believe what she was seeing. In the dim light she saw the woman across from her was completely naked. She had twisted herself into a fetal position, her skin slathered in mud and what looked and smelled like blood and feces.

"Oh dear God," Tess mumbled. "Why didn't you tell me you had nothing on?"

Tess struggled to her feet. Her ankle rebelled, sending her to her knees. Now her pain seemed minor. She forced herself up again, putting all the weight on her other foot. Her fingers frantically pulled at the knot keeping her blanket cape around her shoulders. The woman's body shivered. No, she wasn't just shivering. Her muscles looked to be in some sort of convulsions.

Her teeth chattered and her lower lip was bleeding where she must have bitten herself repeatedly.

"Are you in pain?" Tess asked, realizing how stupid the question sounded. Of course she was in pain.

She ripped the blanket off and draped it carefully around the woman. It was damp but the wool had somehow kept her own body heat from escaping all night long. Hopefully it wouldn't make matters worse. How could it possibly make things worse?

Tess kept a safe distance as she examined the horrible bruises, the raw cuts and torn flesh left from what looked like bites—human bites.

"Dear God. We need to get you to a hospital." Another ridiculous thing to say. If she couldn't get out of this pit, how could she get her to a hospital?

The woman didn't seem to hear Tess. Though her eyes were wide and open, they stared at the mud wall in front of her. Her tangled hair stuck to her face. Tess reached down and wiped a clump away from her cheek. The woman didn't even blink. She was in shock, and Tess wondered if her mind had retreated inside herself, into a deep, unreachable cavern. It was exactly what Tess had done so many times as a child. It had been her only defense in combating the long stays of punishment that had exiled her to the dark storm cellar, sometimes for days at a time.

She caressed the woman's cheek, wiping mud and hair from her face and neck. Her stomach lurched when she saw the bruises and bite marks that covered her neck and breast. A raw gash also circled her neck. It looked like an indentation left from a rope or cord pulled so tight it had dug into the flesh.

"Are you able to move?" Tess asked, but got no response.

She looked up to survey the depths of their hell now that light seeped down to them. It was not as deep as she had initially thought—twelve, maybe fifteen feet at the most, about five feet wide and ten feet long. It looked to be an old trench, partially caved in with uneven sides. Tree roots snaked out and rocks jutted out in places. But there were fresh spade marks that told her he intended for this to be a trap.

What kind of monster did this to a woman and then threw

her into a pit? She couldn't think about him. She couldn't wonder or imagine, or it would completely paralyze her. Instead, she needed to concentrate on getting them out of here. But how the hell could she do that?

She kneeled next to the woman. The blanket seemed to reduce the convulsions. She'd need to examine her for broken bones. There were enough gashes in the walls and jutting rocks that they could climb their way out, but she'd never be able to pull or carry the woman.

Just as Tess reached to touch the woman's shoulder, she saw what it was that the woman's eyes were focused on so intently. Startled, she jumped back. Slowly she forced herself closer for a better look, despite her amazement, despite her revulsion. Directly in front of her, buried in the dirt wall and partially unearthed by the rain was a human skull, the empty eye sockets staring out at them. And then, Tess realized. This wasn't a trap, at all. It was a grave. It was their grave.

# CHAPTER 47

*Saturday, April 4*

She wore another red silk blouse. She looked good in red. It emphasized her strawberry-blond hair. It had become a habit for her to leave off her jacket and stand in front of her desk, half sitting on the corner. Today, she didn't bother to pull down the skirt hem that hiked up just enough to reveal shapely smooth thighs. Lovely, tender thighs that made him wonder what it would feel like to sink his teeth into them.

She waited for him to talk while she scribbled in her notepad, probably not even taking notes on him. If the notes were about him, he wasn't the least bit curious about what they said. He was more interested in what her moans would sound like when he finally stuck himself inside her, thrusting deep and hard until she was screaming. He so enjoyed it when they screamed, especially when he was inside them. The vibration felt like shock waves, like he was causing a fucking earthquake.

It was one of many things he had in common with his old friend, his old partner. At least it was one thing he didn't need to fake. He pushed the sunglasses up on the bridge of his nose and realized she was waiting.

"Mr. Harding," she interrupted his thoughts. "You never answered my question."

He couldn't remember what the fucking question had been. He cocked his head to the side and jutted out his chin in that pathetic gesture that said, "Forgive me, I'm blind."

"I asked if any of the exercises I suggested have helped."

Sure enough. If he waited, people always made it easy, supplying the answer, repeating themselves or getting up and doing whatever it was they had wanted him to do. He was getting good at this. Probably a good thing, in case it became permanent.

"Mr. Harding?"

She didn't have much patience today. He wanted to ask how long it had been since she had been fucked. That was, no doubt, the problem. Or perhaps she needed a few porn movies from his new private collection.

He knew from his personal research that she was divorced, for almost twenty-five years now. It had been a short, two-year marriage, a youthful indiscretion. Certainly there must have been several lovers since, though, of course, those details weren't easily accessible on the Internet.

Now he could see her impatience growing in the way she crossed her arms. Finally, he said politely, "The exercises worked quite well, but that doesn't prove or help anything."

"Why do you say that?"

"What good does it do to get myself...well, excuse the expression...to get my little general all hot, hard and bothered when I'm alone?"

She smiled, the first she had surrendered since they had met. "We need to start somewhere."

"Okay, but I'm afraid I must object if you suggest I move on to blow-up dolls."

Another smile. He was on a roll. Should he tell her he'd like her to be his blow-up doll? He wondered how good a blow job she could give with that sweet, sexy little mouth of hers. He was certain he could fill it quite nicely.

"No, I won't make any more suggestions for the time being," she said, detecting none of what went through his mind. "However, I would encourage you to continue with the exercises. The idea is to have a—excuse the expression—surefire method of arousal to fall back on should you find yourself wanting to perform with a woman but not able to."

She was idly swinging her left foot as she sat on the corner of the desk. Her black leather pump teetered at the end of her toes as she played with it. He wished the shoe would fall off. He wanted to see if she had painted her toenails. He loved red painted toenails.

"Whether we want to believe it or not, many of our preconceived notions about sex," she continued, though he paid little attention, "come from our parents. Boys especially find themselves imitating their fathers' behaviors. What was your father like, Mr. Harding?"

"He certainly had no problems when it came to women," he snapped, and immediately regretted letting her see that the subject was a touchy one. Now she wouldn't leave it alone. She'd insist they poke and probe through it until she found a way to bring his mother into it as well. Unless...unless he turned it around somehow and embarrassed her away from the subject entirely.

"My father brought women home quite frequently. He even let me watch. Sometimes the women let me join in. What other thirteen-year-old boy can say he got his cock sucked by a woman while his dad fucked the shit out of her from behind?"

There it was—that look of utter shock. Soon it would be followed by the pity look. Funny how the truth possessed such remarkable power. A knock at the door made her jump. He stared off into oblivion like a good little blind fucker.

"Sorry to interrupt," her secretary called from the door. "That phone call you've been waiting for is on line three."

"I need to take this call, Mr. Harding."

"That's fine." He stood and fumbled for his cane. "Perhaps we can end early today."

"Are you sure? This really will take but a minute or two."

"No, I'm exhausted. Besides, I think you more than earned your money today." He rewarded her with a smile so that she wouldn't continue to object. He found the door before she could offer to call his make-believe driver. As he waited for the elevator, the anger began to churn inside his guts. He hated thinking about his parents. She had no right bringing them into this. She had overstepped her bounds. Yes, today, Dr. Gwen Patterson had gone too far.

# CHAPTER 48

Assistant Director Cunningham had commandeered a small conference room for them on the first level. Tully was so excited about having windows—two that looked into the woods at the edge of the training field—he didn't care that he had to walk up and down stairs, clear to the other end of the building to bring stuff from his cramped office.

He spread out everything they had gathered in the last five months, while O'Dell followed behind him, insisting on putting it all in neat little stacks, lining it up on the long conference table so that it flowed from left to right in chronological order. Instead of being irritated by her anal-retentive process, he found himself amused. So they approached puzzles differently. She liked to start by finding all the corner pieces and lining them up, while he liked to scatter all the pieces in the center, picking and choosing random sections to piece together. Neither way was right or wrong. It was simply a matter of preference, although he doubted that O'Dell would agree with that assessment.

They had tacked up a map of the United States, marking the recent murders in Newburgh Heights and Kansas City with red pushpins. Blue pins marked each of the other seventeen areas where Stucky had left victims before his capture last August. At least those were the ones they knew about. The women Stucky kept for his collection were often buried in remote wooded areas. It was believed there could be as many as a dozen more, hidden and waiting to be discovered by hikers or fishermen or hunters. All this, Stucky had accomplished in less than three years. Tully hated to think what the madman may have done in the last five months.

Tully continued to examine the map and left O'Dell to her housekeeping. For the most part, Stucky had stayed on the eastern edge of the United States from as far north as Boston to as far south as Miami. The Virginia shoreline seemed to be a fertile ground for him. Kansas City appeared to be the only anomaly. If Tess McGowan was, in fact, missing, that meant Stucky really was playing with O'Dell again, bringing her in, making her a part of his crimes. And by choosing only women who she came in contact with, rather than friends or family members, he made it virtually impossible for them to know who might be next. After all, what could they do? Lock O'Dell up until they caught Stucky? Cunningham already had several agents watching her house and following her. Tully was surprised O'Dell hadn't objected.

Saturday morning and she was already digging in as if it were any other weekday. After the week she had, anyone else would still be at home in bed. Although this morning he did notice that she hadn't bothered to use makeup to conceal the dark, puffy lines under her eyes. She wore an old pair of Nike running shoes, a chambray shirt with the sleeves rolled up to the elbows and the tails neatly tucked into the waistband of faded jeans. Though they were in a secured facility, she kept her shoulder harness on, her Smith & Wesson .38 ready at her side. Compared to O'Dell, he felt overdressed, except when Assistant Director Cunningham stopped by, looking as crisp, spotless and wrinkle-free as usual. That was when Tully noticed the coffee stains on his own white shirt and his loosened and lopsided tie.

Tully checked his watch. He had promised Emma lunch and a total discussion of this prom thing. He had already decided to stand firm on the matter. Emma could call it being close-minded if she wanted to, but he simply didn't want to start thinking about her as being old enough to date. At least not yet. Maybe next year.

He glanced over at O'Dell who stood over the reports they had received earlier from Keith Ganza. Without looking up at him, she asked, "Any luck with airport security?"

"No, but now that Delores Heston has filed a missing-person's report, we can get an APB out on the car. A black Miata can't be that hard to miss. I don't know, though. What if McGowan just decided to take off for a couple of days?"

"Then we ruin her vacation. What about the boyfriend?"

"The guy has a house and business in D.C., and another house and office in Newburgh Heights. I finally tracked down Mr. Daniel Kassenbaum last night at his country club. He didn't sound very concerned. In fact, he told me he suspected McGowan might be cheating on him. Then he quickly added that their relationship was a no-strings sort of thing. That's what he called it. So, I guess if his suspicions are true, maybe she simply took off with some secret lover."

O'Dell looked up at him. "If the boyfriend thought she was cheating on him, can we be certain he didn't have something to do with her disappearance?"

"I honestly don't think the guy cares, not as long as he was getting what he wanted." O'Dell looked puzzled. Tully felt a surge of emotion and knew this was a touchy subject with him. Kassenbaum reminded him too much of the asshole Caroline had left him for. Still, he continued, "He told me the last time he saw her was when she stayed over at his house in Newburgh Heights Tuesday night. Now, if the guy thinks she's cheating on him, why is he still having her stay overnight at his house?"

O'Dell shrugged. "I give up. Why?"

He wasn't sure if she was serious or being sarcastic. "Why? Because he's an arrogant asshole who doesn't care about anyone other than himself. So as long as he's getting his jollies serviced, what does he care?" She was staring at him. He should have known when to quit. "What do women see in guys like that?"

"Getting his jollies serviced? Is that what you call it in Ohio?"

Tully felt his face grow red, and O'Dell smiled. She went back to the reports, letting him off the hook, and evidently not realizing how hot the subject made him. Last night, Daniel Kassenbaum had treated him like some servant he didn't have time for, scolding Tully for interrupting his dinner. Like the guy didn't think maybe Tully was interrupting his own dinner by looking for his girlfriend? Maybe Tess McGowan really did take off with some secret lover. Good for her.

He stood facing the map again. They had circled possible sites, mostly remote wooded areas. There were way too many to check. The only clue they had was the sparkling dirt found in Jessica Beckwith's car and in Rachel Endicott's house. Keith Ganza had narrowed down the chemical concoction that made up the metallic substance, but even that didn't narrow down the sites. In fact, it made Tully wonder if they were looking in the wrong places. Maybe they should be checking out deserted industrial sites instead of wooded areas. After all, Stucky had used a condemned warehouse in Miami to hide his collection until O'Dell found him.

"What about an industrial site?" He decided to try out his theory on O'Dell.

She stopped what she was doing and came beside him, studying the map.

"You're thinking of the chemicals Keith found in the mud?"

"I know it doesn't follow his pattern, but neither did the warehouse down in Miami." As soon as he said it, he glanced at O'Dell, realizing the subject may still be a touchy one. If it was, she made no indication.

"Wherever he's hiding, it can't be far. I'm guessing an hour, maybe an hour and a half at most." She traced the area with her index finger, a fifty-to-seventy-mile radius, with her home in Newburgh Heights at the center. "He couldn't drive too far and still keep watch over me."

Tully watched her out of the corner of his eyes, again looking for any signs of the frenzy, the terror he had witnessed the other night. He wasn't surprised to find it masked. O'Dell wouldn't be the first FBI agent he knew who could compartmentalize her emotions. With O'Dell, however, he could see it was an effort. He wondered just how long she could contain them without cracking at the seams again.

"The map may not show old industrial sites that have been closed. I'll check with the State Department and see if they have anything."

"Don't forget Maryland and D.C."

Tully jotted notes on the McDonald's brown paper sack that had held his breakfast; a sausage biscuit and hash browns. For a brief moment he tried to remember the last meal he had eaten that hadn't come from a bag. Maybe he'd take Emma somewhere nice for lunch. No fast food. Somewhere with tablecloths.

When he turned back, O'Dell was back at the table. He looked over her shoulder at the crime scene photos she had sorted. Without looking at him, she said in almost a whisper, "We need to find them, Agent Tully. We need to find them very soon or it'll be too late."

He didn't need to ask who she meant. She was talking about the McGowan woman, and also her neighbor, Rachel Endicott. Tully still wasn't convinced either woman was missing, let alone taken by Stucky. He didn't share his doubts with O'Dell, nor did he share with her that he had talked to Detective Manx in Newburgh Heights. With any luck Manx would find it in his stubborn, isolationist pig head to share whatever evidence he recovered from the Endicott house. Though Tully didn't expect much. Detective Manx had told him the case was nothing more than a bored housewife running off with a telephone repairman.

He hated to think Manx might be right. Tully shook his head. What was it with married women these days? He didn't like being reminded of Caroline for the second time that morning.

"If you are right about Tess McGowan and the Endicott woman," Tully said, careful to keep his own doubts aside, "that means Stucky has killed two women and taken two others in a span of only one week. Are you sure Stucky could pull that off?"

"It would be tough but not impossible. He would have had to take Rachel Endicott early last Friday. Then come back to Newburgh Heights, watch Jessica deliver my pizza, lure her to the house on Archer Drive and kill her late Friday evening or early Saturday morning."

"Doesn't that seem like a bit much?"

"Yes," she admitted, "but not for Stucky."

"Then somehow he finds out that you'd be in KC. Even finds out where you're staying. Again, he watches you, Delaney and Turner with the waitress—"

"Rita."

"Right, Rita. That was what, Sunday night?"

"Around midnight...actually early Monday morning. If Delores Heston is correct, Tess showed the house on Archer Drive Wednesday." She avoided Tully's eyes. "I know it sounds like a lot, but keep in mind what he's done in the past."

She started sorting through the photos again. "It's never been easy to track. Some of the bodies were found much later, long after they were reported missing. Most of them were so badly decomposed we could only guess at the time of deaths. But the spring before we caught him, we estimated that he killed two women, leaving them in Dumpsters, and that he had taken five others for his collection. That was all in the span of two or three weeks. At least that's the time frame that the women were first discovered missing. We didn't find those five bodies until months later, and they were all in one mass grave. The women had been tortured and killed at different intervals. There were signs that he may have even hunted down a couple of them. We found evidence that he may have used a crossbow and arrows."

Tully recognized the photos. O'Dell had laid out a series of Poloraids that chronicled one victim's wounds. If the photos hadn't been marked, it would be difficult to tell that they were all the same woman. This was one of those five victims who had been found in that mass grave. The corpse was one of the rare ones found before decomposition or before animals had ravaged it. It was one of the few that was intact and whole.

"This was Helen Kreski," O'Dell said without looking up the name. "She was one of the five. Stucky choked and stabbed her repeatedly. Her left nipple had been bitten off. Her right arm and wrist were broken. There was a puncture through her left calf with a broken arrow still intact." O'Dell's voice was calm, too calm, as though she had resolved herself to something beyond her control. "We found dirt in her lungs. She was still alive when he buried her."

"Christ, this is one sick son of a bitch."

"We need to stop him, Agent Tully. We need to do it before he crawls back into a hole someplace. Before he runs off and hides and starts playing with his new collection."

"And we'll do that. We just need to find out where the hell he's hiding." He didn't want to notice that she had used the word *stop* instead of *catch*.

He left her side and checked his watch again.

"I need to leave around eleven. I promised my daughter we'd have lunch together." O'Dell had moved back to the reports they had received from Ganza. She had the fingerprint analysis and was reading it over for the third time. He wondered if she had even heard him. "Hey, why don't you join us?"

She glanced up, surprised by his invitation.

"I still think the print was left by someone who looked at the house earlier," he said, referring to the fingerprint report and taking her off the hook if she really didn't want to accept his invitation.

"He wiped down everything in the bathroom," she said, "but he missed two clean and whole fingerprints. No, he wanted us to find these. He's done it before. It was how we finally confirmed who he was."

He watched her rub her eyes as if the memory brought on a whole new fatigue.

"At that time, we had no name, no idea who The Collector was," she continued. "Stucky evidently thought we were taking too long to figure it out. I think he left us a print on purpose. It was so blatant, so careless, it had to be on purpose."

"Well, if this one was on purpose, why bother to clean up the place at all? He never seemed to care before."

"Maybe he cleaned up because he wanted to use the house again."

"For McGowan?"

"Yes."

"Okay. But why bother to leave us a print that doesn't even belong to him? Just like on the Dumpster behind the pizza place and on the umbrella in Kansas City."

O'Dell hesitated, stopping her hands from shuffling papers and looking at him as if wondering whether or not to tell him something. "Keith hasn't been able to find a match for those prints in AFIS. But he says he's almost certain all three sets of prints belong to the same person."

"You're kidding. He knows that for sure? If that's the case, maybe these murders aren't Stucky, after all."

He stared at her, waiting for some kind of reaction. Her face remained impassive, just like her voice when she said, "Jessica's murder and Rita's in Kansas City are awfully close together. I know I just said that Stucky could pull it off, but the anal penetration with Jessica is not Stucky's M.O. Also, she's much younger than any of his other victims."

"So what are you saying, O'Dell. You think this one was a copycat?"

"Or an accomplice."

"What? That's crazy!"

She buried her eyes in the files again. He could see she was having a difficult time with the theory herself. O'Dell was used to working and brainstorming alone. Suddenly he realized that it probably took a good deal of trust for her to share this idea with him.

"Look, I know you're serious, but why would Stucky take on an accomplice? You have to admit, that's out of character for any serial killer."

In reply, O'Dell pulled out several photocopied pages that looked like magazine and newspaper articles and handed them to Tully.

"Remember Cunningham said he found the name Walker Harding, Stucky's old business partner, on an airline manifest?"

Tully nodded and began sorting through the articles.

"Some of those go back several years," she told him.

They were articles from *Forbes,* the *Wall Street Journal, PC World* and several other business and trade periodicals. The *Forbes* article included a picture. Though the grainy black-and-white copy had obliterated most of the men's features, the two of them could have passed for brothers. Both had dark hair, narrow faces and sharp features. Tully recognized Albert Stucky's piercing black eyes, which he knew to be void of color despite the poor reproduction. The younger man smiled while Stucky's face remained stoic and serious.

"I'm guessing this must be the partner?"

"Yes. A couple of the articles mention how much the two men had in common and how competitive they were with each other. However, they seemed to have ended their partnership amicably. I wonder if they might still be in contact with each other. Maybe still in competition with each other, only with a new game."

"But why now after all these years? If they were to do something like this, why not when Stucky first started his game?"

O'Dell sat down and tucked strands of hair behind her ears. She looked exhausted. As if reading his thoughts, she sipped her Diet Pepsi, which he had noticed was her coffee substitute. This was her third one of the morning.

"Stucky has always been a loner," she explained. "I haven't done any research on Harding except for these articles, but for Stucky to have chosen anyone as a business partner is remarkable. I've never thought about it before, but perhaps the two men had, and still have, some strong connection, a connection Stucky didn't realize until recently. Or perhaps there's some other reason he decided he needed his old friend."

Tully shook his head. "I think you're grasping at straws, O'Dell. You know as well as I do that statistically, serial killers don't take on partners or accomplices."

"But Stucky is far from fitting any of the statistics. I'm having Keith run a check to see if Harding has ever been fingerprinted. Then we can see if we have a match to the fingerprints being left at the crime scenes."

Tully looked over the articles, scanning the text until something caught his eye.

"Looks like there's a slight problem with your theory, O'Dell."

"What's that?"

"There's a footnote to this *Wall Street Journal* article. Stucky and Harding ended their partnership after Harding was diagnosed with some medical problem."

"Right. I saw that."

"But did you finish reading it? This part is blurred at the bottom from the copier. Unless Walker Harding found some miracle cure, he can't be Stucky's accomplice. It says here he was going blind."

# CHAPTER 49

Maggie waited until Tully left to meet his daughter. Then she began unearthing every scrap of information she could find on Walker Harding. She pounded the computer's keys, searching the FBI's files and other Internet sites and directories. The man had virtually disappeared after announcing his ambiguous medical problem almost four years ago. Now she realized Keith Ganza might never find a fingerprint record, either. Perhaps it was simply a gut instinct, but she felt certain Harding was still connected to Stucky, helping him somehow, continuing to work with him.

From what little she had read, she knew Harding had been the brains of their business, a whiz with computers. But Stucky had been the one who had taken all the financial risk, investing a hundred thousand dollars of his own money; money he had joked about winning one weekend in Atlantic City. Maggie couldn't help noticing that the investment capital and the start-up of the business happened the same year Stucky's father died in a freak boating accident. Stucky had never been charged though he had been questioned in what looked like a routine investigation, and only because Stucky had been the sole beneficiary of his father's estate, an estate that made that hundred thousand dollars look like pocket change.

Harding appeared to have been reclusive long before his business venture with Stucky. Maggie could find nothing about his childhood, except that he—like Stucky—had been raised by a single, overbearing father. One directory listed him as a 1985 graduate of MIT, which made him about three years younger than Stucky. The state of Virginia listed no marriage license, driver's license or property owned by a Walker Harding. She had begun a search of Maryland's records when Thea Johnson from down the hall knocked on the open conference-room door.

"Agent O'Dell, there's a phone call for Agent Tully. I know he left for a while, but this sounds important. Do you want to take the call?"

"Sure." Maggie didn't hesitate and reached behind her for the phone. "What line?"

"Line five. It's a detective from Newburgh Heights. I believe he said his name was Manx."

Immediately, Maggie's stomach took a dive. She sucked in a deep breath and punched line five.

"Detective Manx, Agent Tully is at lunch. This is his partner, Agent Margaret O'Dell."

She waited for the name to register. Even after a sigh, there was a pause.

"Agent O'Dell. Barge in on any crime scenes lately?"

"Funny thing, Detective Manx, but here at the FBI we usually don't wait for engraved invitations." She didn't care if he heard the irritation in her voice. If he was calling Tully, he wanted something from them. Besides, what was he going to do? Go tell Cunningham she was mean to him again?

"When's Tully gonna be back?"

So that was the way he wanted to play.

"Gee, you know, I don't remember if he told me. He might not be back until Monday."

She waited out his silence and imagined the scowl on his face. He was probably swiping a frustrated hand over that new buzz hairdo of his.

"Look, Tully talked to me last night about this McGowan woman down here in Newburgh Heights that's supposedly missing."

"She is missing, Detective Manx. Seems you have a problem with women disappearing in your jurisdiction. What's up with that?" She was enjoying this too much. She needed to back off.

"I thought he should know that we checked out her house this morning and found a guy snooping around."

"What?" Maggie sat up and gripped the phone.

"This guy said he was a friend and was worried about her. He had a screen off a back window and looked like he was getting ready to break in. We brought him in for questioning. Just thought Tully might like to know."

"You haven't released him yet, have you?"

"No, the boys are still chatting with him. I think we got him pretty damn scared. First thing, he insisted on calling his fucking lawyer. Makes me think he's guilty of something."

"Don't release him until Agent Tully and I have a chance to talk to him. We'll be there in about a half hour."

"Sure, no problem. Lookin' forward to seeing you again, O'Dell."

She hung up, grabbed her jacket and was almost out the door before she realized she should probably call Tully. She patted her jacket down until she felt the cellular phone in the pocket. She'd call him from the road. No, of course, this wasn't a matter of her running off on her own. It wasn't breaking any of Cunningham's new rules. She simply didn't want to ruin Agent Tully's lunch with his daughter.

That was what she told herself. The fact was, she wanted to check this out on her own. If Manx had Albert Stucky or even Walker Harding, Maggie wanted him all to herself.

# CHAPTER 50

As the sun moved overhead and more light seeped down, Tess could see the hellhole for what it was. The skull that stared out from the earth wall was not the only human remains that surrounded them. Other bones glistened, washed white by the rains, protruding at odd angles from the uneven walls and the muddy floor.

At first Tess told herself it was some ancient burial ground, maybe a mass grave from a Civil War battle. Then she found a black underwire bra and a woman's leather pump with a broken heel sticking out of the ground. Neither looked old enough or deteriorated enough to have been there much longer than weeks, maybe months.

Dirt had been recently thrown into one of the corners. The mound looked fresh despite the rain packing it down. She stared at it, but didn't dare go near it, staying away as if the pile would crumble and reveal some new horror. If that was at all possible.

The rays of sunshine felt wonderful, though they wouldn't last long. She managed to gently drag the woman to the center, so she could be warmed directly. Even the wool blanket had begun to dry. Tess stretched it out across some rocks, leaving the woman naked but bathed in sunlight.

Tess was getting used to the rancid smell of the woman. She could stay close without the urge to vomit. The woman had defecated in her corner several times and had accidentally rolled in it. Tess wished she had some water to clean her. The thought reminded her how dry and raw her mouth and throat were. Surely the woman was already in a state of dehydration. Her convulsions had calmed to a mild shiver and her teeth had stopped chattering. Even her breathing seemed to return to normal. Now with the sunlight on her skin, Tess noticed she had closed her eyes, as though finally able to rest. Or had she finally decided to die?

Tess sat on a broken branch and examined the pit again. She knew she could climb out. She had tried twice, reaching the top both times. Each time she peered over the edge, the relief and satisfaction overwhelming her to tears. But each time, she lowered herself back down, carefully easing the pressure on her swollen ankle.

Though she didn't want to think about the madman, she realized there could be safety in this pit. He must have dumped the woman here, expecting her to die from her wounds and exposure. Eventually, he would return to throw some dirt over her and create yet another mound. When he discovered Tess was gone from the shack, he might not think to look for her down here.

That didn't mean she wanted to stay. She hated feeling trapped. And this hellhole reminded her too much of the dark storm cellar her aunt and uncle had used as punishment for her. As a child, being buried beneath the ground for an hour was terrifying. One or two days, unimaginable. Even as an adult, she could never remember what she had done to deserve such punishment. Instead, she had readily believed her aunt when she called her an evil child and dragged her down to the damp torture chamber. Each time, Tess had screamed how sorry she was and pleaded for forgiveness.

"No apologies accepted," her uncle would always say, laughing.

In the dark, Tess would pray over and over for her mother to come and rescue her, remembering her mother's last words, "I'll be right back, Tessy." But she never came back to rescue Tess. She never returned at all. How could her mother leave her with such evil people?

As Tess grew older and stronger, her aunt was no longer a match for her. That's when her uncle took over. Only, her uncle's form of punishment came late at night when he let himself into her bedroom. When she tried to lock him out, he removed the door to her room. At first she screamed, knowing her aunt could now hear without the door to muffle the sounds. It didn't take long for her to realize that her aunt had always heard, had always known. She just didn't care.

Tess ran away to D.C. when she was fifteen. Quickly, she had learned that she could make quite a bit of money doing what her uncle had taught her for free. Fifteen years old, and she was fucking congressmen and four-star generals. That was almost twenty years ago, and yet she had only recently found her escape from that life. She had finally begun a life that was her own. And she sure as hell would not end it here. Not now. Not in this remote grave where no one would ever notice.

She got to her feet and approached the woman. She squatted next to her and put a gentle hand on her shoulder.

"I don't know if you can hear me. My name is Tess. I want you to know I'm going to get us out of here. I'm not going to leave you here to die."

Tess pulled a branch closer so she could sit next to the woman in the sunlight. She needed to rest her ankle. She buried her toes into the mud. Despite the slimy earthworms against her skin, the mud did soothe the cracks and cuts and bruises on her feet.

She surveyed the jutting rocks and tree roots, trying to come up with a plan. Just when she began to think it would be impossible, the woman moved slightly to her side. Without opening her eyes, she said, "My name's Rachel."

# CHAPTER 51

Maggie wasn't sure what she expected. Could Albert Stucky or Walker Harding be stupid enough to get caught by the Newburgh Heights Police Department? Yet, when Manx showed her into the interrogation room, her heart sank. The handsome young man looked more like a college student than the hardened criminal Manx had described when he had insisted the man was guilty of something.

The kid even stood up when she entered the room, not able to stifle his good manners despite the situation.

"There's been a huge misunderstanding," he told her as if she was the new face of reason.

He wore khakis and a crew-neck sweater. Maybe this was what Manx expected burglars to wear in Newburgh Heights.

"Sit the hell down, kid," Manx snapped at him as though he was jumping up to attack her.

Maggie walked around Manx and sat down at the table opposite the young man. He slid back into his chair, wringing his hands in front of him on the table, his eyes darting from Manx to the other two uniformed officers already in the room.

"I'm Special Agent Margaret O'Dell with the FBI." She waited for his eyes to settle on hers.

"FBI?" He looked worried and fidgeted in his chair. "Something's happened to Tess, hasn't it?"

"I know you may have already explained all this, but how do you know Ms. McGowan, Mr.—"

"Finley. My name's Will Finley. I met Tess last weekend."

"Last weekend? So you haven't been friends for very long. Did she show you a piece of real estate?"

"Excuse me?"

"Ms. McGowan is a real estate agent. Did she show you a house last weekend?"

"No. We met at a bar. We...we spent the night together."

Maggie wondered if it was a lie. Tess McGowan hadn't looked like the barfly type. Plus, she guessed Tess to be close to her own age. She couldn't imagine Tess giving this college kid a second glance. Unless she had been trying to get back at her big-shot, country-club boyfriend. Of course, she also couldn't imagine Tess McGowan with the guy who Agent Tully called an arrogant asshole. But then she realized she really hadn't taken time to get to know anything about Tess McGowan. Nevertheless, she was certain Will Finley had nothing to do with Tess's disappearance. Now she was glad she hadn't dragged Tully away from lunch with his daughter for this.

"What's happened to Tess?" Will Finley wanted to know. He looked genuinely concerned.

"Maybe you ought to be tellin' us," Manx said from behind Maggie.

"How many times do I have to tell you? I didn't do anything to her. I haven't seen her since Monday morning. She hasn't returned any of my phone calls. I was worried about her." He scraped a shaking hand over his face.

Maggie wondered how long they had kept him here. He looked exhausted, his nerves frayed. She knew after enough hours of the same questions, in the same room, sitting in the same position, that the most innocent of men could break down.

"Will." She waited again for his eyes. "We're not sure what happened to Tess, but she is missing. I'm hoping you might be able to help us find her."

He stared at her as though he wasn't sure whether to believe her or if this was a trick.

"Is there anything you can remember?" she continued, keeping her voice calm and steady, unlike Manx's. "Anything you might be able to tell us that could help us find her?"

"I'm not sure. I mean, I really don't know her very well."

"Well enough to fuck her, though, right?" Manx said, insisting on playing out his role as the bad cop.

Maggie ignored him, though Will Finley stared at him and

fidgeted with the appropriate amount of guilt. Manx was right about the kid hiding something. It was the illicitness of the affair, not that he had hurt Tess.

"Where did you spend the night together?"

"Look, I know my rights, and I know I don't have to answer these questions." He sounded defensive now. Maggie didn't blame him, especially since Manx treated him like a suspect.

"No, you don't need to answer any of my questions. I just thought you might want to help us find her." Maggie gently tried to persuade him.

"I don't see how knowing where or when or how or what we did that night is going to help."

"Hey, kid, you banged an older woman. You should be jumping at the chance to share the details."

Maggie stood and faced Manx, trying to maintain her calm and bridle her impatience.

"Detective Manx, do you mind if I have a word with Mr. Finley alone?"

"I don't think that's a good idea."

"And why is that?"

"Well..." Manx hesitated while he manufactured a reason. She could practically hear his rusty gears grinding. "Might not be safe to leave you alone with him."

"I'm an experienced FBI agent, Detective Manx."

"You sure don't dress like one, Agent O'Dell," he said as he purposely let his eyes slide slowly over her body.

"Tell you what. I'll take my chances with Mr. Finley." She glanced over at the officers. "You gentleman can verify that I said that."

Manx stalled, then finally waved the two officers out of the room. He followed but not before shooting a warning look in Finley's direction.

"I'd apologize for Detective Manx, but that would mean I was trying to excuse his behavior, and quite honestly, there is no excuse for his behavior."

She sat back down with a sigh and an absent rub at her eyes. When she looked up at Will Finley, he was smiling.

"I just realized who you are."

"Excuse me?" Maggie asked.

"You and I have a mutual friend."

The door opened again, and Maggie jumped to her feet, ready to snap at Manx. It was, instead, one of the other officers. His entire face seemed to be apologetic.

"Sorry, but the kid's lawyer just got here. He's insisting on seeing him before any more questioning is—"

"You shouldn't be questioning him at all," a voice from the hall interrupted. "At least not without his attorney present." Nick Morrelli pushed past the officer and into the room. Immediately, his eyes found Maggie's and his anger gave in to a smile. "Jesus, Maggie. We have to stop meeting like this."

# CHAPTER 52

Harvey greeted Nick at the door with an impressive growl, teeth bared and his upper lip curled back. Maggie smiled at Nick's surprise even though she had warned him.

"I told you I have my own private bodyguard. Down, Harvey. Actually, we're temporary roommates." She petted the dog's head, and his entire hind end started wagging. "Harvey, this is Nick. He's one of the good guys."

Nick extended an apprehensive hand for the dog to sniff. In seconds, Harvey decided Nick deserved the royal treatment, and the dog stuck his snout in Nick's crotch. Maggie laughed and pulled back on Harvey's collar. Nick seemed more amused than embarrassed.

"So I see you have him checking out other things for you as well."

His comment caught her off guard. She led Harvey into the living room, hoping Nick didn't notice.

"I just moved in last week. I don't have a lot of furniture yet. I barely got some of the blinds up late last night."

"It's an incredible house, Maggie," he said, wandering into the sunroom and looking out at the backyard. "Pretty secluded. How safe is it?"

She looked up from the alarm system she was resetting. "About as safe as I would be anywhere. Cunningham has me under twenty-four-hour surveillance. Didn't you notice the cable TV van down the street? He says it's so we can catch Stucky, but I know he thinks it'll protect me."

"You don't sound convinced."

She opened her jacket to show him her revolver in her shoulder harness.

"This is the only thing that I find convincing these days."

He smiled. "Geez, I get so turned on when you show me your gun."

She found herself blushing from his innocent flirting. Immediately, she looked away. Damn it! She hated that he could get her pulse racing by his simple presence. Had it been a mistake to invite him here? Maybe she should have sent him back home to Boston with Will.

"I'm going to check if dinner is possible. I only have the very basics." She retreated to the kitchen, wondering what she would do if he went beyond flirting. Would she remember to act sensibly? "Would you mind taking Harvey out in the backyard?"

"No, not at all."

"His leash is by the back door. Press the green flashing button on the security system."

"It's a little like living in a fort." He motioned to the sensors and the alarm boxes. "Are you okay with all this?"

"I don't have much of a choice, do I?"

He shrugged and met her eyes. She realized he was feeling helpless, as though there must be something he should be able to do.

"It's part of the job, Nick. A lot of profilers live in gated communities or houses with elaborate alarm systems. After a while you get used to having an unpublished phone number and making certain your address isn't listed in any directory. It's all a part of my life, the part Greg didn't want to deal with. Maybe he shouldn't have had to deal with it. Maybe no one should."

"Well, Greg was a fool," he said as he snapped the leash onto Harvey's collar. Harvey licked Nick's hand in advanced appreciation. "But then, I sorta see Greg's loss as my gain." He smiled at her, then pushed the green button and let Harvey pull him into the backyard.

Maggie watched them, wondering what was it about this man and that lean body and those charming dimples that could so easily stir up feeling and emotions she hadn't accessed in years? Was it just a physical attraction? Did he simply set off her hormones? Nothing more?

When she met Nick last fall in Platte City he was a cocky,

arrogant sheriff with a playboy reputation. Immediately, she had been annoyed with herself for being attracted to his charm and classic good looks. But over the course of that terrifying, exhausting week, she had the opportunity to see a sensitive, caring man who truly wanted to do the right thing.

Before she left Nebraska, he had told her that he loved her. She wrote it off with all the other confusing emotions people think they feel after being thrown together during a crisis. In Kansas City, he said he still cared about her. Now that he knew she was divorcing Greg, she wondered what Nick's intentions were. Did he really care about her, or was she only one more notch he wanted to carve in his bedpost?

It didn't matter. She didn't have the energy to entertain such thoughts. She needed to remain focused. She needed to start listening to her head and her gut, not her heart. And more importantly, she didn't want to care about someone who Stucky could take away from her in a split second.

What Gwen had said last night about Stucky coming after her stayed with Maggie, gnawing at her. Although she honestly didn't believe Gwen needed to worry. They all believed Stucky had chosen women who were mere acquaintances of hers, in order to make it impossible to predict who his next target might be. But the fact of the matter was, Maggie had few people she allowed into her life. Gwen claimed it was because she wasn't over the loss of her father. What a bunch of psychobabble that was. Gwen believed that Maggie purposely made herself off-limits, emotionally, to her friends and co-workers. What Maggie called professional distancing, Gwen called fear of intimacy.

"If you don't let people in, they can't hurt you," Gwen had lectured in her motherly tone. "But if you don't let people in, they can't love you either."

Nick and Harvey were coming back, Harvey carrying the bone Maggie had bought him. She thought he had taken it out and buried it because he didn't want it. Instead, the fresh hole under the dogwood was merely for safe storage. She certainly had a lot to learn about her new roommate.

As soon as Nick unleashed Harvey, he bounded up the stairs.

"He looks like a guy with a mission." Nick watched.

"He'll plop down in the corner of my bedroom and gnaw on that thing for hours."

"The two of you seem to be getting attached to each other."

"No way. The smelly brute goes home as soon as they find his mom." Or at least, that's what she kept telling herself. Fact was, she would feel horribly betrayed when Rachel Endicott showed up and Harvey ran to her without so much as a glance in Maggie's direction. The thought alone felt like a stab. Okay, maybe not a stab—a poke or a pinch.

The point was, Gwen was full of crap. Letting anyone in, including a goddamn dog, usually ended up hurting like hell. So she protected herself. It was one of the few things in her twisted life she could protect herself from. One of the last things she could have control over.

She realized Nick was leaning against the kitchen counter, watching her, concern clouding his crystal blue eyes.

"Maggie, are you okay?"

"I'm fine," she answered, and his smile told her she had hesitated much too long to convince him.

"You know what?" he said as he walked slowly across the kitchen toward her, stopping directly in front of her, his eyes holding hers. "Why don't you let me take care of you for one evening?"

His fingertips stroked her cheek. The familiar current of electricity raced through her, and she knew exactly what he meant by saying he wanted to take care of her.

"Nick, I can't."

She felt his breath in her hair. His lips didn't pay attention to her words as they traced where his fingers had been. Her breathing was already uneven by the time his lips brushed hers. But instead of kissing her, he moved to her other cheek. His lips moved over her eyelids and nose and forehead and hair.

"Nick," she tried again, only she wondered if the word was audible. Her own heart beat so noisily in her ears, she couldn't hear herself think. Not that her thought process was in any kind of working condition. Instead of concentrating on what his hands and lips were doing, she kept thinking about the edge of countertop that was cutting into the small of her back as if that would allow her to hang on to reality and not be swept away.

Finally, Nick stopped, his eyes meeting hers, his face still so close. God, she could easily get lost in his eyes, the warm blue oceans. His hands caressed and massaged her shoulders. His fingers strayed inside her collar to gently touch her throat and then the nape of her neck.

"I just want to make you feel good, Maggie."

"Nick, I really can't do this," she heard herself say while the flutter in her stomach disagreed with her words, screaming at her to take them back.

Nick smiled, and his fingers caressed her cheek again.

"I know," he said, taking a deep breath. There was no disappointment or hurt, only resignation, almost as if her response had been a foregone conclusion. "I know you're not ready. It's too soon after Greg."

It was great that he understood, because Maggie wasn't sure she did. How could she explain it to him?

"With Greg, it was so comfortable." It was the wrong thing to say. She saw the wounded look in his eyes.

"And it's not comfortable with me?"

"With you, it's..." His fingers were distracting her, still exploring, making her breathing uneven. Was he trying to change her mind? Did he realize how easy it could be to change her mind? "With you," she tried to continue, "it's so intense, it scares me." There, she said it. She had admitted it out loud.

"And it scares you because you might lose control." He looked into her eyes.

"God, you know me well, Morrelli."

"Tell you what. When you're ready, and I'm emphasizing when. No ifs," he said, his eyes not letting her go, his fingers still touching her. "I'll let you have all the control you want. But tonight, Maggie, I just want to make you feel good."

The flutter reawakened, immediately kicking into overdrive.

"Nick—"

"Actually, I was thinking maybe I could fix you dinner."

Her shoulders relaxed immediately, and she sighed with a smile. "I didn't realize you knew how to cook."

"There are a lot of things I know how to do that I haven't shown you...yet." And this time, he smiled.

# CHAPTER 53

Maggie couldn't believe such delicious aromas were coming from her kitchen. Even Harvey had come down for a look and a closer sniff.

"Where did you learn to cook like this?"

"Hey, I'm Italian." Nick faked an accent that sounded nothing like Italian as he stirred the tomato sauce. "Don't tell Christine, okay?"

"Afraid you might ruin your reputation?"

"No, I don't want her free dinner invitations to stop."

"Is this enough garlic?" She stopped chopping and mincing long enough for him to examine her progress.

"One more clove."

"How are Christine and Timmy?" Maggie had grown attached to Nick's sister and his nephew in the short time she had spent in Nebraska.

"They're good. Really good. Bruce has taken an apartment in Platte City. Christine's making him earn his way back into their lives. I think she wants to make sure his philandering days are completely over. Here, taste this." He held the wooden spoon out to her, keeping an open palm underneath to catch any drips.

She took a careful lick. "A little more salt and definitely more garlic."

"So can you tell me anything about this Tess who Will is so crazy about? Any idea what happened to her?"

Maggie wasn't sure where to begin, or how much she wanted to share. All of it was still speculation. She watched him take salt in the palm of his hand, make a fist and sprinkle it into the simmering pot. She liked the way he moved around her kitchen, as though he had been fixing her dinners for years. Already Harvey followed him, anointing Nick the new master of the house.

"Tess was my real estate agent. She sold me this house, then less than a week later, she disappeared."

She waited, wondering if it would sink in, if he would make the connection on his own. Or was she the only one who could see that connection so clearly? He came over to the island where she sat on a bar stool and minced garlic. He poured more wine into both their glasses and took a sip. Finally, he looked at her.

"You think Stucky's murdered her?" He said it calmly and frankly.

"Yes. Or if he hasn't murdered her, she may be wishing he had."

She avoided his eyes and pretended to concentrate on the pieces of garlic. She didn't want to think about Stucky carving up Tess McGowan or playing his little torture games with her mind and body. Now Maggie's mincing had turned into vicious chops and hacks. She stopped herself and waited for the beginning fury to settle back down. She handed the cutting board to Nick.

Thankfully, he took it without commenting on the slight tremor in her hands. He scraped the garlic bits into the steaming sauce and immediately the new aroma filled the kitchen.

"Will told me there was a car parked outside Tess's house that morning he left."

"Manx ran the license-plate number through the DMV." It was one of the few things Manx had grudgingly shared with her. "The number belongs to Daniel Kassenbaum, Tess's boyfriend."

Nick glanced over his shoulder. "The boyfriend? Did anyone question him?"

"My partner did, briefly. Manx promised he would question him in more detail."

"If he saw Will leaving her house, then he should be pissed. Maybe Stucky doesn't have anything to do with her disappearing."

"I don't think it's that simple, Nick. Apparently, the boyfriend doesn't much care that Tess is missing or that she may have been cheating on him. My gut tells me Stucky has everything to do with this."

Maggie's cellular phone rang, startling both of them. She grabbed her jacket and searched until she found it in the breast pocket.

"Maggie O'Dell."

"Agent O'Dell, it's Tully."

Damn it! She had forgotten all about Tully. She hadn't called him, hadn't even left him a message.

"Agent Tully." She probably owed him an apology or at least an explanation.

Before she had a chance to say anything he said, "We've got another body."

# CHAPTER 54

At first, Tully had been relieved when he heard the body wasn't in Newburgh Heights. The call came from the Virginia State Patrol. The state patrolman told Tully that a trucker had grabbed a take-out container from the counter of a small café. On the phone, he explained with a quaking voice how the truck driver hadn't made it back to his truck before he discovered the container was leaking. What he thought was his leftover chicken-fried steak was suddenly dripping blood.

Tully remembered the truck stop, just north of Stafford, off Interstate 95 but it wasn't until he pulled into the café's parking lot that he realized this was probably Agent O'Dell's route home from Quantico. His relief quickly dissipated. If this wasn't Tess McGowan, chances were, O'Dell would still recognize the body.

Tully cursed when he saw the media vans and strobe lights already set up for the TV cameras. They had been lucky up to this point. Only local media had taken the time to be interested. Now he could see the national players were here. A group was crowded around a large, bearded man who Tully guessed was the truck driver.

Thank God, the State Patrol had had enough sense to confiscate the take-out container, and restrict the area behind the café. That's where a battered gray, metal trash bin rested against a chain-link fence. The trash bin was one of the extra-large commercial ones. Tully estimated it to be at least six feet tall. How the hell did Stucky dump the body? Never mind that, how had he gone undetected, with the gas pumps and the café open twenty-four hours a day, seven days a week?

He flashed his badge at a couple of uniforms keeping the media behind the sawhorses and yellow crime scene tape. His long legs allowed him to step over the ribbon without much effort. The Stafford County detective Tully had previously met behind the pizza place was already on the scene, directing the commotion. Tully couldn't remember his name, but as soon as the detective saw him, he waved him over.

"She's still in the Dumpster," he said, wasting no time. "Doc Holmes is on his way. We're trying to figure out how the hell to get her out of there."

"How did you find her?"

The detective took out a pack of gum. He unwrapped a piece and popped it into his mouth. The pack was in his pocket before he thought to offer Tully a piece. He started grabbing for it again, but Tully shook his head. He couldn't imagine having an appetite for anything, even gum.

"Probably wouldn't have found her," the detective finally said, "if not for that snack pack he left behind."

Tully grimaced. He wondered how many years it would take before he could refer to body parts in such a nonchalant way.

The detective didn't notice and continued, "Least not until the trash truck dumped this sucker. But you know, these big ones hold a lot. We might never've found her. Not like anyone would complain about the smell. This stuff always smells. So it looks like this guy's on a roll again."

"It appears so."

"I was working in Boston the last time."

Tully would have guessed the accent had the detective not told him. He was keeping an eye on the reporters near the ribbon, constantly looking over Tully's shoulder. Tully had the impression not much got past this guy. Without knowing anything more, he decided he liked him. But whether Tully liked him or not probably would matter little to the detective. And Tully liked that about him, too.

"Yeah, I remember the last time when they found that councilwoman's body in the woods. Bite marks, skin ripped off, cuts in places you don't need to see cuts."

"Stucky's one sick bastard, that's for sure." Tully remembered the photos of Stucky's collection that O'Dell had laid out on the conference-room table. Side by side they looked like a savage pack of wolves had ripped up the bodies and left them for the vultures.

"Wasn't he playing games with one of your agents back then? I remember reading something. That he was messin' with her head, sending her notes and stuff?"

"Yes, yes he was."

"Whatever happened to that agent?"

"If I'm not mistaken, that's her red car pulling into the parking lot."

"Fuck, no kidding? She's still working on this case?"

"She doesn't have much choice."

"She's got some balls."

"I guess you could say that," Tully said, now distracted. "More than likely, Agent O'Dell will be able to identify the victim for us."

He watched O'Dell. Her badge was getting her across the barriers but not without a lot of glances and long looks. He had worked with other attractive women in law enforcement and in the Bureau, but none quite like O'Dell. There was no discomfort and certainly no preening. Instead, she seemed oblivious to the stares, almost as if she had no clue they were aimed at her.

Tully didn't see it until O'Dell was closer to them. She carried a small black bag, not a purse but a case. They couldn't touch the body until the medical examiner got to the scene. He hoped O'Dell didn't have other plans.

Her eyes met his as her only greeting. He could see the exhaustion, the nervous anticipation.

"Detective—" Tully again realized he didn't know the man's name "—this is Special Agent Maggie O'Dell."

She offered him her hand, and immediately Tully could see the detective's tough exterior softening.

"Sam Rosen," he said, more than willing to fill in the blank for Tully.

"Detective Rosen." O'Dell gave him her polite and professional greeting.

"Call me Sam."

Tully resisted the urge to roll his eyes.

"Sam here—" Tully tried to keep the sarcasm to a minimum "—is with the Stafford County Sheriff's Department. He was at the first crime scene with the pizza delivery...with Jessica Beckwith."

"Is the victim still in the Dumpster?" O'Dell appeared anxious and unwilling, or unable, to hide her anticipation.

"We're waiting for Doc Holmes," Sam told her.

"Is there any way I can take a look without disturbing the scene?" She was already taking out a pair of latex gloves from her black case.

"Probably not a good idea," Tully said, knowing that O'Dell wanted to see if she recognized the victim. He saw her eyeing the trash bin. The thing was almost a foot taller than her. She brushed past them for a closer look.

"How were your men able to look inside?"

"We pulled a cruiser alongside. Davis crawled up on the roof. He took a couple of Polaroids. Want me to get them for you?" Sam looked as if he'd do just about anything she asked. Tully couldn't help being amazed. And even more amazing was how oblivious O'Dell seemed to it all.

"Actually, Sam, would you mind pulling the cruiser alongside it again?"

Or maybe she wasn't entirely oblivious. Without hesitation, Detective Rosen shouted at one of the uniforms holding back the reporters. He left them to meet the officer halfway and started telling him what he wanted, with hands gesturing as quickly as he talked.

"There's a chance it might not be her," Tully said while Detective Rosen was still busy giving directions. He knew she was expecting this to be the missing real estate agent.

"I want to assist with the autopsy. Do you think we can convince Dr. Holmes to do it tonight?" She avoided looking at him and kept her eyes on Rosen.

It was the first time she had asked anything of him, and he could tell it was not an easy thing for her to do.

"We'll insist he do it tonight," he promised.

She nodded, still keeping her eyes from him. They stood quietly, side by side, watching the police cruiser drive up as close as possible to the metal trash bin. He heard her take a deep breath as she set down the black case and threw the pair of gloves she had extracted on top. Detective Rosen met her at the bumper, offering her a hand, but she waved it off. She kicked out of her shoes and crawled up on the trunk with bare feet and little effort.

She paused, almost as if preparing herself mentally. Then she carefully stepped up on top of the roof and stood upright, able to stare down into the trash bin.

"Does anyone have a flashlight?" she called out.

One of the officers from the group who had gathered around to watch hurried to the cruiser to hand her a long-handled flashlight. O'Dell shone a stream of light into the bin, and Tully watched her face. She took her time, sweeping the inside, back and forth. He knew she was trying to examine as much of the scene as she could with her eyes since she couldn't use her hands. Her face remained composed, indifferent, and he couldn't tell whether she recognized the victim as the McGowan woman or not.

Finally she crawled down. She handed back the flashlight, tapped the cruiser's window to thank the driver and then found her shoes.

"Well?" Tully asked, still watching her closely.

"It's not Tess McGowan."

"That's a relief," he sighed.

"Not really a relief at all."

Now under a lamppost, he could see she looked agitated, her face tight with tension, the exhaustion clouding her eyes.

"It's not Tess, but I do recognize her."

Tully felt the knot winding around his stomach. He couldn't begin to imagine what O'Dell was feeling.

"Who is she?"

"Her name's Hannah. She's a clerk at Shep's Liquor Mart. She helped me pick out a bottle of wine last night."

She rubbed a hand over her face, and Tully saw the slight tremor in the fingers.

"We need to stop this goddamn son of a bitch," she said, and Tully heard that the tremor had also invaded her normally calm voice.

# CHAPTER 55

Tess felt the panic seeping into her system as the last bit of light turned everything into shadows. She tried to ignore the little voice in the back of her mind that kept telling her to crawl out of this tomb, to run as far away as possible. It didn't matter what direction or where she ended up, at least she would be out of this hell pit, this grave of mutilated bones and lost souls.

She sat next to the woman named Rachel, close enough to hear her ragged breathing. Soon she wouldn't be able to see, but she had made certain the blanket covered her. The woman would not spend another cold night exposed to the elements.

Tess wasn't sure why she had returned. Why hadn't she just left for good? She knew it would be best for Rachel if she went for help. But after an afternoon of roaming the endless woods, she knew help was not close by. She had barely found her way back, trying to leave herself a trail of pinecones. Now she wondered if it had been a mistake to come back. If by doing so, she might be guaranteeing her own death. But for some reason, she couldn't bring herself to leave this woman. She wasn't certain whether she was being gallant or just selfish, because she couldn't bear to spend an entire night out here alone.

Tess had managed to bring back a shoeful of water, using the broken-heeled leather pump she had unearthed. Rachel had to be incredibly thirsty, yet she drank little, most of it dribbling out of her cut and swollen lips and trickling down her bruised chin.

She had said little since uttering her name. Sometimes she answered Tess's questions with a simple yes or no. Most of the time she remained silent as though breathing took all her effort. And Tess had noticed that the woman's breathing had become more raspy, more labored. She had a fever and her muscles went into spasms for long periods racking her entire body, no matter what Tess tried to do to help her.

After hours of analyzing the area, and examining every possible rock step, dirt ledge and sturdy root, Tess had resigned herself to the fact that she could not pull or carry or drag Rachel out. And no amount of rest would cure or repair the damage already done to her body.

Tess leaned her head against the dirt wall, no longer caring that pieces crumbled inside her collar and down her back. She closed her eyes and tried to think of something or somewhere pleasant. A difficult task, considering her empty reservoir of pleasant experiences. Without much effort, Will Finley came to mind. His face, his body, his hands, his voice were all so easily retrieved from her memory bank. He had touched her so gently, so lovingly, despite his urgency and his insatiable passion. It was as though he genuinely felt something deeper than pleasure. And he seemed so intent on pleasing her, as though it truly mattered that she feel what he was feeling.

In all her many experiences with men and sex, she had never thought to associate sex with love. Oh sure, she knew that was the way it was supposed to be, but it had certainly never been a part of her experiences. Even with Daniel, she felt nothing remotely close to love. But she had never expected to—she had never promised or lied to herself that it would ever happen.

She didn't know Will Finley, so how was it possible to feel something remotely close to love? He was a stranger, a one-night stand. How could that be any different than any of the many johns she had serviced? Yet, even here—especially here—she couldn't lie to herself. Will Finley and their one night together had been different. She wouldn't turn it into something cheap and dirty. Not when it could be the closest she may ever get to feeling real love. And not now, when she needed it most. So she tried to remember. She remembered his soft lips, his gentle exploring hands, his hard body, his whispers, his energy, his warmth.

It worked for a short while, carrying her away from the smell of decay and the feel of mud. She thought perhaps she might even sleep. Then suddenly Tess noticed how quiet it was. She held her breath and listened. When the realization came, it swept over her like ice water being injected into her veins. The panic rushed through her, squeezing her heart. Her breathing resumed in quick bursts, frantic gasps. Her body began shaking uncontrollably, and she wrapped her arms tightly around herself, rocking back and forth.

"Oh dear God. Oh God, no," she mumbled over and over like a madwoman. When she could get her body to keep still for a moment, she listened again, straining over the pounding of her heart, straining to hear, willing the truth to be untrue. It was no use. The silence couldn't lie. She knew Rachel was dead.

Tess curled into the damp corner and then allowed herself to do something she hadn't done since she was a child. She cried out loud, releasing years of welled-up sobs and letting them rack her entire body in hysterical convulsions over which she had absolutely no control. The sound pierced the silent darkness. At first she didn't recognize it as something coming out of her, coming up from some deep well inside herself. But there was no stopping, no confining it. And so, she surrendered herself to it.

# CHAPTER 56

Maggie watched from across the metal table as Dr. Holmes sliced into the woman's chest, making a precise Y incision that curved under the woman's breasts. Though she had gowned up, her gloved hands ready, she restrained herself from taking part. Instead, she waited for his permission, participating only when asked, trying to confine her impatience when things took too long. She reminded herself that she should be grateful the medical examiner had agreed to do the autopsy on a Saturday night rather than waiting for Monday morning.

He had allowed her to do the busywork; helping insert the body block, scraping behind the woman's nails, taking the external measurements and then the samples of hair, saliva and body fluids. Maggie couldn't stop thinking that Hannah had put up the fight of her life. Bruises covered her body, the one to her hip and thigh suggesting she had fallen down some stairs in the process.

Now, as Maggie watched Dr. Holmes, she found herself going through the woman's brutal murder, step by step, from the telltale signs her body telegraphed. Hannah had scratched and clawed as Jessica had, only Hannah managed to get pieces of Stucky under her nails. Why had her death not been simple and swift? Why wasn't he able to tie her up, rape her and slit her throat as he had with Jessica and Rita? Had Stucky not been prepared for this challenge?

Maggie wanted to shove her sleeves up. The plastic apron was making her sweat. God, it was hot. Why wasn't there better ventilation?

The county morgue was larger than she had expected, with dingy gray walls and the overpowering scent of Lysol. The counters were a dull yellow Formica rather than stainless steel.

The overhead fluorescent lighting unit hung low over the table, almost brushing the tops of their heads when they stood up straight. Dr. Holmes was not much taller than Maggie, but she noticed he had grown accustomed to the light fixture, ducking automatically each time he came underneath it.

Her forensic and premed background had allowed her to perform many autopsies on her own and assist in plenty of others. Maybe it was her exhaustion or perhaps it was simply the stress of this case, but for some reason she was having difficulty disconnecting from the body on the metal table in front of her. Her face felt hot from the hovering light. The windowless room was threatening to suffocate her, though a hidden fan circulated the stale air in the room. She resisted the urge to swipe at the strands of hair that stuck to her damp forehead. The tension in her neck had spread to her shoulders, and was now knotting its way down to take control of her lower back.

Ever since she had recognized the woman, Maggie couldn't help feeling responsible for her death. Had she simply not asked for help in choosing a bottle of wine, the woman would still be alive. Maggie knew the thoughts were counterproductive. They were exactly what Stucky wanted her to be thinking, to be feeling. But she couldn't shut them off. She couldn't stop the growing hysteria that gnawed at her insides, the exploding anger that whispered promises of revenge. She couldn't control the brewing desire of wanting to put a bullet between Albert Stucky's eyes. This anger, this need for revenge was beginning to scare her more than anything Albert Stucky could do to her.

"She hasn't been dead for very long," Dr. Holmes said, his voice bringing her mind back to where it needed to be. "Internal temperature indicates less than twenty-four hours."

Maggie knew this already, but also realized he was saying this for the tape recorder on the stand next to them, and not for her benefit.

"There appears to be no signs of livor mortis, so she was definitely murdered somewhere else and moved within the span of two or three hours." Again, he said this in a matter-of-fact tone for the recorder.

Maggie appreciated his casual manner, his conversational

style. She had worked with other M.E.'s whose hushed reverence or clinically cold methods acted as a constant reminder of the brutality and violence that had brought them to their task. Maggie preferred to view an autopsy only as a fact-finding mission, the soul or spirit long gone by the time the body lay on the cold metal table. The best thing for the victim at this stage was a search for evidence that could help catch whoever had committed such an act. Although this time, she knew there would be little Hannah could tell them that would bring them any closer to finding Albert Stucky.

"I heard you ended up with the dog."

It took Maggie a minute to realize Dr. Holmes was talking to her and not speaking for the recorder. When she didn't answer immediately, he looked up and smiled.

"He seemed like a good dog. Tough son of a bitch to survive whoever stabbed him."

"Yes, he is."

How could she have forgotten about Harvey? Already she wasn't a very good dog owner. Greg had been right about her. She had no room for anything or anyone else in her life.

"That reminds me. May I use your phone?"

"Over in the corner, on the wall."

She had to stop and try to remember what her new phone number was. Before she dialed, she took off her latex gloves and wiped her forehead with the sleeve of the borrowed gown. Even the telephone receiver smelled of Lysol. She punched in the numbers and listened to it ring, feeling guilty that she had completely forgotten. She certainly wouldn't blame Nick if he had been angry enough to leave. She checked her wristwatch. It was a quarter past ten.

"Hello?"

"Nick? It's Maggie."

"Hey, are you all right?"

He sounded concerned, not a hint of anger. Maybe she shouldn't expect his reactions and responses to be similar to Greg's.

"I'm okay. It wasn't Tess."

"Good. I was kinda worried that Will would flip out if it was."

"I'm at the county morgue, assisting with the autopsy." She paused, waiting to hear some sign of anger. "Nick, I'm really sorry."

"It's okay, Maggie."

"I might be a couple more hours." Again, she paused. "I know I ruined our plans...your dinner."

"Maggie, it's not your fault. This is what you do. Harvey and I went ahead and ate. We saved you some. It'll warm up fine in your microwave whenever you're ready for it."

He was being so understanding. Why was he being so understanding? She didn't know how to respond to this.

"Maggie? Are you sure you're okay?"

She'd left too much of a pause.

"Just very tired. And I am sorry I missed having dinner with you."

"Me too. Do you want me to stay with Harvey until you get back?"

"I can't ask you to do that, Nick. I don't even know for sure how late I'll be."

"I carry around an old sleeping bag in my trunk. Would you mind if I crashed here for the night?"

For some reason the thought of Nick Morrelli sleeping in her huge and empty house brought an incredible feeling of comfort.

"Maybe it's not such a good idea," he added quickly, misreading her hesitation.

"No, it's a good idea. Harvey would really like that." She had done it again, disguising her true emotions—careful not to reveal a thing. It had become habit. "I'd really like it, too," she said, surprising herself.

"Be careful driving home."

"I will. Oh, and Nick."

"Yeah?"

"Don't forget to always reset the alarm system after you've taken Harvey out. And there's a Glock 40 caliber in the bottom desk drawer. Remember to shut the blinds. If you need—"

"Maggie. I'll be just fine. You concentrate on taking care of you, okay?"

"Okay."

"I'll see you when you get back."

She hung up the phone and leaned back against the wall, closing her eyes and feeling the exhaustion and a chill seep into her bones. She needed to ignore the strong urge to leave now. To go home and curl up with Nick in front of a warm, crackling fire. She could still remember what it had felt like to fall asleep in his arms, though it had happened only once and that was over five months ago. He had comforted her and tried to shield her from her nightmares. And for a few hours, it had worked. But there was nothing Nick Morrelli could do to help her escape Stucky. These days Albert Stucky seemed to be in everything she touched and everyplace she went.

She looked back at the metal table with the woman's gray body splayed open. Dr. Holmes was now removing organs, one by one, weighing and measuring them like a butcher preparing different cuts of meat. She tucked her hair behind her ears, pulled on a fresh pair of gloves and joined him.

"Not easy having a life of your own in this business, is it?" He didn't look up as he continued to cut.

"It's certainly not a life for a dog. I'm never home. Poor Harvey."

"Well, he's still better off with you. From what I understand, Sidney Endicott is an idiot. It wouldn't surprise me if he had murdered his wife and stashed her body somewhere so we'll never find it."

"Is that the direction Manx is going?"

"I have no idea. Take a look at the muscle tissue here and here." He pointed to the layers he had cut through.

Maggie only glanced at the area. She was wondering if the medical examiner realized that what he said regarding Mr. Endicott would be caught on tape. But what if he was right? Maybe Stucky hadn't taken Rachel Endicott. Perhaps her husband did have something to do with her disappearance, although it seemed much too easy. Suddenly she realized Dr. Holmes was staring at her over the bifocals that had slipped down to the tip of his nose.

"I'm sorry, what was it you were looking at?"

He pointed again, and immediately she could see that there was hemorrhage in the muscle tissue. She leaned against the counter behind her and felt the anger swelling up inside her again.

"If there's this much hemorrhage in the muscle tissue it has to mean—"

"Yes, I know," she stopped him. "It means she was still alive when he started cutting her."

He nodded and returned to his task, quickly and expertly tying string to each of the arteries as he cut, leaving generous lengths for the local mortician who would later use these same arteries when he or she injected the embalming fluids. Then with both hands, Dr. Holmes carefully scooped out the woman's heart and set it on the scale. "Heart looks to be in good condition," he said for the recorder. "Weight is 8.3 ounces."

While he dunked the organ in a container of formaldehyde, Maggie forced herself to take a closer look at the incision Stucky had made. Now that she could look into the body cavity, she could follow the path. His precision continued to amaze her. He had extracted the woman's uterus and ovaries as though it had been a surgical procedure. On the counter at the other end of the room lay his handiwork, still enclosed in the plastic takeout container that the truck driver had had the misfortune of picking up.

Dr. Holmes looked at what had drawn her attention. On his way back from the sink, he brought the container with him and set it on the table with their instruments. He flipped open the lid and began examining the contents.

The intercom on the wall buzzed, and Maggie jumped.

"It's probably Detective Rosen. He said he'd stop by if they found anything." He headed for the door, removing his gloves.

"Wait, are you sure?" She couldn't believe he'd open the door without checking first. "It's pretty late, isn't it?"

"Yep, it sure is," he said, stopping and looking at her over his shoulder. "But in case you didn't notice earlier, I think Rosen has developed a crush on you."

"Excuse me?"

"No, I didn't think you noticed." He smiled but didn't wait to explain, instead turning the dead bolt without hesitation or caution.

Maggie's fingers dug into her gown, groping to get at her holster and her gun, but Dr. Holmes was already opening the door.

"Evening, Sam."

"Hey, Doc." Detective Rosen's eyes found Maggie without even noticing the corpse. He held up a couple of evidence bags with what looked like dirt in them. "Agent O'Dell, I think we found something kinda interesting."

After Dr. Holmes's comment, she wondered if Sam had really discovered something at the scene or if he would try to pass off dirt as evidence in order to justify his stop. She was being ridiculous. Maybe Greg had been right about that, too. She didn't trust anyone.

He handed her one of the Ziploc bags over the table. This time he glanced down at the body. It didn't seem to bother him. She guessed that Detective Rosen had seen his share of autopsies, which meant he hadn't always belonged to the Stafford County Sheriff's Department.

She took and inspected the bag of dirt and immediately recognized it. She held the bag up to the light. Yes, there were bits of silver and yellow that sparkled under the bright fluorescent.

"Where did you find this?"

"On the side of the trash bin closest to the chain-link fence. There's actually some metal rails, sorta like steps. We found muddy prints from shoes or boots. That's probably how he was able to climb up and toss in her body. It faces away from the parking lot. No one would see him there."

Rosen seemed excited with the discovery, and she wondered why. "Did you show this to Agent Tully?"

"Nope, not yet. But I figure this has gotta be a big break. It should lead us to where this guy has been hiding out."

Maggie waited for the detective to explain. Now he seemed to be distracted by Dr. Holmes, or rather the bloody glob in the take-out container that Dr. Holmes was examining.

"Detective Rosen," Maggie waited for his attention. "Why do think this will lead us anywhere?"

"For one thing, it's mud." He stated the obvious as though he had uncovered a secret. When he realized she didn't see the significance, he continued, "Well, it hasn't rained for quite a while. It's looked like it several times, but nothing. Not around here anyway. Always offshore."

She drummed her fingers on the counter, waiting for something more than this weather report. He noticed her impatience, quickly opened one of the bags and pinched some of the dirt between his fingers, bringing it out and showing her.

"It's a thick, sticky clay. Even smells a bit moldy. Again, nothing like we have around here."

She could put an end to all of this by simply admitting she had seen the stuff before, that they had actually analyzed and broken it down. Instead, she let him go on.

"A couple of the guys who've lived here all their lives said they haven't seen anything like this stuff before. Take a close look. It's unusual, with bits of reddish rock, and that yellow and silvery crap is pretty weird...maybe even man-made."

Finally, she confessed, "We have found similar dirt at two other crime scenes, Detective Rosen, but—"

"Sam."

"Excuse me?"

"Call me Sam."

Maggie brushed annoying, damp strands off her forehead. Had Dr. Holmes been right about Detective...Sam? Was he really only here to flirt and try to impress her?

"Sam, we have analyzed this stuff. It may be from a closed-down industrial site. We do have several people trying to find a possible location."

"Well, I think I can save you some time."

She stared at him, growing more impatient with his cocky smile. He was wasting their time with this grandstanding.

"I think I know where this came from," he said, pleased with himself despite Maggie's look of skepticism. "I went fishing a couple of weekends ago. A little spot about fifty miles from here on the other side of the toll bridge. I was supposed to meet a buddy, but I still don't know this area very well. I ended up getting lost in this isolated wooded area. When I got home I noticed this sticky mud covering my boots. Took me almost two hours to clean them. The mud looked just like this crap. Couldn't figure out what the hell that silver dust was."

Now he had Maggie's full attention. She could feel her pulse begin to race. The area sounded exactly like someplace Stucky would hole up. Detective Rosen was right. This could be their big break.

"Well, I hope this pans out," Dr. Holmes interrupted, only now looking up from the contents of the plastic container. "This guy is one sick bastard. I think this woman may have confessed to him, tried appealing to him, hoping he had one ounce of human dignity in him."

"What are you talking about?" Maggie watched the medical examiner wipe his forehead, suddenly not caring that he smeared blood from his gloves to his face. The calm, experienced professional seemed visibly shaken by his discovery.

"What is it?" she tried again.

"Might not be a coincidence that he chose to extract her uterus." He stepped back from the table and shook his head. "This woman was pregnant."

# CHAPTER 57

Detective Rosen had called and filled in the Newburgh Heights Police Department when they realized Hannah Messinger may have been taken from the downtown liquor store. O'Dell had anxiously accompanied Dr. Holmes, and Rosen had stayed behind at the truck stop, gathering evidence, so Tully decided to accompany Manx and his men. After talking to Detective Manx earlier in the week and not being impressed with his foot-dragging tactics on the Tess McGowan case, Tully knew he should be here if any evidence showed up.

As he waited for one of Manx's officers to jimmy the lock on the back door, he found himself wondering if Detective Manx had been called away from some nightclub. He was dressed in chinos and a bright orange jacket with a blue tie. Okay, maybe the jacket could pass for brown. It was difficult to tell under the street lamps. But he was certain the tie had little dolphins on it. He took a sidelong look at Manx. He looked to be about his age. His buzz cut emphasized his square features, but Tully supposed women probably found Manx attractive in a brutish sort of way. Actually, he had no clue what women found attractive anymore.

From this position in the alley, Tully recognized the back of Mama Mia's Pizza Place on the corner. A shiny new Dumpster replaced the one they had found Jessica Beckwith in. Perhaps it was the owner's way of getting rid of any and all memories. What would they think when they found out that another woman had been taken and murdered only several stores away?

He pulled up the collar of his jacket against the sudden chill of the night. Or perhaps the chill came simply from the memory of that beautiful young woman tangled unceremoniously in a web of garbage. Thinking of young Jessica Beckwith reminded

Tully of Emma. How could he ever make Emma understand he only wanted to protect her? That he wasn't simply being mean. Not that she wanted any explanation. And of course, now she wasn't even talking to him since he had prevented her from going to the prom with Josh Reynolds.

"We tried to get hold of the owner," Manx interrupted Tully's thoughts. "He's out of town, won't be able to get back until late tomorrow. His wife said Messinger was taking care of things."

Tully reached for his eyeglasses and noticed the officer was making a mess of the door's lock. Finally something clicked just as the door handle came loose and fell off.

Manx found a light switch and not only did the back storeroom brighten, but the entire shop lit up, aisle by aisle. It didn't take much time to inspect the small shop and realize nothing seemed to be out of place. The cash register had been shut down and locked up. Even the Closed sign had been turned on. There was no indication of forced entrance.

"He may have grabbed her while she was walking to her car," Manx said, scratching his head, reminding Tully of one of the Three Stooges.

An officer took off out the door to check the alley, while the other started rummaging through the storeroom.

"Rosen filled me in, told me about O'Dell."

Tully stopped and glanced over at Manx from behind the counter. The detective's bulldog features softened. He actually looked sympathetic, if that was possible. Tully decided the jacket was definitely orange. In the bright light of the store there was no doubt.

"Now maybe you'll understand," Tully said, "why she's been overly anxious about your investigation of the McGowan woman's disappearance."

"Well, I figure there might be a reason to rethink the Endicott case, too." Manx hesitated as though making a major concession. "I've got copies of the case file for you in my car."

"Detective," the officer from the storeroom called out. He appeared at the door, his face pale and his eyes wide. "There's a wine cellar below the storeroom. I think you better take a look."

Tully followed Manx. They started down the narrow steps, only a bare lightbulb above to guide the way. But Tully didn't need to see anything to know they had found the murder site. No farther than the third or fourth step, he could smell the blood, and he knew his stomach was not ready for what was below.

# CHAPTER 58

He couldn't believe that she had escaped. How had she been able to unlock the door so easily? He should have felt disappointment rather than exhilaration. But even his fatigue would not deprive him of the thrill and challenge of a good hunt.

The night goggles seemed to make little difference. Sure they helped him see, but there was nothing to see. Where could that little cunt have wandered off to? He shouldn't have left her unattended for so long, but he had been distracted with the cute brunette. She had been so thoughtful, just as she had been with Agent Maggie. She had taken her time, helping him pick out a nice bottle of wine, not minding that it was closing time. In fact, she had already shut off the Open sign and was locking the front door, when he hurried in. Yes, she had been most helpful, insisting he try the crisp, white Italian for his special occasion, all the while not realizing that she herself would be the denouement of his special occasion.

But his little detour had taken its toll on him. He should have simply taken his prize and left her body in the cellar of the liquor store. At least then his muscles wouldn't be aching. His eyes were having problems focusing. The red lines were appearing more frequently, or were the night goggles malfunctioning? He hated to think that his eyesight had gotten worse in less than a week. He hated the idea of depending on someone else. But he would do whatever was necessary to accomplish his goal, to finish this game.

He wandered through the dark woods, annoyed that his feet kept tripping over tree roots and slipping on the mud. He had fallen once, but not again. He bet she hadn't wandered far from the shed. They never did. Sometimes they even came back, afraid of the dark or wanting to get out of the cold or the rain.

Stupid bitches, so gullible, so naive. Usually they followed the same path, hoping the worn trail would lead them to freedom. Never thinking it might lead them, instead, to another trap.

He had to hand it to Tess McGowan. She had managed to hide herself quite nicely. But it wouldn't last. He knew these woods like the back of his hand. There was no way for her to escape unless she was willing to swim. Funny, he thought as he adjusted the goggles to a different setting, none of them ever attempted that. But then, not many of them had had the opportunity. Tess was lucky he had been held up—even luckier that she had found a way to escape from the shack. He should have been angry with her, but her talents excited him. He did so love a challenge. It would make it all the sweeter to finally take her down, to possess her—mind, body and soul.

As he climbed the ridge he hoped he wouldn't find her with a broken neck at the bottom of some ravine. That would be a total waste. He was hoping she would make up for his disappointment in Rachel. She hadn't lived up to his expectations at all. She had been such a flirt as long as she thought he was a lowly utility worker she could tease and control. She seemed to have so much energy and vibrancy, yet she had whimpered like a helpless child when he was fucking her, the fight driven out of her so easily it was pathetic. To make matters worse, she lasted less than a half hour when he released her into the woods. What a shame.

He grabbed onto the vines and pulled himself up to the top of the ridge. Here he'd be able to look down and see for quite a distance. Nothing registered. There was no mass of heat that lit up his goggles. Where the hell had she gone?

He reached under the contraption to rub his eyes. Maybe he needed sleep more than he needed to punish Tess McGowan with a good fuck. With the familiar lethargy taking over his body, he didn't need the added disappointment if he did find her and wasn't able to...fuck her. He didn't even want to think about that. No, he'd start again in the morning, when he had the energy and could enjoy a good hunt. Yes, he'd start bright and early. He looped the rope over his shoulder, picked up the crossbow and headed back. Maybe he'd open that nice bottle of Italian wine that Hannah had promised would delight him.

# CHAPTER 59

Maggie felt numb. It took all her effort to keep her eyes open. She didn't realize until she pulled into her driveway that she had been functioning on autopilot. She couldn't remember leaving the interstate nor winding along Highway 6 with its sharp curves and steep ditches. It was a wonder she had found her way in the dark of night and through the fog of her mind.

Nick had left the light on in the portico for her. His Jeep remained where he had parked it earlier. She pulled up next to it, surprised to find the sight of its dusty sides and huge rugged tires supplied her with a wave of comfort. Now she was glad Detective Rosen had convinced her to wait until morning. How could she have thought to go hunting for Stucky in strange, dark woods in the middle of the night? Yet it had made plenty of sense only an hour ago. She had been prepared to stage a sneak attack, forgetting so quickly that she had lost the last one to Stucky. Why was it so easy for Albert Stucky to destroy all her common sense with a sweep of a hand, or rather a cut of his knife?

She knew Dr. Holmes was right, despite the probability that they would never be able to confirm it. She knew the liquor store clerk must have pleaded with Stucky. Maggie could hear it in her head—it came without warning and she couldn't seem to turn it off.

She could hear Hannah pleading, and when she realized Stucky didn't care, she must have begged for her unborn baby's life. He would have laughed at her. It would not have made any difference to him. But she would have continued to beg and cry. Was that why he started cutting while she was still alive? Had he attempted to show her the unborn fetus? It would have been a new challenge to add to his repertoire of horror. It seemed grotesquely inconceivable, but, for Stucky, she knew it was not.

Maggie tried to shut out the images. She unlocked the door, and she tried to be as quiet as possible. It had been a long time since she had come home to anyone or anything other than a dark, empty house. Even before she and Greg had begun avoiding each other, their schedules conflicted more often than not. In the last several years they had become nothing more than roommates who left behind notes for each other. Or at least there had been notes in the beginning. Gradually, the only signs of double occupancy had been the empty milk cartons in the frig and unrecognizable socks and underwear in the laundry room.

The alarm system beeped only once before Maggie punched in the correct code. Immediately, she felt Harvey's cold nose sniffing her from behind. She reached out a hand in the dark, and his tongue found it.

Though the foyer was dark, the living room was bathed in moonlight. Nick hadn't closed any of the blinds, and she was glad he hadn't. She liked the blue glow that made the room seem magical. She saw him stretched out on the floor, his long body only halfway encased in the sleeping bag. He was bare-chested and the sight of his skin, his knotted arms, his tight stomach brought a flutter to her stomach. And just when she thought she was too tired to feel anything more.

She set down her forensic kit, took off her jacket and began peeling off her shoulder holster, when she heard the sleeping bag rustle. Harvey had returned to Nick's side, laying his head on the bundle of legs.

"Don't get too comfortable here," she told Harvey.

"Too late," Nick said, rubbing a hand over his face and lifting himself up onto one elbow.

"I meant Harvey." She smiled.

"Ah. Good."

He ran his fingers through his short hair, causing it to stick up in places. Suddenly Maggie had an incredible urge to smooth it down for him, to run her own fingers through his hair and along that strong, square jawline.

"How are you holding up?" Even in the blue light, she could see the concern in his eyes.

"I honestly don't know, Nick. Maybe not so good." She leaned against the wall and rubbed her eyes. She didn't want to remember the dead clerk's eyes. She didn't want to see the shriveled-up fetus still clinging to the wall of its mother's uterus.

"Hey," Nick said quietly, "why don't you join Harvey and me." He pulled back the top of the sleeping bag, inviting her inside. In doing so, he also revealed tight jockey shorts and muscular thighs.

Again, the stirrings of arousal surprised her. Her face felt hot, and she was a bit embarrassed by her reaction, because she knew Nick didn't mean the invitation as anything more than to curl up next to him. But now, however, he seemed to be reading her thoughts.

"I promise I'll let you have as much control as you want." His eyes were serious, and she knew he had managed to zoom in on her feelings. Was she that transparent?

All she wanted was to feel something other than the frayed nerves, the exhaustion, the emotions that had rubbed her mentally raw. She could no longer remember what it felt like to feel warm and safe. Earlier, in her kitchen, Nick's presence had reminded her just how few times in the past several years she had felt any stirrings of passion and desire. Ironically, the only times she could remember were when she and Nick had been together back in Nebraska.

Without a word, she slipped off her shoes and started undoing her jeans. She met his eyes and saw a bit of surprise mixed with anticipation. He looked as though he wasn't sure what to expect. She had no idea herself.

She left on her chambray shirt. Her underpants were already damp before she climbed in next to him. Harvey stood up, turned around three times and flopped down with his back up against Nick. They both laughed, and Maggie was grateful for the release of tension.

They lay facing each other, each braced up on an elbow. His eyes held her, but he kept his hands away. She realized he was serious about letting her have control. He looked anxious to see what she might do with him. She touched his face with her fingertips, stroking his cheek, his bristled jaw and lingering at his lips. He kissed the tips of her fingers, his mouth warm and wet and inviting.

She moved down to the scar, the slight pucker of white on his chin. Then, to his throat, watching him swallow hard as though trying to contain his emotions. Her eyes stayed with his as her fingers caressed the muscles of his chest and traced a path over his hard, flat stomach. His breathing was already uneven by the time her fingers made it to the bulge in his jockey shorts. As soon as she touched him, he sucked in air like a man no longer able to stifle himself.

"Jesus, Maggie," he managed breathlessly. "If I'd known this was what it would be like to give you control—"

She didn't let him finish. She kissed him lightly on the lips while her hand slipped into his waistband. His entire body quivered. Then his mouth urged her on. Each of her nerve endings seemed to come alive, though he still touched her nowhere except her lips. She knew she had him close to the edge, but he was holding back. She brought the length of her body against his. The kisses had become deep and urgent, but she left his mouth and moved her lips to his ear. She let her tongue run along his outer ear and then slip inside, rewarded immediately by a groan. She whispered, "Don't hold back, Nick."

It didn't take long and his breathing came in gasps through clenched teeth. Moments later, her hand was wet and sticky. Nick collapsed onto his back, his eyes closed, waiting to gain control over his body again. Maggie's own body was still a live wire, tingling without any stimulation other than in reaction to Nick. How was it possible for this man to make her feel so alive, so whole and full of electricity without even touching her? As she watched him, she realized she had never before felt so sensual or so completely satisfied.

He put his hands behind his neck. Sweat glistened on his forehead. His breathing had almost returned to normal. He was looking up at her now, as if trying to read her thoughts, maybe even wondering what was next. He glanced over at Harvey who had moved to the sunroom.

"Is he giving us some privacy, or is he tired of us waking him up?"

She smiled but didn't answer. She braced herself up on her elbow again, lying on her side and watching him. Why was she suddenly not exhausted anymore?

Nick reached up and touched her hair, pushing back a strand

and letting his fingers caress her cheek. She closed her eyes and absorbed the lovely sensation being sent through her body. When she opened her eyes again, he was on his side, leaning so close she could feel his breath. Yet he kept their bodies from touching while his hand gently made its way down her neck and into the collar of her shirt. He unbuttoned her shirt, hesitating at each button to give her time to protest. Instead, she lay back, inviting his touch. He was going slowly, cautiously, as if that would give her control. As if that would reduce the intensity. It only made her ache.

He sensed her urgency and let his mouth replace his fingers, gently kissing her. He tugged open the rest of her shirt and his mouth wandered, taking his time moving down her body. Suddenly he stopped. She was breathing too hard to notice at first. Then she felt his fingertips on her stomach, lightly tracing the scar that ran across her abdomen. The hideous scar that Albert Stucky had left. How could she have forgotten it?

She sat up abruptly and disentangled herself from the sleeping bag, escaping before Nick could react. In her rush, she almost tripped over poor Harvey. Now, she stood looking out over the backyard, the front of her shirt gathered into a fist. She heard him come up behind her. She realized she was shivering though she wasn't cold. Nick wrapped his arms around her, and she leaned into his warm body, resting her head back against his chest.

"You gotta know by now, Maggie," he whispered into her hair, "there isn't anything you can say or show me that's gonna scare me away."

"You sure about that?"

"Positive."

"It's just that he's with me all the time, Nick." Her voice was hushed, and there was an annoying catch in it. "I can't seem to get away from him. I should have known that there would be some way for him to ruin even this."

He tightened his hug and nuzzled her neck. But he didn't say anything. He didn't try to persuade her that she was wrong. He didn't try to contradict her just to make her feel better. Instead, he just held her.

# CHAPTER 60

Maggie got up before dawn. She left Nick a scrawled note, apologizing for last night and giving him brief instructions for setting the alarm. He had said that he needed to get back to Boston to prepare for a trial, but she knew as he was telling her that he was trying to figure a way out of it. She told him she didn't want him to jeopardize his new job. What she left out was that she didn't want him close by for Albert Stucky to hurt.

She called Agent Tully from the road, but when he answered his door he didn't look as if he expected her. He wore jeans and a white T-shirt and was barefoot. He hadn't shaved yet, and his short hair stuck up. He let her in without much of a greeting and gathered up a scattered edition of the *Washington Post*. He grabbed a coffee mug from the top of the TV.

"I'm brewing coffee. Would you like a cup?"

"No, thanks." She wanted to tell him there was no time for coffee. Why did he not feel the same urgency she was feeling?

He disappeared into what she thought must be the kitchen. Instead of following, she sat down on a stiff sofa that looked and smelled brand-new. The house was small with very little furniture, and most of it looked like hand-me-downs. It reminded her of the apartment she and Greg had right out of college—with milk crates for a TV stand, and concrete blocks and stained two-by-sixes for bookshelves. The only thing missing was a lime green beanbag chair. The sofa and a black halogen floor lamp were the only two new pieces.

A girl wandered into the room rubbing her eyes and not bothering to acknowledge Maggie. She wore only a short nightshirt. Her long blond hair was tangled and her steps were those of a sleepwalker. Maggie recognized the teenager as the little girl in the photo Tully paid homage to on his office desk. The girl plopped into an oversize chair facing the TV, found a remote between the cushions and turned the TV on, flipping through the channels but not paying much attention. Maggie hated feeling that she had gotten the entire household out of bed as if it was the middle of the night instead of morning.

The girl stopped her channel surfing in the middle of a local news report. With the volume muted, Maggie still recognized the truck stop behind the handsome, young reporter who gestured to the gray trash bin cordoned off with yellow crime scene tape.

"Emma, shut the TV off, please," Tully instructed after only a glance at the screen. His coffee mug was filled to the brim and the aroma filtered in with him. He handed Maggie a cold can of Diet Pepsi.

"What's this?" she asked, taken by surprise.

"I remembered Pepsi is sorta your version of morning coffee."

She stared at him, amazed that he would have noticed. No one except Anita ever remembered.

"Did I get it wrong? Is it regular and not diet?"

"No, it's diet," she said, finally taking the can. "Thanks."

"Emma, this is Special Agent Maggie O'Dell. Agent O'Dell, this is my ill-mannered daughter, Emma."

"Hi, Emma."

The girl looked up and manufactured a smile that looked neither genuine nor comfortable.

"Emma, if you're up for the morning, please put on some regular clothes."

"Yeah, sure. Whatever." She pulled herself out of the chair and wandered out of the room.

"Sorry about that," he said while he skidded the chair Emma had vacated around to face Maggie and the sofa rather than the TV. "Sometimes I feel like aliens abducted my real daughter and transplanted this impostor."

Maggie smiled and popped open the Diet Pepsi.

"You have any kids, Agent O'Dell?"

"No." The answer seemed simple enough, but she noticed Tully still staring at her as though an explanation should follow.

"Having a family is a little bit tougher to accomplish when you're a woman in the FBI than when you're a man in the FBI."

He nodded as though it was some new revelation, as though he had never considered it before.

"I hope I didn't wake your wife, too."

"You'd have to be pretty noisy to do that."

"Excuse me?"

"My wife lives in Cleveland...my ex-wife, that is."

It was still a touchy subject. Maggie could see it in the way he suddenly avoided making eye contact. He sipped his coffee, wrapping both hands around the mug and taking his time. Then, as though he remembered why they were here in his living room on a Sunday morning, he stood up abruptly, set down the mug on the overflowing coffee table and started digging through the piles. Maggie couldn't help wondering if there was any part of Agent Tully's life that he kept organized.

He pulled out a map and started unfolding and spreading it out over the surface of uneven piles.

"From what you told me on the phone, I'm figuring this is the area we're talking about."

She took a close look at the spot he had highlighted on the map in fluorescent yellow. Here she had thought he wasn't even listening to her when she had called and woken him.

He continued, "If Rosen was lost, it's hard telling exactly where he was, but if you cross the Potomac using this toll bridge, there is this piece of land about five miles wide and fifteen miles long that hangs out into the river sort of like a peninsula. The toll bridge passes over the top half. The map shows no roads, not even unpaved ones down in the peninsula part. In fact, it looks like it's all woods, rocks, probably ravines. Pretty tough terrain. In other words, a great place to hide out."

"And a difficult place to escape from." Maggie sat forward, hardly able to contain her excitement. This was it. This was where Stucky was hiding out and keeping his collection. "So when do we leave?"

"Hold on," Tully sat down and reached for his coffee. "We're doing this by the book, O'Dell."

"Stucky strikes hard and fast and then disappears." She let

him hear her anger and urgency. "He's already killed three women and possibly kidnapped two others in a week. And those are just the ones we know about."

"I know," he said much too calmly.

Was she the only one who seemed to understand this madman?

"He could pick up and leave any day, any minute. We can't wait for court orders and county police cooperation or whatever the hell you think we need to wait for."

He sipped his coffee, watching her over the rim. "Are you finished?"

She crossed her arms over her chest and sat back. She should never have called Tully. She knew she could talk Rosen into assembling a search team, though the area in question was across the river, which meant not only a different jurisdiction but also a different state.

"First of all, Assistant Director Cunningham is getting in touch with the Maryland officials."

"Cunningham? You called Cunningham? Oh wonderful."

"I've been trying to find out who owns the property." He ignored her and went on. "It used to be owned by the government, which may account for that weird chemical concoction in the dirt. Probably something they were testing. It was purchased by a private corporation about four years ago, something called WH Enterprises. I can't seem to find out anything about it, no managing CEO, no trustees, nothing."

"Since when does the FBI need permission to hunt down a serial killer?"

"We're operating on hunches, Agent O'Dell. We can't send in a SWAT team when we don't know what's there. Even the mud simply means that Stucky may have been in this area. Doesn't prove he's still there."

"Goddamn it, Tully!" She stood up and paced his living room. "This is the only lead we have as to where he might be, and you need to analyze it to death when we could just go find out!"

"Don't you want to know what you might be walking into this time, Agent O'Dell?" He emphasized "this time," and she knew he was referring to last August when she went running off to find Albert Stucky in an abandoned Miami warehouse. She hadn't told anyone else. She had been following up on a hunch then, too. Only Stucky had been expecting her, waiting for her with a trap. Was it possible he'd be waiting for her again?

"So what do you suggest?"

"We wait," Tully said as though waiting was no big deal. "We find out what's there. The Maryland authorities and their resource people can fill us in. We find out who owns the property. Who knows? We certainly don't want to go onto private property if there's some white supremacist group holed up with an arsenal that could blow us off the planet."

"How long are we talking?"

"It's tough getting in touch with everyone we need on a Sunday."

"How long, Agent Tully?"

"A day. Two at the most."

She stared at him, the anger clawing to reveal itself.

"By now you should know what Albert Stucky can do in a day or two." She calmly walked to the door and left, allowing the slamming door to enunciate what she thought about waiting.

# CHAPTER 61

Tully sank into the chair and laid his head back against the cushion. He listened to O'Dell slam her car door and then gun the engine, squealing the tires—taking out her anger on his driveway. He could understand her frustration. Hell, he was frustrated, too. He wanted Stucky caught just as badly as O'Dell. But he knew this was personal for O'Dell. He couldn't imagine what she must be feeling. Three women, all of them acquaintances of hers, all of them brutally murdered simply because they had the misfortune of meeting Maggie O'Dell.

When he looked up, Emma stood in the door to the hallway, leaning against the wall and watching him. She hadn't changed or combed her hair. He was suddenly too tired to remind her. She continued to stare at him, and he remembered that she still wasn't talking to him. Well, fine. He wasn't talking to her either. He laid his head back again.

"Was that your new partner?"

He glanced at her without moving from his comfortable position, trying to keep the surprise of her sudden armistice to himself in case she had temporarily forgotten.

"Yeah, O'Dell's my new partner."

"She sounded really pissed at you."

"Yeah, I think she is. I guess I really have a way with women, don't I?"

Surprisingly, Emma smiled. He smiled back and then she laughed. In two steps she came to him and crawled into his lap the way she used to do when she was a little girl. He wrapped his arms around her and held her tight against him before she could change her mind. She tucked her head under his chin and settled in.

"Do you like her?"

"Who?" Tully forgot what they were talking about. It felt so good to hold his little girl again.

"O'Dell, your new partner."

"Yeah, I guess I like her. She's a smart, tough lady."

"She's really pretty."

He hesitated, wondering if Emma was concerned he would run off with one of his co-workers just as her mother had done.

"Maggie O'Dell and I are only partners at work, Emma. There isn't anything else going on between us."

She sat quietly, and he wished she'd talk to him about any fears she might have.

"She did seem really pissed at you," she finally said with a bit of a giggle.

"She'll get over it. I'm more concerned about you."

"Me?" She twisted around to look at him.

"Yeah. You seemed really pissed at me, too."

"Oh, that," she said, settling in against him again. "I'm over that."

"Really?"

"I was thinking if we don't spend all that money it'd cost me to go to the prom, I thought maybe I could get a really cool CD Walkman, instead?"

"Oh, really?" Tully smiled. Yes, he was quite certain he'd never understand women.

"Don't have a cow. I have enough of my own money saved." She wiggled out of his arms and out of his lap. Now she stood in front of him, arms crossed, waiting for his response and looking more like the teenager he remembered. "Can we go pick one out today?"

Was this any way to raise a teenage daughter, teaching her that she would receive some material thing for good behavior? Instead of analyzing it, he simply said, "Sure. Let's go this afternoon."

"All right!"

He watched her practically skip back to her room while he got up and wandered over to the coffee table. He found the file folder and slid it out from under one of the piles. He flipped it open and started going through the file: a police report, a copy from a DNA lab, a plastic bag with a pinch of metallic-flecked dirt stapled to an evidence document, a medical release form from Riley's Veterinary Clinic.

Last night Detective Manx had given him the file marked Rachel Endicott, the missing neighbor O'Dell suspected Stucky had taken. Now, from the looks of the evidence and a recent DNA lab report, even the arrogant, stubborn Manx had been able to figure out that Ms. Endicott may have indeed been kidnapped. After seeing how close to the edge O'Dell was this morning, Tully wondered whether or not he should show her the file. Because according to the lab's DNA test, Albert Stucky had not only been in Rachel Endicott's house, but he'd helped himself to a sandwich and several candy bars. And now there was no doubt in Tully's mind that Stucky had also helped himself to Ms. Endicott.

# CHAPTER 62

Maggie drove without a destination, hoping only to burn off the mounting anger. After an hour, she pulled into the busy parking lot of a pancake house, thinking some food might settle her nerves and her stomach. She was at the door of the restaurant, her hand on the door handle when she spun around, almost bumping into two customers before hurrying back to the car. She didn't dare have breakfast. How could she possibly risk another waitress's life?

Back on the road, Maggie's eyes darted all around her, checking the rearview mirror and every car alongside her. She pulled off the interstate, drove several miles down a deserted two-lane highway, then returned to the interstate. Several miles later, she exited at a rest stop, circled around, parked, waited, then headed back onto the interstate.

"Come on, Stucky," she said to the rearview mirror. "Where the hell are you? Are you out there? Are you following me?"

She used her cellular phone and tried to call Nick, but he must have already left for Boston. Desperate for a distraction, any distraction, she dialed her mother's phone number. Maybe she could drive down to Richmond. That would certainly take her mind off Stucky. Her mother's answering machine picked up on the fourth ring.

"I can't come to the phone right now," a cheerful voice answered, and Maggie immediately thought she had dialed the wrong number. "Please call back another time, and remember, God watches out for those who can't watch out for themselves."

Maggie snapped the phone shut. Oh God, she thought, wishing the voice had not been her mother's, and that she indeed had the wrong number. However, she recognized the raspy, cigarette-smoking tone despite the false cheerfulness. Then she remembered what Greg had said about her mother being out of town. Of course, she was with Reverend Everett—whoever the hell he was. They were in Las Vegas. Where else would manic-depressed alcoholics go to find God?

She noticed the gas tank getting low so she pulled off the interstate and found an Amoco station. She had the gas cap off when she realized the pumps were not set up for credit cards and a pay-at-the-pumps. She glanced over at the station's shop. As soon as Maggie saw the female clerk's blond curls, she replaced the gas cap and got back into the car.

It took two more attempts and about twenty more miles before she found a pay-at-the-pumps station. By now her nerves were rubbed raw. Her head hurt and the nausea had left her feeling hollow and sick to her stomach. There was nowhere she could go. Running away would not solve anything. Nor could she coax Stucky into coming after her. Unless he was already waiting for her. She decided to take her chances and return home.

# CHAPTER 63

Tess ran, her ankle throbbing. Her feet ached and were now bleeding despite her attempt to wrap them with what once were the sleeves of her blouse. She had no idea where she was headed. The sky had clouded up again, bulging gray and ready to burst. Twice she had come to a ledge that overlooked water. If only she had learned to swim, she wouldn't have cared how far away the other side appeared to be. Why couldn't she escape this eternal prison of trees and vines and steep ridges?

She had spent the morning eating wild strawberries or, at least, that's what she thought they were. Then she drank from the muddy bank of the river, not caring what algae also slipped into her cupped hands. Her reflection had frightened her at first. The tangled hair, the shredded clothes, the scratches and cuts made her look like a madwoman. But wasn't that exactly what she had been reduced to? In fact, she couldn't think of Rachel without feeling something raw and primitive ripping at her insides.

She couldn't be sure how much time had gone by while she cringed in a corner of the hole. She had cried and rocked, hugging herself with her forehead pressed against the wall of dirt. At times she had felt herself slipping into some other dimension, hearing her aunt shouting down at her from the top of the hole. She could swear she had seen her aunt's pinched face scowling at her and waving a bony finger, cursing her. She had no clue whether she had spent one night or two or three. Time had lost all meaning.

She did remember what had brought her out of her stupor. She had felt a presence, someone or something rustling above at the ledge of the hole. She had expected to look up and see him like a raptor, perched and ready to jump down on her. She didn't care. She wanted it to end. But it wasn't the madman, or a predator. Instead, it was a deer looking into the hole. A young, beautiful doe curiously staring down at her. And Tess found herself wondering how something so lovely and innocent could exist on this devil's island.

That's when she pulled herself together, when she decided once again that she would not die, not here, not in this hellhole. She had covered her temporary companion as best she could with branches from a pine tree, the soft needles like a blanket on the battered, gray skin. And then she crawled out into the open. However, there had been no sense of relief in leaving the earthly tomb that, ironically, had become a sanctuary of sorts. Now after running and walking for miles, she felt farther away from safety than she had felt inside that musty grave.

Suddenly she saw something white up on the ridge and through the trees. She climbed with new energy, pulling herself up with tree roots, ignoring the cuts in her palms that she hadn't noticed before. Finally on level ground again, she was gasping for air, but she had a better view. Hidden by huge pine trees was a huge white, wooden frame house.

Tess's pulse quickened. She blinked, hoping the mirage would not disappear. An incredible wave of relief swept over her as she noticed a wisp of smoke coming from the chimney. She could even smell the wood from the fireplace. She heard a wind chime and immediately saw it hanging from the porch. Along the house, daffodils and tulips were in full bloom. She felt like Little Red Riding Hood finding her way through the woods to her grandmother's warm and inviting house. Then she realized the analogy might prove more real than fantasy. An alarm seemed to go off in her head. The panic raced through her veins. She turned to run and slammed right into him. He gripped both her wrists and smiled down at her, looking exactly like a wolf.

"I was looking for you, Tess," he said calmly while she pulled and twisted against his strength. "I'm so glad you found your way."

# CHAPTER 64

*Washington, D.C.*
*Monday, April 6*

Maggie couldn't believe Cunningham had insisted she keep her Monday-morning appointment with Dr. Kernan. It was bad enough that they had to wait for some kind of unofficial permission from the Maryland authorities. How could they be sure Stucky wouldn't find out? If any of the information leaked, they wouldn't need to worry about Stucky setting another trap. No, this time he'd be long gone. It would be another five or six months before they heard from him again.

She had made the trip, angry and on edge—an hour's drive in D.C.'s early-morning rush. And now she had to wait some more. Once again Kernan was late. He shuffled in, smelling of cigar smoke and looking as though he had just crawled out of bed. His cheap brown suit was wrinkled, his shoes scuffed, with one shoestring untied and dragging behind him. He had plastered down his thin white hair with some foul-smelling gel. Or maybe it was the Ben-Gay assaulting her nostrils. The man looked like a poster model for homeless mental patients.

Again, he didn't acknowledge her as he shifted and creaked in his chair, back and forth, until he decided he was comfortable. This time Maggie felt too restless and angry to be intimidated. She didn't care what strange insights he might probe from her psyche. Nothing Kernan could do or say would reduce or heal the chaotic storm ticking away inside her chest like some time bomb ready to explode without warning.

She tapped her foot and drummed her fingertips on the arm of the chair. She watched him sift through his mess. God, she was sick of everyone's messes. First Tully's, now Kernan's. How did these people function?

She sighed, and he scowled at her over his thick glasses. He smacked his lips together in a "tis, tis," as if to scold her. She continued to stare at him, letting him see her contempt, her anger, her impatience. Letting him see it all, and not giving a damn what he thought.

"Are we in a hurry, Special Agent Margaret O'Dell?" he asked as he thumbed through a magazine.

She glanced at his fingers and caught a glimpse of the magazine's cover. It was a copy of *Vogue,* for God's sake.

"Yes, I am in a hurry, Dr. Kernan. There's an important investigation I'd like to get back to."

"So you think you've found him?"

She looked up, surprised, checking to see if he knew. But he appeared engrossed in the magazine's pages. Was it possible Cunningham had told him? How else would he know?

"We may have," she said, careful not to reveal anything more.

"But everyone is making you wait, is that it? Your partner, your supervisor, me. And we all know how much Margaret O'Dell hates to wait."

She didn't have time for his stupid games.

"Could we please just get on with this?"

He looked up at her again over his glasses, this time surprised. "What would you like to get on with? Would you like some special absolution, perhaps? Some sort of permission to go racing after him?"

He put the magazine aside, sat back and brought his hands together over his chest. He stared at her as if waiting for an answer, an explanation. She refused to give him any of what he wanted. Instead, she simply stared back.

"You'd like us all to get out of your way," he continued. "Is that it, Special Agent Margaret O'Dell?" He paused. She pursed her lips, denying him a response, and so he continued, "You want to go after him all by yourself again, because you're the only one who can capture him. Oh no, excuse me. You're the only one who can stop him. Perhaps you think stopping him this time will absolve *you* of his crimes?"

"If I was looking for absolution, Dr. Kernan, I'd be in a church and certainly not sitting here in your office."

He smiled, a thin-lipped smile. Maggie realized it was the first time she had ever seen the man smile.

"Will you be looking for absolution after you shoot Albert Stucky between the eyes?"

She winced, remembering their last session and how out of control she had been. It reminded her that she still felt out of control, only now the anger gave her a false sense of how close the ledge really was. If she remained angry, perhaps she wouldn't see the ledge at all. Would she even feel herself slipping or would the fall be abrupt and sudden when it happened?

"Maybe I've been around evil too long to care about what I need to do to destroy it." She was no longer concerned with what she told him. He couldn't use any of it to hurt her. No one could hurt her more than Stucky already had. "Maybe," she continued, letting the anger drive her, "maybe I need to be as evil as Albert Stucky in order to stop him."

He stared at her, but this time it was different. He was contemplating what she had said. Would he have some smart-ass response? Would he try his reverse psychology on her? She wasn't one of his naive students anymore. She could play at his game. After all, she had played with someone ten times as twisted as him. If she could play at Albert Stucky's game, then Dr. James Kernan's would be nothing more than child's play.

She stared him down, without flinching, without fidgeting. Had she rendered the old man speechless?

Finally he sat forward, elbows on his messy desk, fingers constructing a tent of bent and misshapen digits.

"So that's what concerns you, Margaret O'Dell?"

She had no idea what he was talking about, but she kept the question from her face.

"You're concerned," he said slowly, as if approaching a delicate subject. It was an unfamiliar gesture, one that immediately made Maggie suspicious. Was it another of Kernan's famous tricks or was he genuinely concerned? She hoped for a trick. That, she could handle. The concern, she wasn't too sure about.

"You're worried," he began again, "that you may be capable of the same sort of evil Albert Stucky is capable of."

"Aren't we all, Dr. Kernan?" She paused for his reaction. "Isn't that what Jung meant when he said we all have a shadow side?" She watched him closely, wanting to see how it felt to have one of his students contradict him with his own teachings. "Evil men do what good men only dream of doing. Isn't that true, Dr. Kernan?"

He shifted in his chair. She should have counted the succession of eye blinks. She wanted to smile, because she had him on the ropes, so to speak. But there was no victory in this truth.

"I believe—" he hesitated to clear his throat "—I believe Jung said that evil is as essential a component of human behavior as good. That we must learn to acknowledge and accept that it exists within all of us. But no, that doesn't mean we're all capable of the same kind of evil as someone like Albert Stucky. There's a difference, my dear Agent O'Dell, between stepping into evil and getting your shoes muddy, and choosing to dive in and wallow in it."

"But how do you stop from falling in headfirst?" She felt an annoying catch in her throat as the inner frenzy threatened to reveal itself. Her thoughts of revenge were black and evil and very real. Had she already dived in?

"I'm going to tell you something, Maggie O'Dell, and I want you to listen very closely." He leaned forward, his face serious, his magnified eyes pinning her to the chair with their unfamiliar concern. "I don't give a rat's ass about Jung or Freud when it comes to this evil crap. Remember this and only this, Margaret O'Dell. The decisions we make in a split second will always reveal our true nature, our true self. Whether we like it or not. When that split second comes, don't think, don't analyze, don't feel and never second-guess—just react. Trust. Trust in yourself. You do that—just that—and I'm willing to bet you end up with nothing more than a little mud on your shoes."

# CHAPTER 65

Tully punched at the laptop's keyboard. He knew the computer down in his office was much faster, but he couldn't leave the conference room. Not now that he had had all the calls forwarded, and every last file on the case was spread out over the tabletop. Agent O'Dell would be furious about the mess. Though he doubted she could get much angrier. He hadn't seen or talked to her since she had stormed out of his house yesterday.

Assistant Director Cunningham had informed him that O'Dell would be spending the morning in D.C. at a previously scheduled appointment. He didn't elaborate, but Tully knew the appointment was with the Bureau psychologist. Maybe it would help calm her down. She needed to keep things in perspective. She needed to realize that everything that could be done, was being done, and as quickly as possible. She needed to get past her own fear. She couldn't keep seeing the bogeyman in every corner and expect to handle it by running after him with guns blazing.

Although Tully had to admit, he was also having a tough time waiting. The Maryland authorities were hesitant to go storming onto private property without just cause. And no government department seemed willing to admit or confirm that the metallic mud could have come from the recently closed and sold government property. All they had was Detective Rosen's fishing story, and now that Tully had repeated it over and over to top government officials it was beginning to sound more and more just like a fish story.

It might be different if the property in question wasn't miles and miles of trees and rocks. They could drive down the road and check things out. But from what he understood, this property had no road, at least not a public one. The only dirt road available included an electronic gate, a leftover from when the government owned the property and had allowed no unauthorized access. So Tully searched for the new property owners, hoping to find something that would tell him who or what WH Enterprises was.

He decided to use a new search engine and keyed in "WH Enterprises" again. Then he sat, elbows on the desk, his chin resting on his hand as he watched the line crawl along the bottom of the screen...3% of document transferred...4%...5%... This would take forever.

The phone rescued him. He wheeled his chair around and grabbed the receiver.

"Tully."

"Agent Tully, this is Keith Ganza—over in forensics. They told me Agent O'Dell was out this morning."

"That's right."

"Any chance I could get hold of her? Maybe her cell phone? I was wondering if you had the number."

"Sounds important."

"Don't really know for sure, but I figure that's up to Maggie to determine."

Tully sat up straight. Ganza's voice was a constant monotone, but the fact that he didn't want to talk to him alarmed Tully. Had O'Dell and Ganza been on to something that she wasn't letting him in on?

"Does this have anything to do with the luminol tests you did? You know Agent O'Dell and I are working on the Stucky case together, Keith."

There was a pause. So he was right. There was something.

"Actually, it's a couple of things," he finally said. "I spent so much time analyzing the chemicals in the dirt and then the fingerprints that, well, I'm just getting to that bag of trash you found."

"It didn't look too unusual except for all the candy bar wrappers."

"I might have an explanation for those."

"The candy wrappers?" He couldn't believe Ganza would waste his time with those.

"I discovered a small vial and a syringe at the bottom of the trash bag. It was insulin. Now, it could be that one of the previous owners of the house has diabetes, but then we should have found more. Also, most diabetics I know are fairly conscientious about properly disposing of their used syringes."

"So what exactly are you saying, Keith?"

"Just telling you what I found. That's what I meant about Maggie determining whether or not it was important."

"You said there were a couple of things?"

"Oh yeah..." Ganza hesitated again. "Maggie asked me to do a search of prints for a Walker Harding, but it's been taking me a while. The guy has no criminal record, never registered a handgun."

Tully was surprised Maggie hadn't stopped Ganza after they had read the article and discovered that Harding was going blind. He couldn't possibly be a suspect. "Save yourself the time," he told Ganza. "Looks like we don't need to check."

"I didn't say I wasn't able to find anything. The cold search just took a bit longer. The guy had a civil servant job about ten years ago, so his prints are on file after all."

"Keith, I'm sorry you went through all that trouble." Tully only half listened to Ganza as he watched the computer screen. The search engine must be accessing something on WH Enterprises if it was taking this long. He started tapping his fingers.

"Hopefully, it was worth the trouble," Ganza went on. "The prints I lifted from the whirlpool bath were an exact match."

Tully's fingers stopped. His other hand gripped the phone's receiver. "What the hell did you just say?"

The fingerprints I lifted off the bathtub at the house on Archer Drive...they matched this Walker Harding guy. It's an exact match. No doubt about it."

The pieces of the puzzle were falling into place, but Tully didn't like the picture they were forming. On an obscure Web site designed to look like some clearinghouse run by the Confederacy, he found computer video games for sale. All were wholesale priced, and the search could be completed by clicking on the tiny Confederate-flag icons. The games were available though a company called WH Enterprises. Most of them guaranteed graphic violence and others promised to be of pornographic nature. These were not the types of games kids could pick up at Best Buys or Kids "R" Us.

The sample that could be viewed with a simple click of the

mouse included a naked woman being gang-raped, with the player being able to gun down all the assailants, only to be rewarded by raping the woman himself. Despite the animation, the video clip was all too real. Tully found himself sick to his stomach. He wondered if any of Emma's friends were into this sort of garbage.

One of the Web site's features was the "Lil' General's Top Ten List," including a note from the CEO of WH Enterprises. Tully knew what he'd find before he scrolled down to see the message ending with, "Happy hunting, General Walker Harding."

Tully paced the conference room, walking from window to window. Walker Harding may have been going blind, but he sure as hell could see now. How else could he run a computer business like this one? How else could he be at each crime scene, helping his old pal, Albert Stucky?

"Son of a bitch," Tully said out loud. O'Dell had been right. The two men were working together. Maybe they were still competing in some new game of horror. Whatever it was, there was no denying the evidence. Walker Harding's fingerprints matched those found on the Dumpster with Jessica Beckwith's body. They matched the umbrella in Kansas City, and they matched the prints left on the whirlpool bath at the house on Archer Drive.

Earlier, the Maryland authorities had finally confirmed that there was a large two-story house and several wooden shacks on the property. All government buildings had been bulldozed before the sale. The rest of the property, Tully was informed, was surrounded on three sides by water and covered with trees and rock. There were no roads except a dirt path that led to the house. No electrical lines or telephone cables had been brought in from the outside. The new owner used a large generator system left behind by the government. The place sounded like a recluse's dream come true and a madman's paradise. Why hadn't he realized sooner that, of course, WH Enterprises would belong to Walker Harding?

Tully checked his wristwatch. He needed to make some phone calls. He needed to concentrate. He took several deep breaths, dug the exhaustion out from under his glasses and picked up the phone. The waiting was over, but he dreaded telling Agent O'Dell. Would this be the final thread to unravel her already frayed mental state?

# CHAPTER 66

Tess woke slowly, painfully. Her body ached. Her head throbbed. Something held her down. She couldn't move. Couldn't open her eyes again, the lids were too heavy. Her mouth felt dry, her throat was raw on the inside as well as the outside. She was thirsty and ran her tongue over her lips, alarmed when she tasted blood.

She forced her eyes open and strained against the shackles that clamped her wrists and ankles to the small cot. She recognized the inside of the shack, could feel its dampness and smell its musty odor. She twisted, trying to free herself. She felt a scratchy blanket beneath her and that's when she realized she was naked. Panic rushed through her insides, shoving against the walls of her body. A scream stuck in her throat, but nothing came out except a gasp of air. That was enough, however, to send a scrape of pain down her throat as though she were swallowing razor blades.

She settled down, trying to calm herself, trying to think before terror took control of her mind. She no longer had control over her body, but no one would control her mind. It was a painful lesson she had learned from her aunt and uncle. No matter what they did to her body, no matter how many times her aunt had banished her to the dark cellar or how many times her uncle had shoved himself inside her, she had retained control over her mind. It was the ultimate defense. It was her only defense.

Yet, when she heard the locks to the door clicking open, Tess felt the terror clawing at the flimsy barricades to her mind.

# CHAPTER 67

Maggie swerved around slower-moving traffic, trying to keep her foot from pushing the accelerator to the floor. Her heart hadn't stopped ramming against her chest since Tully's phone call. All the anger she had accessed in Kernan's office had been converted to sheer panic. It no longer ticked quietly like a time bomb. Instead, it pressed against her rib cage like some heavy weight being lowered, little by little, threatening to crush her.

She knew Walker Harding was involved. It made sense that Stucky would call on his old pal. Though she still had a difficult time believing Stucky would allow anyone to help, even his ex-partner—unless the two men were competing at some bizarre game. And from Tully's description of Harding's new entrepreneurial venture, it seemed more than possible that he was capable of the same sort of twisted, perverted evil as Stucky was.

She tucked her hair behind her ears and rolled down the window. The breeze whipped through the car's interior, bringing with it the fumes of exhaust and the scent of pine trees.

Dr. Kernan had said she shouldn't think so much—just trust. All her life she had felt as if she was the only person she could trust. There was no one else. Did he understand how incredibly frustrating, how...hell, why not admit it?—how frightening it was to think she could no longer trust the one person she had trusted her whole life? That she could no longer trust herself?

She had a B.A. in criminal psychology, and a master's in behavioral psychology. She knew all about the shadow side, and she knew it existed in everyone. There were plenty of experts who debated the fine line between good and evil and they all hoped to explain why some people choose evil, while others choose good. What was the determining factor? Did anyone really know?

"Trust in yourself," Kernan had told her. And that the decisions she made in a split second would somehow reveal her true self.

What kind of psychobabble was that? What if her true self really was her shadow side? What if her true self was capable of Stucky's blend of evil? She couldn't help thinking that all it would take was a split second for her to aim and fire one bullet right between those black eyes. She no longer wanted to capture him, to stop Albert Stucky. She wanted him to pay. She wanted—no, she needed—to see fear in those evil eyes. The same kind of fear she felt in that Miami warehouse when he cut her abdomen. The same fear she felt every night when darkness came and sleep would not.

Stucky had made this a personal war between the two of them. He had made her an accomplice to his murders, making her feel as though she had handpicked each woman for his disposal. If he had somehow managed to coerce Walker Harding into his game of horror, then there were now two of them who needed to be destroyed.

She glanced at the map spread out on the passenger seat. The toll bridge was about fifty miles from Quantico. Tully was still making arrangements. It would take several hours before he had everything ready according to his careful, by-the-book standards. There would be more waiting. They'd be lucky to make it to Harding's property by nightfall. Tully was expecting her back at Quantico in the next ten to fifteen minutes. Up ahead a sign indicated that her exit was just ten miles away.

She pulled out her cell phone and slowed the car to the speed limit, allowing her to maneuver more easily with one hand on the steering wheel. She punched in the number and waited.

"Dr. Gwen Patterson."

"Gwen, it's Maggie."

"You sound like you're on the road."

"Yes, I am. Just coming back from D.C. Can you hear me okay?"

"Little bit of static, but not bad. You were in D.C.? You should have stopped in. We could have done lunch."

"Sorry, no time. Look, Gwen, you know how you're always saying I never ask anything of my friends? Well, I need a favor."

"Wait a minute. Who did you say this was?"

"Very funny." Maggie smiled, surprised she was able to amidst all the internal tension. "I know it's out of your way, but could you check on Harvey this evening—let him out, feed him...all those dog things that a real dog owner normally does?"

"You're off fighting serial killers, and you're still worried about Harvey. I'd say you already sound like a dog owner. Yes, I will stop and spend some quality time with Harvey. Actually, that's the best offer I've had in a long time as far as spending an evening with a male companion goes."

"Thanks. I really appreciate it."

"Does this mean you're simply working late or have you found him?"

Maggie wondered how long it had been since her friends and co-workers could simply ask her about "him" and automatically mean Albert Stucky.

"I don't know yet, but it's the best lead we've had so far. You may have been right about the candy bar wrappers."

"Wonderful. Only I don't remember what it was I said."

"We dismissed Stucky's old business partner as an accomplice because the guy was supposedly going blind due to some medical condition. Now the evidence suggests that the condition could be diabetes. Which means the blindness may not have been sudden or complete. In fact, he could be hoping to control it with insulin injections."

"Why would Stucky be working with an accomplice? Are you sure that makes sense, Maggie?"

"No, I'm not sure it makes sense. But we keep finding fingerprints at the scenes that don't belong to Stucky. This morning we found out the prints are a perfect match with Stucky's old business partner, Walker Harding. The two sold their business about four years ago and supposedly went their separate ways, but they might be working together again. We also discovered a remote piece of land just across the river registered to Harding. This place sounds like the perfect hideout."

Maggie glanced down at the map again. The exit to Quantico was getting closer. Soon she'd need to make a decision. She knew a shortcut to the toll bridge. She could be there in less than an hour. Suddenly she realized that Gwen's pause had lasted too long. Had she lost the call?

"Gwen, are you still there?"

"Did you say the partner's name is Walker Harding?"

"Yes, that's right."

"Maggie, last week I started seeing a new patient who is blind. His name is Walker Harding."

# CHAPTER 68

Tully ripped off the fax and began piecing the four sheets together. The Maryland Parks Commission had faxed an aerial view of Harding's property. In black and white not much could be seen through the acres of treetops. The first thing Tully noticed was that, from above, the area looked like an island except for a sliver that connected it to the mainland. The property jutted out into the water with the Potomac River on two sides and a tributary river on the third.

"The SWAT team is assembled and ready to go," Cunningham said as he entered the conference room. "Maryland State Patrol will meet you on the other side of the toll bridge. Are those any help?" He came around the table and looked at the map Tully had just finished taping together.

"Can't see any buildings. Too many trees."

Cunningham pushed his glasses up the bridge of his nose and bent down to examine the map. "From what I understand, the facility housing the generator is in the upper northwest corner." He ran his index finger over the spot that resembled a black-and-gray mass. "I would think the house would need to be close by. Any idea how long Harding has lived here?"

"At least four years. Which means he's settled and knows the area. It wouldn't surprise me if he had a bunker somewhere on the property."

"That seems a bit paranoid, doesn't it?" Cunningham raised his eyebrows.

"The guy was a recluse long before he and Stucky started their business. Some of the computer video games he sells are his own creations. The guy may be a computer genius, but he's weirder than hell. A lot of the games are antigovernment, white supremacist garbage. He even has one called 'Waco's Revenge.' Lots of Armageddon-type stuff, too. Probably sold truckloads of it in 1999, so it wouldn't surprise me if he's well prepared."

"What are you saying, Agent Tully? You mean we might have more problems on our hands than busting a couple of serial killers? You think Harding may have an arsenal in there, or worse, have the property booby-trapped?"

"I don't have any proof, sir. I just think we should be prepared."

"But be prepared for what? A stand-off?"

"Anything. I'm just saying if Harding is as extreme as his games would suggest, he could freak out with the FBI showing up on his doorstep."

"Wonderful." Cunningham stretched his back and walked over to the bulletin board where Tully had tacked up printouts of Harding's Web site next to photos of the crime scenes. "When is Agent O'Dell scheduled to be here?"

Tully glanced at his watch. She was already a half hour late. He knew what Cunningham was thinking.

"She should be here any minute now, sir," Tully said without indicating he thought that she might not show up. "I think we have everything we need. Is there anything I'm forgetting?"

"I want to brief the SWAT team. We should let them in on your suspicions," Cunningham said, looking at his own watch now. "What time did Agent O'Dell leave D.C.?"

"I'm not really sure. Will they need any extra preparations?" He avoided his boss's eyes, just in case he could see that Tully was stalling and changing the subject.

"No extra preparations. But it is important they know what they're in for."

When Tully looked up, Cunningham was staring at him with his brow furrowed.

"You're sure Agent O'Dell is on her way here?"

"Of course, sir. Where else would she be headed?"

"Sorry, I'm late," O'Dell came in as if on cue.

Tully restrained the deep sigh of relief he felt.

"You're just in time," he told her.

"I need a few minutes with the SWAT team, and then you're on your way." Cunningham headed out the room.

As soon as it was safe, Tully asked, "So how close to the toll bridge did you get before you turned back?"

O'Dell stared at him in surprise.

"How did you know?"

"Lucky guess."

"Does Cunningham know?" Suddenly she seemed more angry than concerned.

"Why would I tell Cunningham?" He pretended to look wounded. "There are some secrets only partners should share." He grabbed a bundle from the corner, handed her a bulletproof vest and waited for her at the door. "Coming?"

# CHAPTER 69

"We have to stay back and let them attempt to serve the search warrant," Tully instructed. He wasn't sure that O'Dell was even listening. He could hear her heart pounding. Or was that his own heart? The thumping seemed indistinguishable from the rumble of thunder in the distance.

They had left their vehicles far back on the other side of the electronic gate that blocked the road. Not much of a road, really. Tully had seen cow paths that were more easily accessible. Now as he and O'Dell crouched in the brush and mud, he regretted wearing his good shoes. A crazy thing to be thinking about when they were this close to capturing Stucky and Harding.

The Maryland State Patrol had supplied them with a half-dozen officers—officially for the sole purpose of serving the search warrant to the owner or occupants of the house. If no one responded, the FBI SWAT team would secure the area and accompany Tully and O'Dell in a search of the house and grounds. Tully was quick to notice that all the members of the SWAT team wore sturdy boots. At least O'Dell had remembered the FBI windbreakers. He was sweating under the weight of the bulletproof vest, but that didn't protect him from the wind. Out here in the woods the wind swirled around the trees, crisp and cold. If the thunder was any indication, they would also be wet before the night was over. Night would come quickly in these woods, and with the thick cloud cover they would soon be in the pitch black. Already the twilight was providing eerie shadows that grew darker by the minute.

"There's smoke coming out of the chimney," O'Dell whispered. "Someone must be here."

A faint light appeared in one of the windows, but it could easily be set to a timer. The smoke, however, was a little more difficult to manufacture without someone stoking a fire in the fireplace.

Two of the state patrol officers approached the front door as several of the SWAT team members moved in behind the bushes along the cobblestone path that led to the door. Tully watched, hoping he was wrong about Harding's paranoia and hoping that the patrolmen would not simply be easy targets. He pulled out his own revolver and started scanning the windows of the house, looking for gun barrels peeking through. The house sat nestled in the woods like something out of a fairy tale. There was a porch swing and Tully could hear a wind chime. He couldn't help noticing that there were way too many windows for a man who was going blind.

No one was answering the patrolman's knock. He tried again while everyone else waited quietly. Tully wiped his forehead and suddenly realized that all the chirping birds and rustling forest creatures had also gone silent. Maybe they knew something their human counterparts did not. Even the wind had settled down. The thunder rumbled closer and flashes of lightning streaked across the horizon beyond the wall of trees.

"Perfect," Tully whispered to no one in particular. "Isn't it bad enough that this place already looks like something out of *Dark Shadows?*"

"*Dark Shadows?*" O'Dell whispered back.

"Yeah, the old TV show." He glanced at her, only now she had a blank look on her face. "You know, with Barnabus Collins and The Hand?" There was still no glint of recognition. "Forget it. You're too young."

"Doesn't sound like I missed much."

"Hey, watch it. *Dark Shadows* was a classic."

The two patrolmen looked over their shoulders and into the bushes. Not very discreet. One shrugged. The other put an ear to the door. Then he knocked one last time. For some reason he tried the doorknob, then again looked over to the bushes, pointing and indicating that the door was unlocked. Of course, Tully found himself thinking, why the hell would anyone lock the door out here?

Agent Alvando, who was heading the SWAT team, hurried over to Tully and O'Dell.

"We're ready to go in. Give us a few minutes. I'll come back out and give an all-clear sign."

"Okay," Tully said, but O'Dell was up, looking as if she was ready to go in with the SWAT team.

"Come on, Agent Alvando," O'Dell began to argue, and Tully wanted to pull her back down into the brush. "We're trained agents, too. It's not like you're here to protect us."

She looked to Tully as if for reassurance. He wanted to disagree, but she was right. The SWAT team was here for backup, here to help with the search-and-arrest mission, not to protect them.

"We'll go on in with you, Victor," he reluctantly told Agent Alvando.

There was barely enough light to see inside the house. The entry included a hallway down the middle with a great room to the left and an open staircase over to the right. The second-floor landing was visible, separated only by a balcony railing. The team split up with half of them going upstairs, and the other half covering the main floor. Tully followed Agent O'Dell up the stairs. Before they got to the landing, they noticed the SWAT team members had stopped at the end of the hall. Tully could hear what sounded like a voice on the other side of the door where the three men hesitated. They motioned to each other, getting into position. Tully followed O'Dell's lead and pressed himself against the wall. One of the men kicked the door open, and they stormed the room without a word to each other.

O'Dell looked disappointed when they got to the door and discovered the voice came from one of the half-dozen computers lined up along the wall.

"Click twice for confirmation," the electronic voice said. "Speak into the microphone when ready."

From another computer, an electronic voice gave different instructions. "That order has been shipped. Please check the status in twenty-four hours."

"What the fuck is this?" one of the SWAT team asked.

O'Dell was taking a closer look while the rest of them stayed next to the door watching their backs.

"It's a whole computer system set up to be voice activated." She walked from one computer to the next, examining the screens without touching anything. "Looks like it reports the status of his video-game business."

"Why would anyone want a voice-activated system?" Agent Alvando was at the door.

O'Dell looked back at Tully, and he knew what she was thinking. Why, indeed, unless that person was blind—not just partially, but totally blind.

# CHAPTER 70

Tess squeezed her eyes shut. She could do this. She could pretend she was somewhere else. After all, she had done it many times before. There wasn't much difference really. She needed to convince herself of that. What did it matter whether a paying john fucked her or some madman?

She needed to relax or it would only hurt more. She needed to stop feeling his thrusts, stop thinking about his hands fondling her breasts, stop hearing his groans. She could do this. She could survive this.

"Open your eyes," he grunted between clenched teeth.

She squeezed them tighter.

"Open your goddamn eyes. I want you to watch."

She refused. He hit her across the mouth, whipping her head so violently to the side that she heard her neck crack. Immediately, she tasted blood. She kept her eyes closed.

"Goddamn you, bitch. Open your fucking eyes."

He was gasping, rocking back and forth with such force she thought he'd crack her insides open as well. She felt his hot breath on her neck and suddenly his teeth sank into her skin. His hands clamped down on her breasts, and he was hanging on to her, riding her, every part of him scraping, rubbing and thrusting at her, devouring her like a rabid dog.

She bit down on her lower lip. She forced her eyes to remain shut. Not much longer. She could do this. He would come, and then it would be over. Why the hell didn't he come already? It wouldn't be much longer. It couldn't be. She twisted her head as far away as possible and kept her eyelids closed tight.

Finally, his body jerked, his teeth let go, his hands gave a final squeeze and he relaxed. He crawled off her, jamming his knee into her stomach and slamming his elbow against her head. Finally, it was over. She lay still, swallowing blood and pretending not to feel the sticky mess between her legs. Instead, she reminded herself that she had survived.

He was so quiet, she wondered if he had gone. She opened her eyes to find him standing over her. The yellow glow of the lantern he had brought with him created a halo behind him. When she met his eyes, he twisted his lips into a smile. He looked as calm and composed as he had when he entered the shack. How was it possible? She had hoped that he would be exhausted, spent and ready to leave. But he showed no signs of fatigue.

"This part you will watch," he promised. "Even if I need to cut your fucking eyelids off." He held up a shiny scalpel for her to see.

Her weak, muffled scream made it past the raw pain in her throat.

"Scream all you want." He laughed. "No one can hear you. And quite frankly, I like it."

Oh dear God. The terror rushed through her veins and exploded in her head. She pulled and shoved against the restraints. Then suddenly she noticed him backing away, his head cocked to the side, as though he was listening to something outside the shack.

Tess strained to hear over the pounding in her head and chest. She lay still, watching him, and then she heard it. Unless she had gone mad, it sounded like voices.

# CHAPTER 71

Maggie wondered if they were too late. Had Stucky and Harding escaped into the woods? She looked out the window and watched as Agent Alvando and his men combed the area, disappearing into the woods. Soon they wouldn't be able to see anything without flashlights and strobes, things they hated to use, because the lights made them easy targets for snipers. As much as she wanted to be out there looking with them, she knew Alvando was right. She and Tully weren't equipped or trained to participate in a SWAT team sweep of the woods.

The rain had started softly with a pitter-patter on the metal gutters. The sound was almost comforting, except that the approaching roar of thunder promised a storm. Maggie was grateful the house depended on a generator and not electricity that could easily be knocked out.

"Could we have been wrong about this place?" Agent Tully asked from the other side of the room. He had pulled out some of the cartons from under the computer desks, and with latex gloves on he sifted through what looked like ledgers, mail orders and other business documents.

"All of this could simply be preparation for him losing his sight entirely. I'm not sure what to think." Perhaps it was the impending storm and the electrical current thick in the air. Whatever it was, she couldn't shake the feeling of dread and restlessness. "Maybe we should go check and see if they got that room opened in the basement."

"Alvando told us to stay put." Tully shot her a warning look.

"It could be a torture chamber, not some bunker."

"I'm only guessing it's a bunker. We won't know for sure until Alvando's men can get it opened."

She glanced around the room. It looked like a typical home office except for the talking computers. What a disappointment. What a letdown. She had psyched herself up for a showdown with Albert Stucky, and he was nowhere to be found.

"O'Dell?" Tully was hunched over another of the cartons he had unearthed. "Take a look at this."

She looked over his shoulder expecting to see more X-rated computer software and videos. Instead, she found herself staring at newspaper clippings about her father's death.

"Where the hell do you suppose he got this?" Tully asked.

She was wondering the same thing until she saw her appointment book and childhood photo album. It was her missing carton from the move. She had completely forgotten about it. So Greg had been telling the truth. The carton hadn't been left at the condo. Somehow Stucky had been watching and had managed to take it from the movers. A shiver slid down her back as she thought about him handling her personal possessions.

"Maggie?" Tully stared up at her, concern in his eyes. "Do you think he broke into your house without you knowing?"

"No, I've been missing it since the day I moved in. He must have stolen the box before it made it into the house."

The rage began in the pit of her stomach. She left Tully to dig through the other cartons while she paced the room from window to window.

"That means Stucky has been here," Tully said without looking up.

She kept her eyes on the windows as she walked back and forth. The lightning struck closer, igniting the sky and making the trees look like skeleton soldiers standing at attention. Suddenly she saw a reflection of someone in the hallway walking past the door. She spun around, her revolver gripped firmly, outstretched in front of her. Tully jumped to his feet and had his gun out in seconds.

"What is it, O'Dell?" He kept his eyes ahead watching the doorway. She moved slowly across the room, gun aimed, hammer cocked.

"I saw someone walk by," she finally explained.

"Are any of the SWAT team still in the house?"

"They were finished up here," she whispered. Her heart slammed against her chest. Her breathing was already coming too quickly. "They wouldn't come back up and not announce themselves, right?"

"Do you smell something?" Tully was sniffing the air.

She smelled it, too, and the terror that had begun to crawl up from her stomach started to explode.

"It smells like gasoline," Tully said.

All Maggie could think was that it smelled like gasoline and smoke. It smelled like fire. The thought grabbed hold of her, and suddenly she couldn't breathe. She couldn't think. She couldn't walk the rest of the distance to the door—her knees had locked. Her throat plugged up, threatening to strangle her.

Tully ran to the door and carefully peeked out, his gun ready.

"Holy crap," he yelled, looking out into the hallway in both directions without stepping out. "We've got flames on both sides. There's no way we're getting out the way we came in."

He returned his gun to his holster and hurried to the windows, trying to open one while Maggie stood paralyzed in the middle of the room. Her hands shook so badly she could barely grip her revolver. She stared at her hands as though they belonged to someone else. Her breathing was out of control, and she worried she might start to hyperventilate.

The smell alone sparked images from her childhood nightmares: flames engulfing her father and scorching her fingers every time she reached for him. She could never save him, because her fear immobilized her.

"Damn it!" She heard Tully struggling behind her.

She turned toward him, but her feet wouldn't move. He seemed so far away, and she knew she was losing visual perception. The room began to tilt. She could feel the motion, though she knew it couldn't possibly be real. Then she saw him again, a reflection in the window. She twisted around, but it felt as if she was moving in slow motion. Albert Stucky stood tall and dark in the doorway, dressed in a black leather jacket and pointing a gun directly at her.

She tried to raise her own gun, but it was too heavy. Her hand wouldn't obey the command. The room had tilted to the other side, and she felt herself slipping. He was smiling at her and seemed to be oblivious to the flames shooting up behind him. Was he real? Had her panic, her terror, brought on hallucinations?

"This damn thing is stuck," she heard Tully yell somewhere far off in the distance.

She opened her mouth to warn Tully, but nothing came out. She expected the bullet to hit her squarely in the heart. That's where he was aiming. Everything in slow motion. Was it a dream? A nightmare? He was pulling back the hammer. She could hear wood creaking, giving way in crashes outside the room. She pulled at her arm one more time as she saw Stucky begin to squeeze the trigger.

"Tully," she managed to yell, and just then Stucky slid his aim to the right of her and pulled the trigger. The explosion jolted her like an electrical shock. But she wasn't hit. He hadn't shot her. She looked down. She wasn't bleeding anywhere. It was an effort to move her arm, but she raised it, ready to fire at the now-empty doorway. Stucky was gone. Had it all been her imagination? There was a groan behind her, and before she turned to look, she remembered Tully.

He gripped his bloody thigh with both hands and stared at it as though he couldn't believe what he was seeing. The smoke had entered the room and burned their eyes. She ripped off her windbreaker. She could do this. She had to be able to do this. She ran to the door, forcing herself not to think of the heat and the flames. She slammed the door shut, wadded up her jacket and shoved it into the crack under the door.

She came back to Tully and kneeled next to him. His eyes were wide and beginning to glaze over. He was going into shock.

"You're gonna be okay, Tully. Breathe but not too deeply." Already the smoke was seeping in between the cracks.

She pulled at his necktie, undoing the knot and removing it. Gently she moved his hands away from the wound. She tied the necktie around his thigh, just above the bullet hole, tightening it and wincing when he shouted out in pain.

Smoke was filling the room. The crashing of beams sounded closer. She could hear a commotion of voices outside. Tully hadn't managed to make either window budge. Maggie crawled to her feet, trying to focus only on Tully and getting them out of the room, out of the house. She would not think of the flames on the other side of the door. She would not imagine the hellish heat licking at the floorboards beneath them.

She grabbed one of the computer monitors, yanking the cords and cables until they became unplugged.

"Tully, cover your face."

He only stared at her.

"Goddamn it, Tully, cover your face and head. Now!"

He pulled up his windbreaker and turned to face the wall. Maggie felt her arms weakening under the weight of the monitor. Her eyes burned, and her lungs screamed. She hurled the monitor through the window, and then quickly kicked out the chunks of glass. She grabbed Tully under the arms.

"Come on, Tully. You're going to have to help me."

Somehow she managed to drag him out the window and onto the roof of the porch. Agent Alvando and two other men were down below. It wasn't a great distance to the ground, but with a bullet in his thigh, she couldn't expect Agent Tully to jump. She held on to his arms as he lowered his body over the edge and waited for the men below to grab him. The entire time, his eyes held hers. But there wasn't shock now. There wasn't fear. Instead, what she saw in Agent Tully's eyes surprised her even more. The only thing she saw was trust.

# CHAPTER 72

Tully's leg hurt like hell. Most of the flames were out. He sat a safe distance away, but the heat actually felt good. Someone had thrown a blanket around his shoulders. He didn't remember it happening. He also didn't remember that it was raining until he discovered his clothing wet and his hair plastered to his forehead. Somehow Agent Alvando had managed to get the ambulance past the electronic gate and all the way to the burning house.

"Your ride is here." Agent O'Dell appeared from behind him.

"Let them take the McGowan woman first. I can wait."

She studied him as if she would be the judge of whether he waited or not.

"Are you sure? They might be able to fit both of you."

He looked past O'Dell to examine Tess McGowan himself. She was sitting in one of the SWAT team's trucks. From what he could see of her, she looked to be in bad shape. Her hair was tangled and wild like Medusa. Her body, now wrapped in a blanket, had been covered with bloody cuts and bruises. She could barely stand. Alvando's men had found her locked in a wooden shack not far from the house. She had been shackled to a cot, gagged and naked. She had told them that the madman had left only seconds before they found her.

"I'm not bleeding anymore," Tully said. "She's been through God knows what. Get her out of here and into a nice warm bed somewhere."

O'Dell turned and caught one of the men's attention, then waved to him. He seemed to know exactly what she meant and went directly to the truck to escort Ms. McGowan to the ambulance.

"Besides," Tully said, "I want to be here when they bring them out."

The men had found a fire hydrant in back, probably a leftover from when the property had been occupied by the government. They were dousing the entire house with thick streams of water that were much more efficient than the light rainfall. Firefighters from some neighboring community had stomped their way to the scene about an hour ago, but only after their truck had gotten stuck in the mud about a mile from the entrance. Now they ventured into the burned-out hull of the house as though on a mission. They had discovered two dead and burned bodies in the basement bunker.

Tully rubbed the soot from his face and eyes. O'Dell sat down on the ground next to him. She pulled her knees up to her chest, wrapping her arms around her legs and resting her chin on the tops of her knees.

"We don't know for sure that it's them," she said without looking at him.

"No, but who else would it be?"

"Stucky doesn't seem like the suicidal type."

"He may have thought the bunker was fireproof."

She glanced over at him, not moving from her position. "I never thought of that." She looked almost convinced. Almost.

The firefighters came out of the wreckage, hauling a body on a gurney. It was draped with a black canvas. Two more followed with another gurney. O'Dell sat up straight. Tully heard her suck in air, and he thought she was holding her breath as she watched. The second gurney approached the FBI's truck, when suddenly the dead man's arm slipped out from under the canvas. The arm slipped off the gurney, hanging down, clothed in what looked like a leather jacket. He felt O'Dell stiffen. Then finally, he heard her breathe a deep sigh of relief.

# CHAPTER 73

If it hadn't been so late, Maggie would have offered to take Gwen out for dinner. However, she had spent too much time at the hospital making sure Tess was comfortable and that Agent Tully had no permanent damage to his leg.

Though she should have been completely exhausted, for the first time in a very long time she felt like celebrating. So she searched and discovered a Chinese place that was still open on the north side of Newburgh Heights. She could finally stop by a restaurant again without worrying the waitress would end up in a Dumpster the next day. She picked up kung pao chicken, sweet-and-sour pork and plenty of fried rice. She asked for extra fortune cookies and wondered whether Harvey liked egg rolls.

Maggie arrived home to find the two of them curled up in the recliner watching Jay Leno on the portable TV. The cartons reminded her once again of the carton Stucky had stolen, now gone forever, literally up in flames. The photo album had contained the only pictures she had possessed of her father. She didn't want to think about it right now. Not now when she was enjoying what felt like some sort of liberation.

Gwen saw the bags of takeout and smiled. "Thank God! I'm starved."

She had called Gwen from the road, filling her in on most of the details. Her friend had sounded relieved not only for Maggie but for herself as well. At least she wouldn't have to worry about Walker Harding ever again.

"Why don't you spend the night here?" Maggie suggested over a forkful of chicken.

"I have an early-morning appointment. I'd rather drive tonight.

I'm worthless in the morning." She was examining Maggie while she scooped out more rice. "How are you? Honestly?"

"Honestly? I'm fine."

Gwen frowned at her as though that was too easy an answer.

"I came close to getting Tully and myself killed," she said, now serious. "I panicked with the fire. I couldn't move. I couldn't breathe. But you know what?" She smiled. "I survived. And I got us out of there."

"Very good. Sounds like you passed some major personal test, Maggie."

Harvey shoved his nose under Maggie's arm, insisting on another egg roll. She gave him a half-eaten roll and patted his back.

"I don't think you're supposed to feed dogs egg rolls, Maggie."

"And how would I know that? Is there a book with all these rules?"

"I'm sure there are several. I'll pick one up for you."

"Might not be a bad idea since it looks like Harvey and I are going to be permanent roommates."

"Does that mean you were right about his owner?"

"Tess told us there was another woman. A woman named Rachel who's dead in a pit somewhere on the property. Of course we don't know yet, but I feel certain it's Rachel Endicott." She noticed Gwen's grimace. "They'll continue to search for her tomorrow. Tess said there were other bodies, bones, skulls. Stucky and Harding may have been using this property for years."

"What do you suppose Harding had planned for me?"

"Don't, Gwen," Maggie snapped at her, and immediately she apologized. "I'm sorry, I just don't want to think about it, okay?"

"I suppose it makes sense that the two of them would have eventually moved on to women you knew more intimately. Friends, relatives...oh, speaking of intimately—" she smiled "—that reminds me. You had a phone call earlier. That hunky ex-quarterback from Nebraska."

"Nick?"

"What, you know more than one hunky ex-quarterback?" Gwen looked as if she was enjoying Maggie's annoying blush.

"Did he want me to call him back tonight?"

"Actually, he said he was headed for the airport. I took a message." Gwen pulled herself up off the floor. "You need to shop for a table, Maggie. I'm getting too old to be eating on the floor." She found the note she had left on the desk. She read the message, squinting as though someone else had written it. "He said his dad had a heart attack."

"Oh Jesus." Now Maggie wished she had talked to him. Nick and his father had a complex relationship, one in which Nick had only recently been able to get away from. "Is he going to be okay? He's not dead, is he?"

"No, but I think Nick said they were talking about surgery as soon as possible." Gwen scrunched up her face as she continued to decipher her notes.

"This is something that I didn't understand. He said his dad had received a letter, and that's what they think may have caused the heart attack. But unless I'm mistaken, I could swear Nick said the letter was from South America."

Maggie felt sick to her stomach. Had Father Michael Keller sent Antonio Morrelli some sort of confession? Maggie seemed to be the only one who believed the charismatic young priest was the one who had killed four boys in Platte City, Nebraska. But he had left the country before she had been able to prove it. The last she knew, he was still in South America.

"That's it," Gwen said. "Does any of that makes sense to you?"

The phone startled both of them.

"Maybe this is Nick." Maggie untangled herself out of the cross-legged position on the floor and grabbed the phone. "Maggie O'Dell."

"Agent O'Dell. It's Assistant Director Cunningham."

She checked her watch. It was late, and she had just seen him at the hospital a couple of hours ago.

"Is Tully okay?" It was the first thing that came to mind.

"He's fine. I'm with Dr. Holmes. He was good enough to do the autopsies tonight."

"Dr. Holmes has had his share of autopsies in the past two weeks."

"There's a problem, Agent O'Dell." Cunningham didn't waste any time.

"What kind of problem?" Maggie prepared herself, leaning against the desk and gripping the phone. Gwen watched from her perch on the recliner.

"Walker Harding died of a gunshot wound to the back of his head. He was shot with a .22, execution style. Not only that, but his organs are in an extremely advanced state of decomposition. Dr. Holmes is guessing he's been dead for several weeks."

"Several weeks? That's impossible, sir. We found his fingerprints at three of the crime scenes."

"I think we might have an explanation for that. Several of his fingers are missing, cut off, including his thumb. I'm guessing Stucky did it. Took the fingers with him. Preserved them and used them at the crime scenes to throw us off."

"But Gwen has had two sessions with Harding." She glanced at Gwen and her friend's face showed concern and alarm. Even Harvey started pacing in the sunroom, tilting his head, listening.

"Dr. Patterson has never seen Albert Stucky," Cunningham said, keeping his cool professional tone and ignoring the frantic edge to Maggie's. "If we ask her to describe the man she had the sessions with, I'm guessing she'll describe Stucky. I've only seen one or two photos of Harding, but if I remember correctly, there was an uncanny resemblance between the two men. Stucky must have been using Harding's identity for some time now, pretending to be him. That probably also explains the airline ticket in Harding's name."

"Jesus." Maggie couldn't believe it. Though it all made sense. She wasn't sure she had completely believed Stucky would allow anyone, even Harding, in on his game. "So he had the perfect disguise and the perfect hiding place."

"There's more, Agent O'Dell. The other body has been dead for several weeks, too, and it's not Albert Stucky."

Maggie sat down before her knees gave out from under her. "No, this can't be happening. He can *not* have escaped again."

"We're not sure who it is. Maybe a friend or caretaker of Harding's. Harding was definitely blind. Dr. Holmes says both his retinas were detached, and there were no signs of diabetes."

Maggie was barely listening anymore. She could hardly hear him over the pounding of her heart as she glanced frantically around the room. She noticed Harvey sniffing at the back door, now agitated. Where the hell had she left her Smith & Wesson? She opened the desk drawer. The Glock was gone.

"I've sent several agents back to watch your house," Cunningham said as if that would be enough. "I suggest you not leave tonight. Stay put. If he comes after you, we'll be ready."

If he comes after me, I'll be a sitting duck, but she kept the thought to herself.

She met Gwen's questioning eyes. The fear began invading Maggie's system like cold liquid injected into her veins. Still, she held herself up and pushed away from the solid security of her father's rolltop desk.

"Stucky wouldn't dare come after me again."

# CHAPTER 74

He crawled through the bushes, staying low to the ground. The damn bushes had prickly branches that kept grabbing his sweatshirt. This sort of thing would never happen with his leather jacket. He missed it already, though it had been a worthy sacrifice to see Special Agent Maggie O'Dell's look of relief and know it to be false. He had fooled them all, slipping in and out of hiding places he had specifically prepared for just such an occasion.

He rubbed at his eyes. Fuck, it was dark! He wished the red lines would go away. Pop, pop—no, he wouldn't think of the fucking blood vessels rupturing in his eyes. The insulin stabilized his body, but there seemed to be nothing to stop the exploding blood vessels in his eyes.

He could still hear Walker's tinny laugh, telling him, "You'll be a blind fucker just like me, Al." Walker was still laughing when he put the .22 at the base of his head and pulled the trigger—pop, pop.

The lights were completely out now. He had seen her moving back and forth in what he knew to be the bedroom. He wished he could see her face, relaxed and unsuspecting, but the curtains were drawn and not sheer enough.

He had already intercepted and dismantled the security system with a handheld gadget that Walker had invented for him a few months ago. Blind as a bat, but the man had been an electronics genius. He didn't even know how the thing worked. But he had tested it on the house on Archer Drive, and it did, indeed, work.

He started up the trellis that was hidden by vines and more bushes. He hoped it was sturdier than it looked. Actually, all of this seemed too easy, not much of a challenge. But then, she would be the challenge. He knew she wouldn't disappoint him.

He thought of the scalpel in its thin sheath, tucked safely inside his boot. He'd take his time with her. The anticipation aroused his senses so intensely he needed to stifle what sounded like panting. Yes, this would be well worth the effort.

# CHAPTER 75

Maggie sat in the dark corner. Her back pressed against the wall of the bedroom, her outstretched arms leaning on her knees. Her hands gripped her Smith & Wesson, her finger on the trigger. She was ready for him this time. She knew he had been watching. She knew he would come. Yet, when she heard him at the foot of the trellis, her pulse began to race. Her heart slammed against her chest. Sweat trickled down her back.

In a matter of minutes, he was at the window. She saw his shadow hovering, a black vulture. Then his face was at the glass, startling her and almost making her jump. Don't move. Don't flinch. Stay calm. Steady. Yet the terror hammered away at her, raw and unyielding to any of her mental commands. A slight tremor threatened her aim. She knew she was safe in the dark corner. Besides, he would be looking at the curled-up bundle of pillows he would mistake for his sleeping victim.

Would he be surprised that she had gotten so good at his game? Would he be disappointed that she could predict his moves? Certainly he wouldn't expect that they had already discovered the second body to not be his. He must have realized they would and soon, because he was wasting no time coming after his ultimate victim, his ultimate blow to his nemesis. This would be his grand finale, his final scar to leave Maggie with before the diabetes left him completely blind.

She tightened her grip. Instead of the terror, she concentrated on the faces of his victims, the litany of names, now adding Jessica, Rita and Rachel to the list. How dare he make her an accomplice to his evil. She let the anger seep into her veins, hoping it would replace the crawly feeling that invaded her insides.

He eased the window up, gently, quietly, and before he stepped into the room, she could smell him, the scent of smoke and sweat. She waited until he got to the edge of the bed. She waited for him to draw the scalpel from his boot.

"You won't be needing that," she said calmly, not moving a muscle.

He spun around, holding the scalpel. With his free hand he stripped off the bedcovers, then grabbed for the lamp on the nightstand. The yellow glow filled the room, and when he turned toward her, she thought she saw a flash of surprise in his colorless eyes. He quickly composed himself, standing straight and tall, replacing the surprise with one of his twisted smiles.

"Why, Maggie O'Dell. I wasn't expecting you."

"Gwen isn't here. In fact, she's back at my house. I hope you don't mind me taking her place?" Stucky hadn't dared come for her. That would have been too easy. Just like in that Miami warehouse eight months ago. It would have been easier to kill her. Instead, he left her with a scar, a constant reminder of him. So this time, why wouldn't he do it again? No, Stucky didn't intend to kill her. He simply wanted to destroy her. It would be his ultimate blow, to hurt a woman Maggie knew, one she cared about and loved.

"You're good at our little game." He seemed pleased.

Without warning, she squeezed the trigger, and his hand flew back, the scalpel clinking to the floor. He stared at his bloodied hand. His eyes met hers. This time she saw more than alarm. Was that the beginning of fear?

"How does it feel?" she asked, trying to keep the quiver out of her voice. "How does it feel to have me beating you at your own game?"

There was that smile again, a cocky smirk that she wanted to shoot off his face.

"No, I should be asking you, Maggie. How does it feel to play at my game?"

She felt the hairs on the back of her neck stand up. She could do this. She would not let him win. Not this time.

"It's over," she managed to say. Could he see her hand tremble?

"You like seeing me bleeding. Admit it." He raised his hand

to show her the blood dripping down his sleeve. "It's a powerful feeling, isn't it, Maggie?"

"Is it a powerful feeling to kill your best friend, Stucky? Is that why you did it?"

She thought she saw him grimace. Maybe she had finally found his Achilles' heel.

"Why did you do it? Why did you kill the one man, the only person who could stomach being your friend?"

"He had something I needed. Something I couldn't get anywhere else," he said, holding up his chin and looking away from the light.

"What could a blind Walker Harding possibly have that was worth killing him for?"

"You're a smart lady. You already know the answer to that. His identity. I needed to become him." Now he laughed and squinted.

Maggie watched his eyes. The light was bothering him. Yes, she was right. Whether it was diabetes or something else, Stucky was losing his eyesight.

"Not like Walker was doing much with his identity anyway," Stucky continued. "Sitting in that house in the boonies with his cyberlife. Jacking off to porn videos instead of enjoying the real thing." His lips curled into a snarl as he added, "He was pathetic. Never would I become what he was, at least, not without a fight."

He reached for the lamp again to turn it off. Maggie pulled the trigger. This time the bullet shattered his wrist. He grabbed at his hand, the anger and pain distorting his face while he tried to keep it composed.

"Are your eyes giving you a little trouble?" she taunted him, despite the panic sliding down into her legs and paralyzing her. She couldn't run. She needed to stay put. She couldn't let him see her fear.

He managed another smile, his face void of the pain that had to be shooting up his arm. He started walking toward her. Maggie pulled back the hammer and squeezed the trigger again. This time the bullet ripped into his left kneecap, knocking him to the floor. He stared at his knee in disbelief, but he didn't wince or cry out in pain.

"You like this, don't you? Have you ever felt such power before, Maggie?"

His voice began to unnerve her. What was he doing? If she wasn't mistaken, he was the one taunting her. He wanted her to continue.

"It's over, Stucky. This is where it ends." But she heard the quiver in her voice. Then a new fear rushed through her when she realized that he had heard it, too. Damn it! This wasn't working.

He crawled back to his feet. Suddenly her previous plan seemed ridiculous. How could she incapacitate him enough to bring him down, let alone bring him in? Was it possible to harness someone as evil as Stucky? As he started toward her again, she wondered if it was possible to even destroy him. He barely limped from his shattered kneecap, and now she could see that he had retrieved the scalpel while he had been down on the floor. How many bullets did she have left in the chamber? Had she fired twice or three times? Why the hell could she suddenly not remember?

He held up the scalpel for her to see, flipping it around and getting a better grip on it in his good hand.

"I was hoping to leave your good friend Gwen's heart on your doorstep. Seemed kind of poetic, don't you think? But now I guess I'll have to settle for taking out yours instead."

"Put it down, Stucky. It's over," but even she wasn't convinced by her words. How could she be with her hands shaking like this?

"The game ends only when I say it ends," he hissed at her.

She took aim, trying to steady her hands, concentrating on her target—that space between his eyes. Her finger twitched as she kept it pressed against the trigger. He wouldn't win this time. She forced herself to stare into his black eyes, the evil holding her there, pinning her against the wall. She couldn't let it dismantle her. But as he continued slowly toward her, she felt the wall of fear blocking her, the raw hysteria strangling her and blurring her vision. Before she could squeeze the trigger, the door to the room flew open.

"Agent O'Dell," Cunningham yelled, rushing in with his revolver drawn.

He stopped when he saw the two of them, stunned, hesitating. Maggie was startled, looking away for a split second. Just long enough for Stucky to dive at her, the scalpel plunging down. Gunfire exploded in the small bedroom, in rapid succession—the echoes bouncing off the walls.

Finally, the sound stopped as suddenly as it had started.

Albert Stucky lay slumped over Maggie's knees, his body jerking, blood spraying her. She wasn't sure whether or not some of it was hers. The scalpel stuck into the wall, so close she felt it against her side, so close it had ripped the side of her shirt open. She couldn't move. Was he dead? Her heart and lungs slammed against each other, making it difficult to breathe. Her hand shook uncontrollably as she still gripped the warm revolver. She knew without checking that its cylinder was empty.

Cunningham shoved Stucky's body off her, a thud with no sound of life. Suddenly Maggie grabbed Stucky's shoulder, desperate to see his face. She rolled him over. Bullets riddled his body. His lifeless eyes stared up at her, but she wanted to cry out in relief. With all the holes in his body, there was *not* a single one between his eyes.

# CHAPTER 76

Tess leaned against the glass. Now she realized she should have taken the wheelchair that the Nurse Ratched look-alike had recommended. Her feet burned and the stitches pinched and pulled with little provocation. Her chest ached, and it was still difficult to breathe. She had been wrong about the ribs, two cracked, two bruised. The other cuts and bruises would heal. In time she would forget about the madman they called Albert Stucky. She would forget his cold, black eyes pinning her to the table like the leather shackles that had held her wrists and ankles. She would forget his hot breath on her face, his hands and body violating her in ways she thought were not possible.

She gathered the front of the thin robe in her fist, warding off the shiver, the icy fingers that could still strangle her whenever she thought about him. Why fool herself? She knew she would never forget. It was one more chapter to try to erase. She was so very tired of rewriting her past in order to survive her future. Now she struggled to find a reason why she should even bother. Perhaps that was what had brought her here.

She looked past her battered reflection in the window and watched the wrinkled red faces. Little chunky fists batted at the air. She listened to the newborns' persistent cries and coos. Tess smiled. What a cliché to come here looking for the answers.

"Girlfriend, what are you doing out of bed?"

Tess glanced over her shoulder to find Delores Heston in a bright red suit, lighting up the sterile white corridor as she marched toward her. She wrapped her arms around Tess, carefully and gently hugging her. When she pulled away, the hard-nosed business owner had tears in her eyes.

"Oh mercy, I promised myself I wouldn't do this." Delores

swiped at her eyes and the running mascara. "How are you feeling, Tess?"

"I'm fine," she lied, and tried to smile. Her jaw hurt where he had punched her. She found herself checking over her teeth again with the tip of her tongue. It amazed her that none of them had been chipped or broken.

She realized Delores was studying her, examining for herself whether Tess was fine. She lifted Tess's chin with her soft hand, taking a closer look at the bite marks on her neck. She didn't want to see the horror and pity in Delores's face so she looked away. Without a word, Delores wrapped her arms around her again, this time holding her, stroking her hair and rubbing her back.

"I'm making it my job to take care of you, Tess," she said emphatically as she pulled away. "And I don't want a single argument, you hear me?"

Tess had never had anyone make her such an offer. She wasn't sure what the correct response was. But of all her choices, tears did not seem appropriate. Not now. Delores took out a tissue and dabbed at Tess's cheeks, smiling at her like a mother preparing her child for school.

"You have a handsome visitor waiting for you in your room."

Tess's insides clenched. Oh God, she couldn't handle facing Daniel. Not like this.

"Could you tell him I'll call later and thank him for the roses?"

"Roses?" Delores looked confused. "Looked like a bunch of purple violets he was clutching. He's squeezing those flowers so tight, they're probably potpourri by now."

"Violets?"

She looked over Delores's shoulder, and Tess could see Will Finley, watching, hesitating at the end of the corridor. He looked incredibly handsome in dark trousers, a blue shirt and, if her blurred vision served her correctly, a bunch of violets in his left hand.

Maybe there were a few new chapters in her life that needed writing, after all.

# EPILOGUE

*One week later*

Maggie wasn't sure why she had come. Perhaps she simply needed to see him lowered into the ground. Maybe she needed to be certain that this time Albert Stucky would not escape.

She stood back, close to the trees, looking at the few mourners and recognizing most of them as reporters. The religious entourage from St. Patrick's outnumbered the mourners. There were several priests and just as many altar boys carrying incense and candles. How could they justify sending off someone like Stucky with all the same ceremony given an ordinary sinner? It didn't make sense. It certainly didn't seem fair.

But it didn't matter. She was finally free. And in more ways than one. Stucky had not won. And neither had her own shadow side. In a split second, she had chosen to defend herself, but had not given in to true evil.

Harvey nudged her hand, suddenly impatient and probably wondering what use it was to be out in the open if they were not going to walk and enjoy it. She watched the procession make its way from the grave down the hill.

Albert Stucky was finally gone, soon to be buried six feet under like his victims.

Maggie petted Harvey's soft fur and felt an incredible sense of relief. They could go home. She could feel safe again. The first thing she wanted to do was sleep.

# THE SOUL CATCHER

This book is dedicated to two amazing women—
fellow authors, wise mentors, treasured friends.

For
Patricia Sierra
who insisted I stay grounded, focused and on track
then nagged me until I did.

And for
Laura Van Wormer
who insisted I could soar
then gave me a gentle shove in the right direction.

In a year that asked more questions than provided answers, just having the two of you believe in me has meant more than I can ever express in words.

# CHAPTER 1

*WEDNESDAY*
*November 20*
*Suffolk County, Massachusetts,*
*on the Neponset River*

Eric Pratt leaned his head against the cabin wall. Plaster crumbled. It trickled down his shirt collar, sticking to the sweat on the back of his neck like tiny insects attempting to crawl beneath his skin. Outside it had gotten quiet—too quiet—the silence grinding seconds into minutes and minutes into eternity. What the hell were they up to?

With the floodlights no longer blasting through the dirty windows, Eric had to squint to make out the hunched shadows of his comrades. They were scattered throughout the cabin. They were exhausted and tense but ready and waiting. In the twilight, he could barely see them, but he could smell them: the pungent odor of sweat mixed with what he had come to recognize as the scent of fear.

*Freedom of speech. Freedom from fear.*

Where was that freedom now? Bullshit! It was all bullshit! Why hadn't he seen that long ago?

He relaxed his grip on the AR-15 assault rifle. In the last hour, the gun had grown heavier, yet, it remained the only thing that brought him a sense of security. He was embarrassed to admit that the gun gave him more comfort than any of David's mumblings of prayer or Father's radioed words of encouragement, both of which had stopped hours before.

What good were words, anyway, at a time like this? What

power could they wield now as the six of them remained trapped in this one-room cabin? Now that they were surrounded by woods filled with FBI and ATF agents? With Satan's warriors descending upon them, what words could protect them from the anticipated explosion of bullets? The enemy had come. It was just as Father had predicted, but they'd need more than words to stop them. Words were just plain bullshit! He didn't care if God heard his thoughts. What more could God do to him now?

Eric brought the barrel of the gun to rest against his cheek, its cool metal soothing and reassuring.

*Kill or be killed.*

Yes, those were words he understood. Those words he could still believe in. He leaned his head back and let the plaster crumble into his hair, the pieces reminding him again of insects, of head lice burrowing into his greasy scalp. He closed his eyes and wished he could shut off his mind. Why was it so damned quiet? What the hell were they doing out there? He held his breath and listened.

Water dripped from the pump in the corner. Somewhere a clock ticked off the seconds. Outside a branch scraped against the roof. Above his head, a crisp fall breeze streamed in through the cracked window, bringing with it the scent of pine needles and the sound of dry leaves skittering across the ground like the rattle of bones in a cardboard box.

*It's all that's left. Just a box of bones.*

Bones and an old gray T-shirt, Justin's T-shirt. That was all that was left of his brother. Father had given him the box and told him Justin hadn't been strong enough. That his faith hadn't been strong enough. That this is what happened when you didn't believe.

Eric couldn't shake the image of those white bones, picked clean by wild animals. He couldn't stand the thought of it, bears or coyotes—or maybe both—growling and fighting over the ripped flesh. How could he endure the guilt? Why had he allowed it? Justin had come to the compound, attempting to save him, to convince him to leave, and what had Eric done in return? He should have never allowed Father's initiation ritual to take place. He should have escaped while he and Justin had a chance. Now what chance was there? And all he had of his younger brother was a cardboard box of bones. The memory brought a shiver down his back. He jerked it off, opening his eyes to see if anyone had noticed, but found only darkness swallowing the insides of the cabin.

"What's happening?" a voice screeched out.

Eric jumped to his feet, crouching low, swinging the rifle into position. In the shadows he could see the robotic jerks of the others, the panic clicking out in a metallic rhythm as they swung their own weapons into place.

"David, what's going on?" the voice asked again, this time softer and accompanied by a crackle of static.

Eric allowed himself to breathe and slid back down the wall, while he watched David crawl to the two-way radio across the room.

"We're still here," David whispered. "They've got us—"

"No wait," the voice interrupted. "Mary should be joining you in fifteen minutes."

There was a pause. Eric wondered if any of the others found Father's code words as absurd. Or for that matter, wouldn't anyone listening in find the words strange and outrageous? Yet without hesitation, he heard David turn the knobs, changing the radio's frequency to channel 15.

The room grew silent again. Eric could see the others positioning themselves closer to the radio, anxiously awaiting instructions or perhaps some divine intervention. David seemed to be waiting, too. Eric wished he could see David's face. Was he as frightened as the rest of them? Or would he continue to play out his part as the brave leader of this botched mission?

"David," the radio voice crackled, channel 15's frequency not as clear.

"We're here, Father," David answered, the quiver unmistakable, and Eric's stomach took a dive. If David was afraid, then things were worse than any of them realized.

"What's the situation?"

"We're surrounded. No gunfire has been exchanged yet." David paused to cough as if to dislodge the fear. "I'm afraid there's no choice but to surrender."

Eric felt the relief wash over him. Then quickly he glanced around the cabin, grateful for the mask of darkness, grateful the others couldn't witness his relief, his betrayal. He set the rifle aside. He let his muscles relax. Surrender, yes of course. It was their only choice. This nightmare would soon be over.

He couldn't even remember how long it had been. For hours, the loudspeaker had blared outside. The floodlights had sprayed the cabin with blinding light. While inside the radio had screeched on and on with Father reminding them to be brave. Now Eric wondered if perhaps it was a thin line that separated the brave and the foolish.

Suddenly, he realized Father was taking a long time to respond. His muscles tensed. He held his breath and listened. Outside, leaves rustled. There was movement. Or was it his imagination playing tricks on him? Had exhaustion given way to paranoia?

Then Father's voice whispered, "If you surrender, they'll torture you." The words were cryptic, but the tone soothing and calm. "They have no intention of allowing you to live. Remember Waco. Remember Ruby Ridge." And then he went silent, while everyone waited as if hanging by a thread, hoping for instruction or, at least, some words of encouragement. Where were those powerful words that could heal and protect?

Eric heard branches snap. He grabbed his rifle. The others had also heard and were crawling and sliding across the wooden floor to get back to their posts.

Eric listened, despite the annoying banging of his heart. Sweat trickled down his back. His fingers shook so violently he kept them off the trigger. Had snipers moved into position? Or worse, were agents getting ready to torch the cabin, just as they had done in Waco? Father had warned them about the flames of Satan. With all the explosive ammo in the storage bunker beneath the floorboards, the place would be a fiery inferno within seconds. There would be no escape.

The floodlights blasted the cabin, again.

All of them scurried like rats, pressing themselves into the shadows. Eric banged his rifle against his knee and slid down against the wall. His skin bristled into goose bumps. The exhaustion had rubbed his nerves raw. His heart slammed against his rib cage, making it difficult to breathe.

"Here we go again," he muttered just as a voice bellowed over the loudspeaker.

"Hold your fire. This is Special Agent Richard Delaney with the FBI. I just want to talk to you. See if we can resolve this misunderstanding with words instead of bullets."

Eric wanted to laugh. More bullshit. But laughter would require movement, and right now his body stayed paralyzed against the wall. The only movement was that of his trembling hands as he gripped the rifle tighter. He would place his bet on bullets. Not words. Not anymore.

David moved away from the radio. He walked toward the front window, his rifle limp at his side. What the hell was he doing? In the floodlight, Eric could see David's face, and his peaceful expression sent a new wave of fear through Eric's veins.

"Don't let them take you alive," Father's voice screeched over the static. "You're all heroes, brave warriors. You know what must be done now."

David kept walking to the window as though he didn't hear, couldn't hear. Hypnotized by the blinding light, he stood there, his tall, lean figure wrapped in a halo, reminding Eric of pictures he had seen of saints in his catechism books.

"Give us a minute," David yelled out to the agent. "Then we'll come out, Mr. Delaney, and we'll talk. But just to you. No one else."

He saw the lie. Even before David pulled the plastic bag from his jacket pocket, Eric knew there would be no meeting, no words exchanged. The sight of the red-and-white capsules made him light-headed and dizzy. No, this couldn't be happening. There had to be another way. He didn't want to die. Not here. Not this way.

"Remember there is honor in death," Father's voice came smooth and clear, the static gone now, almost as if he were standing in the room with them. Almost as though he were answering Eric's thoughts. "You are heroes, each and every one of you. Satan will not destroy you."

The others lined up like sheep to the slaughter, each taking a death pill, reverently handling it like hosts at communion. No one objected. The looks on their faces were of relief, exhaustion and fear having driven them to this.

But Eric couldn't move. The convulsions of panic had immobilized him. His knees were too weak to stand. He clutched his rifle, hanging on to it as though it were his final lifeline. David, zeroing in on Eric's reluctance, brought the last capsule to him and held it out in the palm of his hand.

"It's okay, Eric. Just swallow it. You won't feel a thing." David's voice was as calm and expressionless as his face. His eyes were blank, the life already gone.

Eric just sat there, staring at the small capsule, unable to move. His clothes stuck to his body, drenched in sweat. Across the room the voice droned on over the two-way radio. "A better place awaits all of you. Don't be afraid. You are all brave warriors who have made us proud. Your sacrifice will save hundreds."

Eric took the capsule with shaking fingers and enough hesitation to make David stand over him. David popped his own pill into his mouth and swallowed hard. Then he waited for the others and for Eric to do the same. The calm was unraveling in their leader. Eric could see it in David's pinched face, or was it the cyanide already eating its way out of his stomach lining?

"Do it!" David said through clenched teeth. Everyone obeyed, including Eric.

Satisfied, David returned to the window and called out, "We're ready, Mr. Delaney. We're ready to talk to you." Then he raised his rifle to his shoulder, taking aim and waiting.

From the position of the rifle, Eric knew without seeing that it would be a perfect head shot, without risk of wasting any ammo on a bullet-proof vest. The agent would be dead before he hit the ground. Just as all of them would be dead before David's rifle ran out of ammunition and the mass of Satan's warriors crashed through the cabin's doors.

Before the first shot, Eric lay down like the others around him, allowing for the cyanide to work its way through their empty stomachs and into their bloodstreams. It would take only a matter of minutes. Hopefully they would pass out before their respiratory systems shut down.

The gunfire started. Eric laid his cheek against the cold wooden floor, feeling the vibrations and shattered glass, listening to the screams of disbelief outside. And as the others closed their eyes and waited for death, Eric Pratt quietly spit out the red-and-white capsule he had carefully concealed inside his mouth. Unlike his little brother, Eric would not become a box of bones. Instead, he would take his chances with Satan.

## CHAPTER 2

*Washington, D.C.*

Maggie O'Dell's heels clicked on the cheap linoleum, announcing her arrival. But the brightly lit hallway—more a whitewashed, concrete tunnel than a hallway—appeared to be empty. There were no voices, no noises coming from behind the closed doors she passed. The security guard on the main floor had recognized her before she displayed her badge. He had waved her through and smiled when she said "Thanks, Joe," not noticing that she had to glance at his name tag to do so.

She slowed to check her watch. Still another two hours before sunrise. Her boss, Assistant Director Kyle Cunningham, had gotten her out of bed with his phone call. Nothing unusual about that. As an FBI agent she was used to phones ringing in the middle of the night. And there was nothing unusual about the fact that he hadn't awakened her with his call. All he had interrupted was her routine tossing and turning. She'd been awakened once again by nightmares. There were enough bloodied images, enough gut-wrenching experiences in her memory bank to haunt her subconscious for years. Just the thought clenched her teeth, and only now did she realize she had developed a walk that included hands fisted at her sides. She shook the fists open, flexing her fingers as if scolding them for betraying her.

What had been unusual about Cunningham's phone call was his strained and distressed voice. Just one of the reasons for Maggie's tension. The man defined the term *cool and collected.* She had worked with him for almost nine years, and couldn't remember ever hearing his voice being anything other than level, calm, clipped and to the point. Even when he had reprimanded her. However, this morning Maggie could swear she had heard a quiver, a twinge of emotion too close to the surface, obstructing his throat. It was enough to unnerve her. If Cunningham was upset about this case, then it had to be bad. Really bad.

He had filled her in on the few details he knew, still too early for specifics. There had been a standoff between the ATF and FBI and a group of men holed up in a cabin somewhere in Massachusetts on the Neponset River. Three agents had been wounded, one fatally. Five suspects in the cabin were dead. One lone survivor had been taken into federal custody and sent to Boston. Intelligence had not nailed down, yet, who the young men were, what group they belonged to or why they had stockpiled an arsenal of weapons, fired on agents and then taken their own lives.

While dozens of agents and Justice Department officials combed the woods and the cabin for answers to those questions, Cunningham had been asked to start a criminal analysis of the suspects. He had sent Maggie's partner, Special Agent R.J. Tully, to the scene and Maggie—because of her forensics and premed background—had been sent here into the city morgue where the dead—five young men and one agent—were waiting to tell their tale.

As she came to the open door at the end of the hall, she could see them. The black body bags lined up on steel tables one after another, looking like a macabre art exhibit. It almost looked too strange to be real, but then, wasn't that the way so many recent events in her life had been? Some days it was difficult to distinguish what was real and what was simply one of those routine nightmares.

Maggie was surprised to find Stan Wenhoff gowned up and waiting for her. Usually Stan left the early morning call-ins to his competent and able assistants.

"Good morning, Stan."

"Humph." He grunted his familiar greeting as he kept his back to her and held up slides to the fluorescent light.

He would pretend the urgency and stature of this case weren't the reason he had crawled out of bed to be here, when his normal method would have been to call one of his assistants. It wasn't that Stan would want to make certain everything was carried out by the book as much as he wouldn't want to miss an opportunity to be the point man for the media. Most pathologists and medical examiners Maggie knew were quiet, solemn, sometimes reclusive. However, Stan Wenholf, the chief medical examiner for the District, loved being in the limelight and in front of a TV camera.

"You're late," he grumbled, this time glancing over at her.

"I got here as quickly as I could."

"Humph," he repeated, his fat, stubby fingers rattling the slides back into their container to signal his discontent.

Maggie ignored him, took off her jacket and helped herself to the linen closet, knowing there would be no invitation issued. She wanted to tell Stan that he wasn't the only one who didn't want to be here.

Maggie looped the plastic apron's strings around her waist. She found herself wondering how much of her life had been dictated by killers, getting her out of bed in the middle of the night to hunt them down in moonlit woods, along churning black rivers, through pastures of sandburs or fields of corn? She realized that this time, she might actually be the lucky one. Unlike Agent Tully's, at least this morning her feet would be warm and dry.

By the time she returned from the linen closet, Stan had unzipped their first customer and was peeling back the bag, careful that any contents—including liquid contents—didn't fall or run out. Maggie was startled by how young the boy looked, his gray face smooth, having never yet experienced a razor. He couldn't be more than fifteen or sixteen years old. Certainly not old enough to drink or vote. Probably not old enough to own a car or even have a driver's license. But old enough to know how to obtain and use a semiautomatic rifle.

He looked peaceful. No blood, no gashes, no abrasions—not a single mark that explained his death.

"I thought Cunningham told me they committed suicide? I don't see any gunshot wounds."

Stan grabbed a plastic bag off the counter behind him. He handed it to her across the boy's body.

"The one who survived spit his out. I'm guessing arsenic or cyanide. Probably cyanide. Seventy-five milligrams of potassium cyanide would do the trick. Eat through the stomach lining in no time."

The bag held one ordinary red-and-white capsule. Maggie could easily see the manufacturer's name stamped on the side. Though intended to be an over-the-counter headache medication, someone had replaced the contents, using the capsule as a convenient container.

"So they were well prepared for suicide."

"Yeah, I'd say so. Where the hell do kids come up with these ideas today?"

But Maggie had a feeling it hadn't been the boys' idea. Someone else had convinced them they could not be taken alive. Someone who amassed arsenals, concocted homemade death pills and didn't hesitate to sacrifice young lives. Someone much more dangerous than these boys.

"Can we check the others before you start the autopsies?"

Maggie made it sound like a casual request. She wanted to see if all the boys were Caucasian, supporting her initial hunch that they might belong to a white supremacist group. Stan didn't seem to mind her request. Maybe he was curious to get a look himself.

He started unzipping the next bag and pointed a stubby finger at Maggie.

"Please put your goggles down first. They're not doing you any good on top of your head."

She hated the suffocating things, but she knew Stan was a stickler for rules. She obeyed and pulled on a pair of latex gloves. She glanced at the bag Stan had opened as she unzipped the one in front of her. Another blond-haired Caucasian boy slept peacefully as Stan pushed the black nylon material down around his face. Then she looked at the bag her fingers were peeling open. She didn't get very far when she stopped. She snapped back her hands as though she had been stung.

"Oh Jesus!" Maggie stared at the man's gray face. The perfectly round bullet hole was small and black against his white forehead. She could hear the sloshing of liquid behind his head; liquid that she had disturbed but that still remained captured inside the bag.

"What?" Stan's voice startled her as he leaned over the body, trying to see what had upset her. "It must be the agent. They said there was one dead." He sounded impatient.

Maggie stepped back. A cold sweat washed over her body. Suddenly she grabbed onto the counter, unsure of her knees. Now Stan was staring at her, concern replacing impatience.

"I know him" was the only explanation she could manage before she took off for the sink.

## CHAPTER 3

*Suffolk County, Massachusetts*

R.J. Tully hated the *whop-whop* of the helicopter blades. It wasn't that he was afraid of flying, but helicopters made him aware that he was riding hundreds of feet above ground in nothing more than a bubble with an engine. And something this noisy couldn't possibly be safe. Yet he was grateful the noise prevented any conversation. Assistant Director Cunningham had appeared agitated and visibly shaken the entire trip. It unnerved Tully, who had known his boss for less than a year. He had never seen Cunningham reveal much emotion other than a frown. The man didn't even swear.

Cunningham had been fidgeting with the helicopter's two-way radio, trying to get updated information from the ground crew investigating the scene. All they had been told so far was that the bodies had been airlifted to the District. Since the standoff had been a federal matter, the investigation—including the autopsies—would be handled under federal jurisdiction instead of county or state. And Director Mueller had personally insisted that the bodies be brought to the District, especially the one dead agent.

There were still no IDs being issued. Tully knew it was the identity of the fallen agent that had Cunningham jerking around in his seat, looking for things to occupy his hands and readjusting his headset every few seconds as if a new radio frequency would bring him new information. Tully wished his boss would sit still. He could feel the extra motion shake the helicopter, even though he realized it was probably scientifically impossible to do so. Or was it?

As the pilot skimmed the treetops looking for a clearing to land, Tully tried not to think of the rattle under his seat. It sounded suspiciously like loose nuts and bolts. Instead, he tried to remember if he had left enough cash on the kitchen table for Emma. Was today her school field trip? Or was it this weekend? Why didn't he write these things down? Although shouldn't she be old enough and responsible enough to remember on her own? And why didn't this get any easier?

Lately, it seemed as though all his parenting had been learned the hard way. Well, if the field trip was today maybe it wouldn't hurt for Emma to learn a few lessons. If he shortchanged her, maybe it would finally convince her to look for a part-time job. After all, she was fifteen years old. When Tully was fifteen he was working after school and in the summers, pumping gas at Ozzie's 66 for two dollars an hour. Had things changed that drastically since he was a teenager? Then he stopped himself. That was thirty years ago, a lifetime ago. How could it be thirty years?

The helicopter began its descent and Tully's stomach flipped up into his chest, bringing him back to the present. The pilot had decided to take them down on a patch of grass no bigger than a doormat. Tully wanted to close his eyes. He stared at a rip in the back of the pilot's leather seat. It didn't help. The sight of stuffing and springs only reminded Tully of the nuts and bolts rolling loose underneath him, probably disconnecting the landing gear.

For all his anxiety, the helicopter was grounded in seconds with a bounce, a thump and one last flip of Tully's stomach. He thought about Agent O'Dell and wondered if he would rather have traded places with her. Then he thought about watching Wenhoff slicing into dead bodies. Easy answer. No contest. He'd still take the helicopter ride, loose screws and all.

A uniformed soldier had come out of the woods to meet them. Tully hadn't thought about it, but it made sense that the Massachusetts National Guard would be brought in to secure the expansive wooded area. The soldier waited in military stance, while Tully and Cunningham pulled their belongings off the helicopter—an assortment of rain gear, a Coleman thermos and two briefcases—all the while trying to keep their heads down and their necks from being whiplashed by the powerful blades. When they were clear, Cunningham waved to the pilot, and the helicopter didn't hesitate, taking off and scattering leaves, a sudden downpour of crackling red and gold.

"Sirs, if you follow me, I'll take you to the site." He reached for Cunningham's briefcase, knowing immediately which of them to suck up to. Tully was impressed. Cunningham, however, wouldn't be rushed, holding up a hand.

"I need to know names," Cunningham said. It wasn't a question. It was a demand.

"I'm not authorized to—"

"I understand that," Cunningham interrupted. "I promise you won't get in trouble, but if you know, you need to tell me. I need to know now."

The soldier took up his military stance again, not flinching and holding Cunningham's gaze. He seemed determined to not divulge any secrets. Cunningham must have realized what he was up against, because Tully couldn't believe what he heard his boss say next.

"Please, tell me," Cunningham said in a quiet, almost conciliatory tone.

Without knowing the assistant director, the soldier must have recognized what it had taken for him to say this. The man relaxed his stance and his face softened.

"I honestly can't tell you all their names, but the one who was killed was a Special Agent Delaney."

"Richard Delaney?"

"Yes, sir. I believe so, sir. He was the HRT—the Hostage Rescue Team—negotiator. From what I heard, he had them ready to talk. They invited him into the cabin, then opened fire. The bastards. Sorry, sir."

"No, don't apologize. And thank you for telling me."

The soldier turned to lead them through the trees, but Tully wondered if Cunningham would manage the trek. His face had gone white; his usual straight-backed walk seemed a bit wobbly.

With only a quick glance at Tully, he said, "I fucked up big time. I just sent Agent O'Dell to autopsy a friend of hers."

Tully knew this case would be different. Just the idea that Cunningham would use the words *please* and *fucked* in the same day, let alone the same hour, was not a good sign.

# CHAPTER 4

Maggie accepted the cool, damp towel from Stan and avoided his eyes. With only a quick glance, she could see his concern. He *had* to be concerned. Judging from the towel's softness, she could tell it had come from Stan's own privately laundered stash, unlike the institutional stiff ones that smelled like Clorox. The man had a cleaning obsession, a fetish that seemed contradictory to his profession; a profession that included a weekly, if not daily, dose of blood and body parts. She didn't question his kindness, however, and without a single word, took the towel and rested her face in its cool, plush texture, waiting for the nausea to pass.

She hadn't thrown up at the sight of a dead body since her initiation into the Behavioral Science Unit. She still remembered her first crime scene: spaghetti streaks of blood on the walls of a hot, fly-infested double-wide trailer. The blood's owner had been decapitated and hanging by a dislocated ankle from a hook in the ceiling like a butchered chicken left to jerk and drain out, which explained the blood-streaked walls. Since then, she had seen comparable, if not worse—body parts in take-out containers and mutilated little boys. But one thing she had never seen, one thing she had never had to do, was look down into a body bag soaked with the blood, cerebral spinal fluid and the brain matter of a friend.

"Cunningham should have told you," Stan said, now watching her from across the room, keeping his distance as if her condition might be contagious.

"I'm sure he didn't know. He and Agent Tully were just leaving for the scene when he called me."

"Well, he'll certainly understand you not assisting me." He sounded relieved—no, pleased—with the prospect of not having her shadow him all morning. Maggie smiled into the towel. Good ol' Stan was back to his normal self.

"I can have a couple autopsy reports ready for you by noon." He was washing his hands again, as if preparing the damp towel for her had somehow contaminated his precious hands.

The urge to escape was overwhelming. Her empty but churning stomach was reason enough to do just that. Yet there was something that nagged at her. She remembered an early morning less than a year ago in a Kansas City hotel room. Special Agent Richard Delaney had been concerned about her mental stability, so much so that he had risked their friendship to make sure she was safe. After almost five months of him and Agent Preston Turner playing her bodyguards, protecting her from a serial killer named Albert Stucky, it had come down to that early morning confrontation, Delaney pitting his stubbornness against hers all because he wanted to protect her.

However, at the time, she had refused to see it as protection. She had refused to simply see it as his attempt to, once again, play the role of her surrogate big brother. No, at the time, she had been mad as hell at him. In fact, that was the last time she had spoken to him. Now here he lay in a black nylon body bag, unable to accept her apology for being so pigheaded. Perhaps the least she could do was to make certain he received the respect he deserved. Nausea or not, she owed him that.

"I'll be okay," she said.

Stan glanced at her over his shoulder as he prepared his shiny instruments for the first boy's autopsy. "Of course you will be."

"No, I mean I'm staying."

This time he scowled at her over his protective goggles, and she knew she had made the right decision. Now, if only her stomach would agree.

"Did they find the spent cartridge?" she asked as she put on a fresh pair of gloves.

"Yes. It's over on the counter in one of the evidence bags. Looks like a high-powered rifle. I haven't taken a close look yet."

"So we know cause of death beyond a doubt?"

"Oh, you betcha. No need for a second shot."

"And there's no mistaking the entrance wound or the exit wound?"

"No. I imagine it won't be difficult to figure out."

"Good. Then we won't need to cut him. We can make our report from an external examination."

This time Stan stopped and turned to stare at her, then said, "Margaret, I hope you're not suggesting that I stop short of doing a full autopsy?"

"No, I'm not suggesting that."

He relaxed and picked up his instruments before she added, "I'm not suggesting it, Stan. I'm insisting you don't do a full autopsy. And believe me, you don't want to fight me on this one."

She ignored his glare and unzipped the rest of Agent Delaney's body bag, praying her knees would hold her up. She needed to think of his wife, Karen, who had always hated Delaney being an FBI agent almost as much as Maggie's soon-to-be ex-husband, Greg, hated her being one. It was time to think of Karen and the two little girls who would grow up without a daddy. If Maggie could do nothing else, she'd make certain they didn't have to see him mutilated any more than necessary.

The thought brought back memories of Maggie's own father, the image of him lying in the huge mahogany casket, wearing a brown suit Maggie had never seen him in before. And his hair—it had been all wrong—combed in a way he would never have worn it. The mortician had tried to paint over the burned flesh and salvage what pieces of skin were still there, but it wasn't enough. As a twelve-year-old girl, Maggie had been horrified by the sight and nauseated by the smell of some sort of perfume that couldn't mask that overpowering odor of ashes and burned flesh. That smell. There was nothing close nor worse than the smell of burned flesh. God! She could smell it now. And the priest's words hadn't helped: *You are dust and unto dust you shall return, ashes to ashes.*

That smell, those words and the sight of her father's body had haunted her childhood dreams for weeks as she tried to remember what he looked like before he lay in that casket, before those images of him turned to dust in her memories.

She remembered how terribly frightened she had been seeing him like that. She remembered the crinkle of plastic under his clothes, his mummy-wrapped hands tucked down at his sides. She remembered being concerned about the blisters on his cheek.

"Did it hurt, Daddy?" she had whispered to him.

She had waited until her mother and the others weren't looking. Then Maggie had gathered all of her child-size strength and courage and reached her small hand over the edge of the smooth, shiny wood and the satin bedding. With her fingertips she had brushed her father's hair back off his forehead, trying to ignore the plastic feel of his skin and that hideous Frankenstein scar at his scalp. But despite her fear, she had to rearrange his hair. She had to put it back to the way he always liked to wear it, to the way she remembered it. She needed her last image of him to be one she recognized. It was a small, silly thing, but it had made her feel better.

Now, looking down at Delaney's peaceful gray face, Maggie knew she needed to do whatever she could, so that two more little girls wouldn't be horrified to look at their daddy's face one last time.

# CHAPTER 5

*Suffolk County, Massachusetts*

Eric Pratt stared at the two men, wondering which of them would be the one to kill him. They were seated facing him, so close their knees brushed against his. So close he could see the older man's jaw muscles clench every time he stopped chewing. Spearmint. It was definitely spearmint gum he was grinding his teeth into.

Neither looked like Satan. They had introduced themselves as Tully and Cunningham. Eric had been able to hear that much through the fog. Both men looked clean-cut—close-cropped hair, no dirt beneath their fingernails. The older one even wore nerdy wire-rimmed glasses. No, they looked nothing like Eric had expected Satan to look. And just like the others now crawling around the cabin floor and combing the woods outside, these guys wore the navy-blue windbreakers with the yellow letters, FBI.

The younger one had on a blue tie, pulled loose, his shirt collar unbuttoned. The other wore a red tie, cinched tight at the buttoned collar of a brilliant white shirt. Red, white and blue, with those government letters emblazoned across their backs. Why hadn't he thought of it before? Of course Satan would come disguised, wrapped in symbolic colors. Father was right. Yes, of course, he was always right. Why had he doubted Father? He should have obeyed, not doubted, not taken his chances with the enemy. What a fool he had been.

Eric scratched at the lice still digging into his scalp, digging deeper and deeper. Could Satan's soldiers hear the scratching sounds? Or perhaps they were the ones making the imaginary lice dig into his skull. Satan had powers, after all. Incredible powers he could transmit through his soldiers. Powers that Eric knew could easily inflict pain without so much as a touch.

The one called Tully was saying something to him, lips moving, eyes burrowing into Eric's, but Eric had turned down the volume hours ago. Or was it days ago? He couldn't remember how much time had passed. He couldn't remember how long he had been in this cabin, how long he had sat in this straight-backed chair with his wrists handcuffed and his feet in shackles, waiting for the inevitable torture to begin. He had no sense of time, but he did know the exact moment his system had begun to shut down. The exact second his mind had gone numb. It was the instant that David dropped to the floor, the thud of his body forcing Eric to risk opening his eyes. That was when he found himself staring directly into David's eyes, their faces only inches apart.

Eric had seen his friend's mouth open. Thought he heard a faint whisper, three words, no more. Maybe it had been Eric's imagination, because David's eyes were already empty when the words "He tricked us" left his lips. He must have heard his friend wrong. Satan hadn't tricked them at all. They had tricked him, instead. Hadn't they?

Suddenly, the men were scrambling to their feet. Eric braced himself as best he could, closed fists, shoulders hunched, head down. Only there were no blows, no bullets, no wounds inflicted of any kind. And their voices melted together, the hysteria in them breaking through Eric's self-imposed barrier.

"We need to get out of the cabin. Now."

Eric twisted around in the chair, just as one of the men pulled him to his feet and started to shove him toward the door. He saw another man, with some weird contraption mounted on top of his head, come up out of the floorboards. Of course, they had found the hidden arsenal. Father would be disappointed. They had needed that stockpile of weapons to fight Satan. Their mission had failed before they could deliver them back to their home camp. Yes, Father would be very disappointed. They had let everyone down. Maybe more lives would be lost, because all the weapons that had taken months to amass would now be confiscated and put under Satan's control. Precious lives might be lost because they had failed their mission. How could Father protect any of them without these weapons?

The men shoved and pulled at him, hurrying out the cabin door and down into the woods. Eric didn't understand. What were they running from? He tried to listen, tried to hear. He wanted to know what could possibly frighten Satan's soldiers.

They gathered around the man with the strange headgear, who brought out a metal box with blinking lights and odd wires. Eric had no idea what it was, but it sounded like the man had found it down with the weapons.

"There's an arsenal underneath large enough to blow this place to kingdom come."

Eric couldn't help but smile and immediately felt a jab to his kidneys. He wanted to tell Mr. Tully, the owner of the elbow in his back, that he wasn't smiling about them being blown up, but rather at the idea that any of them believed they would ever be allowed into the Kingdom of God.

No one else noticed his smile. They focused on the dark-haired man with the crazy gogglelike contraption now pushed up on top of his head, reminding Eric of some life-size insect.

"Tell us something we don't already know," one of the men challenged.

"Okay. How about this. The entire cabin is wired," the insect man told them.

"Shit!"

"It gets even better. This is only a secondary switch." He showed them the metal box he held. "The real detonator's off-site." Then he pointed to the blinking red button and flipped a switch. The light shut off. Within seconds it snapped back on, blinking again like a pulsing red eye.

The men turned and twisted, craning their necks and looking around them. Some of them had their guns drawn. Even Eric's head pivoted, his eyes suddenly clear and squinting into the shadows of the woods. He didn't understand. He wondered if David had known about the metal box.

"Where is it?" demanded the big guy with no neck, the one everyone seemed to treat as being in charge, the only one dressed in a navy blazer instead of a windbreaker. "Where's the goddamn detonator?"

It took Eric a minute to realize the man was asking him. He met his eyes and stared like he had been taught, looking directly into the black pupils and not blinking, not flinching, not letting the enemy win even one word.

"Hold on a minute," the one named Cunningham said. "Why wouldn't they want the detonator inside the cabin, so they could control when and how to blow it up? We already know they were willing to take their own lives. So why not do it by blowing themselves and the arsenal up?"

"Maybe they still intend to blow us up." And there was more shuffling, more worried heads pivoting.

Eric wanted to tell them Father would never blow up the cabin. He couldn't sacrifice the weapons. Father needed them to fight, to continue to fight. Instead, he simply transferred his stare to Cunningham, who not only held his gaze but bore into him as if his powers could wrench out the truth with only a look. A knot in Eric's stomach twisted, but he didn't blink. He couldn't show weakness.

"No, if they wanted to blow us up, we'd already be dead," Cunningham continued without looking away. "I think the real targets are already dead. I think their leader just wanted to make sure they did the right thing."

Eric listened. It was a trick. Satan was testing him. Seeing if he would flinch. Father wanted to save them from being taken alive and tortured. This was simply the beginning of that torture, and Satan's soldier, this Cunningham, knew his job well. His eyes wouldn't let Eric go, but he wouldn't blink. He couldn't look away. He had to ignore the thunder of his heart in his ears, and the knot tightening in his gut.

"The detonator," Cunningham said without a single blink of his own eyes, "may have been a backup plan. If they didn't swallow their death pills, he was prepared to blow them to pieces. Some leader you have, kid."

Eric wouldn't take the bait. Father would never do such a thing. They had voluntarily given up their lives. No one had forced them. Eric simply hadn't been strong enough to join them. He was weak. He was a coward. For a moment he had dared to lose faith. He had not been a brave, loyal warrior like the others, but he wouldn't show weakness now. He wouldn't give in.

Then suddenly, Eric remembered David's last words. "He tricked us." Eric thought David had meant Satan. But what if he meant…? It wasn't possible. Father had only wanted to save them from being tortured. Hadn't he? Father wouldn't trick them. Would he?

Cunningham waited, watching and catching Eric as he blinked. That's when he said, "I wonder if your precious leader knows you're still alive? Do you suppose he'll come to your rescue, just like he did last night?"

But Eric was no longer sure of anything as he stared at the metal box flashing its strange lights, red and green, stop and go, life and death, heaven and hell. Maybe David and the others were not only the brave ones; now Eric wondered if perhaps they were also the lucky ones.

# CHAPTER 6

*SATURDAY*
*November 23*
*Arlington National Cemetary*

Maggie O'Dell gripped the lapels of her jacket into a fist, bracing herself for another gust of wind. She regretted leaving her trench coat in the car. She'd ripped it off in the church, blaming the stupid coat for her feeling of suffocation. Now, here in the cemetery, amid the black-clad mourners and stone tombstones, she wished she had something, anything, from which she could draw warmth.

She stood back and watched the group huddle together, surrounding the family under the canopy, intent on protecting them from the wind, as though compensating for the mistakes that had brought them all here today. She recognized many of them in their standard dark suits and their trained solemn faces. Except in the middle of this graveyard, even those bulges under their jackets couldn't prevent them from looking vulnerable, stripped by the wind of their government-issue, straight-backed posture.

Watching from the fringes, Maggie was grateful for her colleagues' protective instincts. Grateful they prevented her from seeing the faces of Karen and the two little girls who would grow up without their daddy. She didn't want to witness any more of their grief, their pain; a pain so palpable it threatened to demolish years of protective layers she had carefully constructed to hide and stifle her own grief, her own pain. Standing back here, she hoped to stay safe.

Despite the crisp autumn gusts attacking her bare legs and snapping at her skirt, her palms were sweaty. Her knees wavered. Some invisible force knocked at her heart. Jesus! What the hell was wrong with her? Ever since she opened that body bag and saw Delaney's lifeless face, she had been a wreck of nerves, conjuring up ghosts from the past—images and words better left buried. She sucked in deep breaths, despite the cold air stinging her lungs. This sting, this discomfort, was preferable to the sting the memories could bring.

After twenty-one years, it annoyed her that funerals could still reduce her to that twelve-year-old girl. Without will or warning, she remembered it all as though it had happened yesterday. She could see her father's casket lowered into the ground. She could feel her mother tugging at her arm, demanding that Maggie toss a handful of dirt on top of the casket's shiny surface. And now, in a matter of minutes, she knew the lone bugler's version of taps would be enough to knot her stomach.

She wanted to leave. No one would notice, all of them wrapped in their own memories or vulnerabilities. Except that she owed it to Delaney to be here. Their last conversation had been one of anger and betrayal. It was too late for apologies, but perhaps her being here would bring her a sense of resolution, if not absolution.

The wind whipped at her again, swirling dried and crackling leaves like spirits rising up and sailing between the graves. The howl and ghostly moans sent additional chills down Maggie's back. As a child, she had felt the spirits of the dead, surrounding her, taunting her, laughing at her, whispering that they had taken away her father. That was the first time she had felt the incredible aloneness, which continued to stick to her like that handful of wet dirt she had squeezed between her fingers, squeezing tight while her mother insisted she toss it.

"Do it, Maggie," she could still hear her mother say. "Just do it already and get it over with" had been her mother's impatient words, her concern more of embarrassment than of her daughter's grief.

A gloved hand touched Maggie's shoulder. She jumped and resisted the instinct to reach inside her jacket for her gun.

"Sorry, Agent O'Dell. I didn't mean to startle you." Assistant

Director Cunningham's hand lingered on her shoulder, his eyes straight ahead, watching.

Maggie thought she was the only one who had not joined the group gathered around the freshly cut grave, the dark hole in the ground that would house Special Agent Richard Delaney's body. Why had he been so cocky, so stupid?

As if reading her mind, Cunningham said, "He was a good man, an excellent negotiator."

Maggie wanted to ask, Why then was he here rather than at home with his wife and girls, preparing for a Saturday afternoon of watching college football with the gang? Instead, she whispered, "He was the best."

Cunningham fidgeted at her side, shoving his hands deep into his trench coat's pockets. She realized that, although he would never embarrass her by offering his coat, he stood in such a way that protected her from the wind. But he hadn't sought her out just to be her windbreak. She could see there was something on his mind. After almost ten years, she recognized the pursed lips and furrowed brow, the agitated shifting from one foot to the other, all subtle but telling signs for a man who normally defined the term *professional.*

Maggie waited, surprised that he, too, appeared to be waiting for some appropriate time.

"Do we know anything more about these men—what group they belonged to?" She tried to coax him, keeping her voice low, but they were far enough back that the wind would never allow them to be overheard.

"Not yet. They weren't much more than boys. Boys with enough guns and ammo to take over a small country. But someone else, someone was definitely behind this. Some fanatical leader who doesn't mind sacrificing his own. We'll find out soon enough. Maybe when we dig up who owns that cabin." He pushed at the bridge of his glasses and immediately replaced his hand into his pocket. "I owe you an apology, Agent O'Dell."

Here it was, yet he hesitated. His uncomfortable behavior surprised and unnerved Maggie. It reminded her of the knot in her stomach and the ache in her chest. She didn't want to talk about this, didn't want the reminder. She wanted to think of something else, anything other than the image of Delaney crumpling to the ground. With little effort, she could still hear the sloshing of his brains and see the pieces of his skull in the body bag.

"You don't owe me an apology, sir. You didn't know," she finally said, letting the pause last too long.

Still keeping his eyes straight ahead and his voice quiet, he said, "I should have checked before I sent you. I know how difficult that must have been for you."

Maggie glanced up at him. Her boss's face remained as stoic as usual, but there was a twitch of emotion at the corner of his mouth. She followed his eyes to the line of military men who were now marching onto the cemetery and into position.

*Oh, God. Here we go.*

Maggie's knees grew unsteady. Immediately, she broke into a cold sweat. She wanted to escape, and now she wished Cunningham wasn't right next to her. However, he didn't seem to notice her discomfort. Instead, he stood at attention as the rifles clicked and clacked into position.

Maggie jumped at each gunshot, closing her eyes against the memories and wishing they would stay the hell away. She could still hear her mother warning her, scolding her, "Don't you dare cry, Maggie. It'll only make your face all red and puffy."

She hadn't cried then, and she wouldn't cry now. But when the bugle began its lonesome song, she was shivering and biting her lower lip. Damn you, Delaney, she wanted to curse out loud. She had long ago decided God had a cruel sense of humor—or perhaps He simply wasn't paying attention anymore.

The crowd suddenly opened to release a small girl out from under the tent, a piece of bright blue spilling between the black, like a tiny blue bird in a flock of black crows. Maggie recognized Delaney's younger daughter, Abby, dressed in a royal-blue coat and matching hat and being led by her grandmother, Delaney's mother. They were headed straight for Maggie and Cunningham, and they were about to destroy any hopes Maggie had of trying to isolate herself.

"Miss Abigail insists she cannot wait to use the rest room," Mrs. Delaney said to Maggie as they approached. "Do you have any idea where one might be?"

Cunningham pointed to the main building behind them, hidden by the slope of the hill and the trees surrounding it. Mrs. Delaney took one look and her entire red-blotched face seemed to fall into a frown, as though she faced one more hill than she could possibly endure on this day of endless hills.

"I can take her," Maggie volunteered before realizing she might be the worst possible person to comfort the girl. But surely, bathroom duty was something she could handle.

"Do you mind, Abigail? Would it be okay for Agent O'Dell to take you to the rest room?"

"Agent O'Dell?" The little girl's face scrunched up as she looked around, trying to find the person her grandmother was talking about. Then suddenly, she said, "Oh, you mean Maggie? Her name's Maggie, Grandma."

"Yes, I'm sorry. I mean Maggie. Is it okay if you go with her?"

But Abby had already taken Maggie's hand. "We need to hurry," she told her, without looking up and pulling Maggie in the direction she had seen Cunningham point.

Maggie wondered if the four-year-old had any understanding of what had happened or why they were even at the cemetery. However, Maggie was simply relieved that her only task at the moment was to fight the wind and trek up the hill, leaving behind all those memories and wisps of spirits riding the wind. But as they got to the building that towered over the rows of white crosses and gray tombstones, Abby stopped and turned around to look back. The wind whipped at her blue coat, and Maggie could see her shiver. She felt the small hand squeeze tight the fingers it had managed to wrap around.

"Are you okay, Abby?"

She nodded twice, setting her hat bouncing. Then her chin stayed tucked down. "I hope he doesn't get cold," Abby said. Maggie's heart took a plunge.

What should she say to her? How could she explain something that even she didn't understand? She was thirty-three years old and still missed her own father, still couldn't understand why he had been ripped away from her all those years ago. Years that should have healed the gaping wound that easily became exposed at the sound of a stupid bugle or the sight of a casket being lowered into the ground.

Before Maggie could offer any consolation, the girl looked up at her and said, "I made Mommy put a blanket in there with him." Then, as if satisfied by the memory, she turned back toward the door and pulled Maggie along, ready to continue with the task at hand. "A blanket and a flashlight," she added. "So he'll be warm and not scared of the dark. Just till he gets to God's house."

Maggie couldn't help but smile. Perhaps she could learn a thing or two from this wise four-year-old.

# CHAPTER 7

*Washington, D.C.*

Justin Pratt sat on the steps of the Jefferson Memorial, pretending to rest his feet. Yeah, his feet were sore, but that wasn't why he wanted to escape. For hours they had been walking between the monuments, handing out pamphlets to touring groups of giggling and shouting high school kids. They had hit the city at the right time—fall field trips. There must have been more than fifty groups from across the country. And they were all a fucking pain in the ass. It was hard to believe he was only about a year or two older than some of these idiots.

No, the real reason Justin had excused himself involved much more sinister thoughts than sore feet; illicit thoughts, according to the gospel of Reverend Joseph Everett and his followers. Jesus, would he ever get used to calling himself one of those followers, one of the chosen few? Probably not as long as he took breaks from handing out the word of God, only to sit back and admire Alice Hamlin's breasts.

She looked up and waved at him as if she had read his thoughts. He fidgeted. Maybe he should take off his shoes to play up the sore-feet thing. Or had she already figured him out? She certainly couldn't mind. Why else would she have worn such a tight pink sweater? Especially on a bus trip where they were to spend the day handing out godly propaganda. And then later, in about an hour, they'd be at the fucking prayer rally.

Jesus! He needed to watch his language.

He looked around, checking to see if any of Father's little messengers could hear his thoughts. After all, Father sure as hell made it appear that he could. The man seemed to be telepathic or whatever that term was for reading people's minds. It was downright spooky.

He grabbed one of the pamphlets so Alice would think he took their job seriously and maybe not notice that breast thing. The slick four-color pamphlets were pretty impressive with the word *freedom* in raised letters. What did Alice call it? Embossing? Very professional. It even included a color photograph of Reverend Everett and listed on the back the entire schedule of future prayer rallies, city by city. From the looks of the brochure, you'd think they could afford to eat something better than beans and rice seven days a week.

When he looked back at Alice, a new group of potential recruits had surrounded her. They listened and watched intently as her face and gestures became animated. She was three years older than Justin, an older woman. Just the idea gave him a hard-on. She didn't have much street smarts, but she knew stuff about so many different things. She amazed him. Like all the quotes of Jefferson's she had memorized. She recited them before they got up all the steps to read them off the walls. She kicked ass when it came to that history crap. And she knew that one-two-three thing about Jefferson. That he was the first secretary of something or another, second vice president and third president. How could she even remember that fucking shit?

It was one of the many things Justin admired about her. That had to be a good sign, that he didn't care only about her great pair of tits, which had usually been the case with him and girls in the past. In fact, there was a whole list of things he liked about Alice. For one thing, she could make religion sound almost as exciting as if it were some fucking NASCAR race to heaven. And he liked the way she looked into her listeners' eyes as though they were the only souls on earth for that moment. Alice Hamlin could make a suicidal maniac feel special and forget why he was out teetering on a ledge. Or at least, that's how she made Justin feel. After all, he had been that suicidal maniac just a couple months ago.

Sometimes he still felt it, that restlessness, that urge to just forget about everything and stop trying so hard to make it look like he had his shit together. Especially now that Eric had left him and was off on some mission.

In fact, he had felt the urge as recently as this morning when he found himself wondering how he might take the blades out of his plastic disposable razor. He knew if the veins at the wrists were cut vertically instead of horizontally that a person bled to death much quicker. Most people fucked it up and did the horizontal thing. Cutting himself didn't bother him. Getting his tattoo probably hurt a hell of a lot more than slitting your wrists.

Alice was bringing a group of girls up the stairs toward him. She'd want to introduce him. Earlier she had told him he was cute enough to convince any girl to attend Father's rally. Words didn't usually mean a fucking thing to Justin. Not after a lifetime of people telling him stuff. But when Alice said stuff, it was hard not to believe her. So he didn't mind. Besides, he enjoyed watching girls walk up steps. Of course, he'd much rather be watching from behind, but this view wasn't bad.

It was a chilly day and yet all three wore short-sleeved blouses. One even had on a tight knit top, cut short to show her flat stomach. It was a false indicator of a wanna-be wild side, since even from this distance, Justin could see the belly button was pierce-free. But it was still nice to look at.

Now, if they'd just shut up. Did all high school girls have that same high-pitched giggle? Where the fuck did they learn that squeal? It grated on his nerves, but he smiled, anyway, and offered a cute little tip of his baseball cap that only seemed to set them off again, but an octave higher. Dogs had to be pitching their ears for miles.

"Justin, I want you to meet some of my new friends."

Alice and the three girls stopped in front of him, right at crotch level, and suddenly he forgot about sore feet or even Alice's perfectly shaped tits—for a few minutes, anyway. The tall blonde and her shorter counterpart shielded their eyes from a momentary and rare appearance of the sun. The third one, a short girl with dark eyes, looked older up close. She wasn't afraid to meet his eyes like the blonde and her bookend.

"This is Emma, Lisa and Ginny. Emma and Lisa are best friends from Reston, Virginia. Ginny lives here in the District. They never met each other before today, and see, we're already good friends."

The two blondes giggled and the tall one said, "Actually, her name is Alesha, but she hates that, so we shortened it to Lisa."

"Well, my name is really Virginia," the dark-eyed girl told them, only it came out as though it was a competition, and she needed to outdo her new friends.

"No way," the blondes said in practiced unison.

"My dad thought it would be cute since we're from Virginia. Which, by the way, my dad would kill me if he knew I was attending this sort of thing tonight. He hates this kind of stuff." This she said to Alice, and like the name thing, she made it sound like a challenge instead of a simple statement.

Justin watched for Alice's reaction. This girl wasn't exactly a prize recruit, and Justin wondered why Alice had even invited her to stay for the prayer rally. Already Ms. Ginny-my-name-is-really-Virginia was showing signs of doubt. That was supposed to be a big red flag. Next there would be questions. Father hated questions.

"We can't always rely on our parents to guide us in the correct direction," Alice told her with a smile, sounding like a mother herself, and the girl nodded, pretending to know exactly what Alice meant, because Alice was too cool to disagree with or contradict.

Justin crossed his arms over his chest. It was all he could do to keep from rolling his eyes.

A scuffle at the bottom of the steps made them all jerk around, the girls rocking on ridiculous platform shoes while trying not to fall down the steps. Justin got to his feet, climbing a few more steps to get a better look. Down below, a James Dean look-alike was shoving at an older guy while he tried to yank the man's camera out of his hands.

"Wow! He's really cute," the one called Ginny managed to say without a squeal.

Justin sat back down with a sigh of frustration that no one noticed. Leave it to fuckin' Brandon to steal all the attention.

# CHAPTER 8

Ben Garrison knew a thing or two about causing pain. The kid was younger and taller, but Ben knew he was stronger and definitely wiser. This hothead would last about five seconds if Ben shot a hand to his throat and squeezed in just the right place.

"No fucking reporters, Garrison. How many times do we have to tell you that?" the kid screamed at him.

He grabbed at Ben's Leica, managing to yank the strap wrapped around Ben's neck. The 35 mm camera was almost as old as Ben and probably tougher. Hell, it had survived a stampede of caribou in Manitoba and getting dropped in an Egyptian sand dune. It could certainly survive some pissed off religious freak.

"Why no reporters? What is your precious leader afraid of? Huh?" Ben egged him on. He knew this kid from the short visit he had paid to their camp at the foot of the Appalachian Mountains. Hell, he even kind of liked the kid. From what he had seen in the past, this kid, this Brandon, had a lot of passion, a lot of fire in his belly, but he didn't have a clue as to what to do with it.

Brandon swiped at the camera again, and this time Ben gave him a shove that sent him onto his backside. Now the kid's red face almost matched his red, goop-backed hair. He looked up at Ben like a bull, revving up and getting ready to charge. Ben could see his nostrils flaring and his hands balling into fists.

"Give it up, kid." Ben laughed at him and snapped a couple of shots to prove the kid couldn't rattle him. "Reverend Everett may have tossed me out of his hideout, but he isn't gonna get rid of me that easy. Why doesn't he send a real man to do a real man's job?"

Brandon was back on his feet, his jaw and teeth clenched,

his hands ready at his sides. Ben imagined little clouds of steam coming out of his ears like in the comic strips. The kid would need more than those accompanying bubbles of "Pow" and "Wham" to scare off Ben Garrison. Hell, he had survived an Aborigine's blow dart and a Tutsi's swipe of a machete. Like the Leica, he had seen a few death battles before, and this wasn't one of them. Not even close. Poor kid. And with all his precious little friends watching. But there was no Reverend Everett to swoop in and save the souls of his little lost fools.

A crowd had gathered, hiking up the Jefferson Memorial steps to get a better look, but they kept their distance. Even the gang of young men, the redhead's gang, circled like dogs in heat, but yellow-bellied dogs that stayed out of the way. Ben scratched his bristled jaw, bored with the whole thing. He had spent the afternoon getting some lame shots of tight-assed, hipless nymphettes. A few he had recognized. One he had even followed for a while, hoping for a risqué *Enquirer* shot, to embarrass her big-shot daddy. He'd stay and get a few of the prayer rally, with the precious, fucking Reverend Joseph Everett in action. This poor excuse of a rebel without a cause wouldn't stop him. They couldn't stop him, especially if they insisted on using public property.

He walked up several steps, leaving the hothead to snort and stomp and pretend to be choosing the godly thing of turning the other cheek. In the distance, Ben could see people starting to flock to the FDR Memorial.

It surprised him that Everett had chosen this spot for his rally in the District, especially over the Jefferson Memorial. Jefferson seemed more in tune with Everett's philosophy of individual freedoms and limited government. Hell, hadn't FDR put into place some of the very government programs Everett abhorred? The good reverend was a complicated piece of shit. But Ben was determined to expose the bastard for what he really was. And it would take more than this hotheaded punk to stop him.

# CHAPTER 9

*FBI Headquarters*
*Washington, D.C.*

Maggie waited for Keith Ganza to finish the work she had interrupted. He was used to her barging into his lab at FBI headquarters, whether invited or not—usually not. And although he grumbled about it, she knew he didn't mind, even late on a Saturday afternoon when everyone else had already called it a day and left.

As the head of the FBI crime lab, Ganza had seen more in his thirty-plus years than any one person should ever see. Yet he seemed to take it all in stride, unruffled—unlike his outward appearance—by any of it. As Maggie waited and watched his tall, thin frame hunched over a microscope, she wondered if she had ever seen him in anything other than a white lab coat, or rather a yellowed-at-the-collar, wrinkled lab coat with sleeves too short for his long arms.

Maggie knew she shouldn't be here—she should wait for the official report. But four-year-old Abby's tenacity had only strengthened Maggie's resolve to find out who was responsible for Delaney's murder. Which reminded her—she pulled out a string of red licorice Abby had given her and began unwrapping it. Ganza stopped at the sound of crinkling plastic and glanced up at her over the microscope and over his half glasses that sat at the end of his nose. He looked at her with a familiar frown, one that remained in place, whether he was delivering a joke, talking about evidence or, in this case, staring at her impatiently.

"I haven't eaten today," she offered as an explanation.

"There's half a tuna salad sandwich in the frig."

She knew his offer to be generous and sincere, however, she had never gotten used to eating anything that had spent time on a shelf next to blood and tissue samples.

"No, thanks," she told him. "I'm meeting Gwen in a little while for dinner."

"So you buy licorice to tide you over?" Another frown.

"No. I got this at Agent Delaney's funeral."

"They were handing out red licorice?"

"His daughter was. Are you ready for me to interrupt you yet?"

"You mean you haven't already?"

Her turn to frown. "Very funny."

"I'm getting the file to A.D. Cunningham first thing Monday morning. Can't you wait until then?"

Without answering, she folded the long string of licorice, holding it up in front of her to measure, then pulling it apart at the fold. She handed him one section of candy. He took the bribe without hesitation. Satisfied, he left his microscope, began nibbling at the candy and searched the counter for a file folder.

"It was potassium cyanide in the capsules. About ninety percent with a mixture of potassium hydroxide, some carbonate and a smidge of potassium chloride."

"How difficult is it to get your hands on potassium cyanide these days?"

"Not difficult. It's used in a lot of industries. Usually as a cleaning solution or fixative. It's used in making plastics, some photographic development processes, even in fumigating ships. There was about seventy-five milligrams in the capsule the kid spit out. With little food in the digestive tract, that dose causes almost an instantaneous collapse and cessation of all respiration. Of course, that starts only after the plastic capsule is dissolved, but I'd say within minutes. Absorbs all the oxygen out of the cells. Not a pretty or fun way to die. The victims literally strangle to death from the inside out."

"So why not just stick their guns in their mouths like most teenage boys who commit suicide?" Both images bothered Maggie, and Ganza raised his eyebrows at the impatience and sarcasm in her voice.

"You know the answer to that as well as I do. Psychologically it's much easier to swallow a pill than pull the trigger, especially if you're not so keen on the idea to begin with."

"So you don't think this was their idea?"

"Do you?"

"I wish it were that simple." She ran her fingers through her hair, only now noticing the tangles. "They found a two-way radio inside the cabin, so they were in contact with someone. We just don't know who. And, of course, there was a huge arsenal underneath the cabin."

"Oh, yes, the arsenal." Ganza opened a file folder and shuffled through several pages. "We were able to track the serial numbers on about a dozen of the weapons."

"That was fast. I'm guessing they were stolen instead of bought at some gun show, right?"

"Not exactly." He pulled out several documents. "You're not going to like it."

"Try me."

"They came from a storage facility at Fort Bragg."

"So they *were* stolen."

"I didn't say that."

"Then what exactly did you say?" She came to stand at his side, looking over his arm at the document he had extracted.

"The military never knew they were missing."

"How is that possible?"

"They retired the weapons long ago, sent them to storage. Whoever got ahold of them would have had to have high-level clearance or some type of official access."

"You're kidding!"

"It gets even more interesting." He handed her an envelope stamped Document Department and motioned for her to open it.

Maggie pulled out several sheets of paper, which included a land title from the state of Massachusetts for ten acres of property, as well as for a cabin and docking rights to the Neponset River.

"Great," she said after scanning the copy. "So the land was donated to some nonprofit organization. These guys really know how to hide their tracks."

"Not that unusual," Ganza said. "A lot of these groups filter weapons and money, even property, through bogus NPOs. Saves them from paying taxes and allows them to thumb their noses at the government they profess to hate so much. That's usually all they have the courage to do."

"But this group is into more dangerous stuff than tax evasion. Whoever is behind this, this maniac's willing to sacrifice his own men…boys, really." Maggie flipped through the pages. "So what in the world is the Church of Spiritual Freedom? I've never heard of it before." She looked back up at Ganza, who shrugged his bony shoulders. "What the hell did Delaney get in the middle of?"

# CHAPTER 10

Justin wished he didn't have to stay for the prayer rally. After all, they had worked all day to get a good crowd here. Didn't they deserve a break? He was beat and starving. Would Father really be able to tell if he and Alice ducked out? Except he knew Alice would never go for it. She lived for these yawners and really seemed to get into the singing and clapping and hugging. Actually, he had to admit that he did enjoy the hugging. And tonight they had gathered some serious babes.

He watched Brandon talking to the blond bookends. Brandon was pointing at one of the granite walls. The one that had carved: Freedom of Speech, Freedom of Religion, Freedom From Want, Freedom From Fear. Justin had heard Father repeat those same words many times, especially when he got on a roll about the government and its conspiracies to suppress people. In fact, for a while Justin had thought the reverend had been the one who had come up with the words.

Whatever bullshit Brandon was telling them, Justin could tell the girls were eating it up. The tall one, Emma, kept flipping her hair back and tilting her head in that way high school girls must all learn in Flirting 101. Maybe that's where they learned that fucking giggle, too.

"Hey, Justin."

He felt a tap on his shoulder and turned to find Alice and the dark-eyed Ginny. The first thing he noticed was the big pretzel and can of Coke Ginny was holding. The smell of the pretzel made his stomach rattle. Both girls heard and laughed. Ginny handed him the pretzel.

"Want some?"

He glanced at Alice, checking for her disapproval, but she

was looking in the other direction, looking for someone, and immediately he wondered if it was Brandon.

"Maybe just a bite," he told Ginny.

He bent down and bit into the doughy pretzel, tugging a piece away while Ginny held it and pulled. It tasted wonderful, and he thought about asking for a second bite, but Ginny was already biting off a piece for herself from the same spot, licking her lips while her eyes met his. Jesus! She was coming on to him. He looked to see if Alice had noticed, but now she was waving to someone. He turned to find Father, flanked by his core group: several older women and one black man. Following close behind were three Arnold Schwarzenegger look-alikes, his bodyguards.

Justin thought Father looked more like a movie actor than a reverend. Earlier on the bus, he had even seen Cassie, Father's beautiful black assistant, applying makeup to the reverend's face. She had probably styled his hair, too. Father went way out for these rallies. Ordinarily, he wore his longish black hair slicked back, but today it stayed in place on its own, tucked neatly over his ears and collar just enough to be stylish and not shaggy. Later during the rally, when the man had what he called one of his "passionate moments," strands of hair would fall onto his forehead, sorta reminding Justin of Elvis Presley when he got all shook up. He wondered if Father would mind the comparison. He certainly wouldn't mind having people refer to him as "the King."

The rest of Father looked like a well-paid business executive. Tonight he wore a charcoal-gray suit, white shirt and red silk tie. The suits always looked expensive. Justin could tell. They looked like something his dad would wear, probably several thousand dollars a pop. And there were the gold cuff links, a Rolex watch and gold tie bar, all gifts from rich donors. Sorta pissed Justin off. Why were there always donors to buy expensive jewelry, but when it came to toilet paper, they had to use old newspapers? And it was shreds of old newspaper, at that—pieces too small to even provide any college football scores.

The sun had just set, only pink-purple stains remaining, yet

Father still wore his sunglasses. He took them off now as he approached. He smiled at Alice, reaching both his hands to her, waiting for her to do the same. Justin watched the reverend's hands swallow Alice's, his fingers overlapping onto her wrists and caressing her.

"Alice, my dear, who is your lovely guest?" He was smiling at Ginny, his eyes working their magic.

Ginny seemed flustered by the sudden attention, her hands clumsily trying to dispose of her pretzel and Coke. Justin started to offer to take them when she turned and tossed the precious pretzel into a nearby trash can. He wondered if everyone could hear his sigh of disappointment, but instead they were already mesmerized by Father's charm. Justin moved aside, not wanting to risk being shoved aside by one of the Schwarzenegger triplets. It had happened to him once before.

He sat down on one of the benches. Everyone was watching Father now, including Brandon and the blond bookends. Except that Brandon looked a little pissed. Justin wondered if he hated Father stealing the attention away from him.

Father took each of Ginny's hands, in the same way he had done with Alice, only now, probably because he knew he had everyone's attention, he was making a fucking ceremony out of it. He looked into her eyes, smiling down at her and going on and on about what a beautiful young woman she was. Ginny was even smaller than Alice, so the reverend's large hands practically wrapped around her entire forearms.

The skeptical Ginny, who had told them several times that her father would be so pissed if he knew she had come tonight, appeared to be eating up the attention. Justin had to admit the man was a charmer…a snake charmer. Just then, Father looked over at Justin and frowned.

*Jesus!* Justin thought. *Maybe the guy really could read minds.*

## CHAPTER 11

Ginny Brier could barely hear the clapping and singing from down below. Dried leaves crackled underneath them and a twig poked into her thigh. But all she paid attention to was Brandon panting in her ear as he fumbled with her blouse buttons.

"Careful, don't rip any," she whispered, which only seemed to make his fingers more urgent and reckless.

The back of his neck was wet, but she continued to caress him there, hoping it would calm him, though she liked how hot and bothered she could make him. She wondered if perhaps he hadn't done it in a long time or something. That would explain his fumbling. Or was he nervous they'd get caught? Did he worry that reverend guy would get mad if he found out? Actually, that was what turned Ginny on even more. She liked that this incredibly cool guy, who had been staring at her all evening, had come up behind her, taken her hand and led her around the back of the monument.

The sharp glare of the monument's lights didn't reach up here in the wooded area just above and behind the granite wall. If she listened closely, she could hear the waterfall below. But instead, she concentrated on Brandon's heavy breathing. He had finally gotten through the button obstacle course and was ready to start on her bra. Suddenly, in one quick and rough motion, he grabbed the bottom of her bra and simply shoved it up over her breasts. She almost protested until his mouth devoured her and made her forget.

She reached down and undid his belt buckle, undoing the snap and his zipper in a smooth, almost expert motion. But he didn't wait for her. He was taking himself out while pushing her back into the leaves. She tried to slow him down, whispering in his ear and rubbing his back and shoulders.

"Slow down, Brandon. Let's enjoy this."

But it was already too late. He hadn't even made it all the way inside her when he exploded. In seconds he lay limp on top of her. More panting while he tried to catch his breath, drowning out Ginny's exaggerated sigh of disappointment. Then he sat up, wiped his wet hair off his forehead and pulled his zipper up, all as casually as if he were getting dressed in the morning. Ginny felt as if she had become invisible. Why were the cute ones always the quick triggers and the insensitive shitheads?

"That's it?" She unleashed her disappointment. She no longer cared if anyone heard her, though her voice couldn't compete with the waterfall, the Reverend Yacky-Yack and the mind-numbing clapping.

He finally looked at her, his brown eyes black and empty in the shadows. It felt worse than being invisible. His look made her feel dirty. She pushed her bra back into place and tried to pull her skirt down, noticing that he had ripped the crotch of her underwear.

"You klutz." She showed him the damage. "Now what am I supposed to do?"

"I don't know. What do whores like you usually do afterward?"

She stared at him, stunned by his words. She needed to hold on to her anger, because without it, she would start to be frightened.

"You really are a bastard, aren't you?" Two could play this word game, only his response this time came without words as his fist slammed into her mouth. Ginny fell into the leaves, grabbing at her jaw, and felt the blood trickling down her chin. She crawled out of his reach. Her anger was quickly replaced by fear.

"Leave me alone, or I swear I'll scream."

He laughed, then threw back his head to the stars and laughed louder, as if to prove no one would hear. And he was right. The singing below only made his laughter sound like a piece of the harmony.

He picked up her purse, wiped his hand over it to clear the debris and tossed it to her.

"Don't forget to button your blouse before you come back down," he told her, his voice suddenly calm and polite, almost solemn but so distant it gave her a chill. How was he able to do that? How could he disconnect like that? And so quickly.

She grabbed her purse and scooted farther away, leaning against a tree as if for protection. Without saying anything more, he turned and left, taking the same path they had used to come up.

Down below, she could hear a woman's voice replace the good reverend's, but Ginny didn't pay attention to the words. Pretty soon there was more singing, even louder now, gaining volume as the night went along. They were singing something about coming home to a better place. What a bunch of losers.

Ginny breathed a sigh of relief. God, how stupid she had been this time. She bet that Justin guy wouldn't treat a girl like this. Why was she always choosing the wrong ones? The bad-boy types? Maybe she did it simply because she knew it pissed off her dad and embarrassed the hell out of her soon-to-be step-mom. Not like they cared about her, only about their public images, their precious reputations. They screamed at each other in private and made cow eyes at each other in public. It was pathetic. At least she acted on her real emotions, her real feelings, wants and needs.

Something rustled in the bushes behind her. Did Brandon have a change of heart? Maybe he was coming back to apologize. Then she realized he had taken the path at the opposite end. She jerked around, scrambling to her feet and squinting into the dark.

Something moved. Something in the shadows. Oh, jeez! It was only a branch.

She needed to get the hell out of here before she scared herself to death. She reached down for her purse. Something whipped in front of her, a glowing cord that looped over her head. It pulled tight against her neck before she could grab at it.

Ginny tried to scream but it came out as a gasp, stuck in her throat. She choked and gulped for air. Her hands and fingers clawed at the cord, then clawed at the hands that held it. She dug her fingernails into skin, ripping at her own flesh, and still couldn't breathe. She couldn't stop it. Couldn't keep it from tightening even more. Already she felt herself slipping to her knees. There were flashes of light behind her eyes. No air. She couldn't breathe. Her feet kicked, then slipped out from under her. Now her neck bore all the weight as her body dangled on a single cord.

She couldn't regain her balance. Couldn't see. Couldn't breathe. Her knees wouldn't work. Her arms flayed. Her fingers dug even deeper into her own skin, but nothing helped. When blackness came, it came as a relief.

# CHAPTER 12

*Downtown*
*Washington, D.C.*

Gwen Patterson transferred the strap of her briefcase to the other shoulder and waited for Marco. She squinted into the dimly lit pub, the antique gas-flamed lanterns and candelabras preserving the historic atmosphere of the saloon. This late on a Saturday evening Gwen knew Old Ebbitt's Grill would be free of all the politicos who usually hung out there, which would make getting a booth possible and would please her friend, Maggie O'Dell, who seemed to hate the political atmosphere of the District.

Ironically, the very things about the District that Maggie hated, Gwen thrived on. She couldn't imagine living anywhere more exciting and loved her brownstone in Georgetown and her office overlooking the Potomac. She had lived here for more than twenty years, and though she had grown up in New York, the District was her home.

Marco smiled as soon as he saw her and waved her down the aisle to where he was standing.

"She beat you this time," he said, and pointed to the booth at the end of the aisle where Maggie was already seated, a glass of Scotch on the table in front of her.

"Not like this is a first." She winked at Maggie, who was always on time. Gwen was the late one.

Maggie smiled, watching Marco fawn over her, helping her with her coat, even taking the briefcase. He started to hang it from the brass hook beside their table, then thought better of it and leaned it carefully and safely inside their booth.

"What are you carrying around these days?" he complained. "Feels like a load of bricks."

"Close. It's a load of my new book."

"Ah…yes, I forget that you are now a famous author as well as a famous shrink to the pundits and politicos."

"I'm not sure about that famous-author part," she told him as she smoothed her skirt with both hands and scooted into the booth. "I doubt that *Investigating the Criminal Mind of Adolescent Males* will make it onto the *New York Times* best-seller list anytime soon."

Marco's massive eyebrows rose, along with his hands, in mock surprise. "Such a large and weighty subject for such a small and beautiful woman."

"Now, Marco, every time you flatter me like that I end up ordering the cheesecake."

"Sweets for the sweet. Seems appropriate."

This time Gwen rolled her eyes at him. He patted her shoulder and headed off to greet a pair of Japanese men waiting at the door.

"Sorry," she said to Maggie. "We go through this every time."

"It must pay off. He gave us the best booth in the place."

Gwen sat back and took a long look at her friend. Maggie seemed pleasantly amused by the whole charade. Maybe it was simply the effects of the Scotch, because when Maggie had called earlier, she had sounded depressed, almost pained and stricken. She had told Gwen she was in the city and wanted to know if she had time for dinner. Gwen knew her friend had to be working. Maggie lived in Virginia, almost an hour away, in one of the District's ritzy suburbs. She seldom drove into the city for recreation, least of all on the spur of the moment.

"How did the book signing go?" Maggie sipped her Scotch, and Gwen caught herself wondering if this was her first. Maggie noticed. "Don't worry. This is my one and only. I need to drive home later."

"The signing went well," she said, deciding to bypass an opportunity to lecture Maggie about her newly acquired habit.

The fact was, she worried about Maggie. She rarely saw her anymore without an accompanying glass of Scotch. "I'm always surprised how many people are interested in the strange and twisted minds of criminals." She waved down a waiter and ordered a glass of chardonnay. Then to Maggie, she said, "I've been cabbing it all day, so I get more than one."

"Cheater."

Gwen was relieved that Maggie could still joke about it, especially after their last dinner together when Gwen had suggested Maggie needed the Scotch more than she wanted it. Gwen had gotten off with only a glare that told her to butt out. Useless, really. Maggie was stuck with her friendship, and with it—whether she liked it or not—came a buttinsky maternal instinct that Gwen couldn't even explain to herself.

Gwen was fifteen years older than Maggie, and ever since the two met, back when Maggie was a forensic intern at Quantico and Gwen a consulting psychologist, Gwen had felt a protectiveness toward Maggie that she had never experienced before. She had always believed she didn't have a maternal bone in her body. But for some reason she became the proverbial mama bear, ready to claw the eyes out of anyone who threatened to hurt Maggie.

Now Gwen shoved her menu aside, ready to play psychologist, friend and mother. She hadn't learned how to separate those roles. So what if she never did. Maggie could use someone to look after her, whether she believed it or not.

"What brought you to the city? Something at headquarters?"

Maggie worked out of Quantico in the Behavioral Science Unit and rarely made it to FBI headquarters at Ninth and Pennsylvania Avenue.

Maggie nodded. "Just got back from visiting Ganza. But I was out at Arlington before that. Today was Agent Delaney's funeral."

"Oh, Maggie. I didn't realize." Gwen watched her friend, who was doing an excellent job of avoiding Gwen's eyes, sipping her Scotch, rearranging the cloth napkin on her lap. "Are you okay?"

"Sure."

It came too quickly and too easily, which for Maggie meant

"No, of course not." Gwen waited out the silence, hoping for more. Maggie opened her menu. Okay, so this was going to take some pulling and prodding. Not a problem. Gwen had a Ph.D. in pulling and prodding, though officially her certificate called it a Ph.D. in psychology. Same difference.

"On the phone, you sounded like you needed to talk."

"Actually, I'm working a case and could use your professional insight."

Gwen checked Maggie's eyes. That's not what she meant earlier on the phone or she would have said so. Okay, so if her friend wanted to talk shop and put off the real stuff, Gwen could be patient. "What's the case?"

"The standoff at the cabin. Cunningham wants a criminal profile of these guys, so that we might connect them to whatever organization they belong to. Because six young men certainly didn't do this on their own."

"Right. Yes, of course. I read something about that in the *Washington Times*."

"And the criminal psychology of adolescent male minds is your new specialty," Maggie said with a smile that Gwen recognized as pride. "Why would six teenage boys put down their guns, take cyanide capsules and then lie down and wait to die?"

"Without knowing any of the details, my first reaction is that it wasn't their idea. They simply did what they were told or instructed to do by someone they feared."

"Feared?" Maggie looked suddenly interested, leaning in, elbows on the table, her chin on her hands. "Why do you automatically say *feared*? Why not because they believed so strongly in their cause? Isn't that the reasoning behind most of these groups?"

A waiter delivered Gwen's glass of chardonnay and she thanked him. She wrapped her hands around the glass and set the wine swirling. "At that age they don't necessarily know what they believe. Their opinions, their ideas are still easily molded and manipulated. But boys usually have a natural tendency to fight back. There's actually a physiological reason for that."

Gwen sipped her wine. She didn't want to sound like she was lecturing Maggie on something she already knew, but her friend seemed eager to hear more, so she continued, "It's not just their higher levels of testosterone, but boys have lower levels of the neurotransmitter serotonin. And serotonin inhibits aggression and impulsivity. That could explain why more males—especially adolescent males—than females carry through with suicide, become alcoholics or shoot up school yards as a way to solve their problems."

"Also why their first instinct when trapped in a cabin with an arsenal of guns would be to think they could impulsively shoot their way out." Maggie sat back and shrugged. "Which brings me back to the same question, why lie down and die?"

"Which brings me to my same answer." Gwen smiled. "Fear. Someone may have had them convinced they had no alternative." Gwen watched as Maggie cradled the Scotch. "But you already knew most of that, didn't you? Come on, now, I'm not telling you anything new here. Why did you really call me for dinner? What do you really *need* to talk about?"

The silence continued longer than Gwen normally allowed.

"To be honest—" Maggie grabbed the menu again and avoided Gwen's eyes "—I'm really, really hungry." But she glanced over the top and managed a tense smile at Gwen's frown. "And I needed to be with a friend, okay? A living, breathing, wonderful friend whom I absolutely adore."

This time Gwen got a glimpse at Maggie's deep brown eyes. They were serious, even a tad watery, which was why she went back to hiding them behind the menu. Gwen could see she was trying to cover up a vulnerability that had slipped too close to the surface; a vulnerability that the tough Maggie O'Dell worked hard to keep to herself and harder to conceal from others, even from her living, breathing, wonderful friends.

"You should try the hickory burger," Gwen said, pointing to the menu.

"A burger? The gourmet is recommending a burger?"

"Hey! Not just any burger, but the best damn burger in town." She saw Maggie relax. The smile genuine now. Okay, so Gwen would pull and prod next time. Tonight they would eat burgers, have a couple of drinks and simply be living, breathing friends.

# CHAPTER 13

He needed to sit. The haze seemed thicker this time. Had he taken too much of his homemade concoction? He needed it only to enhance, only to help him see beyond the dark. He certainly didn't need this. He needed to sit. Yes, sit and wait for the haze to move from back behind his eyes.

He'd sit and concentrate on his breathing, just as he was taught to do. He would ignore the anger. Wait. Was it anger? Frustration, maybe. Disappointment, yes. But not anger. Anger was a negative energy. Beneath him. No, it was simply frustration. And why wouldn't he be frustrated? He honestly thought this one would last longer. She had certainly tried. And he was almost sure that on the third time he had seen it. Yes, he was quite certain he had seen the light behind her eyes, that glimmer, that flash, that moment of life escaping the body, just as she drew her final breath. Yes, he had seen it and he had come so close.

Now it would be days, maybe even a week before he could try again. He was running out of patience. Why the fuck did she have to give in so soon? One more chance was all he needed. He had been so close. So close that he didn't want to wait.

He gripped the book and let the feel of its leather binding soothe him. He sat on a hard bench in a dim corner of the terminal, ignoring the screech of hydraulic brakes, the endless clacking of heels rushing, bodies shoving—all of them in such a fucking hurry to get where they were going.

He closed his eyes against the lifting haze and listened. He hated the noise. Hated the smells even more—diesel fuel and something that smelled like dirty wet socks. And body odor. Yes, body odor from the assholes who abandoned their cardboard homes in the alley to venture in and beg for pocket change. Worthless assholes.

He opened his eyes, pleased that his vision was clearing. No more haze. He watched one of the worthless assholes by the vending machines, checking the return slots for change. Was it a woman? It was difficult to tell. She wore everything she owned, layer after filthy layer, pant cuffs dragging behind her, adding to the slow motion of her absent shuffle. Her ragged and stretched-out stocking cap gave a crooked point to her head and made her dirty blond hair stick out like straw. Such a coward. No survival instinct. No dignity. No soul.

He lay the book in his lap and let it fall open to the page where he had left his homemade bookmark—an unused airline ticket, creased at the corners and long expired. He needed to let the book calm him. It had worked before, the words offering guidance and inspiration, even direction and justification. Already his hands grew steady.

He pulled his shirt cuff down over the caked blood. She had scratched him good. It had hurt like hell, but nothing he couldn't ignore for the time being. He'd wash his hands later. Right now, he needed to feel some sense of completion and validation. He needed to calm the frustration and find some reserve of patience. Yet, all he could think about was having come so close to his goal. He didn't want to wait. If only he could find a way so he didn't need to wait.

Just then the pointy-headed loser stuck her smelly, gloved hand in his face. "Can you spare a dollar or two?"

He looked up into her smudged face and realized she was quite young, maybe even once attractive underneath that dirt and smell of decay, of rotten and sour garbage. He searched her eyes—clear, crystal blue and, yes, there was light behind them. No hollow look of despair. Not yet. Maybe he didn't need to wait, after all.

# CHAPTER 14

*Newburgh Heights, Virginia*

The cold wind pricked at Maggie's skin, but she continued running, welcoming the sensation. Delaney's death had triggered a swell of emotions that she hadn't anticipated, that she wasn't prepared to deal with. And his funeral had released an avalanche of memories from her childhood, memories she had worked long and hard to keep safely behind a barrier. The battle to contain them left her feeling numb one minute and angry the next. Amazing that both emotions could be so exhausting. Or perhaps the exhaustion came from keeping them concealed, shoving them down away from the surface, so that no one could witness how easily she could feel nothing one moment and explode the next. No one, that is, except Gwen.

Maggie knew her friend could sense her vulnerabilities, despite Maggie's effort to hide them. It was one of the curses of their friendship, a comfort as much as an annoyance. Sometimes she wondered why the hell Gwen put up with her, and at the same time, she didn't want to know the answer. Instead, she was simply grateful for this wise, loving mentor who could take one look into her eyes, see all the turmoil, sift through the hidden wreckage and somehow manage to inspire strength and good from some reserve Maggie hadn't even known existed. And tonight Gwen had been able to do all that without a single word. Now, if only Maggie could hold on to that strength.

When she first became a criminal profiler she thought she could learn how to compartmentalize her feelings and emotions, separate the horrors and images she witnessed as part of the job from her personal life. Not that Quantico taught them such a thing. But since she had done it all her life with the unpleasant memories and images of her childhood, why wouldn't she be able to do it with her career? The only problem was that every time she thought she had the technique down pat, one of those damn compartments sprung a leak. It was annoying as hell. Especially annoying that Gwen could see it no matter how hard Maggie tried to hide it from her.

She picked up the pace. Harvey panted alongside her. The big dog wouldn't complain. Ever since she had taken him in, he had become her shadow. The pure white Labrador retriever had become a bit overprotective with her, jumping at sounds that Maggie never heard, barking at footsteps whether they belonged to the mailman or the pizza-delivery person. But then Maggie could hardly blame him.

Last spring the dog had witnessed his owner being violently kidnapped from their home, by a serial killer named Albert Stucky, who Maggie had already put in jail once and who had escaped. And though Harvey had put up a good fight, he hadn't been able to stop the attacker. For months after Maggie had taken him in, he looked out the windows of Maggie's huge Tudor home, looking, waiting for his owner. When he realized she wouldn't return, he attached himself to Maggie with such a protectiveness that she wondered if perhaps the dog was determined not to lose a second owner.

What would Harvey think if he knew, if he could possibly understand, that his previous owner had been taken and killed simply because she had met Maggie? It was Maggie's fault that Albert Stucky had taken Harvey's owner. It was one of the things she had to live with, one of the things that caused her nightmares. And one of the things that was supposed to have its own little compartment.

Her breathing came in rhythmic gasps, timed to the pounding of her feet and the beat of her heart, which filled her ears. For a few minutes her mind cleared, and she concentrated instead on her body's basic responses, its natural rhythms, its force. She pushed it to its limit, and when she felt her legs strain, she pushed harder, faster. Then suddenly, she noticed Harvey favoring his front right paw though he didn't dare slow down, forcing himself to stay alongside her. Maggie came to an abrupt halt, surprising him with a tug of the leash.

"Harvey." She stopped to catch her breath, and he waited, cocking his head. "What's wrong with your paw?"

She pointed to it, and he crouched to the ground as if preparing for a scolding. She gently took the big paw in both her hands. Even before she turned it over she felt a prick. Embedded deep between his pads was a clump of sandburs.

"Harvey." She hadn't meant for it to sound like a scold, but he cowered closer to the ground.

She scratched behind his ears, letting him know he had done nothing wrong. He hated having these things pulled out, preferring to hide and endure the pain. But Maggie had learned how to be quick and efficient. She grabbed the clump between her fingernails, instead of fingertips, and gave one quick yank. Immediately, he rewarded those same fingers with grateful licks.

"Harvey, you need to let me know about these things as soon as you get them. I thought we agreed that neither of us would play hero anymore."

He listened while he licked, one ear perched higher than the other.

"So do we have a deal?"

He looked up at her and gave one sharp bark. Then he climbed to his feet, ready to run again, his entire hind end wagging.

"How 'bout we take it easy the rest of the way?" She knew she had pushed it a bit too hard. As she stood and stretched, she could feel a cramp threatening her calf. Yes, they'd walk the rest of the way, despite the wind chilling her sweat-drenched body and making her shiver.

A bulging orange moon peeked from behind a line of pine trees and the ridge that separated Maggie's new neighborhood from the rest of the world. The houses were set far back off the street with enough property and landscaping between them to make it difficult to see the next-door neighbors. Maggie loved the seclusion and privacy. Though without any streetlights, darkness came quickly. It still freaked her out a bit to run after dark. There were too many Albert Stuckys out there. And even though she knew *he* was dead—that she'd killed him herself—she still sometimes ran with her Smith & Wesson tucked in her waistband.

Before she got to her long circular driveway, she saw a glimmer of windshield. She recognized the spotless white Mercedes and wanted to turn around. If he hadn't seen her, she might have done just that. But Greg waved from the portico, leaning against its railing as if he owned the house.

"It's a little late to be out running, isn't it?" This was his greeting, which sounded more like a scolding, and she found herself flinching instinctively, just as Harvey had earlier. The gesture represented a microcosm of their relationship, which had been reduced to instinctive survival tactics, and Greg still wondered why she wanted a divorce?

"What do you need, Greg?"

He looked like he had stepped off the pages of *GQ*. He was dressed in a dark suit, with sharp creases she could see even in the moon's dim light, not a wrinkle in sight. His golden hair was moussed and styled, not a strand out of place. Yes, her soon-to-be ex-husband was certainly handsome, no question about that. She knew he must be on his way home from dinner with friends or business associates. Maybe he had a date, and immediately she wondered how she would feel about that. Relieved, was her quick and easy answer.

"I don't need anything." He sounded hurt, and she saw him shift to his defensive stance, another survival tactic in his own arsenal. "I just thought I should check up on you."

As they got closer, Harvey started growling, his signal that warned of any stranger on their property.

"Good Lord!" Greg backed up, only now noticing Harvey. "That's the dog you took in?"

"Why are you checking up on me?"

But Greg was now preoccupied with Harvey. Maggie knew he hated dogs, though while they were together he had made excuses that he was allergic to them. Seemed the only thing he was allergic to was Harvey's growl.

"Greg." She waited until she had his attention. "Why are you here?"

"I heard about Richard."

Maggie stared at him, waiting for more of an explanation. When one didn't come, she said, "It happened days ago." She stopped herself from adding that if he was so concerned, why did he wait until now.

"Yeah, I know. I did hear about it on the news, but the name didn't ring a bell with me right away. Then I talked to Stan Wenhoff this morning about a case I'm representing. He told me about what happened at the morgue."

"He told you about that?" Maggie couldn't believe it. She wondered who else he had told.

"He was just concerned about you, Maggie. He knows we're married."

"We're getting a divorce," she corrected him.

"But we're still married."

"Please, Greg. It's been a long day and a long week. I don't need any lectures. Not tonight, okay?" She marched past him to the front door, letting Harvey lead, so that Greg moved out of the way.

"Maggie, I really did just stop to see if you're okay."

"I'm fine." She unlocked the door and hurried to reset the buzzing alarm system inside the entrance.

"You could be a little more grateful. I did come all this way."

"Next time, perhaps you should call first."

She was ready to close the door on him, when he said,

"That could have been you, Maggie."

She stopped and leaned against the doorjamb, looking up at him and into his eyes. His perfect forehead was creased with concern. His eyes startled her with flecks of dampness she didn't recognize.

"When Stan told me about Richard...well, I..." He kept his voice low and quiet, almost a whisper, and there was an emotion in it she hadn't heard for years. "The first thing I thought of was, what if it had been you?"

"I can take care of myself, Greg." Her job had been an ongoing debate in their marriage—no, *argument* was a better word. It had been an ongoing argument between the two of them for the last several years. She wasn't in the mood for any "I told you sos."

"I bet Richard thought he could take care of himself, too." He stepped closer and reached to caress her cheek, but Harvey's growl cut the gesture short. "It made me realize how much I still care about you, Maggie."

She closed her eyes and sighed. Damn it! She didn't want to hear this. When she opened her eyes, he was smiling at her.

"Why don't you come with me. I can wait while you get ready."

"No, Greg."

"I'm meeting my brother, Mel and his new wife. We're gonna have a nightcap at their hotel."

"Greg, don't—"

"Come on, you know Mel adores you. I'm sure he'd love to see you again."

"Greg." She wanted to tell him to stop, that she wouldn't be meeting with him and Mel probably ever again. That their marriage was over. That there was no going back. But those watery gray eyes of his seemed to replace her anger with sadness. She thought of Delaney and of his wife, Karen, who had hated Delaney's career choice as much as Greg hated hers. So instead, she simply said, "Maybe some other time, okay? It's late and I'm really wiped out tonight."

"Okay," he said, hesitating.

For a minute she worried that he might try to kiss her. His eyes strayed from hers to her mouth, and she felt her back tense up against the doorjamb. Yet in that moment of hesitation, she realized she wouldn't resist the gesture, and that revelation surprised her. What the hell was wrong with her? There was no need to worry, however. Harvey's renewed growl cut short any attempt at intimacy, drawing away Greg's attention.

He scowled at Harvey, then smiled back at Maggie. "Hey, at least you don't have to worry about security with him around."

He turned to leave, then spun back around. "Oh, I almost

forgot," he said, pulling a clump of torn and wrinkled papers from his jacket's inside breast pocket. "These must have blown out of your garbage can. The wind was nuts today." He handed her what she recognized as several ripped ad inserts, stuffers from her credit card statements and a notice about her *Smart Money* magazine subscription. "Maybe you need tighter lids," he added. Typical Greg, practical Greg, not able to resist the chance to correct or advise her.

"Where did you find these?"

"Just under that bush." He pointed to the bayberry along the side of the house as he headed to his car. "Bye, Maggie."

She watched him wave and waited for him to get inside, predicting his routine of checking his reflection in the rearview mirror, followed by one quick swipe at his already perfect hair. She waited until his car was down the street and out of her sight, then she took Harvey and rounded the garage. Instantly, the lights rigged to the motion detector came on, revealing the two galvanized steel garbage cans, lined up exactly where she kept them, side by side, securely against the garage wall, each can with its lid tightly intact.

She glanced through the pieces of crumpled paper, again. She shredded the important stuff, so she didn't need to worry. She was always careful. Still, it was a bit unnerving to know that someone had bothered to go through her garbage. What in the world had they hoped to find?

# CHAPTER 15

*Washington, D.C.*

Ben Garrison dropped his duffel bag inside the door of his apartment. Something smelled. Had he forgotten to take out the damn garbage again?

He stretched and groaned. His back ached, and his head throbbed. He rubbed the knot at his right temple, surprised to find it still there. Shit! It still hurt like a bitch. At least his hair covered it. Not like he cared. He just hated people asking a lot of goddamn questions that weren't any of their business to begin with. Like that yappy old broad on the Metro, sitting next to him. She smelled like death. It was enough to make him get off early and take a cab the rest of the way home—a luxury he rarely allowed himself. Cabs were for wusses.

Now all he wanted was to crawl into bed, close his eyes and sleep. But he'd never be able to until he knew whether or not he had gotten any decent shots. Oh, hell, sleep was for wusses, too.

He grabbed the duffel bag and spilled its contents onto the kitchen counter, his large hands catching three canisters before they rolled off the edge. Then he began sorting the black film canisters according to the dates and times marked on their lids.

Out of the seven rolls, five were from today. He hadn't realized he had shot so many, though lack of lighting remained his biggest problem. And the lighting around the monuments was often too harsh in places while too dark in certain corners. He usually found himself in the dark corners and shadows where he hated to risk using a flash, but did, anyway. At least the cloud covering from earlier in the day was gone. Maybe his luck was changing.

There was so much left to chance in this business. He constantly tried to eliminate as many obstacles as possible. Unfortunately, dark was dark and sometimes even high-speed film or that new infrared crap couldn't cut through the black.

He gathered the film canisters and headed for the closet he had converted into a darkroom. Suddenly the phone startled him. He hesitated but had no intention of picking it up. He had stopped answering his phone months ago when the crank calls began. Still, he waited and listened while the answering machine clicked on and the machine voice instructed the caller to leave a message after the beep.

Ben braced himself, wondering what absurdity it would be this time. Instead, a familiar man's voice said, "Garrison, it's Ted Curtis. I got your photos. They're good but not much different from my own guys'. I need something different, something nobody else is running. Call when you've got something, okay?"

Ben wanted to throw the canisters across the room. Everybody wanted something different, some fucking exclusive. It had been almost two years since his photos of dead cows outside Manhattan, Kansas, broke the story about a possible anthrax epidemic. Before that, he had been on a roll, as if luck was his middle name. Or at least, that was how he explained being outside that tunnel when Princess Diana's car crashed. Wasn't it also luck that put him in Tulsa the day of the Oklahoma City bombing? Within hours he was there, shooting exclusives and sending photos over the wires to the top bidders.

For several years afterward, everything he shot seemed to be gold, with newspapers and magazines calling him nonstop. Sometimes they were just checking to see what he had available that week. He went anywhere he wanted and shot anything that interested him from warring African tribes to frogs with legs sprouting out of their fucking heads. And everything got snatched up almost as quickly as he could develop the prints. All because they were *his* photographs.

Lately, things were different. Maybe his luck had simply run dry. He was fucking tired of trying to be in the right place at the right time. He was tired of waiting for news to happen.

Maybe it was time to make some of his own. He squeezed the canisters in his hands. These had better be good.

Just as he turned for the darkroom again, he noticed the answering machine flashing twice, indicating a message other than Curtis's. Okay, so maybe Parentino or Rubins liked the photos that Curtis didn't want.

Without emptying his hands, he punched the message-play button with his knuckle.

"You have two messages," the mechanical voice recited, grating on his nerves. "First message recorded at 11:45 p.m., today."

Ben glanced at the wall clock. He must have just missed the first call before he came in.

There was a click and a pause, maybe a wrong number. Then a young woman's polite voice said, "Mr. Garrison, this is the customer service office at Yellow Cab. I hope you enjoyed your ride with us this evening."

The film canisters slipped to the floor and scattered in different directions while Ben grabbed the countertop. He stared at the answering machine. No cab company on this planet called its passengers to see if they enjoyed their ride. No, it had to be them. Which meant they had moved from crank calls to watching him. And now they wanted him to know they were watching.

# CHAPTER 16

Justin Pratt waited outside the McDonald's rest room. Who'd think the place would be this busy at this time of night? But where else were kids supposed to hang out? Shit! What he wouldn't do for a Big Mac. The smell of French fries made his mouth water and this stomach ache.

He had carelessly suggested to Alice that they grab a bite to eat. Even before her nose crinkled and she gave him that exasperated look, he knew she wouldn't agree. That was one of the things he admired: her unflinching self-discipline. Yet, at the same time, what would it hurt to have one fucking cheeseburger?

He needed to watch his language. He glanced around again. It was becoming a habit for him to check that no one could hear his thoughts. What the hell was wrong with him? He was creeping himself out.

He couldn't believe how jumpy he was. It was as if he had no control over his body or his thoughts. He scratched his jaw and combed his fingers through his greasy hair. He hated taking timed showers. The water never got warm, and this morning his two minutes were up before he could get the shampoo out of his hair.

He leaned against the wall and crossed his arms over his chest to stop his fidgeting. What was taking her so long? He knew part of the jumpiness had to be withdrawal from nicotine and caffeine. No cigarettes, no coffee, no cheeseburgers—Jesus! Was he out of his fucking mind?

Just then, Alice came out of the rest room. She had tied back her long blond hair, revealing more of her smooth white skin and her pouty lips, lips cherry-red without the aid of any cosmetics. When her green eyes met his, they sparkled, and she smiled at him like no one had ever smiled at him before. And once again, none of what he had given up mattered, as long as this beautiful angel continued to smile at him like that.

"Any sign of Brandon?" she asked, and immediately Justin felt wrenched from his temporary fantasy.

"No, not yet." He stared out the window, pretending to watch.

Fact was, he had forgotten about Brandon, and even now, didn't care if he showed up. He couldn't figure out how the hell his brother, Eric, had been such good friends with the guy. Brandon wasn't anything like Eric. In fact, he wished Brandon would just sorta disappear off the face of the earth. He was sick of him and his macho Casanova, oh-look-at-me-I'm-so-cool attitude. He didn't care if he was supposedly some precious Father-in-training.

Justin also couldn't understand why Brandon had to tag along everywhere he and Alice went. The guy could have any girl he wanted. Why couldn't he leave Alice the fuck alone? Except that Justin knew Father insisted members never travel anywhere alone. And since Justin wasn't a full-fledged member yet, anyone with him would still be considered traveling alone.

Eric had attempted to explain all the rules and crap to him, but then Father sent Justin out into the woods for almost a week. Father had called it an initiation ritual, and Eric hadn't argued with the man. Although Justin still wasn't sure what camping out, sleeping on the ground and eating cold canned beans had to do with being initiated into anything.

Luckily, he had wandered into Shenandoah National Park, and some campers ended up taking him in—fed him pretty damn well, too. He worried he had put on weight instead of looking the emaciated, frightened fledgling that Father had hoped would return. Unfortunately, when he got back, Eric was gone, off on some top-secret mission that no one could tell him about. He hated all the cloak-and-dagger shit. It felt as goddamn stupid as it sounded.

Alice scooted into a corner booth to wait. Justin hesitated. He really wanted to sit next to her. He could use the excuse that he needed to watch for Brandon, but Alice was already doing that, watching so intently he found himself hating Brandon for drawing away her attention.

Justin slid into the booth on the opposite side. He surveyed the restaurant, checking to see if anyone cared that they take up a booth when they hadn't ordered anything. The place was filled with late-night customers getting their Saturday-night junk-food fix. It was long past dinnertime. No wonder his stomach ached. The bite of Ginny's pretzel was all he'd had since lunch. And not like that gummy rice and beans they fed him would last, despite it feeling like it stuck to the inside walls of his stomach. How the hell did they eat that crap day after day? And since they were on the road, today's ration had been served cold. Yuck! He could still taste it.

Realizing it might take a while, Alice wiggled out of her jacket. Justin followed her lead, trying not to stare at her incredible tits. Yet, he couldn't stop thinking how hot she looked in that tight pink sweater.

She reached into her jacket pocket and brought out the bulging leather pouch, clumping it down on the table and making the quarters chink against one another. Justin thought about asking if they could, at least, get a couple of Cokes. She had used only one quarter for the phone call that seemed to be a big part of their mission. But then Alice had left just a short message, some weird code about a cab ride.

Justin didn't try to figure it out. Truth was, he didn't much care about the group's politics or religious beliefs. Or even their travel arrangements, for that matter. He simply wanted to be with Alice. Not like he had any place better to be.

He had been gone almost a month, and he doubted that his parents gave a fuck that he wasn't around. Maybe they hadn't even noticed he was gone. They certainly didn't seem to care when Eric left home. All his dad said was that Eric was old enough to screw up his own life, if that's what he wanted to do. But Justin didn't want to think about them. Not now. Not when he was sitting across the table from the only person who had ever made him feel like he was someone special.

Alice smiled at him again, but this time she pointed over his shoulder.

"Here he is."

Brandon slid into the booth next to Alice, taking up too much space and squeezing Alice against the wall. She didn't seem to mind, but Justin felt his hands clenching into fists, so he kept them in his lap under the table.

"Sorry I'm late," Brandon muttered, though Justin knew he didn't mean it. He knew guys like Brandon said "sorry" like some people asked "how are you?"

Justin examined the tall redhead, who reminded him of that dead actor in all those rebel movies—James Dean. Brandon's head pivoted, his eyes looking everywhere except at the two of them. Justin glanced over his shoulder. Was Brandon worried someone had followed him? It sure as hell looked like it. His eyes kept darting all over the place. If Justin didn't know better, he'd think Brandon was high on something. Except that was impossible. Brandon pretended to be a rebel, but he wouldn't dare cross Father. And drugs were forbidden.

"We need to get back to the bus," Alice politely and quietly instructed them. "The others will be waiting."

"Give me a chance to catch my breath." Brandon saw the pouch of quarters and reached for it. "I could use something to drink."

Justin waited for Alice to scold Brandon in her soft, strict way. Instead, she stared at his hands. Then Justin noticed what had stopped Alice. Brandon's left knuckle had something caked on it. Something dark and red that looked an awful lot like blood.

# CHAPTER 17

*Reston, Virginia*

R.J. Tully held down the button on the remote and watched the TV's channels flip one after another after another. Nothing on the screen could distract him from the clock on the wall—the clock that now showed twenty minutes after midnight. Emma was late! Another night of breaking curfew. No more Mr. Nice Guy, no matter what her excuse. It was time for RoboDad. If only it were possible to access some mechanical part inside himself and let it take over without emotion getting in the way.

Nights like this made him miss Caroline the most. Probably a sign that parenthood had driven him completely over the edge. After all, shouldn't a red-blooded guy miss his ex-wife's sexy, long legs or even her to-die-for lasagne? There was a whole list of more likely things than missing her ability to sit next to him and reassure him that their daughter was just fine.

Caroline had always been so creative in their plans for punishing Emma, zooming in on the one thing she knew would bug the hell out of their daughter. Simple things like making her sort all the household socks for the entire month. Stuff he'd never dream of in a million years. Sorting socks was fine when Emma was eight or nine and caught riding her bike past the territorial limits they had set. But at fifteen, it was increasingly difficult to get her attention, let alone find meaningful ways of disciplining her.

He scraped a hand over his face, attempting to wipe away the sleep and the brewing anger. He was just tired. That's why he was irritable. He left the TV on Fox News and traded the remote for the bag of corn chips he'd left on the secondhand coffee table. He had to sit up to make the exchange, and only now did he notice the remnants of his previous snack attack crumbling out from the folds of his Cleveland Indians T-shirt. Jeez! What a mess. But he made no effort to clean it up. Instead he sank back into the recliner. How much more pathetic could he get? Sitting here on a Saturday night, eating junk food and watching the late night news?

Most days he didn't have time to feel sorry for himself. However, Caroline's earlier phone call had set him on edge. No, actually, it had pissed him off. She wanted Emma for Thanksgiving, and was sending the airline tickets by FedEx on Monday.

"It's all been worked out and scheduled," she had told him. "Emma's looking forward to it."

All worked out and scheduled before she even checked with him. He had custody of Emma, something Caroline had willingly agreed to when she decided having a teenage daughter had become an inconvenience to her as a CEO and new dating-game member. She knew Tully could say no to a Thanksgiving trip, and she wouldn't have a legal foot to stand on. So, of course, she had planned it beforehand with Emma, getting the girl excited, using her as a pawn. That way Tully had no choice but to agree to the trip. The woman headed an internationally successful advertising agency, why wouldn't she be an expert at manipulation?

Putting his feelings aside, Tully knew Emma needed to spend time with her mother. There were things that only mothers and daughters should discuss, things Tully felt totally inept at, not to mention downright uncomfortable with. Caroline wasn't the most responsible person in the world, but she did love Emma. Maybe Tully was simply feeling sorry for himself, because this would be the first Thanksgiving he would spend alone in more than twenty years.

A car door slammed. Tully sat up, grabbed the remote and turned down the TV's volume. Another car door slammed, and this time he was certain it came from his driveway. Okay, he needed to put on his stern expression, his I'm-so-disappointed-in-you face. But what punishment had he decided on? Oh, crap! He hadn't come up with anything. He slumped into the recliner again, pretending to be caught up in the news as he heard the front door unlock.

There were more than one set of footsteps in his entrance. He twisted around in the recliner and saw Alesha's mother coming in behind Emma. Oh, jeez! What the hell happened this time?

He stood, brushing more crumbs from his T-shirt and jeans, running his fingers through his hair and quickly swiping his mouth. He probably looked like hell. Mrs. Edmund looked impeccable as usual.

"Mr. Tully, sorry to interrupt."

"No, I appreciate you doing the chauffeuring tonight." He watched Emma but couldn't decide if her discomfort was embarrassment or worry. These days anything he said or did in front of her friends or her friends' parents appeared to embarrass her.

"I just wanted to come in and let you know that it's my fault Emma's late *in* getting home tonight."

Tully continued to watch Emma out of the corner of his eyes. The girl was an expert manipulator, just like her mother. Had she put Mrs. Edmund up to this? Finally, he crossed his arms over his chest and gave his full attention to the petite blonde, an older mirror image of her own daughter. If she had hoped to cover for Emma without providing an explanation, she was mistaken.

He waited. Mrs. Edmund fidgeted with her purse strap and pushed back an unruly strand of hair. Usually people didn't act nervous unless they were guilty of something. Tully didn't bother to fill the discomforting silence, despite seeing Emma squirm. He smiled at Mrs. Edmund and waited.

"They wanted to go to a rally at one of the monuments instead of going to a movie. I thought it would be okay. But afterward, traffic was just nuts. I hate driving in the District. I got lost a couple of times. It was just a mess." She stopped and looked up at him as if checking to see if that was sufficient. She continued, "Then I couldn't find them. We crossed wires as to the exact place I'd pick them up. Thank God, it didn't rain. And all that traffic—"

Tully held up a hand to stop her. "I'm just grateful you're all safe and sound. Thanks again, Mrs. Edmund."

"Oh, please, you must start calling me Cynthia."

He could see Emma roll her eyes.

"I'll try to remember that. Thanks so much, Cynthia." He escorted her out the front door, waiting on the steps until she made it safely into her car. Alesha waved at him and her mother joined in, the distraction almost causing the woman to back into his mailbox.

When he stepped back inside, Emma was in his spot, a leg over the recliner arm and channel surfing. He snagged the remote, shut the TV off and stood in front of her.

"You made Mrs. Edmund drive all the way into the District? What happened to going to a movie?"

"We met some kids during our field trip. They invited us to this rally. It sounded fun. Besides, we didn't make Mrs. Edmund drive us. She said it was okay."

"That's almost an hour's drive. And what kind of a rally was this? Were drugs and alcohol being passed around?"

"Dad, chill out. It was some religious revival thing. Lots of singing and clapping."

"Why in the world would you and Alesha even want to go to something like that?"

She sat up and started taking off her shoes, as if suddenly dead tired and in need of getting to bed.

"Like I said, we met some cool kids on our field trip, and they told us we should come. It was sort of a yawner, though. We ended up walking around the monuments and talking to some kids we met."

"Kids? Or boys?"

"Well, there were boys and girls."

"Emma, walking around the monuments at that time of night could be dangerous."

"There were like tons of other people, Dad. Busloads. They have tour groups. Real sight-seeing fanatics, rubbing their little pieces of paper on the wall and taking umpteen pictures with their cheap disposables."

Tully did remember that there were several night tours of the monuments. She was probably right. They were probably just as safe as in the daylight. Besides, didn't the monuments have twenty-four-hour security?

"You were really funny with Mrs. Edmund." She smiled up at him.

"What do you mean?"

"I thought for a minute there you were gonna ground her." She giggled and Tully couldn't help but smile.

The two of them ended up laughing, eating the rest of the corn chips and staying up to watch the last half of Hitchcock's *Rear Window* on *American Movie Classics.* Yes, his daughter was a chip off her mother's block, already knowing what buttons to push. And Tully wondered, once again, if he'd ever get this parenting thing right.

# CHAPTER 18

Justin pretended to sleep. The converted Greyhound bus was finally quiet, the rumble of the engine and tires a welcome lullaby. Thank God! No more fucking "Kumbaya" songs. Getting through that wacky "praise the Lord" and "Yahweh rules" at the too-long prayer rally had been bad enough. But Justin knew his head would surely explode if he had to listen to that crap for the three-hour bus ride home.

He had reclined his bus seat just far enough back that he could keep a half-closed eye on Brandon and Alice. They were sitting together one row behind him and across the aisle. The interior of the Greyhound bus was dark except for the track lighting on the floor, like little-bitty runway lights. He could barely see Alice's silhouette, her head turned to look out the window. She had kept that same pose since they left D.C. Even when the rest of the bus had been wailing at the top of their lungs, he could see Alice's lips move only when she occasionally looked back. Otherwise she kept staring out the window. Maybe she couldn't stand the sight of Brandon, either. Hey, he could hope, couldn't he?

With the seat reclined, he could watch Brandon a little easier. Justin kept his eyes on Brandon's hands. The guy better keep those fucking hands off Alice. Once in while, in the light of oncoming cars, he caught a glimpse of his face. Contentment. Fucking contentment, like he didn't have a worry in the world. It still pissed Justin off that Brandon had rammed his way into the bus, practically shoving him aside and plopping down in the seat next to Alice as if it were marked his. The bastard took anything and everything he wanted without ever thinking of asking.

Justin heard the whispered murmurs before he twisted around and noticed Father coming from his private compartment in the back of the bus. Rumors were that it included a bathroom and bed for Father to catch up on his rest. Now, as he walked slowly up the aisle, holding on to the backs of seats to keep his balance, Justin couldn't help thinking the man looked pretty ordinary in the shadows of the dark bus. What? The guy walked on water, but he had to hang on for a short trek down a bus aisle?

Justin kept his head pressed to the back of his seat, shifting slightly, so no one would think he was fully awake. He even snorted a little under his breath, a sound he had heard himself make other times in a half-conscious state.

Through the slits of his eyes, he could see Father stop, standing right at Justin's head. His dark features made it impossible for Justin to tell through half-shut eyes whether or not the man was looking down at him.

Then he heard him whisper, "Brandon, go sit with Darren up in front for a few minutes. I need to talk with Alice."

Brandon got up and obeyed without a word. Justin wanted to smile. Good, the bastard won't be bothering Alice for a while. Maybe Father had noticed Brandon's obsession with Alice. After all, he preached about celibacy being necessary in order for all of them to fulfill their mission. It was bullshit, of course, but he had witnessed the punishment imposed for disobeying. A couple who had gotten caught the first week Justin came to the compound were still being ostracized by the others.

"Alice, I wanted to commend you," Justin heard Father say, though his voice was hushed. "You did an excellent job recruiting young people to come to the rally."

"Justin and Brandon helped." Alice's voice was a whisper, but Justin's radar seemed to be picking it up. He loved that soft, tender, sweet voice of hers. It sounded like a bird's song, the words melodic, no matter what she said.

"That's just like you to give some of the credit away."

"But it's true. They did help."

Father gave a laugh that Justin didn't recognize. He tried to remember if he had ever heard the man laugh.

"Do you have any idea how special you are, my dear girl?"

Justin smiled, glad that someone else noticed that important fact. Except Alice didn't seem happy—the look on her face was almost a grimace. Too much modesty? She certainly needed to learn how to take a compliment, especially—what the hell?

Now, he could see what had quieted Alice. In the faint light of oncoming traffic, Justin could just make out Father's right hand on Alice's thigh. Justin kept his head against the seat but opened his eyes for a better look. Yes, the bastard's fingers were sliding in between Alice's thighs, moving their way up to her crotch. Shit! What the hell?

He felt a cold sweat wash over him, and a panic hammered in his chest. He looked back up at Alice's face and this time she noticed him watching. She gave just a slight shake of her head, a definite "no." At first, he thought it was meant for Father, but the man seemed fixated on the route his hand was taking. So the "no" was for Justin.

Fuck! Everything on her pained face told him she didn't want what was happening, and yet she was telling him not to interrupt?

Shit! He had to do something. He couldn't see Father's hand anymore. It was too dark again, the stream of traffic having passed. But from the movement of the man's shoulder, Justin figured he must be digging into her. Maybe by now, he had his goddamn hand down the front of her pants.

Justin laid his head back. He had to do something. Fuck! He needed to think. Suddenly he decided. He jerked and twisted, flaying his body back and forth in the seat, faking a nightmare as best he could. Then he slammed his body forward and yelled, "Stop it! Don't do it!"

It was enough to wake everyone, and several people hung over or around their seats to look. Justin shook his head and rubbed his eyes and face.

"Sorry, everybody. Bad dream, I guess. I'm okay."

He glanced at Father. The man was staring at him, the anger easily visible in the dim light. As he stood, he scowled down at Justin, holding that pose as if wanting everyone to witness his disapproval. How could he justify being angry about a nightmare? Of course, no one else would know the real reason for his anger. But Justin didn't care if anyone else knew. He was just glad the pervert had stopped. He simply shrugged at Father. Then he shifted in his seat away from that piercing and condemning stare, mumbling an apology to the zit-faced ditto-head sitting next to him.

Finally, he heard Father turn, but Justin waited until he heard the click of the back compartment's door before he looked over at Alice. Her face was turned to the window again, but, almost as if reading his mind, she glanced at him over her shoulder and again slowly shook her head, only this time she didn't look pained. This time, she looked worried, and he knew he was probably in a whole lot of trouble with their leader, their so-called fucking soul caretaker. How could he take care of their souls when he couldn't even keep his fucking hands to himself?

# CHAPTER 19

*SUNDAY*
*November 24*
*The Hyatt Regency Crystal City*
*Arlington, Virginia*

Maggie checked her watch again. Her mother was fifteen minutes late. Okay, some things never changed. Quickly, she chastised herself for the thought. After all, her mother was trying to change. Her new friends seemed to have had a positive influence on her. There had been no drunken bouts or botched suicide attempts in more than six months. That had to be a record, yet Maggie remained skeptical.

Her mother rarely left Richmond, but lately she was traveling some place new every other week. Maggie had been surprised to get the phone call last night and even more surprised to find her mother had been calling from the Crystal City Hyatt. She couldn't remember the last time her mother had been to the District. She had told Maggie she'd come for a prayer meeting or some such thing, and for a brief moment Maggie had panicked that it was the prayer thing she was being invited to. Now Maggie wondered why she thought having breakfast with her mother would be any less awkward. Why hadn't she just said no?

She sipped her water, wishing it were Scotch. The waiter smiled at her again from across the restaurant, one of those sympathy smiles that said, "I'm sorry you've been stood up." She decided if her mother didn't show, she'd order bacon, scrambled eggs and toast with a tumbler of Scotch instead of orange juice.

She refolded her napkin for the third time when all she

wanted to do was dig the exhaustion from her eyes. She had only gotten about two hours of sleep, fighting images of Delaney's head exploding over and over again. God, she hated funerals! Even Abby's innocent acceptance of her father's death hadn't stopped Maggie's memories from leaking into and invading her sleep. The nightmare that finally convinced her to stay awake was one of herself, tossing handful after handful of dirt into a dark hole. The process seemed endless and exhausting. When she finally looked over the edge, she saw the dirt quickly turning to maggots scattering and crawling across her father's face, his wide eyes staring up at her. And he was wearing that stupid brown suit with his hair still combed the wrong way.

Maggie blinked and shook her head, willing the image out of her mind. She looked for the waiter. There was no sense in putting off the Scotch. Just then she saw her mother come in the restaurant door. At first, Maggie glanced right by her, not recognizing the attractive brunette dressed in a navy coatdress and bright red scarf. The woman waved at Maggie, and Maggie did a double take. Her mother usually wore absurd combinations that confirmed how little she cared about her appearance. But the woman approaching the table looked like a sophisticated socialite.

"Hi, sweetie," the imposter said in a sugary tone that Maggie also didn't recognize, though there was a familiar raspiness, a leftover from a two-pack-a-day habit. "You should see my room," she added with an enthusiasm that continued the charade. "It's huge! Reverend Everett was so kind to let us stay here last night. He's just been so good to Emily, Stephen and me."

Maggie barely managed to utter a stunned greeting before her mother sat down and the waiter was at their table.

"Would you ladies like to start off the morning with some juice and coffee or perhaps a mamosa?"

"The water's fine for now," Maggie said, watching her mother, waiting to see if she would take the waiter up on his invitation to drink before noon. Time of day had never stopped her in the past.

"Is this tap water?" Kathleen O'Dell pointed to the glass in front of her.

"I think so. I guess I'm not sure."

"Could you please fetch me a bottled water? Spring water from Colorado would be good."

"Colorado?"

"Yes, well…bottled spring water. Preferably from Colorado."

"Yes, ma'am. I'll see what I can do."

She waited until the waiter was out of sight, then she leaned across the table and whispered to Maggie, "They put all kinds of chemicals in tap water. Nasty stuff that causes cancer."

"They?"

"The government."

"Mom, I am the government."

"Of course you're not, sweetie." She sat back and smiled, smoothing the cloth napkin into her lap.

"Mom, the FBI is a government agency."

"But you don't think like them, Maggie. You're not part of…" She lowered her voice and whispered, "The conspiracy."

"Here you are, ma'am." The waiter presented a beautiful, crystal stemmed water glass filled to the brim and garnished with a wedge of lemon. His efforts were only met with a frown.

"Oh, now, how do I know this is bottled spring water if you bring it to me already in a glass?"

He looked at Maggie as if for help. Instead, she said, "Could you bring me a Scotch? Neat."

"Of course. One Scotch, neat, and one bottled spring water in the bottle."

"Preferably from Colorado."

The waiter gave Maggie an exasperated glance, as if checking for any other demands. She relieved him with, "My Scotch can be from anywhere."

"Of course." He managed a smile and was off again.

The waiter barely left before her mother leaned over the table again to whisper, "It's awfully early in the day to be drinking, Maggie."

Maggie resisted the urge to remind her mother that perhaps

this was a tendency she had picked up from her. Her jaw clenched and her fingers twisted the napkin in her lap.

"I didn't get much sleep last night," she offered as an explanation.

"Well, then some coffee might be more appropriate. I'll call him back." She started looking for the waiter.

"No, Mom. Stop."

"Some caffeine is just what you need. Reverend Everett says caffeine can be medicinal if not abused. Just a little will help. You'll see."

"It's okay. I don't want any coffee. I don't really even like coffee."

"Oh, now, where did he run off to?"

"Mom, don't."

"He's over at that table. I'll just—"

"Mom, stop it. I want the goddamn Scotch."

Her mother's hand stopped in midair. "Well…okay." She tucked the hand into her lap as if Maggie had slapped it.

Maggie had never spoken to her mother like that before. Where the hell did that come from? And now, as her mother's face turned red, Maggie tried to remember if she had ever seen her mother embarrassed, though there had been plenty of times in the past that would have justified such a response. Like making her daughter drag her half-conscious body up three flights of stairs or waking up in a pool of vomit.

Maggie looked away, watching for the waiter, wondering how she'd get through an entire meal with this woman. She'd rather be anywhere else.

"I suppose that dog kept you awake," her mother said as if there were no dark cloud of the past hanging over their table.

"No, actually it was my government job."

She looked up at Maggie. There was yet another smile. "You know what I was thinking, sweetie?" As usual she conveniently changed the subject, a tactical expert at avoiding confrontation. "I was thinking we should do a big Thanksgiving dinner."

Maggie stared at her. Surely, she must be joking.

"I'll cook a turkey with all the trimmings. It'll be just like the good ole days."

The good ole days? That must be the punch line, but from what Maggie could tell, her mother was serious. The idea that the woman even knew which end of the turkey to baste seemed incomprehensible.

"I'll invite Stephen and Emily. It's about time you met them. And you can bring Greg."

Ah, no punch line. But definitely an ulterior motive. Of course, why hadn't she seen that one coming?

"Mom, you know that's not going to happen."

"How is Greg? I miss seeing him." Again, Kathleen O'Dell continued the charade as if Maggie hadn't spoken.

"I suppose he's fine."

"Well, the two of you still talk, right?"

"Only about the division of our mutually accumulated assets."

"Oh, sweetie. You should simply apologize. I'm sure Greg would take you back."

"Excuse me? What exactly should I apologize for?"

"You know."

"No, I don't know."

"For cheating on him with that cowboy in Nebraska."

Maggie restrained her anger by strangling the cloth napkin in her lap.

"Nick Morrelli is not a cowboy. And I did not cheat on Greg."

"Maybe not physically."

This time her mother's eyes caught hers, and Maggie couldn't look away. She had never told her mother about Nick Morrelli, but obviously Greg had. She had met Nick last year. At the time he had been a county sheriff in a small Nebraska town. The two of them had spent a week together chasing a child killer. Ever since then she hadn't been able to get him out of her mind for very long, a task made more difficult now that he was living in Boston, an A.D.A. for Suffolk County. But she was not even seeing Nick, had insisted, in fact, that they have little contact until her divorce was final. And, despite her feelings, she had not slept with Nick. She had never cheated on Greg, or at least not in a legal sense. Maybe she was guilty of cheating on him in her heart.

Never mind. It wasn't any of her mother's business. How dare she claim that she had some secret access to Maggie's heart. She had no right. Not after all the damage she had done to it herself.

"The divorce papers have already been drawn up," Maggie finally said with what she hoped was enough finality to close the subject.

"But you haven't signed them yet?"

She continued to stare at her mother's concerned look, puzzled by it as much as she was uncomfortable with it. Was her mother sincerely trying to change? Was she genuinely concerned? Or had she talked to Greg, discovered he was having second thoughts and agreed to some secret alliance? Was that the real reason behind this good ole Thanksgiving plan?

"Whether we sign the divorce papers or not, nothing will change between Greg and me."

"No, of course not. Not as long as you insist on keeping that government job of yours."

There it was. The subtle but oh-so-effective jab to the heart. Much more effective than a slap to the face. Of course, Maggie was the bad guy, and the divorce was all her fault. And, according to her mother, everything could be fixed if only Maggie apologized and swept all the messy problems out of sight. No need to solve anything. Just get them the hell out of sight. After all, wasn't that Kathleen O'Dell's specialty? What you don't acknowledge can't possibly exist.

Maggie shook her head and smiled up at the waiter who had returned and deposited in front of her a tumbler of amber, liquid salvation. She picked up the glass and sipped, ignoring the frown on her mother's new and carefully made-up face. Indeed, some things never changed.

Her cellular phone began ringing, and Maggie twisted around to pull it out of her jacket, which hung on the back of her chair. Only two rings and the entire restaurant was now joining her mother to frown at her.

"Maggie O'Dell."

"Agent O'Dell, it's Cunningham. Sorry to interrupt your Sunday morning."

"That's fine, sir." This new apologetic Cunningham could easily start to grate on her nerves. She wanted her old boss back.

"A body's been found on federal property. District PD's on the scene, but I've gotten a request for BSU to take a look."

"I'm already at the Crystal City Hyatt. Just tell me where you need me to be." She could feel her mother scowling at her. She wanted another sip of Scotch, but set it aside.

"Meet Agent Tully at the FDR Memorial."

"The monument?"

"Yes. The fourth gallery. The District's lead on the scene is..." She could hear him flipping pages. "Lead is a Detective Racine."

"Racine? Julia Racine?"

"Yes, I believe so. Is there a problem, Agent O'Dell?"

"No, sir. Not at all."

"Okay then." He hung up without a goodbye, a sign the old Cunningham was still in charge.

Maggie looked at her mother as she wrestled into her jacket and peeled out a twenty dollar bill to leave for the breakfast she hadn't yet ordered.

"Sorry. I need to leave."

"Yes, I know. Your job. It tends to ruin quite a few things, doesn't it?"

Rather than even try to find the correct answer, Maggie grabbed the tumbler of Scotch and drained it in one gulp. She mumbled a goodbye and left.

# CHAPTER 20

*Everett's Compound*
*at the foot of the Appalachian Mountains*

Justin Pratt jerked awake at the sudden blast of music, almost falling off the narrow army cot. Had he done so, he would have crashed on top of several members stretched out in sleeping bags. He knew he should be grateful to have a cot in the cramped sleeping quarters that housed almost two dozen men. After his probationary period—whenever the hell that ended—he was certain he would be on the floor with the rest of them.

It wouldn't matter, with the little sleep they were allowed. And then to wake up to that god-awful music over the loudspeakers. It sounded like an old scratched LP of "Onward, Christian Soldiers." No, he shouldn't complain. He needed to remember to be grateful. At least, until Eric got back. Then they could figure out what to do together. Maybe they could hitchhike to the West Coast. Although he wasn't sure how they'd survive without a fucking dime. Maybe they could go back home. If only he could convince Eric. He wouldn't leave without Eric.

He rubbed the blur from his eyes. Shit! It felt like he hadn't even slept. Out of habit, he looked at his wrist before he remembered that the expensive Seiko watch his grandfather had given him was gone. It had been just one of the hedonistic material things confiscated for his own good. Like knowing what time it was would fucking send him straight to hell.

Now Justin wondered if perhaps the real reason Father didn't allow them to keep anything of value was to make them dependent on him. And they were. For everything. Everything from that buggy rice to the scraps of newspaper they used as toilet paper.

"Get up, Pratt." Someone shoved his shoulder from behind.

Justin felt his hands ball up into fists. Without looking, he knew it was Brandon. Just once he'd like to slam a fist into that smug, arrogant face. Instead, he pulled a clean pair of underwear and socks from the clothesline in the corner. Brandon had been good enough to share it with him, because it seemed that even something like a cheap piece of fucking clothesline was a rare commodity around this place. The socks were still damp, which meant that once again his feet would be cold all day.

He took his time dressing while the others scurried to get in line for the showers. From the small, single-paned window, Justin could see the line forming. It curved all the way around the concrete building's corner. He combed his fingers through his greasy hair. Fuck it! Maybe he could sneak in a shower later. He was tired of waiting in line after line. Besides, he was starving, and his stomach reminded him with a rumble that he hadn't eaten since yesterday's lunch.

Justin headed for the cafeteria, looking around as he walked across the compound. That's what they called it, a fucking compound. The only other time he had heard someone refer to a place as a compound was on a cable special about the Kennedy family and their estate; an estate that they called a compound. So, of course, when Eric had told him about the compound, Justin had imagined something similar with servant cottages and horse stables and a huge mansion. But this place looked like army barracks—stark, metal and concrete buildings surrounded by trees and more trees, secluded in the Shenandoah Valley.

Piles of brush and uprooted trees were stacked on the south side where they had bulldozed and cleared just enough land to set up their compound. It didn't seem very organized, either. Wells hadn't been dug deep enough and many of the buildings didn't have plumbing. There certainly was never enough warm water. And hot water? Forget about it.

The whole place looked temporary, and Justin had heard rumors about Father building a new compound somewhere else, some paradise he was promising everyone. But after last night, Justin wasn't about to trust the asshole or anything he said. The pervert was a fucking hypocrite. Not like he had trusted him much before. Trust was a rare commodity with Justin. He should have known from his first week that the guy was nothing but a fraud.

That first week, Eric had taken him to what Father called a cleansing ritual. All of those who attended had to write down their most embarrassing moment, as well as one of their deepest fears. They were supposed to sign the papers, too.

"No one else will see these confessions," Father had assured them in his smooth, hypnotic manner. "The signatures are strictly an exercise for you to own up to your past and face your fears."

The folded papers were then collected in a black, square metal box. Justin had been asked to collect them and told where to set the dented box, back behind Father's huge wooden chair. A chair that looked more like a throne and was flanked by his Cro-Magnon bodyguards. At the end of the evening, Father brought out the black box with all those confidential secrets. He threw a single lit match into the metal container, setting the confessions on fire. There had been sighs of relief, but Justin couldn't help noticing that the black box no longer had a dent in it.

Later, when Justin told Eric about the miracle of the disappearing dent, his brother had practically snapped his head off.

"Some things require faith and trust. If you can't accept that, you don't belong here," his brother had told him in a pissed-off tone he had never used with him before that night. Justin remembered thinking that Eric sounded like he wasn't just trying to convince him. That maybe he was trying to convince himself, too.

Justin took a shortcut to the cafeteria, hopping over some sawhorses and wandering through a maze of stacked lumber and archaic construction equipment. He couldn't help thinking that a couple of pairs of Father's solid-gold cuff links could probably buy a small new forklift that would put the old John Deere tractor with the front loader and rusted plow hitched behind out of its misery.

He could smell the garbage dump and decided his shortcut wasn't such a hot idea. No wonder everyone avoided this area. Just as he was weaving his way back to the main path, he saw several men digging behind the piles of garbage. Maybe they were finally burying the smelly mess. But as he stopped, he saw that they had several strongboxes they were lowering into the ground.

"Hey, Justin."

He turned to find Alice waving at him over the stacks of lumber. She was making her way through the maze. Her silky hair glistened in the morning sun, and her clothes were crisp and fresh. No way were *her* socks still damp. Suddenly, he wished he had taken the time for that cold two-minute shower. When she looked up at him, her face immediately scrunched into that cute little worried expression.

"What are you doing, Justin? No one's allowed back here."

"I was just taking a shortcut."

"Come on, let's get out of here before someone notices." She took his hand to lead him away, but he stayed put.

"What are those guys doing over there?"

She frowned at him, but put a hand to her forehead and squinted into the morning sun, taking a look at where he was pointing.

"It's none of your concern."

"So, you don't know?"

"It doesn't matter, Justin. Please, you don't want to get caught back here."

"Or what? No one will talk to me for weeks? Or no, maybe I won't get my week's ration of gummy rice and beans."

"Justin, stop it."

"Come on, Alice. Just tell me what those guys are burying, and I'll go nice and quiet like."

She dropped his hand, practically shoving it away, and suddenly he realized how stupid he was being. She was the only person he cared about, and now he was pissing her off, just like he seemed to piss off everyone else.

"They're burying the money we collected at the rally last night."

At the end of each rally, about a half-dozen wicker baskets were passed around for what Father called a "gratitude offering" to God. Those baskets usually ended up overflowing.

"Whaddya mean, they're burying it?"

"They bury all the cash we take in."

"They're putting it in the ground?"

"It's okay. They put mothballs in the boxes, so the bills don't get all moldy."

"But why bury it?"

"Where else would they put it, Justin? You can't trust banks. They're all controlled by the government. ATMs and electronic transfers—all of that stuff is just so the government can monitor and take your money whenever it wants."

"Okay, so why not at least invest some of it, like in the stock market?"

"Oh, Justin, what am I going to do with you?" Alice smiled and patted his arm as though he had made a joke. "The stock market is controlled by the government, too. Remember reading in your history classes about the Great Depression?" She was using her calm teacher voice with him. At least the worry lines had left her face for the time being. "Anytime the stock market takes a plunge, it's the government causing the decline, stealing people's hard-earned money and making them start all over again."

Justin hadn't really thought about it before. He knew his dad got really pissed when he lost money in the market. Alice knew so much more about this stuff than he did. History had never been one of his strongest subjects. He shrugged, pretending it didn't matter to him. This time when she took his hand to lead him away, he let her and enjoyed the feel of her soft skin. He wanted to ask her about last night, about Father and the perverted moves he had made on her. Yet, at the same time, he didn't want to talk about it. He just wanted to forget it had ever happened. Maybe it was best that they both did.

As they walked to the cafeteria, Justin decided instead to think about how much money must be buried in that hole. He couldn't help wondering how many others knew about it. When they decided to leave maybe he and Eric wouldn't need to hitchhike, after all.

# CHAPTER 21

*FDR Memorial*
*Washington, D.C.*

Ben Garrison put his gloves back on and slapped the back of his camera shut on a fresh roll of film. He certainly didn't want to waste any time or give Detective Racine a chance to change her mind. He stepped in closer, focusing on the woman's face. She looked so peaceful, almost as if she were simply sleeping, despite being set up against a tree. Ben was fascinated by the blue tint of her skin. Had it been caused by the cold last night or a delayed reaction to the strangulation?

Even more fascinating were the flies, hundreds of them, persistent despite the activity of officers and detectives examining the area around them. They were huge and black, not your ordinary houseflies, and they seemed to be taking up residence in every one of the body's orifices, especially the warmer, moist areas like her eyes and ears. Her dark pubic hair looked alive with them. Already Ben could see what had to be milky gray eggs nestled in the mass of thick hair.

Death and its rituals and all the natural processes that went along with it amazed him. No matter how many dead bodies he saw, he continued to be fascinated. Less than twenty-four hours ago something warm and pulsating had been housed within this body. In New Caledonia the old men called this a word that meant *shadow soul.* The Esquimaux of Bering Strait referred to it as a person's shade. In Christian faith it was simply referred to as the soul. But now, whatever it was, it was gone. It had disappeared into thin air, leaving behind an empty, hollow carcass for insects to feed upon.

He remembered reading somewhere that in a week's time, a human cadaver could lose about ninety percent of its original weight when left exposed to insects during a hot summer. Insects were certainly efficient and predictable. Too bad human beings weren't. It would make his job so much easier.

"Hey, watch where you're stepping!" a uniformed cop yelled at him.

"Who the hell are you, buddy?" a guy in a navy windbreaker and baseball cap wanted to know. He looked more like a third baseman than a cop. When Ben didn't answer and continued to snap shots, the man grabbed him by the elbow. "Who let this guy back here?"

"Wait a fucking minute." Ben twisted free and was immediately accosted by two uniforms. Now he could see the white letters on the back of the guy's windbreaker: FBI. Shit, how was he supposed to know? The guy looked like a clean-cut, fucking Boy Scout.

"It's okay." Racine finally appeared to rescue him. The knees of her carefully pressed trousers had leaves sticking to them and her short blond hair had been tangled by the wind. "I know the guy. He used to shoot crime scenes for us before he became a big-shot freelancer. Steinberg isn't here yet. He's across town at another scene. We've gotta get some shots before the rain starts. Hell, we lucked out. Garrison just happened to be in the neighborhood."

The officers let go of Ben's arms, giving him a shove just as a reminder that they could. He checked his camera settings to make sure they didn't get all fucked up. Assholes. He was doing them a goddamn favor, and they still treated him like shit.

"Come on, boys. Show's over," Racine told the mobile-crime-lab guys who had stopped crawling around in the grass to watch the commotion. "We've got to hurry up before our evidence gets washed away. That goes for you, too, Garrison."

He nodded but wasn't paying much attention. He had only now noticed that no matter where he stood, the dead woman's eyes seemed to follow him. It had to be one of those strange illusion things, right? Or was he getting paranoid?

"Hey, camera guy," the FBI agent called to him. "Get a shot of this."

The guy stood behind Ben, pointing to a spot on the ground about five feet away from the body.

"The name's Garrison," Ben said, waiting for the guy to meet his eyes, and when he did, Ben made it clear that he wouldn't proceed until the guy acknowledged him with a little respect.

He tipped back his baseball cap and smiled. "And you just happened to be in the neighborhood, is that what Detective Racine said?"

"Yeah. What about it? I was getting some fucking stock shots of the monuments."

"On a Sunday morning?"

"Best time to do it. No oddballs monkeying around, thinking it's funny to screw up my shots. Hey, I'm helping you guys out here. Maybe you could quit busting my balls." Ben kept his tone calm, confining the anger, when he really wanted to tell this guy to go fuck himself.

"Okay, Mr. Garrison, could you please take a shot of these indentations in the dirt?" He pointed to the ground again. He was tall, over six feet, and lanky but athletic-looking. The sarcasm and his eyes told Ben he'd better not push it. Fucking feebie. Ben glanced at the guy's windbreaker and wondered where his gun was hidden. He bet the asshole wouldn't be such a macho prick without his government-issued Glock.

"No problem," Ben finally said. He checked out the area where the agent pointed. Immediately he saw two, maybe three small circular indentations in the ground. They were about five to six inches apart.

"What is it?" Racine joined them, looking over Ben's shoulder just as he felt the first raindrops on the back of his neck.

"Not sure," the agent told her. "Something was set down here. Or maybe it's some sort of signature."

"Jesus, Tully, you're always thinking serial killers, aren't you? Maybe the killer set down a suitcase or something."

"With little circular feet?" Ben laughed and snapped a couple of more shots.

"Everyone's a goddamn expert." Racine was getting pissed.

Ben smiled, his bent back to her and his face to the ground. He liked when Racine got pissed, and he imagined her mouth making that sexy little pout.

"That should be enough photos, Garrison. Now, play nice and hand over the film."

When he glanced up at her, she was holding out her hand.

"I didn't get very many angles of the body," he protested. "And I have a few more exposures left."

"I'm sure we have enough. Besides, the medical examiner's here." She waved to the small, pudgy man in the houndstooth jacket and wool cap making his way up the overgrown incline. The guy took small, careful steps, watching his feet the entire time. He reminded Ben of some cartoon character with a little black bag.

"Come on, Garrison." Her hands had moved to her hips while she waited. Maybe she thought it made her look authoritive. Racine had boyish, straight hips, probably even wore men's trousers with those long legs. What she lacked in hips, she made up for in tits. He stared at them now as she waited. Something about those soft tits next to that holstered metal gave him a hard-on every time. He wondered if she knew and liked it, because she didn't budge to close her jacket. Instead, she stood there, same stance, pretending to get impatient but not denying him access.

"Garrison, I don't have all fucking day."

Reluctantly, he tapped the release button and rewound the film, snapped the camera open and handed her the roll. "No problem. Not like I don't have better places to be."

She stuffed the film into her pocket, then buttoned the jacket as if to tell him the show was over now that she had what she wanted.

"So you owe me one, Racine. How about dinner?"

"In your dreams, Garrison. Just send me a bill." She turned to meet the medical examiner, dismissing Ben as though he were one of her lackeys.

Ben scratched his bristled jaw, feeling like he had been

sucker punched. The ungrateful cunt. One of these days she wouldn't get away with jacking men around. Actually, Ben had heard rumors that she did the same thing to women. Yeah, he could see Racine doing both, maybe even at the same time. The thought threatened to give him another hard-on. He felt the feebie staring at him. It was time to get the hell out of here. After all, he had gotten what he wanted.

He started down the path, knowing without looking where to step so he wouldn't slip. Before he turned around the granite boulders, he glanced over his shoulder. Racine and the rest of them were already occupied with the medical examiner. Ben stuffed his hand deep into his pocket, found the smooth cylinder. Then he smiled as he squeezed the roll of film into the palm of his hand. Poor Racine. It had never occurred to her that he may have taken more than one roll.

# CHAPTER 22

Maggie felt an immediate sense of relief. How awful was that? She preferred examining a dead body to having breakfast with her mother. Surely, that had to be a mortal sin for which she'd burn in hell. Or perhaps she'd be struck by lightning—maybe by one of the thickening gray thunderheads gathering now.

She flashed her badge to the first uniformed officer blocking the sidewalk next to the information center. He nodded, and she ducked under the crime scene tape. It was her first visit to the monument, though it had been finished and dedicated in 1997. She guessed she wasn't much different from other District suburbanites. Who had time to tour monuments except on vacation? And even if she took vacations, she certainly wouldn't choose to stay in the District.

Unlike the other presidential monuments, the FDR Memorial included trees, waterfalls, grassy berms, alcoves and gardens, all spread out over a long, expansive area rather than grouped in one imposing structure. As Maggie walked through the galleries or rooms, she paid little attention to the sculptures and bronzes. Instead her attention went to the granite walls, the ledges above and behind. She noticed plenty of trees and bushes. From down here, the area looked like a private haven for murder. Had the designers not given that a thought or had she simply become cynical after years of trying to think like a killer?

Maggie stopped at the bigger-than-life bronze of the seated Roosevelt with a little bronze dog next to him. She checked the position of the spotlights around it and wondered how far up they would shine. If the sky continued to darken, perhaps she'd soon get her answer. However, the granite walls had to be ten to fifteen feet tall. She doubted the lights illuminated any of the trees and bushes above and behind. From where she stood, craning her neck, she wondered if it was possible to even notice someone in those woods? She could faintly hear the commotion of detectives over the rushing sound of the waterfall. The voices came from above and farther in the bushes, but she couldn't see them. Not a single motion.

"The little dog's name is Fala."

She startled and turned to find a man with a camera hanging from his neck.

"Excuse me?"

"Most people don't know that. The dog. It was Roosevelt's favorite."

"The monument's closed this morning," she told him, and immediately saw his expression change to anger.

"I'm not some fucking tourist. I'm here taking crime scene shots. Just ask Racine.

"Okay, my mistake." But his quick temper drew her attention, and she found herself assessing his bristled jaw and tousled dark hair, the worn knees of his blue jeans and the toe-tips of shiny, expensive cowboy boots. He could easily pass for a tourist or an aging college student.

"See, I could make a snap judgment, too, and wonder what a babe like you was doing here. I thought Racine liked being the only babe on the scene." He returned her assessment by letting his eyes slowly run the length of her.

"New police procedure. We like to have at least one backup."

"Excuse me?"

"I'm the backup babe."

He smiled, more of a smirk than a smile, and his eyes traveled the same path.

"Sorta like cameramen," she continued. "Every police station needs a backup. You know, a second stringer, some lackey they call when they're in a pinch and the real cameraman can't make it."

His eyes shot up to hers, and she could see the flash of anger return. This guy was as much a crime scene photographer as she was a police babe. What the hell was Racine thinking? Or perhaps that was the problem. Racine hadn't been thinking, as usual.

"I'm tired of this fucking treatment," he said, with his hands swiping the air as if to show her what he had endured. "I do you assholes a favor and what do I get? I don't fucking need this shit. I'm outta here."

He didn't wait for a response. Instead, he turned on the heels of his polished boots and left with enough of a strut that Maggie knew he had gotten something for his early morning trouble. Just what, she wasn't sure. Perhaps some promise from Racine, some token quid pro quo. The woman had it down to an art form. Maggie remembered the last time she and Racine had worked a case, not that long ago. It was still too fresh in her memory bank to shrug off the distasteful experience. She had almost found herself on the other end of one of Racine's quid pro quos.

"O'Dell." This time the voice came from above. Agent Tully leaned over the ledge. "I want you to take a look at this before they bag the body."

"What's the best route up?"

"Around the fourth gallery. There's a set of rest rooms. Come all the way around them and to the back." He pointed to a place she couldn't see—too many granite walls. She found her way past another waterfall and more granite, then climbed a path that looked freshly made.

They were waiting for her, keeping their distance from the body, though Stan Wenhoff looked anxious to get on with his job. The forensics team was packing up what they had gathered so far in larger plastic bags. Maggie understood their urgency even before a low rumble of thunder came from overhead.

The girl sat against a tree with her back to the ledge of the monument. Her head lolled on her neck, exposing one side of deep raw tracks. Her eyes stared out despite the mass of whitish yellow in the corner of one. Without closer examination,

Maggie knew the mass to be maggots. Her legs were extended straight out in front of her and spread apart. Black, shiny-backed blowflies were already taking their posts in her pubic area and up her nostrils.

The girl wore only a black bra, still clasped but pushed up to expose her small white breasts. A piece of gray duct tape covered her mouth. Her short dark hair was tangled with bits and pieces of dried leaves and pine needles. Despite the horror of the scene, the girl's hands were folded together, lying neatly and calmly across her lap, resting just below the nest of blowflies. The hands reminded Maggie of someone praying. Was it supposed to mean something?

"We don't have much time, Agent O'Dell." Stan was the first to get impatient.

Poor Stan. Another early morning call-in for him in less than a week.

Tully was alongside her now, pointing to the ground in front of her.

"There's these weird marks, circular indentations."

At first she couldn't see them. It looked as if something may have been set down, though the object had not been very heavy. The marks Tully referred to were not deep, barely leaving impressions on the surface.

"Mean anything to you?" he asked.

"No. Should it?"

"I think so, but I can't figure out what."

"Tully's all gloom and doom today." Julia Racine approached on Maggie's other side. She smiled down at her, hands on her hips. "He's already looking for a serial killer."

Maggie took one last look at the indentations, stood up and glanced at the girl's body again, then she faced the detective. "I think Agent Tully's right. And judging by this scene, I'd say this guy's just getting started."

# CHAPTER 23

"If you ask me, it looks like a rape that got carried away."

Tully winced at Detective Racine's assessment, but he didn't need to argue with her. All he had to do was wait for O'Dell to do it.

"If that's what you think, then why did Agent Tully and I get called in to check it out?"

"Beats me." Racine shrugged, lifting the collar of her jacket as another rumble of thunder echoed through the air. "It's federal property."

"Then someone at the field office would have been called. Still doesn't explain why BSU would be consulted."

Tully stared up at the rolling gray thunderheads. O'Dell was right. The two of them specialized in criminal analysis, coming up with profiles, especially of repeat offenders or serial killers. Someone other than Detective Racine must have thought it important to call Cunningham. Whoever it was hadn't bothered to let Racine in on it. Didn't make much sense.

"The scuffle happened over here." Racine, anxious to prove her theory, pointed to a spot where leaves were smashed and crumbled. The mobile crime lab people had spent a good deal of time sifting and collecting from that area.

"Doesn't look like much of a scuffle." O'Dell squatted at the edge of the perimeter and examined the area without touching anything. "Someone definitely lay down here. Maybe even rolled around. The leaves and grass are packed down. But I don't see any torn grass, any scuffs in the dirt or heel marks for the type of violent scuffle you're talking about."

Detective Racine snorted under her breath, and Tully couldn't help thinking how unladylike it sounded. These two were strutting around each other like a couple of cockfighters. Sort of the equivalent of two men having a pissing contest.

"Look, O'Dell, I know a thing or two about rape scenes." Racine sounded as though her patience was wearing thin. "Posing the body like that is just one more way for him to degrade his victim."

"Oh, really?"

Tully turned away. Oh, Jesus! Here it comes. He recognized that tone of sarcasm. Had even had it launched at him a time or two.

"Did you ever think the unsub may have posed the body to alter the crime scene?" O'Dell asked the detective.

"Alter? You mean like on purpose, to throw us off?"

With his back to the two women, Tully rolled his eyes and hoped that O'Dell didn't say "Oh, duh." Detective Racine was in charge. Just once, couldn't O'Dell remember that?

"Maybe he posed the body," O'Dell was saying slowly as if speaking to a small child, "to redirect the investigation away from himself."

Another snort from Racine. "You know what your problem is, O'Dell? You give criminals too much credit. Most of them are stupid bastards. That's the premise I work from."

Tully walked away. He couldn't take any more. It had been entertaining at first. Now he no longer cared who won the pissing contest, although he'd place his money on O'Dell. He wandered over to Wenhoff, who was finishing his examination of the young woman's body.

"Any guess on time of death?"

"My best guesstimate right now judging from the stage of rigor, the rectal temp and the invasion of only the early feeders—" he batted away a few of the persistent blowflies "—is less than twenty-four hours. Maybe about twelve hours. I'll need to do some other tests. I also want to check with the weather service and see how cold it got last night."

"Twelve hours?" Tully knew enough about dead bodies to have estimated on his own that the murder had been recent;

however, he hadn't expected it to have been that recent. Suddenly, he felt a knot twist in his stomach. "That would make it last night, maybe somewhere between what—eight and midnight?"

"That's a good guess." Wenhoff pushed himself up with great effort and waved over a couple of uniformed officers. "She's ready to bag, boys, but she's stiff as a board. Be careful you don't break something."

Tully moved out of the way, not wanting to watch how they'd get her from a sitting position into the black nylon bag. He looked out over a clearing in the woods. In the distance he could see tourists wandering along the Vietnam Wall. Buses were winding around the police blockade to bypass the FDR Memorial and snake around to the Lincoln Memorial. Last night Emma and her friends had been here, walking those same sidewalks. Had the killer watched them while choosing his target? Hell, this girl didn't look much older than Emma.

"Tully." O'Dell came up beside him, startling him. "I'm heading over to the morgue. Stan's going to do the autopsy today. You want to meet me there, or should I just fill you in tomorrow?"

He only heard about half of what she had said.

"Tully? Are you okay?"

"Sure. I'm fine." He rubbed his hand over his face to cover up the sense of panic he was feeling. "I'll meet you over there." When she didn't move and continued to stare at him, he decided he needed to convince her. No better way to do that than to change the subject. "What's with you and Racine? I get the feeling there's some history there?"

She looked away, and immediately Tully knew he was right. But instead she said, "I just don't like her."

"How come?"

"Do I need a reason?"

"I know I probably don't know you very well, but yeah, I'd say you're the type of person who needs a reason to not like someone."

"You're right," she said, then added, "You don't know me very well." She started to leave but said over her shoulder, "I'll see you at the morgue, okay?" She didn't look back, only waved a hand at him, a gesture that said it was a done deal and that any conversation about her and Racine was over. Yes, there was definitely something there.

Now, as he watched everyone pack up, including the officers with the body bag, he could allow the nausea to take over his stomach. He walked to the ledge and looked out over Potomac Park. This time a rumble of thunder cracked open the sky—as if it had been waiting out of respect—and the rain came pouring down.

Tully stood still, watching the tourists below, scattering for shelter or popping open umbrellas. The rain felt good, and he lifted his face to it, letting it cool the sweaty, clammy feeling that had taken over his body. Yet, all he could think about was—Jesus—how close had his daughter come to being this guy's victim?

# CHAPTER 24

Maggie kicked off her leather pumps and put plastic shoe covers over her stockinged feet. She'd chosen the pumps for breakfast with her mother at the Crystal City Hyatt, not ones she would have picked had she known she would be working. Stan watched but said nothing. Perhaps he didn't want to push his luck. After all, she was wearing her goggles without being told. Usually they stayed on top of her head. But there was something different about Stan's behavior toward her; he seemed quieter. He hadn't yet muttered a single "humph" or heavy sigh. Not yet, anyway. Was he worried she'd freak out on him again?

She had to admit, she wasn't exactly comfortable being back here this soon. With little effort she could still conjure up the image of Delaney's gray death mask. But lately, she was able to do that anytime, anyplace—being back at the morgue probably wouldn't make it any worse. Or at least, that's what she told herself. She needed to stop thinking about Delaney. It wasn't just Delaney, though. It was all the memories his death had unleashed. Memories of her father that, after all these years, still left her feeling empty and hollow and, worst of all, alone.

It made her realize that with her impending divorce from Greg, she was on the verge of losing any sense of family that she had tried to construct. Or had she honestly ever tried? Gwen was constantly telling her that she kept too many people who cared about her at arm's length. Is that what happened with her and Greg? Had she kept her own husband at arm's length, not allowing him access to the vulnerable places inside her? Maybe her mother was right. Maybe the demise of her marriage *had* been all her fault. She felt a shiver. What a thought! That her mother could actually be right about something.

She joined Stan. He had already begun his external examination of the girl's body and was taking measurements. She helped him with the menial tasks of placing the body block and removing fluid samples. It felt good to concentrate on something concrete, something familiar and constructive. She had worked with Stan enough times to know which tasks he'd allowed her to do, and which she needed to stand back and simply watch.

Maggie carefully slipped the paper bags off each of the girl's hands and began scraping under the fingernails. There was plenty of material to scrape, which, ordinarily, would mean the girl might be able to tell them through DNA who her attacker had been. But from a preliminary look at the girl's neck, Maggie could see at least a dozen horizontal crescentic abrasions among the various raw and deep ligature tracks and massive bruising. Horizontal marks meant it was a safe guess that much of the skin behind the girl's fingernails was her own, caused by her clawing at the ligature.

Stan snapped enough Polaroids to fill the corkboard over the main sink. Then he removed his gloves, and for the third time since they had started, he scrubbed his hands, applying lotion and massaging it into his skin before putting on a fresh pair of gloves. Maggie was used to his strange ritual, but once in a while it made her acutely aware of the blood on her own gloves. Today would be one of those times.

"Sorry, I'm late," Agent Tully said from the doorway where he stood, hesitating. He was dripping wet—even the brim of his baseball cap was soaked. He took off the cap and raked the wetness from his close-cropped hair. At first, Maggie thought his hesitancy was because he didn't want to get the floor wet, which was crazy because it was cement with drains strategically positioned for nastier run-off than rainwater. But then, she saw he was waiting for someone. Detective Racine appeared behind Tully, looking too dry and refreshed to have come from the same place as him.

"Are we all here now?" Stan asked with the grumble he had suppressed until now.

"Yep. We're all here and ready," Racine sang out, rubbing her hands together as if they were gathering for a game of dodge ball.

Maggie had forgotten that Racine would be at the autopsy. It was her case—of course she'd want to be here. The last time Maggie worked with Racine the detective had been assigned to the sex crimes unit. Now she couldn't help wondering if Racine had ever watched an autopsy before. Suddenly, Maggie was anxious to get to work.

"Shoe covers, masks, everything's in the linen closet," Stan said, pointing. "No one watches without being properly gowned up. Got it?"

"No problem." Racine whipped off her leather bomber jacket and headed for the closet.

Tully lagged behind, taking more time than necessary to wring out his windbreaker and cap over one of the drains. He glanced several times at the girl's body, splayed out on the aluminum table. Maggie realized suddenly she may have been mistaken. Was it possible Tully was the one who had never witnessed an autopsy?

Before he transferred to Quantico, Tully had been doing criminal analysis at the Cleveland field office for five or six years. But she also knew much of that time was spent viewing crime scenes via photos, digital scans and video. He had admitted once that he hadn't physically attended many murder scenes until the Albert Stucky case. It was altogether possible he had never attended an autopsy until now. Damn it! And she had been so hoping it would be Racine who would upchuck her breakfast.

"Agent Tully." Maggie needed to get his mind off the dead body and onto the case. "Are we sure there was no ID found anywhere at the scene?"

She saw him glance at Racine, but the detective was busy, taking too much time finding a gown her size, like they came in anything other than large, too large and extra too large. At this rate, Maggie knew it would take the woman another ten minutes to accessorize. When Tully realized Racine wasn't paying enough attention to answer, he left his wet gear at the door and came over, grabbing a clean gown off a laundry rack and slipping it on.

"They found her handbag, but no ID. Her clothes were folded and stacked with the purse about ten yards away."

The absence of ID didn't surprise Maggie. Killers often disposed of any tangible identification in the hopes that if the victim couldn't be identified, perhaps neither could the killer. Then, there were always the freaks who took the IDs as trophies.

"Her clothes were folded? What a neat and tidy rapist," Maggie said for Racine's benefit. Now the woman glanced over and frowned at her. So she was listening, after all.

"The girl's underpants were ripped in the crotch area," Racine couldn't resist adding. She padded over to the table, tucking the goggles up onto her spiky blond hair.

Maggie waited for Stan to notice and reprimand Racine, but he was occupied with getting the nests of maggots out of the girl's pubic hair. Then she reminded herself that she needed to concentrate and not let Racine get under her skin. She continued scraping evidence from beneath each fingernail, bagging the findings and labeling each as to which finger it had been taken from.

Besides, why should she care if Racine insisted on sticking with her theory of this being a rape that got carried away? That the District PD hadn't noticed yet that their detective was incompetent shouldn't be Maggie's problem. Yet, it *did* matter if Maggie was going to be on this case, even as a consultant. The last case she'd worked with Racine had left Maggie with a bad taste in her mouth—Racine's mistakes had almost cost them an indictment.

Maggie swatted a strand of hair off her perspiring forehead with the back of her wrist, so as not to contaminate her latexed hands. She caught Racine watching her. Maggie looked away.

Quite honestly, other than the one botched case, Maggie knew little about Julia Racine except what she had heard through rumors. She probably had no right to judge the woman, but if there was any truth to the rumors, Detective

Racine represented a breed of woman that Maggie despised, especially in law enforcement, where playing games could get someone hurt, or even killed.

Since day one of her forensics fellowship, Maggie had worked hard to be just one of the guys and to be treated as such. But women like Racine used their sex as some sort of entitlement or bribe, a means to an end. Now, as she felt Racine's eyes watching her, Maggie hated that Racine still thought she could use that tactic, especially with her. After the last time they had worked together, Maggie thought Racine would know better—pouring on the charm or flirting wouldn't get her any favors from her. But when Maggie glanced up and caught the woman watching her, Racine didn't look away. Instead, she met Maggie's eyes, held her glance and smiled.

## CHAPTER 25

Ben Garrison strung the dripping prints on a short length of clothesline in his cramped darkroom. The first two rolls of film had been disappointing, but this roll…this one was incredible. He was back in the saddle again. Maybe he'd even be able to get a little bidding war started, though he wouldn't be able to waste any time. His fingertips tingled with excitement, but his lungs ached from the fumes. He needed to take a break despite his impatience.

He took one of the prints with him, closing the door on the fumes and heading for the refrigerator. Of course, it was empty except for the regular array of condiments, some kiwi fruit he couldn't remember putting in the back, a container of mystery goop and four long-neck bottles of Budweiser. He grabbed one of the bottles, twisted off the cap and returned to the kitchen counter to admire his masterpiece in the shitty fluorescent lighting.

A knock at the door startled him. Who the hell? He rarely got visitors, and he thought he had trained his meddling neighbors to fuck off. His artistic process was time sensitive. He couldn't be disturbed if he had prints in the fix bath or a roll of film in the developing canister. No respect. What was fucking wrong with people?

He flipped all three locks and yanked open the door.

"What is it?" he growled, causing the small gray-haired woman to step backward and grab the railing. "Mrs. Fowler?" He scratched at his jaw and leaned against the doorjamb, blocking his landlady's wandering eyes. Apparently he hadn't trained everyone in this dilapidated old building to leave him alone. "Why, Mrs. Fowler, what can I help you with today?" He could turn on the charm when necessary.

"Mr. Garrison, I was just wandering by. I've been checking

on Mrs. Stanislov down the hall." Her beady eyes were darting around him, trying to get a glimpse into his apartment.

Several weeks ago, she'd insisted on accompanying the plumber to fix his leaky faucet. The old woman's birdlike head pivoted around, trying to take in the African masks on his wall, the bronze fertility goddesses that adorned his bookcase and the other exotic trinkets he had amassed during his travels. That was when the money was flowing in, and there wasn't a photo he could shoot that someone at *Newsweek* or *Time* or *National Geographic* wouldn't pay top dollar for. He was the hottest new commodity to hit the photojournalism world. Now he was barely thirty and everyone seemed to consider him a has-been. Well, he'd show them all.

"I'm actually pretty busy, Mrs. Fowler. I'm working." He kept his voice pleasant, crossed his arms to stifle his irritation and waited, hoping she could see his impatience through her trifocals.

"I was checking on Mrs. Stanislov," she repeated, waving a skeletal arm toward the door at the end of the hall. "She's been under the weather all week. There's that flu bug going around, you know."

If she was expecting some show of sympathy, they'd be here all night. That was above and beyond his ass-kissing ability, cheap apartment or not. He shifted his weight and waited. His mind wandered back to the print he had left on the kitchen counter. Over thirty exposures to finally capture that one image, that one—

"Mr. Garrison?"

Her small pinched face reminded him of the wrinkled kiwi fruit in the back of his frig.

"Yes, Mrs. Fowler? I really must get back to my work."

She stared at him with eyes magnified three times their size. Her thin lips pursed, wrinkling her skin beyond what he thought possible. Spoiled kiwi. He reminded himself to throw them out. "I wondered if it might be important. That you might want to know."

"What are you talking about?" His politeness had but one level, and she was pushing it past its limits.

This time she backed away, and he knew his tone must have frightened her. She simply pointed at the package he hadn't noticed sitting next to his door. Before he stooped to pick it up, Mrs. Fowler's tiny bird feet shuffled down the stairs.

"Thank you, Mrs. Fowler," he called after her, smiling when he realized he sounded like Jack Nicholson in *The Shining*. Not that she would notice. The old bat probably hadn't even heard him.

The package was lightweight and wrapped in ordinary brown paper. Ben flipped it around. Nothing rattled, and there were no labels, only his name scrawled in black marker. Sometimes the photo lab down the street delivered supplies for him, but he couldn't remember ordering any.

He set it on the kitchen counter, grabbed a paring knife and started cutting the wrap. When he opened the lid of the box, he noticed the packing material's strange texture—it looked like brown packing peanuts. He didn't give it a second thought and stuck his hand into the box, feeling for what was buried inside.

The packing material began to move.

Or was it the exhaustion and too many fumes playing tricks on him?

In seconds the brown peanuts came to life. Shit! The entire contents started crawling out over the sides of the box. Several scurried up his arm. Ben swatted and slapped at them, knocking the box off the counter and releasing hundreds of cockroaches, racing and skittering across his living room floor.

## CHAPTER 26

"Anything found that could have been used as a ligature? And what about handcuffs?" Maggie showed Tully and Racine the girl's wrists, but looked to Tully for answers. The bruises and marks on the wrists were undeniably made by handcuffs. She watched Tully's face, pretending to wait for the answer but really trying to see if he was okay.

This time Tully didn't glance at Racine, but Maggie did, and she could tell the detective wanted to answer, but stopped herself. Tully started pulling out his eyeglasses and pieces of paper from somewhere beneath the gown, tangling his hands in the process. Typical Tully, Maggie noted. He put the glasses on and began sorting through his slips of paper, an odd assortment that included some sort of pamphlet, a folded envelope, the back of a store receipt and a cocktail napkin.

"No handcuffs," he finally answered, and continued to search his scraps of paper.

She wished he would relax. Tully was usually the laid-back one. She was the quick-tempered, hotheaded one, the loose cannon. He was the steady, let's-think-before-we-leap type. It unnerved her how uptight he seemed to be. Something was wrong. Something more than his discomfort with witnessing an autopsy.

"You know, Tully," she said, "they make these really cool contraptions with sheets of paper all tacked together. They're called notebooks, and you can even get them small enough to fit into your pocket."

Tully frowned at her over his glasses and went back to his notes.

"Very funny. My system works just fine."

"Of course, it does. As long as you don't blow your nose."

Racine laughed.

"Humpf." Stan Wenhoff didn't have time for a sense of humor. He motioned to Maggie for help, wanting to hoist the body onto its side for a quick search of any other lacerations.

"Why is her bottom so red?" Racine asked. "The rest of her seems to have this bluish tint, but her ass is all red. Is that weird or what?" Racine attempted a nervous laugh.

Stan sighed, exhaling what sounded like a day's worth of sighs. He was not the most patient medical examiner when it came to explanations. Maggie got the impression he would post No Visitors signs if allowed. They eased the body back. And Stan turned around to peel off his gloves and begin his hand-washing ritual again.

"It's called livor mortis, or the bruising of death," Maggie said when it was obvious Stan wasn't going to answer.

She watched and waited for him to stop her. Instead, he nodded for her to continue. "When the heart stops pumping, the blood stops circulating. All the red cells are literally pulled by the force of gravity to the lowest area, usually the area of the body that's in contact with the ground. The blood cells start breaking down and separating into the muscle tissue. After about two hours, the entire area looks like this, sort of one big reddish bruise. That is, if the body hasn't been moved."

"Wow!" Maggie could feel Racine staring at her. "Does that mean she died sitting up?"

Maggie hadn't thought about it before, but Racine was probably right. Why would the killer have positioned the girl's body while she was still alive? Without asking, she looked to Stan for him to confirm or deny Racine's observation. As the silence stretched out, he finally realized they were waiting for him to respond. He turned around, tugging on a fresh pair of gloves.

"My early guesstimate would be, yes. I'm curious, though. She has almost a pinkish-red tint to her. I'll need to have toxicology check for any poisons."

"Poisons?" Racine attempted another of her nervous laughs. "Stan, this kid was obviously strangled."

"Really, Detective? You believe that to be obvious, do you?"

"Well, maybe not entirely obvious."

Stan took this opportunity to choose a scalpel from the tray of instruments, and Racine's eyes grew wide. Maggie knew they had reached that moment Racine had been dreading since she arrived. Stan started the Y incision.

"Wait." Maggie stopped him, but it wasn't to save Racine. There was something she wanted to check, now curious. If the girl had still been alive when sitting up, maybe strangulation wasn't the cause of death. "Do you mind if we take a look at the ligature marks on her neck first?"

"Fine. Let's take a look at the ligature marks on her neck first." Wenhoff sighed again and set the scalpel aside, purposely clanking it against the other metal instruments.

Maggie knew he was doing his best to restrain his impatience, though his pudgy face betrayed him with its unnatural shade of red. Sweat beads filled his receding hairline. He was used to doing things his own way and his audiences keeping their mouths shut. That he humored her at all, Maggie regarded as Stan's ultimate show of respect. Now he stepped aside, giving her permission to proceed.

"So there was nothing left at the scene that could have been used as a ligature?" Maggie asked Tully while she searched the countertops.

This time she saw him check with Racine, and she was the one to answer. "Nothing. The girl wasn't even wearing panty hose. The purse strap was found intact and clean. Whatever he used, he took with him."

Maggie found what she was looking for and grabbed the tape dispenser from a desk in the corner. She peeled off her gloves so she could handle the tape, then ripped off a piece, holding each end carefully.

"Stan, could you tilt her head, so I can get a better look at her neck?"

Stan handled the girl's head as if it belonged to a mannequin. Rigor mortis was fully established and had stiffened the muscles. After about twenty-four more hours, the muscles would become pliable again, but at the moment, Stan had to twist the head in what looked like an irreverent way, but was, in fact, a necessity.

There were several ligature marks, some overlapping, some deeper than the others. The girl's neck, which probably hadn't contained a single age line, now looked like a road map in 3-D. In addition to the tracks were massive bruises, where the killer must have decided to use his hands, as well.

"Why do you suppose he had such a tough time getting the job done?" Maggie said out loud, not really expecting an answer.

"Maybe she put up a hell of a fight," Racine suggested.

The girl was small, barely sixty-two inches, according to Stan's measurements. Maggie doubted that she could have managed much of a fight.

"Maybe he didn't want to get the job done right away." Tully surprised her with his hushed remark. She could feel him close by, looking over her shoulder.

"You mean he just wanted her unconscious?" Racine asked.

Maggie tried not to get distracted and pressed the transparent tape against the girl's skin, pushing it into one of the ligature grooves.

"He might simply have gotten off on watching her pass out," Tully said, exactly what Maggie had been thinking. "It could have been part of some autoerotic asphyxiation."

"That could explain her dying while sitting up," Maggie said. "Maybe her position was simply a part of his sick game."

"What are you doing with the tape?" Racine asked her.

Ah, so the good detective would finally admit to not knowing something. Maggie lifted the tape while Stan held a slide up for her to attach it to. When it was safely secure, Maggie raised it up to the light.

"Depending on what the killer used, we can sometimes pick up fibers left in the tracks."

"That's if he used a rope or some kind of clothing," Tully added.

"Or any sort of fabric or nylon. Doesn't look like any fibers here. But there is something odd. Looks like glitter."

"Glitter?" Stan was suddenly interested. She handed him the slide and went back to the girl's throat.

"He must have used something strong and thin." Maggie pulled on a fresh pair of gloves. "Probably a cord. Maybe something like a clothesline." She examined the sides of the neck. "Doesn't appear to be a knot."

"Does that mean anything?" Tully asked.

"It could help us if he's done this before. We might be able to match up something already on VICAP. Sometimes killers use the same kind of knot each time. That was one of the identifying factors of the Boston Strangler. He used the same knot on all thirteen of his victims."

"O'Dell, you sure know your trivia about serial killers," Racine jabbed.

Maggie knew she meant it as an innocent joke, but snapped back, "It wouldn't hurt you to know some. You can bet the killers know." As soon as the words were out of her mouth, she regretted them.

"Maybe I need to come to Quantico and take a couple of your classes."

Oh, wonderful, Maggie thought. That was all she needed—to have Julia Racine as a student. Or was that what Racine was hoping for? Did the detective have aspirations of being an FBI agent? Maggie shoved the thought aside and concentrated on the girl's throat.

She ran an index finger over the deep, red scars. As she did this, she noticed a bump. Not just a bump, but a swollen area in the soft underside of the girl's throat. "Wait a minute. Stan, did you check her mouth yet?"

"Not yet. But we'll need to get dental prints if there was no ID."

"I think there's something in her throat."

She hesitated. Both men and Racine hovered over the body and over Maggie, waiting and watching. As soon as Maggie pried open the mouth, she could smell it, a sweet almond scent. Again, she hesitated and glanced up at Stan.

"Do you smell that?"

He sniffed the air. Maggie knew not everyone was capable of smelling the scent, actually about fifty percent of the population. It was Tully who finally answered, "Cyanide?"

Maggie used an index finger to scoop inside both cheeks and removed a partially dissolved capsule. Stan held up an open plastic bag.

"What's with cyanide these days?" Stan said, then noticed the warning look Maggie shot him.

"What kind of crazy son of a bitch gives his victim a cyanide pill after he's strangled her? Or is that the cause of death?" Racine sounded impatient. She didn't seem to notice the exchange between Stan and Maggie, who had both recognized the red-and-white capsule. Enough of it was intact to see that the capsule bore the same brand name they had extracted from the five boys in the cabin just last weekend.

"I haven't gotten that far yet," Stan finally answered.

He was growing impatient, too, but for the moment he was keeping what he knew quiet. Evidently he had read Maggie's urgent look accurately. If there was a connection between this girl and those boys, Racine would know soon enough. For the moment, it was one of the few things they had managed to keep from the media, and Maggie wanted it to remain that way.

"Her mouth was taped shut," Stan continued. "I bagged the duct tape."

"He probably stuck the pill into her mouth and taped it shut while she was unconscious," Tully said, trying to explain the partially dissolved capsule. The girl's saliva glands would have still needed to be working for the capsule to have started dissolving.

Maggie glanced at Tully and could see that he had recognized the capsule, too, and had guessed what was going on. So Racine was the only one in the dark. Not a bad game plan. Maggie refused to feel an ounce of guilt over keeping this from the detective, especially after their last case together.

"Seems like overkill," Racine said.

"Or insurance." Stan was playing along.

"I hate to interrupt your brainstorming, everyone," Maggie said. "But there's something else in here. Stan, could you hand me those forceps?"

She opened the woman's mouth as wide as the rigored jaws allowed, then squinted as she pinched onto an object that was lodged halfway down the girl's throat. What she extracted was covered with blood, folded and crinkled, but still recognizable.

"I think I just found her ID," Maggie told them, holding up what looked like a mangled driver's license.

## CHAPTER 27

Tully sipped his Coke, grateful for the break. Wenhoff had taken the seventeen-year-old's driver's license and fingerprints upstairs to the lab. But Tully knew they wouldn't find any priors or runaway reports on Virginia Brier. From the bikini wax and the girl's mid-November tan lines, Tully knew Virginia was not the typical high-risk victim. She wasn't a prostitute or some throwaway or a homeless street kid. He guessed she came from a good home, a middle- to upper-class family. Somewhere a father and mother were still waiting for her to come home from last night or going crazy because it was too early to file a missing person's report. It reminded him of waiting up for Emma last night. She had been only twenty minutes late, but what if…

"Hey, Tully?"

He realized O'Dell was staring at him again with a look of concern.

"Are you feeling okay?"

"Yeah, I'm fine. Just tired. Stayed up too late last night."

"Oh, really? Hot date?" Racine hoisted herself up onto an empty countertop, her long legs allowing her to do it in one smooth motion.

"My daughter and I stayed up watching *Rear Window*."

"Jimmy Stewart and Grace Kelly? I love that movie. I guess I didn't realize you were married, Tully."

"Divorced."

"Oh, okay." The detective smiled at him as if she was glad. Most people automatically mumbled some sort of apology, which he didn't really understand, either.

He glanced over at O'Dell, who was pretending to be occupied with some evidence bags instead of paying attention to Racine's flirting. Or at least, he *thought* Racine was flirting with him. He'd never been good at it himself or even good at detecting it, for that matter. At least O'Dell was trying to behave herself with Racine, as if being nice to the detective would make up for them keeping her in the dark about the cyanide capsule. He wasn't sure he agreed that they should be withholding information. This was Racine's case, after all. Not theirs. They were here only to assist and offer consultation.

Tully still wondered why Cunningham and BSU had even been called in on this case. Who had made that call and what did they know? Had someone already suggested a connection between this girl and the five young men from the cabin raid? And if so, who was it and how did they know? Evidently, it wasn't anyone at the District PD, because Racine seemed clueless.

His stomach still felt queasy, though the Coke was helping. He was fine as long as he concentrated on the case and not the fact that the dead girl could just as easily have been Emma. He found himself wondering what had made this girl different. Why had the killer chosen her?

"Okay, you two," Racine said. "Tell me what you know."

Tully shot a look at O'Dell. Had Racine finally figured out they hadn't told her something? Before either of them could answer, Racine continued, "Since we have some time, tell me about this guy from what we've learned so far. I have to get out there and start looking for this fucking psycho. You guys are the profilers. Tell me what I'm supposed to look for."

Tully relaxed, almost sighing. O'Dell hadn't flinched. She was good, impressive. They hadn't known each other for very long, but he did know that O'Dell was a better liar than he was. He'd let her have the first shot at Racine's question.

"Everything so far points to him as being organized."

Racine nodded. "Okay, I know about organized versus disorganized. You can save me the textbook stuff. I'm after specifics."

"It's awfully early for specifics," O'Dell told her.

This time Tully could tell O'Dell was not just being difficult with the detective; she was being careful. Maybe too careful. They owed Racine something.

"I'd say he's between twenty-five to thirty years old, Tully said. "Above-average intelligence. He probably holds a regular job and appears to be socially competent to those who know him. Not necessarily a loner. Maybe even a bit arrogant, a braggart."

Racine flipped open a small notebook and was jotting the information down, though what he was giving her could be considered classic textbook generalities, exactly what she had said she didn't want.

"He knows a thing or two about police procedure," O'Dell added, obviously deciding it safe to divulge some of what they knew. "Probably why he likes to use handcuffs. Also, he knew how to ID-proof a body and that delaying her identity might delay us in identifying him, too."

Racine looked up. "Wait a minute. What are you saying? That he could be an ex-cop or something?"

"Not necessarily, but he could be someone who knows a thing or two about crime scenes," O'Dell said. "With some of these guys, it's a fascination. It's part of the cat-and-mouse chase. What they know about police procedure could be from cop shows or even suspense novels."

Tully watched. Racine seemed satisfied and continued writing. At least the two women weren't trying to contradict or outdo each other. For the moment, anyway.

"His posing the body is significant, too. I think it's something more than just gaining control or some sense of empowerment." O'Dell looked at Tully to see if he wanted to venture a guess. He motioned for her to go ahead. "It's possible," she continued, "that he wanted only for us to admire his handiwork, but I think there's something more to it. It may be symbolic."

"You said at the crime scene that it may have been to alter the scene, to throw us off."

"Oh my God, Racine! You mean you were actually listening to me?" This time the women smiled at each other, much to Tully's relief.

"Those circular indentations in the ground mean something, too," Tully reminded them, "but I have no idea what. Not yet, anyway."

"Oh, and he's left-handed," O'Dell added as an afterthought.

Both Tully and Racine stared at her, waiting for an explanation.

O'Dell walked back to the body and pointed to the right side of the girl's face.

"There's a bruise here along her jawline. Her lip is split in this corner. Even bled for a short time. It's her right side, which means, if he was facing her, he hit her from left to right, probably with his left fist."

"Couldn't he have used the back of his right hand?" Tully asked, trying to play out the possible scenarios.

"Maybe, but that would be more of an upward motion." She demonstrated, swiping a backhanded motion toward him. He could see what she meant. A person's natural tendency would be to start with the hand down and to bring it up and across. "This injury," O'Dell continued, "looks like a direct hit. I'd say a fist." She balled up her left hand and swiped again, this time straight in front. "Definitely, a left fist to the right jaw."

Throughout this demonstration Tully noticed Racine watching quietly, almost with awe or perhaps admiration. Then she went back to her notes. Whatever it was Tully had noticed in Racine's expression, it had been lost on O'Dell. She hadn't been paying any attention. But then she was like that when anyone seemed to be amazed by her. Most of the time, she drove him a little nuts with her anal-retentive habits, her hotshot tactics or her tendency to overlook procedure whenever it was convenient to do so. However, this—her ability to be impressive and not take note or make a big deal of it—this was one of the things he really liked about her.

"One thing," O'Dell said, addressing Racine, "and I really am not just saying this to bug the hell out of you. This is not a one-time thing. This guy's going to do it again. And I wouldn't be surprised to find that he may have already killed before this. We really should check VICAP."

The morgue door swung open behind them. All three of them jumped, spinning around to find Stan Wenhoff, his ruddy complexion pale. He held up what looked like a computer printout.

"We're in for a hell of a mess, kids." Stan wiped at the sweat on his forehead. "She's the daughter of Henry Franklin Brier… a goddamn U.S. senator."

# CHAPTER 28

*Everett's Compound*

Justin Pratt felt an elbow poke his side, and only then did he realize he had dozed off. He glanced at Alice, who was sitting beside him, cross-legged like the rest of the members, but her head and eyes were facing ahead, her back straight. Two of her fingers tapped his ankle, her polite way of telling him to stay awake and pay attention.

He wanted to tell her he didn't give a fuck what Father had to say tonight or any night, for that matter. And after last night he wished that Alice didn't give a fuck, either. Jesus! He was so tired. All he wanted to do was close his eyes, just for a few minutes. He could still listen even if his eyes were closed. His eyelids started to droop, and this time he felt a pinch. He sat up and scrubbed a hand over his face, digging a thumb and index finger into his eyes. Another elbow. Jesus!

He glared at her, but she didn't flinch from her appropriately adoring attention on Father. Maybe she liked what the guy did to her last night. Maybe she had really gotten off on it, and what Justin thought was a grimace had actually been her expression of orgasm. Shit! He was just tired. He needed to stop thinking about last night. He sat up straight and folded his hands into his lap.

Tonight Father was going off on the government again, a favorite topic of his. Justin had to admit that some of the stuff the man said did make sense. He remembered his grandfather telling Eric and him stories about government conspiracies. How the government had murdered JFK. How the United Nations was really a conspiracy to take over the world.

Justin's dad had said, "The old man had a couple of loose screws," but Justin loved and admired his grandfather. He had been a war hero, getting the Congressional Medal of Honor for saving his whole squad in Vietnam. Justin had seen the medal, as well as the photos and letters, one from President Lyndon Johnson. It was pretty cool. But it was all stuff Justin knew his dad despised. Probably another reason Justin loved the old man—they had something in common: neither of them had ever been able to please Justin's dad. Then his grandfather up and died last year. Justin still felt pissed at him for leaving him. He knew that was a fucked-up attitude. It wasn't his granddad's fault, but he missed the old man. He didn't have anyone to talk to, especially after Eric left.

He knew Eric missed Granddad, too, even if he was too much of a macho-shithead to admit it. Less than three weeks after the funeral, Eric dropped out of Brown University. That was when all hell broke loose at home.

"Excuse me, am I boring you?" Father's voice boomed across the room.

Justin sat up, but he was already sitting about as straight as he could. He felt Alice gripping his ankle, so tight her fingernails dug into his sock and skin.

Shit! He was in trouble now. Alice had warned him that daydreaming during Father's talks could lead to punishment. Oh, what the hell. So what if he sent him out into the woods again. Maybe this time he'd just take off. He didn't need this shit. Maybe he could meet up with Eric somewhere else.

"Answer me," Father demanded as the room grew quiet. No one dared turn to look at the guilty one. "Do you find what I say so boring you'd rather sleep?"

Justin looked up, ready to take his punishment, but Father's eyes were staring off to Justin's left. And now the old man sitting next to Justin began to fidget restlessly. Justin could see the man's callused hands wringing the hem of his blue work shirt. He recognized him from the building crew. No wonder the poor guy was dozing. The building crew had been working around the clock to remodel Father's living quarters before winter, which was ridiculous if all of them were to be moving to some paradise soon. Surely others on the crew would speak up and remind Father of the long hours they'd been working. But instead, everyone remained silent, waiting.

"Martin, what do you have to say for yourself?"

"I guess I—"

"Stand up when you address me."

The members all sat on the floor during the meetings. Justin couldn't figure out why the hell Father was the only one who got a chair. Alice had tried to explain that no one's head should be higher than Father's when Father spoke. Justin would have laughed out loud at that had it not been for the somber, almost reverent look on her face.

"We have traitors in our midst," Father bellowed. "We have a reporter trying to destroy us with ugly lies. This is no time for any of us to be caught sleeping. I said stand!"

Justin watched the old man untangle his legs and crawl to his feet. He could sympathize with the guy. After three hours, he, too, had problems with muscle cramps. The old guy reminded Justin of his grandfather, thin and small, but wiry. He was probably stronger and younger than his weathered skin suggested. He shot a look at Justin, then looked away quickly, reminding Justin that he shouldn't be watching. Out of the corner of his eyes Justin could see the others with their heads obediently facing the front of the room and their eyes cast down.

"Martin, you're wasting everyone's time. Perhaps instead of offering an explanation, you need a reminder of what happens when you waste everyone's time." Father waved to the two bodyguards, and the men disappeared out the back door. "Come here, Martin, and bring along Aaron."

"No, wait..." Martin protested as he made his way to the front, stepping carefully around the members who sat in an unorganized fashion on the floor. "Punish me," Martin said, weaving his way, "but leave my son out of this."

However, the fair-skinned, blond Aaron was already making his way to Father's side. Justin figured him to be about his age, only small and wiry like his dad, and strangely eager to assist Father.

"Martin, you know there are no fathers and sons here. No mothers and daughters. No brothers and sisters." Father's voice was back to its calm, soothing tone. "We all belong to one unit, one family."

"Of course, I just meant—" Martin stopped when he saw the guards return, carrying what Justin thought was a huge, long hose.

Then the hose moved.

"Shit!" he said under his breath, then quickly glanced around, grateful no one had heard him over their own gasps. Because what the guards carried between them was the biggest fucking snake Justin had ever seen.

He stole a glimpse at Father's face while everyone else returned to silence. Father was smiling, watching the crowd's reaction and nodding as if in satisfaction. Suddenly, Father caught Justin's eyes and the smile turned to a scowl. Justin looked away, lowering his head as well as his eyes. Jesus! Was *he* in trouble now? He waited for his name to be called and realized his heart had begun slamming against his ribs. In this fucking silence would the sound betray him?

"Aaron," Father called instead, "I want you to take this snake and place it around Martin's neck."

There were no gasps, only more silence, as though the entire room of people was collectively holding its breath.

"But Father…" Aaron's voice sounded like a small boy's, and Justin cringed. Stupid kid. Don't show weakness. Don't show him you're scared.

"Aaron, I'm surprised." The reverend's voice was soft and sweet, and it made Justin cringe even more. "Didn't you come to me just last week and tell me you were ready to become one of my soldiers? One of our warriors for justice?"

"Yes, but—"

"Stop your sniveling, then, and do as I say," he yelled, causing everyone to jump at the change in his tone.

Aaron looked from Father to Martin and then at the snake.

Justin couldn't believe the kid was considering it. But what choice did he have if he didn't want that fucking snake around his own neck? Surely, this was only a test. Yeah, that was it. Justin didn't know much about the Bible, but wasn't there some story about God telling a father to kill his own son? Then at the last minute God stopped the guy. That had to be what this was.

Justin took a deep breath, but no relief seemed to come with his sudden realization. Instead, all he felt was Alice's fingernails digging deeper into his ankle.

Aaron took hold of the snake. Martin, who had stood tall and firm all this time, began to sob, so violently he shook as Aaron and one of the guards wound the snake across the old man's shoulders and neck.

"We must not be caught sleeping," Father was saying, his voice calm again as though this was just another one of his instructive lectures. "Our enemies are closer than you think. Only those of us who are strong and obey the strictness of our rules will survive."

Justin wondered if anyone was listening to Father's words. He had difficulty hearing them over the pounding of his own heart, while he watched the snake squeeze and Martin's face swell, turning crimson-red. The old man's fingers clawed at the snake as panic overrode fear.

"All it takes is one person," Father continued, "to betray us, to destroy us."

Justin couldn't believe it. Father wasn't even looking at Martin. Surely, he'd call it off any second now. Wasn't this enough of a test? The old man's eyes started to roll back in his head, his tongue hung from his mouth. His head would explode. It was going to fucking explode all over the place.

"We must remember…" Father stopped and looked down at the puddle forming around his shoes. Martin had peed his pants. Father lifted one foot, his face contorting with disgust. He waved to his guards. "Remove the snake," he said, as if only because he didn't want his shoes soiled any more than they already were.

It took both guards and Aaron to pull off and unwrap the snake. Martin collapsed where he stood. But Father continued as though this had only been a minor distraction, stepping over Martin's body and turning his back to him as the old man crawled away.

"We must remember there are no loyalties, no bonds except for the greater good of our mission. We must free ourselves from petty desires of the material world."

Father seemed to be addressing a specific group, especially one woman, who sat in front. Justin recognized her. She was one of the entourage that the reverend kept close at prayer rallies, one of the group of about a dozen members that was bused in for the meetings. They all still lived and worked on the outside and had not yet entirely joined the community. Alice had explained that these were people with important ties to the outside, or ones who had not yet fully proved themselves to Father.

As the meeting ended, Justin watched Father go to the woman, giving her both his hands to help her stand and hugging her. Probably feeling her up and getting in a few extra squeezes. Justin couldn't help thinking she looked like one of his mom's country club friends, wearing a navy dress and that bright red scarf.

## CHAPTER 29

It was at this time every evening that Kathleen O'Dell still craved a tumbler of bourbon, a stirred—not shaken—martini or even a snifter of brandy. She stared at the tray with the porcelain gold-trimmed pot and watched as Reverend Everett poured a cup of hot tea for her, Emily, Stephen and himself. All the while, she couldn't help thinking how much she hated tea. It didn't matter if it was herbal, spice or served with lemon or honey or milk. Just the aroma made her want to gag.

The tea reminded her of those first weeks from hell when she quit drinking. Father had stopped by her apartment several times a week, generously giving of his precious time to brew for her a pot of his special tea made from leaves shipped from some exotic place in South America. He claimed it had magical powers. Kathleen swore it made her hallucinate, causing painful flashes of bright light behind her eyes. That was before it made her stomach rock violently. Each time, Father stood patiently over her, telling her how God had different plans for her, or more precisely, telling the back of her head while she vomited her guts into the toilet.

Now she smiled up at him as he handed her a cup, pretending this was exactly what she craved. She owed this man so much, and yet he seemed to ask for so little in return. Pretending to enjoy his tea seemed a small sacrifice.

They all sat in front of the roaring fireplace in the soft leather chairs Father had received from a wealthy donor. Everyone sipped the tea, and Kathleen put the cup to her lips, making herself do the same. There had been little conversation. They were still a bit stunned from Father's powerful performance. No one doubted the need for Martin to be taught a lesson. How dare he fall asleep.

She could feel Father watching the three of them, his diplomats to the outside world, as he called them. Each played an important role, assigned tasks that only he or she could deliver. In return, Father allowed them these private meetings, gracing them with his time and his confidences, both rare and special commodities. He had so many obligations. There were so many people who needed him to heal their wounds and save their souls. Between weekend rallies and daily lectures, the man had little time to himself. So many pressures, so much to expect from one person.

"All of you are very quiet tonight." He smiled at them, sitting down in the large recliner set closest to the fire. "Did tonight's lesson shock you?"

There were quick glances between them. Kathleen sipped her tea again, suddenly a preferable action to saying the wrong thing. She watched over the rim of her cup. Earlier, during the meeting, Emily had almost fainted. Kathleen had felt the woman leaning into her while the boa constrictor choked Martin, turning his face into a puffy crimson balloon. But she knew Emily would never admit to such a thing.

And Stephen, with his soft and... She stopped, trying to keep a promise to herself not to think of Stephen in that way. After all, the man was quite smart and certainly had other qualities that had nothing to do with his... Well, with his sexual preference. But she knew Stephen had probably been shocked and too much in awe to say anything. Perhaps that's why Father's eyes now met Kathleen's and stayed there, as if the question had been addressed to only her. But they were friendly eyes, coaxing her, making her feel, once again, as though she was the only one whose opinion he cared about.

"Yes, I was shocked," she said, and saw Emily's eyes grow wide as if she were going to faint again. "But I understood the importance of the lesson. You were very wise in choosing a snake," she added.

"And why do you say that, Kathleen?" Father leaned forward, encouraging her to continue, as if anxious to hear why he was so wise. As if he didn't already know.

"Well, it was a snake, after all, that contributed to Eve's

betrayal and the destruction of paradise, just like Martin's falling asleep could betray all of us and destroy our hopes for building our paradise."

He nodded, pleased, and rewarded her with a pat on the knee. His hand lingered a bit longer than usual tonight, the fingers splaying onto her thigh, caressing her, making her feel warm—so warm she could feel his power radiating through her panty hose, through her skin, almost sending a shiver through her veins.

Finally he removed his hand and turned his attention to Stephen. "And speaking of our paradise, what have you learned about our possible transportation to South America?"

"Just as you thought, we'll need to do it in several waves. Trips, perhaps of two or three dozen at a time."

"South America?" Kathleen didn't understand. "I thought we were going to Colorado."

Stephen wouldn't meet her eyes. He looked away, embarrassed, as if he had gotten caught revealing a secret. She looked to Father for an answer.

"Of course we're going to Colorado, Kathleen. This is merely a backup plan. No one else knows, and it must not leave this room," he instructed. She studied his face to see if he was angry, but then he smiled and said, "You three are the only ones I can trust."

"So we are still going to Colorado?" Kathleen had fallen in love with the slides he had shown them of the hot springs, the beautiful aspen trees and wildflowers. What did she know about South America? It seemed so far away, so remote, so primitive.

"Yes, of course," he reassured her. "This is just in case we need to leave the country."

She must have not looked convinced, because he reached for her hands, taking them delicately in his as though they were fragile rose petals.

"You must trust me, my dear Kathleen. I would never let any harm come to any of you. But there are people, evil people, in the media and in the government who would be pleased to destroy us."

"People like Ben Garrison," Stephen said with an uncharacteristic snarl that surprised Kathleen and garnered a smile from Father.

"Yes, people like Mr. Garrison. He was only able to spend a couple of days inside the compound before we discovered his true mission, but we're still not certain what he saw or what he knows. What lies he might tell the rest of the world."

Absently, he still held Kathleen's hands in his and began caressing the palms while he continued to address Stephen. "What do we know about the cabin? How did the feds even find out about it?"

"I'm still not sure. Perhaps a disgruntled ex-member?"

"Perhaps."

"Everything is lost," Stephen answered, looking at his hands, not able to meet Father's eyes.

"Everything?"

Stephen only nodded.

Kathleen had no idea what they were referring to, but Father and Stephen often talked of secret missions that didn't concern her. Right now all she could focus on was how Father's large hands seemed to be massaging her small ones, making her feel special but at the same time, much too warm and suddenly much too uncomfortable. She wanted to pull her hands away but knew that would be wrong. Father only meant it as a gesture of compassion. How dare she think otherwise. She felt her cheeks flush at the mere thought.

"We have one loose end," Stephen said.

"Yes, I know. I'll take care of that. Will we need to..." Father hesitated as if looking for the correct word. "Will we need to accelerate our departure?"

Stephen pulled out some papers, along with a map, went to Father's side and got down on one knee, showing him the items. Kathleen watched Stephen, concentrating on his gestures. He constantly amazed her. Though tall and lean with flawless brown skin, boyish features and a sharp mind, he appeared timid and quiet, as if always waiting for permission to speak. Father said Stephen was brilliant, but at the same time, he was too humble for his own good, slow to take credit and a little too ordinary in his mannerisms to stand out. He was the type of man who would not easily be noticed. And Kathleen wondered if that made his everyday job more or less difficult.

She tried to remember what it was that he did at the Capitol. Though she spent hours with Stephen and Emily in conversations like this, she knew little about either of them. Stephen's position sounded like an important one. She had heard him mention something about his level of security clearance, and he was always dropping the names of senators and their aides whom he had talked to or whom he would get in touch with. Whatever his position was, it obviously helped Father and the church.

Stephen finished with the papers, stood and retreated. Kathleen realized she hadn't paid attention to a word of the conversation. She looked to Father's face, checking to see if he had noticed. His olive skin and bristled jaw made him look older than his forty-six years. There were new lines at his eyes and at the corners of his mouth. So much pressure he was under, too much for one man. That was what he often told them, but then said he had no choice, really, that God had chosen him to lead his followers to a better life. He finally pulled his hands back, away from Kathleen's, and folded them together in his lap. At first, Kathleen thought it was in prayer until she noticed him kneading the hem of his jacket, a subtle but disturbing gesture.

"Those who want to destroy us draw closer each day," he said in a hushed tone, confiding in the three of them. "There are ways I can destroy some of our enemies, but others can simply be stifled for the time being. Everything stored at the cabin was for our protection, our security. If all is lost, we will need to find some other way to obtain protection. We must protect ourselves from those who wish to destroy us. Those who are jealous of my power. What concerns me most is that I sense betrayal within our own ranks."

Emily gasped, and Kathleen wanted to slap her. Couldn't she

see this was hard enough for Father? He needed their strength and support, not their panic. Although she wasn't sure what Father meant by betrayal. She knew there had been members who had left, several recently. And then, of course, the reporter—that photographer who had pretended to be a lost soul to gain access to their compound.

"No one shall cross me and go unpunished." Instead of angry, Father looked sad when he said this, glancing at each of them as if appealing to them for help, though this strong, miraculous man would never ask for such a thing, at least not for himself. It made Kathleen want to say or do something to comfort him.

"I'm counting on the three of you," he continued. "Only you can help. We must not let lies destroy us. We cannot trust anyone. We mustn't let them break up our church." The calm slowly transformed to anger, his hands turning to fists and his face changing from olive to crimson. Still his voice remained steady. "Anyone who is not with us is against us. Those against us are jealous of our faith, jealous of our knowledge and of our special graces with God."

He pounded a fist on the chair arm, making Kathleen jump. He didn't seem to notice and continued as if the rage had taken control. She had never seen him like this before. Spittle drooled from the corner of his mouth as he said, "They're jealous of my power. They want to destroy me, because I know too many of their secrets. They will not destroy everything I worked so hard to build. How dare they even think they can outwit me. That they can destroy me. I see the end and it will come in a ball of fire if they choose to destroy me."

Kathleen watched, uncomfortable yet unflinching. Perhaps this was one of Father's prophetic fits. He had told them about his visions, his tremors, his talks with God, but no one had witnessed one. Is that what was happening now? Is that what caused the veins at his temples to bulge and his teeth to clench? Is this what it looked like to talk to God? How would she know? She had stopped talking to God ages ago. Right about the time she started believing in the power of Jack Daniel's and Jim Beam.

However, Father did seem to have special powers, certain knowledge, almost psychic abilities. How else was he able to so keenly zero in on people's fears? How else was he able to know so much about things the media and the government kept from everyone?

She had been shocked at first when he told them about the government putting chemicals like fluoride in the water to cause cancer or about the government injecting healthy cows with E. coli to cause a national panic. About the government putting listening devices in cellular phones and cameras in ATM machines, all to record their every move. Even the magnetic strips on the back of credit cards contained personal tracking devices. And now with the Internet, the government could see inside people's homes anytime they went online.

At first she had found it all hard to believe, but each time, Father read to them articles from sources he said were unbiased, some in prestigious medical journals, and all backing up his knowledge.

He was one of the wisest men Kathleen had ever known. She still wasn't sure she cared whether or not her soul had been saved. What Kathleen O'Dell did care about was that, for the first time in more than two decades, she believed in someone again and that she was surrounded by people who cared about her. She was an integral part of a community, an integral part of something larger and more important than herself. That was something she had never experienced.

"Kathleen?"

"Yes, Father?"

He was pouring more tea for them and frowned when he noticed she had hardly touched hers. But instead of lecturing her on the healing qualities of his special tea, he said, "What can you tell me about breakfast with your daughter?"

"Oh, that. It was nice," she lied, not wanting to confess that they hadn't even ordered breakfast before Maggie bailed out on her. "I told Maggie that perhaps we could do Thanksgiving."

"And? I hope she won't make an excuse that she has to be off profiling some important case, will she?" He seemed so concerned that her relationship with her daughter work out. With all these other problems to deal with, Kathleen felt guilty that she had given him one more concern.

"Oh, no, I don't think so. She seemed very excited about it," she lied again, wanting to please him. After all, he often said the end justified the means. He had so many pressures of his own. She couldn't add to that. Besides, it would all work out just fine with her and Maggie. It always did.

"I'm excited about cooking a real holiday meal. Thanks so much for suggesting it."

"It's important for the two of you to repair your relationship," he told her.

He had been encouraging her to do so for months now. She was a bit confused by it. Usually, Father emphasized that members needed to let go of family. Even tonight with Martin and Aaron, he had lectured that there were no fathers and sons, no mothers and daughters. But she was sure Father had a good reason—if he was insisting it must be for her own good. He probably knew that she needed to repair the relationship before they left for Colorado. Yes, that was it. So that she could truly feel free.

Just then, she wondered how Father knew that Maggie was a profiler for the FBI. She was quite certain she hadn't told him. Half the time, she couldn't even remember what it was called. But, of course, Father would have taken it upon himself to know. She smiled to herself, pleased that he obviously cared a great deal about her to bother with such a small detail. Now she really would need to make an effort to have Thanksgiving with Maggie. It was the least she could do if it meant that much to Reverend Everett.

# CHAPTER 30

*Newburgh Heights, Virginia*

Maggie leaned her forehead against the cool glass and watched the raindrops slide down her kitchen window. Wisps of fog descended upon her large, secluded backyard, reminding her for a second time in two days of swirling ghosts. It was ridiculous. She didn't believe in ghosts. She believed in things she knew, black-and-white things she could see and feel. Gray was much too complicated.

Yet each time she viewed a dead body, each time she helped slice into its flesh and remove what were once pulsating organs, she found herself reaffirming—or perhaps it was hoping—that there had been something eternal, something no one could see or even begin to understand, something that had escaped from the decaying shell left behind. If that's the way it worked, then Ginny Brier's spirit, her soul, was in another place, perhaps with Delaney and Maggie's father, all of them sharing the horrific last moments as they swirled in wisps of gray fog around the dogwoods in her backyard.

Jesus! She grabbed the tumbler of Scotch off the kitchen counter and drained what was left, trying to remember how many she had drunk since getting home from the morgue. Then she decided if she couldn't remember, it didn't matter. Besides, the familiar buzz was preferable to that annoying hollow feeling she couldn't shake off.

She poured another Scotch, this time noticing the wall calendar that hung alongside the small corkboard above the counter. The board was empty except for a few pushpins with nothing to hold up. Was there not one goddamn thing she needed to remind herself about? The wall calendar was still turned to September. She flipped the pages, bringing it to November. Thanksgiving was only days away. Had her mother been serious about cooking a dinner? Maggie couldn't remember the last time they had attempted a holiday together, though whenever it was, she was sure it had been disastrous. There were plenty of holidays in her memory bank she would just as soon forget. Like four years ago when she spent Christmas Eve on a hard, lumpy sofa outside the critical care unit of St. Anne's Hospital. While others had been buying last-minute gifts or stopping at parties for sugar cookies and eggnog, her mother had spent the day mixing red and green pills with her old friend, Jim Beam.

She stood at the window again, watching the fog swallow entire corners of her landscape. She could barely see the outline of the pine trees that lined her property. They reminded her of towering sentries, standing shoulder to shoulder, shielding her, protecting her. After a childhood of feeling lost and vulnerable, why wouldn't she spend her adulthood looking for ways to be in control, to protect herself? Sure, in some ways, it had also made her cautious, a bit skeptical and untrusting. Or as Gwen would put it, it made her inaccessible to anyone including those who cared about her. Which made her think of Nick Morrelli.

She leaned her forehead against the glass again. She didn't want to think of Nick. Her mother's accusation that morning still stung, probably because there was more truth in it than she wanted to admit. She hadn't talked to Nick in weeks, and it had been months since they had seen each other. Months since she had told him she didn't want to see him until after her divorce was final.

She checked her watch, took another sip of Scotch and found herself reaching for the phone. She could stop at any second, she could hang up before he answered. Or maybe just say hi. What harm was there in hearing his voice?

One ring, two, three… She would leave a brief and friendly message on his answering machine. Four rings…five—

"Hello?" It was a woman's voice.

"Yes," Maggie said, not recognizing the voice. Maybe she had the wrong number. It had been months, after all, since she had dialed it. "Is Nick Morrelli there?"

"Oh," the woman said, "is this the office? Can't it wait?"

"No, this is a friend. Is Nick there?"

The woman paused as if she needed to decide what information a friend was entitled to. Then finally she said, "Umm…he's in the shower. Can I take a message and have him call you back?"

"No, that's okay. I'll try back another time."

But when Maggie hung up the phone, she knew she would not try back anytime soon.

# CHAPTER 31

*Reston, Virginia*

Tully hoped his gut instinct was wrong. He hoped he was being an overprotective father who was simply overreacting. That's what he kept telling himself, yet before he left the morgue he made a copy of Virginia Brier's driver's license photo and stuck it in his back pocket.

He had called Emma earlier to let her know he wouldn't be home until later, but if she wanted to wait for dinner, he'd pick up a pizza. He was pleased when she asked for lots of pepperoni on her side. At least they would be sharing a meal together, perhaps one they could both enjoy. Between the two of them, their culinary skills didn't extend much beyond grilled cheese sandwiches with soup. Sometimes when Tully was feeling a bit adventurous he'd throw a couple of chunks of meat on the grill. Unfortunately, he had never been able to figure out how to keep it from becoming a shrunken, charred hockey puck, and there wasn't much treat in that.

Their small two-bedroom bungalow in Reston, Virginia, was a far cry from the two-story colonial they'd lived in in Cleveland. Caroline had insisted on keeping the house, and now Tully wondered if Emma would ever want to come back here after spending Thanksgiving vacation in her old room. Only recently had this house begun to feel like home, though it had been almost a year since they'd made the move. No matter how much he complained about this parenting stuff, he couldn't imagine what this house, the move, the new town and new job—what any of it would have been like without Emma.

Thanks to his daughter, the house didn't have that bachelor look or smell to it, though, as Tully weaved his way through the living room clutter to the kitchen clutter, he wondered if there was a difference between bachelor clutter and teenager clutter. Maybe what he liked was having some feminine things around, even if the pink lava lamp on the bookcase, the purple Rollerblades sticking out from under the sofa or the smiley-face magnets on the refrigerator were not his style.

"Hey, Dad." As he stepped through the front door Emma appeared. He didn't kid himself. It was the power of pizza that drew her, not his lovable presence.

"Hi, sweat pea." He kissed her cheek, a gesture she tolerated only when they were alone.

She wore her headphones wrapped around her neck, a compromise that had taken much drilling and constant reminders, but was well worth it, although he could still hear the music blaring. The music, however, he couldn't complain about, since he still enjoyed some head-banging rock 'n' roll once in a while, only in the form of the Rolling Stones or the Doors.

Emma got out the paper plates and plastic cups that they had agreed long ago would be part of any take-out treat. What was the use of having someone else prepare the meal if you still had to wash dishes? As he scooped up pieces of pizza and watched her pour their Pepsis, he wondered when would be a good time to broach the subject about the dead girl.

"Kitchen or living room?" she asked, picking up her plate and cup.

"Living room, but no TV."

"Okay."

He followed her into the living room, and when she decided to sit on the floor, he joined her despite his thigh still being a bit tender. It reminded him that Agent O'Dell never once mentioned or complained about *her* scar, a memento from the legendary serial killer Albert Stucky. Although he had never seen it, Tully knew from rumors that the scar crossed the length of her abdomen, as if the man had tried to gut her. Now he and O'Dell had something in common. Tully had a scar of his own, a constant reminder of the bullet Albert Stucky had put into him last spring as he and O'Dell tried to recapture him.

The bullet had caused some damage, but he refused to let it stop him from his daily ritual run. Lately he hated to admit that it qualified more as jogging than running. That one bullet had messed up a lot of things, including his ability to sit cross-legged on the floor without feeling the muscles sting and pinch. There were some things worth a little pain, and having pizza on the floor with his daughter was one of them.

"Mom called," Emma said as if it were an everyday occurrence. "She said she talked to you about Thanksgiving and that you were cool with everything."

He clenched his jaw. He wasn't cool with everything, but then Emma didn't need to know that. He watched her swipe a strand of long blond hair from her face to keep it away from the strings of cheese that hung from the pizza slice.

"Are you cool about spending Thanksgiving in Cleveland?" he asked.

"I guess."

It seemed like a typical Emma response, a hint of indifference mixed with that you'd-never-understand-anyway shrug of the shoulders. He wished someone had told him long ago that he'd need a degree in psychology to be a parent of a teenager. Maybe that's why he enjoyed his job. Figuring out serial killers seemed like a piece of cake compared to figuring out teenage girls.

"If you don't want to go, you don't have to." He gulped his Pepsi, trying to replicate the art of indifference that his daughter seemed to have perfected.

"She's got it all planned and stuff."

"Doesn't matter."

"I just hope she didn't invite him over."

Tully wasn't sure who the new "him" was in his ex-wife's life. Maybe he didn't want to know. There had been several since their divorce.

"You have to understand, Emma, if your mom has someone new in her life, she's probably gonna want to include him for Thanksgiving."

Jeez! He couldn't believe he was defending Caroline's right to screw yet another guy. Just the thought made him angry, or worse, lose his appetite. Two years ago his wife decided one day that she was no longer in love with him, that the passion in their marriage was gone and that she needed to move on. Nothing better to destroy a guy's ego than to have his wife tell him she needed to move on and away from his passionless, unlovable self.

"What about you?"

For a minute Tully had forgotten what exactly they had been talking about.

"What do you mean?"

"What will you do for Thanksgiving?"

He caught himself staring at her, then grabbed for another piece of pizza, feeling his indifference slipping. Yet he couldn't help but smile. His daughter was worried about him spending Thanksgiving alone. Could there be anything more cool?

"Hey, I'm planning on a full day of fun, sitting in my underwear watching football all afternoon."

She frowned at him. "You hate college football."

"Well, then maybe I'll go to the movies."

This made her giggle, and she had to set her Pepsi aside so as not to spill it.

"What's so funny about that?"

"You, go to the movies by yourself? Come on, Dad. Get real."

"Actually, I'll probably need to work. There's a pretty important case we're working on. In fact, I wanted to talk to you about it."

He pulled the photocopy from his back pocket, unfolded it and handed it to Emma.

"Do you know this girl? Her name's Virginia Brier."

Emma took a careful look, then set the copy aside and began on another piece of pizza.

"Is she in some kind of trouble?"

"No, she's not in trouble." Tully felt a wave of relief. It looked like Emma didn't recognize the girl. Of course he had been crazy. There had been hundreds of people at the monuments Saturday night.

But before he could relax, Emma said, "She doesn't like to be called Virginia."

"What?"

"She uses Ginny."

Jesus! The nausea grabbed hold again.

"So you do know her?"

"Actually, Alesha and I just met her Saturday when we were on the field trip, but yeah, she was there Saturday night, too. She sorta made us mad, because she was flirting with this boy Alesha really liked. He was really cool and he seemed to be having a good time with us until that reverend guy fawned all over Ginny."

"Hold on a minute. Who was this boy?"

"His name's Brandon. He was with Alice and Justin and the reverend guy."

Tully got up and went to where he'd left his windbreaker. He started pulling everything out of his pockets and finally found the pamphlet he had picked up blowing around the FDR Memorial. He handed it to Emma.

"Is this the reverend guy?" He pointed to the color photograph on the back.

"Yeah, that's him. Reverend Everett," she read off the pamphlet. "Except they were all calling him Father. Seemed kinda creepy. I mean it's not like he's their dad or anything."

"It's not that weird, Emma. Catholics call priests Father. It's sort of a title, like pastor or reverend or Mr."

"Yeah, but it wasn't like they were using it as a title. They really were all talking about him as if he were their father, 'cause he's their leader and like he knows what's best for them and stuff."

"This Brandon guy, did you see him go off with Ginny?"

"You mean like to be alone?"

"Yes."

"Dad, there were like tons of people. Besides, Alesha and I left before the rally thing was over. It was so lame, all that singing and clapping."

"You think you might be able to give a detailed description of Brandon?"

She looked at him as if realizing for the first time there might be some connection to the questions about Ginny and his job as an FBI agent.

"Yeah, I guess I could," she said, her indifference changing to concern. "I thought you said Ginny wasn't in trouble."

He hesitated, wondering what to tell her. She wasn't a little girl anymore, and chances were she'd hear about it soon on TV. No matter how much of a protective father he wanted to be, he couldn't protect her from the truth. And she'd be upset with him if he lied.

He reached across the floor and took her hand, then said, "Ginny's dead. Someone murdered her Saturday night."

## CHAPTER 32

*MONDAY*
*November 25*
*FBI Academy*
*Quantico, Virginia*

Maggie stole a glance at Agent Tully as they watched Agent Bobbi LaPlatz scratch several pencil lines. Magically the face on her sketch pad developed a thin, narrow nose.

"Does that look close?" she asked Emma Tully, who sat beside her, hands in her lap, her eyes examining the line drawing.

"I think so, but the lips aren't quite right." Emma glanced at her dad, as if waiting for him to comment. He only nodded at her.

"Too thin?" LaPlatz asked.

"Maybe it's the mouth, not the lips. You know, like he never smiled. He sorta had this…um…frown, but not like he was mad. Just maybe like he was too tough to smile." She flipped her hair back and gave her dad another glance. "Does that make sense?" she asked, turning back to Agent LaPlatz, her eyes darting back to check Tully's face before returning to the paper.

"I think so. Let me give it a try." And LaPlatz's hand went to work, making quick, short movements. A line here, one there, transforming the entire face again with her simple number two pencil, a magic wand with teeth marks embedded in its sides.

Maggie could see Tully had that worried indent in his forehead. She had noticed it earlier, even before he now started rubbing at it as if he could make it disappear. Earlier when he stopped by her office he seemed more than just worried. *Disoriented* was the best word Maggie could come up with.

His daughter, Emma, had never been to Quantico before, and this morning, unfortunately, was not going to be one of those fun tours to see where Daddy worked. Emma seemed to be handling the situation just fine, but Tully was still fidgeting. His toe kept tapping. When he wasn't rubbing the indent off his forehead, he was pushing up the bridge of his glasses. He remained silent, saying not a word since Agent LaPlatz had sat down. Once in a while his eyes strayed from the face materializing on the paper to Emma's. Maggie watched as his fingers found a paper in his breast pocket and he began an accordion fold. His fingers worked without the aid of his eyes, as if on a mission of their own.

Maggie had a good idea why her normally laid-back partner looked like he had been injected with caffeine. It wasn't just that Emma had known the dead girl, but that she had also been at the rally Ginny had supposedly attended. Some rally held at the monument Saturday evening. This was probably why he had been on edge at the crime scene and at the autopsy. Was Tully wondering how close Emma had come to being the killer's target?

"How's that?" LaPlatz asked.

"Close. Is there any way I can see it in color?" Emma looked back at Tully again, as if waiting for an answer from him.

"Sure." LaPlatz stood. "Let me scan it into the computer. I like to use the old-fashioned method first, but if you think we're close, we can let the computer mess around with what we have." She started for the door with Emma alongside of her, but turned just as Tully was getting to his feet to follow. "Why don't you two wait here," LaPlatz said casually, but her eyes looked from Tully to Maggie.

When Tully looked like he might still follow, Maggie put a gentle hand on his arm. He looked down at it, a sleepwalker suddenly waking.

"We'll wait here," he said, and watched the door close before sitting down again. Maggie stood in front of him, leaning against the table, studying him. He didn't seem to mind. If he even noticed. He was off somewhere else, if not in the other room with Emma, then back conjuring up that horrible murder scene.

"She's doing an excellent job."

"What?" He looked up at her as if only now realizing she was still there.

"Emma might be providing the only clue we have as to who this killer is."

"Yeah. I know." He rubbed his jaw, pushed up his glasses for the tenth time.

"Are you okay?"

"Me?" This time there was surprise in his tone.

"I know you're worried about her, Tully, but she seems to be okay."

He hesitated and took off his glasses, rubbed his eyes. "I just worry about her." Back went the glasses. The hands found the pamphlet again and the folds began in the other direction, putting new creases in a picture of a man's face. "Sometimes I feel like I don't have a clue how to do this parenting thing."

"Emma's a brave, smart girl, who came here today to help in a murder investigation. And she's doing a great job while remaining calm and diligent. Judging from that alone, I'd say you've done a damn good job with her."

He looked up at her, met her eyes and managed a weak smile. "Yeah? So you don't think it's totally obvious that I'm winging it?"

"If you are, it'll be our secret. Okay? Hey, didn't you tell me once that there are some things, some secrets, that only partners should share?"

Finally a real smile appeared. "I said that? I can't believe I would ever encourage secrets or withholding information."

"Maybe I'm becoming a bad influence on you." She checked her watch and started to leave. "I need to go rescue Gwen from Security. I'll see you in the conference room."

"Hey, Maggie?"

"Yep?"

"Thanks."

She stopped at the door and gave him a quick glance over her shoulder, just enough to check his eyes, and was immediately relieved to see that deer-in-the-headlights daze gone. "Any time, partner."

# CHAPTER 33

Gwen Patterson hurried up the steps of the Jefferson Building. As usual, she was late. Kyle Cunningham and BSU hadn't called her in as a consultant on a case for more than a year. She knew this time it was probably only at Maggie's request. In fact, it had been such a long time since her last visit to Quantico that she almost expected to be strip-searched at the guard hut. But apparently Maggie had seen to it that her credentials had been updated and kept on file. She stopped at the counter to sign in, but before she picked up the pen the young woman sitting at the computer stopped her.

"Dr. Patterson?"

"Yes."

"Here you are." The woman handed her a visitor's badge. "I do still need for you to sign in with your check-in time."

"Yes, of course." Gwen signed the sheet as she noticed the badge. It had her name printed on it—Dr. and even Ph.D. at the end—instead of the standard Visitor. Okay, so Maggie was trying hard to make her feel at home. Gwen still wasn't convinced, though, she'd be much help with the investigation.

That Cunningham had even agreed to Maggie's request for Gwen to be a part of the case meant he was feeling desperate. He usually didn't call in outsiders. In the early days, yes, but not now, not since the FBI had come under considerable scrutiny. Gwen knew Cunningham well enough to detect a hint of desperation in his voice yesterday when he called. He had asked if she would share her new research and expertise. Her response was that he had some amazing agents in his Behavioral Science Unit, including Maggie, who could tell him just as much, if not more, about the criminal workings of the adolescent male's mind. She told him she wasn't sure she could add much to the investigation.

"As an outsider, you might be able to point out things we're missing," he countered. "You've done that with some of our cases in the past. I'm hoping you'll be able to work your magic on this one."

Flattery. Gwen smiled as she clipped on her badge. The man could be charming as hell when he wanted to be. Then she read the words on the badge under her name and immediately frowned: Member, Special Task Force.

*Task force.* Gwen hated the term. It reeked with bureaucracy and brought to mind visions of red tape. Already the media had trounced every tidbit of information that had been released on this case, hounding poor Senator Brier from outside his apartment to the Capitol. When Gwen checked her office this morning for messages, her assistant, Amelia, had already received calls from the *Washington Times* and the *Post* wanting to know about Gwen's involvement. How the hell did they find out these things so quickly? It had been less than twelve hours since Cunningham had even called her.

Supposedly, it was one of the reasons they were meeting at Quantico instead of in the District. The murder of a senator's daughter—let alone having it occur on federal property—warranted a federal investigation. Yet, it surprised Gwen that Cunningham had been asked to head the task force. Now she wished she had been able to get ahold of Maggie last night. Her friend may have answered some of the questions Cunningham wouldn't.

"Gwen, you're here."

She leaned around the counter to find Maggie coming down the hall. She looked good, dressed in burgundy trousers, matching jacket and a white turtleneck sweater. Only now did Gwen notice that her friend had finally put back on some of the weight she had lost last winter. She looked more her athletically trim but strong self rather than the emaciated waif Albert Stucky had driven her to become.

"Hi, kiddo," Gwen said while she managed a one-armed hug, her briefcase and umbrella occupying her other arm.

She knew Maggie only tolerated the gesture, but this morning she felt the younger woman hugging her back. As Maggie pulled away, Gwen kept a hand on her shoulder, keeping Maggie from escaping too quickly. The hand moved to Maggie's face, gently lifting her chin for a closer inspection. Maggie put up with this, too, even managing a smile while Gwen examined the red lines in Maggie's eyes and the puffiness underneath that was concealed with makeup to fool those who were less adept at reading this intensely personal and private woman.

"Are you okay? You look like you didn't get much sleep."

This time she casually shifted away from Gwen's touch. "I'm fine." There went the eyes—someplace, anyplace, as long as they could no longer be scrutinized.

"You didn't return my call last night," Gwen said, treating it like no big deal and trying to keep the concern from her voice.

"Harvey and I didn't get back from our run until late."

"Jesus! Maggie, I wish you wouldn't go out running that late at night."

"It's not like I was alone." She started back down the hall. "Come on, Cunningham's waiting.

"I figured as much. I can feel him frowning at me through the walls."

As they walked, Gwen found herself absently patting at her hair, which felt in place, and smoothing her skirt, which began the day without a single wrinkle, but after an hour-long drive… She caught Maggie watching her.

"You look sensational as always," Maggie told her.

"Hey, it's not every day I meet a United States senator."

"Oh, right," Maggie said with just enough sarcasm for Gwen to smile.

Of course, Maggie wouldn't let her get away with a comment like that. Gwen's past and present clients included enough embassy, White House and congressional members to start her own political caucus. Okay, so her friend was not getting enough sleep. Probably still upset about her fallen colleague—a certain amount of depression could develop from such a circumstance. But that Maggie was feeling up to some repartee was a good sign. Maybe Gwen had been worried for no reason.

Two blue-polo-shirt academy recruits held a set of doors open for them. Gwen smiled and thanked them. Maggie only nodded. They started down one of the walkways. Gwen knew they had a long way to go. What would it hurt to make another attempt at finding out if Maggie was, indeed, okay?

"How did breakfast go with your mom yesterday?"

"Fine."

Too short, too easy. This was it. She knew it.

"It was fine? Really?"

"We didn't actually have breakfast."

A group of law enforcement officers in green polo shirts and khakis moved to the side of the walkway and let the two women pass. Used to living in the hustle and bustle of the District, Gwen always felt the treatment she received at Quantico was over the top on the polite-and-courteous Richter scale. Maggie waited for her at the next door before they started down another hallway.

"Let me guess," Gwen continued as though there had been no interruption, "she didn't show up."

"No, she showed up. Boy, did she show up. But I had to leave early. For this case, as a matter of fact."

Gwen felt that annoying maternal instinct begin to stir—the one that only reared its ugly head when she was feeling protective of her friend. She didn't dare ask the question for fear she'd get the answer she expected. She asked, anyway. "What do you mean, boy, did she show up? She wasn't drunk, was she?"

"Can we talk about this later?" Maggie said, then greeted a couple of official-looking men in suits.

Gwen recognized them as other agents. Yes, this probably wasn't the best place to air the family laundry. They turned a corner and approached another walkway, this one empty. Gwen took advantage of it.

"Yes, we can talk later. But just tell me now what you meant, okay?"

"Jesus! Did anyone ever tell you you're a pain in the ass?"

"Of course, but you must admit, it's one of my more endearing qualities."

She could see Maggie smile, though she kept her attention and her eyes ahead and safely away from Gwen's.

"She wants us to have Thanksgiving together."

It was the last thing Gwen expected. When the silence lasted too long, she felt Maggie glance over at her.

"That was sort of my response, too," Maggie said with another smile.

"Well, you've been saying for some time now that she's trying to change."

"Yes, her friends and her clothes and her hair. Reverend Everett seems to have helped her change quite a few things in her life, many of them for the better. But no matter what she does, she can't change history."

They got to the end of the walkway, and Maggie pointed to the last door on their right. "We're here."

Gwen wished they had more time. If she wasn't eternally late, maybe they would have. As they entered the conference room, the man at the end of the table stood, though it took effort and he leaned on a walking cane. His gesture prompted the other men around the table to stand, as well; Agent Tully, Keith Ganza, whom Gwen recognized as the head of the FBI crime lab, and Assistant Director Cunningham. Detective Julia Racine shifted impatiently in her chair. Maggie ignored her colleagues' clumsy attempt at courtesy and walked ahead, directly to the senator, her hand outstretched to him.

"Senator Brier, I'm Special Agent Maggie O'Dell and this is Dr. Gwen Patterson. Please excuse us for being late."

"That's quite all right"

He shook both their hands with a brisk but bone-crushing strength, as if making up for his disabled left leg. It had been the result of a car accident, Gwen remembered, not a war injury as the media seemed quick to point out during the last election.

"I'm so sorry for your loss, Senator," Gwen said and immediately saw him flinch, uncomfortable with the rise of emotion her simple condolence seemed to spark.

"Thank you," he said quietly in a tone that suddenly lacked the control and strength that his greeting had projected.

Other than the dark circles under his eyes, Senator Brier

looked impeccable, dressed in an expensive navy suit, crisp white shirt and purple silk tie with an initialed gold tie bar. Hoping to put him back at ease, Gwen noticed four initials—WWJD—instead of the traditional three engraved there.

"That's a lovely tie bar," she said. "If you don't mind me asking, what are the initials?"

He looked down as if needing a reminder. "Oh, no, I don't mind at all. It was a gift from my assistant. He said it's supposed to help me make important decisions. I'm not much of a spiritual man, but he is, and well, it was a gift."

"And the initials?" Gwen insisted, despite Cunningham's frown of impatience.

"I believe it's the acronym for What Would Jesus Do."

"Let's get started," Cunningham announced, waving them to their places before there could be any more wasted chitchat.

Gwen took a seat close to the senator and noticed that Maggie walked clear around the table, taking a seat next to Keith Ganza and avoiding the empty one next to Racine. However, in doing so, she now sat directly across from the detective. Racine smiled at her and nodded. Maggie looked away. Gwen had forgotten why Maggie disliked the woman so much. She was certain it had something to do with a previous case they had worked together, but there was something else. Something more. What was it? She studied Racine, trying to remember. The detective was a little younger than Maggie. Maybe in her middle or late twenties, fairly young for a detective.

"Senator, I know I speak for all of us when I say I'm sorry for your loss," Cunningham said, interrupting Gwen's thoughts and bringing her back to the group in front of her.

"I appreciate that, Kyle. I know having me here is out of the ordinary. I don't want to get in the way, but I want to be involved." He pulled at the cuffs of his shirt and leaned his arms on the table. A nervous gesture of a man trying to keep himself together. "I need to be involved."

Cunningham nodded, began opening file folders and distributing handouts across the table to each of them. "This is what we know so far."

Before looking at the papers, Gwen knew this would be a watered-down version of the real story. She would need to wait until later to be filled in on the details, which only made her fidget in her chair. She hated not being prepared and wondered why Cunningham hadn't scheduled a later meeting with the senator, after the task force had had time to discuss the case. Or didn't he have a choice? Already Gwen could feel there was something about this case that didn't fit neatly into any of the regular rules and procedures. She glanced at Cunningham and found herself wondering if he really was in charge of this case.

Gwen flipped through the pages and with only a glance began picking out the ambiguous terms, the safe posts that specified approximate time and cause of death, giving information without giving details. Whatever clearance or special permission Senator Brier may have gotten from Director Mueller himself, Gwen knew he would be spared the real facts. Yes, Cunningham would do his best to dilute the gruesome details, no matter who might be calling the shots. And Gwen didn't blame him. Senator or not, no father should hear about the frightening and brutal last minutes of his daughter's life.

"There is one thing I need to ask up front." The senator stopped riffling through the papers, but did not look up. "Was she…was she raped?"

Gwen watched all the men's faces, their eyes avoiding the senator's. This was something that fascinated her about men who were close to a victim, whether it be husband, father or son. Their loved one could have been beaten and stabbed beyond recognition, tortured, mutilated and brutally murdered, but somehow none of that was as awful to them as the mere thought that she may have been raped, that she may have been violated in a way incomprehensible to them.

When nobody spoke, Maggie said, "The evidence is inconclusive."

Senator Brier stared at her, then shook his head. "You need not spare me. I need to know."

Like hell he needed to know. Gwen stopped herself as Maggie caught her eyes. Maggie looked to Cunningham as if for permission to proceed. He sat, eyes straight ahead, his hands folded over each other on the table, no indication that he wanted her to stop.

Maggie continued, "We did find some vaginal semen, but there was no bruising, no tearing. Is it possible Ginny may have been with someone earlier in the evening?"

Gwen saw Cunningham shoot Maggie a look of warning. He obviously hadn't expected her to ask the question. But now Maggie was no longer paying attention. Instead, she focused on the senator, waiting for his answer. Gwen wanted to smile. Good for you, Maggie. The senator looked flustered. He seemed more willing and comfortable talking about his daughter's possible rape than he did about her normal sex life.

"I don't know for sure. Some of her friends might know."

"It would be helpful for us to find out," Maggie continued, despite Cunningham fidgeting at the end of the table.

"You can't possibly believe some boyfriend of hers did this to her, can you?" Senator Brier leaned forward, a hand twisting into a fist, crumpling a piece of paper. "That's absolutely absurd."

"No, we don't believe that. Not at all, sir," Cunningham said, jumping in. "That's not what Agent O'Dell meant." He looked at Maggie, and Gwen recognized the scowl that barely transformed his always stoic face. "Is it, Agent O'Dell?"

"No, of course not." Maggie appeared calm and unflustered, and Gwen was relieved. "What I meant was that we will need to determine whether or not Virginia did, in fact, have consensual sex that evening. Otherwise the semen could be important evidence in finding her murderer."

The senator finally nodded, then he sat back an inch, maybe two. Gwen imagined this was his style on the Senate floor, too, always ready, never relaxed.

"On that same note, Senator Brier," Cunningham said, pushing up his glasses and planting his elbows on the table, "I have to ask you, is there anyone you know of who would want to hurt you or your daughter?"

The senator flinched, stunned by the question. He rubbed at

his temple as if warding off a headache. When he finally spoke there was an unmistakable quiver. "So you *are* saying this wasn't random? That it may have been someone Ginny knew?"

Chairs creaked with the shifting of uncomfortable bodies. Nervous fingers rustled papers. Without knowing much about the case, even Gwen realized that, whether it was a crazed boyfriend or not, no one around the table believed Virginia Brier had simply been in the wrong place at the wrong time. No one, that is, except for Senator Brier, who either believed it had been random, or wanted badly to convince himself that it had been. Gwen watched the man wring his hands as he waited for Cunningham to tell him the obvious.

"We don't know anything for certain, Senator. We need to eliminate all possibilities. And, yes, we'll need a list of all your daughter's friends, anyone who may have seen or talked to her Saturday or even Friday."

There was a muffled knock at the door and a tall, handsome black man came in, apologizing as he went to the senator's side without waiting for an invitation. He leaned down and whispered something in his boss's ear, a gesture that appeared familiar and comfortable for both men, despite the audience that waited quietly around the table.

The senator nodded and without looking up at his assistant said, "Thank you, Stephen." Then he looked across the table to Cunningham while he stood, leaning on the young man's outstretched arm. "I apologize, Kyle. I must get back to the Capitol. I expect you'll keep me informed."

"Of course, Senator. I'll give you all the details you need to know, as soon as we know them."

Senator Brier seemed satisfied. Gwen smiled at Cunningham's choice of words—"all the details you *need* to know." Cunningham should have been a politician. He was good at this, telling people what they wanted to hear while telling them absolutely nothing at all.

## CHAPTER 34

*Richmond, Virginia*

Kathleen O'Dell shoved the papers aside and grabbed for her mug of coffee. She took a sip, closed her eyes and took another. This was much better than that god-awful tea, although Reverend Everett would be scolding her if he knew how much caffeine she had poured into her system, and it wasn't even noon. How could she be expected to give up alcohol *and* caffeine?

She shuffled through the pages again. Stephen had been very considerate in getting all the government forms she needed. If only it didn't take so long to fill them out. Who would ever guess that it took so much work to transfer what little assets she had: a meager money market and savings account along with Thomas's pension. She had even forgotten about Thomas's pension, a small monthly amount, but enough that Reverend Everett seemed quite pleased when she had remembered it. That was when he'd told her once again she played an integral part in his mission. That God had sent her to him as a special favor. She'd never before been an integral anything to anyone, let alone to such an important man as Reverend Everett.

After spending the morning sorting through her assets, she realized that she also had never had much of anything. But then, she had never really expected much, either. Just what was necessary to get by—that was enough.

After Thomas's death, Kathleen had sold their house and all their belongings so that she could move Maggie as far away as possible and as soon as possible. With Thomas's life insurance, she thought they would be okay, and they had been comfortable in the small Richmond apartment. They never had much, but it wasn't like Maggie went hungry or wore rags.

Kathleen looked around her current apartment, a sunny one-bedroom she had recently decorated herself with bright and cheerful colors that she no longer saw through blurry, hungover eyes. She hadn't had a drink in ten months, two weeks and… She checked the desk calendar—four days. Though it still wasn't easy. She reached for the coffee mug again and took a swallow.

Looking at the calendar reminded her how close Thanksgiving was. She checked her watch. She would need to call Maggie. It was important to Reverend Everett that she and Maggie have a family Thanksgiving together. Surely they could do it, just this once. How difficult could it be to get through one day together? It's not like they hadn't done it before. They had spent plenty of holidays together, though at the moment, Kathleen couldn't remember any vividly enough to feel reassured. Holidays had usually been sort of a blur to her.

She checked the time again. If she called during the day, she'd get Maggie's voice messaging service, and she wouldn't get to talk to Maggie.

Kathleen thought about their breakfast yesterday. The girl had fidgeted as if she couldn't wait to leave, and now Kathleen wondered if Maggie really had been called away. Or had she simply not wanted to spend another minute with her own mother? How did they ever get to this place? How did they ever get to be enemies? No, not enemies. But not friends, either. And why could they not even talk to each other?

She checked her watch again. Sat quietly. Tapped her fingers on the papers, then glanced at the phone on the counter. If she called while Maggie was at work, she'd only be able to leave a message. She sat for a while longer, staring at the phone. Okay, so this wasn't going to be easy—she was still a coward. She got up and went to the counter. She'd leave a message, and she picked up the phone.

# CHAPTER 35

Maggie stood up to stretch her legs and automatically began her ritual pacing. The real meeting hadn't begun until the senator was safely in his limousine and on his way back to the District. Now the uncensored reports and photos were strewn across the conference room's table alongside coffee mugs, cans of Pepsi, bottles of water and sandwiches Cunningham had ordered up from the cafeteria.

The old easel-backed chalkboard Cunningham liked to use was almost filled. On one side were the words:

duct tape
cyanide capsule
semen residue
handcuff marks: none found on the victim
ligature tracks: possible cord with glittery residue
possible DNA under nails
scene posed/staged
unidentified circular marks in dirt

On the other side under the heading Unsub was a shorter list, the beginning of a profile:

left-handed
organized, although a risk-taker
knows police procedure
prepared: brought weapon to scene
may interact well with society, but no regard for others
draws satisfaction from seeing his victim suffer
strong sense of grandiosity and entitlement

Cunningham had peeled off his jacket and gotten down to work as soon as Senator Brier had left the conference room, yet he still hadn't explained why they had gathered out here at Quantico instead of at FBI headquarters. Nor had he bothered to explain why he had been chosen to head the task force rather than the Special Agent in Charge (SAC) of the District's field office or why BSU had even been called in to take a look at the scene before they knew the victim was a daughter of a United States senator. He hadn't bothered to explain any of it, and neither Maggie, nor the rest of them, seemed willing to call him on it.

There was plenty he wasn't telling them. Yet, what he had told them, at least three times, was that all information was to remain shared with only the six members of the task force and with absolutely no exceptions. Redundant, really. They were all professionals. They knew the rules. Well, maybe all of them except Racine. Maggie wondered if perhaps Cunningham didn't trust Racine, either. Could that be why he was holding back on an explanation? Of course, he had no choice about including Racine. The task force had to have someone from the District PD, and since Racine had already been assigned to the case, it made sense she would continue as liaison.

"According to Wenhoff, cause of death was asphyxiation due to manual strangulation," Keith Ganza said with his usual monotone, continuing their list.

Cunningham found the word *ligature* on the chalkboard and scrawled underneath *manual strangulation—COD*.

"Manual strangulation? What about all the ligature marks?" Tully pointed them out in the autopsy photos of the young woman's neck.

Keith reached for several of the photos, pulled one out and slid it back to Tully. "See that bruising and the vertical crescent marks? The bruising was made by the pressure of his thumbs. The vertical crescentic abrasions were made by his fingernails. The horizontal ones are all hers. The bruising and the abrasions are in the perfect position to break the hyoid bone. That's the curved bone at the base of the tongue." He indicated the area in one of the photos. "There were also fractures to the cartilage of the windpipe and the larynx. All are signs of excessive force and signs of manual strangulation."

"The guy obviously had been using some kind of cord, over and over again." Racine stood now to look over Tully's shoulder at the photos. "Why the hell would he suddenly decide to use his hands?"

Maggie noticed that Racine was leaning close enough into Tully to brush her breasts against his back. She looked away and caught Gwen watching. Gwen's eyes told her she knew exactly what she was thinking, and Gwen's sudden frown warned Maggie to be careful and keep any sarcasm to herself.

"Maybe he used his hands when he was finished with whatever little game of pass out and wake up he was playing with her. He may have felt like he had more control with his hands to complete the job," Maggie said, then turned away from them and stared out the window. She remembered the girl's neck without looking at any photos, and she could easily conjure up an image of how it came to its mangled black-and-blue state. Black and blue, almost the color the sky had now turned, swollen with dark clouds. A light rain began tapping against the glass. "Maybe the cord simply wasn't personal enough," she added without looking back at any of them.

"She may have gotten personal enough to get a piece of him under her fingernails," Ganza said, and immediately had Maggie's attention. "Most of the skin was her own, but she managed to get in a scratch or two. Enough for DNA. We're checking to see if it matches the semen."

"Also, what about the cyanide capsule?" Racine asked. "And that pinkish tint. Stan made it sound like it could have been the poison."

Now Maggie turned and glanced at Tully. The two of them looked to Cunningham. Yes, what about the cyanide capsule? They had avoided discussing the possible connection between the senator's daughter and those five suicidal boys from the cabin in the Massachusetts woods. No way was it a coincidence—not that Maggie even believed in coincidences.

Someone had gone to an awful lot of trouble to make sure they made a connection. Someone, perhaps, wanting to point out his deed, or rather, his revenge.

"Poison does leave a pinkish tint. Some of the cyanide had been absorbed into her system, but very little," Keith answered, though no one except Racine seemed interested.

"So," Racine said, rubbing her temple as if genuinely trying to figure it out. "Why strangle her if you've put cyanide in her mouth and taped it shut? Am I the only who thinks that doesn't make sense?"

"The capsule was strictly for show," Cunningham finally offered without looking at the detective, making the explanation sound commonplace. He wiped the chalk from his hands, taking a break and picking up his ham on rye. He took a bite without looking at the sandwich, concentrating instead on the diagrams and police reports spread out on the table.

Racine, now back in her chair, shifted impatiently, waiting.

"You must have heard about the standoff last week in Massachusetts." Cunningham, still wouldn't meet her gaze and flipped through the reports. "Five young men used the same kind of capsule filled with cyanide to commit suicide before they opened fire on ATF and FBI agents. For some reason, someone wants us to know there's a connection with Senator Brier's daughter."

Racine looked around the table, only now realizing this was news only to her. "You all fucking knew about this?"

"The information about the cyanide is classified and so far has been successfully held back from the media." Cunningham's tone made Racine sit back. "We need to keep it that way, Detective Racine. Is that understood?"

"Of course. But if I'm to be a part of this task force, I don't expect information to be held back from me."

"Fair enough."

"So was this some sort of revenge killing?" Racine caught on quickly. Maggie couldn't help but be impressed, and she turned back to the window when Racine looked her way.

"Or is that too obvious?" Racine asked. "The life of a senator's daughter in exchange for five?"

"Revenge certainly can't be discounted," Cunningham answered between bites of his sandwich.

"Maybe now you can also tell me how you knew about it before we discovered it was the senator's daughter?"

"Excuse me?"

Maggie looked back at Cunningham. Racine dared to ask the question all of them had been thinking. The woman certainly had more guts than brains.

"Why was BSU called in on this?" Racine asked, apparently unaffected by Cunningham's position of power or his scowl. Maggie couldn't help thinking that if Racine did have aspirations of getting into the FBI, she may be squashing an important reference.

"A homicide on federal property is a federal matter," he told Racine in his best cool, authoritarian tone, "and therefore, the FBI is in charge of the investigation."

"Yeah, I know that. But why BSU?" Racine didn't flinch. Maggie watched to see if Cunningham would. By now, everyone was watching to see if Cunningham would.

He pushed up the bridge of his glasses and looked around at each of them. "There was an anonymous phone call early yesterday morning," he finally confessed, digging his hands into his pockets and leaning against a seldom-used podium next to the chalkboard. "It was traced to a pay phone at the monument. The caller simply said we'd find something interesting at the FDR Memorial. The call came in on my direct line."

No one said anything.

"I'm not certain why the caller chose to tell me," Cunningham added when no one, not even Racine, dared to ask. "Perhaps they knew I was at the crime scene at the cabin. Perhaps they knew we had been asked to profile that case." He looked over at Maggie. "You were quoted in the *Times*. Anyone could have made the assumption we were on the case."

Maggie felt a sudden flush, regretting that she had said anything. That morning a reporter had caught her off guard, coming down the steps of the J. Edgar Hoover Building. He had asked about Agent Delaney. She hadn't been able to mask her anger and simply told him that they would catch the responsible party. That was all she had said, but in that evening's edition of the *Washington Times,* the reporter had identified her as a criminal profiler, insinuating that BSU was somehow involved.

"It doesn't matter." Cunningham tried to relieve her discomfort with a wave of his hand. "The important thing is for us to find this bastard. Agent Tully, how did it go with Emma and Agent LaPlatz?"

"I think it went well." Maggie noticed Tully seemed back to his normal self. He pulled out a copy of the line drawing from a folder and added it to the mess in the middle of the table. "Whether this Brandon is involved or not, Emma knows she saw him with Ginny Brier that evening. Agent LaPlatz is in the process of faxing the sketch to all law enforcement within a hundred-mile radius with a note that he's wanted for questioning."

"Questioning and perhaps a voluntary DNA sample. We need to find him. Detective Racine," Cunningham said, picking up the sketch, "perhaps you could have some officers take a copy of this and check if anyone saw this Brandon around the monuments Sunday morning. Maybe he's also our mystery caller."

Racine nodded.

"And we need to know what group those boys in that cabin belonged to. We keep coming up empty-handed." He looked to Gwen. "There's one survivor. He's refused to talk to anyone. He may have important information. Would you give it a shot?"

"Of course," Gwen said without hesitation.

Just then, Tully pulled out the pamphlet Maggie had seen him folding earlier. It still had the accordion folds, and he tried smoothing out the creases on the side with the man's picture. "I forgot about this. I found it at the monument Sunday morning. It's from the group that held the prayer rally Saturday night. Emma thinks Brandon might be a member. And in fact, if Wenhoff's time of death is accurate, the murderer was killing the Brier girl while the rally was still taking place down below."

Cunningham leaned over the table to take a look. Maggie left her perch at the window.

"That's it," Maggie said as she read the block type: Church of Spiritual Freedom. "That's the nonprofit organization that owns the cabin."

"Are you sure?"

She nodded, looking to Ganza for confirmation as they all stood, leaning over Tully for a closer look. Now Maggie glanced at the man's photo, a handsome, dark-haired man in his forties with a movie star's slick looks. Then she read the caption, and she felt her stomach flip. Reverend Joseph Everett. Jesus! The man who might be at the center of these murders was her mother's savior.

## CHAPTER 36

Justin couldn't believe his eyes. Compared to the rest of the compound, Father's small cottage looked like a fucking palace. There was a fireplace and expensive leather chairs. Bookcases were filled with books, something members were not allowed to own or keep, except for a personal copy of the Bible. The walls were covered with framed artwork and the windows with flowing drapes. A bowl with fresh fruit, another rare commodity, sat on a hand-carved sofa table. Next to the bowl was a can of Pepsi. Shit! Alice had led him to believe that junk food was like the Antichrist or some fucking thing.

He sat in one of the leather chairs, waiting as he had been instructed to do by Cassie, Father's personal assistant. He should have been nervous about being asked here—no, summoned. That was the word Darren had used when he came to get him. Had to be Father's word. Not likely an idiot like Darren would come up with a word like that all on his own.

He could hear Father's voice in the room next door, Father's office. He couldn't hear another voice, though it was obvious Father was having a conversation with someone. He had to be on the phone. Another surprise. Had to be a cellular phone, since there weren't any fucking phone lines running into the compound.

"I don't like the sounds of this, Stephen," Father was saying.

Yeah, he had to be on the phone, 'cause Justin wasn't hearing Stephen answer.

"How could this have happened?" Father asked, sounding impatient. He didn't wait for an answer. "He made a big mistake this time."

Justin wondered who'd fucked up. Then he heard Father say, "No, no. Brandon's being taken care of. Don't worry about him. He won't make the same mistake twice."

Brandon? So it was the golden boy who fucked up? Justin smiled, then caught himself. There could be cameras.

He tried to sit still, but his eyes kept pivoting around at the amazing surroundings. Office, bedroom, huge fucking living room. He knew Father even had his own bathroom. Now he wondered if the man had a fucking whirlpool bath and… Oh, shit. He hadn't even thought about it before—the man probably had toilet paper. Not just toilet paper but that white, soft, cushiony stuff. And no way was he restricted to two-minute showers. The thought had Justin raking his fingers through his hair. At least this morning he had gotten all the shampoo out before the water shut off. Maybe he was finally getting the hang of it. But he would never get used to brushing his teeth without water. The antiseptic taste of that generic paste stayed with him throughout the day.

"Justin." Father entered the room without a sound, no footstep, no warning. He wore a black turtleneck sweater and dark trousers that looked freshly pressed.

Justin jumped at the sound of his voice, then automatically stood, wondering if he would need to sit on the floor now. Hadn't Alice told him that Father's head had to be above everyone else's? Or did it not count when no one else was around to see? Shit! He wished he had talked to Alice before coming.

"Sit down," Father said, pointing to Justin's chair. "I've been meaning to talk to you since Saturday night." He sat in the leather chair facing Justin's.

He watched the reverend's face, looking for signs of anger or that scowl he had perfected, the one that could turn men to stone and probably make women sterile. Who knew what powers this guy possessed. But, instead, Father's face was calm and serious but friendly.

"I know you must be confused by what you think you saw on the bus coming back Saturday evening."

Oh, shit! He was actually going to make them discuss this.

Justin shifted, making the leather of his chair crackle. "I was sorta half-asleep," he attempted.

"Yes, I thought perhaps you had been. That's why I think you may have misunderstood what you saw." Father sat back and crossed his leg with his right ankle resting on the knee of his left leg, making himself comfortable yet looking in complete control. "You know, Justin, I must constantly test all my followers. Just one among us who shows weakness could destroy us all."

Justin nodded, pretending to understand this bullshit.

"It's not something I enjoy, and sometimes my tests probably look odd to those who don't fully understand. But no one can be exempt. No one, not even sweet, dear Alice." He folded his hands together as if trying to decide whether or not to proceed. "There are things you don't know about Alice. Things no one else knows."

Justin had to admit he didn't know much about Alice's past. She never talked about it or mentioned her family, even though she was always trying to get him to talk about his. It had taken days of probing to finally get her to tell him she was twenty years old, three years older than he was. Now that he thought about it, he didn't even know where she had grown up.

"Alice was a very troubled girl when she came here. Her parents had thrown her out of the house. She had nowhere else to go. I took a special interest in her, because I knew there was such good inside her, wanting to come out. But there were things she has done in her past, things that…well, all I will tell you, Justin, is that she has been used to receiving anything she wanted in exchange for sexual favors."

Justin felt a knot twisting in his stomach. Father's eyes were searching his, making sure Justin understood what he was saying.

"I know it's hard to believe." Father seemed satisfied with what he saw and sat back, shaking his head as if he, too, still couldn't believe it. "Looking at her now and seeing what progress she's made, yes, it is so hard to believe what a slut she was."

Justin caught himself from grimacing at the word. He blinked and swallowed hard. His mouth had gone dry and suddenly the room had grown much too hot. He remembered that tight pink sweater Alice had worn Saturday and how inappropriate he thought it was. Then he remembered her shaking her head no the entire time Father had his hand in her crotch. But there had also been such a pained look on her face, almost a sort of fear in her eyes. Had he imagined all that? Or had she simply been afraid of failing Father's test? Jesus!

"So now you understand the manner of testing I must use with Alice. It's so important to make certain that she has grown beyond that lifestyle, that she isn't continuing to lead other members into temptation. That she recognizes she has so much more to offer. That's also why I put her in charge of recruiting, so that she can experience successes from using her other talents and not just her body."

Justin didn't know what to say. Father was watching him, waiting, but what the hell kind of response did he expect?

"You must never speak of this, Justin. It must never leave this room. Do you understand?"

"Sure. No, I won't tell anyone."

"Not even Alice. It would devastate her to realize that anyone knows. Can I trust you, Justin?"

"Yeah, sure. I mean…yes, you can trust me."

"Good." He smiled, and Justin couldn't remember Father ever smiling at him. It actually felt pretty good. "I knew you could be trusted. You're a good man, just like your brother, Eric." He sat forward, suddenly serious. "I knew you were special, Justin, when you survived my test."

Justin stared at him, looking for signs that the man knew he hadn't really survived but had spent the time with some campers. But Father was serious, his eyes warm and friendly.

"You must never repeat this, Justin, not even to your brother, but I knew from the day you stepped onto the compound that God had sent you."

"Sent me?"

"Yes. You're not like the rest. You see things, know things. You're not easily fooled."

Maybe the man honestly could read minds. Justin swallowed and nodded.

"You were sent by God to play an integral part in this mission, Justin. God sent you to me as a favor. You are a blessing."

Justin wasn't sure what to say. He couldn't help feeling... Hell, he couldn't help feeling special. He had never heard Father say such things to anyone else.

"That's why I want you to join the ranks of my warriors. I have the feeling you will be a very special warrior." He leaned even closer and lowered his voice. "I need your help, Justin. There are those who would like to destroy me, even here within our ranks. Are you willing to help me?"

Justin didn't know much about Father's warriors, except that they did get special treatment, rewards. Eric was a warrior and took great pride in the title. Justin tried to remember if anyone had ever told him they needed him before. It felt good. It felt damn good.

Father was waiting for an answer.

"Yeah," Justin said, and found the answer came quite easily. "Yeah, I guess I could help."

"Good. Excellent." He smiled and slapped Justin on the knee, then sat back in the recliner. "Brandon and I are taking a group to Boston for initiation. I'd like you to go, too.

"Sure, okay." He had no idea what he was getting himself into, but maybe it was a good idea to be away from Alice for a while. Just to think and sort through everything Father had told him. Besides, he really was kind of excited about this. Eric would be so proud when he heard the news. "About Eric," he said, "any idea when he'll be back?"

"Could be any day now," Father said. But his eyes suddenly drifted off to look out the window, as if his mind had wandered somewhere else.

# CHAPTER 37

*John F. Kennedy Federal Building*
*Boston, Massachusetts*

When the guard told Eric Pratt he had a visitor, Eric knew Father had sent someone to kill him. He sat down next to the thick glass partition and stared at the door on the other side, waiting to see who his executioner would be. His best friend, Brandon, walked through the door, stopped to be patted down by a guard then waved a hello. He sat in the yellow plastic chair and scooted as close as allowed to the barrier. Brandon was clean shaven, his wild, red hair wet with some sort of gel, combed and plastered to his head. He smiled at Eric as he picked up the telephone receiver.

"Hi, buddy," Brandon said, his voice muffled, though he sat right across from him. "They treatin' you okay in here?" His eyes flicked everywhere except to meet Eric's, and right then, Eric knew. It was Brandon. Brandon had come to deliver his death warrant.

After those first days of questioning when Eric refused to answer any questions, they had thrown him into solitary confinement. What they hadn't realized was that they were giving him exactly what he wanted—to be left alone. After months of being surrounded by people, of not being able to go anywhere without a tagalong, the solitary confinement was a reward, not a punishment. But he wouldn't dare tell Brandon. That would only give his friend more reason to want him dead.

"I'm fine," Eric said, not caring that his tone probably didn't back up his words.

"Heard the food in here is worse than the crap we eat every day." Brandon laughed, but it was a manufactured one.

Had he forgotten that Eric would be able to recognize it as such? Did he really believe he could dupe him into exchanging confidences? Oh, Father was good. Of course, he would send Eric's best friend to do the job. What sweet poetic justice, like sending Judas to betray Jesus, or rather, Cain to slaughter Abel.

"The food's okay."

Brandon glanced around, then leaned close to the glass. Eric stayed put, sitting straight-backed in the hard plastic chair. This was it. But how…how would he choose to destroy him?

"What the hell happened out there, Eric? Why didn't you take the pill?" He kept his voice hushed, but there was no mistaking the anger. Eric had expected nothing less than anger. And no matter how honest he tried to be with him, Brandon would never understand, because *he* would not have hesitated. Brandon would have swallowed ten cyanide capsules for Father. And now he wouldn't hesitate for a second to kill his best friend, whose only sin had been that he wanted to live.

"I did take it," Eric offered as a weak defense.

It was the truth, or at least part of the truth. Besides, hadn't Father taught them that it was okay to lie, cheat and steal as long as the end justified the means? Well, the end was now Eric's own survival. Then he realized something for the first time. How stupid of him to not realize it sooner. Neither Brandon nor Father had any idea what had happened after the shoot-out. They had no idea what the agents had asked him or what he had told them. How could they? All they knew was that he was still alive and in the midst of the enemy.

But maybe they didn't care about what had happened. They certainly didn't care about him or it wouldn't have taken this long for Father to send someone. No, the only thing they cared about was what he might confess, though there was nothing he could say. What could he tell them? That Father had tricked them? That he cared more about guns and his own protection than he did about his own followers? And why would the FBI care to hear about that?

"I don't get it," Brandon whispered. "Those capsules are supposed to be enough to drop a horse."

Eric looked into his friend's eyes. He could see Brandon didn't believe him. His friend's jaw was taut. One hand clenched the phone, the other was a fist on the small ledge.

"Maybe mine didn't have as much," Eric said, continuing the lie. "Lowell packs dozens of those. Maybe he didn't pack enough into the one I got." But even Eric wasn't convinced by his own emotionless voice.

Brandon looked around again. Two seats down a large, greasy-haired woman began to sob in loud, sloppy gulps. He leaned even closer to the glass, and this time he didn't bother to hide the anger. "That's bullshit!" he spat in a low, careful voice.

Eric didn't blink. He didn't answer. He could be silent. He had done it for two whole days while prosecutors and FBI agents screamed into his face. He continued to sit quiet and straight, telling himself, commanding himself not to flinch, while his heart pounded against his rib cage.

"You know what happens to traitors," Brandon whispered into the phone. Those same eyes that only moments ago couldn't meet Eric's were now holding him, pinning him to his chair with their hate. When had Brandon's eyes become so black, so hollow, so evil? "Look for the signs of the end," Brandon said, "and just remember, this could be the day."

Then Father's messenger slapped the phone's receiver into its cradle. He shoved back the chair, its metal legs screeching against the floor. But he walked out with his usual calm, cocky strut, so that no one else would notice that he had just personally delivered Father's curse of death.

Eric should have felt relief that he had survived Brandon's visit. Instead he felt sick to his stomach. He knew what Father was capable of doing. The man seemed to have special powers. In the past, there had been members who had left, all of them traitors. No one left without being a traitor. Eric had heard plenty of stories, and then there were the ones he knew firsthand.

The most recent one to leave was Dara Hardy. She had given

the excuse that her mother had cancer and Dara wanted to spend her last days with her. But Father insisted that if her story had been true, Dara certainly would have taken him up on his generous offer to bring the ill woman to the compound. Never mind that Father didn't allow any medications and preached that doctors were a selfish indulgence. After all, he alone could heal and would take care of his members. Dara Hardy left. Exactly one week later, she was killed in a car accident. Her mother died without Dara at her bedside.

Eric wondered what freak accident they would use with him. Would another prisoner accidently scald him in the shower? Would more cyanide find its way into his food? Or would a guard come into his cell late at night and make it look like he had hanged himself? One thing he knew for certain; his killer would be someone he least expected. Just as his messenger of death had been his best friend. How could he survive in this snake pit of the enemy and constantly be looking over his shoulder?

But it wasn't his enemy who wanted him dead. It was the man who, even as he killed Eric, would still claim to be his savior, the redeemer of his soul. No, he had that wrong—the owner of his soul, not the redeemer. Because that was the price Father charged all his followers in order for them to come into his fold. Their soul.

For the first time, Eric felt grateful that Justin was dead, reduced to a cardboard box full of unidentifiable bones. At least Father could no longer pull the two brothers apart, make them wage war against each other like he had with so many other family members. And, perhaps, just maybe, he had not had time to steal Justin's soul. If that was true then Justin was, indeed, the lucky one.

# CHAPTER 38

"You don't know it's the same Joseph Everett," Tully said from the doorway, watching O'Dell's fingers fly over her computer keyboard.

"Unlikely that there are two Reverend Joseph Everetts in the Virginia area," she said without a glance, but he recognized that anxious tone in her voice, and he couldn't help thinking, "Here we go again."

He became a little nervous whenever O'Dell got that tone in her voice and a certain look in her eyes, like she was on a personal mission. The last time it happened, the two of them ended up in a burning house with O'Dell saving his life—*after* he took a bullet to his thigh.

He was relieved however, that they might actually have some answers. And also relieved that Emma had gotten through the morning. O'Dell was right. Emma was an incredibly brave and smart girl. And before Agent LaPlatz volunteered to drive her back to Reston High, he embarrassed his brave, smart daughter with a hug and told her how proud he was of her.

Tully watched as O'Dell brought up some sort of document and began scrolling through it. He looked over at Dr. Patterson, who sat in the overstuffed lounge chair O'Dell had managed to squeeze into her small office. There had been several late nights when he had found his partner curled up and asleep in it. All of their offices in BSU were small, but O'Dell had a knack for organizing, using every inch of the floor-to-ceiling bookshelves and little cubbyholes to keep piles off chairs and off the floor, so that even with the lounge chair, her office looked cozy but not overcrowded. Not like his own, which reminded him some days of a storage closet with walking paths to his desk.

Dr. Patterson had removed her heels, and Tully watched absently as she made herself comfortable, tucking her legs underneath her. In doing so, she hiked up her skirt. She had great legs. Trim ankles. Firm, smooth thighs. Jeez! What the hell was wrong with him? He looked away as if caught doing something he shouldn't.

Usually Gwen Patterson bugged the hell out of him. There seemed to be nothing they agreed on. The last time he and O'Dell were working late, they stopped at her huge Tudor in Newburgh Heights, where Dr. Patterson had been dog-sitting. The three of them decided to order takeout. If he remembered correctly, he and Patterson had gotten into an argument over Chinese or pizza, debating each food's nonnutritional value. Of course, she was supposed to be the expert, being a so-called gourmet cook. Yeah, she irritated the hell out of him. Didn't mean she couldn't have great legs, though. Maybe thinking about Caroline over the weekend had simply reminded him—

"Here's something." O'Dell interrupted his rambling thoughts. "It's a court document. It's old—1975. That's over twenty-five years ago. Everett would have been…what do you think…in his twenties?"

"We don't even know yet if Everett is involved."

"Cunningham must think so or he wouldn't be sending you and Gwen to Boston to interview the lone survivor. And he didn't hesitate when I asked to arrange a meeting with someone from Everett's organization. Maybe even an ex-member. In fact, he told me he'd call Senator Brier and see if he had any connections."

O'Dell kept her back to them while she read. Dr. Patterson was ignoring the two of them, rolling her shoulders and slowly massaging her temples—perhaps some relaxation routine she was used to doing to unwind. Tully found it distracting as hell. He finally gave in and came to O'Dell's side to look at what she had found.

"Not like a trip to Boston will do much good," Tully said. "The kid wasn't willing to talk at the cabin when we had him scared out of his wits. I can't imagine he'll spill anything now after he's had a nice warm place to sleep and three square meals."

"What makes you think that fear can be the only motivating force to get a suspect to talk?" Dr. Patterson asked without disturbing her temple rubbing.

Now that Tully was out of her line of vision he could safely steal a glance at her shiny, strawberry-blond hair. The woman was definitely attractive. Suddenly, she turned to look up at him.

"No really, what makes you think fear is the only way to go?"

"Fear's usually what works best on that age group," he told her.

This time O'Dell looked over her shoulder. "Isn't that exactly what you told me the other day, Gwen?"

"Not exactly. I said fear most likely made them think they didn't have an alternative when their natural instinct should have been to fight. But from what I understand, this boy spit his cyanide capsule out. Which would tell me that fear might not be a motivating factor for him."

"That's not necessarily true," Tully said, and realized he was already feeling defensive. Why did she do that to him? He wasn't a defensive kind of guy. But now both Patterson and O'Dell were waiting for an explanation. "I know you think spitting the cyanide out could be a sign of him wanting to stick around to fight. But maybe he was simply scared to die. Isn't that possible?"

"Whoever convinced these boys to take cyanide certainly would have convinced them that they would be tortured and killed if taken alive." Dr. Patterson was no longer relaxing. Even her legs had come out from under her. "That this boy was willing to take that chance tells me that he's looking for and hoping for a safe haven."

"Really? You can tell all that even before you've met the kid."

"Okay, you two." O'Dell put up her hands in mock surrender. "Maybe I should be going to Boston with you, Gwen."

"You need to talk to your mother," Gwen answered, keeping her eyes on Tully as if planning her next offensive.

"You promise you two won't kill each other?" O'Dell smiled.

"I'm sure we'll be fine," Gwen said, smiling at O'Dell. However, O'Dell seemed to be waiting for confirmation from Tully.

"We'll be fine," he said, now anxious to change the subject, because even though Patterson made him defensive, she hadn't realized her skirt was still hiked up to her thighs. He turned back to the computer screen. "What did you find?"

"I have no idea if it's the same Joseph Everett, but at twenty-two years of age and from Arlington, Virginia, it could very well be. He was charged with rape. The nineteen-year-old girl was a second-year journalism student at the University of Virginia."

The phone suddenly rang, and O'Dell grabbed it. "O'Dell."

Tully pretended to read the computer screen, trying to keep his attention away from Patterson.

"What makes you think that?" O'Dell asked, then waited. Whoever it was hadn't given much of an explanation. O'Dell frowned as she said, "Okay, I'll be there."

She hung up the phone. "That was Racine," she said, swiveling her chair back to the computer. "I'll print out copies," she told Tully as she hit the print icon, listened for the printer to groan into action, then started closing down the Internet site. "She thinks she has something I need to take a look at."

There was an emphasis on "she thinks" and enough sarcasm to prompt Tully to try again. "What is it with you and Racine?"

"I told you. I don't trust her."

"No. You told me you didn't like her."

"Same thing," she said as she whipped two copies from the printer tray, handing one to Tully and folding the other for herself. "Any chance you could check if this is our Joseph Everett before you leave?"

"Sure. If he has a criminal conviction for rape, it'll be easy to track."

"Unfortunately, this is all we've got." She held up her copy. "There won't be any other documents. The girl dropped the charges." She put on her jacket, then stopped and looked from Tully to Gwen. "Everett must have been good at instilling fear, even back then."

# CHAPTER 39

He knew he shouldn't be taking the concoction in between kills. Too much recreational usage would water down the effects, but he needed something to calm him. He needed something to battle the anger and fear…no, not fear. They couldn't scare him. He simply wouldn't allow it. They were out to stop him, to keep him from his mission, but he couldn't let them get to him. He was stronger than that. He simply needed a reminder that he was stronger. That was all this was. A simple reminder.

He sat back and waited. He knew he could count on the exotic concoction's special effects, its healing magic, its hidden strength. Already he was using almost twice the original dosage. But right now, none of that mattered. Right now, all he wanted to do was sit quietly and enjoy the psychedelic light show that always occurred afterward. Yes. After he accessed the strength and the rush of adrenaline, then came the light show. It flashed behind his eyes and caused the zinging inside his head. The flashes looked like tiny little angels shaped like stars, flitting from one side of the room to the other. It was absolutely beautiful.

He grasped the book and caressed the smooth leather. The book. How could he have done any of this without it? It had inspired the heat, the passion, the anger, the need, the justification. And it would provide the validation, as well.

He took deep breaths and closed his eyes, enjoying the warm, calm sweep through him. Yes, now he was prepared for the next step.

# CHAPTER 40

The moon peeked over the District skyline just as Maggie pulled her Toyota into the empty parking lot. She could see the yellow crime scene tape, flapping in the wind, blocking off the entrance to the viaduct. Several officers paced and waited, but she couldn't see Racine. A mobile crime scene lab passed by as Maggie finished the last bite of her drive-thru dinner, a McDonald's Quarter Pounder and fries. She got out of the car and brushed the excess salt from her knit shirt, then exchanged her suit jacket for her navy FBI windbreaker.

She dug under the front seat and pulled out a pair of rubber boots, low-tops that she slipped over her leather shoes. Out of habit, she started to reach for her forensic kit, too, then stopped. The medical examiner's station wagon was already parked alongside the concrete wall, next to the opening of the viaduct. No sense in ticking off Stan any more than she already had.

However, as Maggie walked toward the scene, she wasn't surprised to see Wayne Prashard emerging from the viaduct entrance instead of Stan. Not only had Stan probably had his share of after-hours call-ins for one week, but he certainly wouldn't make the trip himself for some homeless woman. Maggie wasn't quite sure why Racine was so certain she should be here, either. She hoped it wasn't some ploy. Who knew what Racine could be up to.

Prashard nodded at Maggie as he opened the back of the wagon. "She won't let me touch a goddamn thing until you take a look."

"Good to see you, too, Wayne."

"Sorry." He surrendered a smile and his normal bulldog face creased into friendly lines. "It's just that sometimes she can be such a pain in the ass, you know what I mean?"

Yes, she knew exactly what he meant, but she only smiled. Prashard wasn't finished, though. "She never used to be that way."

"Really?" Maggie couldn't imagine Racine any other way.

"All she cares about now is making sure everyone knows she's in charge. But before she made detective she was actually nice," he said while he brought out a body bag from the back of the wagon. "Maybe a little too nice, if you know what I mean." He glanced at Maggie and winked.

She ignored his invitation to join in trashing the detective. She might not like Racine, but she had never resorted to idle gossip about other law enforcement officers. She wasn't about to start now. And it did look as if Prashard had a story or two he wanted to share. Instead, she turned to leave. "I wouldn't know," she said. "I didn't know Racine before she made detective." And she left it at that.

As she continued toward the entrance, she checked the area, aware of the noisy traffic overhead, flashes of headlights between six-foot guardrails. The smell of diesel emanated from the bus terminal on the other side of the small empty parking lot where engines were left running and several mechanics climbed in and around the Greyhound buses. About a half-dozen broken-down buses lined the chain-link fence, blocking a direct view of the viaduct's entrance.

Except for where the mechanics worked, the place was badly lit. It was dark and noisy, but deserted, and Maggie wondered why anyone would come here voluntarily. Except that the arch of concrete—more a tunnel than an arch—would provide shelter from the wind, if not some warmth. She could understand why it might be an enticing spot for someone looking to set up her cardboard home. Also an enticing spot for someone looking for a victim.

"Oh, good! You're here." Racine appeared and held up a section of crime scene tape for Maggie to crawl under.

Maggie could smell the body as soon as she walked into the tunnel. Racine led the way, carefully stepping around two crime lab technicians, one crawling the grid pattern with a flashlight, brush and plastic bags while the other set up several spotlights.

At the other opening, leaning against the cold concrete wall, sat a naked woman, stark and gray in the sharp glare of a spotlight. Her eyes were wide open, the corners already filled with white clusters of maggot larvae. Her head lolled to one side, revealing several ligature marks across her neck. Her dirty-and-smudged face was bloated, her mouth duct-taped shut. Her hands were folded into her lap, the wrists facing forward as if to show off the welts from where handcuffs had restrained her. Maggie noticed the insides of her elbows were clean, no track marks from needles. She hadn't been lured here by the promise of drugs. There was no cardboard box, no shopping cart, no other personal belongings, other than the carefully folded rags stacked about a yard away.

"What do you think?"

She realized Racine was watching her and waiting while Maggie examined the scene, careful where she stepped and letting her eyes collect the evidence.

"The posing of the body looks very similar."

"Looks fucking identical," Racine said. "Although I get the idea we won't find any ID stuffed down her throat."

"She certainly doesn't fit the victimology of our guy," Maggie said, squatting in front of the body to get a better look. She was staring directly into the corpse's empty eyes. The woman had been dead for more than thirty-six hours, the rigor mortis already leaving the body pliable again. Maggie could tell this by gently lifting one hand and carefully letting it fall back into place.

"I wish the hell you wouldn't touch the stiff," Prashard said from the entrance, making his way inside, staying close to the concrete wall.

"But she's not stiff anymore. She's been dead for a while. You have any estimates?" Maggie asked without getting up.

"I'm guessing forty-eight hours, but it's a major guess since I haven't been able to touch a fucking thing yet." He shot a look at Racine, but she wasn't paying attention. Instead, she was still watching Maggie.

"Check this out," Racine said, bringing out a penlight and shining it at the dirt floor of the tunnel.

Maggie got up and went to Racine's side. About five feet in

front of the body was what looked like a circular indent in the dirt, although it and the area around it looked scuffed on purpose as if in an attempt to erase it and possibly other marks like it.

"Tully's signature," Racine said. "I don't know what the hell it is, but tell me that's not the exact weird imprint we found at the monument yesterday morning."

Maggie looked around the tunnel again. The scene looked too similar to be a coincidence. "Forty-eight hours ago would put time of death at Saturday night. Why in the world would he target and kill a senator's daughter and then some random homeless woman?"

"Maybe the guy's just really fucked up?" Racine suggested.

"No. Both scenes are much too organized." Maggie looked to Prashard. "Wayne, would you mind checking the victim's mouth?"

"Out here?"

"Yes. It would be helpful and speed things up if we can check to see if anything is left inside her mouth."

"I don't know." Prashard shrugged and scratched his head as though Maggie was asking him to do the autopsy out in the field. "It's highly unusual."

"Oh, for fuck's sake, Prashard," Racine yelled at him. "Just do it."

To Maggie's stunned surprise, Prashard started getting out latex gloves and a pair of forceps from his bag. Then he took position over the body, bending stiffly at the waist instead of getting down on his knees.

Maggie glanced at Racine, who seemed neither pleased nor angry with the assistant medical examiner. Instead, the detective came in closer, crossed her arms over her chest and waited, pointing the penlight, ready to peek inside. Suddenly moonlight streamed into the exit, just above the arch, and illuminating the woman's whole face, making her eyes glitter.

"Jesus!" Racine said. "That's pretty freaky." She glanced back at Maggie, and Maggie tried to remember when there had been a full moon, or if it was still to come. And did it mean anything?

"What exactly are we looking for?" Prashard asked, ignoring Racine and the sudden moonlight as he continued to peel back the gray duct tape, inch by inch, taking care to not lift away any skin. Maggie grabbed a plastic evidence bag from Prashard's case and held it open for him to put the tape in.

"Should be a capsule," Racine answered. "Check the inside of her cheeks."

"You mean like poison?"

"Just check, Prashard. Jesus!" The detective seemed a bit unnerved and impatient.

Prashard finally opened the woman's mouth, but before he could insert a gloved finger, quarters came spilling out.

"What the hell?" Racine shined the penlight, so that even standing over Racine's shoulder, Maggie could see quite clearly. The woman's mouth looked like a black, decaying slot machine filled with shiny coins, spilling out like she'd just hit the jackpot.

# CHAPTER 41

*TUESDAY*
*November 26*
*Boston, Massachusetts*

From his corner suite at the Ritz-Carlton, Ben Garrison could see the Boston Common in one direction and the Charles River in the other. The lush suite was a long-overdue reward to himself and hopefully a good-luck charm for more good things to come. Not that he was superstitious, but he did believe that attitude could be a powerful tool. There was no harm in a few rewards and props now and then to boost that attitude. It made all the crap he had to deal with worthwhile; crap like crank phone calls and cockroaches. Small stuff compared to what he had dealt with in the past.

He remembered several years ago living out of a leaky one-man tent in a smelly, rat-infested warehouse in Kampala, Uganda. It had taken him months to learn Swahili and gain the locals' trust. But it paid off. In no time, he had enough explicit photographs to break the story about a mad scientist luring homeless people from the streets of Kampala for his radical experiments.

Ben still had several of those photos tacked up on the walls of his darkroom. In order to feed her family of five kids, one woman had allowed the so-called scientist to remove her perfectly healthy breast, leaving a scar that looked like the asshole had chopped it off with a machete. An old man had sold the use of his right ear, now mutilated beyond repair, for a carton of cigarettes.

Ben had chosen a slow-speed black-and-white film to bring out the textures and details with natural side lighting. When he developed the prints, he had used high-contrast-grade paper to accentuate the dramatic effect, making the blacks dense and silky and the whites blindingly bright. Through his magic, he had managed to transform those hideous scars into art.

He was a genius when it came to catching hopelessness, that flicker of despair that, if he waited long enough, would always reveal itself in his subjects' eyes. All it took was patience. Yes, he was truly a master at capturing on film the whole spectrum of emotions, from terror to jealousy to fear and evil. After all, the eyes were the window to the soul, and Ben knew he could one day capture the image of the soul on film. Patience.

At the time, both *Newsweek* and *Time* had been working on the mad scientist story, but neither of them had photos, not ones like Ben's. His reward to himself after selling those photos for a nice chunk of change had been a week on a yacht with some waitress whose name he couldn't remember. He did, however, still remember the cute rose tattoo on her tight little ass. Even had a photo of her on his darkroom wall, or rather a photo of her tattoo.

That was back in the days when kinky sex gave him a rush and kept him satisfied for a while. But there wasn't anything that could equal the rush of these past several weeks.

Of course, the best rush of all would be to see the Reverend fucking Everett's smug face when he finally got a visit from the FBI. Surely, even Racine and her bunch of Keystone Kops would make the connection and soon. Although if and when the feebies attempted to raid Everett's precious compound, there probably wouldn't be much left to investigate. If Everett truly believed he was in danger of being arrested, Ben knew the good reverend's blind little sheep would be prepared for a suicide drill, like during the raid on that shitty little cabin on the Neponset River.

He had heard about the cyanide capsules from an ATF agent who had been on the scene. Couple more drinks and the guy probably would have given Ben more details. But mentioning the capsules had been enough. Besides, he had seen them firsthand when he spent two days inside Everett's little compound, that concrete barricade that looked more like a prison than the utopia Everett professed it to be.

He'd also discovered that Everett had enough explosives to blow a nice-size hole in the Appalachian Mountains. The crazy thing was, Everett didn't have the explosives for some terrorist attack. Just like the stockpile at that cabin in the woods—no complex, intricate conspiracy takeover. No, not at all. Instead, it was all for protection, all to protect his fucking fortress if anyone dared try to come in and take away his flock. It would be sort of a cross between Jim Jones's purple Kool-Aid and Timothy McVeigh's fertilizer bomb. What a mess the feebies would have to clean up. And boy, would they have some explaining to do. Probably make Waco look like a cakewalk.

That's if the FBI even made it past all of Everett's booby traps. The asshole had the entire woods filled with Viet Cong-like surprises. Ben couldn't help wondering if his making shingle-nail pipe bombs and chemical-burn grass rags were a few of the reasons the guy had gotten kicked out of the military. Oh, but for good measure, the thoughtful reverend had posted what he probably believed to be disclaimer signs outside the area. Signs that said stuff like Survivors Will Be Prosecuted and Step Beyond This Point Only at Your Own Risk.

It was when Ben had seen the signs that he'd made the decision to gain entrance as a pathetic lost soul rather than as a renegade journalist sneaking through the woods. Weeks before he began his pathetic lost soul's charade, he had muddied himself up like the Three Hills tribe of Mozambique had shown him, covering every inch of his body with a paste mixture, surprised that he could still remember its basic recipe. Even Everett's ex-World Wrestling Federation bodyguards hadn't seen him sliding through the tall grass and blending in with the tree bark. He had learned a lot that visit. The main thing had been that no one could sneak in—or out, for that matter—without getting his fucking head or leg blown off.

Ben checked his wristwatch. He had plenty of time. From what he had overheard at the District rally Saturday night, Everett's boys wouldn't be ready yet for a few hours. He decided to call down to room service. Maybe even check out the whirlpool bath. He'd enjoy himself, reward himself for a short time, then get back to work.

# CHAPTER 42

*John F. Kennedy Federal Building*
*Boston, Massachusetts*

Gwen Patterson watched Agent Tully wrestle their suitcases out of the taxi cab's trunk while the driver stood beside him. He was directing Tully, just as he had when he picked them up at the airport in Boston, pointing with a gnarled right hand, his excuse for not lifting the cases himself. Tully didn't seem to mind. Instead, he simply asked for a receipt while he dug in his trench coat's pockets, pulling out a wad and separating dollar bills from other crumpled receipts and a couple of McDonald's napkins.

Gwen waited, her patience wearing thin. She wanted to snap open her handbag and pay the fare herself. It would be quicker. It was bad enough she was wasting two days, volunteering her services to the bureau and to Kyle Cunningham. Why was it that her colleagues wrote books and garnered interviews with Matt Laurer and Katie Couric? She wrote a book and what did she get? An interview with an adolescent killer.

She reached for her overnight case, but Tully snatched it away.

"No, I've got it," he insisted, tucking it under his arm while he wrapped the strap of her laptop computer's case around his other shoulder and grabbed his duffel bag.

Rather than argue with him, she led the way up the steps, letting him pass her at the last stretch so he could shuffle the bags and still open the heavy door. She wondered if he was overcompensating after Maggie had pointed out that perhaps the two of them couldn't do this trip without being at each other's throats the entire time. Whatever his reason for all the chivalry, Tully had been nothing but polite since they boarded their flight for Boston.

Maggie had assured Gwen time and again that Tully was one of the good guys, a smart, decent agent who wanted to do the right thing. Maggie always added that he was simply a little green, having spent much of his short time with the bureau behind a desk in Cleveland. But that his instincts and his motives were genuine. Yet, there was still something about the tall, lanky agent that rubbed Gwen the wrong way.

What she did know was that his polite, Midwestern manner grated on her. Perhaps he seemed too good to be real. Too honest. Too much of a Boy Scout. The kind of guy who would never drive over the speed limit or have one too many drinks. The kind of guy who went out of his way to open doors for women, but couldn't remember to keep his dollar bills in a money clip or take time to shine his shoes. Maybe that was why she insisted on ruffling his feathers, pushing his buttons. Maybe she wanted to expose that calm, polite, naive Boy Scout's facade, rip it just a bit and see what was underneath, discover what he was really made of. Had too many years as a psychologist made her cynical?

"Dr. Patterson?"

Gwen and Tully stopped and looked up at the man leaning over the second-floor railing. When he realized he was right, he bounded down the stairs with an athletic gait. Gwen knew immediately, before any introductions, that this had to be Nick Morrelli, the man who managed to make Maggie O'Dell blush at just a mention of his name. And now Gwen could understand why. He was more handsome than Maggie's description, the epitome of the cliché tall, dark and handsome, with a strong square jaw, warm blue eyes and dimples when he smiled.

"You must be Nick Morrelli," she said, offering her hand as he got to the bottom of the steps. "I'm Gwen Patterson."

"And I'm Agent R.J. Tully." Tully had to reshuffle the bags to free a hand, nearly dropping her overnight case in the process.

"Here, let me take one of those," Nick said, helping Tully

peel the laptop case's strap from his shoulder. "District Attorney Richardson is still in court, so you're stuck with me. I'll take you upstairs. We can put your bags in a safe place. Why don't we take the elevator." He led them farther into the lobby to a bank of elevators and pushed the up button. "How was your flight?"

"It was fine," Gwen said. She hated small talk, but Nick made it seem as if he was genuinely interested, so she humored him. "Not much of a lunch, so I hope you have some good coffee waiting for us."

"There's a Starbucks across the street. I'll send someone out. What would you like?"

"A café mocha would be lovely." She smiled at Nick as he held the elevator door open and let her squeeze past him. As she did so, she noticed Tully watching her, and from his frown, she knew exactly what he was thinking. But she didn't care if he was disgusted by her shameless flirting. The least she could get out of this trip was a good cup of coffee.

"How about you, Agent Tully?"

"Just regular coffee is fine," he said, in what almost sounded like a grumble. Gwen watched him lean against the far corner of the elevator car with his eyes glued to the numbers above the door. What happened to the polite Boy Scout?

Now Gwen did the same—watched the numbers light up, one floor at a time—suddenly uncomfortable with the tension between the two men and feeling somewhat responsible.

"How's Maggie?" Morrelli asked without taking his eyes from the numbers above the door.

"She's good." She waited for him to ask more, but he didn't. Maybe he wasn't comfortable asking for more information with Agent Tully sulking nearby. She glanced at Tully and wondered if he knew about Nick and Maggie. Although, what was there really to know, since Maggie herself didn't seem to know what to do with the handsome assistant district attorney?

With Nick being in Boston and Maggie living in Newburgh Heights, Virginia, the two of them had little opportunity to spend any time together. It had been months since they had seen each other. Months since Maggie had even mentioned him. Even knowing that he'd been assigned this case and that Gwen would be seeing him today, Maggie had barely acknowledged the fact. Hadn't even given Gwen any messages to relay.

Gwen knew Maggie's divorce from Greg was dragging on, and that Maggie had purposely kept things from progressing with Nick, or as she would say, "getting messy." But there was something more, something her friend was keeping to herself. Why did Maggie insist on doing that? She had real problems with intimacy but refused to see it. Instead, she called it professional distancing and used her career as an excuse to keep everyone in her life at a safe distance.

"He's had only one visitor since he's been here," Nick was telling them, and Gwen forced herself to refocus on the reason for their trip. "He's refused to talk to a public defender and hasn't even made his one phone call."

"Who was the visitor?" Tully asked.

"I'm not sure. D.A. Richardson is personally handling this case. I haven't been involved until now, so I don't know all the details. I think the kid—the visitor—checked out as a college friend of Pratt's."

The elevator's doors opened and Nick held them again for Gwen to pass. Tully stayed for a moment, leaning in the corner of the elevator car, then trailed behind them as though he didn't need anyone's help, keeping his distance while Nick led them down a busy corridor. She hated how men played their territorial games, especially in the presence of a woman. If she hadn't been here, they'd be exchanging football scores and pretending to be old buddies.

"How did he know he was here?" Tully asked, now catching up with them.

"Excuse me?"

"How did the college friend know Pratt was here if Pratt hadn't made any phone calls?"

Nick slowed and glanced at Tully over his shoulder. The look on his face told Gwen Nick wished he had had more time to equip himself with the details of the case. She found herself wanting to defend him and at the same time wondered if Tully ever tried to make a good first impression.

"Good question. I can find that out for you." Nick finally said. "Here we are." He pointed to the door at the end of the hall.

This time Tully was on the right side, grabbing the handle before Nick had a chance and opening it wide for both Gwen and Nick. She stopped herself from rolling her eyes at him. It would probably only encourage him.

"We've got him ready to see you," Nick explained, "but if you'd like to take some time to unwind—"

"No," Gwen stopped him. "Let's go ahead."

He led her down another hallway to a door where a uniformed guard stood.

"Agent Tully and I will be watching from next door," Nick said, pointing to another door. "Burt, here, will be right outside, so you start feeling uncomfortable or want to stop and get the hell out, just say the word, okay?"

"Thanks, Nick." She smiled at him, hoping to relieve his concern. "I know the drill, so don't worry. I'll be fine."

She did know the drill. She had interviewed numerous criminals, tougher, cruder men than this boy. She slipped out of her London Fog trench coat, unsnapped her watch, plucked off her earrings and pearls, placing the items in her handbag, then surrendered the coat and handbag to Nick. She checked her suit jacket and unlatched a gold pin of a dove from her lapel. Nick opened the handbag for her, and she carefully placed it inside.

After inspecting her skirt and shoes and buttons, making certain there were no sharp edges, she bent down to her overnight case and pulled out a plain yellow legal pad—no wire spiral notebooks—and a simple number two lead pencil. She had learned the hard way that the simplest pen could be dismantled in seconds, its insides used to pick the lock of even the best set of handcuffs.

Finally prepared, she took a deep breath and nodded to Burt to open the door. Yes, she knew the drill. Don't show any signs of vulnerability. Let him know immediately that she wouldn't be intimidated by any of his bullshit, crude comments or lewd glares. However, when the young man sitting across the wooden table looked up at her, Gwen saw something that threatened to unravel her calm more than any obscene gesture or wolf-call whistle. What she saw in Eric Pratt's eyes was pure, undeniable fear. And that fear seemed to be directed at her.

# CHAPTER 43

*FBI Headquarters*
*Washington, D.C.*

Maggie spread out the files on the counter Keith Ganza had cleared for her, shoving high-tech microscopes out of the way and setting empty racks of vials clinking.

"Should we wait for Detective Racine?" Ganza asked, glancing at his watch.

"She knew what time we were going to get started." Maggie tried to keep the impatience out of her voice. Just when she was starting to be impressed with Racine, the detective did something to annoy her all over again. "The only case I could find on VICAP," Maggie began, "is a floater fished out of Falls Lake just north of Raleigh. They found her about ten days ago." She pulled out the scanned photos she had downloaded. "She was a twenty-two-year-old college student at Wake Forest."

"A floater?" Ganza hovered over her shoulder. "How long had she been in the water?"

"Coroner's report says several days." She showed him a faxed copy. "But you know as well as I do that it's pretty tough to figure time of death with a floater."

"This doesn't sound like our guy. What was VICAP's match?"

"Actually there're quite a few things. Her mouth was taped shut with duct tape and a piece of paper was found shoved down her throat. There're handcuff marks on the wrist and several ligature tracks on her throat." Again, she pulled out more scanned photos, close-ups of a mutilated neck and welted wrists.

"Was the hyoid crushed?"

Maggie ran her index finger down the coroner's report until she came to the notation. "Yes. And check the photo. There's a lot more bruising than from a cord. This guy likes to use his hands when he's ready for the kill."

Ganza held up a full-length scan. "Looks like livor mortis on her backside. She may have been sitting when she died. Would have had to be sitting for hours before he came back and tossed her in the water. But why toss her? Our guy likes to pose his victims."

"He may not have tossed her," Maggie said. "The Wake County sheriff told me they had some flooding in that area about two weeks ago. The lake came up over its banks."

"Well, she's washed pretty clean. Any DNA samples found at all? How 'bout under her nails?"

"Nope. All washed away."

"I have the preliminary DNA results from the Brier girl," Ganza said while he shifted through the documents Maggie had laid out.

"And?"

"There was some foreign DNA under her fingernails, but it doesn't match the semen." Ganza didn't sound surprised. Maggie wasn't, either. Whether Senator Brier wanted to believe it or not, the evidence seemed to point to consensual sex, probably earlier in the evening.

"Also found some foreign fingerprints on the Brier girl's purse. We'll check them against what we have in AFIS," Ganza continued. "'Course, the way you girls share your belongings with one another, it might not lead us anywhere."

"Goes to show you what you know about girls, Ganza. I don't share my things with anyone, let alone something as personal as a purse."

"Goes to show what you know about girls, O'Dell. When was the last time you carried a purse?"

"Okay, good point." She felt her cheeks flush, surprised that he had noticed such a detail about her. Yes, she hated to admit it, but it was true that she had been anything but the typical teenage girl, and it looked like she was far from the typical woman. Still, it was embarrassing that this scruffy, weathered, forensics relic knew more about women and their accessories than she did.

"One other thing." This time he went to the metal cabinet in the corner and brought back a plastic evidence bag. Inside, Maggie recognized the slide with a piece of transparent tape attached. It was the slide she and Stan had made from the residue found on Ginny Brier's neck. "Hang on to that for a minute," he told her as he walked to the door and reached for the light switch. "Now, keep in mind that whatever cord or wire or rope this guy is using has to be covered with this crap, okay?"

He shut off the light and the glittery substance on the slide began to glow in the dark.

"What in the world?"

"If we can figure out what it came off of, it might be able to tell us something about our guy."

He snapped the lights back on.

"What about something used in a magic act or for a theater production?" Maggie asked. "Maybe some novelty store or costume shop might be able to tell us."

"Could be. But I'm wondering, does he use it because it's a nifty prop or because it's something he has handy all the time?"

"My guess is it's a nifty prop." Maggie held up the slide again. "This guy likes attention. He likes putting on a performance."

When she looked back at Ganza, he was picking through the assortment of documents again. He pointed to the fax copy of the crumpled piece of paper found in the floater's throat. "No ID, no cyanide capsule, no quarters. What was this?"

Despite the wrinkles and creases, it looked like some kind of schedule with a list of dates and cities. Maggie pulled out another piece of paper from her jacket pocket.

"Recognize this?" she asked as she unfolded a copy of the Church of Spiritual Freedom's pamphlet. The one Tully had found after Reverend Everett's Saturday night rally. On the inside was listed the dates and cities for the organization's fall schedule of rallies. "Take a look at the first of November. That week's designated rally was at Falls Lake State Recreation Area in Raleigh, North Carolina. Don't tell me it's a coincidence, because you know—"

"Yeah, yeah, I know. You don't believe in coincidences. So how does the homeless woman fit into all this? There was no rally close by. And if Prashard's early assessment is correct, she was also killed Saturday night."

"I haven't figured that out yet."

"Maggie, you know all this means is that someone wants us to make a connection to Everett. The murder of Senator Brier's daughter looked like it could be revenge for the deaths of those boys in the cabin. But the rest—the floater, the homeless woman…" Ganza waved his hand over the spread of photos and reports and faxes. "All it means is that someone wants us to make a connection to Everett. Doesn't mean he's involved."

"Oh, he's involved," Maggie said, surprised by the hint of anger in her voice. "I don't know how or why, but my gut tells me the good Reverend Joseph Everett is somehow responsible. Maybe not directly."

"Or maybe even directly," Racine said, appearing at the doorway. Her spiky blond hair looked windblown, her face flushed, and she seemed a bit out of breath. She came in and held up a copy of the *National Enquirer.* The front-page photo showed Ginny Brier holding hands with Reverend Everett. Without looking at the newspaper, Racine read the headline aloud. "Moments Before Her Death, Senator's Daughter Attends Prayer Rally. Photo credit by our good pal Benjamin fucking Garrison."

"Garrison?" Maggie wasn't surprised. Though she had met him only briefly at the monument Sunday morning, she hadn't trusted him or his reasons for being there. "Okay, so Everett met Ginny Brier. No incriminating evidence there. And no harm done. We already knew she was at the rally. Why so steamed, Detective Racine?"

"Oh, it gets much better." Racine practically ripped the pages, flipping to the inside, creasing the fold before turning it back around. This time both Maggie and Ganza came in for a closer look.

"Son of a bitch," Ganza muttered.

"I should have known I couldn't trust that bastard," Racine said through gritted teeth.

Maggie couldn't believe it. The page was filled with crime scene photos, photos of Ginny Brier's dead body, black boxes strategically placed over her private parts, but nothing to hide the horrible, brutal rest. Nothing to cover those terrified eyes—frozen in time, eyes wide open.

# CHAPTER 44

Eric Pratt could hear and feel the chipping and splintering of his fingernails as he dug them into the grooves of his handcuffs. It had become a new habit, useful only in that it prevented him from digging the jagged nails into his own flesh.

He should have been grateful that the guard had let him keep his hands together instead of locking them at his waist to each side. He knew his captors had misread his polite behavior, perhaps even thought he was harmless. Though not entirely harmless—he rattled the shackles on his ankles, reminding himself they were there, readjusted himself in the chair. He needed to stop squirming. Why couldn't he sit still?

As soon as the woman entered the room, Eric had felt a wet chill sweep over his body. She had introduced herself as a doctor, but Eric knew better. The woman was small, well dressed, about his mother's age, but very attractive. She carried herself with confidence and ease despite the high-heeled shoes she wore. He found himself watching her legs as she crossed them, making herself comfortable in the steel folding chair. She had smooth, firm calves, and from what he could see of her thighs, she was really nothing like his mother.

She was explaining why she was here. He glanced at her mouth, but he didn't need to listen. He knew exactly why she was here. He had known the second she walked in the door.

She was the woman clothed with the sun. Her reddish-blond hair had been a dead giveaway. It circled her face like the rays of the sun. Of course, she would possess warm green eyes and a quiet, captivating manner, a polite and hypnotic voice and a body that could distract and tempt. Father Joseph had outdone himself this time. He had sent a vision straight out of John's description of the Apocalypse. Had he honestly believed Eric wouldn't recognize her?

Sweat trickled down his back. Her voice hummed in his ears, the words no longer separate but strung together as melody—Satan's death song, lovely and mesmerizing. He wouldn't let it hypnotize him. He wouldn't let her draw him in and incapacitate him. But she was good. Oh, she was clever with that kind smile and those sexy legs. If Brandon's visit hadn't prepared him, he may very well have been taken into her web, ensnared before he realized what the true purpose of this visit really was.

*Click, click*—his fingernails picked at the metal. One of them was bleeding. He could feel it, but he kept his hands in his lap, pretending to be calm, pretending the fear wasn't clawing inside him, ripping at the walls of his stomach and trying to race up his throat to strangle him.

He looked into her eyes, saw her smile and quickly looked away. Was that her secret weapon? If she couldn't hypnotize him with her voice, would she use her eyes? He wondered how she might kill him, and his eyes scanned the length of her, looking for bulges in her clothing.

The guards would have allowed her in with anything she cared to conceal. They would want no part of the mess, even if they were able to stop her. After all, Father had told them the woman clothed with the sun had special powers, according to the gospel of John, St. John the Divine, Revelation 12:1–6. She was light. She was dark. She was good and evil. She was a messenger of Satan and could disguise herself easily.

Suddenly, Eric remembered a newspaper article Father had read them just months ago. No member was allowed newspapers or magazines. There was no need when Father took the burden upon himself to relay those news items that were relevant and from sources that could be trusted.

But now Eric remembered the story of a foreign diplomat who had been visiting the States from some evil empire. Eric couldn't recall the country. The diplomat had been slain in his hotel bed and reports were that the woman who killed him did it while straddling him, waiting for him to come and then slitting his neck. Father Joseph had used it as an example of justice being done. Was that where he had gotten the idea of sending this woman?

Eric noticed her tapping the pencil, the eraser smacking the notepad—the notepad, a decoy left on the table, not a single note scrawled on it. The pencil had been freshly sharpened, its lead a dagger's point. He could distinguish some of the words that came out of her mouth, words like *help* and *cooperate.* He knew better. He refused to be sucked in by her code words. They could just as well have been words like *kill* and *mutilate.* He knew their true meaning.

*Tap-tap, tap-tap*—he watched the pencil and tried to ignore the panic squeezing the air out of his lungs. The room felt smaller. Her voice droned on. *Tap-tap, tap-tap.* His heart pounded in his ears. Or was that the pencil?

He made himself look into her eyes. He had cheated Satan once before. Could he do it again?

# CHAPTER 45

Gwen shifted in her chair and recrossed her legs. Pratt was watching her again, staring at her legs. The horny bastard wasn't listening to a word she was saying. Had she misread his initial reaction, that look of absolute fear in his eyes when she entered the room? If it hadn't been fear, what the hell had it been? Had she been wrong about him wanting to survive, wanting to find a safe haven?

He hadn't answered a single one of her questions. Instead, he looked everywhere except into her eyes, as if she were Medusa and doing so would turn him to stone. Or did he simply hate psychologists? Maybe the kid was sick of shrinks or didn't trust any authority figures. Yet deep down she wondered if the real reason for his distraction, for his avoidance, was because he was worried she wielded some sort of power he couldn't stand up to.

If their theory was correct, Eric Pratt had been manipulated and controlled by someone other than himself for some time now. He had been a puppet willing to kill and be killed. Perhaps that someone—the Reverend Joseph Everett, most likely—still had a strong hold on him, despite Eric being locked away. But something had made the boy spit out that cyanide capsule. Self-preservation had won. She needed to follow her instinct. And she needed to believe his instinct to live was stronger than his fear of Everett.

"You are a survivor, Eric. That's why you're still here. I want to help you. Do you believe I can help you?"

She waited, tapping out her impatience with the pencil against her notepad. The kid seemed mesmerized by the motion. She tried to remember the reports she had glanced at, whether or not toxicology had shown any drug use. Yet that was what he reminded her of; some spaced-out coke-head. If he'd look at her, she might be able to tell from the dilation of his pupils. Was that why he kept his eyes away from hers?

"You don't need to be in this all alone, Eric. You can talk to me." She kept her voice low and soft, careful not to sound like she was addressing a small child. She didn't want to insult him. And if he was afraid, she needed to convince him he could trust her. Right now that looked like a dim prospect.

She noticed drops of sweat on his forehead and his upper lip. A glimpse into his eyes made her wonder if he was even here in the room with her. An annoying clicking came from under the table. This would be a wasted trip, she realized, and she thought of all the billable hours she had rescheduled back at her office.

Then she accidentally dropped the pencil.

His chair screeched as he lunged for the floor. The leg shackles clattered and his body flew so quickly, all Gwen saw was the streak of his orange jumpsuit. Her own impulse was to dive for the pencil, as well, sending her chair tumbling behind her. But she was too late. He had beaten her to it. She scrambled on hands and knees, trying to get to her feet. But just as she heard running footsteps and locks sliding open, she felt her head jerked backward.

He was sprawled on the floor but had managed to grab a handful of her hair before she could pull away. He yanked her hard, throwing her off balance. He yanked her again, and she slammed against his chest. All she could see were three sets of shoes come sliding to a halt. That's when she felt the pencil at her throat, the sharp point pressed against her carotid artery, threatening to penetrate through flesh and veins. And, despite the fear that shot through her, the first thing that came to mind was how stupid she had been to have sharpened the pencil just that morning.

## CHAPTER 46

Tully kept his Glock aimed at the kid's head. At this angle, it would be a clean shot. He could do it, but would the bastard's jerking muscles still plunge the pencil into Dr. Patterson's neck. Shit! Why hadn't he thought of that damn pencil?

"Eric, come on now." Morrelli was trying to talk sense to the kid. From the crazed look in Pratt's eyes, Tully knew there would be no talking him out of anything. But Morrelli continued. "You don't want to do this, Eric. You're in enough trouble. We can help you, but not—"

"Stop it! Shut the fuck up!" the boy yelled, and yanked Dr. Patterson's head back, exposing her neck even more.

His cuffed hands only allowed him to hang on to a clump of her hair with one hand, keeping her close to him while his other hand held the pencil, its razor point pressing into her skin. So far Tully could see no blood. But one good shove, and he knew it would be a major gusher. Jesus!

Tully tried to figure out the doctor's position without taking his sight off Pratt. One of her legs was twisted under her body. One hand had instinctively shot up to grab at her assailant's arm, and she kept her fingers tightly grasping the sleeve of the orange jumpsuit. Pratt either didn't notice or didn't care. That was good. She had some sense of control, though she was holding on to the arm that held her hair and not the pencil. He glanced at her face. She seemed calm and steady. But then her eyes caught his, and he could see the fear. Fear was good. Panic was not.

"What do you want us to do, Eric?" Morrelli tried again.

It was obvious he was bugging the hell out of the kid, but at least he was keeping him distracted. Tully was impressed with

Morrelli's demeanor, hands quietly at his side, despite two men with guns drawn on either side of him. He talked to the kid as if he had a jumper on a ledge.

"Just talk to us, Eric. Tell us what you need."

"Eric," Dr. Patterson said quietly, "you know you don't want to hurt me." She said it slowly—making a noticeable effort to say the words without moving or swallowing—but she managed it without a trace of fear.

Tully couldn't help wondering if she had been through this before.

"No, I don't want to hurt you," Pratt answered. But before any of them could relax, he added, "I need to kill you."

Out of the corner of his eye, Tully saw Morrelli shift just slightly, and he hoped to God the prosecutor wasn't thinking of doing something stupid. He glanced at Dr. Patterson again, this time trying to draw her eyes to his. When she did, he gave her a slight nod, hoping she would understand. She watched him, keeping her eyes on his face, then finally moving her gaze down the length of his arm and to his trigger finger.

"Eric." Morrelli had decided to try one more time. "So far there's no murder charge against you. Only weapons charges. You don't want to do this. Dr. Patterson only wants to help you. She isn't here to hurt you."

Tully focused his aim and kept it steady. His finger wanted to squeeze now. He waited, checked Dr. Patterson's grip on the orange sleeve.

"She's Satan," Eric whispered this time. "Can't any of you see that? Father Joseph sent her." He adjusted his grip on the pencil, puncturing the skin and drawing blood. "She's come to kill me. I need to kill her first."

Tully heard Burt's safety click off. Shit! He couldn't signal the guard with Morrelli standing between them. Instead, he found Dr. Patterson's eyes again. She was ready despite the fear. He gave her another slight nod.

"I have to kill her," Eric said, and something in his voice told Tully he meant it. "I have to kill her before she kills me. I have to. I don't have a choice. It's kill or be killed."

Tully saw her fingers tighten on the orange sleeve. Good. She was getting a better grip. He watched her fingers while still looking down the sight of his Glock. Then suddenly she yanked downward and hard. Pratt didn't let go of her hair, and the motion caused her head to twist down and away from the pencil. Tully wasted no time. He squeezed the trigger, shattering Pratt's left shoulder. The boy's fingers opened. The pencil dropped. Dr. Patterson slammed an elbow into his chest, causing him to release his grip on her hair. She scrambled away on hands and knees. In seconds, Burt was on Pratt, smashing his face against the floor. The angry guard had a huge black boot pressed on top of Pratt's bleeding shoulder and a gun to the kid's temple.

"Easy, Burt." Morrelli was at the guard's side, keeping him in line.

Tully hesitated before going to Dr. Patterson. She remained hunched on her knees, sitting back on her feet as if waiting for the strength to stand. He knelt down in front of her, but she avoided his eyes. He touched her cheek, cupped her jaw and lifted it gently, to get a good look at her neck. She allowed him the examination, now watching his eyes and gripping his arm as though she didn't want to let go.

He wiped the drops of blood away. The puncture had only broken the skin.

"You're gonna have a hell of a bruise, Doc." He met her eyes and looked for the fear he could see her already stowing away. Or trying to, anyway.

"We should get you to an emergency room," Morrelli said from behind them.

"I'll be fine," she reassured Morrelli while giving Tully a quick and restrained smile before she pulled away from him, removing her hand from his arm. She didn't, however, resist his help as she climbed to her bare feet. Sometime during the scuffle she had lost both shoes.

"She's Satan, she's the Antichrist. Father Joseph sent her to kill me," Pratt was still yelling. "Why can't any of you see that?"

"Get him the hell out of here," Morrelli told Burt, who swung the kid up to his feet and shoved him along, pushing harder when Pratt began to mutter again.

Tully picked up the folding chair and brought it over for Dr. Patterson. She waved him off, looking around the room in search of her shoes. Tully saw one and crawled under the table for it. When he stood up again, Morrelli was on one knee placing the other shoe on the good doctor's foot, holding her ankle and looking like Prince Charming. It only reminded Tully how much he didn't like this guy or guys like him. Morrelli turned to him, staying on his goddamn knee and gesturing for the other shoe. Tully surrendered it.

However, when he glanced at Dr. Patterson's face, she was watching him and not Morrelli.

# CHAPTER 47

*West Potomac Park*
*Washington D.C.*

Maggie stopped at the drinking fountain and took long, slow gulps. The afternoon had turned unseasonably warm for November. She hadn't been far into her run when she peeled off her sweatshirt and knotted it around her waist.

Now she pulled the sweatshirt loose and wiped the dripping sweat from her forehead and the water from her chin as she scanned the surroundings. She looked up and down the Mall, watching for the woman she had talked to earlier, who had given her a long list of instructions but failed to include a single description of what she looked like.

Maggie found the wooden bench on the grassy knoll overlooking the Vietnam Wall, exactly where the woman told her it would be. Then she put a foot up on the bench's back rail and began her leg stretches, something she seldom did after running, always feeling like she didn't have time. But this, too, had been requested, as well as the strict instructions to wear nothing that would give her away as a law enforcement officer: no FBI T-shirts, no bulging holsters, guns or badges, no navy-blue. Not even a baseball cap or sunglasses.

Maggie wondered—and not for the first time—what good it would do to talk to someone so paranoid. Chances were, she'd get some delusional perspective, some skewed vision of reality. Yet she felt fortunate that Cunningham and Senator Brier had found someone willing to talk. An aid in Senator Brier's office had tracked the woman down, and although she had agreed to meet Maggie, she had insisted on remaining anonymous. The cloak-and-dagger game didn't bother Maggie. As long as this woman, an ex-member of Everett's church, could provide a view of Everett that Maggie knew she'd never find in any FBI file. And certainly a view she'd never get from her mother.

High school kids outnumbered tourists, scattered all along the sidewalks, hiking up the Lincoln Memorial steps and winding around the bronze sculptures of the Korean Veterans and Vietnam Women's Memorials. More field trips. Wasn't that why Emma Tully had been at the monuments the other day? November must be prime time for school field trips, though the educational significance seemed to be lost on most of them. Yes, other than the students there were very few tourists.

Then Maggie saw her. The woman wore faded blue jeans, too loose for her tall, thin frame, a long-sleeved chambray shirt and dark aviator sunglasses. Her long brown hair was pulled back into a ponytail, and Maggie could see that she wore little, if any, makeup. A camera hung from her neck and a backpack from her shoulder while she stopped and reached with paper and pencil to do a rubbing against the Wall.

She looked like any other tourist, a family member completing her journey and paying homage to a loved one, a fallen soldier. The woman took three rubbings before she came over and sat on the bench next to Maggie. She started pulling out of her backpack a sandwich wrapped in wax paper, a bag of Doritos and a bottled water. Without a word, she began eating, looking out over the park and watching. For a minute, Maggie wondered if she had been wrong about this being her mysterious contact. She took another look at the tourists at the Wall. Was it possible the woman had changed her mind and not come?

"Do you know anyone on the wall?" the woman asked without looking at Maggie while she sipped her water.

"Yes," Maggie answered, expecting the question. "My uncle, my father's brother."

"What was his name?"

The exchange was casual, an everyday occurrence between two complete strangers sitting on a park bench in front of the one monument that seemed to touch every American's life somehow. An everyday exchange and yet so very clever. No way to mistake the details of this question.

"His name was Patrick O'Dell."

The woman seemed neither pleased nor especially interested and picked up her sandwich again. "And so you are Maggie," she said with a slight nod, taking a bite and keeping her eyes on a game of tag that had broken out between several of the teenagers up on the hill.

"What should I call you?" Maggie asked, since she'd been given only the woman's initials.

"You can call me..." She hesitated, took another sip of water and glanced at the bottle. "Call me Eve," she said.

Maggie caught a glimpse of the bottle's label: Evian. This was ridiculous. But names didn't matter as long as she answered her questions.

"Okay, Eve." She waited. No one was within earshot, and the game of tag was drawing everyone's attention. "What can you tell me about Everett and his so-called church?"

"Well." She crunched several chips, offering the bag to Maggie. Maggie accepted. "The church is a ruse to get donations and stockpile money and arms. But he's not interested in taking over the world or the government. He preaches the word of the Lord only to get what he wants."

"So if it's not to overtake the government or even terrorize the government, what is it he wants?"

"Power, of course. Power over his own little world."

"So he doesn't even believe?"

"Oh, he believes." Eve set aside her sandwich and dug in her backpack until she found another bottle of Evian water and handed it to Maggie. "He believes he is God." She hesitated, picking up her own bottle, wrapping both hands around it, cradling it as if looking for something to hang on to. "He preys on those of us who have no clue who we are, those who are weak and searching and have nowhere else to go. He tells us what to eat, what to wear, who we can and can't talk to, what we should believe.

"He convinces us that no one outside the church understands or loves us and that those who are not with us are against us and only want to hurt us. We're told we must forsake family and friends and all worldly materialistic things in order to find true peace and be worthy of his love. And by this time, he's stripped us of every single individual thing that defined us, until we are absolutely nothing without him and without his church."

Maggie listened quietly. None of this was news. It only followed the same profile of every other cult she had read about. It simply confirmed their beliefs that Everett's church was a bogus organization, a smoke screen for his own power-hungry maneuvers. But there was something she didn't understand. Something she needed to ask. A hint of impatience seeped out in her question. "Why in the world does anyone join?"

"In the beginning," Eve said in a calm voice, taking her time, appearing to be neither insulted nor intimidated by the question, "you want to believe that you've found a place where you finally belong. Where you're a part of something bigger than you. In not so different ways, we're all lost souls, looking and searching for something that's missing in our lives. Self-identity or self-esteem—whatever you want to call it—it's such a fragile commodity. When you have no idea who you are to begin with, it's so easy and tempting to become your surroundings. When you feel lost and alone, sometimes you're willing to give anything to belong. Sometimes you're even willing to give your soul."

Maggie fidgeted, growing weary and suspicious of the woman's overly calm manner. It seemed too well rehearsed. Was this meeting a ploy, maybe even orchestrated by Everett to convince her the organization, though definitely screwed up, was not dangerous? Maggie was looking for a murderer, and this woman was talking like Everett's only crime was snatching souls.

"It doesn't sound so bad," she told Eve, and took a sip of her water, watching the woman from the corner of her eye. "Everett takes good care of you, feeds and clothes you, makes all your decisions and gives you a place to stay free of charge.

All he asks for in return is for you to indulge in his delusions of grandeur. Nope. Doesn't sound bad to me. And quite honestly, no one can really take away your soul without your permission, can they?"

She waited out the silence, helping herself to the bag of chips left on the bench between them. Finally, the woman looked over at her, pushed her sunglasses on top of her head and examined Maggie, holding her gaze as if searching for something hidden within her. She looked older than Maggie had guessed. Now without the dark glasses, Maggie could see the wrinkles at Eve's eyes and lines around her mouth. There was another smile, again just a twist at the corner of her mouth. It occurred to Maggie that this woman was used to keeping her expressions and emotions in check. Even her eyes refused to show any hint of feeling, though they were not cold, just empty.

Eve looked away suddenly, as if she had exposed too much, and flipped the dark glasses back down into place.

"You look a lot like her," she said in that same even tone.

"Excuse me?"

"Kathleen. She's your mother, isn't she?"

"You know my mother?"

"She joined just before I escaped."

Maggie felt herself wince at Eve's use of the word *escape,* though she had said it as casually as if they were talking about going home after a day at work.

"Don't think for a minute—" Eve began unbuttoning and rolling up the sleeves of her shirt as if suddenly too warm "—that there is anything harmless about Everett. He saves you, builds you up, tells you he loves you, trusts you, that you are special, a favor to him from God. Then he turns on you and rips you to shreds. He discovers your weaknesses and your fears, then uses them to humiliate you and to destroy any last piece of self-respect you think you deserve."

With her shirtsleeves now rolled up, she held out her wrists in front of her for Maggie to see.

"He calls it being sent to the Well," she said, her voice still annoyingly calm and level. Red welts circled both her wrists where the skin had flayed and bled from rope or handcuffs cutting into the flesh. The wounds looked recent. Eve's head pivoted around, and she pulled the sleeves back in place, picking up her sandwich and unwrapping it to continue her lunch as though there had been no interruptions.

Again Maggie waited, this time out of respect and not impatience. She followed Eve's lead and sipped at her own water and managed a few more chips.

"It's an actual well," Eve said. "Though I doubt he ever intended to use it for anything more than a punishment chamber. He knew I was terrified of the dark, closed places, so it was a perfect punishment."

She stared out at the teenagers up on the hill, though Maggie wondered what the woman really saw. Her voice remained calm but now almost disconnected. "He had them tie me by the wrists and lower me into the well. When I kicked and clawed and tried to climb out, he had them spill buckets of spiders down on top of me. At least that's what I think they were. It was too dark to see them. But I could feel them. I could feel them all over me. Every inch of my hair and face and skin seemed to be crawling. I couldn't even scream anymore because I was afraid they'd crawl inside my mouth. I closed my eyes and tried to stay still, so they wouldn't bite me as much. And for hours I tried to retreat to somewhere else inside my mind. I remember reciting an old Emily Dickinson poem over and over again in my head. It was probably the one thing that saved me from losing my mind. 'I'm nobody. Who are you?' Do you know it?"

"'Are you nobody, too?'" Maggie answered with the next line of the poem.

"'Then there's a pair of us,'" Eve continued. "'Don't tell. They'd banish us.'"

"The mind's a powerful tool," Maggie said, thinking of her own childhood and how many times she had resorted to going away—far, far away inside her own mind.

"Everett took everything away from me but still wasn't able

to take away my mind." Eve looked over at her and this time when she spoke there was a spark of anger. "Don't let anyone tell you Everett is harmless. He makes them believe he only wants to take care of them while he has them sign over their homes and property, their social security and pension and child support checks. He rewards them with fear. Fear of the real world. Fear of being hunted down if they betray him. Fear of the FBI. So much fear that they're more willing to go through his suicide drills than be captured alive."

"Suicide drills?" Despite Eve's story, Maggie couldn't help thinking this didn't sound like the man who had gotten her mother to stop drinking. All the changes she'd seen in her mother seemed so positive. "My mother doesn't seem frightened," she told Eve.

"He may still be looking for ways to use her. Is she living at the compound yet?"

"No. She has an apartment in Richmond and has made no mention of leaving it." Only now did that realization bring relief to Maggie. Perhaps her mother wasn't in too deep. She couldn't possibly be in as much danger as this woman had been. "She loves her apartment. I doubt very much she'll be willing to move to the compound."

The woman shook her head and there was that smile again. "She's more valuable to him on the outside," she said, without looking at Maggie. "He's hoping to find a way to use you."

"Me?"

"Believe me, he knows Kathleen has a daughter who is an FBI agent. He knows all about you. He knows everything. It could be why he's been so good to her. But if he finds out you're of no use to him, or if he finds out you're trying to hurt him… Well, just be careful. For your mother's sake."

"I just need to convince my mother to stay the hell away from him."

"And, of course, she'll listen to you because the two of you are so close."

Maggie felt the sting of Eve's sarcasm, despite Eve's calm, friendly tone.

"I need to go," the woman said, suddenly packing up her things and getting to her feet.

"But wait. There's got to be something you can tell me that could help me bring down Everett."

"Bring him down?"

"Yes. Exactly."

"You'll never get him. Most of what he does is legit, and what he does that isn't.... Well, you don't see any of us lining up to press charges, do you?"

"Only because you're still afraid of him. Why let him control your life? We can protect you."

"We? You mean the government?" She laughed, a true, genuine laugh. Then she slung her backpack over her shoulder. "You can't protect me until you get Everett. And you'll never get him. Even if you try, he'll know. He'll have them all lined up for their cyanide capsules and dead before you step foot inside the compound." She hesitated, glancing around the park as if making certain it was safe. As if she expected Everett to appear from behind a monument or a tree.

"What did you do?" Maggie asked.

"Excuse me?"

"What was it that you did to deserve the Well?"

"I wouldn't stop trying to take care of my mom. She was the only reason I was there. And she was sick. I kept sneaking her my food. The breaking point was when I stole some of her heart medicine to give to her. It was her own medicine that had been confiscated from her, because, of course, Father's love is the only medicine anyone needs."

"Where is your mom now?"

Maggie watched Eve disconnect as she stared out over her head. It was like turning an on-off switch.

"She died the day after he put me in the Well. I think she felt so guilty, she had a heart attack. I'll never know for sure." She looked at Maggie through her dark glasses, reflecting back the Wall. "In the end, he always wins. Just be careful for yourself and especially for your mom."

Then she turned and left.

# CHAPTER 48

*Boston, Massachusetts*

Maria Leonetti took a shortcut through Boston Common, wishing she had brought a pair of running shoes. But she hated wearing them with her expensive suits and thought the other women at the brokerage firm gave up a piece of their credibility as soon as they put on their Nikes and Reeboks at the end of the day. After all, none of the male brokers changed their shoes just to walk home. Why couldn't women simply buy comfortable shoes? And why the hell couldn't shoe designers create something both stylish and comfortable?

She noticed a crowd at the fountain and wondered what kind of celebration could be taking place on a Tuesday afternoon. The day had been unseasonably warm, bringing out in-line skaters, joggers and all sorts of riffraff, too. This group of rowdy young guys looked like a fraternity party. Maybe college kids were out already for the Thanksgiving holiday. She probably should have taken another trail, but she was exhausted. Her feet hurt. All she wanted to do was get home, snuggle with Izzy, her calico cat, and veg out. Maybe put on an old Cary Grant movie and make popcorn. That was as much of a party as she wanted.

Suddenly, she felt someone grab her elbow.

"Hey," she yelled, and jerked away. Before she could turn around, two men were on either side of her, each grabbing an arm. One of them pulled at her purse, ripping the strap and tossing it to the ground. Jesus! They weren't interested in robbing her. A fresh panic took hold.

"Hey! Look what we found," one of them shouted to the others.

"Get your fucking hands off me," Maria screamed, pulling and tugging as they dragged her into the crowd.

Arms and hands and faces came at her from all directions. They were laughing and egging one another on, chanting, "Bitch, bitch."

She screamed and kicked, losing a shoe but connecting with one groin. It only infuriated them into holding her feet as well as her arms. Someone sprayed her with beer, dousing her face and blouse. Then she heard the rips of her clothing, and she screamed louder. No one seemed to care—or could they just not hear over the laughter and yelling? Hands squeezed her breasts and ran up her thighs. Fingers poked and prodded into her underpants, and soon they were being ripped off her, too. She could see a glint of a camera lens and then saw its owner, pushing between shoulders to get a better view.

Oh, dear God. They were going to kill her. They were going to rape her and then they were going to kill her. And it would all be on film for someone's entertainment.

She clawed at their faces and got slapped so hard, blood trickled down her mouth. She managed to pull one hand free, and clung to her bra as the rest of her blouse was ripped away. Her shoes were gone. She could feel her panty hose shredded around her ankles, where they were using them to hold her down. They gripped her so tight she could already feel the bruises and her skin rubbed raw.

"Hey, here comes another bitch."

One by one, they let go. They left her as suddenly as they had attacked, rising up and moving like a swarm. She lay heaped on the grass in only her bra and her skirt, which was slit up the side seam, hanging together only by the waistband. Her underpants were gone. She hurt everywhere and couldn't see through the tears. She wanted to curl up and die. Then she heard the woman's scream and realized they had found another victim. Her stomach knotted up and she felt dizzy, but she knew she needed to leave before they decided to come back to her.

She tried to stand, but her knees collapsed as her head began to spin. Another hand grabbed her arm, and she jerked away, falling back on the grass.

"No, wait. I just want to help."

She stared up at the young man, but the spinning in her head wouldn't let her eyes focus. All she could see was that he wore a blue baseball cap, jeans and a T-shirt that smelled of beer. Oh, God! He was one of them. She tried to crawl away, but he took her by the arm and lifted her to her feet.

"We need to get you away from here." He was holding her up and wrapping her in a scratchy jacket.

She had no energy left to fight him. She walked as best she could as he led her up the trail and away from the crowd, away from the laughter and that continuous scream for help that made her sick to her stomach. They barely got to the edge of the park before she pulled away from him, retching and vomiting behind a nearby bush. When she turned around, he was gone.

Maria sat down, safely hidden behind the trees, trying to calm her stomach and catch her breath. The rumble of nearby traffic seemed to soothe her, as if reminding her that civilization was, indeed, close by. That she hadn't fallen off the edge of the world. A breeze chilled her wet body, and she could smell the stale beer that had doused her skin. It made her gag again, but she was able to contain the urge to vomit. She hugged herself, listening to the sound of car horns and the hydraulic screech of brakes, listening for anything that would help shut out the sounds of laughter, the chants of "bitch, bitch" and the poor woman's stifled cries. Why couldn't anyone else hear that? Why wasn't anyone stopping them? Had the whole world suddenly gone mad?

She pushed her arms into the jacket sleeves and discovered most of the buttons were missing. Still it was better than nothing. It smelled of peppermint. She dug into the pockets and found two quarters, a McDonald's napkin and half a roll of peppermint Life Savers. God, her fingers were still shaking so bad, it took a concentrated effort to unwrap one of the mints and pop it into her mouth. Hopefully it would settle her stomach.

As soon as her knees were strong enough, she'd get out of the park, onto the street, and find a cop. Where the hell were the cops, anyway? It was getting dark. There was usually at least one hanging around in the evenings.

Then from behind her, something came over her head and around her neck. Maria clawed at it. It dug into the skin of her throat. She gasped for air, kicking and twisting her body. Her fingers tried to get hold of the cord. God! It was so tight. It was already embedded into her neck, so deep that her fingernails were ripping at her own skin as she tried to dig it out.

She couldn't breathe. Couldn't pull away. My God, he was strong. And now he was pulling her back farther into the trees, dragging her, because her feet wouldn't work. She had no energy left.

Air. She needed air. She couldn't breathe. Couldn't focus. Couldn't even see straight. Her head was spinning again, a blur of trees and grass and sky. She felt herself slipping away. She could no longer hear the chants or the laughter or even the woman's screams. Where were the sounds of traffic? Why did everything sound so muffled? So far away? The cord drew tighter, and soon she couldn't hear anything at all.

## CHAPTER 49

Justin's hands were still shaking when he got back to the bus. He hadn't bothered to wait for the rest of them. He still couldn't believe this was what Father had meant by an initiation trip. He imagined it to be some test of survival like his so-called week alone in the woods. Or some marathon lecture series like their weekend revival meetings. But, Jesus! He had never imagined something like this.

He felt sick to his stomach, remembering that poor woman vomiting and all those screams. He yanked off his cap and wiped the sweat from his forehead with the back of his arm. The bus was empty. Thank God! Though he could see Dave, their driver, inside the McDonald's, keeping an eye on things as he probably wolfed down an illicit Big Mac.

Justin slumped into one of the seats, crossing his arms over his chest and trying to stop shaking. He was sweating up a storm, so why was he shivering like he was cold? Fuck! He couldn't get those screams out of his head. Those poor women. That wasn't the way his grandfather had taught him to treat women. Even his dad could be an asshole sometimes, but he was good to Justin's mom. No woman deserved to be treated that way. He didn't care what the hell Father's instructions were.

While he handed out Quarter Pounders and beer, Brandon had told them that they were about to learn an important lesson. All Justin had cared about was that finally he had some decent food and that being a warrior wasn't such a bad thing. He'd hardly paid attention to what Brandon was saying. He must have eaten three Quarter Pounders and drunk four or five beers.

He had been feeling a pleasant buzz by the time Brandon led them to the park, where he continued his lecture about how they needed to put all bitches in their place, make them understand that men were still in power. He said women were the reason everything was going so haywire in the world. Women thought they didn't need men, were off being lesbos, having babies on their own, taking good jobs away from family men and then crying to the government to protect them. The sluts and whores were responsible for spreading AIDS. They needed to be punished. They needed to be taught a lesson.

They sprayed the first woman who came by with beer, and Justin remembered laughing at her. By the third woman, they were grabbing and fondling and ripping. Her screams shook Justin as if waking him from a nightmare. He couldn't believe what he was doing. That was when he started to think about Alice. What if Alice had been one of the women walking through that park? What if the others knew about her past? Jesus! Would they swarm her like a pack of wolves?

No one had seen him slip behind the trees to vomit up all those precious hamburgers. He stayed there, and when they were finished with the third woman and heading for a fourth, Justin helped her away, trying to make up for his part in the nightmare. When he knew she was safe, he left, sneaking back to the bus, still hearing the laughter and the screams ringing in his ears.

He didn't want to think about it. He brought his knees up and hugged them to his chest. He needed to think about something, anything else.

He had only been to Boston once before when Eric was still at Brown. It had been one of their last family trips together. They had stayed at the Radisson. He and Eric had even gotten a room to themselves. Their dad let them order room service, which blew them away because he'd always been so tight with money.

They spent one day at a Red Sox game, then the Metropolitan Museum to satisfy his mom. But even that didn't suck. It had actually been a good time, one of the few that hadn't ended in a huge argument of some kind. It had left Justin with good feelings about Boston; feelings that now were replaced with sounds of women's screams for help and the smell of warm beer.

He jumped off the seat and into the aisle, pulling off his T-shirt, wadding it up and kicking it under seat. Then he peeled off the rest of his clothes until he was standing in the bus aisle, wearing only his jockey shorts. That was when he saw Brandon standing in the bus's door, staring at him. But instead of getting angry, Brandon started laughing.

"I knew it," he finally said as Justin wrestled back into his blue jeans. "I knew you didn't have the stomach for this. You're a coward, just like your fucking brother, Eric. I need to get back and finish things like a real man."

Then he turned and left, heading toward the park.

# CHAPTER 50

Calm. He needed to stay calm and let the liquid coarse through his veins. Let it do its magic. Already he could feel its strength, its power.

Not that he needed much physical strength. The woman was small, easy to drag. And with the noise and excitement still going on close by, no one would notice the rustling of leaves and snapping of twigs.

But he needed to hurry. He needed to find a more isolated area. The sun was sinking behind the buildings. He didn't have much time to set up, to get ready. Tonight would be different. He could feel it. Tonight would be the night. Somehow he just knew it.

He stopped, turned and waited while he stared at the woman's half-naked body, leaves and brush dragging along between her legs. He smiled when he finally saw her exposed chest move just slightly, shallow breaths, barely noticeable. Oh, good. She was still alive. Then he continued dragging her. Yes, tonight he felt quite certain it would happen. He would finally see it tonight.

# CHAPTER 51

Maggie drove with the windows rolled down, hoping it would squelch the churning in the pit of her stomach. As she drove, she tried to make sense of all that she had learned from the woman called Eve about the Reverend Joseph Everett. She needed to prepare herself before she confronted her mother. She'd need to arm herself with information for when her mother started to defend the man, because Maggie knew her mother would defend him.

She tried to put aside the horrible images Eve had conjured up. Instead, she should concentrate on the facts. Most of her arsenal of facts was general biographical stuff. As a young man, Everett had been kicked out of the army, an honorable discharge with no further explanation. There was no police record, despite the rape charge that was later dropped by the journalism student herself. At thirty-five he ran for the Virginia state senate and lost. Then three years later he started the Church of Spiritual Freedom, a nonprofit organization that allowed him to amass stockpiles of tax-free donations. Everett finally found his calling, but there seemed to be no information on where or if he had actually been ordained as a minister.

In less than ten short years, the Church of Spiritual Freedom claimed more than five hundred members with almost two hundred of them living on a compound he had built in Virginia's Shenandoah Valley. Ironically, the area was only a few miles from where the journalism student had been raped twenty-seven years earlier. Everett had either been innocent and had nothing to hide, or perhaps, Maggie couldn't help thinking, he was superstitious and didn't think lightning could strike in the same place twice.

If it was the latter, he had good reason to believe it. In the past ten years, he and his church had not been in any kind of trouble with the law—no IRS audits, no weapons violations, no building permit or zoning violations. The illegal-weapons summon at the Massachusetts cabin was the first violation, and even that could only loosely be connected to Everett's church. In fact, everything seemed to be going quite nicely for the good reverend. He had even made some close and powerful friends in Congress, permitting him to buy a parcel of government land in Colorado for a sinfully low price. If things were going so well, why did he want to uproot and move to Colorado?

Maggie wasn't certain what her mother's involvement was with Everett and his so-called church. One thing Maggie did feel certain about, however, was that the man could be a time bomb waiting to explode. And despite only circumstantial evidence, she knew he was somehow involved in, at least, Ginny Brier's death and possibly the floater in North Carolina. It was too much of a coincidence that these women died while Everett's rallies were taking place just footsteps away. As for the nameless transient, well, she was still a mystery.

The crisp autumn air chilled her, but she kept the windows down. She took deep breaths, filling her lungs with the scent of pine and the exhaust fumes of the traffic on I-95. She'd need to have all her senses on alert and in overdrive for this mission. Even without a confrontation, being in the same room with her mother was difficult enough. There were too many memories. Too much past left behind, and that's just the way Maggie preferred it.

It had been more than a year since she had visited her mother's apartment, although she doubted her mother would remember that visit. How could she remember? She had been passed out for most of it. Now Maggie wondered how she would begin to explain this visit. What did she think she could do, just drop by and say, "Gee, Mom, I was passing through and thought I'd stop and see how you were? Oh, and by the way, did you realize your precious Reverend Everett may be a dangerous maniac?" No, somehow she didn't think that would get her anywhere.

Maggie tried to put aside what she had learned in the FBI file and what she had just learned from Eve. Instead, she tried to remember everything in the past year that her mother may have told her about Reverend Joseph Everett. She was embarrassed to admit that she hadn't paid much attention. In the beginning she had simply been relieved that there was someone else to watch over her mother. Months went by without a suicide attempt, and Maggie hoped that the woman had finally found a less destructive addiction. Perhaps she had finally found a way to get the attention she so craved, and it didn't include a trip to the ER.

Later, when she discovered that her mother had stopped drinking, Maggie was skeptical. It seemed too good to be true. There had to be a catch. And, of course, there was one. The sudden sobriety had changed the habits but hadn't changed Kathleen O'Dell's personality. She was still as selfish, needy and narrow-minded as she had always been, only now Maggie couldn't explain it away as drunken drivel.

It didn't make sense that her mother had suddenly found God. Maggie could count on one hand the times her mother had insisted they attend mass. Her entire childhood, she couldn't remember her mother doing or saying anything that could remotely be misconstrued as religious.

The only time Maggie remembered her mother mentioning religion was when she was drunk, often times joking that she was a recovering Catholic from which there was no cure. Then she would snort and laugh, telling anyone who would listen that being a little bit Catholic was like being a little bit pregnant.

For Kathleen O'Dell, being a Catholic was something she had held on to simply as a party favor. Which led Maggie to believe that Everett's Bible-thumping would probably be lost on the woman. In the last several months, she had not heard her mother suddenly start spouting off psalms or scripture. There certainly hadn't been a miraculous religious conversion. At least not one Maggie could see.

What she did see was the same compulsive, judgmental, addictive woman finally finding someone or something to blame for all her hardships and bad luck. And Reverend Everett provided for her the sinister, evil culprit in the form of the United States government, a faceless entity, an easy target as long as Kathleen O'Dell could reason that her daughter was not a part of that entity.

Now that Maggie thought about it, why would she find it odd that her mother be attracted to Everett's brand of religion, to Everett's version of reality? After all, hadn't Kathleen O'Dell spent years worshipping at the altar of BCD: Beam, Ceurvo and Daniel's? There had been times in the past when the woman would have sold her soul for a bottle of Jack Daniel's. Just because she was no longer drinking didn't necessarily mean her soul was no longer for sale. She had handed in one skewed sense of reality for a different one, one addiction for another.

Maggie could understand the seductive lure for her mother, whose version of current events came from the *National Enquirer* or watching *Hard Copy.* What a rush it must now be for her to believe that she had the inside scoop on national issues; that she was respected and trusted by someone with the charisma and charm of the good reverend; and that she could have the easy answers to questions so many people spent a lifetime in search of.

She had heard some of those answers, the paranoid delusions that men like Reverend Everett spread. There was power in hate, and control by fear was one of the most successful manipulations. Why had Maggie shrugged off her mother's comments about chemicals in her drinking water, hidden government cameras in ATM machines and oh, yes, several weeks ago a hysteria about not wanting to talk to Maggie if she was calling on her cellular phone because "they had ways of listening in to those conversations?"

Why hadn't she seen the danger signs long ago? Or had she seen them but been so relieved to no longer be picking up the shattered pieces her mother left behind that she didn't care, or that she simply didn't want to know?

Somewhere Maggie had read that alcohol only emphasized an alcoholic's personality, bringing out and highlighting characteristics that already existed. It made sense with her mother. The alcohol only seemed to make her more needy, more hungry for attention. Yet, if that was indeed true, Maggie realized the irony in her own drinking habits. She usually drank to forget the empty feeling inside her, and to not feel so alone. If the alcohol only emphasized those very same things, then no wonder she was so fucked up.

*Like mother, like daughter.*

Maggie shook her head, trying to prevent the memory.

*You two could be sisters. I never fucked a mother and daughter before.*

Those goddamn crumbling walls. She grabbed the Pepsi can in her cup holder and gulped the warm, flat remainder. Why was it that she could not remember the sound of her father's voice, but she could still feel this stranger's breath on her face? With little effort, she could smell the sour odor of whiskey and feel the scrape of his beard as he pinned her small body to the wall and tried to kiss her. She remembered his hands fondling her preadolescent breasts, laughing and telling her he bet she was "gonna have some big tits just like her mama."

And all the while her mother stood back with her glass of Jack Daniel's, watching and telling him to cut it out but not making him stop. She didn't make him stop. Why didn't she make him stop?

Somehow Maggie had escaped on her own. She couldn't even remember how. That was when her mother started insisting her men friends take her to a hotel. She stayed out all night, sometimes was gone for days at a time, leaving Maggie home alone. Alone. It was good to be alone, a little scary but less painful. She had learned early on how to be a survivor. Being alone was simply the price of survival.

As she approached Richmond, she started paying attention and watching for her exit. She tried to ignore the growing nausea in the pit of her stomach and was annoyed that it was there at all. What the hell was wrong with her? She chased killers for a living, examined their gruesome handiwork and traveled into their worlds of evil. What could be so difficult about one goddamn visit to her mother's?

# CHAPTER 52

*Richmond, Virginia*

Kathleen O'Dell finished packing the last of her grandmother's porcelain figurines. The man from Al and Frank's Antiques and Secondhand Treasures would be picking them up in the morning with the other items. Now she couldn't remember if the man's name was even Al or Frank, although he had told her, while he appraised her things, that he was one of the co-owners.

It bothered her that she felt sad about giving up the items. She still remembered her grandmother letting her handle the figurines when she was just a child, allowing her to gently turn them around in her small hands in order to admire and touch them.

Several of the figurines had come over with her grandmother from Ireland, stuffed in an old suitcase with few other belongings. They were a part of her family's heritage, and it seemed wrong to sell them for something as meaningless as money. But then, Reverend Everett constantly reminded them that they needed to divorce themselves from the materialism of the world in order to be truly free. That it was sinful to admire and covet material items even if they held some sentimental value.

More important, Kathleen knew she couldn't very well cart all these things with her when they left for their new paradise in Colorado. Besides, she wouldn't need them. Reverend Everett had promised that everything would be provided for them, their every need and desire would be attended to. She hoped that meant it would be much cleaner and luxurious than the compound. Most of the time the place smelled bad. And on her last trip there, she could swear she had seen a rat scurrying along the side of the conference hall. She hated rats.

She left the boxes and walked through the rooms, looking to see if she had forgotten any of the items she had agreed to sell to the man from Al and Frank's. The man whose name she couldn't remember. She decided she would miss this apartment, though she hadn't lived here very long. It was one of the few places she had bothered to decorate and make into a home. And it was one of the few places that didn't remind her how trapped and alone she could feel. Although some evenings nothing could prevent her from feeling the walls closing in on her.

She told herself that it would be nice to live in a community where her new friends lived just across the hall. But hopefully not Emily. Dear God, Emily's constant complaining would drive her nuts if she had to live across the hall from the woman. It would also be nice to have people she could talk to, rather than spending her evenings answering Regis Philbin's million-dollar questions. Yes, she was tired of being alone, and she certainly didn't want to grow old alone. So if the price was a few rare figurines her grandmother had willed to her, then so be it. It wasn't like those silly things had done anything for her lately.

There was a knock at the door, and for a moment she wondered if perhaps she had gotten the days mixed up. Was it possible the man from Al and Frank's meant to come today and not tomorrow? She'd just have to tell him that she'd changed her mind. That's what she would do. She couldn't possibly sell them to him today. She needed time, after all, to get used to the idea.

She opened the door, ready to say just that, and found herself staring at her daughter, instead.

"Maggie? What on earth are you doing here?"

"Sorry I didn't call."

"What's wrong? Did something happen? Is Greg okay?"

She saw Maggie flinch. It was the wrong thing to say. Why did her daughter always have to make her feel like she was saying the wrong thing?

"Nothing's wrong, but I do need to talk to you. Is it okay if I come in?"

"Oh, sure." She opened the door and waved her in. "The place is a mess."

"Are you moving?" Maggie walked over to the stacked boxes.

Thank God the boxes weren't labeled. Her daughter would never understand about the materialism and divorcing it to feel free or not coveting, or whatever it was… Oh, it didn't matter. Maggie would never understand, and no one outside the church was supposed to know about Colorado.

"I'm just cleaning out some old stuff."

"Oh, okay."

Maggie gave up her questioning and stood at the window, looking out over the parking lot. Kathleen couldn't help wondering if the girl already wanted to escape. Well, it wasn't like it was a day at the circus for her, either. At least, she didn't expect anything from Maggie. Not anymore, that is.

"Would you like some iced tea?"

"Only if it's no trouble."

"I just brewed some. It's raspberry. Is that okay?" But she didn't wait for an answer. She retreated to her small kitchen, hoping its cozy warmth would soothe her nerves.

When she reached for the tall iced tea glasses, she noticed a bottle in the far corner of the cupboard. She had forgotten she even had it. It was for emergencies. She hesitated, then stretched to grab it. This was feeling like an emergency day. First her grandmother's figurines and now an unexpected visit from her daughter.

She poured a quarter of a glass for herself, closed her eyes and gulped it, savoring the burning sensation sliding down her throat and all the way to her stomach. What a wonderful, warm feeling. She had another, then filled her glass one last time about halfway, tucked the bottle back into its hiding place, and poured iced tea in to fill the rest of the glass. The tea was almost the same color.

She grabbed both glasses, remembering that hers was in her right hand. She glanced around the small kitchen. Yes, she was going to miss this place, the welcome mat at the sink and the yellow curtains with little white daisies. She still remembered the day she found those curtains at a garage sale down the street. How could she be expected to leave this place without some sort of help?

When she came back into the living room, Maggie had discovered one of the figurines she had left half wrapped on the window bench

"I remember these," she said, handling the statue and gently turning it just as she had taught her to do, just like Kathleen's grandmother had taught her.

She had forgotten that she had even shown them to Maggie. But now seeing one in her hands, the memory came back as though it were yesterday. She was such a beautiful little girl, so curious and cautious. And now she was a beautiful young woman, still curious and oh, so very cautious.

"You're not getting rid of them, are you?"

"Actually, I've had them in storage. I was just getting them out to take a look and…and well, decide just what to do with them." It was partly the truth. She couldn't be expected to get rid of all her things, move from her nice little apartment *and* tell the truth. That was just too much to expect.

She watched as Maggie carefully returned the figurine to the window bench. She took the glass of tea Kathleen handed her from her left hand. Yes, her left hand had Maggie's tea. She couldn't mix them up now.

Maggie sipped her drink and continued to glance around the room. Kathleen gulped hers. She wasn't sure she wanted Maggie examining any more of her things, stirring up more memories. The past belonged in the past. Wasn't that what Reverend Everett always said? He said so many things. Sometimes it was just too hard to remember them all. She was almost finished with her tea. Perhaps she would need more.

"What did you need to talk about that couldn't wait until Thursday?" she asked Maggie.

"Thursday?"

"Thanksgiving. You didn't forget, did you?"

Another flinch.

"Oh, jeez, mom. I'm not sure I'll be able to make it."

"But you must. I've already bought the turkey. It's in the frig. Practically fills up the entire damn thing." Oh, Jesus, she shouldn't cuss. She needed to watch her language or Reverend Everett would be upset. "I'm thinking we'll have dinner at five o'clock, but you can come earlier, if you like."

She remembered that she still needed to buy cranberries and that bread stuff. Where did she leave her list? She started searching the tabletops.

"Mom, what are you doing?"

"Oh, nothing, sweetie. I just remembered a few things for Thursday. I wanted to write them—oh, here it is." She found the list on the lamp stand, sat down and jotted *cranberries* and *bread stuff* at the bottom. "Do you know what that bread stuff is actually called that you use to make the stuffing?"

"What?"

"The bread. You know those small pieces of dry bread that you use to make stuffing." Maggie stared at her like she didn't know what she was talking about. "Oh, never mind. I'm sure I'll figure it out."

Of course, Maggie probably didn't know. She was never much of a cook, either. She remembered the girl trying to bake sugar cookies one Christmas and ending up with rock-hard, burnt Santas. Then she refused to be consoled when one of the guys from Lucky Eddie's suggested they paint them and use them for coasters. Poor girl. She never had much of a sense of humor. She was always so sensitive and took too many things to heart.

When she finally looked up from the list, Maggie was staring at her, again. Uh-oh. Now she looked pissed.

"What else should we have for our Thanksgiving dinner?" Kathleen asked.

"Mom, I didn't come here today to talk about Thanksgiving."

"Okay, so what did you come here to talk about?"

"I need to ask you some questions about Reverend Everett."

"What kind of questions?" she asked. Father had warned them about family members wanting to turn them against him.

"Just some general stuff about the church."

"Well, I have an appointment I need to get to," she lied, glancing at her wrist only to find no watch. "Gee, Mag-pie, I wish you would have called. Why don't we talk about all this on Thursday."

She walked to the door, hoping to lead Maggie out, but when she turned back, Maggie stood in the same spot, clear across the room. Now Maggie frowned at her. No, not a frown. It was that worried, angry look. No, not anger. Well, yes, anger but also sadness. She had the saddest brown eyes sometimes. Just like her father, just like Thomas. Yes, she knew that look. And yes, Kathleen knew exactly what her daughter was thinking even before Maggie said it.

"I don't believe this. You're drunk."

# CHAPTER 53

Maggie knew as soon as her mother called her "Mag-pie." It had been her father's nickname for her. One her mother had adopted, but only when she was drunk. Instead of a nickname, it had become a signal, a warning, a grate on her nerves like fingernails on a chalkboard.

She stared at her mother, but the woman didn't flinch. Her hand stayed firmly planted on the front doorknob. God! She had forgotten how good her mother was at this game. And how god-awful she was, because she let the emotion rule and carry her away—the emotion of a twelve-year-old. Suddenly, she found herself pacing the short length of her mother's living room.

"How could I have been so stupid to believe you?" Maggie said, annoyed that her lower lip was quivering. A quick glance showed no change in her mother's face. That perfected combination of puzzlement and innocence, as if she had no clue what Maggie was talking about.

"I have an appointment, Mag-pie…and lots of packing to do." Even her voice had not shifted, not even a notch. There was still that sugary cheerfulness that came with the alcohol.

"How could I have believed you?" Maggie tried to ward off the anger. Why did this always feel so personal? Why did it seem like a betrayal? "I thought you stopped."

"Well, of course, I stopped. I stopped packing to talk to you." But she stayed by the door, hand still planted—maybe she hoped if Maggie didn't leave, she could simply escape. She watched Maggie pace from one end of the room to the other.

"It was the tea," Maggie said, slapping her forehead like a child finally getting an answer to a quiz. She snatched up her mother's glass and took a whiff. "Of course."

"Just a little something to take the edge off." Kathleen O'Dell waved it away, a familiar gesture that reminded Maggie of some form of alcoholics' absolution.

"To take the edge off? For what? What did you need to take the edge off of? So you could get through one goddamn visit with your own daughter?"

"A surprise visit. You really should have called first, Mag-pie. And please don't swear." Even that tone, that Pollyanna tone, grated on Maggie's nerves. "Why are you here?" her mother asked. "Are you checking up on me?"

Maggie tried to slow down, tried to focus. Yes, why had she come? She rubbed a hand across her face, again annoyed that there was a bit of a tremor in her fingers. Why did she have so little control over her reaction, over her body's response? It was as if the hurt little girl inside of her came to the surface to deal with this, because the adult woman had not yet found a sufficient way.

"Maggie, why are you here?"

Now her mother had come back into the room, suddenly anxious for an answer.

"I needed to…" She needed to remember the investigation. She was a professional. She needed answers. Answers her mother could provide. She needed to focus. "I was worried about you."

It was her mother's turn to stare. Suddenly, Maggie wanted to smile. Yes, she did know a thing or two about playing games, about the power of denial or in her mother's world, the power of pretend. Her mother wanted to pretend one drink to take the edge off was not a fall off the wagon? Well Maggie could pretend she was simply worried about her, afraid for her safety, instead of looking for answers about Everett. That was what brought her here, wasn't it? The investigation and trying to solve it. Of course it was.

"Worried?" her mother finally said, as if it had taken this long for her to formulate a definition for the word itself. "Why in the world would you be worried about me?"

"There are some things about Reverend Everett that I don't think you know."

"Really?"

Maggie saw suspicion slipping in past the bewilderment. Careful. She didn't want her to get defensive. "Reverend Everett is not who he seems to be."

"How do you know? You've never met him."

"No, but I did some research and—"

"Ah, research?" her mother interrupted. "Like a background check?"

"Yes," Maggie said, keeping her voice calm and steady now. The professional kicked back into gear.

"The FBI has always hated him. They want to destroy him."

"I don't want to destroy him."

"I didn't mean you."

"Mom, I am the FBI. Please, just listen to me for a minute." But her mother was fidgeting with the living room blinds, wandering from one window to the next, shutting each and taking her time. "I've talked to others who have told—"

"Others who have left the church." Another interruption, but still with that annoying distracted cheerfulness.

"Yes."

"Ex-members."

"Yes."

"Well, you simply can't believe a word they say. Surely, you must know that." This time she looked at Maggie, and there was something in her eyes, an impatience Maggie didn't recognize. "But you'd rather believe them, wouldn't you?"

Maggie stared at her again. Her mother's mind was already made up. Nothing Maggie could say would change what she believed or didn't believe. No surprise there. What exactly was it that she had expected to find out? Why had she come? It wasn't likely her mother had any damning information about Everett. To warn her mother, perhaps? Why did she believe her mother would suddenly listen to anything Maggie had to say or to advise? This was ridiculous. She shouldn't have come.

"I shouldn't have come," she said out loud, and turned to leave.

"Yes, you'd rather believe them, strangers you've never met before." Her mother's tone was no longer cheerful, a cruel sarcasm edging in. This, Maggie recognized. This, she remembered. "Not like you would ever believe me. Your own mother."

"I didn't mean to suggest that," Maggie said calmly, facing her mother and trying to ignore the change, not only in her mother's tone but even in her gestures—nervous swipes of fingers through her hair. Her eyes darted around the room, looking for a tumbler or bottle and finding the tea glass. She grabbed it and emptied it in one gulp, satisfied and not realizing it had been Maggie's glass by mistake.

"You never believed in me."

Maggie continued to stare at her. How could the insertion of one little word like "in" make such a world of difference? "I've never said that."

But her mother didn't seem to hear her. She was going back around the room, opening the window blinds that she had just shut, one after the other. "It was always him. Always him."

She was ranting, and Maggie knew it was too late to have any semblance of a conversation with her now. But she had no idea who she meant by "him." This was a new rant. One she didn't recognize.

"Maybe I should go," Maggie said, but made no attempt to leave. She only wanted to get her mother's attention. But her mother was no longer listening. No longer paying attention. This was a mistake.

"It was always him." This time her mother stopped in front of her, facing her with accusation. "You loved him so much, you have nothing left for any of the rest of us. Not for me. Not for Greg. Probably not even for your cowboy."

"Okay now, that's enough." Maggie wouldn't put up with this. It was ridiculous. The woman didn't know what she was even saying.

"He was no saint, you know."

"Who are you talking about?"

"Your father."

Maggie's stomach took a plunge.

"Your precious father," her mother added as if she needed clarification. "You always loved him more. So much love for him that there was never enough left for the rest of us. You buried it all with him."

"That's not true."

"And he was no saint, you know."

"Don't you dare," Maggie said, immediately disappointed to find the quiver return to her lower lip.

"Dare to tell the truth?" Her mother managed a cruel smile.

Why was she doing this?

"I need to leave." Maggie turned toward the door.

"He was out fucking his girlfriend the night of the fire."

It was like a knife had been thrust into her back, stopping her in her tracks, making her turn to face her mother again.

"I had to call her house," she continued, "when the fire department's dispatcher called looking for him. Everyone thought he was up sleeping in our bed, but he was in her bed. Her bed, fucking her."

"Stop it," Maggie said, but it came out as a whisper, because all the air had suddenly been sucked out of her.

"I never told you. I never told anyone. How could I after he went out that night, ran into that burning building and died a fucking hero."

"You're making this up."

"He got her pregnant. She has a son. His son. The son I never could give him."

"Why are you doing this? Why are you making this up?" Maggie said, trying to keep the twelve-year-old hurt little girl from surfacing, though in her head, her voice sounded exactly like a child's. "You're lying."

"I thought I was protecting you. Yes, I lied then. But not now. Why would I lie now?"

"To hurt me."

"To hurt you?" Her mother rolled her eyes, the sarcasm having overpowered any other emotion or response. "I've been trying to protect you from the truth for years."

"Protect me?" Now the anger began to unleash itself. "You call moving me halfway across the country protecting me? You call bringing home strange men to fondle me, protecting me?"

"I did the best I could." The eyes were darting around the room again, and Maggie knew she had said what she wanted to say and was now looking to retreat, searching to escape.

"You lost a husband that night. But I lost both my parents."

"That's ridiculous."

"I lost both my father *and* my mother. And what did I get in their place? A drunken invalid to take care of. A drunken slut instead of a mother."

The slap came so suddenly, Maggie didn't have time to react. She wiped at the sting and was more unnerved by the tears already dampening her cheek.

"Oh, Jesus! Maggie." Her mother reached for her and Maggie pulled away. "I'm sorry. I didn't mean—"

"No, don't." Maggie raised a hand in warning. She stood straight, avoided her mother's eyes. "Don't apologize," she said, allowing one more swipe at the tears. "This was the perfect response from you. I wouldn't have expected anything less."

Then she turned and left, making it to her car, managing to drive through the blur before stopping at the entrance to I-95. She pulled off on the side, killed the headlights and switched on the car's flashers, shoved the emergency brake into place, left the engine running and the radio blaring while she let the sobs pour out of her. While she gave in and let those damn leaky compartments burst wide open.

# CHAPTER 54

Gwen needed to slow down, but she gulped the remainder of her wine, anyway. She could feel Tully watching her from across the small round table with a polite look of concern while he fumbled with his spaghetti and meatballs.

He had chosen a lovely Italian restaurant with crisp white tablecloths, candles in every window and an array of wait staff that treated them with a kind and friendly manner, then screamed at each other in Italian as soon as they got behind the swinging kitchen door.

She had barely touched her fettuccine Alfredo with fresh cream sauce and portobello mushrooms. It smelled wonderful; however, right now the wine and its anesthetizing effect was all she wanted. She needed something to wipe away the feel of that pencil stabbing into her throat and the desire to kick herself for being so stupid. She was beginning to understand why Maggie resorted to Scotch so often. Maggie had a much longer and more grisly list of images to wipe out of her memory bank.

"I'm sorry," she finally said. "You probably should have left me in my hotel room. I'm afraid I'm not very good company tonight."

"Actually, I'm used to women not talking to me at the dinner table."

It wasn't at all what she expected him to say, and she found herself laughing. He smiled, and it only then occurred to her how awful this afternoon must have been for him, too.

"Thanks," she said. "I really needed to laugh."

"Glad I could help."

"I certainly messed up this trip. We didn't get anything."

"I wouldn't say that. Pratt thought that Father Joseph sent you. He said it. That's more than we knew before, and it may be all we need to connect him and the others to Reverend Joseph Everett. It will be a wasted trip, though, if you don't eat something."

He smiled at her again, and she wondered if he wanted to forget about this afternoon as much as she did. He was still looking at her as if expecting an answer.

"If you'd like, we could go somewhere else, if this isn't quite what you had in mind," he offered.

"Oh, no, this is fine. It smells wonderful. I'm just waiting for my appetite."

She hadn't told him she helped herself to a glass of champagne while she changed for dinner. The hotel had mistakenly sent up a newlywed basket to her room. When she called down to the front desk, the clerk was so embarrassed, he insisted she keep and enjoy it, that they would send another to the intended couple. Well, she wouldn't be able to enjoy all of it. The basket included massage oils and an assortment of condoms. She'd have to settle for the champagne and chocolates.

She watched Tully wrestle with his spaghetti, mutilating it into small pieces instead of wrapping it around his fork. It was painful to watch.

"Mind if I show you how to do that?" she asked.

He looked up, saw what she meant and immediately turned red. Before he could answer, she slid her chair over, so that she was sitting next to his right arm. Without making a big deal or fuss, she gently put her hand over his, barely getting her fingers around his large hand in order to show him how to hold his fork.

"The secret," she said, while reaching across his lap and taking his other hand, "is in the spoon." She nodded for him to pick up his spoon in his left hand. "You pull just a little spaghetti with your fork to release it from the pile, and then you wrap it, slowly in a smooth gentle motion, against the bowl of the spoon."

She could feel his breath in her hair and could smell the subtle scent of his aftershave. His hands complied with her every command, and it surprised her how good they felt against her own palms. When the task was complete, she let go, sat back into her chair and scooted to her side of the table, all the while avoiding his eyes.

"Mission accomplished." She pointed to the perfectly wound spaghetti still on his fork. "You're a quick learner."

He hesitated, then brought it to his mouth. He tried the process again while he chewed, lifting his fork to show her when he managed it on his own. This time their eyes met and neither of them looked away until one of the wait staff interrupted, offering to refill their wineglasses, which Gwen accepted. She was sure it was probably a good idea to also anesthetize the unfamiliar arousal she was suddenly feeling.

With this glass of wine, she did manage to eat some of her fettuccine and even clean up her half of a cannoli dessert. Through coffee and during a long cab ride back to the hotel, she found herself telling Tully about her practice and the old brownstone she was restoring, while he told her about Emma and the trials and tribulations of raising a fifteen-year-old girl. She hadn't realized he had custody of his daughter. Somehow his being a devoted single father only completed the annoying image she already had of him as the perfect Boy Scout.

At her hotel door, she invited him in for a glass of her complimentary champagne, sure the Boy Scout wouldn't accept and that she was safe. The Boy Scout accepted. Before she poured the champagne, she turned to him, needing to say what she had avoided saying all evening.

"I need to thank you," she said, meeting his eyes and holding him there, so he couldn't joke his way out of this. "You saved my life today, Tully."

"I couldn't have done it without your help. You have really good instincts, Doc." He smiled at her, obviously still uncomfortable with taking any of the credit. Okay, so he was going to make this difficult.

"Could you just let me thank you?"

"Okay."

She came to him, stood on tiptoe and still had to tug on his tie to bring him down to her height so she could kiss his cheek. As she did this, she noticed that his eyes were now serious. Before she pulled back, his mouth caught hers in a gentle but passionate kiss that was no longer about gratitude.

She rocked back on her feet, feeling a bit out of breath and staring up at him.

"That was unexpected," she said, surprised that she was feeling light-headed. It had to be all the wine.

"I'm sorry," he said, restoring her image of the Boy Scout. "I shouldn't have—"

"No, you don't need to apologize. Actually, it was…it was quite nice."

"Nice?" He looked wounded, and she smiled though his eyes were still serious. "I think I can do better than nice."

In two steps he was kissing her again, only this time it wasn't long before his mouth refused to be confined to her lips. Gwen leaned against the back of the sofa and her fingers slid across its texture, looking for something to grab hold of while Tully continued to convince her that he could, indeed, do better than nice.

# CHAPTER 55

Ben Garrison didn't get back to the Ritz-Carlton until late. He found the employee door at the back alley and took the freight elevator up to the fourteenth floor. This morning he had argued with the desk clerk about getting moved to a different floor. No matter how anyone looked at it, the fourteenth floor was still the thirteenth floor. Surely there had to be another corner suite available. But now, it looked like it wouldn't matter. His luck was back. Nothing could go wrong. After these photos hit the newsstands, he would be king of the fucking world again.

As soon as he got back to his room he threw his duffel bag on the bed and stripped out of his clothes, bagged them in one of the plastic hotel laundry bags and tossed the bag next to the other trash he'd dump in the morning. He set his boots in the whirlpool tub to clean later and slipped on the plush terry-cloth robe that the wonderful housekeeping staff had left fresh and clean on the back of the bathroom door.

He had packed his developing tank and enough chemicals to develop the film. He could make a contact sheet of the exposures he wanted to sell. That way he wouldn't have to take them to a local twenty-four-hour photo shop and have some pimply faced kid freaking out by what he saw.

While he pulled out everything he'd need, he called down to room service. He ordered their roast duck with raspberry chocolate cheesecake and the most expensive bottle of Sangiovese on their wine list. Then he dialed his own number to retrieve his messages. After the *National Enquirer* had hit the stands, he expected some calls from news editors he hadn't heard from in years, suddenly pretending to be his best buddies again.

He was right. There were fifteen messages. His damn machine could take only eighteen. He grabbed the notepad with the hotel's embossed logo and began going through the list. He could hardly contain the smile and finally laughed out loud at the two messages from Curtis, the first wanting to know why he hadn't brought the exclusive to him and the second telling him he'd beat anyone's price for whatever else Ben had. Oh, yes, life was good again. It was very good.

One of the messages was from his old pal, Detective Julia Racine—he had been hoping to hear from her. Unlike the other messages, Racine didn't waste her breath sweet-talking or befriending him. Instead, she threatened to arrest him and charge him with obstruction of a police investigation. Jesus! She could turn him on just with her voice, especially when she talked dirty. Hearing her call him a "fucker" gave him an incredible hard-on. He played the message again, just to enjoy the sensation. Then he decided to save it for future use, rather than erase it.

He flipped through his little black book, and it occurred to him that he might be able to make it up to Detective Racine. As much as he enjoyed her calling him a fucker, he wouldn't mind cashing in on one of the quid pro quos she was so famous for. From the tone of her voice, the poor woman probably hadn't been laid for some time, be it male or female. And he had to admit, tonight had sorta put him in the mood. He was quite certain he could come up with a proposition that might be as interesting to Racine as it was to him.

Finally, he found the phone number he was looking for and started dialing Britt Harwood's number at the *Boston Globe*. It was late, but he'd go ahead and leave a message. Hell, might as well give the hometown boy a first shot at this exclusive. He smiled, thinking of Harwood's face when he showed him the contact sheet of a dozen good little Christian boys mauling and ripping the clothes off women in the middle of Boston Common.

# CHAPTER 56

Tully still couldn't believe it. If it hadn't been for cellular technology, he'd be back at the hotel with Gwen, perhaps even making their way through that gift basket of champagne and condoms. How close had they come to making a huge mistake? Yet, he'd give anything to be back there with her instead of standing under a moonlit sky, up to his ankles in mud, listening to a chain-smoking detective mangle the English language as they waited for the medical examiner.

At first, he'd wanted to strangle Morrelli for the interruption, even if there really had just been a murder similar to the one at the FDR Memorial. He caught himself wondering if Morrelli had done it on purpose, which he knew was crazy. After all, how could Morrelli have known what he was interrupting? Hell, Tully hadn't known what was going to happen. Fact was, he still couldn't believe he had even kissed her, let alone... What was he thinking? Maybe it was for the better that they had been interrupted. Otherwise...otherwise, it could have been...hell, otherwise, it would have been pretty incredible.

"Here's maybe the marks you talkin' about?" Detective Kubat shined the flashlight on an area six feet from the body.

Tully bent down and examined the circular indentations. One was clearly stamped in the mud. A possible second one looked rubbed out. They did look like the marks at the FDR Memorial. What the hell did they mean?

"Did someone get a photo of these?"

"Hey, Marshall," Kubat yelled. "Get your ass over here and shoot a couple of Polaroids of this here."

"What about her clothes?"

"Folded all nice like and piled up over there." He swung the flashlight to highlight the spot, though the clothes had already been bagged and taken by the mobile crime unit. "Weird thing, though, they'd been all ripped up and ripped pretty good."

Tully stood and looked around. They appeared to be in a fairly secluded area of the park. On one side were trees, on another a brick wall, and yet the girl's body was sitting against a tree and staring out at a clearing with a wooden bench and lamppost. In fact, it looked like she was staring right at the bench, posing for some admirer sitting there.

"What about ropes or cords? Anything?"

"Nope, nothin'. But get a load of this.

He led Tully closer to the body. A police spotlight lit up the area around her, its stark light transforming her into a white-faced puppet. She was bruised much worse than the Brier girl, a black eye and bruising from what looked like a left hook to the jaw. Her head tilted to one side, revealing three or four tracks of ligature marks. Without saying anything more, Kubat bent down and snapped off the spotlight. At first, Tully couldn't figure out what he was doing and then he saw. The girl's neck lit up, the track marks glowing in the dark.

"What the hell?"

"Pretty fuckin' weird, huh?" Kubat said, and snapped the spotlight back on. "Anything like that with your victim?'

"There was some sort of glittery stuff found on her neck. I guess I didn't realize it glowed in the dark."

"Oh, hey. Here's Doc Samuel," Detective Kubat said, waving to the tall, distinguished-looking woman in a trench coat and black rubber ankle boots. She looked like the only one who'd come prepared. "Doc, this here's that FBI guy, J.R. Scully."

"Actually, it's R.J. Tully."

"Really? You sure?" Kubat looked at him as if it were possible Tully could have gotten his own name wrong. "I was thinking it was like that *X-Files* lady. Ain't her name Scully?"

"I wouldn't know."

"Yeah, I'm sure it's gotta be Scully."

"Agent Tully," Dr. Samuel said, ignoring Detective Kubat and holding out her hand. "I've been told you might know a thing or two about this killer."

"Maybe. It looks like the same guy."

"So the victim's ID might be in her throat?"

"Yeah, sorry, Doc," Kubat said. "If that's the case, it sure would speed up things on our end."

"As long as we can do this without compromising any evidence," the medical examiner told him with a stern tone that sounded more like a schoolteacher's. "You mind putting out your cigarette, Detective?"

"Oh, yeah, sure thing, Doc." He stabbed it against a tree, pinched the end off with his fingers and tucked the unused portion behind his ear.

Dr. Samuel found a dry rock big enough to set her case on. She began pulling out latex gloves, forceps and plastic bags. She handed Tully a pair of gloves.

"You mind? I may need another pair of hands."

He took the gloves and tried to ignore the knot forming at the pit of his stomach. He hated this part and missed the days when he could stay in his office and do his own style of analysis from photos and digital scans.

Suddenly, he found himself wondering why the hell he hadn't shut off his cellular phone. He had honestly considered it after that spaghetti-twirling lesson, but then was embarrassed that he had even considered it. He probably would have turned off the damn phone if he hadn't been worried about Emma and her trip to Cleveland. But she had called to say she'd arrived safe and sound at her mother's early that afternoon, so why was he still worried about her?

Dr. Samuel was ready. He followed her instructions, being careful where to kneel and keeping out of the spotlight. He tried to not think about the girl's eyes staring at him or the smell of decomposing flesh. Flies were already buzzing, despite the night being chilly. Tully couldn't help thinking they were the insect world's version of vultures. The damn things could sense blood and set up shop in a matter of hours, sometimes minutes.

Kubat stood to the side. He handed Tully his flashlight. "Might need that to see inside her mouth."

The medical examiner used the forceps to tug gently at the duct tape, peeling it off easily and bagging it. She had to use her gloved fingers to pry open the mouth, then she nodded for Tully to shine the flashlight while she picked up the forceps again. Tully pointed the light.

Something moved inside.

"Wait a minute," he said. "Did something just move?"

The medical examiner leaned in for a closer look, tilting her head while he positioned the light. Then suddenly she jerked back.

"Oh, dear, God!" she said, scrambling to her feet. "Get a couple of bags, Detective."

Tully stayed where he was, stunned and motionless, still holding the flashlight in position and listening to Kubat and Dr. Samuel. They scurried around, trying to find something, anything to capture the huge cockroaches that started pouring out of the dead woman's mouth.

# CHAPTER 57

Maggie knew she should get up and go to sleep in her bed for a change, but to do so would disturb Harvey's huge snoring head, which was nestled in her lap. So she stayed put. The old La-Z-Boy recliner had become a sort of sanctuary. It sat in her sunroom, facing the floor-to-ceiling windows that looked out over her backyard, though there wasn't much to see in the dark. The moonlight created dancing shadows and skeletal arms waving at her, but thankfully no wisps of fog ghosts tonight.

She wished she could erase from her mind the visit to her mother's, like rinsing out a bad taste from her mouth, but the Scotch wasn't cooperating. It wouldn't stop the memories. It couldn't fill that goddamn hollow feeling. And for some reason, she kept hearing that voice, over and over again in her head.

*Your father was no saint.*

Why in the world had her mother made up such a lie? Why did she want to hurt her?

Memories kept replaying in her head, some in slow motion, some in short, quick flashes, others in painful stings. Her mother had been with so many men, so many losers, bastards. Why then would she insist on putting Maggie's father in that same category? What kind of cruel joke was she trying to play? Was this something Everett had planted? Something he had convinced her mother to do? Whatever the reason, it managed to bring the walls—those carefully constructed barriers—crashing down, and now the flood of memories wouldn't stop.

Maggie sipped her Scotch, holding it in her mouth and then letting it slide down her throat as she closed her eyes and relished the slow burn. She waited for its heat to warm her and to erase that tension in the back of her neck. She waited for it to fill that hollow gap deep inside her, though she knew it would need to travel to her heart to accomplish that feat. Tonight for some reason the pleasant buzz had simply made her feel a bit light-headed, restless and…and admit it, damn it. Restless and alone. Alone with all those goddamn memories invading her mind and shattering her soul piece by piece.

How could her mother try to take away, to tarnish, the one thing from her childhood that Maggie still held so dear—her father's love? How *could* she? Why would she even try? Yes, perhaps she was slow to love and trust, quick to suspect, but that had nothing to do with her father, and everything to do with a mother who had abandoned her for Jack Daniel's. Maggie had done the only thing a child knew how to do. She had survived, making herself strong. If that meant keeping others at arm's length, then so be it. It was necessary. It was one of the few things in her life she had control over. If people who cared about her didn't get that, then maybe it was their problem and not hers.

She reached for the bottle of Scotch, then paused when its neck clinked against the lip of the glass, waiting to make sure her movement and the noise hadn't disturbed Harvey. An ear twitched, but his head stayed solidly in her lap.

Maggie remembered her mother telling her after her father's death that he would always be with her. That he would watch over her.

*Bullshit! Why even say that?*

And yet, she knew she should have found some comfort in the thought that her father was still with them somehow, perhaps watching. But even as a child she remembered wondering that, if her mother truly believed that, why then had she acted the way she had? Why had she brought strange men home with her night after night? That is, until she moved her recreation to hotel rooms. Maggie wasn't sure what had been worse, listening through the paper-thin walls of their apartment to some stranger fucking her drunk mother or being twelve and spending the nights home all alone.

*That which does not destroy us, makes us stronger.*

So now she was this tough FBI agent who battled evil on a regular basis. Then why the hell was it still so difficult to deal with her childhood? Why were those memories of her mother's drunken bouts and suicide attempts still able to demolish her and leave her feeling vulnerable? Leave her feeling like the only way she could examine those memories was through the bottom of a Scotch glass? Why did visions of that twelve-year-old little girl tossing handfuls of dirt onto her father's shiny casket remind her of how hollow she felt inside?

She thought she had risen above her past long ago. Why did it keep seeping into her present? Why could her mother's words, her lies, crumble away that solid barrier she had created?

*Goddamn it!*

Somewhere deep inside, Maggie knew something was broken. She hadn't ever admitted it to anyone, but she knew. She could feel it. There was a hole, a wound that still bled, an emptiness that could still chill her, stop her in her tracks and send her reaching, searching for more bricks to build up the wall around it. If she could not heal the wound, perhaps she could at least seal it and keep it off-limits from anyone else, maybe even herself.

She knew about the syndromes, the psychology, the inevitable scars from growing up with an alcoholic parent. How a child could be left feeling there was no one to trust. Happiness was as allusive as the fleeting moment of the parent making promises one minute and then breaking them within hours. The child learns not to trust today, because tomorrow his or her world could be turned upside down again. And then there were the lies. Jesus! All the lies. This was just another one. Of course it was.

She sipped her Scotch and watched the moonlight bring shadows to life in her backyard, while the memories, the voices kept coming.

*Like mother, like daughter.*

No. She was not like her mother. She wasn't like her at all.

Her cellular phone suddenly began chirping inside her jacket pocket. Only now did she remember she had unplugged her regular phone, in case her mother felt some need to call.

Maggie stretched to grab the jacket off a nearby stand without disturbing Harvey, whose eyes were open but whose head was still claiming her lap.

"Maggie O'Dell."

"Maggie, it's Julia Racine. Sorry to call so late."

She closed her eyes and took a deep breath. Racine was the last person Maggie wanted to talk to right now.

"I need to talk to you," she said, her voice uncommonly humbled. "Do you have a few minutes? I didn't wake you, did I?"

"No, it's okay." She petted Harvey, who closed his eyes again. "I haven't made it to bed yet, partly because my dog's oversize head has taken up residence in my lap."

"Lucky guy."

"Jesus! Racine."

"Sorry."

"If that's what this conversation—"

"No, it's not. Really, I'm sorry." Racine hesitated, as if there was something more on the subject she wanted to add before going on. Then she said, "I'm in deep shit with the chief. Senator Brier wants my ass kicked off the force because of those photos Garrison managed to get in the *Enquirer.*"

"I'm sure things will cool down as soon as we figure out who is responsible for his daughter's death."

"I wish it was that easy," Racine said, only this time there was something different about her voice. Not anger, not frustration. Maybe a bit of fear. "Chief Henderson is seriously pissed. I may lose my badge."

Maggie didn't know what to say. As much as she disliked Racine and questioned her competency, she knew this was harsh.

"To make matters worse, that asshole Garrison called me." The anger returned. "He said he has some photos to show me that might help the case."

"Why would he suddenly want to help?"

Silence. Maggie knew it. There had to be something in it for Garrison. But what?

"He wants something from me," Racine admitted, going from fear to anger to embarrassment.

"He wants something like what? Sorry, Racine, but you're not getting off that easy. What does he want?"

"He wants photos."

"What photos could he possibly want from you?"

"No, he wants to take photos *of* me." Racine let the anger slip out.

"Oh, Jesus!" Maggie couldn't believe it. No wonder Racine sounded like an emotional wreck. "And why would he think that's possible?"

"Cut the crap, O'Dell. You know why he thinks it's possible."

So the rumors were true. The stories about Racine exchanging favors weren't just crude locker-room talk.

"Does he realize we could already have him arrested for obstructing a police investigation?"

"I told him."

"And?"

"He laughed."

"Let's do it, then."

"Are you kidding?"

"No. I'll talk to Cunningham. You talk to Henderson. Let's bring him in."

"I'm in enough trouble, O'Dell. If Garrison is bluffing—"

"If Garrison's as arrogant as I think he is, and he does have something, then we'll just convince him it's in his best interests to share that information."

"And just how do we convince him?"

"I'm gonna give Cunningham a call. You talk to Henderson and call me back. Let's bring this asshole in."

Maggie hung up the phone, put the Scotch aside and felt a renewed energy. Gently she nudged Harvey awake. Suddenly, she found herself grateful for bastards like Garrison.

# CHAPTER 58

*WEDNESDAY*
*November 27*
*Washington, D.C.*

Ben Garrison pretended to keep his cool while he sat and waited in the middle of the twelfth precinct, handcuffed to a fucking chair. Officers shoved their way around him, ignoring him. A stoned, toothless hooker kept smiling at him from across the room. She even winked at him once, uncrossed her legs and gave him a Sharon Stone view of her merchandise. He wasn't impressed.

His wrists itched under the too-tight handcuffs. The chair's wobbly legs drove him nuts, and he shoved it back against the wall, drawing scowls from the two bastards who brought him in. He still couldn't believe Racine would do this. Who would have thought she had it in her? Oddly, it only made him want to fuck her all the more.

He returned from Boston to find two of the District's finest waiting for him at his apartment. At first, he thought Mrs. Fowler was having him evicted, especially if she smelled the fumigator crap he had left for the cockroaches to enjoy. And if the little bastards had escaped into the rest of the building, the poor old woman probably would have a coronary. But, no, it wasn't Mrs. Fowler. It was Racine. What a surprise. The little cunt had a game plan all of her own. And part of it, obviously, was to make him wait.

Well, he refused to let her ruin his lucky streak, especially after he had just spent the morning blowing away Britt

Harwood with yet another Garrison exclusive. Ben smiled. Not much Racine could do about the photos that would be in this evening's *Boston Globe.*

Hell, he had done what he wanted with the prints, so, no, he didn't mind sharing them with Racine. He had planned to, anyway. She couldn't blame a guy for wanting a little treat in return.

"They're ready for you, Garrison," one of the thick-necked Neanderthals in blue said as he undid one handcuff to release Ben from the chair, then quickly snapped it onto his wrist again. When Ben stood, the guy grabbed his elbow and led him down the hall.

The room was small, with no windows and several pockmarks in the bare walls, some small enough to be bullet holes, a couple of large ones that looked like someone had tried to put a fist or head through the plaster. The room smelled like burnt toast and sweaty gym socks. The officer sat him down in one of the chairs that surrounded the table. Then he did his little weaving trick again with the handcuffs and the steel folding chair.

Ben wanted to point out that if he really wanted, he could fold up the chair and simply take it with him, maybe even knocking some heads with it on his way out. But now probably wasn't a good time to be a smart-ass, so he sat quietly, expecting to be in for another wait.

Surprisingly, Racine came in within minutes, stopping to consult the Neanderthal at the door before she even acknowledged Ben's presence. She was followed in by an attractive dark-haired woman in an official-looking navy suit. He thought he recognized her. Surely, he'd remember. What a treat! Two police babes.

Racine looked pretty good, too. If she wanted to look butch, she would need to try harder. Although he had to admit her spiky blond hair looked like she had just gotten out of the shower, and she had no fashion sense. Today she had on blue jeans and a sweater that he wished was tighter. But with no jacket—thank goodness—it was still a rush seeing her in the leather shoulder holster with the butt of her Glock tucked nicely under her left breast. Yes, indeed, he could already feel the effect. Poor Racine. She probably thought hauling him in here would be some sort of punishment.

The Neanderthal brought in Ben's duffel bag and set it on the table. Then he left, closing the door behind him. Racine pulled out a chair and put up one foot, trying to look tough. The other woman leaned against the wall, crossed her arms and began examining Ben.

"So, Garrison, glad we could finally arrange that little meeting you wanted," Racine said. "This is Special Agent Maggie O'Dell with the FBI. Thought maybe you wouldn't mind if we made this a threesome."

"Sorry, Racine. If this is your idea of intimidation then you're gonna be really disappointed when I tell you you're giving me an incredible hard-on."

She didn't blush, not even slightly. Maybe Detective Racine was tougher than Officer Racine.

"This case is a federal investigation, Garrison. It could mean—"

"Cut the crap, Racine," he stopped her, glancing at O'Dell, who stayed put, looking official while she continued to lean against the wall. He knew who the real power broker was, so when he spoke again, he addressed O'Dell. "I know you just want the photos. I always intended to hand them over."

"Really?" O'Dell said.

"Yeah, really. I have no idea what Racine misunderstood. Probably all that sexual tension from not knowing who or what to fuck this week."

"Oh, I think you'll certainly feel fucked, Garrison, when we're through with you," Racine said without so much as a blink, playing out her role as the bad cop.

O'Dell, also, remained cool and calm. "You have the photos with you?" she asked, nodding at the duffel bag.

"Sure. And I'm more than willing to show them to you." He lifted his hands and clanked the handcuffs against the steel chair. "Hell, I'll give them to you. As soon as all the charges are dropped, of course."

"Charges?" Racine glanced at O'Dell, then back at him. "Did the boys give you the impression you were under arrest? I'm sure you must have misunderstood, Garrison."

He wanted to tell her to go fuck herself, but instead he smiled and held up his hands again for her to remove the cuffs.

O'Dell reached over and knocked on the door, bringing in the thick-necked cop to unlock the handcuffs. Then he left again, without a word to either woman.

Ben rubbed his wrists, taking his time before he pulled over the bag and began digging through his equipment. He didn't want them messing with his stuff. He set his camera, lens and collapsible tripod out on the table. Then he removed a couple of T-shirts, a pair of sweatpants and a towel to get the manila envelopes at the bottom. He opened one and spilled its contents on the table: negatives, contact sheet and the prints Harwood's people had developed and given him copies of. He laid five eight-by-tens on the table, putting them in chronological order for the full effect.

"Jesus!" Racine said. "Where and when was this?"

"Yesterday. Late afternoon. Boston."

From one of the other envelopes, he pulled out several prints from the Brier girl's crime scene along with about a dozen from Everett's rally in the District. One showed Everett with a young blond-haired girl and Ginny Brier, alongside two of the same boys in the Boston photos. He slid them across the table.

"Pretty easy to recognize some of these good Christian boys," Ben told them. "When I was at the District rally, Saturday night, I heard them talking about some kind of initiation they were planning in Boston Common on Tuesday. I played my hunch that it might be something interesting."

"Funny how you didn't mention that to me. You didn't even mention that you had been at that rally," Racine said.

"Didn't seem important at the time."

"Even though you knew you had photos of the dead girl attending the rally?"

"I took lots of photos over the weekend. Maybe I didn't know exactly what or who I had shot."

"Just like you didn't know that you hadn't turned over all the film you shot at the crime scene?"

He smiled again and shrugged.

"Was Everett in Boston?" O'Dell asked as she picked up each photo, carefully scrutinized it, then moved on to the next.

"No sign of him, but I heard them talking like maybe he was." He pointed to Brandon in several of the Boston photos and in the District one. "This one seemed to be in charge. They were all drunk. You can see in one of the photos that they had beer bottles and were spraying the women."

"I don't believe this," Racine said. "Where were the cops?"

"It was a Tuesday afternoon. Who knows? I didn't see any around."

"And you just watched?" O'Dell was staring at him now as if she was trying to figure him out.

"No, I took pictures. It's my job. It's what I do."

"They were attacking these girls, and you just stood around and took pictures?"

"When I'm behind the lens, I'm not there as a participant. I'm there to record and capture what's going on."

"How could you do nothing?" O'Dell wasn't going to give it up. He could hear the anger in her voice.

"You don't get it. If I had put down my camera, you wouldn't have these fucking photos so you can now go out and charge these motherfuckers."

"If you had put down your camera and tried to stop them, maybe we wouldn't need any photos. Maybe those girls wouldn't have had to go through this."

"Oh, right. Like this is my fault. Let me tell you, it takes a lot more work and planning to make news happen, Ms. FBI Agent. I record the images. I capture the emotions. I'm not a part of what happens. I'm a part of the instruments. I'm fucking invisible when I'm behind the camera. Look, you've got your photos. I'm outta here."

He grabbed his duffel bag, stuffed his camera and lens inside and started to leave, expecting one of them to stop him. Instead, they were both busy examining the photos. Racine was already jotting down notes.

Fuck them! If they didn't get it, he didn't need to explain it. He left, a bit disappointed that even the Neanderthal wasn't around for him to shove or at least flip off. Guess Racine won this round.

# CHAPTER 59

"Do you believe this?" Racine said, standing over the pictures and shaking her head as if she was truly having a tough time believing it. "You think this is what happens to them?"

Without any more of an explanation, Maggie knew Racine was talking about the murdered women: Ginny Brier, the transient they had found under the viaduct and the floater in Raleigh. And now, after talking to Tully, they could add this poor woman whom the Boston PD had just identified as a stockbroker named Maria Leonetti to their list.

"Is it possible?" Racine continued when Maggie didn't answer. "Could it be some savage initiation? Some rite of passage for Everett's young male members?"

"I don't know," Maggie finally said. "I almost hope not."

"It would sure answer a lot of questions. Like why they weren't killed right away. You know. Some crazy game they play with them. And it makes sense that it would coincide with the rallies."

"But there was no rally in Boston," Maggie reminded her.

The two women fell silent again, standing side by side, staring at the photos scattered across the table, neither touching them.

"Why do you say you almost hope not?" Racine broke the silence.

"What?"

"You said you almost hope it's not the way the murders happened."

"Because I hate to believe one man can incite a group of boys to do something like this. That one man could convince a group of boys to rape, brutalize and possibly murder women simply on command."

"Wouldn't be the first time in history. Men can be such bastards," Racine said, letting some anger slip through.

Maggie glanced at her. Perhaps her anger came from personal experience. Perhaps it came from spending several years on the sexual assault unit. Whatever the reason, it seemed a bit personal, and not something Maggie wanted to know.

"It means Everett is much more dangerous than we ever thought," Maggie said, then added in almost a whisper, "Eve was right."

"Who's Eve?"

"An ex-member I talked to. Cunningham and Senator Brier were able to set up the meeting. I thought she was being silly for being so paranoid."

"So what do we do now?"

Maggie finally began to sort through the pile of stuff Garrison had left behind when he'd emptied the duffel bag. He had been in such a hurry to leave that he had taken only his camera and a lens. She pushed aside the strange metal contraption, a smelly T-shirt and sweatpants and reached for the manila envelope. She opened it and spilled its contents—more photos—onto the table alongside the Boston ones. These all looked like shots from Ginny Brier's crime scene. They had to be from the roll of film he had kept for himself—leftover prints from what he had sold to the *Enquirer.*

"I still can't believe I was so stupid," Racine said as soon as she saw what the prints were. "Chief Henderson is so pissed."

"You made a mistake. It happens to all of us," Maggie told her without accusation. She felt Racine staring at her.

"Why are you being so understanding? I thought you were still pissed at me, too."

"I'm pissed with Garrison. Not you," Maggie said without looking over at Racine. Instead, she sorted through the photos of Ginny Brier. Something about the close-ups bothered her. What was it?

"I meant the DeLong case."

Maggie stopped at a close-cropped shot of Ginny Brier's face, but she could feel Racine's eyes on her. So the DeLong case was still bothering her, too.

"You were pretty upset with me." Racine wouldn't let it go. Maybe she was feeling she needed some absolution. "I made a mistake and some evidence got leaked. Is that why you're still so pissed at me?"

This time Maggie glanced at her. "It almost cost us the conviction." She went back to the shot of Ginny Brier's face, the eyes staring directly out at her. Something was different about this photo, about her eyes. What the hell was it?

"But it didn't cost us the conviction," Racine insisted. "It all worked out." She wasn't finished. "Sometimes I wonder..." she hesitated. "Sometimes I wonder if that's really why you got so pissed at me."

Now Maggie looked at her, meeting her eyes and waiting for Racine to get whatever it was she needed off her chest, although she had a pretty good idea what it was. "What exactly are you talking about?"

"Are you still pissed at me because I made a mistake and leaked evidence? Or are you still pissed at me because I made a pass at you?"

"Both were unprofessional," Maggie said without hesitation and without any emotion. "I have little patience for colleagues who are unprofessional." She went back to the photos, but she could feel the detective still watching, still waiting. "That's it, Racine. There really isn't anything more to it. Now, can we get on with this case?" She handed her the photo. "What's different about this one?"

Racine shifted her stance, but Maggie could tell the woman wasn't quite comfortable about moving on. "Different how?" she asked.

"I'm not sure," Maggie said, rubbing at her own eyes and feeling the effects of too much Scotch from the night before. "Maybe I need to see the other crime scene photos. Do we have those handy?"

But Racine didn't make an attempt to search. "Do you still think I'm unprofessional? I mean with this case?"

Maggie stopped and turned to face the detective. They were eye level, almost the same height. The normally cocky detective waited for an answer with one hand on her hip and the other tapping the photo on the table's surface. She held Maggie's eyes in that same tough stare she probably thought she had perfected, but there was something—a slight vulnerability in her eyes as they blinked, darted to one side then quickly returned, as if it took a conscious and silent reminder not to flinch.

"I haven't had any complaints," Maggie finally said. Then she relinquished a smile and added, "Yet."

Racine rolled her eyes, but Maggie could see the relief.

"Tell me what you know about Ben Garrison," Maggie said, hoping to get back to work, despite the nagging sensation she had about Ginny Brier's dead eyes, staring out from Garrison's illicit photos.

"You mean other than that he's an arrogant, lying bastard?"

"It sounds like you worked with him before."

"Years ago, he sometimes moonlighted for second shift as a crime scene photographer when I was with Vice," Racine said. "He's always been an arrogant bastard, even before he became a big-shot photojournalist."

"Any famous shots I may have seen?"

"Oh, sure. I'm sure you've seen that god-awful one of Princess Diana. The blurred one, shot through the shattered windshield? Garrison just happened to be in France. And one of his Oklahoma City bombing ones made the cover of *Time*. The dead man staring up out of the pile of rubble. You don't even see the body unless you look at the photo closely, and then there's those eyes, staring right out at you."

"Sounds like he has a fascination with photographing death," Maggie said, picking up another photo of Ginny Brier and studying those horrified eyes. "Do you know anything about his personal life?"

Racine shot her a suspicious look with enough distaste that Maggie knew it was the wrong thing to ask. But Racine didn't let it stop her. "He's hit on me plenty of times, but no, I don't know him outside of crime scenes and what I've heard."

"And what have you heard?"

"I don't think he's ever been married. He grew up around here, maybe someplace in Virginia. Oh, and someone said his mom just died recently."

"What do you mean, someone said. How did they know?"

"Not sure." The detective squinted as if trying to remember. "Wait a minute, I think it was Wenhoff. When we were waiting for you at the FDR scene, right after Garrison left. I don't know how Wenhoff knew. Maybe somehow through the medical examiner's office. I just remember he made the comment that it was hard to believe someone like Garrison even had a mother. Why? You think that means something? You think that's why he's suddenly so reckless and anxious to be famous again?"

"I have no idea." But Maggie couldn't help thinking about her own mother. What kind of danger was she in just by being a part of Everett's group? And was there any way Maggie could convince her she *was* in danger? "Are you close to your mother, Racine?"

The detective looked at her as though it were a trick question, and only then did Maggie realize it wasn't a fair question, certainly not a professional one. "Sorry. I didn't mean to be personal," she said before Racine could answer. "Mine's just been on my mind lately."

"No, I don't mind," Racine said, appearing relaxed and casual with the subject even when she added, "My mom died when I was a girl."

"Racine, I'm sorry. I didn't know."

"It's okay. The bad part is, I have few memories of her, you know?" She was flipping through the crime scene photos, and Maggie wondered if perhaps Racine wasn't as comfortable with the topic as she pretended. She seemed to need to have her hands occupied, her eyes busy somewhere else. But still, she continued, "My dad tells me stuff about her all the time. I guess I look just like her when she was my age. Guess I need to be the one to remember the stories, because he's starting to forget them."

Maggie waited. It felt like Racine wasn't finished, and when she glanced up, Maggie knew she was right. Racine added, "He's starting to forget a lot of stuff lately."

"Alzheimer's?"

"Early symptoms, but yeah."

She looked away again, but not before Maggie caught a glimpse of vulnerability in the tough, wise-cracking detective's eyes. Then she began sorting through Garrison's stuff as if looking for something and asked, "What do we do about Everett? Everett and his little gang of boys?"

"Are the photos enough for an arrest warrant?"

"For this Brandon kid, I'd say definitely. We have these photos and an eyewitness that puts him with Ginny Brier in the hours before her murder."

"If we can get a DNA sample, I bet we've got a match to the semen."

"We'll need to have the warrant served at the compound," Racine said. "We might not have any idea what we're walking into out there."

"Call Cunningham. He'll know what to do. It'll probably require an HRT unit." As soon as she said it, Maggie thought of Delaney. "Hopefully this won't get messy. How long do you think it'll take to get a warrant?"

"For the possible murder suspect of a senator's daughter?" Racine smiled. "I think we should have one before the end of the day."

"I need to make a quick trip down to Richmond, but I'll be back."

"Ganza said he needed to talk to you. He left a message earlier."

"Any idea what about?" But Maggie was already headed for the door.

"Not sure. Something about an old police report and a possible DNA sample?"

Maggie shook her head. She didn't have time. Besides, maybe it was a different case. "I'll call him from the road."

"Wait a minute." Racine stopped her. "Where are you going in such a hurry?"

"To try to talk some sense into a very stubborn woman."

# CHAPTER 60

Gwen slid into the window seat while Tully shoved their bags into the overhead compartment. During the cab ride to Logan International Airport, they had managed to fill the awkward silences with niceties about the weather and some details about the crime scene. So far they had avoided talking about last night and what Nick Morrelli's phone call had interrupted. She caught herself thinking that it might be best if they pretended it had never happened. Then she realized how stupid that probably was for a psychologist to even consider. Okay, so she wasn't good at practicing what she preached.

He took the seat next to her, fumbling with his seat belt and watching the other passengers file onto the plane. It looked like it wouldn't be a full flight. With no one to occupy the aisle seat there would be more opportunity for them to talk. Oh, wonderful!

Tully mentioned that he hadn't gotten back to the hotel until almost sunrise. Maybe he would want to sleep. She wasn't ready to talk about what had happened between them last night.

She knew it wasn't unusual for two people who had just gone through a crisis to be drawn together in a way they ordinarily would never consider. And yesterday's attempt on her life could certainly be considered a crisis. Of course that was exactly what had happened.

The flight attendants began the preflight procedure, and Tully watched as though he was captivated and had never flown before, an obvious giveaway that he, too, was uncomfortable. Now Gwen wished she had bought a paperback at the airport bookstore. At this rate, the sixty-minute flight would be excruciatingly long.

Once they were in the air, Tully brought his briefcase out from under the seat. With it in his lap, he suddenly seemed more comfortable, a sort of this-is-strictly-business security blanket.

"I talked to O'Dell," he said while he flipped through a mess of papers, shoving pens, a day-planner and a clump of paper clips out of the way.

Gwen immediately wondered if he actually used the day-planner. Then she caught herself wondering what Maggie would think when she found out about last night, and about Gwen breaking her own golden rule of not getting involved with a man she worked with. But nothing had happened. They hadn't had time to get…involved.

Tully brought out some copies of crime scene photos and was pointing out similarities. "O'Dell said that photographer, the one who sold the crime scene photos to the *Enquirer,* has photos of Reverend Everett's boys mauling women in Boston Common yesterday."

"You're kidding. Yesterday?" Now he had her attention. "How did he just happen to be in Boston?"

"Supposedly, he overheard something about an initiation rite when he was shooting photos at the District's prayer rally. O'Dell said last night's victim is one of the women, and that it should be easy to identify the young men, too. Several of the boys show up in photos with Everett at the prayer rally, so there's our connection."

"This is starting to sound too easy. If Everett's boys are involved in the murders, why would Everett allow them to be photographed?"

"Maybe he didn't know they were."

"How did Maggie manage to get these photos from Garrison?"

Tully shook his head, and Gwen could see a slight smile. "Not sure, and I don't even want to know."

Gwen laughed. "So I gather you already know my good friend quite well."

"Let me just say that sometimes she's a little more willing than I am to skip over procedure."

"You're a by-the-book kind of guy?"

"Yeah, I try to be. Something wrong with that?"

"I didn't say there was."

He looked over at her as if he expected more of an explanation, then he said, "It sounded like you wanted to attach a *but* to that."

"No, not at all. I was just wondering how last night played into your rules-and-procedure book."

He actually turned a slight shade of red and quickly looked away. Gwen followed his lead and looked in the other direction, out the window. Oh, smooth move, Patterson, she scolded herself. Who would ever guess she had a doctorate in psychology.

"I suppose we should talk about last night," he finally said.

"We don't need to talk about it," she found herself saying, all the while thinking that yes, they did. What was wrong with her? "I just don't want it to get in the way of us working together."

God, how pathetic. Where did she come up with this stuff? She should stop and yet she found herself continuing. "It was simply the crisis."

He was looking at her, waiting. She didn't think she had to explain it to him, but obviously she would. "A crisis can often make people act in a way they might not normally act."

"We weren't in the middle of a crisis then."

"No, of course not. It doesn't have to be during the crisis. It's the effect of the crisis."

He went back to his computer and punched at a couple of keys to close a file he had just opened. Without looking up at her, he said, "Sounds like you'd rather we pretend it didn't happen."

She glanced at him, looking for some sign of what he wanted. But with the computer screen to distract him, he kept his eyes ahead, now watching the flight attendant's serving cart coming down the aisle as if he couldn't wait for his beverage and package of pretzels.

"Look, Tully, I have to admit—" She stopped herself, something only now occurring to her. "Should I be calling you R.J.? And what does R.J. stand for?"

He grimaced. Another wrong thing to say. Oh, she was definitely good at this.

"All my friends call me Tully."

She waited, then realized that was all she was getting. So much for intimacy. Last night had been about sex and nothing more. Why did that suddenly surprise her? Wasn't that all it had been to her? Thank God for Morrelli's interruption.

"What were you going to admit?" he asked, looking over at her. "You started to say that you had to admit something?"

"Just that I had to admit I wasn't quite sure what to call you. That's all," she said, while some inner voice told her what a good liar she was.

But how could she admit that last night had been surprising and incredible and then say, So let's forget it, okay? She had managed to keep her life uncomplicated for years now. Seemed a shame to throw all that away for one surprisingly pleasant encounter.

"So we chalk it up to the crisis of the moment," Tully said with a casual shrug, not able to hide just a hint of…a hint of what? Disappointment? Sarcasm?

"Yes. I think it's best that we do that," she told him.

She imagined Freud would have a perfect word for what she was doing, for what she was telling herself, for how she was handling this situation. Although she couldn't quite imagine Freud actually saying the word "bullshit" out loud.

# CHAPTER 61

This time Maggie remembered to exit I-95 before she reached the turnpike. She ended up on Jefferson Davis Highway, and as she crossed the James River she realized she would probably need to do some backtracking to get to her mother's. Two trips in two days—she should be able to do this without a hitch. After all, she had spent her adolescent years here until she left for good to go to the University of Virginia in Charlottesville. Yet this city had never felt like home. At that point in her life, no place on earth would have felt like home. No place, that is, without her father.

After his death, Maggie had never understood why her mother insisted they move from Green Bay to Richmond. Why wouldn't they want to stay in their home surrounded by people who knew and loved them, comforted by the memories? Unless, of course, there had been an affair and gossip, rumors… No, it had to be a lie. She wouldn't allow the thought, wouldn't dignify it with… Except *why* had they moved? Had her mother ever given her a reason?

Kathleen O'Dell had plopped them down in the middle of a strange and unfamiliar place, a place she had never visited nor even heard of before. And her mother's only explanation… What? What had it been? Something about a fresh start, a new beginning. Right. A fresh start after every failed suicide attempt. So many of them Maggie had stopped counting.

But here she was again, trying to rescue her mother once more.

She pulled up in front of her mother's apartment building, driving around the huge white paneled truck that took up five prime parking spaces. Several men were loading the truck with furniture while a small gray-haired man propped open the apartment building's security door. So much for security.

It wasn't until Maggie walked up the front sidewalk and past the truck that she recognized the flowered love seat the men were shoving into the back. Immediately, she glanced up at her mother's second-floor apartment and noticed all the curtains gone from the windows. The stab of panic caught her off guard.

"Excuse me." She stopped the small gray-haired man who seemed to be supervising the move. "I recognize some of these items. What's going on?"

"Mrs. O'Dell is selling out."

"You mean moving out?"

"Well, I'm sure she's moving someplace else, but no, I meant selling out."

The confusion must have shown on her face, because he went on to explain, "I'm Frank Bartle." He dug into his jacket pocket and handed her a business card. "Al and Frank's Antiques and Secondhand Treasures. We're down on Kirby. If you see something here you like, we'll have it ready to sell next week."

"But I don't understand why she would sell everything. I guess I should go up and ask her myself, rather than bother you."

"'Fraid you won't be able to do that."

"I promise I won't get in your men's way." She smiled and started for the door.

"No, I just meant that she's not there."

Now Maggie felt a clammy chill. "Where is she?"

"Don't know. I was gonna buy a few of her antiques. You know some trinkets, a few figurines and things like that. She gave me a call early this morning and asked if I wanted the whole lot."

Maggie leaned against the doorjamb. "Where did she go?"

"Don't know."

"But she must have left you a forwarding address."

"Nope."

"What about payment?"

"I came over this morning. Gave her an estimate and then a check. She gave me a key. Said to hand it in to the landlady when we're through."

How could all this happen in less than twenty-four hours? And what had happened to make her mother do this? Or had she planned it and just didn't tell Maggie? Yesterday there had been quite a few boxes packed and stacked. But why make a production of Thanksgiving dinner if she hadn't planned on being here? What the hell was going on?

"I have a receipt, if you don't believe me." Frank Bartle was digging in his jacket pocket again.

"No, that's fine." She stopped him with a wave of her hand. "I believe you. It's just very strange. I saw her yesterday."

"Sorry, but that's all I know," he said, but his attention wandered to one of the moving men who was coming out the apartment building. "Be careful with that one, Emile. Put it someplace safe, okay?"

On the side of the carton the man carried Maggie could see scrawled in black marker the single word, Figurines. Her grandmother's figurines, the one prize possession her mother owned. Suddenly, Maggie felt sick to her stomach. Wherever her mother had gone, she didn't intend on coming back.

# CHAPTER 62

Ben Garrison kicked the unlocked door open. He wanted to strangle Mrs. Fowler. How dare she come into his apartment without letting him know. In the past, the old lady had usually been good about locking up after herself and her string of handymen, almost compulsive about it, in fact. Maybe she had developed a few loose screws in her old age.

He set down his duffel bag on the kitchen counter and out of the corner of his eye he could see them. Quietly, slowly, he picked up the closest thing he could find, pulled back his arm and flung the old tennis shoe at the moving row of black skittering up his living room wall.

Shit! He was sick of these things. Would he ever be rid of them? Is that why Mrs. Fowler let herself in? Maybe the simple solution would be to move to a new apartment. He could certainly afford it now that his lucky streak had returned. He'd need to wait and decide. Right now he barely had enough time to take a quick shower, repack his bags, load up on more film and head to the airport.

He dumped his duffel bag onto the counter, sifting through the contents, tossing empty film canisters and doing a quick inventory. It still pissed him off that he had left all the Boston negatives with Racine. But he couldn't afford to have her trip him up. Not now. Not when he was on a roll.

As he sorted through everything he realized he must have left his collapsible tripod at the police station. Damn it! How could he have been so careless? It happened every time he got a little too cocky. Now he wondered what else he may have left behind. The T-shirts and sweatpants he could do without, but the tripod he couldn't. He'd need to stop and pick up another. No way would he go back to the police station.

He checked his phone messages, jotting down the names of editors and phone numbers he had never heard of or from before. Suddenly everyone wanted a Garrison exclusive. In no time, he'd be back to shooting whatever he wanted, although it would be difficult to beat the rush of adrenaline this little project was producing. Maybe he could find a gallery that would display his outtakes. Those, after all, were the true rush, his true genuine works of art.

There were five hangups on his answering machine, definite hangups with a pause and then a click. Probably Everett's little warriors checking up on him. But why the hangups and no more clever messages? Were they running out of intimidation ammunition?

Poor Everett. He'd finally get what he deserved, what he had coming to him. Perhaps Racine and that FBI chick would be smart enough to put the puzzle pieces together. Hopefully, that wouldn't happen before Cleveland. Ben needed this one last trip, one last rally.

He headed for the bathroom, peeling off his clothes and leaving a trail, not caring whether the cockroaches took up residence in his old worn jeans. Maybe he'd burn them when he got back. Yeah, he'd wrap them all up in a plastic bag, so he could watch the fucking roaches squirm while he set the jeans on fire. He wondered if cockroaches made any kind of noise. Did they scream?

When he stepped into the bathroom, he immediately noticed that the smudged glass door to his shower was closed. He never left it closed. The trapped fog and steam ended up producing a crop of mildew, so he always left it open. He couldn't see through the milky glass, but surely there would be a shadow or silhouette if someone was hiding inside. Maybe Mrs. Fowler's handyman had been screwing around with the plumbing. That had to be it.

He pulled a towel from the rack and shook it out, making sure it was cockroach-free. He opened the shower door and reached in to turn on the water. One glance inside the tub made him jerk backward hard and fast, tangling his feet and sending him crashing to the bathroom floor. He scrambled to his feet, grabbed the shower door and slammed it shut, but not before he took one last look to make sure he wasn't imagining things.

They had gone too fucking far this time.

Coiled inside his bathtub was a snake that looked big enough to swallow him whole.

# CHAPTER 63

*The Compound*

Kathleen O'Dell sat on the floor next to Reverend Everett in his high-backed chair as they waited for the meeting hall to fill. Stephen sat on his other side with Emily. Stephen nor Emily had said much to her since they picked her up. Not a word of explanation the entire trip to the compound, just short, almost curt nonanswers to her questions. Kathleen wasn't sure if it was anger or urgency. She hadn't been able to read either one of them. Now as they sat, she stole a glance at Reverend Everett. He didn't seem angry, either, but earlier there had been something in his voice and in his mannerisms. Kathleen wondered if it was panic.

No, of course not. She was being paranoid. There was no reason to panic. And yet, his morning phone call sounded just frantic enough to set her on edge. All morning, as she waited for Frank from Al and Frank's and then for Stephen and Emily, she kept wishing she hadn't finished that entire bottle from the back of her cupboard.

Reverend Everett hadn't given much of an explanation as to why they had to leave so soon. When they arrived at the compound, they found the others scurrying around, preparing for another stretch of prayer rallies, the first being in Cleveland, the following night. That was all it was—preparation. But then, why did Reverend Everett call this emergency meeting? Why did Emily's face look pinched with panic?

Kathleen wasn't even supposed to be here. She wasn't supposed to be going to the Cleveland rally. It had been Reverend Everett's recommendation that she spend the holiday with

Maggie. Except that she hadn't had the chance to tell him about Maggie. Now it was best she didn't mention it at all. Because now, it seemed as if everything had changed. Something terrible had happened. Something terrible enough to make Emily speechless. Something terrible enough that prevented Stephen from meeting Kathleen's eyes.

Kathleen felt like she was in a fog, where nothing seemed to be quite clear. She still couldn't believe all her things were gone, her apartment, her cheerful yellow curtains and her grandmother's figurines. Perhaps that's why her head had been throbbing all day. It was just too much to expect a person to handle in one day. Surely Reverend Everett understood that. Perhaps by the time they reached Cleveland, he would change his mind. Yes, she was certain he would be able to calm down and realize that everything would be just fine.

As he stood, the room grew silent, despite the nervous tension that spread through the crowd as they sat crossed-legged on the floor and waited.

"My children," he began, "before those of us who are going on our mission to Ohio leave, I'm afraid we have some disturbing news. I've warned many times that we have traitors who wish to hurt us. Those who hate us because we choose to live free. Now I must tell you that one of those among us has betrayed us, has become a traitor. Has exposed us to those mongrel media hounds. And you know how the media can lie."

He waited for the appropriate response, nodding at the few hisses that grew when he encouraged them. Kathleen looked around, hoping there would be no snake tonight. She wasn't sure her nerves could handle that.

"I'm afraid this matter is much too personal and painful for me, and so I'm asking Stephen to take over from here." Reverend Everett sat back down and looked to Stephen, who seemed surprised and perhaps a bit embarrassed by the request. Evidently, this part was unplanned. Poor timid Stephen. Kathleen knew he hated having attention drawn to him. She could see the discomfort taking over his entire face.

He stood, slowly, reluctantly. "It's true." His voice cracked, and he cleared his throat. "We have a traitor among us."

He glanced back at Reverend Everett and the reverend waved a hand at him to proceed, indicating that Stephen knew the drill. Yes, Kathleen looked around at the crowd, now silent and waiting. They all knew the drill. The traitor must be brought forward. Must be taught a lesson. But she was so exhausted tonight that all she wanted was for it to be over.

"The traitor has exposed valuable information to the FBI and the *Boston Globe,*" Stephen continued. "Information that has them talking to ex-members. Information that could tarnish the church's reputation and distract from our mission. This is why the rally in Ohio is even more important now. We cannot be intimidated."

He looked to Reverend Everett as if for approval. Then Stephen's voice grew stronger, deeper. "But traitors must be punished. I ask the guilty person to stand. You know who you are." Another glance back at Reverend Everett. "Stand before us and take your punishment."

They all remained silent. No one dared to look around for fear that they might be the one. No one stirred or dared to shift. Then Stephen turned and pointed his finger.

"Stand up right now and face your punishment," he said.

Kathleen thought she heard a hint of a quiver as he pointed his finger in her direction. No. There had to be a mistake. She looked to Reverend Everett, but he kept his eyes straight ahead. He was the only one who wasn't staring at her.

"Kathleen, come face your punishment for betraying us all." Stephen now managed an angry, stern tone.

"But there must be a mistake," she said, getting to her feet. "I haven't—"

"Silence!" Stephen yelled. "Arms at your sides, stand up straight, eyes forward." When her only response was to stare at him, he grabbed her arms and shoved her to the front of the room where several others, including Emily, had gathered. "Your selfishness could have destroyed us," he screamed into her face. Then he looked to the others to take their turn.

"You betrayed us," shouted an old woman Kathleen had never met.

"How could you?" Emily screamed into her face.

"You should be ashamed," came another.

"Traitor!"

"What makes you think you're special?"

"Ungrateful bitch!"

"What makes you think you're better than the rest of us?"

"Shame!"

One after another, they circled her, hurling insults, screaming at her, poking and shoving.

"How dare you."

"Traitor!"

Kathleen's eyes were already blurred and stinging with tears by the time the first one spit at her. Then came another and another. She attempted to wipe her face, only to have Stephen slap down her arms.

"You know the rules. Arms at your sides," he yelled, only it wasn't Stephen anymore. Those were not Stephen's eyes. It was some creature, some ugly entity who had taken over his body.

She stood, closing her eyes to the spittle and trying to shut her mind to the angry words, absorbing the blows and shoves that reminded her to stand up straight. It went on forever until her eyes burned and her ears were ringing, her feet hurt and the bruises were visible. Then suddenly, they stopped. Suddenly, it got quiet again. Everyone filed out in an orderly fashion, as if they had come for dinner and were now finished. And Kathleen found herself alone, standing in the empty meeting hall.

She was afraid to move, afraid her knees would collapse. The silence inside the hall surrounded her, and she listened to sounds outside—ordinary sounds of preparation for the impending trip. It was as if nothing had happened. As if her biggest fear had not just been played out for everyone to witness; her fear of being humiliated in front of those she thought respected her. What was worse was that they went about their punishment as if it was nothing unusual. As if it wasn't out of the ordinary for her to have her soul ripped out in front of them.

That's when she saw the young man, standing in the shadows, next to the back exit. When he realized he had been discovered, he came to her, slowly, head down, one hand in his pocket, the other holding out a towel to her.

A towel. She wanted to laugh. What she really needed was a bottle, a fucking bottle of anything…Jack Daniel's, Absolut… Hell, rubbing alcohol would do the job. But she took the towel and began gently wiping her face and then her arms, working her way over her body, trying to not think about the black-and-blue marks, trying to pretend… How the hell could she pretend? No, she could do it. She had done it before. She'd be okay. She just needed to steady herself. Was the room spinning? Or was it her imagination?

He was helping her sit. He was saying something to her, taking the towel and leaving. Was he gone? Did he decide she was a lost cause? Had he left her, just like the rest of them? But suddenly, he was back at her side. Two of him this time, handing her the towel. A fresh one, but this one damp.

She dabbed her forehead, the back of her neck, and then pulled up her sleeves and dabbed at the insides of her wrists. Already she was feeling better. This time when she looked up she found only one of him. And thank God, the room…it finally sat still. The young man seemed preoccupied. He was staring at her wrists. Or rather, he was staring at the hideous horizontal scars she had uncovered when she pulled up the sleeves of her knit cardigan.

"Believe me," she said to him, "I'll know how to do it right the next time."

# CHAPTER 64

Justin wanted to tell the woman that he understood, that he had thought about offing himself so many times he had the methods categorized. But he had never known someone older, someone who reminded him of his mother—and she *did* remind him an awful lot of his mother—who had actually tried it.

"Ma'am, are you okay now?" he asked. "Because I really should be helping load and haul stuff."

"I'll be fine." She smiled at him and pushed down the sleeves. "My name's Kathleen. No need to call me ma'am. But then, I guess you should already know my name after tonight."

"I'm Justin," he said.

"Well, thanks for your help, Justin."

He nodded at her. "I know you didn't do anything wrong."

Then he turned and left out the back exit. He needed to get back to the kitchen. Back to packing boxes with cans of beans and soup and enough rice to gag a small nation. Maybe he was trying too hard to be helpful, but he knew he had fucked up big time in Boston. Since they returned, he was half expecting to end up with that boa constrictor around his neck. He knew how close he had come to being the one standing in front of the room. Maybe that's why he had to go back and help this woman, this Kathleen. That and because she reminded him of his mom. He hadn't realized until tonight that he actually missed his mom. And he missed Eric. Now he wondered if Eric was ever really coming back.

At first, he thought he wouldn't be allowed to go to Cleveland, to the next prayer rally. That would have been okay by him. In fact, he was thinking maybe he'd just leave the compound while the others were away. He was pretty sure he could find his way back into Shenandoah National Park. He had done it last time without really trying. But then Alice told him he was on the list, the fucking anointed list that got to go.

He found the old lady named Mavis and helped her load the steel cart full of cartons into the buses' storage compartments. Some of the compartments were already loaded with other boxes. Inside both buses, the overhead compartments looked filled beyond capacity. A woman from the laundry room instructed Justin to place all the boxes she had brought on another steel cart under the seats.

"They have to fit. Make them fit," she told him, and left.

These were labeled: Shirts, Undergarments, Towels. Why would they be needing all this crap for a two-night trip? He stuffed the last one under the driver's seat just as Alice came up the bus steps with an armful of blankets. He helped her find space for them, avoiding her eyes and any other contact. He hadn't been alone with her since his meeting with Father. It shouldn't matter, but he had a hard time looking at her. He couldn't believe how much of a phony she was, pretending to be all pure and good and stuff. To think she had tried to lecture him on his bad habits. Well, at least he wasn't a fucking whore.

Shit! He promised himself he wouldn't think that way, especially after seeing those poor girls yesterday, screaming and kicking. He still couldn't get those images out of his mind.

"You've been really quiet since you got back from Boston," Alice said, staring at him with that look of concern that he used to believe was genuine. Now he wasn't sure what to think. Nobody seemed to be what he thought they were. Including himself. "Are you okay?"

"Yeah, I'm fine. Just tired." He pretended to be inspecting all the boxes, making sure they were secured under the seats.

"Well, you should be able to get some sleep once we get on the road," she said, sounding sympathetic—but how did he know that was real?

When he still didn't look at her, she put her hand on his arm, stopping his bogus inspection.

"Justin? Did I do something to make you angry with me?"

"No, why?"

"Why won't you look at me?"

Shit! He had forgotten. She really could see inside his soul. He looked into her eyes just to prove to her that he could. It was a mistake. She could see something was wrong, and now he was the one responsible for the sadness looking back at him from her eyes.

"Please tell me," she said, "if I've done something wrong. I couldn't stand the thought of you being angry with me."

He used to think she was the only one who was being straight with him, the only person he could trust. Now he didn't know. Fuck! He was so tired, and he still felt sick to his stomach. He hadn't eaten anything since he had thrown up the Quarter Pounders and beer.

"I'm not angry at you," he finally said. "I told you, I'm just really tired." He could see he hadn't convinced her, but he squeezed past her, anyway. "I'll see you later." He escaped, walking away from the bus in quick, long strides, hoping to discourage her from following him.

As he walked past the administrative building, he could see the office staff. It looked like they were shredding papers and taking apart computer hard drives. Back behind the building, three women had started a small bonfire and were tossing into the flames what looked like file folders and stacks of papers. Far off in the trees, Justin could see a spotlight and the broad-shouldered silhouettes of some of Father's bodyguards. He couldn't tell what they were doing. It almost looked like they were laying cable. Something really weird was going on. This didn't look like the ordinary preparation for a road trip.

Justin stopped suddenly and stared. At the construction site, everything had been cleared away—no stacked lumber, no crates, no sawhorses. Even the old John Deere tractor was gone. He went over for a closer look. How the hell did they get rid of it all? How could they move all that crap in such a short time?

Then he saw the flashlight back behind the garbage dump. Two men were digging while one held a flashlight. Justin leaned against an old outhouse where he could hide in the shadows. He saw them bring up four strongboxes out of the ground. It took all three of them to carry one box all the way around the corner, taking slow, deliberate steps as they hauled it down the road to where the bus was parked.

As he watched, it only now occurred to Justin. They weren't going to all this trouble just to prepare for the prayer rally. He couldn't believe it had taken him this long to figure it out. They were doing it because they weren't coming back.

# CHAPTER 65

On her way back from Richmond, Maggie's cellular phone began ringing.

"Hello?"

"O'Dell," Racine said with enough urgency to set Maggie on edge even more than she already was. "Where the hell are you?"

"I'm on I-95, heading back to the District."

"We're all meeting out at Quantico."

"Okay, then I'm only about ten minutes away."

"Good." Racine sounded relieved. "You didn't call Ganza."

"Damn! No, I forgot. Is he there?"

"He's here someplace. I'm not sure where."

Maggie could hear background noise. She knew Racine was pacing. A nervous habit Maggie quickly recognized.

"What is it, Racine? What's going on? Did you get the arrest warrant?"

"Actually, that's now multiple warrants, thanks to Ganza. There was some old police case Tully was checking out. It's one you found about Everett raping…or excuse me, allegedly raping that journalism student?"

"That was over twenty years ago. And the charges were dropped."

"Yeah, well, Rappahannock County has this thing about keeping evidence on file. I guess Ganza knows some boys out there in the sheriff's department and they managed to FedEx some samples to him."

"I can't believe he's wasting time on that old case. We can't get Everett on that case, no matter what he thinks he found. The charges were dropped, the case closed. Besides, the statute of limitations on rape—"

"The sample was old," Racine interrupted her, and continued as if not hearing her. "There was some degradation so he says he couldn't get an exact match. But there're enough hits that it's close."

"What are you talking about?"

"The sample Ganza took from the old case? The sample from Everett? The DNA matches the DNA sample of foreign skin found under Ginny Brier's fingernails. Remember you said most of the skin was her own, but that she managed to get a piece of him? Well, she got a piece of him, all right, and Ganza swears it's Everett."

Maggie slowed and pulled her car to the side of the interstate, eliciting a blare of horns behind her before she was safely stopped and out of the way. She couldn't believe this. It couldn't be Everett. Could it? "Wait a minute. What about the gang thing?"

"It's all starting to make sense, O'Dell. Maybe it's some sick initiation ritual. Who knows how it works. But this also explains why the semen found in the Brier girl doesn't match the DNA of the skin under the nails. One of Everett's boys may have had that duty, while Everett took care of the rest."

"I don't believe this," Maggie said, and felt a new sense of tension instead of relief. Why was there no relief in knowing Everett and his gang were behind the murders? What was still nagging at her? Why did this all seem so easy? She could see Everett orchestrating all of this, but somehow she couldn't see his getting his hands dirty or getting close enough to get under Ginny Brier's fingernails.

"Cunningham's kinda pissed you're not here yet. He's been looking for you." Then Racine's voice came almost in a whisper as she added, "Actually, he looks more worried than pissed. Where did you say you were?"

"Getting to exit 148 now."

"Good. An HRT unit and some agents are headed out to Everett's compound now. The Rappahannock County officials are meeting them out there. In fact, they might already be there."

"Oh, Jesus! They're on their way to the compound now?" The panic slipped. "Racine, my mom's a member of Everett's organization," Maggie said over the lump that suddenly obstructed her throat. "She may be out there at the compound."

# CHAPTER 66

*Quantico, Virginia*

Tully stood over the table, sorting through a mess of photos, documents, police reports and computer printouts. Garrison's T-shirt and sweatpants were starting to smell. Why the hell did Racine bring this stuff out here? He tossed it beside the strange metal contraption set on the far corner of the table.

"Where is everyone?" O'Dell came rushing into the conference room, breathless, her hair tousled, her face flushed and her FBI windbreaker hanging off one shoulder.

He glanced at his watch. "Ganza went to get some dinner. Racine's around here somewhere. Cunningham's down in his office. He's been looking for you. Where the heck have you been? You look like hell."

"What about the HRT unit? Have they made it to the compound yet?"

"Haven't heard."

She went to the window and stared out at the darkness, as if hoping she could see the unit from there.

"They'll be careful," he said, and she glanced at him over her shoulder. "Why didn't you say anything sooner about your mom being a part of Everett's church?"

She came back from the window, stood on the opposite side of the table, in front of him. "Guess I didn't want to believe it myself. And then I thought I could just talk some sense into her. You know, warn her. Pretty stupid, huh?"

"Nah. I think we all like to believe we have some sort of powers of influence over family members. Like, of course they'd want our advice, our suggestions. Sometimes I think the only thing natural about families is that we happen to share some of the same DNA."

She managed a weak smile, and he was pleased that he could help. But then he realized it wasn't enough when she asked, "Is Gwen around?"

Of course, she'd want her best friend.

"No, I don't think Cunningham called her in. She was headed for her office when we got back from Boston. Maybe she's still there." He pretended not to care, but found himself wondering if Gwen was working late or home fixing some gourmet meal for herself in her cozy brownstone. Maybe spaghetti. He smiled, then caught himself, glanced at O'Dell to see if she noticed. She was looking over the mess. He was safe. Besides, Gwen wanted to forget it happened. And it probably was better that they do just that. He knew she was right.

He flipped through one of the many documents scattered over the table but wasn't taking any of it in. He should probably go home. Even if they brought in Everett and that kid, Brandon, there was nothing more they could do tonight. But he didn't want to go home. With Emma in Cleveland at her mom's, the house was too empty, too quiet. It would probably just give him time to think about Boston. That wasn't good—he was supposed be forgetting about Boston.

O'Dell started pacing, close to the table so she could review the messy pile. He watched her as her eyes darted over the crime scene photos, but instead of stopping, she kept pacing, looking at them with each sweep. Had she not been worried about her mother, she'd be straightening out the mess, organizing and sorting and putting things into her neat little piles, trying to create order out of everyone else's disorder. He wished she was doing just that. It unnerved him to see her like this.

Suddenly, she noticed something and stopped. She picked up two of the photos from Ginny Brier's crime scene and started looking from one to the other.

"What is it?"

"Not sure." And she set the photos down. The pacing began again.

"Do you have any idea what this stuff is and what it's doing here?" Tully pointed to the heap on the corner of the table. More than anything, he just wanted her attention. She was starting to spook him.

"Garrison left those things behind. Guess he was in a hurry this morning."

"And we're keeping them because…?"

She shrugged and this time stopped to pick up the lightweight contraption, turning it over in her hands. She fidgeted with it and accidently popped what was a security latch. The thing sprung open.

"It's a tripod," she said, setting it on the table.

Now Tully could see the small plate where a camera could be attached and the lever to tilt and swivel it around. Suddenly, he was beside her, staring at the tripod. He rushed around the table and started riffling through photos, plucking three, one from each crime scene out of the mess. Still not saying a word, he came back around to Maggie's side and placed the photos on the table next to the feet of the tripod. The photos were of the strange circular marks left in the dirt. In the photo from the FDR Memorial crime scene, there had been two, possibly three circular marks, spaced in such a way they could form a triangle.

"Is it possible?" he asked.

He had the tripod in his hands and was examining its feet and the length between them. Why hadn't he thought about it before? The tripod's feet would certainly leave similar marks in the dirt. While he turned the thing over, Maggie suddenly grabbed the two photos of Ginny Brier—the ones she had picked up earlier—and slapped them down on the table in front of Tully.

"Look at these two photos," she said. "Do you see anything different from one to the other?"

He set the tripod aside and picked up the photos to study them. They looked almost exactly the same, same pose, same angle. There was a flash mark at the bottom of one print where the photo ended just above Ginny Brier's hands, almost exactly where her wrists were. Tully wondered if perhaps it was some mark caused by the developing process, though he knew little about film or print processing.

"You mean this white mark at the bottom? This one has it, but the other doesn't."

"What do you think it is?"

"Not sure. Could just be a smudge from developing, couldn't it?"

"Doesn't it look more like the flash reflecting off of something?"

He looked again. "Yeah, I guess so. It's hard to tell. A reflection off of what, though?"

"How about handcuffs?"

He stared at the photo again, then remembered. "She wasn't wearing handcuffs when we found her."

"Exactly," she said, now excited as she grabbed two other photos and slapped them down. "Now look at these two." They were close-ups of the Brier girl's face, the dead eyes wide open, staring directly at her audience. They, too, looked the same.

"I'm not following, O'Dell."

"One is from the roll of film Garrison kept for himself. The roll he used to sell shots to the *Enquirer.*"

"Okay. How can you tell? They look identical. Same angle, same distance. Seems like he was trying really hard to duplicate what he took for himself and what he took for us."

"Both photos are the same angle, same distance, same shot, but taken at different times," O'Dell said, slowing down her excitement, as if she was figuring out the puzzle as she spoke.

"What are you talking about?"

"The eyes," she said. "Take a close look."

As she pointed to the corners of the eyes in each photo Tully finally saw what she was talking about. In one photo there were small clumps of the whitish-yellow eggs in the corners of her eyes. Tully wasn't an expert, but he knew blowflies usually arrived within minutes to a few hours after death and began laying their eggs immediately. Yet in the photo Garrison had kept for himself, the dead girl's eyes were completely clear. There wasn't even the hint of infestation.

"That's impossible," he said, looking to O'Dell. "This photo had to have been taken shortly after her death."

"Exactly."

Tully picked up the tripod again, now more certain than ever that its feet had caused the strange indentations found at the three crime scenes. "Which would mean he's on the scene before the cops are. Just what the hell is Ben Garrison up to?"

"More important, how does he know about the murders before we do?"

"O'Dell, you're back," Cunningham interrupted. He carried a mug of coffee, sipping as he walked, as if he had no time or patience to do only one thing at a time.

"Any word if the agents arrived at the compound yet?" she asked him.

"Why don't you sit down," he told her, pointing to a chair.

Tully immediately felt his own muscles tense as he saw O'Dell's back straighten.

"It's another standoff, isn't it?" she wanted to know.

"Not exactly."

"Eve told me that Everett would never allow himself to be taken alive. He has them prepared for suicide drills. Just like those boys at the cabin." Her voice seemed calm, but Tully could see her right hand twisting the hem of her windbreaker into her fist. "He's refusing to give up, isn't he?"

"Actually..." Cunningham pulled off his eyeglasses and rubbed his eyes. Tully knew their boss wasn't the type to stall, but lately the man seemed a bit unpredictable. "Everett isn't there. He's gone. We think he might already be on his way to Ohio, maybe Colorado."

O'Dell looked relieved until Cunningham put a hand on her shoulder and said, "That's not all, Maggie. There were people still at the compound. Between the short time that the Hostage Rescue Team announced its presence and then actually gained access to the compound there must have been a panic. You're right about the suicide drill. HRT's not sure how many, but there are bodies."

# CHAPTER 67

He closed his eyes and leaned his head back, but the nausea remained. How the hell could he have motion sickness? It was impossible. It had to be something else. Perhaps just the excitement, the anticipation for the inevitable climax.

The engines continued to rumble. He hated having them so close. He tried to let the sound relax him. He tried to concentrate on the next step, the last step. He just needed to keep steady. He was almost out of his homemade concoction. He couldn't afford to take any until it was absolutely necessary. He'd need to wait. He could do that. He could be patient. Patience was a virtue. His mother had written that somewhere in one of her journal entries. So much patience. So much wisdom.

Then he realized he didn't have the book. Damn it! How the hell could he have forgotten it?

# CHAPTER 68

Kathleen O'Dell lay her head back against the seat and tried to let the rumbling of the bus lull the throbbing at her temples. She knew exactly what would get rid of the pain, but unfortunately, there hadn't been a drop of alcohol in sight. She had even raided the cafeteria's medicine cabinet, hoping to find some cough medicine. Instead, all she had found was a plastic bag full of red-and-white headache capsules. Now she wished she had taken several of them to stop this insistent banging in her head.

The girl named Alice sat quietly in the aisle seat beside her, but her eyes kept looking over at the young man who had helped Kathleen earlier in the cafeteria. Now she couldn't remember his name. Why did she have such a problem remembering names? Or was it just because too much was happening? Her eyes still stung. Her ears were still ringing with the memory of those insults, those verbal jabs. And, of course, the physical jabs—she could feel the bruises. She just wanted to forget. She just wanted to sleep, to pretend everything was okay. And maybe everything would be as soon as they got to Colorado.

She noticed Alice's glances getting longer, braver now that all the inside lights on the bus had been extinguished, except for the bright green floor tracking lights. "You like him, don't you?" she whispered to Alice.

"What?"

"The boy across the aisle that you keep looking at. Justin."

Even in the dim light, Kathleen could see Alice blush, the freckles even more pronounced.

"We're just friends," Alice said. "You know Father doesn't allow anything more. We must keep ourselves chaste and our bodies pure." It sounded like she was reading the words off a pamphlet.

"I think he's very nice." She ignored Alice's benediction and nodded her chin in his direction. "And quite handsome."

Another blush, but this time it came with a smile. "I think he's upset with me, but I don't know why."

"Did you ask him?"

"Yes."

"And what did he say?"

"He told me he was just tired. That everything was fine."

Kathleen leaned closer to the girl. "It's been my experience with men that they're just as confused as we are. If he says he's just tired, he may just be tired."

"Really? You think so?"

"Sure."

It seemed to bring the girl relief and she relaxed in her seat. "I was worried, because I really don't have very much experience with boys."

"Really? A pretty girl like you?"

"My parents were always very strict. They never even let me date."

"Where are your parents now?"

Alice got quiet, and Kathleen wished she hadn't pried.

"They died in a car accident two years ago. A month later, I went to one of Father's rallies. It was like he could see how lost and alone I was. I don't know what I would have done if I hadn't found the church. I have no other family." She was quiet for a while, then she looked at Kathleen. "Why did you join the church?"

Good question, she wanted to tell the girl. For the last twenty-four hours she had been asking herself that very same thing. She needed to remember all the good things she had found since joining, like self-respect and dignity. Things the alcohol had stolen from her. Yet, after tonight's humiliation… It was hard to think of anything except sleep.

"I'm sorry," Alice said. "You probably don't want to talk about stuff like that after tonight's meeting."

"No, it's okay." She wanted to tell the girl that she hadn't betrayed the church. That she hadn't told Maggie anything and she wasn't sure why Stephen thought she had. But she knew it wouldn't matter to Alice or probably any of the other members. Most of them were simply relieved they hadn't been the ones called up. "I suppose I was lost in a different sort of way," Kathleen finally said.

"You don't have any family, either, huh?"

"I have a daughter. A beautiful, smart, young woman."

"I bet she looks a lot like you. You're very pretty."

"Well, thank you, Alice. It's been a long time since someone has said that to me." Tonight she certainly didn't feel pretty.

"So why aren't you with your daughter?"

"We have a...well, a strained relationship. She's been angry with me for more years than I can remember."

"Angry? Why would she be angry with you?"

"Lots of reasons. But mostly because I'm not her father."

"What?"

She saw the confusion on Alice's face and smiled. "It's a long, boring story, I'm afraid." She patted Alice's hand. "Why don't you try to get some sleep?"

She rested her own head against the seat again, but now her mind was filled with thoughts about Maggie and thoughts about Thomas. Dear God, she hadn't thought of him in years. At least, not without getting angry all over again. Maggie still idolized the man. And Kathleen had promised herself years ago to never tell Maggie the truth about her father. So why had she? Why now after all these years?

She remembered the disbelief, the hurt on Maggie's face. The surprise when she slapped her. Those sad, brown eyes—they were the eyes of a twelve-year-old little girl who still loved her daddy so much. How in the world could she have tried to destroy that? And why would she want to? What was wrong with her? No wonder her own daughter didn't love her. Maybe she didn't deserve her love. But Thomas didn't, either.

Kathleen still remembered getting the phone call from the fire station in the middle of the night. The dispatcher had been calling in every available man to answer the three-alarm blaze. She had lied to the dispatcher and told her Thomas was upstairs, asleep. And then she had to call him. She hated that she knew exactly where he was. And she hated even more that she had to call him at that woman's apartment. But she had to. She had no choice but to call and give him the message, so that no one else would know the lie.

She had always imagined she had interrupted their lovemaking, their passionate sex-fests, which Thomas had told her she wasn't capable of. Maybe that was why she had spent the last twenty years trying to prove him wrong, sleeping with any man who wanted her, and unlike Thomas, there had been plenty of men who *had* wanted her. But back then, that particular day, she had vowed to herself that she wouldn't take it anymore, that she would take Maggie and leave. And then the son of a bitch had to go and get himself killed. Not only killed but made into a hero.

There had been many times she'd wondered what Maggie would think of her saintly, heroic father if she knew the truth. So many times in a drunken fit, she had come close to telling her. But somehow she had always managed to stop herself.

After Thomas's death, she had moved as far away as she could. It was part of the pact she had made with the devil, with the whore who claimed she was carrying Thomas's child. In order to keep Maggie from knowing the truth about her father, she had to also keep Maggie from knowing her half brother. At the time it seemed a small price to pay. It had seemed like the right thing to do. But now she wasn't sure.

The other day Maggie had been so angry, so unwilling to accept the truth about her father. Would she also not want to accept that she had a brother, a half brother who had been kept from her for all these years? Would she be too angry to believe?

The woman had even named the boy Patrick, after Thomas's brother who had been killed in Vietnam. Kathleen wondered if he looked like Thomas. He'd be a young man now—twenty-one years old, the same age Thomas was when they first met.

Kathleen felt a tap on her shoulder and looked up to find Reverend Everett standing in the aisle. He smiled at Alice, and then to Kathleen he said, "There are some things we need to discuss, Kathleen. Perhaps we can discuss them in my compartment."

She crawled over Alice and followed him to the small space at the back of the bus. Her knees were unsteady and her stomach tense. He hadn't said a word to her since her punishment ceremony. Was he still upset?

The compartment was small, with a bed that filled most of the area and a tiny bathroom in the corner next to a desk. She could hear the roar of the engines. He closed the door behind them, and Kathleen heard him turn the lock.

"I know how painful that was for you tonight, Kathleen," he said in such a soft, gentle voice that she immediately felt relieved. "I would have stepped in, but it would have looked as though I was playing favorites, and that would have only made it harder on you. I do care about you and that's why I'm willing to do this special favor for you."

He motioned for her to sit on the bed and make herself comfortable. Despite his soft and gentle voice, she saw a coldness in his eyes that she didn't recognize, that unnerved her. She sat, anyway, not wanting to make him upset, especially if he was willing to do some special favor for her. He had been so kind in the past.

"I'm very sorry," she offered, not knowing what explanation he hoped to receive. She knew he didn't like it when members made excuses, and no matter what she told him, he might misconstrue it as an excuse.

"Well, that's in the past. With my special graces, I'm sure you'll not betray us like that again."

"Of course," she said.

Then with that same cold look in his eyes, he began unzipping his pants while he said to her, "I'm doing this for your own good, Kathleen. Now you must take off all your clothes."

# CHAPTER 69

Gwen found Maggie down in her office, curled in the overstuffed chair, her legs thrown over an arm, a stack of files resting on her chest, her eyes closed. Without saying a word, she let go of Harvey's leash and gave him a pat on the hind end, telling him it was okay to go to his master. He didn't hesitate and didn't ask for permission to put his huge paws up on the chair to reach Maggie's face and begin licking.

"Hey, you!" Maggie grabbed the dog's head and hugged him. He jumped back when the file folders opened and the contents started sliding down on top of him. "It's okay, big guy," Maggie reassured him, but she was already out of her comfortable position and on her feet by the time Gwen came over to help pick up crime scene photos and lab reports.

"Thanks for bringing him," Maggie said. She stopped and waited until Gwen met her eyes. "And thanks for coming."

"Actually I was glad you called." The truth was Gwen had been surprised, not by the call but by the request. Harvey may have started out as a good excuse, but Gwen had heard the vulnerability in Maggie's voice immediately, long before her friend quietly told her, "I need you here, Gwen. Can you please come?"

Gwen hadn't hesitated. She had left linguine in a colander in the sink, a pot of homemade Alfredo sauce probably now congealing on a cold stove. She was out the door and in her car, heading for Quantico by the time Maggie finished giving her what scant details were available. "So what's the plan?" she asked. "Or do you even know?"

"You mean since I don't get to participate?"

Gwen studied her friend's eyes. There was no anger. Good. "You know it's best that you don't. You do know that, right?"

"Sure." But Maggie was watching Harvey investigate the corners of her office, pretending to be distracted by his curiosity. "Cunningham says the government has an informant. Someone who just recently came forward. He works in Senator Brier's office and he's also a member of Everett's church. His name's Stephen Caldwell."

Gwen helped herself to a Diet Pepsi from the minifrig in the corner of Maggie's office. She looked up at Maggie. "No Scotch?" Maggie smiled at her and held out her hand, so Gwen grabbed another Pepsi. "This informant," she said, "how do we know he's not double-crossing us, too? How do we know that he can be trusted?"

"I'm not convinced that he can be. For one thing, it may have been Caldwell who used his high-level security clearance to gain access to those retired weapons, the ones found at the cabin. But Cunningham tells me it was Caldwell who arranged my secret meeting with Eve." She saw Gwen's question before she asked. "Eve is an ex-member. I talked to her when you and Tully were in Boston."

"Ah, yes. Boston." Gwen felt uncomfortable at the mere mention of the trip, but Maggie didn't seem to notice. As far as Gwen knew, Maggie hadn't even heard about Eric Pratt's attempt on her life. No sense in bringing it up now. "If Caldwell has been stealing weapons and possibly leaking classified information to Everett, why is he suddenly willing to help the government?"

"Evidently, he's grown attached to Senator Brier and his family." Maggie wrestled a tennis shoe away from Harvey. "Ginny's murder shook up Caldwell's loyalties. He claims he's convinced Everett that they need to proceed to Cleveland, that Everett doesn't know about the arrest warrants, only about the negative media attention. Caldwell claims we can safely arrest Everett and Brandon in Cleveland at the prayer rally, in public with little resistance and no threat of Everett being able to stage a standoff. That Everett won't be expecting such a public arrest and will be taken completely by surprise."

"Wait a minute," Gwen interrupted. "If Everett didn't know about the warrants, then what about the dead bodies the FBI's Hostage Rescue Team found?"

"Cunningham said the unit announced themselves. Too many booby traps around the compound to sneak in. They think those left behind got scared, did the one thing they were prepared to do when the FBI came knocking at their door."

"Jesus! Are we sure they weren't in contact with Everett?"

"That we don't know for sure. But there wasn't a whole lot of time. It happened quickly."

"But what about Caldwell?"

"He was informed about the arrest warrants. He wasn't tipped off about the raid. It was meant to be a surprise. A surprise so no one would get hurt."

At this, Maggie avoided Gwen's eyes again. She noticed Harvey scooting under her desk and reached down, rescuing the tennis shoe's mate. She set the pair on the bookcase, out of his reach. The big dog sat and watched as if waiting for compensation. Gwen watched, too, quietly waiting for Maggie to continue. She knew the distraction was intentional. Maggie was doing an excellent job of giving her all the difficult details while sidestepping the subject of her mother. Even Gwen remembered the countless times Maggie had mentioned her mother's new friends, Emily and Stephen. This Stephen Caldwell had to be the same Stephen.

"And Caldwell's conflicted loyalties," Gwen finally said, "how do they affect your mother and her safety?"

"That I don't know. As far as we know, Caldwell is still with Everett. And so is my mother." She sat back down in the chair and Harvey went to her, laying his head in her lap as if this was an expected routine. Maggie absently petted him while leaning her head back into the soft cushion. "I tried to talk to her about Everett. We ended up…it was pretty awful."

Gwen knew to be quiet. Maggie had shared very little about her childhood, and what Gwen knew of Maggie and her mother's relationship came from hints, personal observations over the years and a few rare and accidental admissions from Maggie. She knew about the alcohol abuse and learned about the suicide attempts only after the fact, even though there had been several attempts within the time since Gwen and Maggie had become friends. But Maggie had kept her mother and their relationship off-limits, and whether it was right or wrong, Gwen had allowed it, hoping that one day Maggie would decide on her own to share that obvious struggle. Even tonight and under the present circumstances, Gwen expected little insight, little sharing. She leaned against the corner of Maggie's desk and waited, just in case.

"She always does and says such hurtful things," Maggie said quietly without moving her head from the back of the cushion, avoiding Gwen's eyes. "Not just to me but to herself. It's like she's been spending a lifetime trying to punish me."

"Why in the world would she want to punish you, Maggie?"

"For loving my father more than I love her."

"Maybe it's not you she's trying to punish."

Maggie looked up at her with watery eyes. "What do you mean?"

"Could be she's not trying to punish you at all. Did it ever occur to you that all these years she may have been trying to punish herself?"

# CHAPTER 70

*THURSDAY*
*November 28*
*Thanksgiving Day*
*Cleveland, Ohio*

Kathleen looked out over Lake Erie and for the first time in years found herself homesick for Green Bay, Wisconsin. An unseasonably warm breeze ruffled her hair. She wished she could forget everything and leave it all behind her like one more black mark in her past. She wished she could take off her shoes, run down to the beach and spend the rest of the day, the rest of the week, the rest of her life walking with no destination, no intention other than to feel the sand between her toes.

"Cassie will begin to lead the prayer rally," Reverend Everett said from behind her.

She looked over her shoulder without moving from her place in front of the open patio door. Reverend Everett had checked into a ritzy hotel in order to shower, shave and have access to a telephone to finalize their arrangements. Earlier, when she used the bathroom, Kathleen had been amazed at the wonderful luxuries: perfumed soaps, a shoe-shine kit, a real razor with a real blade instead of the disposable kind, a shower cap and even a jar filled with Q-Tips.

Now, while Stephen and Emily took notes and concentrated on everything Reverend Everett was telling the three of them, Kathleen stood quietly, enjoying the sunshine and the breeze.

She felt like she needed to learn how to breathe again after last night's humiliating ritual and then the cramped bus ride.

She hoped the fresh air and sunlight would help wipe away the feel of Everett's hot breath, the sounds of his grunts and groans while he thrust himself into her over and over again. When he was finished, he had pointed to her clothes, instructing her to get dressed with a coldness in his voice that she had never heard before. He had told her she needed this cleansing ritual in order for him to be able to trust her again.

Without a word, she had slipped her clothes on over her sticky flesh, the smell of his aftershave so pungent she wanted to gag. And as she left his compartment to return to her seat, she couldn't help thinking he had also cleansed her of every last remaining bit of her self-respect.

"The FBI will most likely be surrounding the park," Stephen said. "Father, you can't possibly think of showing up at the prayer rally."

"What time will the cargo plane be ready?"

"It's scheduled for a seven o'clock takeoff. We must be there early to board."

"How can we be certain the FBI won't be waiting at the airport?"

"Because I told them you would be at the rally. That you wouldn't expect an arrest in such a public arena. Even if they do suspect something, they might be waiting at the international airport. However, they won't even think to check a government relief-aid cargo jet leaving from Cuyahoga County Airport."

Reverend Everett rewarded Stephen with a smile. "Very good. You're a good man, Stephen. You will be justly rewarded when we get to South America. I promise you that."

The reverend sat down to finish the platter he had ordered from room service; a platter with several different cheeses, fresh fruits, shrimp cocktail and a loaf of French bread. He made no offer for the others to join him. Instead, Kathleen thought he looked as though he enjoyed having them watch him, and before he had even gotten started on this tray, he had called down to place a whole new order.

None of them had eaten since yesterday's lunch, and it was

almost dinnertime. Was this yet another important lesson, another important sacrifice that they were supposed to willingly accept? She turned back to the tranquil view of the water. At the moment, it seemed to be the only thing that didn't threaten to rip away at her sanity.

"You honestly don't intend to go to the rally?" Stephen asked again.

"I suppose I can stay here until it's time to leave." He waved a hand as if making do with his current surroundings. "But the three of you will need to be my eyes and ears at the rally. You'll need to gather those on the list when the time comes. Cassie will keep the rally going so as to give the appearance that everything is as scheduled."

Kathleen turned at this, stunned by the realization. "You don't want Cassie to come with us?"

The woman had attended to Reverend Everett's every command and probably desire for as long as Kathleen could remember.

"She's a lovely woman, Kathleen, but I'm quite certain there are many beautiful dark-skinned women in South America who would probably give anything to be my personal assistant."

She turned back to the sunshine, wondering if it would have been any different had they been able to go to Colorado. If Reverend Everett would have been any different. Or had he always been this way, and she was the one who was changing, who was seeing things differently?

"Now, you all must go," he said while still chewing. He took a drink of wine as if to cleanse his palate. It was certainly not to be polite, because he took a bite out of a huge strawberry, the juice dripping down his chin, his mouth full again as he said, "Go now. The rally will be getting started soon. No one will be suspicious if my faithful counsel is there waiting for me."

Stephen and Emily didn't hesitate. They waited at the door for Kathleen.

"Oh, Kathleen." Reverend Everett stopped her. "Find Alice

and send her up to my room. I have some things I need to discuss with her before the trip."

Kathleen stared at him for a minute. Did he honestly have something to discuss with the girl or did he have another of his cleansing rituals in mind? Did she dare say anything? Could she afford to make him angry with her again? Did she even care? She decided she would conveniently forget to tell Alice, but she nodded and followed Stephen and Emily out.

She slipped her hand into the pocket of her cardigan. She caressed the metal razor she had stolen from the bathroom. It gave her an odd sense of relief and calm to know it was there, a comfort as if it were an old friend. Yes, an old friend, this simple metal razor with the real metal blade.

This time she would finally get it right.

# CHAPTER 71

"Come in," Everett yelled, not even bothering to check whom he was allowing to enter his hotel room. Could it possibly be any easier?

He smiled and rolled the room service tray into the room. Then he waited. The excitement, the anticipation was better than any homemade concoction the Zulu tribe could brew. After all, this was the moment he had been waiting for all along. And so he stood patiently and waited as if expecting a tip.

Finally Everett turned, his hand ready to wave him away, when his eyes swept across his face, then back. A quick double take.

"You? What the hell are you doing here?"

"Thought I might bring you a treat, a surprise before your last rally."

"I would think you'd be down wandering around, looking for another young girl. Looking for ways to destroy me."

"I can't take all the credit."

Everett shook his head, discounting him, unafraid as if he were one of his ordinary followers. "Go away," he told him. "Go and leave me alone. I'm tired of your shenanigans. You're lucky to have gotten away with only warnings."

"Right. Only warnings. Is that because you wouldn't dare hurt your own son? Is that the only reason I've been so lucky?"

Everett stared at him. But there was no surprise. Had he known all along? No. It was impossible. It was simply another one of his performances.

"How did you find out?" His voice was calm, steady.

Oh, Jesus! He did know. Did it make this more difficult? Or no, it would make it easier. The bastard knew. All these years and he knew.

"She told you before she died," Everett said, as if he had

known all about it, as if her death was something he shared. He had no right and yet he continued, "I read about her death. I think it was in the *New York Times* or perhaps the *Daily News*. You know I did care about her. Did she tell you that, too?"

He wouldn't listen. It was lies. "No, she didn't tell me that. She managed to leave that part out of her journal." He needed to confine the anger, but the concoction had already begun to seep into his system, and Everett's words felt like hot, liquid lava scalding his brain, contaminating his memories. "But she did mention what you did to her. There are pages and pages about that. About what kind of a bastard you really are."

He felt his fingers twisting into fists. Yes, he'd let the anger fuel him. The anger and the precious words of his mother, that mantra he had memorized from her journal entries. Her words had empowered him throughout his mission. They wouldn't fail him now.

"I wondered when you would find out." Everett's voice still sounded too calm, not a hint of fear. "I knew it was only a matter of time. I thought perhaps that was what all this was about—all those young girls. You were trying to get back at me, weren't you?"

"Yes."

"You wanted to hurt me." Everett smiled as he gave him a nod of confirmation, almost acceptance, as if it was exactly what he had expected from a son of his. "Maybe you even wanted to punish me?"

"Yes."

"Destroy my reputation."

"Destroy you."

The smile disappeared.

"There's only one thing left now," he said, picking up the tray from the room service cart. He held it out to Everett, and with his other hand lifted the insulated cover. The tray was empty except for one small red-and-white capsule, sitting on a perfectly folded cloth napkin.

# CHAPTER 72

Justin looked for Father or even his henchmen. Already, the pavilion was jam-packed with giggling teenagers mixed in between the others, an odd assortment with little in common except that they all looked like lost souls. They were fucking pathetic, is what they were. Though he had to hand it to Father. There were plenty who looked like they would be ideal recruits and gullible donors.

He had spent the night on the bus trying to plot a strategy and the entire afternoon scoping out as much as he could see of Cleveland. Someone had told him that Edgewater Park was on the west side of Cleveland. There was a circular lot adjacent to the upper section of the park, overlooking the downtown area. Still, he had no idea where the hell he would go. All he knew was that he had to escape while the rally was going on. He'd need to find a way to duck out without Alice or Brandon noticing. Where he'd go seemed a small detail at the moment.

He dug his hands into both his jeans pockets and made sure the wads of bills hadn't disappeared. Then he pulled down the hem of his T-shirt to make sure the bulge couldn't be seen. He wasn't even sure how much he had taken.

While the men who were digging up the strongboxes hauled each box to the bus, Justin stole two fistfuls. He was in such a hurry, all he took time to do was open one of the boxes, reach in and grab and stuff his pockets. Later, he tried to pick out the mothballs and smooth the bills into a neat, folded wad. Then he helped the women at the bonfire, standing in the smoke so he would smell like burnt trash and not mothballs.

He couldn't help wondering what good the money would do

if he had no fucking place to go. He saw Cassie walking to the stage. She waved to the crowd, and the sight of the long purple choir robe she wore got them clapping. Soon she'd have them singing, too. This might be a good time.

Justin looked down at the bike trail and the beach below. There was a statue near the pavilion and some playground equipment. There wasn't much cover, all the trees were back behind. But he'd already checked. There was a six-foot fence on the other side of the trees, a dead end.

Down by the beach he could see a fishing pier and about ten boat ramps, all empty this time of year. He wondered how hard it would be to take a boat without anyone noticing. Except on the bus ride to the park, he thought he had noticed a Coast Guard station not far from here. Shit! This wasn't going to be easy.

"Hey, Justin." Alice waved to him as she weaved her way through the crowd to join him.

Shit! It just got harder.

"I've been looking for you." She smiled.

Why did she have to be so fucking pretty? And damn, she had on another tight sweater, this one blue, and he couldn't help noticing how fucking beautiful blue her eyes were.

"Why were you looking for me? Do you need something?" He needed to play out the role of complete asshole, or he'd never be able to pull this off.

The wounded look in those blue eyes just about ripped his heart out.

"No, I don't need anything. I just wanted to…you know, be with you. Is that okay?"

Shit! Double shit! He couldn't do this.

"Yeah, I guess," he said, and felt like he had just tossed away his entire plan.

"Hi, Alice, Justin." The woman named Kathleen squeezed through to get to them. Justin couldn't believe she remembered his name. She hadn't been in very good shape last night during their introductions. "I'm glad to see you kids together." She smiled at Alice, and Justin thought he saw Alice blush. Then suddenly, Kathleen looked sad, the smile replaced with almost a frown as she squeezed Alice's shoulder and said, "You kids take care of each other, okay? No matter what happens."

Then she left them, only she was headed in the wrong direction back toward the exit. Maybe she needed to use the rest room. Justin thought he had seen them back that way.

"She's really a nice woman. We talked about a lot of stuff last night," Alice said in her soft voice. "She helped me see a lot of things.'

"What kinds of things?" he asked, but his eyes were scanning the surroundings again, looking, hoping for a miracle.

"Things like how much you mean to me and how I don't want to lose you."

He stopped and stared at her. She reached for his hand and intertwined her fingers with his.

"I care about you, Justin. Please just tell me what I can do to make things right with us again."

God, her hand felt good in his, like it belonged. Was she being straight with him, or was this another of Father's tricks? Before he could say anything Brandon appeared from out of nowhere.

"Alice," he said, scowling down at their hands with some kind of power that made Alice pull hers away. "Father wants to see you before the prayer rally. You need to come with me."

She looked up at Justin, apologetic, almost pained. He immediately wondered if Father had yet another lesson for her. Nah, there wasn't much time. Cassie already had the crowd all revved up.

He watched Brandon lead Alice away, taking some weird shortcut up through the trees. What the hell was Father doing up there, anyway? Probably some strange ritual he does to prepare.

He scanned the crowd again. How much time did he have before Brandon, Alice and Father came back down? Could they see him from up above? Shit! He was fucked.

Then, just as he turned, he recognized a tall blonde at the

edge of the bike trail, waving at him. It took him a minute. He probably would have remembered who she was sooner if she was with her short, blond bookend. He smiled and waved, noticing that she was away from the stage and with an older woman who looked enough like her to be her mother. Maybe that meant they had come in a car.

He started toward them, feeling a surge of excitement again, starting to actually believe in miracles.

# CHAPTER 73

Tully tried to blend into the crowd. It took him a minute to pick out the plainclothes agents from the Cleveland field office. They were scattered throughout the park. If Everett expected to find the place crawling with men in black, he wouldn't be able to pick them out. All of them were in place, and they were ready. Tully knew most of the agents, though he could hardly recognize them in their ordinary, everyday disguises. He had worked with this group on plenty of cases before his transfer to the District. In fact, it felt comfortable being back home.

He looked for Racine and spotted her close to the rest rooms at the back exit of the park. He had to admit, in her baseball cap, worn blue jeans, a borrowed Cleveland Indians T-shirt and her leather bomber jacket, she looked like one of the locals, checking out the pavilion's excitement. No one probably even noticed her mumbling into the cuff of her jacket or the bulge at the back of her waistband. Whatever O'Dell's misgivings about Racine, the detective was doing a hell of a job. Maybe it was simply the threat of suspension or possible demotion. Chief Henderson was still adamant about a discipline review board. Perhaps Racine was trying to make up for past mistakes. Whatever it was, Tully didn't care. The important thing was that she not screw this up.

The prayer rally had started without Reverend Everett, but according to Stephen Caldwell, the good reverend would be here anytime now. Although none of them had seen Everett or even Caldwell, for that matter. In the meantime, a beautiful black woman in a purple choir robe had the crowd stomping, clapping and singing at the top of their lungs. Tully could barely hear the other agents, checking in. He tapped his earpiece just to make sure it was functioning properly.

"Tully," he heard Racine whisper in his right ear. "Any sign of him?"

"No, not yet." He glanced around just to make certain no one noticed he was talking to himself. "But it's early. Any sign of Garrison?"

There was a buzz, then, "I thought I saw him when we first got here. Not sure if it was him, though."

"Keep an eye out for him. He can probably lead us to the action."

Just then, he noticed the kid, the tall redhead, going up the hill on the opposite side from him. He had a girl with him, a girl with long blond hair. Immediately, he was reminded of Emma.

"Here we go," he said into his cuff. "Southeast end of the pavilion, headed for the trees on the hill. I'm going up. I'll wait for backup."

He glanced over at Racine, who seemed distracted, looking in the opposite direction toward the rest rooms.

"Is everyone clear?" Tully whispered to all the agents but meant it for Racine.

Hers was the only voice he didn't hear check in. And now he couldn't see where she went. Damn it! What the hell was she up to? He didn't have time to rein her in. The kid, Brandon, was already leading his next victim up into the trees. Tully squeezed through the crowd, not taking his eyes off the pair. He remained so focused that he practically slammed into an attractive blond woman without stopping. It wasn't until she grabbed his elbow that he turned back.

"R.J. What in the world are you doing here?"

"Caroline?"

Then Tully saw Emma and his stomach began to knot.

"What are you doing in Cleveland?" his ex-wife demanded.

"I'm here on business," he said quietly, trying not to draw attention. Caroline's face already sprouted lines of anger. Yet, all Tully could think about was getting his daughter as far the hell away from this park as he could.

"I just can't believe you'd pull a stunt like this," Caroline was saying now, but she was looking at Emma instead of him. "So is this the reason you wanted to come here tonight, because you knew your father would be here?"

Tully looked at Emma, and her face went red. He could be dense sometimes, but evidently, he knew his daughter better than her mother did. He knew Emma was here because of the athletic-looking young man beside her. The young man whose eyes had been darting around everywhere as if he wanted to be anyplace but here.

"Please, Caroline," he tried again, taking her by the elbow to lead her away from the crowd.

"You two think this is funny?"

"No, not at all." He kept his voice as calm as he could while trying to yell over the noise. "Can we talk about this later?"

"Yeah, Mom, you're really embarrassing me."

Tully glanced around, looking to see if anyone was watching them. But everyone seemed fixated on the stage. His eyes scanned the area, and suddenly he could no longer see Brandon or the girl. Jesus! It was happening.

He couldn't use his mike or Caroline would really blow his cover. Instead, he turned back to Emma and the young man, meeting the boy's eyes and addressing him more than Emma.

"Please, get out of this area now."

Then he left them, ignoring the new list of names Caroline called him in front of their daughter. He pushed through the crowd, whispering into his cuff to the others, letting them know what he was doing and trying to find out what the hell Racine was doing.

Again, she was the only one not to respond.

# CHAPTER 74

Kathleen checked all the bathroom stalls. Good. The place was empty. She wished she could lock the door. But there was no lock on the inside. No chair to shove against the handle. Maybe it wouldn't matter. She could hear the rally had already begun. Hopefully, she wouldn't be interrupted.

She starting filling one of the sinks with lukewarm water. The water kept stopping. One of those conservation faucets. Damn it! At this rate, it would take forever. She punched the "on" faucet again and laid out paper towels on the counter. Silly, really. Why would she need paper towels?

She reached into her pocket and pulled out the razor blade she had confiscated from Reverend Everett's hotel bathroom, a real razor with a real metal blade. Her fingers shook as she tried to pop the blade out of the razor. It took several attempts. Why couldn't she keep her fingers from shaking? This was ridiculous. It wasn't like it was her first time.

Finally!

She laid the blade carefully, almost reverently, on one of the paper towels. The stupid water had shut off again. Another punch. The sink would never fill at this rate. Maybe she didn't need it to. Maybe she didn't care whether it hurt or not. Maybe she just didn't care anymore about anything.

She glanced around the bathroom and stopped when she saw her reflection in the mirror, meeting her own eyes, almost afraid to look too closely. She didn't want to see the betrayal, the accusations, the guilt or even the failure. Because this time she had tried to make things work. She really had. She had stopped drinking. She thought she had found some sense of direction, some sense of self-respect. But she was wrong. She had even tried telling Maggie the truth, the painful truth that made her own daughter only hate her more. There was nothing left.

She picked up the razor between her thumb and index finger just as the bathroom door opened.

The young woman stopped when she saw Kathleen, letting the door slam shut behind her. She wore a baseball cap over short blond hair and a leather bomber jacket with blue jeans and old scuffed boots. She stood exactly where she stopped, staring at Kathleen and recognizing the object in her hand. But the woman didn't look surprised or alarmed. Instead, she smiled and said, "You're Kathleen O'Dell, aren't you?"

Kathleen's heart began pounding, but she didn't move. She tried to place the young woman. She wasn't a member of the church.

"I'm sorry," the woman said, stepping forward, then stopping abruptly when Kathleen shifted. "We've never met before." She kept her voice friendly and calm despite her eyes which kept darting to the razor blade in Kathleen's hand. "I'm Julia Racine. I know your daughter, Maggie. I can see the resemblance." She smiled again. "She has your eyes."

Kathleen felt the panic twisting in her stomach. Damn it! Why couldn't they all just go away and leave her. She gripped the blade tighter, felt it against her wrist, the sharp edge promising such warm silence, promising to shut off the throbbing in her head and plug up the hollow place deep inside her.

"Is Maggie here?" she asked, glancing at the door, almost expecting her daughter to come barging in to rescue her once again. Always the savior, pulling her up out of the darkness, even when Kathleen wanted, needed, longed for the darkness.

"No. Maggie's not here. She's back in the District." The woman, this Julia, looked unsure of herself now. Like maybe she shouldn't have told a truth when a lie would have sufficed. "You know I never got a chance to know my mother," she said, changing the subject quickly, but with such a smooth, steady voice that Kathleen didn't mind. She wasn't stupid. She knew what the woman was doing. But she was better at it than most.

Almost as if she had some experience with talking people down off ledges.

Is that what she was doing? Trying to talk her off this ledge? It only worked if the person wanted to be talked down. Kathleen glanced at her wrist and could see blood dripping where she had started to cut. She hadn't realized she had done that. She certainly hadn't felt it. It surprised her that it didn't hurt. Was that a good sign? That it didn't hurt? When she looked back up she saw the woman had noticed, too, and before Julia Racine could snap back to her professional calm, Kathleen caught a glimpse of something else in the woman's eyes. Something…maybe doubt, maybe fear. So she wasn't as cool and calm as she pretended.

"My mom," the woman continued, "died when I was a little girl. I remember things, you know, pieces of things, really. Like the scent of lavender. I guess it was her favorite perfume. Oh, and her humming. Sometimes I can hear her humming to me. But I never recognize the tune. It's soothing, though. Kinda like a lullaby."

She was rambling but still calm. It was distracting and Kathleen knew that was part of the game. It was a game, after all, wasn't it?

"You know, Maggie's really concerned about you, Kathleen."

She stared at her, but the blue eyes were strong, unflinching, no longer playing or maybe just very good at lying.

"She's so angry with me," Kathleen found herself saying without really meaning to.

"Just because we get angry with people we love, it doesn't mean we want them gone forever."

"She doesn't love me." She said this with almost a laugh, as if letting this Racine woman know that she could see through her lies.

"You are her *mother.* How could she not love you?"

"I've made it very easy. Believe me."

"Okay, so she's angry with you."

"It's more than that."

"Okay, sometimes she doesn't even like you very much. Right?"

Now Kathleen did laugh and nodded.

Julia Racine remained serious and said, "It doesn't mean she wants you gone forever."

When it looked like that sentimental stuff wouldn't work, the young woman smiled and added, "Look Mrs. O'Dell, I'm already in a shitload of trouble with your daughter. How 'bout giving me a break?"

# CHAPTER 75

Tully almost stumbled over a jacket.

*Jesus! He had already started.*

Darkness had just begun to take over, and up here in the trees, it was hard to see. He waited. He tried to slow down his pulse. He needed to give his eyes a chance to adjust. The moon cast some light, but it also added an eerie blue tint to shadows.

Tully held his breath. He got down on his knees. He couldn't hear with all the noise from below. Did that mean anyone up here couldn't hear him, either? He couldn't take any chances. He heard the other agents checking in, whispering their positions into his ear, but he couldn't answer them. He had to ignore them. But they knew that, and they were still getting into position. It was so quiet. What if he was already too late?

He pulled out his gun and started crawling on hands and knees. That's when he saw them, only twenty feet away. He saw them on the ground, scuffling. He was on top. She was fighting, struggling.

But it looked like they were alone. Tully carefully looked around, examining the surroundings. There was no one else. No other young men, waiting or guarding the area. No Reverend Everett. Or did that come later? Did the good reverend wait until the struggle was over? And could Tully wait? Jesus! He was ripping her clothes. There was a slap, a whimper, more wrestling. Did he dare wait for Everett to show himself? Could he risk it?

He thought he heard a belt buckle, maybe a zipper. Another whimper. He thought of Emma. This girl wasn't much older. His eyes searched the trees. Movement on the right. One of the agents moving in. But no Everett.

*Damn it!*

He couldn't see any glowing clothesline. No handcuffs. Maybe all that stuff was Everett's job. If he interrupted now?

This time she cried out and Brandon slapped her again.

"Shut the fuck up and hold still," he hissed at her.

Without hesitation, Tully was on his feet. In just a few rushed steps he had the barrel of his Glock pressed at the base of Brandon's head even before the boy had a chance to flinch.

"No, you shut the fuck up, you bastard," Tully yelled into his ear, so he wouldn't miss a word. "Game's over."

# CHAPTER 76

*Washington, D.C.*

Maggie drove down several unfamiliar streets but found the old building easily. It was an unsavory neighborhood where she'd probably need to worry about her little red Toyota. Three teenage boys watched her the entire time she parked her car and walked to the front door. It made her want to flash her holstered Smith & Wesson nestled under her jacket. Instead, she did the next best thing—she ignored them.

She wasn't sure why she was here, except that she was tired of waiting. She needed to do something, anything. She was just so tired of those old memories taunting her, making her feel guilty, that she was somehow responsible—once again—for her mother being in harm's way. She knew she wasn't responsible. Of course she knew that, but what she knew and what she felt were two entirely separate things.

The inside of the old building surprised Maggie. It was clean, better than clean, with the scent of Murphy's Oil. As she climbed the wooden staircase, she noticed the walls had been freshly painted and the second-floor landing's carpet, though threadbare, showed not a spot of dirt. On the third level, however, she could smell something like a disinfectant, and the odor grew as she progressed down the hall. It seemed to be coming from number five, Ben Garrison's apartment.

She knocked and waited, though she didn't expect him to be here. He'd still be in Cleveland, only hopefully this time he hadn't gotten to the crime scene before everyone else. Tully and Racine had probably already arrested Everett and his accomplice, Brandon. They had DNA to prove Everett's guilt, eyewitnesses and photos to put Brandon with two of the victims minutes before their deaths. Case closed. So what was still nagging her? Maybe she simply hated that Garrison—that the "invisible cameraman"—had gotten away with screwing up crime scenes. Maybe she was curious about his apparent obsession with death, his voyeurism. Perhaps she simply needed to keep her mind preoccupied.

Maggie glanced down the hallway and knocked again. This time she heard scuffles on the staircase. A little gray-haired lady appeared on the landing, staring up at her through thick glasses.

"I think he's out of town," she told Maggie. But before Maggie could respond, she asked, "Are you from the health department? I don't have anything to do with those roaches. I want you to know, it was his doing."

Maggie's suit must have looked official. She didn't say a word, and yet the woman was scooting in front of her to unlock Garrison's door.

"I try to keep the place clean, but some of these tenants... Well, you just can't trust people these days." She opened the door and waved a hand at Maggie as she headed back to the staircase. "Just close up when you're finished."

Maggie hesitated. What would it hurt to take a look?

The first thing to catch her eyes were the African death masks, three of them, on the wall over the cracked vinyl sofa. They had been carved from wood with paint-smeared tribal symbols across the forehead and cheeks and under the eyeholes. On the opposite wall were several black-and-white photographs, labeled portraits: Zulu, Three-Hill Tribe, Aborigine, Basuto, Andamanese. Garrison seemed obsessed with his subjects' eyes, sometimes cropping the forehead and chin in order to draw more focus to the eyes. A bottom photo, labeled: Tepehuane, showed what looked like the back of his subject's head, perhaps a defiant stance, a denial. One meaningful enough for Garrison to keep.

Maggie shook her head. She didn't have time to psychoanalyze Garrison, nor was she certain she would if she had the time. There was something odd about a man who could be so fascinated by ancient cultures and their people and yet stand back and watch young women be attacked in a public park. Or did Garrison consider everyone to be simply a photographic subject and nothing more?

At the police station, when she questioned him about the incident in Boston Common, he had said something strange about her having no idea what it took to stop or to make news happen. Yet, wasn't that exactly what he had been doing with Everett? His photos had broken the story about the church's members and their possible connection to the murder of the senator's daughter and the murder in Boston. But it went further than that. It was his photographs that caused Everett to initially even become a suspect. In a sense Garrison's photos had led them directly to Everett. He had made news happen.

Something skittered across the floor behind her. Maggie spun around. Three huge cockroaches escaped into a crack half their size under the kitchen counter.

*Damn it!*

She tried to settle her nerves. Cockroaches. Why did it not surprise her that Garrison would be surrounded by them?

But the landlady was correct in that Garrison's apartment did not match the spotless hall and the staircase, nor the rest of the aging but clean building. Discarded clothes trailed to the bedroom and bathroom. Crusty dishes and empty beer bottles littered the kitchen counter. Stacks of magazines and newspapers created leaning roach hotels in almost every corner. No, she shouldn't be surprised to see Garrison's roommates were cockroaches.

She wandered through the rooms, finding nothing interesting in his clutter. Although she wasn't sure what she expected to find. Suddenly, she stepped on a book that lay in the middle of the floor, as if someone had dropped it. The leather binding was clean and smooth. It was definitely not something he usually kept on the floor. On closer inspection she realized it was a journal, the pages filled with a lovely, slanted penmanship that sometimes took on a frantic urgency, easily visible by the dramatic changes in jagged lines and curves.

She picked it up and it opened to a page bookmarked with what looked to be an old unused airline ticket, the corners worn and creased. Destination was Uganda, Africa, though it certainly was long expired. The entry it marked was also dog-eared, the only page with its gold-trim creased.

"Dear son," the entry began, "this is something I could never tell you. If you're reading it now, it's only after my death, and I apologize that this is the manner in which I have resorted to tell you. A coward's manner—it would certainly embarrass any Zulu tribe member. Please forgive me for that. But how could I possibly look into your sad and already angry eyes and tell you that your father had brutally raped me? Yes, that's right. Raped me. I was only nineteen. It was my first year in college. I had a brilliant career I was preparing for."

Maggie stopped and flipped to the beginning of the journal, looking for a name, a reference to the owner, and finding none. But she didn't need a name. She already knew whose journal it was. It certainly couldn't be a coincidence. But how had Garrison come across the book? Where in the world had he found it? Among Everett's personal belongings, perhaps? Would Everett have kept the journal of a woman he had raped more than twenty-five years ago? And how would he have gotten it?

She slipped the book into her jacket pocket. If Garrison had stolen it, he couldn't mind her borrowing it. She was ready to leave when she noticed a small room off the kitchen. It wouldn't have attracted her attention except that a faint red light glowed from inside. Of course, Garrison would have his own darkroom.

No. She was wrong, she realized as she opened the door. It wasn't just a darkroom. It was a gold mine.

Prints were strung on a clothesline that stretched the length of the small room. Chemicals had been left in the plastic trays, lining the inside of an oversize sink. Bottles and canisters and developing tanks filled the shelves. And there were prints everywhere, overlapping one another and covering every bit of space on the walls and counter.

There were more prints of tribes doing their ceremonial dances. Prints of Africans with hideous scars. Prints of strange mutant frogs with legs coming out of their heads.

And then she saw them—prints of dead women.

There must have been about a dozen prints. Women naked and braced against trees, eyes wide open with duct tape across their mouths and their wrists handcuffed. Maggie recognized Ginny Brier, the transient they had found under the viaduct, the floater pulled from the lake outside of Raleigh and Maria Leonetti. But there were others. At least a half dozen others. All in the same pose. All with their eyes wide open, looking directly at the camera.

Jesus! How long had this been going on? And how long had Garrison been following Everett and his boys?

Her hand reached for the light switch without looking to find it. She couldn't take her eyes away from the dead women's eyes. Surely there was a light other than the red safelight. She found the set of switches and flipped one, causing the entire room to go black. But before she could flip the other one on, she stood paralyzed, staring in disbelief. The clothesline that stretched across the room glowed in the dark.

She leaned against the counter. Her knees went weak. Her stomach plunged. The clothesline glowed in the dark. Of course, what a perfect invention for a darkroom. What a perfect weapon for a killer.

How could she have been so stupid! Garrison didn't just photograph the dead women. It wasn't dead eyes that interested him. The eyes are the windows to the soul. Why hadn't she thought of it before? Was Garrison trying to photograph the fleeting soul?

She flipped on the red light again and took a closer look at the photos, the track marks on the victims' necks. Over and over again, he must have brought them back to consciousness, posing them, waiting, patiently waiting for that one moment while he watched with his camera ready on a tripod nearby, waiting. Waiting over and over again to catch a glimpse, to photograph that moment when the soul left.

Garrison. It was Garrison and his obsession with that last moment of death.

Maggie heard the creak of floorboards in the living room. She grabbed for her gun. No cockroach was that fucking big. Was it the landlady? Maybe the real health inspector had arrived. It couldn't be Garrison. He was in Cleveland.

She inched her way to the darkroom's door, edging along the counter. Another creak, this time louder, closer, just on the other side of the door. She took aim, holding the gun with both hands and ignoring the slight tremor in her knees. Then in one quick motion she kicked open the darkroom door and rushed out, pointing her gun and yelling "Freeze!"

It was Garrison.

He stood in the middle of his apartment over the frightened landlady, holding a length of clothesline around her neck, yanking on it like a leash. The old lady was on her small bony knees, gasping for air, her glasses gone, her eyes glazed over as her skeletal arms flayed and struggled against him. He seemed unfazed by it all as he looked up at Maggie. It was as if he didn't even notice Maggie's gun pointed at his chest. Instead, he held out his free hand and demanded, "If she doesn't have it, then you must. Hand over my mother's journal."

## CHAPTER 77

Tully had a bad feeling about this whole mess. Yes, they had caught a rapist, but had they caught a murderer? The kid, Brandon—the tough guy, the asshole who beat up and raped young girls—broke down into a sniveling crybaby when they arrested him for the murders of Ginny Brier and Maria Leonetti. But now, as he and several agents followed Stephen Caldwell into the hotel where Everett was supposedly staying, now Tully wasn't too sure anymore.

The desk clerk had given them a card key. No questions were asked when the badges came out. Caldwell claimed he didn't know why Everett hadn't shown up at the park. There was something in the polite black man's manner that told Tully he was lying through his teeth. It didn't help matters that Caldwell himself seemed in a rush to get somewhere when they finally found him outside the pavilion, gathering certain members together. No, Tully had a feeling this Caldwell, this stool-pigeon asshole, had his own agenda. Now he wondered if they were wasting time. If that was also Caldwell's agenda. Was the hotel a distraction? Was Everett on his way to some airfield?

The elevator opened at the fifteenth floor and Caldwell hesitated. Agents Rizzo and Markham gave him a shove, not even bothering to wait for Tully's instructions. They were pissed, too. None of them had to say a word to one another to know something was not quite right.

Caldwell hesitated again at the hotel room door, and Tully noticed the man's hand tremble as he missed the slot for the card key twice. Finally the door unlocked.

Rizzo and Markham had their weapons drawn but at their

sides. Tully gave Caldwell another shove for the man to go in ahead of them. He could see the perspiration glistening on his forehead, but Caldwell opened the door and entered.

Caldwell came to an abrupt halt, and Tully could see he was just as surprised as the rest of them. In the center of the room, Reverend Everett sat in a chair, his wrists handcuffed, his mouth taped shut and his dead eyes staring directly at them. Tully didn't need a medical examiner for this one. He recognized the pinkish tint to the skin and would need only one guess. Cause of death would be cyanide poisoning.

## CHAPTER 78

"Just let her go," Maggie said, not flinching, keeping the gun pointed directly at Garrison's head.

"You have the fucking book, don't you?" His eyes held hers while his hand tightened the noose around the old woman's neck. Maggie heard her sputter, and out of the corner of her eye she could see her bent and misshapen fingers clawing at the clothesline, clawing at her own neck.

"Yes, I have it." She wouldn't move, even to give him the book. "Let her go and I'll give it to you."

"Oh, right!" He laughed, but it was a nervous, angry laugh. "I let her go, you give me the book and we both just go our separate ways. What do you think! I'm some fucking idiot?"

"Of course not." A few more minutes and none of it would matter. The old woman was gasping, her fingers making a pathetic attempt. Maggie knew she could take him but it would need to be a head shot and there could be no missing. But then they'd never have all the answers.

"It makes sense now," she told him instead, hoping to distract him. "Everett's your father. That's why you wanted to destroy him."

"Not my father. Just a sperm donor," he said. Suddenly he yanked the woman up in front of him, as if only now realizing he needed a shield and taking away Maggie's clean head shot. "I can't do anything about biology, but I could make sure that fucker paid for what he did to my mother."

"And all those women," Maggie said calmly. "Why did they have to pay? Why did they have to die?"

"Oh, that." He laughed again and got a better twist on the

clothesline. "It was a study, an experiment…an assignment. You might say for the greater good."

"Like father, like son?"

"What the hell are you talking about?"

"Everett stole lost souls. You wanted to capture them, too. Only on film."

"We are nothing alike," he insisted, a rash of red spreading across his face and betraying his calm. She had struck a nerve.

"You're more alike than you want to believe." Maggie watched closely as he listened, his fingers forgetting as he did so. "Even your DNA was close enough to throw us off. We thought Everett killed those girls."

He smiled, pleased by this. "I really did have everyone fooled, didn't I?"

"Yes," Maggie said, playing along. "You certainly did."

"And I have photos of his unfortunate demise. Just got back from Cleveland with the exclusive." He waved a free hand at the duffel bag on the counter that separated the kitchen from the living room.

He pulled the old woman with him, getting close to the bag. She was breathing more steadily now. Garrison seemed unaware of the loosened noose as he tried to find his precious film. "Haven't decided yet who I'll give the exclusive to. Looks like it might be a bigger story than I thought. Especially now. Now that you're here. Now that you've changed everything."

He didn't seem angry about this. No, he seemed resigned. Perhaps he was just as happy to be caught, so that he could finally share all his illicit photos, all those horrible images, and get the credit, receive the fame—no matter what the cost—just to stroke his overactive ego. It wasn't that unusual. Maggie had known of other serial killers who purposely got caught, just to show off their handiwork, just to make sure they didn't go unrecognized.

She found herself releasing the tension in her arm. She kept the gun pointed at him, but her trigger finger relaxed. Garrison's mind was preoccupied, his only concern on the film, on his fame.

"Three fucking rolls in living color," he said, reaching into the duffel bag as if to show her, dragging the old woman with him.

She expected to see black film canisters. The pistol was in his hand and he fired before she could duck. It ripped through her shoulder, knocking her into the wall. She tried to regain her balance. Instead, she felt her body sliding down the wall. She couldn't move her arm. Tried to raise her gun. The arm and the gun wouldn't move.

Garrison was pleased.

"Yes, looks like I'll be very famous, indeed," he said, smiling. Then he shoved the woman aside and at the same time raised the gun.

"No!" Maggie screamed at him.

In one smooth, easy movement he shot the old woman. Her small body slammed against the wall with a sickening snap of bones and flesh as her body crumpled into a heap.

Maggie tried to raise her own gun again. Damn it! She couldn't feel her fingers. She couldn't even feel the gun. It was still gripped in her hand, but she couldn't feel it, couldn't move it. The bullet had paralyzed her arm from shoulder to fingers.

He came at her, his gun aimed at her chest. She needed to lift the goddamn gun. She needed to point, to squeeze, but her arm wasn't obeying. Just as she reached for her weapon with her left hand, Garrison was there, standing above her. His black boot kicked at her useless fingers, knocking the gun out and sending it skidding across the floor.

There was a stinging pain in the side of her neck, but still no feeling in her right arm. She could feel blood trickling down her sleeve and could see several spots on the floor. She still couldn't move the goddamn hand.

"Where's the book?" he said, standing over her. Then he saw it in her jacket pocket and pointed at it.

"You'll need to get it yourself," she told him. "I honestly can't move." She would make him get it. She still had one good hand. She could grab him, grab the gun.

But he didn't make a move toward her. In fact, he no longer

seemed to care about the precious book. He glanced back at the old woman, then looked around his apartment as if assessing the damage, as if trying to decide what his next move should be.

"You keep it," he said, to Maggie's surprise, and he went back to the kitchen counter, rummaging through his duffel bag. "Just remember it goes with the photos," he told her as he took out several black canisters and set them on the counter. "This can't be anything less than a front-page exclusive—above the fold, continued inside."

Then he started bringing out the rest, and Maggie's stomach took a plunge. Out came the handcuffs, duct tape, more clothesline, a camera and another collapsible tripod. She tried her feet. What the hell was he doing? She steadied herself and eased herself up, using the wall as an anchor and her good arm to balance her. Garrison swung back around, gun pointed and ready, stopping her in half-stance.

"It's best you stay right where you are," he said, grabbing the handcuffs. "Back down." He pointed to the floor, and moved in front of her, waiting as she eased her body down the wall.

He snapped the handcuffs on, pinching the wrist of her already wounded hand. And still she could not feel it. He shoved her shoulders against the wall, as if straightening her posture, carefully posing her with restrained hands in her lap. It was all a part of the staged look. He was preparing her for her own death photo.

He took the extra length of clothesline and bound her feet, pulling her legs out in front of her, safely away from her hands. Then he dropped three of the film canisters into her jacket pocket, so that now she had the film in one pocket and the book, his mother's journal, in the other.

"They'll be sending backup here any minute, Garrison," she told him, trying desperately to remember if she had told anyone about stopping at his apartment. But she hadn't. Not even Gwen. The old woman was the only one who knew.

"Why would you need backup?" He wasn't even concerned, almost humored by the idea. "You said yourself, everyone is convinced that Everett is the murderer. He and his accomplice Brandon. Poor boy. His Achilles' heel is that he doesn't know how to fuck a woman."

Garrison was back at the counter. He spoke with no sense of panic, no sense of urgency. Instead, he put the gun down and began assembling the tripod with careful, deliberate movements. "This isn't exactly what I had in mind," he said almost absently as if talking to himself now. "But what better way to go out than with one last hurrah."

She needed to do something. He was setting the tripod up five feet directly in front of her, just as he had done with each of his victims.

"Yes, you really did have us all fooled," she told him, hoping to get the attention of his overworked ego while she scanned the surroundings. Her gun lay against the opposite wall, about ten feet away. Too far away. With her hands in front—well, one good hand—she could grab something, anything and use it as a weapon. Her eyes searched. A lamp to her left. In the messy pile of clothing, a belt with a buckle. On the coffee table, some kind of African pottery.

Garrison snapped a new roll of film into the camera. Not much time. Damn it! She needed to concentrate. Needed to think. Needed to ignore the throbbing in her shoulder and the blood that continued to trickle down her sleeve. The camera was loaded. He began attaching it to the tripod and then unwinding some sort of cable, plugging one end in to the camera. A trip-cable, a release cable—that's what it was—so he could snap the picture from several feet away. He didn't need to be behind the camera, he didn't need to even touch the camera. He could be strangling her into unconsciousness while he shot the picture.

She shifted her back closer to the wall. How long would it take to bend her knees? To shove against the wall and get to her feet? Even with them tied together, she could do it. But how long would it take?

He was checking the camera's sight, tilting the tripod's platform to adjust the camera's angle. Maggie tried to ignore his preparations, his ritual, trying not to be alarmed by his calculating calm, by his steady and intent hands. Instead, her mind raced. Her eyes darted. Her damn arm throbbed and so did her heart, filling her ears with the constant thump, threatening to dismantle her thought process.

"I'll go down in history for sure," Garrison mumbled, adjusting shutter speed, assessing, then twisting the camera's lens. Focusing, making another change. Readjusting the aperture. Checking again, preparing.

Maggie edged her knees up toward her chest, quietly, slowly. Garrison was too involved to notice, at times his back to her, blocking her view of the camera. He seemed lost in his process. He was quickly becoming the invisible cameraman.

"No one has attempted this. A self-portrait along with a fleeting soul caught on film…all in the timing." His voice continued, his words becoming a sort of mantra of encouragement to himself. "And the angle," he said. "It's definitely the timing and the angle. Oh, yes, I'll be famous. That's for sure. Beyond my wildest dreams. Beyond my mother's dreams." He was caught up in the process, forgetting his victim, or rather reducing her to just another subject, waiting—hopelessly waiting to become a part of his bizarre process.

But Maggie wasn't waiting. She scooted her feet up, straining to be quiet, straining to pull them up as close as possible. Just a little more. Close enough. Yes, she could reach the clothesline. But not the knot. She shifted her weight and a pain shot through her arm, stopping her, almost bringing her to tears. Damn it!

She checked on Garrison. He was unwinding the cable, untangling it as he marched back to the counter. Jesus! He was almost ready. She tried for the knot again, her fingers reaching, her wrists scraping against the metal of the handcuffs. If she could get her feet free she might have some defense when he came at her, ready to strangle her. With the pain throbbing in her arm, she knew consciousness would be difficult to hang on to. She couldn't let him get that far. She couldn't let the clothesline even get around her neck, or else—or else she would be gone.

He stood at the counter, the air bulb of the release cable in one hand. Maggie watched him pick up the gun in his other hand. Her entire body froze. He wasn't going to use the clothesline. Was he actually considering the gun, instead?

He turned to face her. Her knees stayed at her chest. Her fingers stopped at the knot. It didn't matter that he noticed. It was too late. He was ready. And suddenly the rest of her body had become as paralyzed as her right arm. Even her mind came screeching to a halt.

Without a word he walked toward her, carefully dragging the cable. He stood directly in front of her, hovering over her, less than a foot away. He looked back at the camera, checking the angle. He readjusted the cable in his hand, positioning between his thumb and index finger the small plastic bulb—the gizmo that with one quick squeeze would click the photo.

He was ready.

"Just remember," he told her without taking his sight off the camera lens, "front-page exclusive."

Before she could move, before she could react, Garrison lifted the gun barrel to his right temple. Both hands squeezed, trigger and air bulb in morbid unison. Maggie closed her eyes to the spray of blood and brain matter, hitting her in the face, splatting against the wall. The sound of the camera's shutter got lost in the explosion of the gun. The smell of discharge filled the air.

When she opened her eyes, it was just in time to see Garrison's body thump to the floor in front of her. His eyes remained open. But they were already empty. Ben Garrison's own soul, Maggie decided, had left long before this, long before his death.

# EPILOGUE

*MONDAY*
*December 2*
*Washington, D.C.*

Maggie waited outside the police chief's conference room. She leaned her head against the wall. Her neck still ached, even more than the shoulder she had in a sling. Tully sat quietly next to her, staring at the door as though willing it to open, ignoring the newspaper he had spread out on his lap. The front-page headline of the *Washington Times* spoke of yet another new and improved piece of airport security equipment. Somewhere below the fold was a sidebar story about a photojournalist's suicide.

Tully caught her glancing at the newspaper. "*Cleveland Plain Dealer* kept Everett's suicide below the fold, too," he said, as if reading his partner's mind. "Probably would have made top headlines if there had been photos to go along with the stories."

"Yes." Maggie nodded. "Too bad there were no available photos."

He gave her one of his looks, the raised brow and the unconvincing frown. "But there *were* photos."

"Unfortunately, they're considered evidence. We certainly can't release photos that are considered evidence, right? Aren't you always trying to get me to play by the rules?"

At this, he smiled. "So this evidence is being stored in a proper place?"

She simply nodded again, sitting back and adjusting her sling. It was her own personal attempt at justice—that Ben Garrison's horrifying images would not win him the notoriety he so longed for. A notoriety that he had become so obsessed with that he had even been willing to include himself as one of those horrifying images.

"Have you heard from Emma?" Maggie asked, a transparent attempt at getting Tully to put an end to the subject of evidence, of photos and film canisters that remained safely stashed in her file cabinet back at her Quantico office.

"She's staying an extra week with her mom," he answered, folding the newspaper and willingly abandoning the subject along with the newspaper next to a pile of outdated *Newsweek*s on the table beside him. "She invited Alice to stay with them. She wanted to invite Justin Pratt, too."

"Really? What did Caroline have to say about that?"

"I don't think Caroline would have cared. The house is huge, but I said no boys allowed." He smiled as if he was glad he had some say. "Didn't really matter, though. As soon as Justin heard about Eric, he wanted to be in Boston."

"So there are actually some happy endings to this, after all?"

As the words left her mouth, Maggie saw her mother coming down the hall. She was dressed in a conservative brown suit, wore heels and makeup and was drawing a few looks from police officers in the hall and doorways. Her mother looked good, in control, not at all like some lost soul, and yet Maggie felt her muscles tense and her stomach knot.

"Hello, Mrs. O'Dell," Tully said, standing. He offered her his chair and she sat next to Maggie with only a nod to her daughter and a quiet "thank you" to Tully.

"I think I'm gonna get some coffee," Tully said. "Can I get a cup for either of you?"

"Yes, please," Kathleen O'Dell said with a smile. "With cream."

He was waiting. "Maggie? How 'bout a Diet Pepsi?"

She glanced up at him and shook her head, but caught his eyes to show him she appreciated the gesture. He simply nodded and started down the hall.

"I'm not sure why you're here," Maggie said, looking straight ahead, following her mother's lead.

"I wanted to be here to put in a good word." Then as if she

remembered something, she set her purse on her lap, opened it and removed an envelope. She hesitated, tapping it against her hand. She set the purse back down. More tapping. Then she handed the envelope to Maggie with only a glance.

"What's this?"

"For when you're ready," her mother said in a soft, gentle voice that made Maggie look over at her. "It's his name, address and phone number."

The knot in Maggie's stomach twisted even tighter. She looked away and laid the envelope in her lap. She wanted to hand it back and forget about it. And yet at the same time, she couldn't wait to open it. "What is his name?" she asked.

"Patrick." Her mother managed a smile. "After Thomas's brother. I think your father would have liked that."

The door opened, startling both women. Chief Henderson held it open while Julia Racine stepped out, her face immediately showing surprise at seeing Maggie and her mother. Today the detective wore a well-pressed navy suit and heels, her blond hair tamed and styled. She was even wearing lipstick.

"Agent O'Dell? Mrs. O'Dell?" Racine made an effort to hide her astonishment and be polite. Maggie couldn't help thinking the detective would have felt more comfortable asking what the hell the two of them were doing. But Racine was on her best behavior this morning. She had better be. Henderson wasn't taking any of these discipline hearings lightly.

"We'll hear from you first, Agent O'Dell," Henderson said, still holding the door, waiting.

Maggie could feel Racine watching, wondering whose side she would take. She stopped in front of her, met Racine's questioning eyes and said, "You mind keeping my mom distracted, just one more time?"

She waited for Racine's smile, then she walked past Chief Henderson and into the conference room.

# AT THE STROKE OF MADNESS

This book is dedicated to
Amy Moore-Benson,
who believed and coached and encouraged
and never gave up on me.

And to
Deborah Groh Carlin,
who listened and inspired and cared
and never allowed me to give up on me.

# CHAPTER 1

*Saturday, September 13*
*Meriden, Connecticut*

It was almost midnight, and yet Joan Begley continued to wait.

She tapped her fingernails on the steering wheel and watched for headlights in her rearview mirror. She tried to ignore the streaks of lightning in the distance, telling herself the approaching storm was headed in the other direction. Occasionally, her eyes darted across the front windshield. She barely noticed the spectacular view of city lights below, more interested in getting a glimpse in the side mirrors, as if she could catch something the rearview mirror may have missed.

"Objects may be closer than they appear."

The print on the passenger-side mirror made her smile. Smile and shiver at the same time. Not like she could see anything in this blasted darkness. Probably not until it was right on top of her car.

"Oh, that's good, Joan," she admonished herself. "Freak yourself out." She needed to think positively. She needed to keep a positive attitude. What good were all her sessions with Dr. Patterson if she threw out everything she had learned so easily?

What was taking him so long? Maybe he had gotten here earlier and had given up on her. After all, she was ten minutes late. Not intentionally. He'd forgotten to mention the fork in the road, right before the final climb to the top. It had taken her on an unexpected detour. It was bad enough that it was pitch dark up here, a canopy of tree branches overhead so thick even the moonlight couldn't penetrate it. What moonlight was left. The thunderheads would soon block out, or rather they would replace, the moonlight with what promised to be a hell of a lightning show.

God, she hated thunderstorms. She could feel the electricity in the air. Could almost taste it, metallic and annoying, like leaving the dentist with a fresh filling. And it only added to her anxiety. It pricked at her nerves like a reminder that she shouldn't be here. That maybe she shouldn't be doing this… that she shouldn't be doing this, again.

Those stupid, distracting thunderclouds had even caused her to lose her sense of direction. Or at least that's what she was blaming, though she knew full well all it took was getting into a rent-a-car. As soon as she closed the car door her ability to tell direction flew right out the window. It didn't help matters that all these Connecticut cities were made up of streets that ran every which way except at right angles or in straight lines. She had gotten lost plenty of times in the last several days. Then tonight, on the entire trip up here, she kept taking wrong turns, despite telling herself over and over that she would not, could not, get lost again. Yet, if it hadn't been for the old man and his dog, she would have been driving around in circles, looking for the West Peak.

"Walnut hunting," he had told her, and she hadn't thought anything of it at the time, because she was too anxious, too preoccupied. Now, as she waited, she remembered that he wasn't carrying a bag or bucket or sack. Just a flashlight. Who went walnut hunting in the middle of the night? Odd. Yes, there had been something quite odd about the man. A lost, faraway look in his eyes, and yet he didn't hesitate in giving her animated directions to the top of this wind-howling, branch-creaking, shadowy ridge.

Why in the world had she come?

She grabbed her cell phone and punched in the number from memory, crossing her fingers, only to be disappointed when the voice-messaging service picked up after the second ring. "You've reached Dr. Gwen Patterson. Please leave your name and phone number and I'll get back to you as soon as possible."

"As soon as possible might be too late," Joan said in place of a greeting, then laughed, regretting the words because Dr. P. would try to read between the lines. But then wasn't that what she was paying her the big bucks for? "Hey, Dr. P., yes, it's me again. Sorry to be such a pain in the ass. But you were right. I'm doing it again. So no, I guess I haven't learned my lesson, because here I am in the middle of the night, sitting in my dark car and waiting for…yeah, you guessed it, a man. Actually Sonny is different. Remember I told you about him in my e-mail? We've been getting together to talk, just talk. At least so far. He really does seem like a nice guy. Definitely not my type, right? Not like I'm a good judge of character when it comes to men. For all I know he could be an ax murderer, huh?" Another forced laugh. "Look, I was just hoping. I don't know. Maybe I was hoping you would talk me out of this. Save me from…oh, you know… Save me from myself, like you always do. Who knows, maybe he won't even show up. Anyway, I'll see you Monday morning for our usual rendezvous. You can yell at me then. Okay?"

She hung up before the string of prerecorded options, one of which would have allowed her to review her message, revise it or even delete it. She didn't want to be faced with any more choices, not tonight. She was sick and tired of making decisions. That's all she had done the last few days: The Serenity Package or the Deluxe-in-case-you're-feeling-guilty Premium Package? White roses or white lilies? The walnut casket with brass trim or the mahogany with silk lining?

Good heavens! Who would have thought there were so many stupid decisions involved in burying someone?

Joan tossed the phone into her bag. She drew her fingers through her thick blond hair, batted impatiently at damp strands to push them off her forehead. She glanced in the rearview mirror, turning on the overhead light to get a look at her dark roots. She needed to take care of those soon. Being a blonde sure took a lot of work.

"You've become high maintenance, girlfriend," she told the eyes in the mirror. Eyes she hardly recognized some days with new ravens cutting into what were once cute little laugh lines. Would that be her next project? A part of the new image she was creating for herself? God! She had even visited a plastic surgeon. What was she thinking? That she could re-create herself like one of her sculptures? Mold a new Joan Begley out of clay, dip it in brass, then solder on a couple of new attitudes while she was at it?

Maybe it was hopeless. Yet she did seem to be gaining control over the yo-yo dieting. Okay, *control* might not be the right word, because she wasn't totally convinced she did have control, but she had to admit that her new body felt good. Really good. It allowed her to do things she could never do before. She had more energy. Without the extra weight she could get back to maneuvering around her metal sculptures and didn't get winded every five minutes, waiting like her blow torch for more fuel to pump through before she could get going again.

Yes, this new slender self had an impact on her work, too. It made her feel like she had a whole new lease on work, on life. So why in the back of her mind was she unable to stifle that damn annoying little voice, that constant nag that kept asking, "How long will it last this time?"

The truth was, no matter how wonderful things were, she didn't trust this new person she was becoming. She didn't trust it like she didn't trust sugarless chocolate or fat-free potato chips. There had to be a catch, like a bad aftertaste or chronic diarrhea. No, what it came down to was that she didn't trust herself. That was it. That was the real problem. She didn't trust herself and that was what got her into trouble. That was what had brought her to the top of this ridge in the middle of the fricking night, waiting for some guy to make her feel good, to make her feel—Jesus, she hated to admit it—waiting for some guy to make her feel complete.

Dr. P. said it was because she didn't think she deserved to be happy. That she didn't feel worthy, or some psychobabble crap. She had told Joan over and over again that it didn't matter that there was a new improved exterior as long as the old interior didn't change.

God! She hated when her shrink was right.

She wondered if she should try calling her again. No, that was ridiculous. She glanced at the rearview mirror. He probably wouldn't show up, anyway.

Suddenly Joan realized she was disappointed. How silly was that? Maybe she really did think this guy was different. He was different from her regular fare—quiet and shy and interested. Yes, actually interested in listening to her. She hadn't imagined that part. Sonny did seem interested, maybe even concerned about her. Especially when she gave him that load of bull about her weight problem being caused by a hormone deficiency, like it was something out of her control that made her overeat. But instead of treating it like the gutless excuse it was, Sonny believed her. He *believed* her.

Why kid herself. That's why she was up here in the middle of nowhere, waiting in the dark. When was the last time a man had taken an interest in her? A real interest in her and not just in her new slender exterior with the artificial blond hair?

She shut off the overhead light and stared out at the city lights below. It was quite beautiful. And if she would relax, she might be able to see that it was quite romantic, despite that annoying rumble of thunder. Was that a raindrop on the windshield? Great! Wonderful! Just what she needed.

She tapped her fingernails on the steering wheel again and went back to her vigil, checking the side mirrors, then the rearview mirror.

Why was he so late? Had he changed his mind? Why would he change his mind?

She grabbed her handbag and searched inside, digging to the bottom until she heard the crinkle. She pulled out and ripped open the bag of M&M's, poured a handful and began popping them, one after another, into her mouth, as if they were Zoloft tablets, expecting the chocolate to calm her. It usually worked.

"Yes, of course, he'll come," she finally announced out loud with a mouthful, as if the sound of her voice was necessary for confirmation. "Something came up. Something he had to take care of. He's a very busy guy."

After all he had done for her in the last week.... Well, surely she could wait for him. She had been kidding herself to think that losing Granny hadn't had a tremendous impact on her. Granny had been the only person who truly understood and supported her. She was the only one who had stood up for her and defended her, insisting Joan's predicament of still being single and alone at forty was due to her independent nature instead of just being pathetic.

And now Granny, her protector, her confidant, her advocate, was gone. She had lived a long and wonderful life, but none of that could fill the void Joan was feeling. Sonny had been able to see that loss in her, that void. He had gotten her through the last week, allowing and encouraging her to grieve, even encouraging her to "rant and rave" a little.

She smiled at the memory of him, that serious look creasing his forehead. He always looked so serious, so in control. It was strength and a sense of authority that she needed in her life right now.

Just then a pair of headlights magically appeared as if they were her reward. She watched the car weave through the trees. It rounded the twists and curves with a smooth, steady ease, finding its way to this hideaway far above the city as if the driver knew the dark road. As if the driver came here often.

She felt an unexpected flutter in her stomach. Excitement. Anxiety. Nervous energy. Whatever it was, she chastised herself. Such emotions befitted an immature schoolgirl and not a woman her age.

She watched his car drive up behind her, feeling on the back of her neck the startling, powerful glare of his headlights as though they were his strong hands, hands that sometimes had just the slightest scent of vanilla. He said the vanilla removed the other pungent odors he worked with on a regular basis. He had said it as if embarrassed by it. She didn't mind. She had come to like that scent. There was something comforting about it.

The thunder rumbled overhead now and the droplets grew in number and size, splatting on the car's windows and blurring her vision. She watched his shadow, a hat-brimmed, black silhouette, get out of the vehicle. He had cut the engine but left on the headlights, making it difficult for her to see him against the glare and through the wet splotches.

He was getting something out of the trunk. A bag. A change of clothes? Perhaps he had brought her a going-away gift? The thought made her smile again. But as he approached, she noticed the object was long and narrow. Something he could carry by a handle…a duffel bag, perhaps?

He was almost at her car door. In a flash of lightning she caught a glimpse of metal. She recognized the chainlike mechanism around a blade. She saw the dangling pull cord. She had to be wrong. Maybe it was a joke. Yes, a joke. Why else would he bring a chain saw?

Then she saw his face.

Through the flickering lightning and now a steady rain, his features looked dark and brooding. He stared at her from under the hat's brim. He wore an angry scowl, piercing eyes she didn't recognize, eyes that held hers despite the rain-streaked glass between them. There was something wrong, horribly wrong. He looked as though he were possessed.

Joan's mind scattered into fragments as panic took hold of her. He stood at her car door, staring in at her. A clap of thunder startled her, making her jump and sending her body—like electric shock treatment—into action. Instinctively, her hand flew to the locks. Her fingers fumbled in the dark, searching, feeling, racing. Her heart throbbed in her ears. Or was that more thunder? Her fingers pushed, punched, clawed at buttons. A wheeze as the glass lowered. The wrong button—damn rent-a-car—and she punched again.

Oh, Jesus! Too late.

He was pulling the car door open. The car's dinging sound joined the tap-tap-tapping of the rain. That annoying dinging sound, warning her that the keys were still in the ignition, warning her that it was too late.

"Good evening, Joan," he said in his gentle tone, but now combined with the scowl on his face, it only seemed to telegraph his complete madness. That was when Joan Begley realized no one would hear her rant and rave this time. No one would hear her final scream.

# CHAPTER 2

*Monday, September 15*
*Wallingford, Connecticut*

Luc Racine pretended it was a game. That was how it had started a couple of months ago. A silly guessing game that he played with himself. Except now, standing in his stocking feet at the end of his driveway, he stared at the plastic-encased newspaper on the ground as if it were a pipe bomb left just to trick him. What if today was the day? What if he got it wrong today? What the hell would it mean?

He turned around, full circle, to see if his neighbors were watching. Not an easy task for any of them. From atop his lane, Luc could barely see their houses, let alone their windows, well hidden by thick foliage. The sun, which had just broken free over the mountain ridge, couldn't penetrate the thick canopies created by huge oak and walnut trees along Whippoorwill Drive. And it was impossible to see anything up or down the lane, even cars, which were there one second and gone the next.

The road twisted and curved—surrounded by trees and vines on both sides and sometimes twisting together overhead—showing only the next fifty feet, if that. It took anyone who drove it on a winding roller-coaster ride, climbing and climbing, only to send drivers plunging down and around ninety-degree corners. Like some ancient NASCAR track, it could be three to four seconds of exhilaration, shoving your stomach up into your throat while your foot hovered over the brake pedal. The beautiful surroundings, as well as the dramatic plunge, literally took your breath away. It was one of the things Luc Racine loved about this area, and he told anyone who would listen. Yes, they had it all, right here in the middle of Connecticut: mountains, water, forest and the ocean minutes away.

His daughter often ribbed him, saying that he could be "a fucking ad for the tourism department." To which he gave his usual answer, "I didn't raise you to swear like a sailor. You're not too big I can't still wash your mouth out with soap."

He smiled, thinking about his little girl. She did have a mouth on her, more so now that she was a big-shot detective in…blast it! Why couldn't he remember the city? It was easy. It was where all the politicians were, the White House, the president. It was on the tip of his tongue.

Just then he realized he was almost all the way to his front door and both his hands were empty.

"Shoot!" He looked back down the lane. The newspaper lay exactly where the carrier had tossed it. How in the world could he guess what day it was if he couldn't remember to pick up the stupid newspaper? That couldn't be a good sign. He dug a small notepad and pen out of his shirt pocket, jotted down the date—or at least, the date he believed it to be—and wrote, "Walked to end of lane and forgot newspaper."

As he put the notepad back he noticed he had buttoned his shirt wrong—two buttons off this time. He loved his cotton oxford-cloth shirts—short sleeves for the summer, long for the winter—but unfortunately, they would need to go. And as he padded out to the end of the lane he tried to envision himself in a T-shirt or polo shirt, untucked over his trousers. Would it look silly with his black beret? And if it did, did he care?

He scooped up the *Hartford Courant,* pulled it out of its plastic bag and unfolded it, swinging it open like a magician. "And the date today is…yes, Monday, September 15." Pleased, he folded it without glancing at a single headline and tucked it under his arm.

"Hey, Scrapple," he yelled to the Jack Russell terrier coming out of the woods. "I got it right again." But the dog paid no attention, focusing instead on the huge bone he had in his mouth, losing what looked to be a balancing act as he half carried, half dragged his prize.

"One of these days, Scrap ole boy, those coyotes are going to catch up with you for stealing their kill." Just as Luc said it, a loud noise came from the other side of the woods, sounding like metal slamming against rock. Startled, the dog dropped the bone and raced to Luc's feet, tail between his legs as though the coyotes *were* coming.

"It's okay, Scrapple," Luc reassured the dog as another slam shook the earth. "What the hell?"

Luc headed down the footpath that led into the woods. There was about a quarter of a mile of trees and brush that separated his property from what had once been a working rock quarry. The owner had gone out of business years ago, deserting the place, leaving behind equipment and piles of rock waiting to be crushed and hauled away. Who'd have guessed that the precious brownstone would someday not be able to withstand all the gas emissions of New York City?

Someone had started using the secluded quarry as a free dumping ground. Luc had heard that Calvin Vargus and Wally Hobbs had been hired to remove the garbage and clean up the area. So far, Luc had only seen additional huge yellow equipment parked alongside the old rusted stuff. He remembered thinking that perhaps Vargus and Hobbs—or Calvin and Hobbs as many of the townspeople called them—had taken advantage of using the quarry for safe, private and cheap equipment storage.

Now on the other side of the trees, Luc could see the earthmover with its heavy bucket shoving rocks the size of Rhode Island from side to side. He had forgotten how secluded the area was and could barely see the one dirt road through the woods that acted as the only opening. Otherwise, this overgrown pasture was completely boxed in by a stripped mountain, bled of its precious brownstone on one side and thick with woods on the other three sides.

He recognized Calvin Vargus at the monster machine's controls inside the open-air cab. He could see Calvin's bloated forearms shove and grab and pull at the levers, making the machine's bucket scoop up rock like a giant mouth. Another lever shoved forward and the huge yellow body twisted to one side and spit out the rock with a slam and thump.

Calvin's head bobbed, the orange baseball cap shielding his eyes from the morning sun, but he still caught a glimpse of Luc and waved. Luc waved back and took it as an invitation for a closer inspection. The machine drummed in his ears. He could feel its vibration all the way from his toes to his teeth. It fascinated Luc. It scared the dickens out of Scrapple. What a wuss. Stealing bones from coyotes and yet here he was scared by a little noise, following close behind Luc, bumping his nose into the back of Luc's leg

The machine's giant yellow mouth took another bite of rock and debris—debris that looked to be part crushed rock, part brush and garbage. This time a discarded rusted barrel broke free and came rolling down the pile of boulders. It crashed against the sharp rock edges, splitting open and sending the lid flying like a Frisbee.

Luc watched the lid, amazed by its speed and distance, so that he only saw the spilled contents out of the corner of his eye. At first he thought it was old clothes, a bunch of rags. Then he saw an arm and thought maybe a mannequin. It was a garbage dump, after all.

Then he noticed the smell.

It wasn't what ordinary garbage smelled like. No, it smelled different. It smelled like…it smelled like something dead. It didn't really scare him until Scrapple began to howl, an uncontrollable, high-pitched howl that broke through the noise of the equipment and sent a chill up Luc's spine.

Calvin stopped the bucket in midair. He cut the engine. And suddenly, Scrapple's howl came to an abrupt stop, too, leaving an unsettling silence. Luc could see Calvin push back his cap. He glanced up at the big man who now sat paralyzed in the cab. Luc stood still.

The vibrations from earlier seemed to be replaced by throbbing in his ears. Only now did Luc realize the throbbing wasn't the aftereffects of the equipment. The throbbing was his own heart pounding, hammering so hard he could barely hear the geese overhead. There were dozens of them, a flood of squawking as they made their daily pilgrimage to or from the McKenzie Reservoir. In the distance he could hear the hum of rush-hour traffic on I-91. All the routine sounds of an ordinary day.

An ordinary day, Luc thought as he watched the morning sun peek through the trees and highlight the bluish-white flesh that had spilled from the fifty-five-gallon barrel. Luc caught Calvin's eyes. He expected to see his own panic mirrored on Calvin's face. And there may have been a little panic, maybe even a little disgust at the sight. But what struck Luc Racine as odd was what he didn't see. What Luc didn't see on Calvin Vargus's face was surprise.

# CHAPTER 3

*The FBI Academy*
*Quantico, Virginia*

Maggie O'Dell reached for the last doughnut, a chocolate-frosted number with bright pink and white sprinkles, and already she heard a "tsk-tsk" sound scolding her. She glanced over her shoulder at her partner, Special Agent R. J. Tully.

"That's what you're having for lunch?" he asked.

"Dessert." She added a cellophane-wrapped platter of one of the cafeteria's daily specials. Something listed on the chalkboard as a "tacorito" supreme. Maggie couldn't help thinking even the FBI couldn't screw up something as good as Mexican food.

"Doughnuts are not dessert," Tully insisted.

"You're just jealous because it's the last one."

"I beg to differ. Doughnuts are breakfast. Not dessert," he told her as he held up the line, waiting for Arlene's attention behind the counter, waiting for her to put down the steaming hot-out-of-the-oven pot of creamed corn, before he pointed to the roast beef. "Let's ask the expert. Doughnuts are breakfast. Wouldn't you agree, Arlene?"

"Sweetie, if I had Agent O'Dell's figure you'd see me eating doughnuts at every meal."

"Thank you, Arlene." Maggie added a Diet Pepsi, then indicated to the cashier, a little mole-faced woman she didn't recognize, that she'd pay for the tray coming behind her, too.

"Wow!" Tully said when he noticed her generosity. "What's the special occasion?"

"Are you saying I never buy unless there's a special occasion?"

"Well, there's that…that and the doughnut."

"Couldn't it be that I'm having a great day?" she said while leading him to a table next to the window. Outside on one of Quantico's many running trails, a half-dozen recruits were finishing their daily run, weaving through the pine trees single file. "Classes just ended for this session. I have no nightmare cases keeping me awake nights. I'm taking a few days off for the first time in…oh, about a hundred years. I'm actually looking forward to working in my garden. I even bought three dozen daffodil bulbs to add to the southwest corner. Just Harvey and me, enjoying this amazing fall weather, digging in the dirt and playing fetch. Why wouldn't that put me in a good mood?"

Tully was watching her. Sometime around the daffodil bulbs she realized he wasn't convinced. He shook his head and said, "You never get this excited about time off, O'Dell. I've seen you before a three-day federally approved weekend, and you're chomping at the bit for everyone to get the hell back in their offices first thing Tuesday morning so they don't hold you up on whatever case you're working. I wouldn't be surprised if your briefcase is stuffed and ready for the backyard breaks. So really, what gives, O'Dell? What has you grinning like the cat that swallowed the parakeet?"

She rolled her eyes at him. Her partner, ever the profiler, always "on" and solving puzzles. Hard to argue with him for something she did herself. Perhaps it was simply an occupational hazard. "Okay, if you must know, my lawyer finally got the last—the very, very last—of the divorce papers back from Greg's lawyer. This time everything was signed."

"Ah. So it's all over. And you're okay with that?"

"Of course, I'm okay with that. Why wouldn't I be okay with it?"

"I don't know." Tully shrugged as he tucked his tie—already stained with morning coffee—into his shirt, then scooped up mashed potatoes, gravy and all, and dumped them on top of his roast beef.

Maggie watched as he dipped his shirt cuff into the gravy, completely unaware while he concentrated on building a dam out of his mashed potatoes. Maggie only shook her head and restrained herself from reaching across the table to wipe at his newest stain.

Tully continued, fork and now knife working at his lunch creation, "I just remember having lots of mixed feelings when mine was final." He looked up, checked her eyes and paused with fork in midair, as if waiting for a confession that might be prompted by his own admission.

"Yours didn't drag on for almost two years. I've had plenty of time to get okay with this." He was still looking at her. "I'm fine. Really. It's understandable that you had mixed feelings. You and Caroline still have to raise Emma together. At least Greg and I didn't have kids. That's probably the only thing we did right in our marriage."

Maggie started unwrapping the tacorito, wondering at Arlene's overuse of cellophane. She stopped. She couldn't help herself. She took her napkin from her lap, reached across the table and dabbed at the gravy on Tully's cuff. He no longer got embarrassed when she did these things, and this time he even held up the errant wrist for her.

"How is Emma, by the way?" she asked, going back to her lunch.

"Good. Busy. I hardly ever get to see her anymore. Too many after-school activities. And boys…too many boys."

Maggie's cell phone interrupted them.

"Maggie O'Dell."

"Maggie, it's Gwen. Is this a good a time to talk?"

"Tully and I are just having an early lunch. What's wrong?" Maggie knew Gwen Patterson well enough to recognize the urgency in her friend's voice, despite Gwen's attempt to disguise it with a clipped professional tone. She and Gwen had known each other for almost ten years, having first met when Maggie was in Quantico's forensic program and Gwen was a consulting psychologist frequently called in by Maggie's boss, Assistant Director Kyle Cunningham. The two women, despite their age difference—Gwen was thirteen years Maggie's senior—had become instant friends.

"I was wondering if you might be able to check on something for me."

"Sure. What do you need?"

"I'm concerned about a patient. I'm afraid she might be in some kind of trouble."

"Okay." Maggie was a bit surprised. Gwen rarely talked about her patients, let alone asked for help with one. "What kind of trouble?"

"I'm not sure. It may be nothing, but I'd feel better if someone checked on her. She left a disturbing voice message late Saturday night. I haven't been able to reach her. Then this morning she missed our weekly session. She never misses a session."

"Have you tried contacting her employer or any of her family?"

"She's an artist, self-employed. No family that I know of other than her grandmother. Actually she was out of town for her grandmother's funeral. Another concern. You know how funerals can be emotional triggers."

Yes, Maggie did know. Over a decade later and she still wasn't able to go to one without visions of her heroic, firefighting father lying in that huge mahogany box, his hair combed to the wrong side, his burnt hands wrapped in plastic and tucked at his sides.

"Maggie?"

"Could she simply have decided to stay an extra day or two?"

"I doubt she would do that. She didn't even want to be there for the funeral."

"Maybe her car broke down on the trip back?" Maggie couldn't help wondering if Gwen was overreacting. It made sense that the woman may have wanted to be away from everyone and everything for a day or two without running back here for a session with her shrink to dissect how she was feeling. But then Maggie knew not everyone reacted to stress and tragedy like she did.

"No, she rented a car up there. See, that's another thing.

The car hasn't been turned in yet. The hotel told me she was scheduled for departure yesterday but she hasn't checked out, nor has she contacted anyone about staying longer. And she missed her flight yesterday. She's not like this. She has problems, but organization and reliability are not on the list."

"You said yourself that funerals can be emotionally draining. Maybe she just wanted a few more days before coming back to the everyday routine. By the way, how were you able to find out that she missed her flight?" Airlines didn't just hand out their passenger manifest. After years of Gwen lecturing her about playing by the rules, Maggie waited for an admission of guilt. Now that she thought about it, Gwen had managed to get a lot of information that wasn't usually handed out freely.

"Maggie, there's more to it." The urgency returned to Gwen's voice, dismissing any confession to rule breaking. "She said she was meeting someone…a man. That was the message and she was calling me to talk her out of it. She has this…this tendency…" She paused. "Look, Maggie, I can't share the intimacies of her case. Let's just say that in the past she's made some bad choices when it comes to men."

Maggie glanced across the table to find Tully watching her, listening. He looked away quickly as if caught. She had noticed recently—although he tried to disguise it—that he seemed interested in anything related to Gwen Patterson. Or was it simply her imagination?

"What are you saying, Gwen? That you think this man may have done something to her?"

Silence again. Maggie waited. Was Gwen finally realizing that perhaps she was overreacting? And why was she being so overprotective with this particular woman? Maggie had never known Gwen to baby-sit her patients. Her friends, yes, but not her patients.

"Maggie, is there some way you could check on her? Someone you might be able to call?"

Maggie looked at Tully again. He had finished his lunch and now pretended to be watching out the window, another group of recruits down below in sweaty T-shirts and jogging shorts snaking through the woods.

Maggie picked at her own lunch. Why had Gwen suddenly decided to become this patient's caretaker? It seemed like a simple case of a grieving woman shutting herself away from her world for a while, perhaps even finding solace in a friendly stranger. Why didn't Gwen see that?

"Maggie?"

"I'll do what I can. Where was she staying?"

"The funeral was in Wallingford, Connecticut, but she was staying at the Ramada Plaza Hotel next door in Meriden. I have the phone numbers and addresses right here. I can fax over some other information later. All I know about the man she was meeting was that she called him Sonny."

Maggie's stomach gave a sudden flip while she took down the information. All the while she kept thinking, "Not Connecticut."

# CHAPTER 4

Sheriff Henry Watermeier shoved his hat back and swiped at the sweat on his forehead.

"Fuck!" he muttered, wanting to walk, to pace off his frustration, but reminding himself to stand in one place. And so he did, hands on his belt buckle, waiting and watching and trying to think, trying to ignore the stench of death and the buzzing of flies. Jesus! The flies were a pain in the ass, miniature vultures, impatient and persistent despite the plastic tarp.

It wasn't the first body Henry had seen stuffed into a strange and unusual place. He had seen more than his share during his thirty years with the NYPD. But not here. Crimes like this weren't supposed to happen in Connecticut. This was exactly the kind of stuff he had hoped to escape when his wife talked him into moving to the middle of nowhere. Yeah, sure, Fairfield County and the shore got its share of this kind of thing all the time. There were always plenty of high-profile cases—big fucking cases—like that stupid publicist driving her SUV over sixteen people, or even the Martha Moxley murder that took decades to solve, or Alex Cross, Connecticut's very own preppy rapist. Yeah, there were plenty of crimes on the shore and closer to New York, but in the middle of Connecticut things were quieter. Crap like this wasn't supposed to happen here.

He had instructed his deputies to set up a wide perimeter, having them string up yellow crime-scene tape. It was going to take a hell of a lot of tape. He watched two of his men stretching it from tree to tree, Arliss with a fucking Marlboro hanging from his lips and that kid, Truman, screeching like a banshee at any of the outsiders who dared come within ten feet.

"Arliss, make sure your butts don't end up on the ground." The deputy looked up, startled, as if he had no idea what his boss was talking about. "I mean the damned cigarette. Get it out of your mouth. Now."

Finally, a look of recognition crossed Arliss's face as he grabbed at the cigarette, stubbed it out on a tree, started to fling it but stopped with his hand in midair. Henry could see the red start at his deputy's neck as he tucked the rest of the cigarette under his hat and over his ear. It almost made Henry as mad as if Arliss had flung it. First major crime scene as New Haven County sheriff, maybe his last major crime scene of his career, and these goddamn screwups were going to make him look like a fucking idiot.

Henry glanced over his shoulder, pretending to assess the scene when all he really wanted to know was if Channel 8 still had their camera on him. Should have known, the fucking lens was still pointed at his back. He could feel it like a laser beam slicing him in two. And that's exactly what it could do if he wasn't careful.

Why the hell had Calvin Vargus called the goddamn media? Of course, he knew why, and he didn't know Vargus except by reputation. The son of a bitch was living up to that reputation in spades, flapping his yap to that pretty little reporter from Hartford even after Henry told him to shut the fuck up. But he couldn't make Vargus shut up. Not without locking him up. Although that wasn't entirely out of the question.

He needed to concentrate. Vargus was the least of his worries. He lifted the tarp and forced himself to look at the body again, or at least at the part sticking out of the barrel. From what he could see the blouse looked like silk with French cuffs. The fingernails were once professionally manicured. The hair may have been dyed—the roots were a bit darker. It was hard to tell since it was now matted and caked with blood. A shitload of blood. Definite death blow. Didn't have to be a forensic scientist to know that.

He dropped the tarp and wondered again if this poor woman was a local. Was she some bastard's mistress? Before he left the station he had run the list of missing persons, highlighting those in New Haven County, but none of them fit the preliminary description. The list included a male college student who had skipped out on classes last spring, a teenage drug addict who had probably run away from home, and an elderly woman who supposedly went out for milk one morning and hadn't been seen since. Nowhere on the list had Henry found a forty-something-year-old female with long hair, an expensive silk blouse and manicured fingernails.

Henry took a deep breath to clear his mind, to help him think. He looked up into the cloudless blue and watched another flock of geese. Lucky bastards. Maybe he was getting old and tired. Maybe he was simply ready for that fantasy retirement of endless days fishing off the banks of the Connecticut River with a cooler full of Budweiser and a couple of smoked turkey sandwiches with salami and provolone. Yeah, a sandwich, but not just any sandwich. One with the works from Vinny's Deli, wrapped all neat and tight in that white paper that Vinny used. He could go for one now.

He glanced at the barrel again. The flies were sneaking under the tarp, their buzzing amplified instead of muffled. Goddamn vultures. They'd be swarming the moist areas and taking up residence before the M.E. arrived. Nothing worse than flies and their fucking offspring maggots. He'd seen the damage they could do in a matter of hours. Disgusting. And here he was thinking about Vinny's sandwiches. Well, hell, it took a lot for him to lose his appetite.

His wife, Rosie, would say it was because he had become "jaded." Jesus! She actually talked like that, using words like *jaded.* Henry claimed instead that he was simply pissed dry, burned out. This short stint as New Haven County's sheriff was supposed to help him make some sort of transition. It was supposed to help him ease his way from the head-banging stress of New York to the laid-back routine of Connecticut to finally the peace and quiet of retirement.

But this… No, he hadn't signed up for this. He didn't want or need a messy unsolved murder to screw up his reputation.

How the hell were he and Rosie going to retire here if he had to listen to the stories, the second-guessing, the snickers behind his back?

He glanced at Arliss again. The goddamn idiot had some crime-scene tape stuck to the bottom of his shoe, a stream of it following him like toilet paper and fucking Arliss completely unaware.

No, this was definitely not the way he wanted to end his career.

# CHAPTER 5

R. J. Tully watched O'Dell sort through some file folders stacked on her desk.

"So much for vacation," she said, her good mood put on hold.

He thought her mood had changed because of the phone call from Dr. Patterson, but O'Dell seemed to be ignoring the fax machine behind her as it spit out page after page of details about Patterson's missing patient. Instead of retrieving and examining those pages, O'Dell was searching for something already lost in her stacks. Perhaps a case she had planned on taking home with her to peruse during those backyard digging breaks. What was one more if she added Dr. Patterson's?

Tully sank into the overstuffed chair O'Dell had managed to cram into her small but orderly office. It always amazed him. Their offices down in BSU—Behavorial Science Unit—were Cracker Jack boxes, yet hers included neatly stacked bookcases—not one errant hardcover squashed on top. Now that he had a closer look, he could see they were categorized. And alphabetized.

His office, on the other hand, looked like a storage closet with stacks of files and books and magazines—not necessarily each in separate piles—on his shelves, on his desk and guest chair and even on the floor. Some days he was lucky to find a path to his desk. And underneath his desk was a whole other matter. That's where he kept a duffel bag of running shoes, shorts and socks, some of which—especially the dirty ones—never managed to stay put in the bag. Now that he thought about it, maybe that was the mysterious smell that had recently begun to take over the room. He missed having a window in his office. In Cleveland he had left behind a corner office on the third floor in exchange for a Cracker Jack box three floors underground. He missed the fresh air, especially this time of year. Fall used to be his favorite season. Used to be. Back before the divorce.

Funny, but that was how he kept track of time these days—before the divorce and after the divorce. Before the divorce he had been much more organized. Or at least he hadn't been such a mess. Since his transfer to Quantico he hadn't been able to get back on track. No, that wasn't true. It had little to do with the move. Ever since his divorce from Caroline his life had been a mess. Yes, it was the divorce that had caused this nosedive, this spiral into disorganization. Maybe that's what bothered him right now about O'Dell's attitude. She really seemed to be taking this finalization of her divorce as a form of liberation. Maybe he envied her just a little.

He waited while O'Dell continued her search, still ignoring the wheeze of the fax machine. He wanted to say something to retrieve her good mood, something like, "What? No color-coded filing system?" But before he could say it he noticed the files she had pulled out of the stack all had red tabs. He rubbed at the beginning of a smile. For as predictable as his partner was, why couldn't he figure out what the hell she was up to most of the time? Like, for instance, how long did she intend to taunt him with that last doughnut? She had brought it down from the cafeteria with her, still wrapped in cellophane, untouched and now sitting on the corner of her desk—yes, sitting on the edge of her desk, tempting him.

Finally she slipped the file folders into her briefcase and turned to collect the faxed pages. "Her name is Joan Begley," O'Dell said, looking over the information as she put the pages in order. "She's been a patient of Gwen's for more than ten years."

Gwen. Tully still hadn't allowed himself to call her by her first name. To him she was Dr. Gwen Patterson, D.C. psychologist, best friend to his partner and sometimes consultant to the FBI and their boss, Assistant Director Cunningham. Usually the woman drove Tully a little nuts with her arrogant, know-it-all psychobabble. It didn't help matters that she had strawberry-blond hair and nice legs.

He and Dr. Patterson had gotten carried away on a case last November. Exchanged a kiss. No, it was more than that. It was…it didn't matter. They had decided it was a mistake. They had agreed to forget about it. O'Dell was looking at him as if expecting an answer, and only then did Tully realize he must have missed a question. Patterson's fault.

"I'm sorry, what did you say?"

"She was up in Connecticut for her grandmother's funeral and no one's seen or heard from her since late Saturday."

"Seems odd that Dr. Patterson would be so concerned about a patient. Is there a personal connection?"

"Now, Agent Tully, it would be highly unprofessional of me to ask Dr. Patterson that question." She looked up at him and smiled, which didn't prevent him from rolling his eyes at her. O'Dell might be organized, but when it came to protocol and procedure or sometimes even common courtesy, she conveniently forgot to look at whose toes she might be stepping on. "Actually, just between the two of us, I think it's a bit odd, too."

"So what are you going to do?"

"I told her I'd check it out, so I guess I'll check it out." But O'Dell sounded nonchalant about it. "Do you know any law enforcement officers in Connecticut I could call?" she asked him, her attention already on another red-tabbed file folder she had missed on her desk. She picked it up, opened it for a quick glance, then added it to her briefcase.

"Where in Connecticut?"

"Let's see. I know she told me." O'Dell had to flip through the faxed pages, and Tully wondered why she didn't remember the basic details from the phone call. Or was her mind simply already focused on her backyard retreat? Somehow he doubted that. His bet was that she was focused on the contents of those red-tabbed file folders, stuffed safely in her briefcase. "Here it is," she finally said. "She was staying in Meriden, but the funeral was in Wallingford."

"Wallingford?"

O'Dell double-checked. "Yes. Do you know anyone?"

"No, but I've been through that area. It's beautiful. You know who might be able to tell you who to call? Our buddy Detective Racine is from there."

"Our buddy? I think if you know where she's from, she's your buddy."

"Come on, O'Dell, I thought you two made nice…or at least called a truce." The D.C. detective and O'Dell clashed like night and day, but on a case almost a year ago, Julia Racine ended up saving O'Dell's mother. Whatever their differences, the two women now seemed to have what he'd call a healthy tolerance of each other.

"You know my mother has lunch with Racine once a month?"

"Really? That's nice."

"*I* don't even have lunch with my mother once a month."

"Maybe you should."

O'Dell frowned at him and went back to the faxed pages. "I suppose I could just call the field office."

Tully shook his head. For a smart woman his partner could be annoyingly stubborn.

"So what was this Begley woman seeing Dr. Patterson for?"

O'Dell looked at him over the faxed pages. "You know Gwen can't tell me that. Patient confidentiality."

"It might help to know how kooky she is."

"Kooky?" Another frown. He hated when she did that, especially when it made him feel like he was being unprofessional, even when she was right.

"You know what I mean. It could help to know what she's capable of doing. Like, for instance, is she suicidal?"

"Gwen seemed concerned that she may have gotten involved with a man. Someone she met up there. And that she might actually be in some danger."

"She was there for how long?"

O'Dell shuffled through the pages. "She left the District last Monday, so it's been a week."

"How did she get involved with a man in less than a week?

And you said she was there for a funeral? Who meets someone at a funeral? I can't even pick up a woman at the Laundromat."

She smiled at him, quite an accomplishment. O'Dell hardly ever smiled at his attempts at humor. Which meant the good mood lurked close to the surface.

"Let me know if you need any help, okay?" he offered, and now she looked at him with suspicion and he wondered, not for the first time, if Dr. Patterson had confided in O'Dell about their Boston tryst. Geez, tryst wasn't right. That made it sound…tawdry. Tawdry wasn't right, either. That made it sound…O'Dell was smiling at him again. "What?"

"Nothing."

He got up to leave. Wanting her to believe his offer had been genuine, he added, "I'm serious, O'Dell. Let me know if you need any help. I mean with any of your cases, not with the backyard digging. Bad knee, remember?"

"Thanks," she said, but there was still a bit of a smile.

Oh, yeah, she knew. She knew something.

# CHAPTER 6

*Wallingford, Connecticut*

Lillian Hobbs loved her Mondays. It was the one time she left Rosie alone during the busy rush hours, steaming milk for lattes, collecting sticky quarters for cheese Danishes and the *New York Times.* Not a problem. According to Rosie, the busier, the better. After all, it had been Rosie's idea to add a coffee bar to their little bookstore.

"It'll bring in business," Rosie had promised. "Foot traffic we might not get otherwise."

Foot traffic was just the thing Lillian had dreaded. And so at first she had revolted. Well, maybe *revolted* was too strong a word. Lillian Hobbs had never really revolted against anything in her forty-six years of life. She simply hadn't seen the wisdom in Rosie's side enterprise. In fact, she worried that the coffee bar would be a distraction. That it would bring in the gossipmongers who would rather make up their own stories than purchase one off their shelves.

But Rosie had been right. Again. The coffee crowd had been good for business. It wasn't just that they cleaned them out of the daily *New York Times* and *USA TODAY.* There were the magazine sales, and the occasional paperbacks that got picked up on impulse. Soon the regular coffee drinkers—even the mocha lattes with extra whipped cream and the espresso addicts—were browsing the shelves and wandering back into the store after work and on the weekends. Sometimes bringing their families or their friends. Okay, so foot traffic hadn't been such a bad thing, after all.

Yes, Rosie had been right.

Actually, Lillian didn't mind admitting that. She knew Rosie was the one with a head for business. Business was Rosie's forte and books were Lillian's. That's why they made such excellent partners. She didn't even mind Rosie rubbing her nose in it every once in a while. How could she mind when she was allowed to revel in her own passion every single day of the week? But Mondays were the best, like having Christmas once a week. Christmas sitting in a crammed, dark storage room, soothed by her cup of hazelnut coffee and armed with a box cutter.

Opening each box was like ripping into a precious gift. At least that's what it felt like for Lillian, opening each new shipment of books, pushing back the cardboard flaps and taking in that aroma of ink and paper and binding that could so easily transport her to a whole different world. Whether it was a shipment of eighteenth-century history books or a boxful of Harlequin romances or the latest *New York Times* bestseller, it didn't matter. She simply loved the feel, the smell, the sight of a box of books. What could be more heavenly?

Except that this Monday the stacks of ready and waiting cartons couldn't keep Lillian's mind from wandering. Roy Morgan, who owned the antique store next door, had raced in about an hour ago, breathless, ranting and raving and talking crazy. With his face flushed red—Lillian had noticed even his earlobes had been blazing—and his eyes wild, Roy looked as though he would have a stroke. Either that, or he was having a mental breakdown. Only Roy was probably the sanest person Lillian knew.

He kept stumbling over his words, too. Talking too fast and too choppy. Like a man panicked or in a frenzy. Yes, like a man who was losing his mind. And what he was saying certainly sounded like he had gone mad.

"A woman in a barrel," he said more than once. "They found her stuffed in a barrel. A fifty-five-gallon drum. Just east of McKenzie Reservoir. Buried under a pile of brownstone in the old McCarty rock quarry."

It sounded like something out of a suspense thriller. Something only Patricia Cornwell or Jeffery Deaver would create.

"Lillian," Rosie called from the door of the storage room, making Lillian jump. "They have something on the news. Come see."

She came out to find them all crowded around a thirteen-inch TV set that she had never seen before. Someone had slid it in between the display of pastries and the napkin dispenser. Even Rosie's coveted antique jar that she used for the pink packages of Sweet'n Low had been shoved aside. As soon as Lillian saw the TV, she knew. First a coffee bar, now a TV. She knew that whatever was happening would change everything. Not for the better. She could feel it, like a storm brewing. Could feel it coming on like when she was a child, and she had been able to predict her mother's temper tantrums before they started.

On the small TV screen she saw Calvin Vargus, her brother's business partner, standing in front of the petite news reporter. Calvin looked like a plaid railroad tie, solid and stiff and bulky but with a silly boyish grin as if he had discovered some hidden treasure.

Lillian listened to Calvin Vargus describe—although they were getting his bleeped version—how his machine had dug up the barrel out of the rocks.

"I dropped it. Bam! Just like that. And its *(bleep)* lid sort of popped off when it hit the ground. And *(bleep)* if it wasn't a *(bleep bleep)* dead body."

Lillian checked the huddled crowd—about a dozen of their regulars—and looked for her brother. Had he come in yet for his daily bear claw and glass of milk? And his opportunity to complain about today's aches and pains. Sometimes it was his back, other times it was the bursitis in his shoulder or his ultrasensitive stomach. She wondered what he would think about his partner's discovery.

Finally, she saw Walter Hobbs sipping his milk as he sat at the end of the counter, three empty stools away from the frenzy. Lillian took the long way around and sat on the stool next to him. He glanced at her and went back to his copy of *Newsweek* opened in front of him, more interested in the headlines about dead Al Qaeda members found a world away than the dead body in their own back yard.

Without looking up at her and without waiting for her question, Walter Hobbs shook his head and mumbled, "Why the hell couldn't he have stayed away and left that fucking quarry alone?"

# CHAPTER 7

Luc Racine felt sick to his stomach. And embarrassed—because the dead body hadn't made him as nauseated as the TV camera did. He had been fine before they turned the camera on him, before the girl reporter had simply asked him questions. He had been more fascinated by the way her eyes bulged behind the thick glasses. Huge and blue, they reminded him of some exotic fish eyes stuck behind a glass tank. But then the glasses came off and the camera went on and it was pointed right at him, right at him like a high-powered rifle sight.

The girl reporter's questions came faster now. Already he couldn't remember her name, though she had just introduced herself to the camera lens. Maybe it was Jennifer…or Jessica…no, it was Jennifer. Maybe. He needed to pay closer attention. He couldn't think and answer as fast as she could ask. And if he didn't answer quick enough, would she turn her attention to Calvin again?

"I live right over there," Luc told her, his arm waving high over his shoulder. "And no, I didn't smell anything unusual," he added, almost spitting on her. "Not a thing." She stared at him instead of asking another question. Oh, crap! He had *spit* on her. He could see it—a little glistening spot on her forehead. "The trees sorta block this area off." He waved again in the other direction. Maybe she hadn't noticed the spit. Why did his arm go up so high? "All this area is very secluded."

"Very remote," Calvin said, and Luc glanced at him in time to catch the scowl meant especially for Luc, though hidden from the camera by the girl reporter's back.

But Calvin's comment caught her attention and now she was

turning in his direction again, reaching the microphone up to him. It was a stretch. Calvin Vargus stood well over six feet. Earlier inside the big earthmoving machine, Luc thought Calvin looked like part of the machine—thick, heavy, strong and durable like a giant chunk of steel. Yeah, a chunk of metal with few defining marks, like a neck or waist.

She looked like a dwarf next to Calvin, practically standing on tiptoes to reach the microphone up to his fleshy lips, but content to give Calvin her full attention now, despite his earlier colorful description of the morning's discovery. Of course she preferred Calvin's version, especially since he would only say it and not spray it. Who wouldn't prefer a giant no-neck to an arm-waving spitter?

Luc watched. What else could he do? He'd had his chance and he blew it. And this wasn't even his first time. He had been on TV before. Once during the anthrax scare. A woman on his route had gotten sick, and Luc had delivered the letter. For a week they closed down the postal station in Wallingford, tested all facilities and grilled the carriers about precautions they should take. Luc had been interviewed on TV, though he hadn't been allowed to say much. That woman died. What was her name? How long ago was that? Last year? The year before? Certainly it hadn't been long enough ago that he couldn't remember her name.

Now he would be on TV again because some other woman was dead. And he didn't know her name, either. He looked back. They were a safe distance from the crime-scene tape and the deputy who screamed at them anytime they ventured an inch or two closer. Yet Luc could still see the barrel toppled over, its side dented in. One big chunk of brownstone kept it from rolling down the pile of rocks. A blue plastic tarp now covered her, but he could still see the image of that gray-blue arm flung out of the barrel, protruding halfway, as if the body were trying to crawl out. That was all he had been able to see—all he needed to see—that arm and a hunk of matted hair.

Luc felt a nudge at the back of his leg and, without looking, he reached down for the dog to lick his hand. Only there was no lick. He glanced at Scrapple, who immediately went into his defensive stance, gripping harder on the prize he had brought to show his owner. Another bone. Luc ignored him, and his attention went back to the excitement beyond the trees.

Suddenly, it hit Luc. Why hadn't he thought of it before? He looked back at the dog working his paws to hold his large treat as he chewed on the fleshy end and tried to get his teeth around the perimeter. Luc's knees went weak.

"Holy crap, Scrapple. Where in the world did you get that?" he said to the Jack Russell, but now everyone around him went silent as they twisted and turned to see.

Luc glanced at the girl reporter and asked, "You think that's what it looks like?"

Instead of answering—or as if confirming it—she began vomiting on Calvin Vargus's size-thirteen boots. Her hand went up to block the camera and in between gags she yelled, "Shut it off. For God's sake, shut off the camera."

# CHAPTER 8

Sheriff Henry Watermeier didn't need a forensic expert to tell him what he was looking at. The larger bone Luc Racine held out to him had enough tissue to keep the smaller bones attached. And although some of the smaller bones were missing and the flesh was now black and deteriorated, there was no question as to what the Jack Russell terrier had dug up. What Luc Racine held out in shaking hands—his palms faceup as if making an offering—was definitely a human foot.

"Where the hell did he find it?"

"Don't know," Luc said, stepping closer, his eyes never leaving Henry's as if willing himself not to look at the dog's discovery any more than necessary. "He brought it to me. But I don't know where he found it."

Henry waved over one of the mobile-crime guys, a tall, skinny Asian man with a name tag reading "Carl" on his blue uniform. He reminded himself that it wasn't a bad thing he didn't know all the mobile-crime guys by name, even if they were from up the road at Meriden's Police Crime Lab. Just meant the really sick bastards were committing their crimes somewhere outside the boundaries of New Haven County. For the second time today, Henry found himself hoping this sick bastard didn't seriously fuck up his own retirement plans. He had come this far with a perfect record—no unsolved mysteries during his reign—and he'd sure as hell like to keep it that way.

"That didn't fall out of the barrel, did it?" Carl asked as he shook open a paper evidence bag, then held it under Luc's outstretched hands, positioning it for Luc to drop the bones into the bag.

But Luc, who had seemed anxious to get rid of the thing, now only stared at Henry. He nodded at Luc to put it into the bag, and like a sleepwalker waking suddenly, Luc jerked—almost as if snapping back to reality—and he dropped the bone.

Henry kept an eye on him, studying him. Luc Racine had been one of the first people Henry had met when he and Rosie moved here. Hell, everyone knew Luc. He was the best, friendliest postal carrier in the area, making it a habit to remember his customers by name. Henry remembered a package that Luc had delivered when Henry wasn't home, wrapping it in plastic and leaving it on Henry's front portico with a note explaining that it had looked like rain. That wasn't so long ago, and now Luc Racine had taken early retirement. Word was he had early-onset Alzheimer's disease.

How was that possible? The man looked younger than Henry. Though his hair was silver-gray, he had a full head of it, not like Henry's, which seemed to get thinner and thinner and receded away from his forehead more each day. Racine looked fit and trim, too, arms tanned and twisted with muscles from lifting and carrying years' worth of junk mail. Although Henry had a bit of a paunch around the middle, he prided himself on the fact that he could still fit into his NYPD police uniform that he had worn…God, had it been thirty-some years ago?

As Henry assessed the man standing in front of him, he couldn't help thinking that Luc Racine appeared the picture of health for a man in his sixties. Except for that blank stare, the one that came out of nowhere. The one staring back at him right now that looked lost, gone, miles away.

"I think there are others," Luc said, reaching under his trademark black beret and scratching his head, his fingers digging into the shaggy hair as if penetrating his scalp would help him remember.

"Others?" Henry checked Luc's eyes. Was this part of the disease? What was he talking about? Did he forget where he was? Did he forget what had just happened? "Other what?"

"Bones," Luc said. "I think ole Scrap maybe brought me

some others. He's always bringing me stuff, scraps, bones, old shoes. But the bones…I just thought he found leftovers from the coyotes' kill. You know, from down by the pond."

"Do you still have any of them?"

"I don't."

"Damn."

"But Scrapple probably does. I'm sure he's got some of them buried around our place somewhere."

"We'll need to look. You don't mind us doing that, do you, Luc?"

"No, no. Not at all. Do you think the bones belong to that lady in the barrel?"

Before Henry could answer, one of his deputies, Charlie Newhouse, yelled for everyone's attention. Charlie and two of the crime lab guys had been trying to carefully lift the barrel with the woman still inside down off the rocks. All the photos had been taken, the evidence gathered, and the assistant M.E. had made his initial examination. It was time for the transport, but Charlie seemed all excited about something. Charlie Newhouse, the one guy Henry remembered never getting excited except after a few beers and then only when the Yankees managed to make a triple play.

"Okay, you got our attention." Henry joined the others and looked up at Charlie, putting his hand to his forehead to block out the sun. "What the hell is it, Charlie?"

"Might not mean a thing, Sheriff," Charlie said, securing his balance as he paced from rock to rock, looking down into the pile as if trying to locate lost change. He then squatted to get a better look. "Might not mean a thing at all, but there're more barrels under here. And something sure smells to high heaven."

# CHAPTER 9

Adam Bonzado shoved aside Tom Clancy with one hand while he maneuvered the winding road with the other, twisting and pulling at the stubborn and cracked vinyl steering wheel. At each incline the old El Camino pickup groaned as if there were another gear it needed to be shifted into. Adam stirred up the pile of cassettes strewn across the passenger seat, the pile that somewhere included the other three cassettes for Tom Clancy's *Red Rabbit*. He searched with stray glances for something else, something that fit his mood. All he knew was that Clancy wasn't going to cut it. Not today.

Sheriff Henry Watermeier had sounded strained, maybe even a bit panicked. Not that Adam knew Henry all that well. They had worked a case last winter. A skull found under an old building that was being demolished in downtown Meriden. All Adam could determine was that it was a small Caucasian man older than forty-two but younger than seventy-seven who had died about twenty-five to thirty years ago. It was difficult to tell with only the skull. The body must have been buried somewhere else. With all their digging, they had found nothing more, and so, the time of death had been a major guess, based more on architectural facts than archeological ones. Despite the lack of evidence, Watermeier seemed convinced it had been a mob hit.

Adam smiled at the idea. He couldn't imagine the mob operating in the middle of Connecticut, although Watermeier had quickly filled him in with a couple of tall tales. Or at least that's what they sounded like to Adam, who had grown up in Brooklyn and figured he knew a little something about mob hits. But he also knew Henry Watermeier had begun his career as a New York City beat cop, so maybe ole Henry knew a thing about mob hits, too.

Adam Bonzado couldn't help wondering if that was what they had on their hands this time. Dead bodies stuffed in rusted fifty-five-gallon drums and then buried under several tons of brownstone in a deserted rock quarry sounded like something the mob might come up with. But if there were bones scattered around the area, as Henry reported, somebody didn't do a very good job of disposing of the victims. The mob wasn't usually that careless.

Adam reached for the cassette caught between the door and the seat. He read the spine. Perfect. His fingers fumbled with the plastic container. He slowed down to wind around another S in the road as he pried open and freed the Dixie Chicks from their confinement. Then he gave them a gentle shove into the cassette drive and cranked up the volume.

Yes, this was exactly what he was in the mood for. Something upbeat to get the feet tapping and the blood flowing. He couldn't help it. Digging up bones got him excited. Pumped up his adrenaline. There was no better puzzle. Sure, he enjoyed teaching, but that was only to make a living. This—dead bodies in barrels and scattered bones—this was what he lived for.

Unfortunately, after ten years, his parents still didn't get it. He had a Ph.D. in forensic anthropology, was a professor and department head at the University of New Haven, and his mother still introduced him as her youngest son who was single and could play the concertina, as if those two things were his most admirable characteristics. He shook his head. When would it no longer matter? He was a grown man. He shouldn't care what his parents thought. The fact that he cared—no, not cared but worried about what they thought—he could even track back to their influence. For Adam Bonzado knew he had inherited his quiet, rebellious spirit from his Spanish father and his stubborn pride from his mother's ancestral Polish blood.

After creeping up the S in the road, it was time to come back down, and the old pickup flew. Adam didn't brake. Instead, he sat back and enjoyed the roller-coaster ride, working the rigid steering wheel, twisting, turning and pulling to the sexy rhythm of the Dixie Chicks. The intersection appeared suddenly. Adam slammed on the brakes. The pickup came skidding to a halt inches in front of the stop sign and seconds before a UPS truck rolled through.

"Crap! That was close."

His hands were fisted, his fingers red and still gripping the steering wheel. But the UPS driver simply waved, full hand, no choice fingers extended, no lips moving to the tune of "fuck you." Maybe the guy simply hadn't realized how close Adam had come to plowing into him. He reached over as an afterthought and turned down the volume on the Dixie Chicks. As he did so, he noticed the metal pry bar that had slid out from under the passenger seat.

Adam checked his rearview mirror to make sure he wasn't holding up traffic, then he leaned down, grabbed the pry bar, slid open the rear window and tossed the tool into the enclosed pickup bed. It clanked against the lining and he cringed, hoping he hadn't cracked the makeshift shell he'd just installed. It was a tough, waffle-weave polyurethane that was supposed to be easy to clean and would protect the bed from rust and corrosion, no matter how much mud and bones and blood he stuffed back there. It was just another measure he took to keep his pickup from becoming a smelly mobile morgue.

He checked the floor for more tools. He needed to remind his students to put their tools back whenever they borrowed his pickup. Maybe he shouldn't complain. At the least the pry bar was clean. That was a start.

# CHAPTER 10

Maggie juggled her briefcase in one hand, a pile of mail under her arm and a can of Diet Pepsi and a rawhide chew bone in the other hand as she followed Harvey out onto their patio. Harvey had convinced her as soon as she walked in the front door that they should spend their first afternoon of vacation in the backyard.

She had only planned on making a brief visit to her office at Quantico to finish up some paperwork. She'd had no intentions of bringing work home with her. Now, as she unloaded the files from her briefcase onto the wrought-iron patio table, she wished she had left these back on her desk, hidden under the stacks where they had been for the last several months.

She watched Harvey, nose to the ground, doing his routine patrol of the fence line. Her huge two-story, brick Tudor house sat on almost two acres, protected by the best electronic security system money could buy, as well as by a natural barrier of pine trees that made it difficult to see even her neighbors' roofs. Yet the white Labrador went into guard duty every time they stepped out of the house, not able to relax or play until he checked out every inch.

He had been this way ever since Maggie adopted him. Okay, *adopted* wasn't quite right. She had rescued him after his owner had been kidnapped and murdered by serial killer Albert Stucky, targeted only because she happened to be Maggie's new neighbor. Of course, Maggie had rescued poor Harvey. How could she not? And yet, the ironic part was that Harvey had rescued her, too, giving her a reason to come home every evening, teaching her about unconditional love, forgiveness and loyalty. Lessons she had missed out on growing up with an alcoholic, suicidal mother. Important qualities that had also been missing from her marriage to Greg.

Harvey was at her side now, having performed his routine patrol and nudging her hand for his reward. She scratched behind his ears and his big head lolled to the side, leaning against her. She gave him the rawhide chew bone and he pranced off, flopping himself down into the grass, monster paws holding the bone as he chewed while he kept one ear perched, listening, and his eyes on Maggie. She shook her head and smiled. What more could a girl want? Loyalty, affection, admiration and constant protection. And Tully wondered why she was content to have her divorce settlement over with, behind her. In ten years of marriage she had never felt any of those things with Greg.

Maggie grabbed the file folders, hesitating and glancing at the can of Diet Pepsi. She hadn't gone through these before without a glass of Scotch in hand. There was a bottle in the cabinet, the seal unbroken. It was supposed to be there only as proof that she didn't need it. Proof that she wasn't like her mother. It was supposed to be proof, not temptation. She caught herself licking her lips, thinking one short drink wouldn't matter. She wouldn't have it neat. It could be on the rocks, watered down, hardly a drink at all. It would take the edge off, help her to relax.

Just then she realized she had bent the corner of the first file folder. Bent it, hell, she had mutilated it into an accordion fold. This was ridiculous. She grabbed the Diet Pepsi, took a long gulp and opened the folder.

It had been a while since she had sorted through these papers. She had added to them, piece by piece, but avoided sitting down to review all the information. She had treated this profile—she had treated *him*—like a project. No, she had treated him like one of her cases, even leaving the folders stacked on her desk alongside profiles of serial killers, rapists and terrorists. Maybe it was the only way she could deal with his existence. Maybe it was because she didn't want to believe he really did exist.

In the collection of documents, articles and downloaded records there wasn't a single photo. She probably could have found one, had she tried. All she would have had to do was send for a high school yearbook or request a copy of his driver's license. Certainly someone in the Wisconsin Department of Motor Vehicles would have accommodated her, especially with a simple mention of her FBI badge number. But she hadn't done any of those things. Maybe because seeing a photo would have made him too real.

Maggie found the envelope her mother had given her last December, the envelope that had started all this…this spiral…this…whatever this was. Last year, when she first learned that she had a brother, she immediately thought her mother had been lying, that it was another drunken ploy, another way to punish Maggie for loving and missing her father so much. And why wouldn't she believe her mother capable of such cruelty? Maggie had been raised with a double dose of Kathleen O'Dell's punishments. Even the woman's failed suicide attempts felt as if she had been lashing out at Maggie, punishing her. So when her mother, in a fit of anger, told Maggie that her father had been having an affair right up until the night he died, Maggie had refused to believe it. That was until she gave her this envelope.

She opened the envelope the way she had so many times before and carefully pulled out the single index card inside, handling it like fragile material, touching it only by the corner. She stared at her mother's handwriting, the cute curlicues and circles above the "i's." He had been named for Maggie's uncle, her father's only brother, Patrick, whom Maggie had never met, the legendary Patrick who had never come home from Vietnam. It seemed heroism ran in the O'Dell family. The same kind of heroism that had taken Maggie's father away from her when she was twelve. Heroism that she continued to curse.

She slipped the card back into the envelope. She didn't need to see it. She had the address memorized by now. And though her mother had given it to her almost a year ago, Maggie's current research indicated that it was still accurate. He was still in

West Haven, Connecticut, only twenty-five miles away from where Gwen's patient had gone missing.

Her cellular phone started ringing, startling her and making Harvey leave his bone to come sit in front of her. Habit, she supposed. To Harvey, the phone ringing usually meant Maggie would need to be leaving him.

"Maggie O'Dell," she said, wishing she had shut the damn thing off. She was on vacation, after all.

"O'Dell, have you been listening or watching the news?" It was Tully.

"I just got home. I'm on vacation."

"You might want to check this out. AP is reporting a woman was found dead outside of Wallingford, Connecticut."

"A homicide?"

"Sounds like it. Early reports say she was found in a quarry, stuffed in a fifty-five-gallon drum and buried under rock."

"Oh, God. You think it's Gwen's patient?"

"I don't know," he admitted. "Just weird that it's the same town. Almost too much of a coincidence, don't you think?"

Maggie didn't believe in coincidences, either. But no, it couldn't be. Tully was jumping to conclusions and so was she. Maybe she was simply feeling guilty, and yet, she wanted to kick herself. She hadn't taken Gwen seriously this morning. In fact, she hadn't even called anyone to see if she could track down Joan Begley or file a missing persons report. "Why is it making the news down here?"

"Because it might not be the only body. There might be others. Maybe a dozen more."

She recognized that tone in Tully's voice. She could tell that his mind was already working, mulling over the possibilities, another occupational hazard. No, more than an occupational hazard. It was hard to describe, but she could already feel it taking hold of her. It was like an itch, a drive, an obsession. Like Tully, her mind sorted through the possibilities, raising questions and wanting answers. But one nagging question pushed to the forefront. What if one of the bodies was Joan Begley's?

In all the years Maggie had known Gwen, she had never asked anything of her. Not until now. And instead of doing everything she could, instead of doing anything, Maggie had shrugged off her friend's panicked request because it had reminded her of someone and someplace she didn't want to be reminded of.

"Hey, Tully."

"Yeah?"

She knew he wouldn't be surprised. Instead he would understand. Why else would he have called to tell her the news? "Do you think you and Emma might be able to take Harvey for a couple of days?"

# CHAPTER 11

This was bad. Really bad. How could this have happened?

He rode the brakes. Watched the car in front. He needed to keep his distance. Needed to keep his eyes straight ahead, only allowing quick glances to check the rearview mirror. A monster SUV followed, right on his tail, with two idiots straining their necks to get a better look. But there was nothing to be seen. Too much distance. Too many trees. Nothing could be seen from the road. He knew that and yet he had to force himself to not look. *Don't look.*

There had to be a dozen patrol cars. And media vans. How could this have happened? And he hated hearing about it on the news. Hearing it from that anorexic bimbo reporter, sounding so cheerful as she broke the news that the sky was falling.

What the hell was Calvin Vargus thinking? Why did he need to clear that property now? It had been sitting vacant for more than five years. The owner didn't care about it. He wanted it only for a tax write-off. He didn't even live around here. Some hotshot attorney from Boston who probably hadn't seen the place. So why the hell did Vargus suddenly start moving stuff around? Or did he know? Had he suspected something? Had he seen something? Was Vargus trying to destroy him? Did he know? Know? How could he know? *Know, know, know—no!* Impossible. Not possible. Simply inconceivable. He didn't know. He couldn't know.

Breathe. He needed to breathe. He couldn't breathe. He felt a cold sweat breaking out, and it wasn't even midnight. The tingle began in his fingers. The chill slid down from his neck to the small of his back. He needed to stop it. *Stop, stop, stop it.* Stop the panic before it grabbed hold of his stomach.

He fumbled through the duffel bag on the passenger seat,

fingers searching while his eyes stayed on the road. The car in front moved too slowly. Heads still turned. Stupid gawkers. What could they see? By now they should know they couldn't see anything beyond the trees. Assholes! Stupid assholes! *Move it, move it, move it!*

Already he could feel the nausea. The panic was starting, a cramp deep in his bowel. Soon it would slice across his abdomen, a sharp knife piercing him from the inside out and slowly slitting its way along the same course. His muscles tightened, a stiff reflex to prepare for the pain, the dread, the agony. Sweat slid down his back as his fingers grew more desperate, shoving, clawing, searching.

Finally, his fingers found and grabbed on to the plastic bottle. He wrenched it free from the bottom of the stuffed bag. He fumbled, angry with the shaking in his hands, but still he managed to twist off the child-protective cap while steering. Like a man dying of thirst, he guzzled the white chalky liquid, not bothering to stop at the recommended dose. Once the pain had begun, it was a race to squelch it. He took another swallow just for good measure, wincing at the taste. The stuff made him want to gag, and he would if he thought about it.

*Don't think. Stop thinking.*

It was a taste he associated with childhood, with a dark stuffy bedroom, his mother's cold hand on his forehead and her soft voice cooing, "You'll feel better soon. I promise."

He put the cap back on the bottle and wiped his mouth with the sleeve of his shirt. He waited. Stared at the road ahead. Stared at the flaming-red taillights of the car in front. Demon red eyes blinking as the idiots inside continued to gawk. He wanted to tap his car horn, but he couldn't. Couldn't draw attention to himself. He would need to wait. Stay in line and wait. He needed to *stay, stay, stay* put.

Maybe it wasn't Vargus. His mind began racing again. What about the other guy—Racine. Luc Racine. Luc with a "c" was how they had spelled it at the bottom of the TV screen. That name sounded familiar. Had he seen him before? Yes, he was sure that he had. But where? *Where, where, where?* Where had he seen him before? Had the old man been following him? Was he the one who got Vargus interested? What could the two of them be up to? Had they gone to the quarry digging? Digging for something…or no, digging for someone?

But how? How could they have found out? Vargus was stupid, a brute, but that Racine guy. Maybe he wasn't. Maybe he knew something. Luc Racine knew something.

But how? He had been careful. Always very careful. *Careful, careful, careful.* Yes, he had been careful. Even when he used the equipment, he left everything as he found it. Nobody could know. Yes, he had been careful. Always very careful.

It didn't matter, though. Not now. He'd never be able to use that old quarry again. *Never, never, never.* The whole area was crawling with cops and reporters. And here he was, stuck in line, like one of the gawkers. This was worse than the idiots who jammed the roads every fall looking at the trees. And they would be starting up soon, within weeks. Long lines winding the byroads, gawking like they'd never seen leaves turn colors before. *Stupid, stupid, stupid idiots.* But he pretended to be one of them. Just this once. Just so he could see the commotion, scope things out, figure out what was going on.

Finally he could turn off, escaping onto a side road. No one followed. They couldn't. They wouldn't miss any of the excitement. He made his way up the winding road, and felt the tension in his back ease. But only a little. He still had things to worry about. Things to take care of. He needed to settle down, calm himself. He couldn't let the panic return. Couldn't handle the pain. Not now. Not when he needed to think. That panic, that pain could paralyze him if he let it. *Couldn't let it. Couldn't let it.* That pain, the same pain from when he was a kid, could still come out of nowhere, sharp and intense stabs as if he had swallowed a pack of shingling nails or maybe even a fillet knife.

He needed to stop thinking about it. He needed to get to work. How could he work, thinking about this? How could he function? What would he do? What could he do now that he no longer had a safe dumping ground?

# CHAPTER 12

Adam Bonzado looked over the bits and pieces the crime-scene tech named Carl had spread out on a plastic tarp. He had already bagged and labeled some according to where they had been found and what he guessed they might be. From his preliminary once-over Adam could already tell the specimens were from at least two different corpses.

"The dog brought this one," Carl said, pointing to what looked to be a left foot.

Adam picked it up carefully in double-gloved hands and examined it from all angles. Most of the phalanges were gone. The metatarsals and some of the tarsals were held together by what little tissue remained. Even the calcaneus, the heel bone, appeared to be still attached.

"Have you found the rest of the body?"

"Nope. And I doubt if we will. A couple of the barrels look like they rusted through. Coyotes probably helped themselves. There might be pieces scattered all over this county."

"How much do you need to identify a person?" Sheriff Henry Watermeier asked, looking over the assortment.

"Depends on a lot of things. This has some tissue left," Adam said, handing the foot back to Carl, who placed it in a brown paper sack. "We probably have enough for DNA testing. But it won't matter if we don't have anything to match it to."

"So let me see if I can remember how this works," Watermeier said in a tone that Adam thought already sounded exhausted. "If a person is missing, we couldn't test for DNA to see if this is that missing person unless we already had something from that person, like hair samples, to match?"

"Exactly. You can do reverse DNA when you're looking for someone in particular. We did it to identify some of the World Trade Center victims."

"What do you mean, reverse DNA?"

"Say a person is missing, but we have nothing of his to match our DNA sample to. We could do a DNA test on one or both parents, and in some cases siblings, to see if there are enough hits. It can be a bit complicated, but it does work."

"So in other words," Watermeier said, "we may never know whose fucking foot that is."

"If we find more parts and identify them as belonging to the same person I might be able to piecemeal a profile. You know, narrow it down to male or female. Maybe give you a ballpark age. That way you have something to check against the missing persons lists."

"You know how many people go missing every year, Bonzado?"

Adam shrugged. "Yeah, okay, so you're right. We might not ever know whose fucking foot that is."

Carl brought several more pieces, some Adam could tell had been buried, absorbing the soil and turning the bone reddish black. He pointed to a small white one. "I don't think that one's a bone."

"No?" Carl picked it up for a closer look. "You sure? It looks like bone." He handed the piece to Adam.

"There's an easy way to tell," Adam told them, and took the piece, lifting it to his mouth and touching it with the tip of his tongue.

"Jesus Christ, Bonzado. What the hell are you doing?"

"Bone, unlike rock, is porous," Adam explained. "If it's bone it sticks to your tongue." He tossed the piece to the ground. "This one's just a rock."

"If it's okay with everyone else," Carl said, still wincing from Adam's demonstration, "I'll just pick up stuff and let you figure it out."

"Which reminds me—" Adam looked to Watermeier "—you mind if I bring a few of my students to help me sort through some of this stuff?"

"I can't have you teaching class out here, Bonzado."

"No, of course not. Come on, give me a break. Just two or three graduate students. Looks like you could use the help. I mean help, real physical help to dig up and bag what might be out here. We'll only touch what you tell us we can touch. Look, Henry, if Carl's already gathered up this much crap just from looking on the surface, think what might be buried in the rubble."

"You got that right." Watermeier reached under his hat and scratched at thin wisps of graying hair. Adam could see a slight slump of shoulders in the tall sheriff's normal rod-straight posture.

"How many barrels are there?" Adam asked.

"Don't know for sure. Could be almost a dozen. I'm having the crime-scene guys go over the area first, take their pictures and pick up stuff. 'Cause once we start digging out barrels, anything lying around here could get buried or trampled."

"Makes sense."

"We're gonna need one of those fucking earthmovers to get at some of the barrels. And we have to wait for Stolz. He's testifying up in Hartford, probably won't be able to get here until tomorrow morning. He had an assistant pick up the first barrel. That was before we realized there were more. Now he says he better be here himself for the rest. I don't blame him. I've asked the state patrol to bring in a few guys to stand guard tonight. That's all I need, one of these media mongrels sneaking in here. I'm not taking any chances. We're likely to have the governor up our asses on this one."

"That bad?"

Watermeier moved in closer to Adam and looked around, making sure the others were out of earshot, "There're a few barrels with the sides rusted open enough to take a peek inside."

"And?"

"It doesn't look good, Bonzado," Watermeier said in a low voice. "I've never seen anything like it, and I've seen some pretty freaky shit over the years. This is one fucking mess."

# CHAPTER 13

Luc Racine stared at the TV. He really liked this show. It was on every night at the same time. Syndicated repeats, but each episode seemed new to him. He couldn't remember the characters' names, except the old guy, the father, reminded him of himself. Perhaps only because he had a Jack Russell terrier, too. Eddie—that was the dog's name. Figures he'd remember the dog's name.

He looked around the living room, thinking he needed to turn on a light, the TV screen the only illumination in the darkening room. When had it started to get dark? It seemed like he had just sat down for lunch. He hated the dark. Sometimes he worried that he might eventually forget how to turn on the lights. What if he honestly couldn't figure out how they worked? It had already happened with that box in the kitchen. That thing, that box…that food-warmer thing. Shoot! See, he couldn't even remember what the damned thing was called.

He reached over and switched on two lamps, glancing around, wishing he knew what had happened to the remote control. He was always misplacing it. Oh well, he liked this show. No need to change the channel. He sat back and watched, absently scratching Scrapple behind the ears. The dog was worn out from their day's adventure. It was still Monday, wasn't it?

The phone startled Luc. It always did, only because he received few phone calls. Still, for some reason it was close by, within reach.

"Hello?"

"Hey, Pops. The department sergeant told me he saw you on the evening news."

"How did I look?"

"Pop, what the fuck's going on?"

"Jules, you know I don't care for that language."

"He said you found a dead body in McCarty's old rock quarry. Is that true?"

"Calvin Vargus was moving some rocks and a woman fell out of a barrel."

"You're kidding. Who the hell is she?"

"Don't know. Sounds like something you'd have down there in D.C., huh?"

"Just be careful, Pop. I don't like the sound of this. And I don't like you being out in the middle of nowhere by yourself."

Luc stared at the TV screen. "*Frasier,*" he said, seeing the show's title on the screen.

"What's that, Pop?"

He felt it this time like a flipping of a switch. He blinked several times, but it didn't help. He looked around the room and the panic caught him off guard. Outside the windows it looked dark. He hated the dark. Inside there were shelves with books, a pile of newspapers in the corner, pictures on the walls, a jacket by the door. None of it looked familiar. Where the hell was he?

"Pop, are you okay?" Someone was yelling in his ear. "What the hell's going on?"

Yelling, but it sounded like it had come through a wind tunnel. There was a bit of an echo. An echo with words jumbled and then interrupted by a bark. A bark followed by another and another.

Sometimes it felt like jerking awake suddenly from a deep sleep. This time it was Scrapple sitting in front of him, looking up at him and barking as if in Morse Code.

"Pop, are you there?"

"I'm here, Jules."

"Are you okay?"

"Oh, sure."

Now there was silence on the other end. He didn't want to worry her. What was worse was that it was embarrassing. He didn't want her to know, to see what her father was becoming.

"Listen, Pop—" her voice was soft, reminding him of when

she was a little girl, so sweet and shy "—I'm gonna try to get up there as soon as I can. Maybe in a couple of days, okay?"

"Jules, you don't have to do that. I'm fine."

"I'll let you know what my schedule is as soon as I check it."

"I don't want you changing your schedule for me."

"Damn! They're paging me, Pop. I gotta go. You stay out of trouble. I'll talk to you soon."

"You stay out of trouble, too. I love you, Jules." But she was already gone, a dial tone buzzing in his ear. Next time she called he'd convince her he was fine. He had to. As much as he loved seeing her, he couldn't risk her seeing him fumble and forget. He couldn't stand her being embarrassed of him, or worse, feeling sorry for him.

Luc glanced around the room again, comforted and calmed by the simple recognition of his things. He looked back at the TV, but as he did so he thought he saw someone move outside the window. He stopped. Had he imagined it? Had there been movement? A shadow walking right by the back window?

No, it was crazy. He hadn't heard a car door. No one would be out walking around in the dark. It was the stress of the day. He had to have imagined it. But as he crossed the room to pull the blinds shut and make sure the door was locked, he saw that Scrapple was still watching the window. The dog's ears were pitched, listening, and his tail was tucked between his legs. Luc had assumed the dog had barked to get him out of his daze. But had Scrapple seen someone, too?

# CHAPTER 14

It was almost midnight.

He watched from the top of the ridge, crouched low and hidden in the trees. From here he could see down into the rock quarry, although most of the action was now limited to state patrol officers waving flashlights and setting up flares. Some of the media vans had left. Those that stayed had mounted glaring strobe lights atop the vans. What the hell did they think they would see?

His anger had given in to exhaustion for the time being. His stomach ached from all the retching. He hadn't thrown up that much since he was a boy. He hated when he lost control. *He hated, hated, hated it*. Even now, as he watched his hiding place being invaded and desecrated, he couldn't control the cramps, the slicing sensation that ripped at his guts.

And to think it was all because of one man. One man who must want to destroy him. He could see the old man's house in the distance. Actually all he could see was the diffused yellow light through the blinds in the front room, what he knew from a closer inspection to be the living room. He had memorized where the sofa sat in the middle of the large space. How it faced the main window with a TV set on a cheap rolling cart right in front of the window, where he imagined the old man could watch the news and still catch anyone coming up the long driveway.

When he had seen Luc Racine earlier on TV he knew the old man looked familiar. He knew he had seen him around town, but still there was something that nagged at him all day. Then suddenly he remembered as if in a flash of lightning. Yes, lightning, the storm.

The old man had been there Saturday night. He had been in Hubbard Park, wandering around with that stupid little dog. Wandering around despite the dark and despite the storm. How could he have forgotten? Yes, he remembered seeing him with that strange little black hat on his silver head. He had even watched him give Joan directions to the West Peak. He had taken extra precautions so the old man wouldn't see him. He had waited until he was gone, making him late, and he hated to be late.

Yet, despite all the precautions, the old man knew. He knew something. Had he seen him that night? Had he been hiding in the shadows? What had the old man seen? And how in the world did he find out about the rock quarry?

*No, no, no.* It didn't make sense.

If the old man knew, then why hadn't the sheriff arrested him? What kind of game was he playing? Did he simply want to destroy him? Was that it? *Why, why, why?* Why would the old man do that?

Another mess, and he hated messes. *Hated, hated, hated them.* His mother had always made him clean up his own messes, standing over him, pushing him down into his own vomit—face first—if he wasn't quick enough.

"You made it, you clean it." He could still hear her screech.

He needed to start cleaning up this mess and quickly.

# CHAPTER 15

*Tuesday, September 16*

Maggie picked up her keys, badge and cellular phone from the airport security conveyor belt while shoving the plastic basin aside and trying to grab her laptop off the oncoming tray all at the same time. She pushed several buttons on the cell phone and tucked it between her neck and shoulder while she slid her laptop back into its case. She should be an expert at this by now, but still she struggled with the Velcro straps that held the computer in place.

"Hello?" said a voice in her ear.

"Gwen, it's Maggie. I'm glad I caught you."

"Where in the world are you? It sounds like you're calling from the bottom of the Potomac River."

"No, no. Not the bottom of the Potomac. Worse. Airport security at National." She smiled when she saw one of the security officers scowl at her words. The woman wasn't amused. She waved Maggie to the side with her wand. "Oh, shoot, hold on a minute, Gwen."

"Arms at your sides and out," the woman barked at Maggie. She set her laptop case on a nearby chair, the cell phone on top, and followed the instructions she knew by heart. It never failed. She was always getting pulled aside. And as usual she immediately set the security wand chirping. She dug her keys and badge out of her pocket and tossed those on the case, too.

"Sit down and remove your shoes, please."

Maggie slipped off the leather flats and held up the soles of her feet for the wand. The entire time she still smiled at the woman, who refused to return the gesture. With only a nod of release, she left Maggie and went back to the trenches to capture the next potential terrorist or the next wiseass.

Maggie picked up the cell phone. "Gwen, are you still there?"

"You'll never learn, will you?" her friend started the lecture. "You're an FBI agent. You of all people know how important airport security is, and yet you insist on egging them on."

"I don't egg them on. I just don't understand why I have to check my sense of humor with my luggage at the ticket counter."

"I thought you were taking some time off. Where's Cunningham sending you this time?"

"I'm going to Connecticut."

Silence. Such a long silence that Maggie thought she may have lost the connection.

"Gwen?"

"You found something out about Joan?"

"No, not yet." Maggie searched for Gate 11. Of course, it was the one with the line already boarding. "I thought I'd go check on her myself. Who knows, maybe I'll find her at the Ramada Plaza Hotel's pool, drinking piña coladas."

"Maggie, I didn't expect you to do that. I just thought you might be able to make a few phone calls. I didn't mean for you to go to Connecticut, especially on your vacation."

"Why not? You're always telling me I need to get away." Where had she put her boarding pass? Usually she slid it into her jacket pocket.

"Yes, get away and go on a real vacation. When was the last time you took a real vacation, Maggie?"

"I don't know. I was in Kansas City last year." She started to search her computer case's many pockets. Somewhere she knew she had a boarding pass. Maybe Tully's disorganization was rubbing off on her.

"Kansas City? That was two years ago and it was for a law enforcement conference. That's not a vacation. Do you even know what a vacation is?"

"Of course, I know what it is. It's that thing where you sit around on a beach somewhere, getting drunk on piña coladas with those little pink umbrellas and ending up with a miserable sunburn and sand in places where I really don't like to have sand. That's just not something that interests me."

"And looking for a missing person on your vacation does interest you? You know, if you're going to Connecticut, maybe you could finally look up a certain man in the vicinity?"

"Here it is," Maggie said, relieved to find that the boarding ticket must have slipped behind her laptop when she was mastering the Velcro straps. She ignored Gwen's comment about "a certain man," knowing full well she meant a certain assistant D.A. in Boston. "Gwen, if there's anything you haven't told me about Joan Begley, now would be a good time."

Her friend was silent again.

"Gwen?"

"I've faxed you everything I could."

She noticed Gwen's careful choice of words.

"Look, Gwen, before you hear about it on the news, there's something you should know. Yesterday morning a woman's body was found outside of Wallingford in a rock quarry."

"Oh, my God! It's Joan, isn't it?"

She hated hearing the panic in her friend's voice. This was a woman Maggie always looked to for strength.

"No, I don't know that. I wouldn't have even told you, but it's made the national news already. They haven't identified her yet. I'm trying to get in touch with the sheriff who's heading the investigation. He's supposed to be calling me back, but I'm sure I'm on the bottom of a very long list." Maggie tucked the phone into her neck again as she prepared her ID and ticket for the attendant. "Look, my flight's boarding, Gwen. I'll give you a call as soon as I know something, okay?"

"Maggie, thanks for doing this. I hope it's not Joan, but I have to tell you, I just don't have a good feeling about this."

"Try not to worry until it's time to worry. I'll talk to you later."

She shoved the phone into her pocket just as the attendant reached for her ticket.

On board, Maggie unzipped pockets, searching—why was she suddenly so disorganized?—for the paperback she had bought in the airport bookstore: Lisa Scottoline's latest legal thriller. Past titles had succeeded in keeping her mind off being 38,000 feet above control. With the paperback came the envelope she had shoved into the side pocket at the last minute while deciding to leave the file folders behind.

She slid her case into the overhead compartment and squeezed into the window seat. A small gray-haired woman fussed and fidgeted into the seat next to her, and Maggie opened the paperback to read but, instead, stared at the envelope.

Maggie knew Gwen had meant Nick Morrelli when she asked if she would attempt to see "a certain man in the vicinity." And why wouldn't she? Nick was in Boston, probably only an hour's drive from the middle of Connecticut. Whatever had started between Nick and Maggie several years ago while they worked on a case together in Nebraska had fizzled out during Maggie's prolonged divorce. She had refused to start a relationship before her divorce was finalized, not so much out of legalities or principles, but perhaps because she couldn't risk the emotional drain. Quite honestly she had never trusted her feelings for Nick—too much heat and intensity. What they lacked in common interests, they made up for in chemistry. It was the exact opposite of her relationship with Greg. Maybe that's what had attracted her to Nick in the first place.

Then last year, sometime before Thanksgiving, she had called Nick's apartment, except a woman answered, telling Maggie Nick couldn't come to the phone because he was in the shower. Since then, Maggie had kept the distance between them, increasing it by increments with shorter phone conversations replaced by missed phone calls and then never-returned voice messages. She hadn't expected Nick to wait for her to be free. And, though she had been surprised—and yes, a bit hurt—to discover that he had moved on, in the days that followed, she felt an unexpected sense of relief that only galvanized her decision. It was better to be alone, she had decided. At least for a while.

The flight attendant interrupted her thoughts with preflight instructions, something Maggie politely ignored. The woman beside her seemed frantic to find the laminated guide in the seat pocket in front of her. Maggie took out her own and handed it to the woman, who thanked her quickly as she searched with an index finger to catch up.

Maggie opened her paperback again and began to read, using the envelope as a bookmark.

# CHAPTER 16

Lillian Hobbs carried an armful of paperbacks and gently placed them on the front table where Rosie had started setting up the new display. Rosie had another excellent idea, only Lillian's mind was off somewhere. How could she concentrate with a different media van driving by almost every half hour? It was much more exciting than her regular view of the gray, bleak headstones peeking up over the brick fence from the Center Street Cemetery.

This morning they had served half a dozen out-of-town reporters while watching *Good Morning America* on their new portable TV. Maybe it was only a matter of time before Diane Sawyer and Charlie Gibson showed up at their little coffee counter. In fact, Lillian was certain she recognized the reporter ordering a double espresso. She had seen him on Fox News, but she just couldn't remember his name.

She sorted through the books, keeping one eye on the front store window. Rosie had suggested they do a table display with murder mysteries, maybe even a serial killer novel or two. It certainly fit the current atmosphere, although a bit macabre, perhaps. Rosie considered it a business opportunity. Lillian worried that someone might find it offensive, until she realized that she would be able to showcase some of her favorite suspense-thriller authors.

For Lillian, so much of what she saw in real life reminded her of something she had read in a book. This mess at the quarry was no different. Besides that, it truly sounded like it had been concocted by the imagination of Jeffery Deaver or Patricia Cornwell. Fiction Lillian could grasp, like a puzzle with pieces waiting to be fit together or simply sorted through, usually leading to an exciting climax and a neat and tidy conclusion. Or if not neat and tidy, then, at least, one that made sense. Real life, however, wasn't as easy to figure out and oftentimes made no sense at all. Wouldn't it be nice if real-life situations could be summed up in a two- to three-page epilogue?

She stopped arranging the paperbacks and thumbed through the top one. She knew all the characters in this series by heart. Knew the major plots and the killers' MOs. She could even quote some of her favorite lines. But these murders out at the quarry were strange. Lillian shook her head. Truth really was stranger than fiction. She realized she was treating these brutal findings much as she did a new mystery novel—especially by a new and unfamiliar author. She found herself reading, looking for and gathering as many clues as possible and putting the pieces of the puzzle together. She had even started to create a profile of the killer, using images and details, personality traits and deviations she had learned from the masters. Yes, the masters, meaning Cornwell, Deaver, Patterson. Anyone else might think it silly, which is why she hadn't shared her findings with even Rosie. Instead, she casually pumped Rosie for information, any tidbits her husband, Henry, may have mentioned.

Lillian stacked the paperbacks, making a creative pyramid, then chose a half dozen to stand up, using some of the innovative new plastic stands she had convinced Rosie they needed. She sandwiched the stark white and ice blue of Dennis Lehane's *Mystic River* between the black and red of Jan Burke's *Bones* and the black-and-white, hard-to-find copy of *The Prettiest Feathers* by John Philpin and Patricia Sierra. This would be an excellent opportunity for her to prove to Rosie that her compulsive buys were wise financial moves, after all.

The store's front door chimed and she looked over her shoulder. Her brother, Wally, gave a one-finger wave. Lillian returned the wave, then stiffened when she saw Calvin Vargus following behind. Immediately, Calvin seemed to fill the store with his wide shoulders, thick neck and booming laugh. He patted Wally on the back, more of a slap with a hand that looked like a racket. Lillian returned to her display. She didn't want or need to know what the private joke was between the two of them. There was always something. And she hated watching her brother take Calvin's abuse. Of course, Wally would never call it abuse.

Her brother and his business partner had a strange relationship. Calvin had grown up to be a bigger and meaner version of the bully he was when the three of them knew one another in junior high school. Wally, the eternal nerd, seemed content, almost pleased to have the bully now on his side, despite the ramifications or the cost. Lillian gave her glasses a quick, nervous nudge and shook her head. She wasn't the only one who noticed the men's strange arrangement. Why else would they have been anointed with the nickname Calvin and Hobbs after the comic strip of an imaginative and sometimes strange little boy and his pet tiger? A tiger that came to life only in Calvin's presence.

Lillian Hobbs watched the regular performance of the bully and his willing patsy. Only today it wasn't just with distaste. Today she watched with embarrassment. Embarrassed that her brother was weak. Embarrassed that he didn't seem to mind. No, it almost appeared as if he enjoyed the attention, attention at whatever the cost. Why else would he put up with it? Or had it been all those years of training? All those years of growing up with a mother who bullied and praised, often in the same sentence.

Maybe it wasn't embarrassment she felt. Perhaps it was regret, regret that as the older sibling she should have also been her brother's protector. But how could she? It wasn't as though their mother had spared her from the same ritual. Lillian, however, had found solitude in books. She had learned how to escape to her own world of imaginary friends and fantastic places. But Wally. Well, he hadn't been so lucky. Funny how a murder could dig up such things. Dig up! Oh, dear, what a pun. But it made Lillian smile.

Calvin was bragging about how he had found the first body, bragging and telling. How many times had it been? And in only a matter of twenty-four hours. Yet, each time the story became more elaborate with new details added, ones he seemed to have forgotten in the original telling.

"I knew right away that she was dead," Calvin boomed to a new audience, waiting for every gruesome detail. "I could see that her fucking skull had been bashed in. There was blood all over. Still spilling out of the barrel. Buckets of it. Good thing ole Wally wasn't with me. He's such a wuss, he would have upchucked a week's worth of breakfasts. Ain't that right, Wally?" Calvin tousled Wally's hair with that huge hand that made Wally look even more like a child.

Lillian rolled her eyes just as she noticed her brother watching her. Despite his partner's abuse, Wally remained perched at his side by the coffee counter, with a stupid, lopsided grin.

"Our own coffee house entertainment," Rosie said, coming up beside Lillian and pulling out a couple of paperbacks from the shelf behind them.

"Should we ask them to leave?" Lillian asked, then felt her stomach flip when she realized Rosie might ask her to do it.

"Nah, don't bother. People are hungry for details. Look at them." She pointed to the growing crowd around Calvin and Wally. "Not such a bad thing for our little bookstore to be the place to come to for the latest gruesome details. It doesn't bother you, does it?"

"No, of course not. But won't Henry mind?"

"It's not Henry's store," Rosie said abruptly, and Lillian knew she shouldn't have said it. "Besides, maybe if they have someplace to go for information, they'll stop hounding Henry."

Lillian decided not to mention that it might be false or fabricated information from Calvin Vargus. She saw Rosie's face suddenly soften into a smile. The concern of the last twenty-four hours had already started to show in new lines around her friend's mouth and in her forehead. Whenever Lillian studied her partner's face, she was immediately reminded of how beautiful the woman had been. She could see the remnants of the high school prom queen. Rosie was still an attractive woman—even the lines made her face interesting, not marred.

Then Lillian realized what had softened her partner's expression. Her big, strapping, good-looking John Wayne of a husband had walked in the door. All the attention shifted to Henry as he fielded questions while trying to make his way to the coffee bar.

"I better go rescue him," Rosie said with a smile.

As she watched Rosie greet her husband, Lillian noticed her brother, Wally, sneaking out the bookstore's back entrance. And he hadn't even had his daily bear claw and glass of milk.

# CHAPTER 17

Henry shoved his way past the cameras and yelling reporters. The pretty, little one with the thick glasses had been following him everywhere. Earlier she had been at the bookstore, waiting for him as if she knew that he stopped by there every morning. Except now she had a camera guy with her and the camera was rolling. He could tell, because her thick, Coke-bottle glasses came off as soon as the camera went on. He wondered how the hell she had gotten into broadcast journalism with those things.

"Sheriff Watermeier, is it true there may be more than a hundred bodies buried in the quarry?"

"A hundred bodies?" He laughed. Not an appropriate response, but this was ridiculous. "Let's hope not."

"What about the rumors that some of the victims have been cannibalized? Can you elaborate on that, Sheriff?"

This time Henry avoided rolling his eyes. "We'll try to answer some of your questions later today when we know more."

He kept walking, not looking back, despite the questions that continued and despite the clicks of shutters and the hum of video cameras. He knew he would need to address the media, and soon. Earlier he had gotten a call from Randal Graham, the assistant to the governor, and good ole Randal advised him that he needed to somehow calm things down a notch. According to Randal, the governor was tremendously concerned about the national media calling these the worst serial killings in Connecticut's history. Henry wanted to tell that weasel Graham that those reports were probably accurate, and if he wanted things toned down a notch maybe he should get his ass down here and tone them down himself. But, instead, he told the governor's assistant that he had things under control. So, in other words, he had lied.

The tall grass was slick with dew, glittering in the morning sun. Once he got into the mouth of the quarry he couldn't hear the reporters. The rocks and trees insulated the area. Henry took in the surroundings. The leftover, rusted conveyor system that hovered over Vargus and Hobbs's shiny yellow earthmover looked out of place in this sanctuary. It really was beautiful, giant stepping stones all the way up the mountain, sheltered by thick evergreens alongside yellow-and-orange-leafed oak and walnut trees. It only now occurred to him that the killer had chosen wisely when he made this his graveyard.

He stayed back from the commotion and watched Bonzado with his students unloading equipment from the shell of his El Camino. The three students—one woman and two men—looked like typical nerds with none of the flamboyance of their professor, who today wore a pink-and-blue Hawaiian shirt, khaki shorts and brown hiking boots. Henry managed a smile. He actually liked Bonzado. He trusted the kid, which was more than he could say about some of his own men. Most of these guys hadn't seen a bloodied body outside of a car accident. He knew he could depend on the police lab techs, but his own deputies were another story. As if on cue he saw Truman screaming at a reporter. Shit! Henry recognized the guy from NBC News. Wonderful! That would look great tonight on the *Nightly News* with Tom Brokaw.

This really was a fucking mess. Even Rosie couldn't put a positive spin on this one. What he needed was someone he could blame if things went south. Some expert that no one would second-guess. That certainly wouldn't be Dr. Stolz. He watched the medical examiner making his way through the reporters. He was dressed as if for court again in his suit and tie and expensive leather shoes. Shoes that would send him—yup, sure enough, Stolz slipped on the wet grass, almost losing his balance and ending up on his skinny little ass. Henry wiped at his smile, almost breaking out into a laugh when he noticed Bonzado doing the same.

His cell phone vibrated in his shirt pocket, and he grabbed it. Beverly had instructions to forward only the important calls. He hoped this wasn't Graham again. He should have put him on the nonimportant list.

"Watermeier," he barked into the phone.

"Sheriff Watermeier, this is Special Agent Maggie O'Dell with the FBI."

"I don't remember calling the FBI for help, Agent O'Dell."

"Actually, I think we might be able to help each other, Sheriff Watermeier."

"How do you figure?"

"I'm a criminal profiler and it sounds like you might have a serial killer on your hands."

Henry stopped himself from automatically shrugging off this unexpected offer, another in a long list of know-it-alls wanting a piece of the action. Maybe this was exactly what he needed. The local yokels would have a tough time arguing with him about bringing in federal assistance, no matter how uptight they were about outsiders. He did need some help. And this Agent O'Dell might come in handy if he needed a scapegoat.

"You said we could help each other. What is it you want from me, Agent O'Dell?"

"I'm looking for a missing person."

"I don't have a whole lot of time for wild-goose chases right now. I've got my plate full, if you know what I mean."

"No, you don't understand, Sheriff Watermeier. I'm hoping I'm wrong, but I think you may have already found her."

# CHAPTER 18

Maggie slowed the rental car, wishing she had noticed the squeaky brakes before she left Bradley International Airport. She should have insisted on something other than the freshly washed white Ford Escort. She hated rental cars. They always looked good from the outside, but the insides couldn't conceal the last occupants. The Escort's last driver was a smoker with sweaty hands. Easy enough to fix by rolling the windows down, swiping a couple of wet napkins around and introducing some aromatic McDonald's French fries. But squeaky brakes were a whole other matter, especially since it looked like she would need them.

The winding roads that took her up made her as nervous as on the plunges down. And there seemed to be an abundance of them. A small detail both Watermeier and Tully had forgotten to mention when giving her directions. Although Tully's directions had sounded more like a lecture. She remembered thinking at the time that he really must miss his daughter, Emma, because he was treating her like a teenager on her first outing alone, certain that she would get lost without his step-by-step road assistance. She had stopped him once, saying she could pick up a map from the AAA. His scowl told her it would be wise to not interrupt him again.

Who would have guessed that, when it came to road-trip instructions, the same R. J. Tully who used scraps of paper—receipts, napkins, the back of a dry cleaning ticket—would become Mr. Anal Retentive? Actually, it made her smile. After two years of working together, he was finally feeling comfortable enough to take off the kid gloves and treat her like a true partner. She liked that.

She glanced at Tully's homemade map stretched out on the passenger side of the Escort and tried to find the spot according to Watermeier's instructions. Before she could find it on the map, however, she saw the water around the next turn. A sign identified it as McKenzie Reservoir, and immediately she saw the road, Whippoorwill Drive, that would take her over the water. It took two more climbs and one more plunge before she saw the commotion alongside the two-lane road. One of the lanes was clogged with black and whites, media vans, a mobile crime unit and several unmarked sedans.

A uniformed officer waved for her to continue on, and even as she pulled up and stopped beside him, he continued shaking his head.

"Keep moving, lady. Nothing to see and I'm not answering any of your questions."

"I'm with the FBI, Special Agent Maggie O'Dell." She handed her badge out the car window, but he stood with his hands on his gun belt, looking not the least impressed. She tried again. "I just talked to Sheriff Henry Watermeier a few minutes ago."

The officer pulled a walkie-talkie from his shoulder and took her badge, holding it up to the light as if making sure it was authentic. "Yeah, this is Trotter. I've got a woman in a rental, says she's FBI and that Sheriff Watermeier *just talked* to her." He spit out the words, as if he didn't quite believe them.

Through the static came a garbled question. Maggie couldn't make a word out of it, but Officer Trotter seemed to have no problem interpreting static. Without hesitation, he held up the badge again and answered, "A Margaret O'Dell."

There was a crackled response, and this time Maggie saw the transformation in Officer Trotter's face. He handed her badge back through the car window and politely showed her where she could park the car. "You'll need to walk to the scene," he told her, pointing to an overgrown dirt road she may not have noticed otherwise. "Sheriff Watermeier will be waiting for you at the perimeter." Then he was off to wave on the next passersby, tourists in a black Jeep Cherokee with Rhode Island license plates, checking out Connecticut's latest wonder.

She would have recognized Watermeier even without the uniform. He reminded her of John Wayne—the trimmer version from his earlier movies—with a sheriff's hat in place of the ten-gallon cowboy hat. No dusty kerchief at his neck. Instead, his collar was open and his necktie gone. His brown shirtsleeves were rolled up to his elbows and his hat was pulled low on his brow. When he saw her, he waited patiently, raising the crime-scene tape for her to crawl under. There was no smile, no introduction, no raised eyebrow at her appearance. He simply started in as though the two of them had been working together forever.

"We're still scouring the scene, so we haven't started opening any more barrels yet. We'll need to move some rocks to get to some of them. I don't want us jumping in and destroying evidence."

"Sounds like a good idea."

"This missing person—" he shot her a look of suspicion "—she's not someone that's gonna cause all hell to break loose, is she?"

"I'm not sure what you mean."

"I checked you out, O'Dell." He waited as if expecting her to protest. When she didn't, he continued, "My office isn't exactly in the Stone Age. We can do that pretty quickly."

"I'm sure you can, Sheriff Watermeier."

"Well, point being that I know you're out of Quantico. FBI's looking for a missing person, and I'm thinking that missing person must be someone important, right?"

"Every missing person we look for is important to someone, Sheriff Watermeier."

He stared at her and this time she thought she saw the beginning of a smile at the corner of his mouth. He didn't press the issue.

"You ever have a case like this?" He started walking, slowing down when he realized his long strides were keeping her a step behind him. "I mean, there's not some crazy bastard who's been doing this in other states, too, is there?"

"I did check, but nothing registered on VICAP."

"Dr. Stolz—" he pointed to a small-framed, balding man in a suit "—hasn't gotten to the autopsy yet of the woman we found yesterday. You can join us for that later, if you'd like. She's a mess, though. I'm not sure you'll be able to do a visual ID."

"I have some of her physical characteristics that might, at the very least, rule her out."

"Right now, the M.E.'s having a hell of a time. We're trying to figure out how the hell to contain the barrels that have cracked open. He's thinking we may need to set up some kind of temporary morgue out here. On the other hand, if we just pull them out…hell, who knows. My quick reference check said you'd been with the bureau for about ten years. Have you come across anything like this before?"

"There was a case in Kansas. I believe 1998 or '99, John Robinson."

"I think I remember that one. The Internet wacko, right?"

"Yes, that's right. He lured women via the Internet to his farm, killed them and stuffed their bodies into fifty-five-gallon drums." Maggie watched her feet. Rocks protruded out of the ground and were hidden by knee-high grass. "I didn't work that case, but if I remember correctly, I think the drums were found in a storage shed, so there wasn't as much risk of jostling things around as you're dealing with here. Do you have any idea how many barrels there are? And how many are filled with bodies?"

"Could be as many as a dozen barrels. Maybe more. Doesn't mean they all have dead bodies. But we've seen inside several of them. Weird crap, really weird." He tilted his hat back and wiped the sweat from his forehead. "In one, it looks like there's just a pile of bones, but in the other one…" He shook his head and pointed to the barrel he wanted her to see first. "In the other one, the body looks pretty well preserved. From what we can see. Either way, we've got one sick son of a bitch on our hands."

He stopped in his tracks and Maggie waited. They were about a hundred feet from the commotion. A group was hunched over a barrel that had been brought down from the rock pile. Close by, several crime-scene techs searched the area on their latexed hands and padded knees, working their grid over the rocky surface. Maggie was impressed with the sheriff's careful handling of the scene. Too often small-town law enforcement officers allowed unnecessary civilians within the perimeter. They couldn't see the harm in letting the mayor or a local city councilor take a look. What they considered a smart move politically—sheriffs were elected, after all—oftentimes ended up contaminating a crime scene.

Suddenly, Maggie realized Watermeier was waiting, as if weighing what he wanted to ask or tell her before they joined the others.

"I spent over thirty years with the NYPD, so I'm not a rookie to messes, okay?" He met her eyes and held them, waiting for acknowledgment—a brief nod from Maggie—before he went on. "My wife and I moved here about four years ago. She's part owner in a nice little bookstore in downtown Wallingford. The locals elected me because they wanted somebody with some real experience. We like it here…a lot. This is where we wanna retire in a few years."

He stopped to watch his men, looking around him as if to take count. Maggie crossed her arms and shifted her weight from one leg to the other. She knew he didn't need a response from her. And more important, she knew he wasn't finished. She waited.

Finally he looked at her, his eyes meeting hers again. There was something in them Maggie recognized. There was determination, frustration, a bit of anger, but what Maggie recognized was just enough panic—just a glimpse—to tell her that the experienced Sheriff Henry Watermeier was also scared.

"This is one fucking mess," he said, pointing to the barrel the group was focused on. "Whoever did this may have been doing it for years. I'm not gonna bullshit you, O'Dell. Even if we don't find your missing person, I could use your help. I'm going to need it to find this goddamn psycho. I'm not a betting man, but if I were, I'd say he still lives around here. And if I don't find him and haul his ass in, I can kiss my dream of retiring in this community goodbye."

Watermeier waited for her response. But this time he avoided her eyes, looking, searching, assessing, all in an effort to downplay the enormous level of trust he had laid at Maggie's feet. Trust and confidence he had invested in a woman he was meeting for the first time, a woman who had insinuated herself into his investigation. Whether out of desperation or simple strategy, Maggie could tell this was not something a tough, independent sheriff like Watermeier did easily.

She turned toward the group surrounding the barrel, and simply told him, "Then I guess we better get to work."

Maggie didn't glance back for his reaction, but soon he was beside her, restraining his long strides so that they walked side by side.

# CHAPTER 19

Henry introduced Special Agent Maggie O'Dell to the rest of the group and watched the casual exchange and assessment. Of course, Bonzado got the longest look. Bonz looked like some California surfer dude instead of a professor in that goddamn Hawaiian shirt. But the kid was brilliant in a humble, nonarrogant way, and despite his getup, he was good at magically attributing an identity to a pile of bones. But Henry already knew what Dr. Stolz, the medical examiner, was thinking. He had shot Henry one of those famous "what the hell?" looks when he first saw Bonzado. And now, without saying a word, Henry could feel Stolz's scowl saying, "The feds? You brought in the fucking feds already?"

Stolz was probably worried that it was a direct reflection on his own competence. Actually, Henry didn't care what Stolz or any of the rest of them thought. He had learned a long time ago to live by one simple philosophy—CYOA—cover your own ass.

They had a body bag spread out under the lip of one of the barrels that had cracked open during Vargus's shake-up. Henry would just as soon load it up and have the poor sucker join the woman from yesterday at the morgue. But this was Stolz's call. He wanted to process the fractured barrels out here at the scene, worried that jostling around the fragile remains might compromise them. This process didn't look any more efficient to Henry. But again, he reminded himself, it was Stolz's call, Stolz's risk to take. In other words, Stolz's ass. He could only be concerned about one ass at a time, and right now it was his own.

All that could be seen of the corpse inside the barrel was the head and shoulders, a tuff of peppered gray hair and what looked like the lapels of a navy blue suit. Stolz and Bonzado, their hands covered in latex gloves, carefully groped inside, grabbing hold of anything solid that hopefully wouldn't rip or tear or crack. At the other end of the barrel, two of Henry's deputies held tight to a rope that had been secured around the cracked middle. They were ready to play a sort of macabre game of tug-of-war.

Henry handed Agent O'Dell a small jar of Vicks VapoRub. The smell would only get worse once they pulled the unlucky bastard out. But the agent declined with a polite "no thanks." Something told him it had nothing to do with her pretending to be tough. No, she really didn't need it. She was used to the stench of death, not that anyone could get used to that sour, pungent odor. There was something different about the smell of a human corpse, different from any other animal. He hated that smell. Had never gotten used to it and didn't want to. Yet, without taking a swipe of Vicks for himself, Henry dropped the jar into his pocket. He knew better than to offer any to Stolz or Bonzado. And Bonzado's students stayed back, probably at Bonzado's instructions, his way of assuring Henry that they wouldn't get in the way.

They started slowly easing the corpse out of the barrel and immediately there came a low, sickening noise, a sucking sound that made Henry cringe. This one was fresh. This one would be messy. Henry glanced at O'Dell. Maybe he hoped to see her cringe, show at least a twinge of discomfort. There was nothing like that. Anticipation, but certainly not discomfort. Hell, she had probably seen lots worse.

O'Dell stood maybe five five, had an athletic but slight frame and was a bit too attractive to fit Henry's stereotype of an FBI agent. But her self-assured manner revealed an air of confidence that put him at ease. He had noticed it during their phone conversation, too. Confident, not cocky. Hell, he wouldn't have confided what he had if she had come off with that government-issued cockiness that seemed to run rampant at the federal level.

Maybe he was crazy to be putting so much trust and faith in someone he hardly knew, but Special Agent Margaret O'Dell would come in useful if things went south. Bottom line—he wasn't about to piss away a thirty-year career because of some psycho. O'Dell seemed nice enough, but if the governor came looking for answers, Henry needed to be ready. Hell, it wasn't such a bad idea to have someone else he could blame if answers didn't come quick enough.

"Hey, watch it," Stolz yelled at Bonzado as the corpse came loose from the barrel with what almost sounded like a pop. The lower extremities swung free. The M.E. lost his grip and the corpse slid out of their control, falling onto the body bag, the torso slamming hard against the rocks. It fell flat on its face with a hollow thud. And, as it hit against the hard surface, the top of the head cracked open.

"God Almighty," Stolz yelled again. "We're gonna need a better way to do this. We may have just given this guy a new head injury. How am I supposed to figure out what the killer did and what we did?"

Henry practically bit his tongue to avoid saying, "This was your idea." Only the second barrel and already Stolz's incompetence showed in his blatant contradictions. This only reassured him about his decision to bring in Bonzado and O'Dell, two outsiders to witness and document any irregularities.

While the others backed away to regroup and rethink this archaic method, O'Dell came in for a closer look, kneeling on the rocks. Despite the fractured and now-open skull, the corpse appeared to have no other injuries, no mess. Even the navy blue suit had few wrinkles.

"This guy looks in good shape," Henry said.

"Too good a shape. I don't see any blood," Bonzado pointed out. He moved aside for Carl, who came in closer with a camera.

Bonzado's students now dared to come closer, the woman being the bravest of the group, looking over her professor's shoulder. Both of the male students looked as though they might be sick. The older guy limply held a camera at his side and didn't attempt to take a single picture. Maybe he was waiting for Carl to finish. Henry wondered if the two guys were having second thoughts about their choice of career.

"Nice suit," Carl said, setting aside his camera and pulling out a forceps to retrieve a stray thread from the back of the corpse's jacket.

"Doesn't look like the body has begun to liquefy." Stolz squatted on the opposite side of O'Dell.

"I think the skull's been cut open," she said, now on hands and knees.

"Probably sliced right open on these rocks," Stolz said.

"No, I don't think so. Take a look at this." O'Dell moved aside for Stolz to get a better angle, looking up at Henry as she did. For the first time he thought he noticed something in her eyes. Maybe that bit of discomfort he had been searching for earlier. "It looks like someone may have used a saw. Maybe a bone saw or even a Stryker saw."

"A Stryker saw?" Now Stolz seemed interested.

O'Dell got up and came around the rocks to peer inside the top of the skull. The flap that came loose hung over, like a lid or a dismantled toupee. O'Dell practically had her nose to the scalp when she said, "Whatever he used it's left very fine marks. There's no blade chattering."

"Blade chattering?" Henry asked, and glanced around at the others, noticing Bonzado giving O'Dell a look of admiration.

"It's sort of a technical term." It was Bonzado who jumped in with an explanation. "It's when a thin blade jumps slightly from side to side while you're using it. You know, like a hacksaw, especially when you're just starting to cut." Ever the professor, Henry thought, though the kid had a genuine desire to provide information. There was no intention to upstage anyone or condescend to anyone, not like Stolz might do.

"From what I can see," O'Dell continued, "I think the skull is empty."

"A Stryker saw? Empty? What the hell are you talking about? Are you saying the brain is missing?" Stolz shot up, stepping over the corpse to get to O'Dell's side.

Ordinarily, Henry would have laughed at the little man who rarely became animated or allowed an outburst of emotion. He usually confined his emotions to those famous facial expressions. He shouldn't be focused on Stolz. But focusing on Stolz's incompetence and his rising panic was a hell of a lot better than dealing with his own. This crap only got stranger by the minute.

"If you've got enough pictures, let's try to flip him and get all of him on the body bag," Stolz instructed.

Henry stood back. He hated to admit it, but he was starting to enjoy watching the little man get all worked up. Plus, Stolz had more than enough help with Bonzado and two of the students joining in. Even O'Dell had her jacket sleeves pushed up and was grabbing hold of a shoulder. This time the group wasn't taking any chances on having the corpse slip out of their control. They barely had the body turned and Henry's stomach took a plunge.

"Jesus Christ," he said under his breath, and everyone stopped, looking up at him, and then back at the corpse. "It's Steve Earlman."

"You know this man?" O'Dell asked.

Henry found the nearest boulder to lean on before his knees buckled. "Not only do I know him, I was a goddamned pallbearer at his funeral last May."

# CHAPTER 20

Maggie could now see the tacks and pins holding Mr. Earlman's tie and jacket lapels in place. She lifted an eyelid and found a small, convex plastic disk in the eye socket, something morticians used to give definition to the eye area and to keep the eyelids closed.

"It looks like an autopsy incision," Dr. Stolz said, taking his glasses completely off and pocketing them.

"Can't be," Sheriff Watermeier said. "There was no autopsy."

"You're sure?" Maggie was back on her feet, inspecting the rest of the body while the M.E. poked at the flap of skull. The suit looked awfully clean, almost as if it had gone directly from the casket to the sealed barrel. "It certainly looks like a Stryker saw."

"It definitely was a bone saw of some kind," Stolz insisted.

"I know for a fact there was no autopsy," Watermeier said.

"How about surgery?" Adam Bonzado was beside Stolz now, on hands and knees, peering into the top of the dead man's head.

"No surgery," Watermeier answered quietly. "Steve died of an inoperable brain tumor."

Maggie glanced at Watermeier to make sure he was okay. She knew what it was like to discover a friend had been a victim of some heinous crime. Almost a year had gone by since she unzipped a body bag to find a friend of her own with a bullet hole in his forehead. She was sure she would never forget Special Agent Richard Delaney's empty eyes staring up at her. None of the law enforcement workshops and no amount of experience could prepare someone for that shock, that helplessness, that sick feeling in the bottom of the stomach.

Watermeier removed his hat. He wiped the sweat from his face with the sleeve of his shirt, despite what Maggie had noticed was a chill in the air now that the sun was disappearing behind the ridge of rock and trees. Watermeier put the hat on and this time pushed it back. Maggie surveyed the equipment the crime-lab technicians had carefully stacked out of the way on one of the boulders. Finally she saw a red-and-white water jug. She reached and grabbed it, glanced at Carl and waited for his nod of approval. Then she unscrewed the top, took a long slow drink and, as casually as possible, handed the jug to Sheriff Watermeier as if handing it down the line. He didn't hesitate, took a generous swig and passed it on.

"Was it public knowledge?" she asked Watermeier.

He looked at her, knew she was addressing him, but his eyes drew a blank. "What's that?"

"Did Mr. Earlman tell people about the tumor? Friends, family, acquaintances?"

"Oh, yeah. He didn't hide it," Watermeier said. "But he didn't complain about it, either."

"Was there any public mention of it? Was it listed as COD in the obituary?"

Watermeier scratched his head, reaching under his hat. "I don't remember about the obituary, but almost everyone knew Steve. He owned the butcher shop in downtown Wallingford. Bought it from old Ralph Shelby years ago but still kept the name. Figured everybody already knew it as Ralph's. That was Steve. He was a pretty humble guy. And a good guy, fair and honest. Even after he got sick he was going in to work every day. Still did the custom cuts himself. After Steve died, the store closed. Someone bought all the equipment but didn't want to run the shop. It's some kind of knickknack shop now."

Dr. Stolz looked up at Maggie from his perch. "What exactly are you thinking, Agent O'Dell?"

"If it's not a surgery cut, it had to have been made postmortem, right?"

"Yes."

"Was his funeral an open casket?" she asked Watermeier, who now only nodded. "So it had to be after the funeral."

"Someone dug up his grave?" Henry asked, but from the look on his face, Maggie could tell he didn't really want to think about it.

"When and how would they able to do that?" Stolz said. "A sealed vault isn't the easiest thing to break into."

"Not all caskets are put into vaults," Bonzado offered. "Depends on whether or not the family wants to add that extra expense. If I remember correctly it's about $700 to $1,000."

"There's another possibility," Maggie said. "The body could have been taken before the casket was buried."

"You mean someone may have snatched the body right from the funeral home?" Bonzado said as he stood, brushing his knees clean.

His sartorial get-up was an odd uniform for a forensic anthropologist, even for a professor. Maybe not for an eccentric professor with muscular, tanned legs. As Maggie caught herself admiring Bonzado's legs, she also noticed his knees were covered with the rust-colored dust from the rocks and a green weed had latched onto the tops of his socks. It reminded Maggie to take a closer look at the dead man's clothes for any similar debris.

"If someone had access they could have made a switch," Maggie answered as she examined the suit, a lightweight wool, damp and sticky with what she guessed to be embalming fluid.

The skull cut had definitely been made after the body had been embalmed and prepared for its casket. There would be no way to hide leaking embalming fluid for an open-casket viewing without repairing the gaping hole, and the cutter hadn't felt the urgency to make any such repairs. Now that she got a closer look at the blue suit, she could tell there were no signs of green weed, no brown rock dust on the wool. The cut hadn't been made out here. In fact, other than the sticky embalming fluid, the suit looked clean.

"I helped carry his casket," Watermeier said, sounding quiet and far away. "It was heavy. He had to be in there."

Maggie glanced up at the sheriff. He rubbed his temple, not like a man puzzled in thought, but pressing hard—hard enough to wince—as if he wanted the image before him to disappear.

"I'm just saying we need to consider all the possibilities," Maggie said. "In any case, we should find out who had access to the casket and the grave. Maybe his suit might tell us more." She found Stolz watching and met his eyes, ignoring their skepticism and what she immediately recognized as a trace of suspicion. Not even an hour into the investigation and Stolz had already decided to label her an intruder. It didn't matter. She was used to it. "Usually funeral clothes are clean when a mortician puts them on a corpse, right?" She continued, "So anything the clothes came in contact with would have to be from the mortuary or a destination that came later."

Stolz simply nodded.

"We might find something on the suit, some debris from the killer like hair or fibers. He couldn't have done this without making contact with the body."

"He went to a lot of trouble just to take the brain. Maybe he sells parts to teaching colleges," Bonzado's female student suggested, as she helped Carl, who had been quietly collecting evidence that may have spilled from the barrel. The woman seemed overly anxious to help and held open a plastic bag while Carl dropped small particles in with forceps.

Maggie was impressed that Carl already had two bags in his other hand, one containing what looked to be a swatch of hair or fur and in the other, a small, crumpled piece of white paper.

"What is this?" She pointed to the crumpled piece of paper.

"Not sure," Carl said as he handed her the bag. "It's not a note, if that's what you were hoping. It's not even writing paper."

Maggie held it up, examining it in the sunlight. "Looks like a waxy texture."

"Getting back to more important matters," Stolz grumbled. "Like missing brains. Serial killers often take things, clothing, jewelry, even body parts." He looked from Bonzado and Carl to Watermeier and finally—lastly—to Maggie. "As trophies, right?"

"Yes, serial killers often do that. There's only one small problem here," Maggie said, stopping all of them, waiting for their attention. "Mr. Earlman wasn't murdered."

# CHAPTER 21

Adam Bonzado helped Simon with the bags of sandwiches and sodas, keeping an eye on his student. Ramona and Joe had literally dug into this project, but Simon… Well, it was hard to tell. His pasty complexion and quiet demeanor were typical. So when he volunteered to get lunch for the group, Adam knew it was Simon just being Simon, always the first to offer when there were errands that needed to be run.

They made their way through what seemed to be a growing crowd of reporters and cameras. Officer Trotter with the state patrol had the media trained to stay back behind the crime-scene tape, but that didn't stop the barrage of questions.

"Professor, Jennifer Carpenter with WVXB Channel 12. When will we have an official update?"

Adam recognized the attractive blonde behind the glasses.

"I'm not in charge, Ms. Carpenter. You'd have to ask Sheriff Watermeier."

"I've been asking Sheriff Watermeier. What exactly are you finding? And why are you hiding it?"

"We're not hiding anything," Adam said, and when she whipped off her glasses, he realized the cameraman behind her was now running film. Jesus! Just what he needed. Why hadn't he kept his big mouth shut? "We're simply trying to assess the situation. I'm sure we'll let all of you know what's going on as soon as we can."

He turned his back to them and headed for the quarry. Simon waited for him on the other side of the tree line.

"Vultures," he told his student, hoping for a smile.

"I think she likes you."

Adam glanced at him, expecting some smart aleck comment to follow. His students were always razzing him about being single. But Simon looked serious. Adam knew Simon was older than most of the other graduate students, having come into the program late. "Yeah? You think so? I'm not sure she's my type."

Now, Special Agent Maggie O'Dell was another story. From their first introduction Adam couldn't help thinking that if he did actually have a type, she would be in the running. Forget that the woman had amazing brown eyes and could make an FBI-approved navy-blue suit look official as well as make it come alive, the woman was smart. She actually knew what blade chattering was. Definitely a woman who could steal his heart. It had been a long time since any woman had gotten his attention enough for him to check out her ring finger.

According to his mother, it had been an abnormally long time. "It's not good for such a young man to be so alone," she would tell him at every opportunity. But after Kate he had chosen to be alone. Besides, how could he begin to fill the void that Kate had left? When she drowned it was as if she had taken him down under with her. Even now he couldn't think about her without remembering, without feeling her cold, lifeless body, without remembering all those hands trying to pull him away as he continued over and over to pump her chest and try to breathe life into her blue-lipped mouth.

Suddenly Adam realized Simon was staring at him, waiting for him.

"You okay, Professor Bonzado?"

"I'm fine." He turned back to the road, pretending to be distracted, then realized he had actually forgotten something. "What time do you need to get to your job?"

Simon checked his wristwatch. "Not until later this afternoon."

"You still have my keys?"

"Oh, yeah, sorry." Simon shifted the sandwich bags to one hand while he dug in his jeans pockets for the keys.

"You mind going back to the El Camino?"

Simon looked eager to please.

"There's a pry bar that might help us open up some of the barrels. You mind getting that?"

"No, not at all." He started handing the bags to Adam, making sure he had a grasp of everything. "Is it still under the seat?"

"I tossed it into the bed, but I bet it got shoved clear to the back when we loaded everything else."

As Simon headed back, Adam took a deep breath, hoping to wipe out the images of Kate he thought he had buried long ago. Henry waved at him, then met him halfway, rescuing several of the bags before Adam dropped them.

"Hey, everybody. Lunch," Henry yelled.

Adam watched the group stop, setting tools down and placing evidence bags in containers. They gathered around as if there was nothing unusual about sitting down to eat sandwiches and drink Cokes in the middle of a rock quarry surrounded by barrels stuffed with dead and rotting bodies.

"Where did you get these?" Agent O'Dell asked, unwrapping a sandwich.

"Vinny's Deli."

"Vinny's has the best sandwiches in Connecticut, O'Dell," Henry told her, but Adam could tell she hadn't asked because it looked absolutely mouthwatering. If she had, she wouldn't be so interested in the white paper it had been wrapped in.

"This looks like the same stuff you found with Mr. Earlman," she said, looking at Carl.

"I think you're right."

"What the hell are you two talking about?" Henry seemed a little pissed off that they weren't paying attention to their sandwiches.

"This white, waxy paper," she explained, and now Adam remembered it. "We found something like this in the barrel with Mr. Earlman."

"Lots of people use this stuff, O'Dell."

"Actually, I don't think so, Sheriff. I've never seen this stuff on the shelves of your regular grocery store. I bet it's a specialty item."

"So what the hell are you two saying? That the killer has himself a sandwich while he's slicing and dicing his victims?"

Adam wondered if it was simply the exhaustion that had Henry's face flushed and his voice raised. Maybe the fall sunshine that heated up the rocks and caused the beads of sweat on his upper lip had taken a toll on the aging sheriff. Or was Henry's panic slipping out? So far he had almost appeared too calm.

Whatever it was, Henry was waiting for an answer, standing in front of O'Dell, towering over her. She didn't look the least bit intimidated by the big man, and instead ripped off a piece of the paper to stick in her pocket. Everyone else stood watching, waiting, as if for permission to return to their lunches. Adam couldn't figure out why Henry was suddenly being so tough on Agent O'Dell. After all, he had invited her into the investigation, hadn't he?

"You think this could be important?" Henry finally asked, his tone almost back to normal. He must have realized he couldn't rattle O'Dell so easily.

"When a killer uses something out of the ordinary like this it's often because he has it handy. It may be a way for you to track him down."

"A piece of paper?"

"Sometimes it's the simplest things that lead us to a killer. What we might otherwise think is an insignificant piece of evidence. A serial killer named John Joubert used a strange piece of rope. It had unusual fibers. I think it was made in Korea, not something just anyone would have around the house. He tied up his young victims with it. When they arrested Joubert they found more of the rope in the trunk of his car. The rope was something he had access to as a scoutmaster. He had plenty of it handy and he never considered that it might be something that would be used to finger him. Whatever this white paper is, I'm guessing this killer has plenty of it available to him."

"Okay." Henry still didn't sound convinced. "But what the hell is he using it for?"

"I need to see more of the victims, but my guess right now…" O'Dell hesitated, looking around the group as if deciding whether or not to share her opinion. "My early guess is that he's using it to temporarily wrap things."

"Things," Henry chided as if impatient.

"Yes, things like Mr. Earlman's brain."

# CHAPTER 22

Maggie accepted the Diet Coke Sheriff Watermeier offered. She preferred Diet Pepsi, but knew this was a sort of peace offering. As the others finished their lunches, Watermeier sat down next to her on the boulder.

"When we finish later this afternoon, I need to take a minute and throw a bone to those media piranhas." He smiled, pleased with his own pun. "Then Stolz says he'll do the autopsy of the woman we found yesterday. That suit your time schedule?"

"Yes, of course."

He continued to sit quietly at her side, and she wondered if there was something more he needed to tell her, something more he wanted to share.

"It's beautiful here, isn't it?"

She glanced at him, surprised. That wasn't exactly what she expected from the rough-and-tough, ex-NYPD-turned-small-town sheriff.

She followed his eyes, taking it in for the first time since she had arrived. Maggie couldn't help thinking how quiet it was. The trees were still thick with splashes of orange and yellow with flaming red vines licking up the trunks. And the sky seemed so blue it looked artificial. Even the ankle-high grass was dotted with tiny yellow flowers.

"Yes," she finally agreed. "It is beautiful."

"Everybody ready?" Watermeier broke the momentary peace, standing suddenly as though he needed to snap back to attention.

They joined the others where Adam Bonzado and his students had brought down another cracked barrel. This time Maggie pulled her jacket up over her nose. Already the stench was overbearing and the pry bar had only broken the seal. Despite Bonzado's effort the drum's lid came undone bit by squeaky bit, reminding Maggie of opening a lid off a vacuum-sealed can of coffee.

"Man, oh man, this one is ripe," the professor said, and stopped, his hands still clenching the pry bar while he wiped at his face with the bottom of his shirt, revealing for a second or two rock-hard abs. Maggie looked away, realizing that this was the second time in only hours that she had taken notice of his physique.

The rest of them waited. No one offered to take over for the poor professor. Not any of his three students. The one named Joe kept a safe distance, while the woman, Ramona, seemed interested but cautious. The older student Simon, stood quietly, almost rigid with a trowel in one hand and a camera in the other, making no effort to use either. He seemed stunned or perhaps overwhelmed by the sight. Maybe it was the stench.

"Should we be cutting these barrels open?" Watermeier suggested.

"With what?" Stolz swabbed at his forehead, which had been constantly shiny with sweat. "Anything we use could contaminate what's inside more than it already is. Let's at least see what's in these barrels before we go hauling all of them away. I don't want a dozen barrels of garbage in my lab, Henry. Is that okay? Can we at least see what the hell's in them before we do that? I know it's time consuming and I know it's a pain in the ass."

"Whatever you want. That's your call."

"I never said—" But Stolz stopped as a mass of black flies swarmed out the small opening of the barrel. "What the hell?"

"Son of a bitch." Watermeier took a step back.

Bonzado hesitated for a second, then slammed the lid back down. "We should probably collect a few of these, right?" He looked to Maggie and then to Carl, who was already searching for a container.

"Ramona and Simon, could you give Carl a hand?"

The woman practically jumped to Carl's side, but Simon stood there as if he hadn't heard Bonzado.

"Simon?"

"Yeah, okay."

Maggie watched him set the trowel and camera down so slowly it seemed as if in slow motion. Perhaps Bonzado was expecting a bit much from his students, who had imagined their careers examining clean, fleshless bones in sterile, warm and dry laboratories.

Bonzado pried at the lid again and this time Carl and Ramona held the opposite corners of a makeshift net and caught several flies. Simon held the wide-mouth container for them to shake the flies into, slapping the lid on quickly. He handed the container back to Carl and returned to his previous stance, trowel back in one hand, camera in the other.

Now Bonzado proceeded, ignoring the rest of the flies. Finally, the lid came loose, thumping to the ground. More flies were freed and so was the smell, a sour pungent odor like rotten-egg gas. Maggie watched Joe and one of Henry's deputies hurry away. Joe didn't make it to the trees before he began retching. Even Watermeier and Carl backed away, the sheriff's hat now over his nose.

"Holy fucking crap," Watermeier said, his words muffled through his hat.

Maggie climbed onto the rocks, putting some space between herself and the smell, while attempting a look down into the barrel. "Anyone have a flashlight?"

Pry bar now tossed aside, Bonzado shuffled through his toolbox, setting metal clanking. Maggie couldn't help wondering if it was to distract attention from his nervousness. But when he reached up to hand her the penlight, she realized his sudden clumsiness was no disguise. His hand was perfectly still and he had no trouble meeting her eyes.

"How the hell would flies get inside?" Watermeier asked. "That barrel was sealed good and tight. Did they squeeze through the crack?"

"Possibly," Maggie said. "It's also possible the body was exposed to the elements for a while before it was stuffed inside the barrel." Maggie shot the penlight into the black hole and wished she could see more than the spots of lights. The afternoon sun cast shadows that didn't help matters. Swaying branches overhead created dancing shadows that almost made it look like there was movement down inside the barrel.

"But they couldn't have lasted that long," Watermeier insisted.

"They would have laid their larvae," Maggie said while concentrating on the spots of light showing pieces of torn fabric, a tangle of hair, maybe a shoe.

"Blowflies are pretty quick and efficient," Bonzado joined in. "They can sense blood from up to three miles away and be on a body before it's even cooled, sometimes before it's dead."

Maggie checked faces, but the pallor from moments ago was gone, no one wincing at the gruesome details the professor described. In fact, now everyone seemed ready.

"This one's gonna be a mess," Bonzado said, using another flashlight to take a look for himself into the barrel. "Lots of tissue already gone."

"Wonderful," Stolz said, slipping on his jacket against a breeze that suddenly came out of nowhere. Despite his insistence to open the barrels and make certain they did, indeed, contain bodies, he made no attempt to look for himself. "Let's load it up."

"This is interesting," Bonzado said, still examining the contents. "The back is facing up—at least I think it's the back. There's a strange pattern on the skin."

"You mean a tattoo?" Stolz became interested and Maggie came in for a look, too.

Bonzado's flashlight showed what looked like bright red welts crisscrossed into the corpse's back, at least what was left of the back. The flies had already devoured patches of tissue, though Maggie guessed the majority of their feeding frenzy was on the other side, starting in the moist areas first.

"It's just livor mortis," Stolz said as if it didn't matter. "She…or he died lying on something that had this pattern. All the blood settles. Jesus! This one smells." He backed away, disgusted and shaking his head. "Henry, let's call it a day. I need to get back to start doing some autopsies."

"What about this other one?" Henry pointed to the dented barrel off to the side. Maggie hadn't seen the contents of this one. They must have opened it before her arrival.

"Give it to Bonzado." Stolz waved a hand over his head as he headed for the road. "It's nothing but bones. Not much I can do with that."

Maggie buttoned her jacket, also noticing the chill. The sun had begun to sink behind the mountain though it still seemed early. Bonzado and his students were preparing the barrel for transport as Henry gave directions and pointed to the clearing in the trees, the dirt path where the other vehicles had come in. That's when she noticed something flapping in the breeze, something white sticking out from under the discarded lid.

"Carl," she said, waving the tech over. "Take a look."

He squatted down by her side. "I'll be damned." He pulled out an evidence bag and forceps. Gently he tugged the torn white paper from under its trap while Maggie lifted the lid.

It was the same white, waxy paper.

Just then Maggie felt a nudge at her elbow. She turned to find a Jack Russell terrier ready to lick her hand.

"Speaking of burying things," Carl said, "if Watermeier sees that dog here again—"

"Goddamn it, Racine."

"Too late."

"What did I tell you, Racine?" Watermeier yelled at the old man hurrying down from a footpath in the trees. "You've got to keep that mutt the hell away from here."

"Sorry, Sheriff. He has a mind of his own sometimes. Come here, Scrapple."

But the dog was already sitting and leaning against Maggie's hand as she scratched behind his ears.

"Well, you convince him," Watermeier continued, "to stay the hell out of here, Racine. We can't have him dragging off evidence."

"I take it he's been finding scraps?" Maggie smiled up at the old man who seemed embarrassed and agitated, shifting from one foot to the other. Then she remembered what Tully had said about Detective Racine being from this area. "Racine? Do you have daughter named Julia?"

"I don't know," the man mumbled, and Maggie stood up, sure she must have misunderstood him.

"Excuse me?" she said.

"Yes, I do. Jules. Her name's Julia," he said, his eyes meeting hers though making an effort to do so. His daughter possessed the same blue eyes. He scratched his head, reaching up under the black beret. "That's right, Detective Julia Racine with the…with the D.C. police force. Yes, ma'am. That's my daughter, Jules."

# CHAPTER 23

Luc Racine fumbled with the tangle of keys he found in his pocket. Scrapple waited impatiently, staring at the door as if that might help open it. He knew the terrier was upset with him. He had ducked several attempts Luc had made to pet him.

"I'm not gonna have you eating people, okay?" he told the dog for the third time. "Even if they are dead already." Only now Scrapple ignored him—not a flinch, not even a perk of an ear, no indication that he was listening—and he continued to stare at the door.

Luc would make it up to him. Surely there was something in the refrigerator besides sour milk. He sorted through the keys again, trying to concentrate, trying to remember. He used to be able to pull out the house key automatically without a second thought. These days it seemed to take all his deductive reasoning, or at least, all that remained.

Then as if in a sudden flash he remembered. He grabbed at the doorknob and smiled when it turned easily. He had stopped locking the door, afraid he would eventually forget to take the keys and lock himself out. Relief washed over him, so much so that he could feel a chill. It was becoming a typical response, his body reacting, first with surprise and disappointment then relief that the mind could still participate.

Losing his memory wouldn't be so bad if he didn't know it was happening. That was the worst part. Laboring over shoestrings, unsuccessfully looping worthless knots and all the while knowing that tying his shoes was once something he did without a thought, let alone without a struggle. Learning to tie your shoes. How hard could that be? Easy enough for a five-year-old. Easy. Right. Only now Luc Racine wore slip-on loafers.

But forgetting Jules's name. That was unforgivable. How could he have forgotten? He could hear what Julia would say to that, "You never forget the fucking dog's name, but you can't remember your own daughter's."

The house was cold, as if a window had been left open. Summer was certainly over. He didn't need to see the flaming red of the turning oak leaves. He could feel it in the evening chill, hear it after dark in the chirp of crickets.

He stopped in the middle of the living room. He stopped and looked slowly around. Something didn't feel right. It wasn't like last night when he couldn't recognize anything. No, something felt out of place. A clammy shiver swept through him. He felt the hairs on the back of his neck rise.

Coming back from the quarry he had gotten the same chill. He had followed the footpath, watching his feet so he wouldn't trip over the protruding rocks hidden in the tall grass. All the way back it felt like someone had been watching him. Not just Watermeier or one of the others making sure he left, but someone watching. Watching and following. He had heard twigs snap behind him. Thought it was his imagination, but Scrapple heard it, too, growling once, then putting his tail between his legs, his ears back and hurrying home. He barely waited for Luc, only slowing because the wuss of a dog counted on Luc as his protector. There was something wrong with that. Something backward. Weren't dogs instinctively supposed to be protective of their masters?

Now Luc checked around his own living room, looking for signs that he wasn't alone. He looked out the windows, checking for anyone hiding in the trees. His only assurance was that Scrapple seemed content, stretched out on his favorite rug. Luc hurried to the front door, turned the dead bolt, then made sure the kitchen door was bolted, too. It was probably all in his imagination, although he couldn't remember reading a thing about the disease causing hallucinations or paranoia. But then, how the hell would he remember reading about it when he couldn't remember his own daughter's name?

He shook his head, disgusted with himself. He stopped to check the meager possibilities for dinner, opening the refrigerator. There had to be something he and Scrapple could eat. He stared at the top shelf.

A twinge of panic rushed through him again. What the hell? Calm down, he told himself. It was nothing. Nothing at all. Nothing but his own stupid forgetfulness. And he grabbed the TV remote from the top shelf of the refrigerator.

"I've been looking all over the place for this."

# CHAPTER 24

Henry told O'Dell she could follow him to the morgue. She probably thought he was being considerate. He really just wanted her beside him when they walked out of the quarry together, when the media piranhas attacked. He already knew Stolz wouldn't be any help. The M.E. seemed to have an allergic reaction to reporters and was long gone.

"So tell me, Agent O'Dell, from what you've seen, any ideas who I need to start looking for? And you can spare me the basics."

"The basics?"

"Yeah, white male, twenty-something recluse whose mama abused him so now he doesn't know how to respond to a woman except with violence."

"How does Steve Earlman's mutilation fit into that profile?"

Damn! He'd forgotten about Steve, didn't even want to think about poor Steve.

"Okay, so let's hear your basics on this one."

"It's too soon to give you a physical description, except that yes, he is most likely a white male in his twenties or maybe early thirties. He drives an SUV or pickup or has access to one. He probably lives alone on an acreage outside of the city, but he lives within fifty miles of this quarry."

Henry glanced down at her, trying not to show his surprise or that he was impressed.

"This is all premature," she continued without him prompting her, "but just from looking at the place he chose to dump the bodies says a lot about him. Most serial killers leave their victims out in the open, some even display their handiwork. It's part of their ritual or, in some cases, part of their thrill to see others shocked by what they're capable of doing. This guy goes through a lot of trouble to hide the bodies. He didn't want them found. I'm wondering if he might even be embarrassed about what he's done. Because of that, I'm guessing he has a paranoid delusional personality, which means he'll feel threatened by us discovering his hiding place. He'll think we're out to get him, and it might make him do something irrational."

"In other words, he might screw up, and we'll be able to catch him?"

"He might panic and kill someone he thinks is out to destroy him. In other words, a panic kill. Yes, that could mean he screws up and leaves something behind for us to use to catch him, but it also means someone else could be killed."

"Not at all what I wanted to hear, O'Dell," Henry said, almost wishing he hadn't asked. He already had the governor up his ass. What the hell would happen if this madman started killing again? Jesus! He hadn't even thought of that.

As they got to the road, Henry noticed that the state patrol had arrived, two fresh officers to relieve Trotter and set up guard posts for the night. Earlier Randal Graham, the governor's gopher, had offered the local National Guard. All Henry could think of at the time was that the locals would panic if they started seeing the fucking National Guard moving in. This was bad enough. He didn't need to draw more attention.

"Sheriff Watermeier—" the media mongrels began the barrage as soon as he and O'Dell were in earshot "—what's going on?"

"How many bodies are there?"

"Is it true a serial killer is on the loose?"

"When will the victims' names be released?"

"How long has this been going on?"

"Hold on a minute." Watermeier raised one hand and stopped O'Dell with his other by gently taking hold of her arm. She shot him a look, part surprise and part irritation, just enough for him to know that this was not in her plans. He didn't care. What he did care about was retiring in a community that respected him. And that community damn well better think he was doing everything he could to protect it.

"I can't tell you any details, except to say that yes, there are fifty-five-gallon drums, sealed barrels that have been buried under some rock," he told them, slowing his words so that no one had an excuse to misquote him. "And yes, some of those barrels do have bodies inside. That's all I can say about that right now. But I will tell you that we have everything under control. We have experts on the scene collecting evidence and we have—"

"But what about the killer, Sheriff?" someone from the back yelled, interrupting him. "You have a serial killer on the loose. What are you doing about that, Sheriff?"

Jesus! These assholes were hell-bent on starting a panic. Henry tucked his hat lower over his brow, as if to ward off further blows and hopefully to let them know he couldn't be goaded into their hysteria.

"We're working on that," he lied. It was only the second day. How the hell was he supposed to have a list of suspects already? "That's why we have Special Agent Maggie O'Dell here." He gave her a slight shove forward. "She's a criminal profiler with the FBI, up here from Quantico, Virginia. Her specialty is catching guys like this. So you see we've got the very best working on our team. That's all for now."

This time he grabbed O'Dell's arm to lead her out of the crowd, Officer Trotter clearing a path for them.

"Have you brought in any suspects yet, Sheriff?"

"When will you give us more information? Like a profile of the killer?"

"That's it, folks. That's all I have for today." He waved a hand at them and continued to plow through, shoving the cameras aside when they refused to move.

As soon as they were across the road, O'Dell wrenched her arm from his hold and without a word marched to her Ford Escort. He didn't care if she was pissed. Tomorrow she would probably be long gone. All she wanted was to find her precious missing person, and there was a good chance the woman was waiting for them in the morgue.

# CHAPTER 25

Maggie waited, gloved hands at her sides, while Dr. Stolz unzipped the body bag. She was used to participating in autopsies. Her forensic and medical background had prepared her for doing everything from helping place the body block to taking fluid samples to weighing organs. But she knew when not to participate, too, and this was one of those times. Dr. Stolz had made that clear. So she waited, alongside Sheriff Henry Watermeier, still angry with him for blindsiding her, but anxious to have this trip over and done with.

She was trying to be patient despite her anger and her urge to help. She wanted to help clean the woman's chest wound so they could see the incision, the puncture marks, the rips and tears. There had to be multiple ones to have caused such an eruption.

Stolz must have sensed her restlessness when he said, "The chest wound is not the cause of death. Not as far as I can tell from my preliminary exam." He began parting the long tangled hair, his gloved fingers carefully splitting dried, bloody clumps to reveal a large crescent-shaped wound to the side of the corpse's head. "I'm betting this is what knocked her lights out for good."

"There was an awful lot of blood in the chest area," Maggie said, trying not to contradict the doctor. "Are you sure she wasn't just knocked unconscious?"

Stolz looked at Sheriff Watermeier and pursed his thin lips as if showing him that he was purposely refraining from what he'd like to say. Then he began sponging the woman's chest, cleaning the wound, the mess. "If he started cutting her immediately after he killed her, there would still be a boatload of blood. Especially here in the chest where there's some major gushers. And he cut deep. May have even punctured the heart."

"Wait a minute. Deep wounds sound like fatal wounds," Watermeier said, which drew a scowl from Stolz.

"Not stab wounds." The medical examiner lifted skin he had just cleaned. "She's cut open. Nothing pretty about this handiwork, though. At least not as precise and detailed as with Mr. Earlman."

"What did he remove?" Watermeier asked before Maggie got the chance.

"I'll show you." Dr. Stolz began opening the wound with one hand and with the other flushed the wound with the sprayer hose attached to the side of the stainless steel table. "My first guess would have been the heart, maybe a lung. You know, stuff like the usual crazies take. But this one sort of defies anything I've ever seen."

With the wound now washed clean, Stolz pressed the mangled skin to the side and moved back for Watermeier and Maggie to take a closer look.

Watermeier stared, scratching his head, puzzled and not recognizing the scarred tissue. But Maggie knew immediately. And without getting out the photo Gwen had given her, Maggie also knew that this was not Joan Begley.

"I don't understand," Watermeier finally said, looking from Maggie to Stolz and realizing he was the only one in the dark.

"This woman must have been a breast cancer survivor," Stolz explained. "The killer took her breast implants."

Maggie had already prepared herself, had already planned what she would say to Gwen when she called with the news that her patient had been murdered. She should have felt relief. But for some reason she felt beginning panic instead. If Joan Begley wasn't dead, where the hell was she?

# CHAPTER 26

Joan Begley woke to the sound of doves cooing. Or at least that was what it sounded like through the spiderweb in her brain. Her eyes felt matted at the lashes, stuck down with webs. Her mouth was cotton dry. But the cooing reminded her of summer mornings, waking up at Granny's dairy farm outside of Wallingford, Connecticut. A distant humming lulled her in and out of sleep. The breeze over her head felt and smelled like dew-laced grass, the fresh air wafting in from the meadow. Along with the breeze and the cooing came a feeling of contentment.

A click startled her awake. A click and then a low rumble of a motor coming to life. She sat up, her eyes flying open, her arms straining. It was the leather wrist restraints that renewed the panic, that brought her back to reality. Or rather brought her back to her nightmare.

She stared down at the restraints clamping her to the bed rails, and for a brief moment she thought she might be in a hospital. Had he taken her to a hospital? The room was dimly lit, darkness filled the huge windows. She looked around the area and could see walls made of sturdy timber, rafters of the same, more windows with thick glass, none of which were open. The breeze she had dreamed of was only the ventilation fan above the bed, the hum of a chest freezer in the corner. It looked like she was in a cabin or converted shed. As frightened as she was she had to admit this place had a warm and almost cozy feeling, despite the smell of disinfectant laced with, of all things, the scent of lilac.

Where in the world had he taken her? And why?

She looked around again, her vision still blurred, distorting the items on the shelves, elongating and swirling them like something out of a van Gogh painting. Maybe she was hallucinating. Yes, maybe this was all a dream, a nightmare.

She tried to think through the cobwebs in her brain. She needed to stay calm. No good would come from panic. And she didn't seem to have any energy left. She couldn't allow the panic to take control of her again, to exhaust her. Last night…or was it days ago? How could she be sure? He had drugged her. Asked in his polite tone that she drink a bottle of some concoction.

"It won't hurt," he had promised her in that little-boy voice that she had once found endearing. "It tastes like cough syrup."

But when she refused, she remembered how he grabbed her, shoving her into a headlock. She had been surprised by his strength, by his frenzy, by his…his madness. He had forced the liquid down her throat despite her clawing at him, despite her kicking and coughing and gagging. Yes, he had become a madman, totally out of control. Someone she didn't recognize, and certainly not the Sonny she thought she had gotten to know.

She began to cry, thinking about it. Why had he done this? Why had he brought her here? What did he intend to do with her? If she screamed would anyone hear her?

She looked around the room again. The door was certainly bolted even if she could escape her restraints. Now she noticed that there were leather bindings attaching her ankles to the bed rails, as well. She couldn't focus on that. She wouldn't panic. She would talk to him. Yes, they would talk. Where was he? Had he left her? What in the world did he intend to do with her? She knew he hadn't sexually assaulted her. If that wasn't what he wanted, then what was it?

As if trying to find the answer, she began examining the room. There were shelves with jars of all sizes, crocks with metal-clasp lids, plastic containers, bottles and gallon glass containers. Close to her bed was a table with a lighted aquarium, illuminated jellyfish floating along the surface. On the other side was another table with what looked like bowls made of bits and pieces of shells.

There were pictures on the wall. Black-and-white photos of a boy and his parents. She couldn't tell if the boy was Sonny. This was definitely someone's work space or hideaway. There was no need to feel frightened, she tried to convince herself. She could talk to Sonny. Yes, talk and see what he wanted from her.

She lay back down, feeling better. The pillows were so soft. He had gone to some trouble to make her comfortable, despite whatever drug he had forced down her. But even the drug had simply made her sleepy. No headache, no hangover. She would just wait. Eventually he would come in and they would talk. She could feel herself relaxing. That was when she saw the shelf above her head.

She bolted up in bed, straining against the leather and twisting to get a better view, making herself look despite a fresh panic and the urge to flee. On the shelf above her were three skulls, hollow eye sockets staring out at her.

Oh, dear God! Why? What was this place?

She tried to focus on what was in the jars across the room, but it was too far to see anything more than blobs. Then she stared at the jellyfish in the aquarium next to the bed. They were transparent, illuminated from the backlighting, floating on the surface. There was nothing else in the aquarium. No little rocks at the bottom, none of the colorful greenery. She pulled herself closer for a better look. Did jellyfish always float on the surface like that?

Then in the light she noticed that both jellyfish had numbers imprinted on their surfaces. A string of numbers like a serial number, some sort of identification.

"Oh, my God!" Suddenly, she recognized them from a visit she had made to a plastic surgeon. These weren't jellyfish at all. They were breast implants.

# CHAPTER 27

Dr. Stolz didn't bother to hide his displeasure. Maggie saw the scowl he gave Sheriff Watermeier—it was the third or fourth one of the day, Maggie had lost count. The sheriff announced he needed to leave but that she was welcome to stay. For a brief moment she expected Stolz to forbid it. But how could he? Instead, he muttered something into his mask about outsiders. Maggie got the impression he didn't just mean her, but Watermeier, as well.

She wasn't sure why she stayed. The only reason she was here was to identify Joan Begley. Perhaps she hoped that this victim, this woman, might be able to provide some answers of where Maggie could start looking for Gwen's missing patient.

She watched from beside the stainless steel table. Her hands stayed in her pockets beneath the gown. It was an effort to keep them from helping, part instinct and part annoying habit. Already once she had reached for a forceps, stopping herself before Stolz could see.

He was slow. Slow but not necessarily meticulous. In fact, his movements seemed a bit sloppy, slicing here and there around the edges of the body cavity, reminding Maggie of a fisherman severing all the linings before gutting a fish in one swift scoop. It wasn't the usual reverence she was accustomed to seeing medical examiners use. Perhaps it was simply a performance for her benefit. At first she worried that he would use the less-popular Rokitansky procedure where all the organs come out at once—one block of the internal system—instead of the Virchow method where each organ was removed separately to be examined.

She watched him cut with his elbow bent, hand zigging

back and forth, a strange, almost sawing motion. But then she was relieved to see his gloved fingers reach in and scoop out the lungs, one at a time. First the right lung, which he plopped on the scale, then he yelled over the utensil tray to the recorder on the counter, "Right lung, 680 grams." He dropped it into a container of formalyn and scooped up the left one. "Left lung, 510 grams. Color in both, pink."

Maggie disagreed. She wanted to mention that the left lung was not quite as pink as the right, but kept quiet. It wasn't enough to note. No signs of foul play, at least none that had affected the lungs. In the killer's mutilation to get at the breast implants, he hadn't even punctured the lungs. And there wasn't enough discoloration to indicate that the woman had ever been a smoker. The darker pink of the left lung may have only suggested that she had spent a good deal of her life as a city dweller.

Dr. Stolz picked up a needle and syringe off the tray, looked it over, then exchanged it for a larger one. He inserted the needle into the heart, drawing blood into the syringe. The heart showed definite signs of being punctured by the killer. Maggie could easily see a cut that didn't belong, next to the area where Stolz took his sample. Satisfied, he labeled the sample and set aside the syringe, but he didn't bother to remove the heart. Instead, he moved down to the stomach.

Maggie didn't let him see her impatience. Okay, so he had his own way of doing things.

Of all the incredible workings and mysteries of the human body, Maggie always thought the stomach to be one of the most whimsical of the organs. It resembled a small, saggy pink pouch. A simple and soft touch of a scalpel was usually all that was needed to slit it open, and Stolz, despite his bull-in-a-china-shop approach, handled this organ with a gentleness that surprised Maggie. He laid it on a small stainless steel tray of its own, slit it open slowly and carefully. Using just his fingertips, he spread back the walls. Then, reverting to his normal routine, he grabbed a stainless steel ladle and began scooping out the contents, pouring them into a small basin on the tray.

Maggie moved around the table for a closer look. Stolz didn't seem to mind. Now he seemed excited and anxious to share.

"Still lots here," he said, continuing to scoop and stir the contents, clanking the metal ladle against the metal side of the basin with each pour. "This might be our best estimate of time of death. Being in that barrel threw off too many of the other indicators."

So that was why he was so interested. Finally, something to show off his expertise.

"Is that green pepper?" Maggie asked.

"Green pepper, onions, maybe pepperoni. Looks like she had pizza. Lots still here, which means she was most likely murdered shortly after her meal."

"What do you think? Two hours?" Maggie knew that almost ninety-five-percent of food moved out of the stomach within two hours of being consumed. However, it wasn't an exact science, either. There were things that sped up digestion, just as there were things that slowed it, stress being a major factor.

"Not much has made it into to the small intestine yet," he said, his fingers back in the body cavity examining the coil of intestine. "I'd guess less than two hours. Closer to one."

"So the next question, can you tell whether or not it was frozen or restaurant style?"

He looked up at her with raised eyebrows. "The pizza? Why in the world would that matter?"

"If it was restaurant style, chances are she ate out that night. Maybe even with someone. We might be able to track where she was—and with whom—right before she was murdered."

"Well, that's simply impossible to know," he told her, shaking his head. "But—" he seemed to reconsider as he stirred the contents with what looked like an ordinary butter knife "—the colors, especially of the vegetables, seem brighter than normal, which from my experience could indicate that they were fresh and not frozen."

Maggie brought out a pocket notebook and jotted down the contents. When she looked back up, Stolz was staring at her, his arms folded over his chest. The scowl had returned and was now directed at her, the only person left to try his patience.

"You can't be serious?" he said. "You think the killer took her out for pizza first, then bashed in her head and sliced out her breast implants? That's absurd."

"Really? And why do you say that, Dr. Stolz?" It was her turn to grow impatient with his questioning of her expertise, his distrust that an outsider might have an answer.

"For one thing, that would suggest it could be someone local."

"And you don't think that's possible?"

"This is the middle of Connecticut, Agent O'Dell. Maybe on the coast or closer to New York. This guy, whoever he may be, is using the quarry as a dumping ground for his sick game. My guess is that he lives miles away. Why would he risk dumping bodies in his own backyard?"

"Didn't Richard Craft do that?"

"Who?"

"Richard Craft, the guy who killed his wife and then put her dismembered body through a wood chipper." She watched Stolz's expression go from arrogance to embarrassment. "In the middle of a snowstorm, if I'm not mistaken, and not far from his home in Newtown. Newtown, Connecticut—isn't that just west of here?"

## CHAPTER 28

Lillian sat quietly, listening in disbelief as Henry told her and Rosie about the bodies they had found so far. Of course, it was all confidential, and she knew there were things he wasn't telling them, couldn't tell them. When he came in earlier, his distraught and exhausted demeanor had been enough for Rosie to suggest they close the store early, something Lillian thought she would never hear her partner suggest. Now they sat, sipping decaf among thousands of the best stories captured in print, and yet Lillian couldn't help thinking Henry's story had them all beat. Forget Deaver and Cornwell, this was something only Stephen King or Dean Koontz could concoct.

"Sweetie," Rosie said to her husband, keeping her small hand on top of his large one. "Maybe it's some drifter. Maybe this has scared him off."

"No, O'Dell says he has a paranoid personality. Usually those guys stick to familiar territory because they are paranoid. I've been trying to think of everyone I know who lives alone out on acreages in this area. But those I can think of don't seem like the type."

"The profiler says he lives close by?" Lillian wasn't sure why that made her heart skip a beat. Perhaps it made it all too real. She liked thinking about this case in terms of fiction.

"He's probably watching the news coverage every day, getting his kicks."

"But if he's paranoid, Henry, he's not getting kicks," Rosie said. "Wouldn't he be devastated that you discovered his hiding place? Maybe even ticked off?"

Henry looked at his wife, surprised, as if he hadn't expected her to hit the nail right on the head. But it seemed like common sense. You didn't need to be a rocket scientist or Sherlock Holmes to know this guy would be upset. Lillian added to Rosie's thesis, "Yes, very upset. Are you concerned that he might come after one of you?"

"That's what O'Dell suggested." He didn't look happy that someone else would suggest the same. "She said the guy might panic, but I don't think he would risk screwing up."

Lillian couldn't help feeling elated that she could have come up with the same idea the profiler had come up with. Maybe she was good at this. Who said you had to have life experiences to figure these things out, when all she had done was read about it.

"I'm guessing the profiler says he's a loner, a plain sort of man who goes about his business without much notice." She liked playing this game. She tried to remember some of her favorite serial killer novels. "Perhaps he's someone who doesn't draw much attention to himself in public," she continued while Henry and Rosie listened, sipping their coffee, "but ordinarily, he seems to be a nice enough guy. He works with his hands, a skilled worker who has access to a variety of tools. And, of course, his penchant for killing will most likely be somehow tracked to the volatile relationship he probably had with his mother, who no doubt was a very controlling person."

Now the pair was looking at her with what she interpreted as admiration or maybe amazement. Lillian liked to think it was admiration.

"How do you know so much about him?" Henry asked, but Lillian had been wrong about his look of admiration. It appeared instead to be laced with a hint of suspicion.

"I read a lot. Novels. Crime novels. Suspense thrillers."

"She does read a lot," Rosie said, as if she needed to vouch for her partner.

Lillian looked from Rosie back to Henry, who seemed to be studying her now. It caught her off guard and she felt a blush starting at her neck. She gave a nervous shove to her glasses and tucked her hair behind her ears. Did he really think she knew something about this case, about this killer?

"Maybe I should read more," he finally said with a smile. "I could probably crack this case faster. But I have to tell you, for a minute there you sounded like you were describing someone, someone you knew fairly well."

"Really?" she said, and tried to think of a character who might fit the bill. And suddenly her stomach did a somersault. She did know someone who fit her description, but it wasn't anyone in a novel. The person she had described could very easily be her own brother, Wally.

# CHAPTER 29

It was late by the time Maggie got to the Ramada Plaza Hotel. She started to feel the exhaustion of the day. A tight knot throbbed between her shoulder blades. Her eyes begged for sleep. And she wondered if her mind was playing tricks on her. In the parking lot, while she unloaded her bags, she felt someone watching her. She had looked around but saw no one.

As she waited for the desk clerk—or rather, according to Cindy's plastic clip-on badge, "desk clerk in training"—Maggie tried to decide what she'd tell Gwen. After everything that had happened today, she wasn't any closer to knowing where Joan Begley was. For all she knew the woman was still here at the Ramada Plaza Hotel, lying low and simply escaping.

Maggie watched the desk clerk as she plugged in her credit card information. Hotel policy wouldn't allow them to give out Joan's room number. And Maggie didn't want to draw attention to herself or cause alarm by whipping out her FBI badge. So instead she said, "A friend of mine is staying here, too. Could I leave a note for her?"

"Sure," Cindy said, and handed her a pen, folded note card and envelope with the hotel's emblem.

Maggie jotted down her name and cell phone number, slipped the card into the envelope, tucked in the flap and wrote "Joan Begley" on the outside. She handed it to Cindy, who glanced at the name, checked the computer and then scratched some numbers under the name before putting it aside.

"Here's your key card, Ms. O'Dell. Your room number is written on the inside flap. The elevators are around the corner and to your right. Would you like some help with your luggage?"

"No thanks, I've got them." She slung her garment bag's

strap over her shoulder and picked up her computer case, taking several steps before turning back. "Oh, you know what? I forgot to tell my friend what time we're supposed to meet tomorrow. Could I just jot it down quickly?"

"Oh, sure," Cindy said, grabbing the note and sliding it across the counter to Maggie.

She opened the envelope and pretended to write down a time before slipping the card back in, this time sealing the envelope and handing it back to Cindy. "Thanks so much."

"No problem." And Cindy put the card aside, not realizing she had just shown Maggie Joan Begley's room number.

Maggie threw her bags onto the bed in her own room. She kicked off her shoes, took off her jacket and untucked her blouse. Then she found the ice bucket, grabbed her key card and headed up to room 624. As soon as she got off the elevator, she stopped at the ice machine to fill the plastic bucket, and she padded down the hall in stocking feet to find Joan's room. Then she waited.

She popped an ice cube into her mouth, only now realizing she hadn't eaten since the sandwich at the quarry. Maybe she would order some room service. And as if by magic she heard the elevator ding from around the corner. Sure enough a young man clad in white jacket and black trousers with a tray lifted over his head turned the corner, walking away from her to deliver to the room at the far corner. She waited until he came back and saw her, before she slipped her key card into the slot.

"Darn it," she said loud enough for him to hear.

"Is there a problem, miss?"

"I can't get this key card to work again. This is the second time tonight."

"Let me try."

He took her card and slipped it into the slot, only to get the same red-dotted results. He tried again, sliding it slower. "You'll probably need to have them give you a new card down at the front desk."

"Look, I'm beat, Ricardo," she said, glancing at his name badge. "All I want to do is watch a little Fox News and crash.

Could you let me in, so I don't have to go all the way back down tonight?"

"Sure, hold on a minute." He dug through his pockets and pulled out a master. In seconds he was holding the door open for her.

"Thanks so much," she told him. She was getting good at this. She stood in the doorway and waved to him, waiting for him to round the corner. Then she went inside.

Maggie's first thought was that Joan Begley must do quite well as an artist. She had a suite, and from first glance Maggie guessed that she hadn't been here for at least the last two days. Three complimentary *USA Today's* were stacked on the coffee table. On the desk was a punch card for a week's worth of complimentary continental breakfasts. Every day was punched except for Sunday. There was also an express checkout bill dated Sunday, September 14, with a revised copy for Monday and another for Tuesday.

Several suits and blouses were hung in the closet by the door. A jacket remained thrown over the back of the bedroom chair. Maggie patted down the jacket pockets and found a leather checkbook. She flipped it open, pleased to find Joan Begley kept track of her transactions. There were few since she had arrived in Connecticut. The first was to Marley and Marley for $1,000, listed as a "funeral down payment." There was one at the Stop & Shop with the notation, "snacks." Another at DB Mart, "gas."

The last entry was on Saturday, September 13. At first she thought nothing of it. The check had been made out to Fellini's Pizzeria with a notation, "dinner with Marley." She glanced at the earlier notation. Dinner with one of the funeral directors? Would they meet for dinner to discuss funeral business? Yes, that was possible. If it were something else, a date, perhaps, Mr. Marley probably would have paid.

Saturday, September 13. If Gwen was right, Joan Begley may have disappeared later that night. But obviously she had come back to the room or the checkbook wouldn't be here. Had she come back to change? Was Marley the man she was meeting again when she called Gwen?

She started to replace the checkbook when she thought about the autopsy. Whoever the poor woman was from barrel number one, she had been murdered shortly after having pizza, maybe at Fellini's. Maybe shortly after meeting someone, perhaps even the killer for pizza. Maggie slipped the checkbook into her own trouser's pocket.

She continued to survey the suite. A Pullman was spread open on the valet table. Two pairs of shoes lay tipped underneath where they had been kicked off. In the bathroom, various cosmetics and toiletries were scattered. A nightshirt hung on the back of the bathroom door.

Maggie stood in the middle of the suite, rubbing at her tired eyes. There was no doubt that Joan Begley hadn't just picked up and escaped to the shore or somewhere. Even if she had run off with some new man in her life, she wouldn't have left her things. No, it looked as if Joan had intended to come back to her suite. Yet it was obvious that she hadn't done so for several days. So what happened?

She looked around the two rooms again for any clues, and this time she remembered to check the notepad alongside the phone. Bingo! She could see some indentations on the top page. It was an old trick, but she found a pencil in the drawer and with its side, shaded over the top page of the notepad. Like magic the indentations in the page turned into white lines, forming letters and numbers. Soon she had an address and a time: Hubbard Park, Percival Park Road, West Peak, 11:30 p.m.

Maggie ripped off the page and pocketed it. She stopped at the door for one last look. And before she turned out the light, she said to the empty room, "Where the hell are you, Joan Begley?"

# CHAPTER 30

"Tell me about your illness," he said while sitting on the edge of the bed.

Joan had been asleep. It had to be the middle of the night. But when the light snapped on she woke with a jerk. And there he was. She had to squint to see him, sitting at the foot of the bed, watching her. Staring at her.

She could smell him, a combination of wet dirt and human sweat, as if he had just come in after digging in the woods. Oh, God! Had he been digging her grave?

"What did you say?" She tried to wipe at the sleep from her eyes, only then remembering the leather restraints. Alarm spread through her body. Her muscles ached. She strained to reach her face, to push the strands of hair from her mouth, noticing how very dry her skin had gotten, almost crusty at the corners of her eyes and mouth. Perhaps there were no more tears, was no more saliva inside her. Was that possible? Could a person cry herself dry?

She felt the fear already clawing at her. Felt his eyes examining her. Her stomach growled and for a brief moment she realized she was hungry. "What time is it?" She tried to stay calm. If she didn't panic maybe it wouldn't trigger the madman in him.

"Tell me about your disease, your hormone deficiency."

"What?"

"You know, the hormone deficiency. Which hormone is it?"

"I'm not sure what you're talking about," she lied, but she knew exactly what he was talking about. She had told him that a hormone deficiency was the cause of her struggle with her weight. She had lied, embarrassed to admit that it had only been a lack of self-discipline. Oh, dear God. What had her lies gotten her into? She glanced around the room, at the containers and the skulls above her. Is that what he wanted from her?

"Tell me what gland. Is it the pituitary? Or did you say the thyroid?" He continued in almost a singsong tone, as if trying to coax her into sharing. "You know the hormone that makes you fat? Or I guess it's the lack of a hormone, right? You told me about it. Remember? I think you said it had something to do with your thyroid, but I can't remember. Is it the thyroid?"

She looked over his shoulder at the jars that lined the shelves. There were a variety of shapes and sizes: mason jars and pickle jars with the labels scratched out and taped over with new labels. From a distance she could see only globs, but after recognizing the breast implants, she now realized these containers must hold other specimens, bits and pieces of human tissue. And now he was asking about her thyroid. Oh, Jesus! Was that why he had always been interested? Did he have a jar ready to plop it into?

"I don't know," she managed to say over the lump in her throat. "I mean, they don't know." Her lips quivered and she pulled the covers up over her shoulders as best she could, pretending it was because of the cold and not the fear.

"But I thought you said it was your thyroid?" He sounded like a little boy, almost pouting.

"No, no, not the thyroid. No, not at all." She tried to sound sure of herself. She needed to convince him. "In fact, they discounted the thyroid. Discounted it altogether. You know, it may just be a lack of self-discipline."

"Self-discipline?"

His brow furrowed—puzzled, not angry—as he thought about this. Maybe it was only the tinge of blue fluorescent light from the aquarium, but he reminded her of a little boy again. Even the way he was sitting, cross-legged with one foot tucked under himself, his hands in his lap, his eyes hooded with exhaustion and his hair tousled as if he, too, had just been awakened.

She wondered if he was trying to figure out how he might bottle her self-discipline, or rather lack of self-discipline.

Would he try to find another answer? Then she caught a glimpse of shiny metal. Her empty stomach plunged. In his folded hands that sat quietly in his lap, he held what looked like a boning knife.

Her muscles tightened. Her eyes darted around the room. The panic crawled up from her empty stomach, on the verge of becoming a scream.

He had come for her thyroid. He planned to cut it out. Would he even bother to kill her first? Oh, dear God.

Then suddenly he said, "I never thought you looked fat at all." He was looking down at his hands and glanced up at her with a smile, a shy, boyish smile. It reminded her of the way he had been when they first met, polite and quiet with interested eyes that listened and wanted to please.

"Thank you," she said, forcing herself to smile.

"Sometimes doctors make mistakes, you know." He looked sad now as he stood up, and every nerve in her body prepared itself. "They don't know everything," he told her.

And then he turned and left.

# CHAPTER 31

*Wednesday, September 17*

Midnight had come and gone, but the nausea had not.

He had an hour before he needed to leave. Today would be a long day. He had done these double-duty days before, hadn't minded, but not like today. Last night sleep never came, reminiscent of his childhood, when he waited for his mother to come in at midnight, administering her homemade concoction of medicine only to leave him with even more pain. Today he'd be forced to hide that same nausea, that relentless nausea that had lived with him day after day during his childhood. But he had done it before. He had survived. He could do it again.

If only he had taken care of her that first night like he had planned. He had even brought the chain saw with him, expecting to cut her up piece by piece, hoping to somehow find the prize. Instead, he had decided at the last minute to wait.

It was the wrong decision, a *stupid, stupid, stupid decision.*

He thought he could wait, thinking she'd tell him where her precious hormone deficiency resided, saving him a mess, because he hated messes. *Hated, hated, hated them.* And the chain saw was the messiest of all to clean. But here he was with an even bigger mess on his hands. Not only did he need to worry about those who wanted to destroy him, all those digging in the quarry, but now he needed to figure out a way to dispose of her body when he was finished.

He couldn't think about it now. He needed to get ready for the day. He needed to stop worrying or his stomach would make it impossible to get through this day.

He scraped the mayonnaise from inside the jar, the clank-

clank of the knife against glass only frustrating him, grating on his nerves, which already felt rubbed raw. How could he function? How could he do this?

*No, no, no. Of course he could. He could do this.*

He spread the condiment on the soft white bread, slow strokes so he wouldn't tear it, taking time to reach each corner but deliberately not touching the crust. He unwrapped two slices of American cheese, laying them on the bread, making sure neither slice hung over the edge, again, not touching the crust, but letting them overlap in the center. Then carefully he cut the top slice of cheese exactly at the overlap and set aside the unneeded section.

He reached up into the cabinet, back behind the Pepto-Bismol and cough syrup, grabbing hold of the brown bottle his mother had kept hidden for years. He opened it, carefully sprinkled just a few of the crystals on the cheese, then replaced the bottle to its secret place.

He topped the sandwich with the other slice of bread, but not before slathering it with just the right amount of mayonnaise. Last, but most important, he cut away the crust, then cut it in two, diagonally, not down the middle. There. Perfect.

*Perfect, perfect, perfect.*

He wrapped his creation in white wax paper, putting it on a tray that already included a can of Coke, an individual-size bag of potato chips and a Snickers candy bar. It was the exact lunch his mother had packed for him every day of his childhood, or at least, every day for as long back as he could remember. The perfect lunch. Rarely a substitution. It always made him feel better, but this lunch wasn't for him. It was for his guest.

He smiled at that—his guest. He had never had a guest before. Especially not an overnight one. His mother would never allow it. And despite this being an accident, a mistake, a mess… Well, perhaps, yes, just perhaps, he liked the idea of having a guest. He liked having someone he could control for a change. At least for a little while. At least until he decided how to dispose of the parts he didn't need.

That was when he remembered. He might be able to use one of the freezers. Yes, maybe there was room for her in the freezer.

# CHAPTER 32

Luc Racine sat in the second row of folding chairs. The first row was reserved but remained empty, so Luc had a perfect view of the coffin at the front of the room. Too perfect a view. He could see the woman's makeup-caked face with cheeks too rosy. He wondered if she had ever worn lipstick that deep a shade of red. It almost made her look as if she wore a mask.

Luc pulled out the small notebook and pen from his shirt pocket, flipped it open and jotted down the date. Then he wrote, "No makeup. Absolutely no makeup," and he underlined "absolutely." He kept the notebook out and glanced around.

Marley stood by the door waiting for someone coming down the hallway. Perhaps it was that girl reporter. Luc had seen her in the reception area when he came in. Thank goodness she didn't recognize him, but then she probably couldn't see without her glasses.

Marley was in what Luc called his funeral director position, shoulders squared, back straight, his hands coming together below his waist, folded almost reverently as if in prayer, but his chin was up, showing an amazing amount of strength and authority. And there was the look that went with the posture.

Luc had observed Jake Marley so many times that he could catch the transition process though it happened quickly, within a blink of an eye. The man was an expert. He could go from any range of facial expressions, whether it be anger with an employee, sarcasm or even boredom, then within seconds the man could transform his entire face into an expression of *complete* compassion and sympathy. Complete, but Luc knew complete didn't necessarily mean *genuine*. In fact, he knew Jake

Marley's expression wasn't genuine. It was just a part of his job, a skill honed and perfected. One necessary for his profession, like a fine craftsman's eye for detail, or in Luc's case, like a mail carrier's ability to memorize strings of numbers. But there was something about this skill of Marley's that seemed… hmm…Luc couldn't remember the word. Sometimes he had trouble remembering the right words. He scratched his jaw, trying to remember.

Holy crap! He had forgotten to shave.

Then he glanced down at his feet—dad blasted! He still had his slippers on.

He looked back at Marley to see if the funeral director had noticed him. Maybe he could slip out the back. He twisted around in his seat. Shoot! This room didn't have another door. And now Marley was escorting two women in, directing them to the coffin. He gave Luc a slight nod of acknowledgment but nothing more. Marley's attention was, instead, on the two mourners, and Luc knew he didn't have to worry about Marley paying any more attention to him.

The elderly woman had artificial silver hair and big red-framed glasses that swallowed her small pigeonlike face. She leaned on her companion with every step. It was the companion who assured Luc he didn't have to worry about Marley. The woman wore a tight-fitting blue suit that accentuated her full figure in all the right places. She wore her long dark hair pulled back to reveal creamy, flawless skin.

Yes, she would have Jake Marley's full attention. She already had his hand on her lower back as he escorted them to the front of the room. Luc wondered if Marley was imagining his hand a few inches lower. Of course, he'd never slip. He was one smooth operator. Luc had observed him many times. Just as he had caught the sudden subtle face transformations, Luc had also watched Marley smooth talk and literally handle the pretty ones with a touch on the arm, the half pat, half stroke of the shoulder, the hand on the lower back. Luc had seen all of Marley's moves.

Maybe the women found it comforting, Luc told himself.

Marley wasn't obnoxious about it. He wasn't a bad-looking guy, either. Sort of plain, but put him in one of his five hundred dollar black suits and the guy seemed to ooze strength, comfort and yes, authority. And women seemed to love guys with authority, especially when they were at their most vulnerable.

Luc watched the two women now at the casket, gazing at their loved one, whispering to each other as if not to wake her.

"Her hair looks beautiful," the older woman said, then added, "She wouldn't have worn that color of lipstick."

Luc smiled. See, he knew it wasn't her shade. He flipped his notebook open again and jotted down, "No whispering. Make people talk in normal tones."

The young woman glanced back at Luc and smiled. Her eyes were puffy, though she wasn't crying anymore. He smiled back and gave her a nod. In his notebook he wrote, "No crying allowed. And maybe some cheerful music. None of this…this funeral home music."

He tried to remember what kind of music he liked and drew a blank. Surely he could remember a particular song or maybe a singer. How could he not remember music?

Just then he noticed the two women whispering again, only this time the older woman was looking back over her shoulder at him as the young woman said something to Marley. There were talking about him. Wondering who he was. Why they didn't recognize him.

Time to leave.

He got up and took his time shuffling through the long second row of chairs. By the time he got to the door he heard one of them say something about bedroom slippers and realized that yes, they were talking about him.

Luc made it to the end of the hallway, out the door and down the street. Still no Marley. Of course, he wouldn't leave that beautiful brunette. So Luc took a moment to catch his breath and scratch in his notebook, "Bedroom slippers. Bury me in my bedroom slippers. The blue ones, not the brown ones."

He flipped the notebook closed and put it and the pen in his pocket. In the reflection of the store window he saw a man watching him from behind, from across the street. Was it Marley? He didn't want to turn around to look. Didn't want the man to know. He stood still, pretending to look at the knick-knacks in the store that used to be Ralph's Butcher Shop. He looked between the hanging wind chimes and colorful wind socks, the same area where the rows of salami used to hang. He looked for the man's reflection and couldn't see it. Luc stole a quick glance over his shoulder. The man was gone.

Luc stared at his feet, at the slippers that he couldn't remember putting on that morning. Had there even been a man following him? Or was he really just imagining things?

# CHAPTER 33

Maggie moved her room service tray aside, snatching one last piece of toast. She glanced at her watch. She had plenty she needed to do today, places to go, people to talk to. Adam Bonzado had tracked her down first thing this morning, inviting her to his lab at the university to take a look at one of the victims. He seemed under the impression that she was officially on this case. Maybe Sheriff Watermeier had even told him so. She wasn't sure why she was considering it. Most likely it wouldn't help her find Joan Begley. Except that his lab was at the University of New Haven, the same university where Patrick was.

She glanced at her watch again and dug out her cell phone. She had been putting this off long enough. She punched in the number from memory.

Gwen answered on the second ring as if she was expecting the call.

"It's not her," Maggie said without stalling, then waited out her friend's silence, letting it sink in.

"Thank God!"

"But she is missing," Maggie said, not wanting Gwen to misunderstand. She shoved aside a file she had thrown on the hotel desk. She opened it, but only to retrieve a photo. A photo of Joan Begley that Gwen had given her last week.

"Tell me," Gwen said. "Tell me whatever you've found out."

"I was in her hotel room last night."

"They let you in?"

"Let's just say I was in her hotel room last night, okay?" She didn't have the patience this morning for a lecture from her friend, the same friend who had managed to finagle someone into telling her Joan Begley had missed her flight. "It looks like she's been gone since Saturday. But I don't think she just left. Her things are scattered around the room like she intended to come back."

"Is it possible he may have talked her into running off without her things?"

"I don't know. All her cosmetics? And her checkbook? You tell me, Gwen. Is she the type who would do that?"

There was silence again and Maggie used it to examine the photo. The photographer had interrupted Joan Begley, making her look up from a metal sculpture, her welding hood's protective glass mask pushed up, revealing serious brown eyes and porcelain-white skin. In the background were framed prints, bright splashes of red and orange and royal blue, beautiful explosions of colors with black streaks and slashes through the middle. And in the reflection of the glass, Maggie could almost make out another image. Sort of ironic. A portrait of the artist with a self-portrait of the photographer.

"No," Gwen Patterson finally answered. "She's not the type who would run off and leave her things. No, I don't think she would do that."

"I'm going to need your help, Gwen." She hesitated again, making sure she had her friend's attention. "Now's not the time to be holding back any client-patient confidentiality."

"No, of course not. No, I wouldn't do that. Not if it was something that might help find her."

"You said you had an e-mail from her that mentioned this man she may have been meeting. You said she called him Sonny, right?"

"Yes, that's right."

"Can you forward that e-mail to me?"

"Sure, I'll do it as soon as I get off the phone with you."

"I talked to Tully earlier. He's going to see if he can get into Joan's apartment."

"Can he do that?"

"She's been gone long enough to file a missing persons report. I want him to look around her place. Maybe see if she has a computer and if he can get into her e-mail. We need to find out if there's anything more about Sonny. If possible, Tully'll be going over later today. Would you be able to go over with him?"

More silence. Maggie waited. Had Gwen even heard her? Or had she asked too much?

"Yes," she finally said, and this time her voice was strong again. "I can do that."

"Gwen, one other thing." Maggie examined the photo again. "Did Joan ever mention a man named Marley?"

"Marley? No. I don't think so."

"Okay. I'm just checking. Call me if you think of anything."

"Maggie?"

"Yes?"

"Thank you."

"Thank me when I find her. I'll talk to you later, okay?"

She barely clicked off and the phone started ringing. Gwen must have forgotten something.

"You remembered something?" Maggie said in place of a greeting.

"Agent O'Dell, why the hell am I seeing you on TV?"

It wasn't Gwen. It was her boss, Assistant Director Kyle Cunningham. Damn!

"Good morning, sir."

"It says a rock quarry in Connecticut. I thought you were supposed to be in your backyard and I see you're profiling a case in Connecticut. A case I don't remember assigning you to."

"I'm here on personal business, sir. It was a mistake yesterday when Sheriff Watermeier said I was profiling this case."

"Really? A mistake? But you were there at the quarry?"

"Yes. I stopped by to check on—"

"You just stopped by? O'Dell, this isn't the first time you've just stopped by, but it better be the very last time. Do you understand?"

"Yes, sir. But they may actually need a profiler. This certainly has all the signs of a serial—"

"Then they need to request a profiler. Perhaps their own FBI office has someone available."

"I'm already familiar with—"

"I believe you're on vacation, Agent O'Dell. If you have personal business in the area, that's on your own time, but I better not see you on TV again. Do you understand, Agent O'Dell?"

"Yes, sir. I understand." But there was already a dial tone.

Damn!

She paced the room, stopping to watch the morning traffic down on Pomeroy Avenue and Research Parkway. She checked her watch again. There was still time for one stop. She swung on her jacket, slipping her key card into the pocket, and grabbed her notebook with directions already scrawled inside. She started out the door when she hesitated. What would it hurt? She went back to her computer case, unzipped the pockets until she found it. Then without giving it any more thought she shoved the envelope into her notebook and left.

## CHAPTER 34

Lillian did something that she had never done in all the years she had owned the bookstore—she called Rosie and told her she'd be late. Now as she sat in her car looking at the old house where she had grown up she couldn't help wondering if this was a mistake.

The entire place looked worn and run-down, from the peeling paint on the other buildings to the rusted old cars deserted in the yard like some graveyard for unwanted vehicles. There were a few she didn't recognize, added since her last visit, alongside the old panel station wagon, the one that had been first to be exiled after their mother's death. Somehow it had seemed inappropriate for either of them to use it without her permission.

Lillian stared out her own car window, her hands still on the steering wheel as she tried to decide whether to stay or leave. How in the world did her brother, Wally, live out here? Why did it not bother him to do so? That was something she had never understood. All those years growing up here and wanting, needing to escape. She couldn't imagine staying here, living here and not remembering, not being haunted by those memories. But Wally didn't seem to mind.

She tried to hold on to the courage, the determination she had started the morning with. She tried to imagine herself as one of the sleuths in the many mysteries she so enjoyed. She tried to go back to last night when she was putting pieces of the puzzle together and coming up with theories and ideas that even Henry admitted were exactly what the FBI profiler had come up with. And if all else failed, she needed to at least put to rest her nagging suspicion that Wally had anything to do with those bodies they were finding stuffed into barrels. If anything, maybe he was covering something up for Vargus. Yes, that would make sense. That was something Wally would do.

By the time she stepped up to the front door, she was having second thoughts. Yet, she reached under the nearby flowerpot for the spare keys. She wasn't sure why he bothered to lock the door. What could he possibly have that anyone would want? But that was Wally. Always suspicious of others. Always paranoid that someone was out to hurt him.

The house smelled musty, almost as if it had been closed up and unused except for the pungent smell of burnt food, quickly contradicting her initial impression. He had piles everywhere. Piles of newspapers and magazines and videotapes. But the kitchen looked spotless. No dirty dishes in the sink. No crusted pots and pans on the stove. No trash in the corner. She couldn't believe it.

She should check the refrigerator. She braced herself and opened the refrigerator's freezer, ready to wince. Henry had mentioned missing body parts but hadn't elaborated. She wasn't sure what she might find. But there was nothing unusual. Some frozen pizzas and hamburger patties. What did she expect? What in the world was wrong with her?

She shook her head and glanced into the laundry room off the side of the kitchen. This looked more familiar, piles of dirty clothes on the floor in no order of separation, such as whites from darks or delicates from heavy duty. She turned back to the kitchen when she noticed a white T-shirt crumpled and tossed into the corner on top a black trash bag.

This was silly, she told herself. She needed to get to the bookstore. She was getting carried away, lost in her imagination as usual. But she went to the corner and picked up the T-shirt, gasping as she unfolded it. It was caked and crusted and reddish-brown. And Lillian was convinced that it was blood. Her hands were shaking as her mind tried to reason it away.

Wally got nosebleeds as a child all the time. He probably still got them. He was always complaining about some ache or pain. The man was not healthy. Of course, he probably still got nosebleeds.

"Lillian?"

She jumped at the sound of his voice at the door, dropping the T-shirt and turning to find him scowling at her.

"What the hell are you doing here?"

"I was looking for you," she lied, immediately recognizing what an awful liar she was. For someone who lived inside her imagination, she should be better at coming up with stories.

"You never come out here."

"I guess I was feeling nostalgic. Maybe a little lonely for the old place." The lies only got worse. Even she wouldn't believe them. "Can I be honest with you, Wally?"

"That would be a good idea."

"I was looking for…I wanted to see if I could find…that old blue vase Mom had."

"What?"

"Yes, that blue ceramic one. Do you remember it?" Now, this was good. She could see that she had him trying to remember. "It was the one Aunt Hannah gave her."

"I don't know why you want that now." But the suspicion was gone from his voice. "I think it's up in the attic. I'll go see if I can find it."

He was a good guy. A good brother despite everything their mother had put them through. He couldn't possibly have done any of the things Lillian had imagined in her overzealous imagination. It simply wasn't possible. But as she heard him on the stairs, Lillian plucked the bloodied T-shirt up from out of the corner and stuffed it into her handbag.

# CHAPTER 35

*Washington, D.C.*

R. J. Tully paced in front of the brick apartment building, his hands in his pocket jingling change. He made himself stop. Leaned against the handrail and glanced up at the dark clouds. Any minute now they would surely burst open. Why didn't he own an umbrella?

In his younger days it had been a macho thing. Men didn't use umbrellas. Now as the breeze turned chilly and he lifted his jacket collar, he decided staying dry was more important than being macho. He remembered Emma telling him once that there was a fine line between being macho and being a dweeb. When had his fifteen-year-old daughter become so wise?

Tully checked his wristwatch and searched the sidewalks and street. She was late. She was always late. Maybe she'd decided she didn't want to be alone with him. After all, they had done a good job avoiding that since Boston.

Boston…that seemed like ages ago. Then he saw her, walking a half block up the street, black trench coat, black heels, black umbrella and that silky strawberry-blond hair, and suddenly Boston didn't seem so long ago.

He waved when she finally looked his way. One of those wide, open-palmed, counterclockwise waves, like some idiot directing traffic. Something like a total dweeb might do. What was wrong with him? Why did he get all nervous around her? But she waved back. There was even a smile. And he tried to remember why they had decided to forget Boston.

"Sorry I'm late," Dr. Gwen Patterson said. "Have you been waiting long?"

"No, not at all." Suddenly he easily discounted the twenty minutes of pacing.

The building superintendent had given him the security code and key to Apartment 502, but he failed to mention the open freight elevator they needed to take up to the loft. Tully hated these things, metal gates instead of doors and nothing to hide the cables or muffle the groan of the ancient hydraulic system. None of it seemed to faze Dr. Patterson.

"Have you ever been to her apartment before?" he asked, offering chitchat to fill the silence and take his mind off the screech of a pulley in need of a good oiling.

"She had a show about six months ago. I was here then. But that was the only time."

"A show?"

"Yes. Her loft is also her studio."

"Her studio?"

"She is an artist."

"Oh, okay. Sure, that makes sense."

"I'm surprised Maggie didn't tell you that."

Tully thought she sounded almost pissed at O'Dell. He had to be mistaken, and he studied her profile as she watched the number at the top, indicating each floor as they ground past the levels. He decided to leave it alone.

He would have known soon enough about Joan Begley's profession. The loft looked more like a studio than living quarters, with track lighting focused on pedestals of sculptures and walls of framed paintings. In the corner, piles of canvases leaned against easels and more pedestals. Some of the canvases were filled with bright colors, others were whitewashed, waiting their turn. Chrome shelves held clusters of supplies, brushes still in jars of purple-green solution, paint tubes with missing caps, soldering tools and what looked like drill bits, alongside pieces of twisted metal and pipe. Interspersed among this mess were miniature clay figurines, thumbnail models of their larger finished counterparts. The only signs of living were an overstuffed sofa with matching pillows that tumbled onto the hardwood floor and in the distant corner a kitchen separated by a counter with empty take-out containers, discarded bottles of water, dirty tumblers and a stack of paper plates.

"Looks like she may have left in a hurry," Tully said, but was wondering how someone could live in the middle of her work space. He knew he couldn't.

"You might be right. She seemed very upset about her grandmother's death."

"So you spoke to her before she left."

"Just briefly."

Tully ignored the art stuff, a challenge in itself, and began searching for a desk and computer. O'Dell had given him a list of things she needed him to check out.

"Where the heck did she keep a computer?" He glanced back at Dr. Patterson, who stayed at the wall of paintings, looking with a tilted head as if she could see something in the random splashes of paint. Tully could never figure out art, despite his ex-wife Caroline having dragged him to gallery after gallery, pointing out social injustices and brilliant interpretations of individual pain and struggle where Tully could see only blobs of black paint with a mishap of purple splattered through the center.

"Do you have any idea where she may have kept her computer?" he asked again.

"Check the armoire."

"The armoire? Oh, okay." The cherry wood monstrosity took up almost one wall, and when Tully began opening doors and drawers it grew, spreading out into the room with swiveling shelves and sliding hideaways and, yes, a small laptop computer that seemed to be swallowed up inside.

"Do you know if this was her only one?"

Dr. Patterson came over and ran her fingertips over the armoire's surface, almost a caress.

"No, I think she had a couple of them. She liked the mobility of laptops. Said she could go to the park or coffee shop."

"So she may have had one with her in Connecticut?"

"Yes, I'm sure she did. She e-mailed me from Connecticut."

He opened its lid, carefully, touching it on the sides with the palms of his hands, purposely not disturbing fingerprints or adding his own. Then he used a pen to press the on key.

"I should be able to get into her e-mail with a few tricks. It may take a while," he said, as he brought up her AOL program. He hesitated when the screen asked for a password. "I don't suppose you could save me some time. Any idea what she may have used as a password?"

"She wouldn't have used her name or any derivative of it." She stared at the screen and Tully thought he had lost her attention again when she added, "Try Picasso. I believe it's one 'c' and two 's's. He was her favorite. She used to say she was a whore to Picasso and his work. You may have noticed some of his blue-period influence in her paintings and the cubism influence in her sculptures. Especially her metal sculptures."

Tully nodded, though he wouldn't know cubism from ice cubes, and keyed in P-I-C-A-S-S-O, again using the tip of his pen. "No go."

"Hmm…maybe his first name, then."

Tully waited, then realized she thought he knew this. Geez! He should know this. If ever there was a time to impress her, this would be it. What the hell was it? She wasn't helping. Was it a test? He stole a glance her way only to discover that her eyes had been distracted again, her face with the expression of someone lost in thought and trying to find the answers in the wall of paintings. And so even Tully's flash of brilliance was lost on her when he finally keyed in "Pablo."

"Nope. Pablo doesn't work, either," he announced, perhaps a bit too proud for someone who had just keyed in the wrong password. He waited. He glanced up at her again and waited some more. Finally he stood up, stretching his back, towering over her.

"I know what it is," she said suddenly, without turning her eyes from what looked like an anorexic, pasty self-portrait, a nude with the metal frame cutting her below the emaciated breasts. "Try Dora Maar," she told him, spelling it slowly while he keyed in the letters.

"Bingo." Tully watched AOL come to life, announcing, "You've got mail." "How did you know that?"

"Joan started signing some of her paintings as Dora Maar. It's complicated. She was complicated. That one," Patterson pointed out, "reminded me."

"Why Dora Maar?"

"Dora Maar was Picasso's mistress."

Tully shook his head and muttered, "Artists." He clicked on the New Mail. Nothing had been opened since Saturday, the day Joan Begley supposedly disappeared. He clicked on Old Mail. One e-mail address stood out from the rest because there were so many, appearing every day, sometimes twice a day, but stopping the day she disappeared.

"This could be helpful," he said as he opened one of the e-mails from the Old Mail queue. "She has quite a few from someone with an e-mail address of SonnyBoy@hotmail.com. Any idea who that might be?"

"That's what Maggie and I are hoping you'll be able to find out."

# CHAPTER 36

Joan felt sick to her stomach.

She had been famished, devouring the food he brought her earlier. Perhaps she had made herself sick, eating too fast. She had even been embarrassed. Here he was holding her captive, possibly hoping to slice out her thyroid at any moment, and she couldn't wait to wolf down the cheese sandwich and potato chips. But she had always taken solace in food. Why would a time like this be any different?

Her wrists and ankles burned from a night of trying to pull and twist out of the restraints. Her throat felt raw and her voice had gone hoarse from her yells and screams for help. Where was she that no one could hear her? And if Sonny didn't kill her, would anyone ever find her? No one was probably even looking for her. How pathetic was that? But true. There was no one in her life who would miss her if she disappeared. No one who would notice. All that hard work, losing weight and making herself look good, and for what? When it came right down to it she was still alone.

All along that had been her greatest fear, that she would lose all the weight and still not be happy. Oh, she certainly tried. Over and over again she tried, expecting happiness to arrive with the next man she met. And now she met plenty of men, each time hoping this one would somehow make her feel special, complete. And each time they left her feeling more empty and miserable.

It was something that Dr. P. had warned her about. That she could make a wonderful-looking package who would attract men just like she had always desired, but that someone would still be miserable on the inside.

Damn! She hated when Dr. P. was right, because yes, she was still miserable, but now she no longer had the extra weight to blame. Before, she could fall back on that excuse. If she couldn't attract a man, it was because of her weight. If she had no friends, it was because of her weight. If she wasn't a successful artist it was because no one wanted a contract with a fat artist.

She had transferred her tendency to find comfort from food to trying to find it in men. Maybe she could try explaining that to Sonny the next time he stopped by. Would that stop him from trying to slice out her hormone deficiency?

Oh, God! What had she done?

Suddenly her stomach felt as if she were being sliced in two. She tried to curl up to stop the pain but the restraints wouldn't let her. This pain was not from eating too fast. Could it be food poisoning? Had the mayonnaise in the sandwich gone bad? Now every muscle in her body tensed as she cringed against the cramp that turned her stomach inside out. What was happening to her? She had never felt like this before.

Finally the pain eased. She began to relax. Maybe it was from the panic. Maybe she just needed to stay calm. But not a minute later, her entire body braced itself for a second wave of cramps. And that's when she knew Sonny had poisoned her.

# CHAPTER 37

Maggie let Jacob Marley lead her to his office, down the hallway to the rear of the funeral home. Each time he attempted to place his hand on the small of her back she found a way to make him remove it, either by turning toward him or simply stopping short. She recognized the tactic as a leveling tool, a way for him to gain the upper hand. She couldn't help thinking that it was probably an occupational hazard. Maybe it worked with his clients, not the dead ones, of course, but the ones who would be vulnerable and making the spending decisions.

Now she watched as he offered his office's guest chair while he took a seat on the front corner of his desk where he would tower over her. That was when Maggie decided there was something about Jacob Marley she didn't like. What was worse, there was something about him she didn't trust.

She remained standing, pretending to be interested in the black-and-white photos that took up one wall, photos of a small boy, presumably young Jacob, an only child, with his mother and father.

"What is it that I can help you with, Maggie? You don't mind if I call you Maggie, do you?"

"Actually, when it's official business I prefer Agent O'Dell, thank you."

"Official business." He attempted a laugh, but it ended up sounding like a nervous cough. "That sounds serious."

Before she could bring up Joan Begley, he asked, "Is this about Steve Earlman?"

She had forgotten about the town butcher and only now realized Marley and Marley may have been the funeral home that hadn't managed to bury him. Or at least, not keep him buried. She leaned against the wall, studying Mr. Jacob Marley. She guessed him to be in his early thirties, a plain-looking man with a weak chin and narrow eyes, but in the expensive black suit and sitting high on the corner of his desk, he looked in control and poised. And he was concerned about Steve Earlman.

"I know it hasn't been released," he continued, "but rumor is that Steve's body showed up in one of those barrels. It's true, isn't it? That's what you're here to check on, right?"

He was fidgeting, swinging one foot. Marley didn't look like the type of man who allowed himself to perspire, and yet if she wasn't mistaken, there were beads of sweat forming on his upper lip. Now Maggie was curious. What exactly was Jacob Marley worried about?

"I really can't go into any details," she told him. "But if that were true, what explanation could there be for something like that happening?"

Maggie still believed the killer had access to the body before it made it out to the graveyard. Perhaps he had sneaked into the funeral home after hours. Had there been a break-in that Marley failed to report? Was that what had him worried?

"We buried him in a vault," he said, then quickly added, "the family requested a vault. You can see for yourself." He picked up a folder from his desk, handing it to her.

It was Steve Earlman's file with copies of his funeral arrangements and an itemized invoice. Marley had pulled it. He had been waiting for this visit. He was worried about something and it wasn't poor Steve Earlman's corpse.

She flipped through the file, not sure what she should be looking for. The charges looked standard. No extravagances stood out. And yes, there was a charge of $850 for a vault, not just a vault but something called a "Monticello vault."

"Our vaults are sealed tight," he continued. "They're guaranteed against cracking or seepage."

"Really? Has anyone ever complained?"

"Excuse me?"

"Has anyone ever asked for their money back?"

He stared at her then finally laughed, this time a loud, hearty, rehearsed one. "Oh, goodness, no. But that's a good one, Maggie."

"Agent O'Dell."

"Excuse me?"

"I really would prefer if you called me Agent O'Dell, Mr. Marley."

"Oh, sure, of course."

Maggie searched the rest of the documents in Steve Earlman's file.

"Actually, I was curious about another client of yours. I understand you worked with Joan Begley to make arrangements for her grandmother's funeral. Is that right?"

"Joan Begley?"

This seemed to throw him off completely.

"Yes, of course, I worked with Joan last week. We finished the last of the paperwork on Saturday. Was there a problem?"

Jacob Marley seemed more surprised than concerned this time.

She wanted to ask about their dinner out at Fellini's. She wanted to ask him if he knew she was missing. But the look on Marley's face answered her questions. Whatever hope she had that Jacob Marley may have had something to do with Joan Begley's disappearance, Maggie knew that hope was squelched by the look of total confusion and surprise. Jacob Marley was hiding something, but it didn't have anything to do with Joan. Instead, it was probably right in front of her inside this file.

Marley's phone began ringing. He grabbed the receiver. "Yes?"

What should she be looking for? What was Marley nervous they would find?

"I'm with someone right now," Marley said into the phone, unable to hide his irritation. "No, I won't be able to pick up the body for at least another hour. Is Simon working today? Good. Send him when he gets in."

He hung up the phone and turned back to Maggie. "Worst

part of this job is that we always have to be on call and keep some strange hours."

"Yes, I suppose it would be very unpredictable," Maggie said, flipping through the pages. Then she noticed something that caught her attention. If she remembered correctly, Calvin Vargus was one of the men who had discovered the first body at the rock quarry. "You contract out with Calvin Vargus and Walter Hobbs to dig the graves?"

"Yes, that's right." He shifted his weight and the other leg began swinging this time. "They have the equipment to do it."

"How long have they been doing it?"

"Oh, gosh—" Marley folded his arms over his chest "—I think as far back as when Wally's father ran the business and he contracted with my father. So it goes back a ways. My father was a very loyal man, working with the same people for years." He pointed to one of the photos on the wall, a portrait of the older Marley, looking somber as if ready for a funeral. "People felt the same way about him, too, God rest his soul. Even now when I try to do something different, make a few changes here and there, I can't seem to do it without someone telling me, 'That's not the way Jacob Marley would do it.'"

Suddenly it struck Maggie. Maybe she was wrong after all. "Your father's name was Jacob, too?"

"Yes, that's right."

"So you're a junior?"

"Yes, but please, I really hate being called Junior. Anything but Junior."

# CHAPTER 38

Tully let her wait on him. She had insisted. It was the first time he had been inside her brownstone. The first time he had been invited. By default, of course, he reminded himself, but still, an invitation was an invitation.

She had decided they would be more comfortable here than at Joan Begley's loft. There, she had been distracted. Tully had noticed her walking, stepping lightly, quietly, reverently. He knew Joan Begley was a client of Dr. Patterson's, but he didn't have to be a profiler to guess she had also been somewhat of a friend. Or if not a friend, then someone Dr. Patterson genuinely cared about. There was a connection. Even he could see that, feel that.

He studied her face while she poured the coffee into mugs, preoccupied with the task, and so it was safe to study her. He sat at the counter that separated her living room from her kitchen—a spic-and-span kitchen with hanging utensils and pots and pans in more sizes and shapes than Tully could think of uses for. Here, among her own things, she looked less vulnerable than she had at Joan Begley's. But even here, she still looked…it was hard to explain. She looked tired. No, that wasn't right. She looked…sad.

"Cream or sugar?" she asked with only a glance over her shoulder.

"No, thanks. I take it black." He knew before she reached for the cream that she would pour a healthy dollop of it into hers, making it look like milky chocolate. Cream, but no sugar. And if available she preferred a café mocha.

The realization startled him. These days he couldn't remember what color socks he had put on in the morning—hopefully they at least matched. And yet, here he was remembering how Dr. Gwen Patterson took her coffee.

"So you think Maggie's right? That this Sonny has something to do with Joan's disappearance?"

"He sends her e-mails every day that she's in Connecticut, obviously every day after they met. Sometimes two and three a day. Then all of a sudden they just happen to stop on Saturday, the day she disappeared. Too much of a coincidence, don't you think?"

"But from the e-mails we read, they sounded like friends, confidants. He didn't sound like someone who would want to hurt her."

Her cell phone interrupted them and Dr. Patterson managed to grab it before the second ring, like someone expecting news, any news.

"Hello?" Then her entire face softened. "Hi, Maggie," she greeted her friend. "No, I'm okay. Yes, I did meet Tully at Joan's apartment. Actually, he's here. No, here at my brownstone." She listened for a few minutes then said, "Hold on." She handed him the phone. "She wants to talk to you."

"Hey, O'Dell."

"Tully, can you tell me anything about Sonny?"

"Well, we were able to get into her e-mail."

"Already?"

"Dr. Patterson figured out the password. There're daily e-mails from this guy, but we were just talking about that. They sound pretty chummy, in a friendly way, not a romantic way. Right?" He looked at Gwen for her agreement. "But here's the thing. His e-mails stop the day she disappeared."

"Can you track him?"

"I've got Bernard working on it. So far it looks like he uses a free e-mail account and there's no customer profile on him anywhere that I can find. I'm betting he uses a public computer. Probably the local library or maybe one of those cafés that have computers available."

"Have you talked to Cunningham today?"

"No, he's in meetings all day. Why?"

"He managed to get out of a meeting long enough to call me."

“Uh-oh. You’re busted?”

“Not sure. Look, Tully, I just don’t want you getting into trouble for helping me out on this.”

Tully glanced up at Dr. Patterson. She stood on the other side of the counter, sipping coffee and watching him, thinking he was focused on listening to O’Dell when he couldn’t take his eyes off of her.

“Tully, do you hear me?” O’Dell was saying in his ear. “I don’t want you getting into trouble over this.”

“Don’t worry about it, O’Dell.”

# CHAPTER 39

He fixed her soup, hearty chicken noodle. It was just canned—that's all he had—but it smelled good even after he had dissolved the crystals in it. She'd never notice the tiny white residue. Especially after he crumbled saltine crackers into it.

He placed the small bottle back behind his mother's secret stash, her array of "home remedies" that included molasses and honey and vinegar alongside cough syrup and plenty of children's aspirin. The brown bottle contained the magic crystals she insisted would make him well. It wasn't until after she was gone, her control over him broken only by death, that he discovered the brown bottle with the real label hidden underneath an old expired prescription. The real label simply read in bold, black letters, "Arsenic." He had kept it just as he had found it, realizing that some day he might need that kind of control over someone. And he had been right.

He found her sitting at the window, exactly where he had left her with the restraints now wrapped around the chair. She stared out at the woods through the tempered glass. He had specially ordered and installed the custom-made glass himself. Thick and unbreakable, it allowed a view and let the sunshine in, but on the outside it simply looked like a mirrored solar panel for heat. It provided an excellent work environment—sunny and cheerful, yet private and quiet, protecting his specimens.

She looked up at him. This time her hand didn't move, though he could see the red welts on her wrists where she must have fought the leather restraints again. And then he saw the scratches and grooves in the chair's arm. She had ruined the wood. She had done it on purpose. His mother's chair, a Duncan

Phyfe he had reupholstered himself, and she had ruined it by rubbing the buckles of the leather restraints into the wood.

He felt the anger rising but it came with bile, threatening to back up from his stomach. He could taste it. No, no. He couldn't be sick. He wouldn't. He mustn't think about the chair. No anger. He couldn't afford to make himself sick.

He placed the tray on the table next to her and avoided looking at the scarred chair arm.

"You must be hungry," he said, as he pulled up a stool from his workbench.

"I don't feel so good, Sonny," she mumbled. "Why are you doing this?"

"Why? Why? Because you must be hungry," he said in a singsong voice, a fake happy voice he had learned so well from his mother. "You ate all of your sandwich but that was hours ago."

"Can't we just talk for a while?" she insisted. And he thought her voice sounded whiny. He hadn't noticed before how whiny her voice was.

He scooped up a spoonful of soup and held it in front of her, waiting for her to open her mouth. She only stared at him.

"Open wide," he instructed.

She continued to stare.

He brought the spoon to her lips and began to wedge it in, but she kept her lips pursed tight. Suddenly she jerked her head away to the side, so abruptly that she almost knocked the spoon out of his hand and did end up spilling it on his shirt-sleeve.

He tasted the bile again. Oh, God! He couldn't be sick. He felt his face grow hot. But he scooped up another spoonful and held it in front of her again.

"Come on, now, you have to eat."

She turned her head slowly to look at him, this time the glaze clearing a bit, revealing her defiance.

"Not until we talk."

"Look, we can do this the easy way or the hard way," he told her, continuing to keep his happy voice, despite the turmoil brewing in his stomach. "Now, open up."

He brought the spoon to her lips again, but this time she raised her restrained hand just enough to knock his elbow. It spilled all over his trousers. He'd have to change before work.

He rose slowly to his feet, taking his time to roll up the soiled sleeves of his shirt. A difficult task when his hands were shaking and his fingers were balling up into fists. He could feel the transformation, a lead-hot iron stabbing into his guts. And he could see the transformation in the way she looked at him. Whatever drugged courage had possessed her was gone now. She struggled against the restraints, kicking at the chair legs and smacking the ankle shackles against the wood, leaving more grooves in the precious wood.

"I guess you've chosen to do this the hard way," he said through gritted teeth. This time he left the spoon on the tray, and he picked up the bowl of soup.

# CHAPTER 40

*West Haven, Connecticut*

Maggie wasn't sure what she was doing here. There were other places she needed to check out, coincidences she needed to follow up on. Like Jacob Marley Jr. and whether or not anyone called him Sonny. Or if Wally Hobbs's contract to dig graves for the funeral home had anything to do with Steve Earlman not staying buried. Not to mention the address she had found imprinted on Joan Begley's hotel notepad, and whether or not it was the meeting place for a rendezvous that may have been her last. There were plenty of places where she needed to look for answers and she wasn't sure this was one of them. Yet, here she was at the University of New Haven.

The aroma filled the classroom laboratory. Maggie thought it smelled like beef broth. And annoyingly good. Professor Adam Bonzado stood over the industrial-size stove, lifting the lids of several steaming pots, stirring one with a wooden spoon before replacing the lids and turning down the gas flame. Today he wore a purple-and-yellow Hawaiian shirt with blue jeans and high-top sneakers. His plastic goggles were down around his neck, sharing swing space with a paper surgical mask. He glanced at her over his shoulder. Then did a double take, surprised to see her.

"You're early," he said.

"I didn't have as much trouble finding the campus as I thought I might. Would you rather I go wander and come back?"

"No, no, not at all. I've got lots to show you." He checked the pots one more time and turned to give her his attention. "Welcome to our humble lab." He waved a hand over the area. "Come take a look."

Maggie let her eyes take in the shelves of specimen jars and vials, odd assortments and sizes, some makeshift baby-food jars alongside bell jars and pickle jars with scientific labels covering the name brands. From a corner came the soft whirr of a dehumidifier. The room felt cool, and beneath the aroma of soup broth there was a trace of cleaning supplies, perhaps a hint of ammonia. The countertops were filled with microscopes and a scattered, strange collection of tools, from an impressive jawlike clamp without teeth to small forceps and an array of every sized brush imaginable.

In another corner were two huge plastic bubbles. Maggie guessed they were odor hoods. She could hear the quiet wheezing of ventilation fans from inside the contraptions that reminded her of old-fashioned beauty parlor dryers. The contents below, however, quickly dispelled that image. In the double sink underneath the two hoods Maggie could see skeletal remains, soaking in what appeared to be a sudsy solution. A hand stuck up out of the foam as if waving to her, most of the flesh gone.

And then there were the tables, six-foot-long tables, three of them between the aisles, a fleshless village of skulls and bones. Several skulls stared back at her. Others, too wounded to sit up, lay with hollow sockets staring at the wall or gazing at the ceiling. The bones were a variety of sizes and shapes and pieces, as well as colors. Some were sooty black, others creamy white, some dirty gray and still others a buttery yellow—butterscotch came to Maggie's mind. Some were laid out carefully as if reconstructing a puzzle. Others were tangled in cardboard boxes at the edge of the tables, waiting to be sorted, waiting to tell their story.

"Let me finish this, okay? Then I want to show you a few interesting things I've discovered."

Bonzado put on a pair of latex gloves, then put another pair over the first. He pulled the plastic goggles and mask in place, then grabbed what looked like an oven mitt and lifted the lid off one of the pots. He waited for the steam to clear, then took an oversize wooden spoon and began fishing out what looked like chunks of boiled meat and fat and carefully placed them into an open, waiting plastic bag.

"We save as much of the tissue as we can," he explained, raising his voice to get through the mask in what sounded like a practiced tone, perhaps his teaching voice. "These bags are great. They're like 4.5 mil thick so we can heat-seal them, make them airtight and throw them in the freezer. Plus, they can go directly from the freezer to a boiling pot or the microwave."

Maggie couldn't help thinking he sounded like a chef on one of those cable cooking shows.

"The periosteum is what takes the longest to remove," he said, holding up a long thin piece of what looked like gristle. "I'm sorry—" he looked at her over his goggles "—I hope I'm not being condescending. You probably know all this stuff."

"No, no. Go on. I'm quite sure there's a thing or two I don't know." The truth was, despite all the time she'd spent hanging around the FBI's crime lab to pester Keith Ganza, she had never been to an anthropological lab, least of all, a teaching one. The surroundings fascinated her. And Bonzado's enthusiasm and style were far from condescending. He simply seemed excited to share. His excitement could be contagious.

"We try to get all the way down to the bone," he continued while he filled one plastic bag and then another. "Usually using some dishwashing detergent. My personal preference is Arm & Hammer's Super Washing Soda," he said, holding up the container and sounding like a commercial, "and a good long, slow boil. That usually does the trick. But this stuff takes forever."

"The periosteum?"

"That's right." He smiled at her, another practiced response for his students, but practiced or not, Adam Bonzado's smiles always seemed genuine, even to a trained FBI profiler. "All our bones are covered with it. It's this tough fibrous material. I tell my students that a really gross comparison is when you eat barbecue ribs and there's that tough part that sticks to the ribs. You know the stuff I'm talking about?"

She simply nodded.

"That's the pig's periosteum."

This time she rewarded him with a smile and he seemed pleased, all the while she was thinking she probably wouldn't be eating barbecue ribs any time soon. It surprised her that little things like that would make a difference, considering what didn't bother her. But to this day she still couldn't eat anything Keith Ganza offered her from the small refrigerator he kept in his lab. Maggie looked at it as a good sign. A sign that she hadn't grown so jaded she could eat a tuna salad sandwich after it had shared a shelf with human body tissue.

"I'll let these others boil," he told her while he heat-sealed the two newly filled plastic bags and crossed the room to place them in the freezer. He stopped at the sink to pull off the gloves and wash his hands. He reached for a small bottle of what Maggie could see was vanilla extract, dabbing some onto his hands and rubbing it in. Then he started removing his goggles and mask, but hurried back to the stove when one of the pots started boiling over.

He lifted the lid and grabbed a clean wooden spoon to stir. He turned down the flame and then absently scooped out a spoonful and brought it to his lips, blowing on it before he did the unthinkable—he took a sip from the spoon.

"What the hell are you doing!"

He glanced at her, then quickly back at the stove and pot before his face flushed with embarrassment. "Oh, jeez! I'm sorry. I didn't mean to freak you out. It's my lunch." But her look mustn't have convinced him, so he scooped up more as evidence, showing her what she could now identify as carrots, green beans, maybe some potatoes. "It's just vegetable beef soup. Really." He fumbled around the countertop and finally held up the can. "See. It's just soup. Campbell's. Mmm-mm… good."

# CHAPTER 41

"I guess I get so used to being around this all day, I forget. Sorry about that," Bonzado apologized for the third time. "Let me make it up to you. How 'bout I take you out to dinner?"

"You don't have to do that. Really. It's not a problem. It just surprised me, is all."

"No, really, I insist. There's a place called Giovani's close to the Ramada."

"Okay, if you insist."

"Now, let me show you some stuff." He finished peeling off the mask and shoved the goggles up atop his head, messing his hair and not caring. Finally he returned to his enthusiastic self. "On to our body-snatcher case."

"Body snatcher?"

"That's what the kids are calling him. Actually, I think that's what they're calling him in the news media, too. You have to admit, it has a ring to it. Don't you FBI types nickname your killers?"

"I think everyone watches too much TV." But it was true. They often did give killers nicknames. She remembered some of her most recent ones: the collector and the soul catcher. But it wasn't a matter of policy or even morbid name-calling. Perhaps it came out of a need to define, maybe a need to understand and control the killer. Body snatcher seemed appropriate. Appropriate but too easy.

Bonzado waved her over to a table where freshly cleaned bones lay on a white drop cloth.

"This is the young man from barrel number three." The numbering was one of those things that unfortunately had come from necessity. She had watched Watermeier request the number be painted onto the barrel and its lid. And now she saw that all the paper tags with strings attached to each of the skeletal remains were also given the number three.

"Young man? How can you tell?" This was one of the barrels that she hadn't seen inside. The one Stolz had said was a bunch of bones. She wondered if there could have been enough tissue to indicate sex, let alone age.

Bonzado picked up what Maggie recognized as a thigh bone, or the femur. She did, after all, have a medical background, not that bones had been a favorite subject.

"At birth there are several places where there is an epiphysis, or a separate element, separate pieces of bone that throughout childhood and into young adulthood end up getting larger and slowly ossify…or rather, it eventually joins or unites. The end of the femur is one of those places. Right here—" he pointed "—at the knee. Can you see the slight separation? It's just a groove now, sorta looks like a scar on the bone where the growth has occurred. In adulthood it disappears."

He bent over the bone so that his forehead almost touched hers, his elbow brushing her side. For a brief moment his closeness distracted her. She seemed suddenly and acutely aware of his scent, a fresh deodorant soap perhaps with a subtle hint of aftershave lotion, despite being surrounded by the ghastly odors of the lab.

"Do you see it?" he asked again.

She quickly nodded and shifted her weight to put some distance between them.

"Now, because the groove hasn't totally disappeared, I'd say he was a young adult, between eighteen and twenty-two, maybe twenty-three or twenty-four at the oldest. Sometimes with adolescents and young adults it's difficult to determine sex, but this was definitely a young man. You'll notice his bones are thick, the joints are knobby, the skull has a square jaw and a low, heavy brow."

"Which means this killer has chosen a forty-something-year-old woman, an elderly man who had already been dead and embalmed, and a young man. What about the fourth barrel? The one with the waffle pattern imprinted on the back? Do we know anything more about that victim?"

"Not much. Stolz faxed me the head wound, only because I asked. It's a woman. He's having a tough time determining age."

"Most serial killers choose a particular type of victim. Ted Bundy even went as far as choosing young women with long, dark hair, parted in the middle. This guy is all over the place. There doesn't seem to be a pattern to the victims he chooses."

"Oh, I think there is a pattern. But not the kind we're used to seeing. That's why I think you'll find this interesting." Bonzado put down the femur and reached for its pair or a part of what was once its pair. This one looked like it had been sawed above the kneecap. "Take a look at the end of his right femur." He handed it to Maggie and she examined the bulbous growth of bone or cartilage that stuck out at the end. Part of it had been sawed away as well.

"What is it?"

"It's probably been there from birth. I'm guessing it was some form of bone spur. Maybe it's a progressive disorder that they may have been waiting to remove or correct after he finished growing. This part on the femur would have been a small part of the problem so it's difficult to tell. He probably would have had a limp. I'm not sure how pronounced a limp. Depending on what shape the tibia and fibula is in I could probably tell you more."

"But let me guess," Maggie said. "You can't tell me because that part of his leg is missing, right?"

"I'm afraid so. That's your pattern. The first woman's body was missing her breast implants, right? And the old guy had a brain tumor and the killer took the brain. This kid's bum leg must have been what the killer wanted. The barrel was sealed when we found it. As far as I can tell, everything else is here." He indicated the tabletop with the man's skeletal remains stretched out and in place.

"Even the woman with the waffle pattern on her back from livor mortis," he continued. "Stolz hasn't been able to figure it out yet because the maggots made a mess of her, but I bet he finds something, some imperfection or deformity missing. That's got to be our connection. He wants to remove the deformity. Maybe he's a perfectionist? Maybe he feels like he's cleansing the earth of imperfections."

He stopped and waited. She could feel him watching her, gauging her response. "So there's your victim-ology. That's what they all had in common. It can't be coincidence, right?"

"No, you're right," she said. "I don't believe in coincidence. But there's something else they all had in common."

"What's that?"

"They all knew the killer."

# CHAPTER 42

R. J. Tully cleared away the dirty dishes, putting them in the sink, and wiped up the crumbs. He pulled out the laptop computer and set it on the kitchen table, connecting the power cord to the outlet and the cables for Internet access. The lid showed a trace of dusting powder, otherwise the lab guys had been tidy, quick and efficient.

Bernard was still trying to track down the e-mail address, though it looked like Tully had been right. SonnyBoy used only public computers. They had tracked him back to the Meriden Public Library and the University of New Haven. At this rate they might never be able to identify him or narrow down a user profile. It looked like he used this address strictly for chat. There were no accounts, no member profiles, no credit cards or online purchases. Nothing except dead ends.

Tully accessed Joan Begley's AOL account, using the password and going through her file cabinet. He read the e-mails that hadn't been opened yet, but saved each, clicking on "Keep as new" just in case someone else was checking them, too.

Harvey jumped up from under the table, startling Tully. He had forgotten the dog was there. Within seconds he heard the front door unlock. This dog was good.

"Hi, Dad," Emma said, coming in the front door, her friend, Aleesha, her constant companion, following.

"You're home early," he said, trying not to sound as pleased as he was feeling. These days he barely saw her and that was only in passing.

"We thought we'd study here tonight. Is that okay with you?"

She had already thrown her armful of books on the sofa and

squatted down to hug Harvey's thick neck. She laughed at her friend, who had to move or risk getting swatted by the dog's tail.

"You can pet him," she told Aleesha, who seemed to be waiting for permission. "Could we order a pizza later for dinner?"

She let Harvey lick her hand while she looked up at Tully. He thought he saw something in his daughter's eyes—a sparkle, a glint—something that he hadn't seen in a very long time. And that was pure and unadulterated happiness.

"Sure, sweet pea. But only if I get to have some."

"Well, duh, of course you get some. Especially since you're paying for it." She rolled her eyes but was still smiling.

If only he had known that all it took to make his daughter's eyes sparkle was the simple lick and wag of a dog. Who'd ever have guessed? Teenaged girls—he'd never be able to figure them out.

Sometimes it didn't surprise him so much that Emma was almost sixteen as much as it surprised him that he was supposed to be the father of a sixteen-year-old. What did he know about teenaged girls? He had no experience in this category. The father of a little girl, now, that he could handle. He was good at protecting, providing and admiring, but those all seemed qualities his teenaged daughter considered lame.

"Come on, Harvey." Emma called the dog from the hallway. "Watch him, Aleesha," he heard Emma tell her friend as they went back to her bedroom. "This is so cool. He lies at the foot of my bed like he's watching out for me. And those big, sad brown eyes. Aren't they the best?"

Tully smiled. Evidently protecting and admiring were annoying characteristics in a father, but prime qualities for a dog. Was he being replaced in his daughter's life? Better by a dog than by a boy.

He went back to Joan Begley's e-mail. O'Dell had said that the rock quarry killer may be paranoid and delusional. She suggested that he hid the bodies because he didn't want anyone to see his handiwork, unlike some serial killers who put the bodies on display to show their control, their power. So this killer, according to O'Dell, got what he wanted from something other than torturing and killing his victims. There may be no gratification in the actual kills for him. If she was correct, the killing was only a means to the end result, what O'Dell called his trophies. But if this was the same man who had taken Joan Begley, what did he want from her?

Tully scanned the contents of one of SonnyBoy's e-mails to Joan Begley. He sounded genuinely interested and concerned about her. Yes, it might be necessary to lure the victim, get her to trust. But this seemed more than that.

The e-mail read, "You need to let yourself mourn. Let yourself be sad. It's okay, you know. You don't have to be embarrassed. No one will think of you as being weak."

Did SonnyBoy connect with his victims in some way, actually feel for them? Or perhaps feel sorry for them because of their imperfections? Was it part of his game? Or was Joan Begley different?

Tully wondered if O'Dell was right. If on some level, the killer hid the bodies because he was embarrassed by what he was doing. Could that be? A killer embarrassed by his need to possess these deformities that others had? Perhaps even embarrassed that he must kill? Was that possible? It would make sense that he started out with people who were already dead. According to O'Dell, there was an old guy with a brain tumor who had been embalmed and buried. Maybe SonnyBoy started with the dead and worked up his courage. Or maybe his need to possess what they had finally overrode any qualms he may have had about murder.

Tully sat back and stared at the computer screen, the last e-mail that SonnyBoy had sent Joan Begley still open on the screen. Just how paranoid and delusional was good ole SonnyBoy? Tully was tempted to find out.

He probably should check out his theory with O'Dell. Probably shouldn't do anything silly or reckless. And yet, what did he really have to lose? Maybe O'Dell was rubbing off on him. Maybe she was a bad influence on him, tempting him to stray from his by-the-book approach.

He scooted the chair closer to the table. His fingers hovered over the keyboard. What the hell. He hit the reply icon, which brought up Joan Begley's response screen. Before he could change his mind he typed in the message and hit the send icon. What if SonnyBoy did have Joan Begley, bound and gagged? Or what if he had already killed her? Then wouldn't he be surprised to receive an e-mail from her, even if it was just one word:

"Why?"

# CHAPTER 43

Maggie left Bonzado's lab. It had been another warm day, but crispness filled the air as the sun began setting. She walked across campus, trying to enjoy the sights and smells of fall despite her mind flipping over the puzzle pieces Bonzado had added. She pulled out her cell phone as she checked the directions she had scrawled in her notebook. The building had to be close by. As she dialed, she looked around, wondering if perhaps it was on the other side of campus.

"Dr. Gwen Patterson."

"Gwen, it's Maggie. A quick question. Does Joan have anything wrong with her, like a physical handicap of any kind?"

"A handicap? No, not at all. Why?"

"I'm still trying to figure out if there's a connection between her disappearance and this rock quarry killer."

"But you said none of the victims matched Joan's description."

"Okay, now is not the time to worry," she said, hearing the panic in her friend's voice. "I'm just wondering if it's possible he may have taken her. You have to be upfront with me, Gwen. This is no time for secrets."

"Secrets? You think I've been keeping secrets about her?"

"Maybe not secrets, but something she may have told you in confidence."

"I've told you everything that could possibly help find her."

"Are you sure?"

"What's this about, Maggie?"

"The rock quarry killer has been taking...pieces from his victims. Imperfections. Deformities."

"Like what?"

"One woman's breast implants were missing. There's what looks to be a crippled leg bone missing from another. And a man's brain with an inoperable tumor was also taken. But if Joan didn't have any physical deformities or any disease, I don't think we need to worry that she was taken by this killer."

She pulled the envelope from her notebook, fumbled with the index card and double-checked the address. How could she not find this place? Gwen still hadn't responded.

"Gwen?"

"There may be something, Maggie. Joan's lost a lot of weight in the last two years, but when she talks about it she sometimes tells people her weight problems were due to a hormone deficiency."

"What do you mean, a hormone deficiency? You mean a problem with her thyroid?"

"Yes."

"Okay, it may be time to worry. I'll call Sheriff Watermeier as soon as I get back to Meriden."

"Where are you now?"

"I'm sort of taking care of some personal business."

"You're finally going to see him?"

"No, I'm not in Boston, Gwen. I'm not seeing Nick Morrelli. I'm not sure I'll be seeing him ever again."

"Actually, I didn't mean Boston. I meant West Haven."

Maggie almost tripped over the curb. She had never told Gwen about her brother. "How did you know?"

"Your mother asked for my advice before she gave you his name and address last December."

"You've known all along? Why didn't you say anything?"

"I was waiting for you to tell me. Why didn't you tell me, Maggie?"

"I suppose I was waiting, too."

"Waiting for what?"

"Courage."

"Courage? I don't think I understand. You're one of the most courageous people I know, Margaret O'Dell."

"We'll see how courageous I am. I'll talk to you later, okay?"

She dropped the phone into her pocket and was ready to give up—so much for courage when she couldn't even find the place. Then she saw the sign pointing to Durham Hall. She stared at the building, hesitating. What the hell. She was here. It was silly to not go in.

She stopped at the front desk where a brunette with a nose piercing and pink eye shadow held an open textbook in her lap, a phone in one hand and a bottled water in the other.

"I know it'll be on the exam. He only mentioned it about a thousand times." She looked up at Maggie and without putting down the phone, asked, "Can I help you?"

"I'm looking for Patrick Murphy."

The girl glanced at a sign-out sheet on the corner of the desk. "He's out until late this evening, but umm… You know, I think he's working. You might be able to catch him there." She pointed across the street.

At first Maggie wasn't certain where she meant. Then she saw it, Champs Grill. A job to work his way through college, of course. It was one of the details she didn't have in any of her files.

Champs Grill smelled of greasy fries, was dark and noisy and smoky with tall-backed booths, all packed with students. Maggie found a stool at the bar and began her search, looking out into the dining area and watching the waiters, wondering if she would be able to recognize him. And if she did, what would she say? How did you tell someone you'd never met before that you were his big sister? Maybe she should have sent a Hallmark card first. Didn't Hallmark have a card for every occasion?

She saw a tall, dark-haired waiter at the corner table, laughing with the group as he took their order. Did his profile look familiar? He seemed to be the one making them all laugh and Maggie smiled, remembering how her father had been able to make her laugh so hard it hurt. She hadn't laughed as hard since. So many of her memories of her father were overshadowed by his death. Instead of remembering his jokes and his hugs, she woke up in the middle of the night able to smell the scorched scent of his flesh, despite all the efforts the funeral home had made. Instead of remembering that medallion he had given her to wear for protection, one that matched his, all she could think about was that his hadn't protected him when he ran into the inferno, only to be carried out a hero.

She fingered her own medallion now, though she kept it under her blouse. There were memories she needed to allow, reminders that didn't need to be painful. She watched the waiter in the corner and she wondered if Patrick even knew who his father was. Had his mother shared that with him? Or had that been part of the bargain Maggie's mother had made with his mother after their father's death?

"Can I get you something to drink, ma'am?" she heard the bartender ask.

"A Diet Pepsi, please," she said, when what she really wanted was a Scotch. She turned just enough to glance at him.

"Would you like that with a twist of lemon?"

"No, I really don't—" She stopped in midsentence, staring at the bartender as if she were seeing a ghost. She *was* seeing a ghost. It was as if she were looking at her father, the exact same brown eyes, the same dimpled chin.

"No lemon?" he asked, smiling at her with her father's smile.

"No, thanks."

She tried not to stare while he tossed ice into a glass and poured her soda, setting it in front of her.

"It's a buck fifty, but no hurry. There's free refills on soda."

She seemed to have been rendered speechless and could only smile and nod. He left her to serve others and she watched, feeling like a voyeur, studying his every move, mesmerized by his hands, the long fingers. He wore his hair the same, a pronounced cowlick giving him few choices.

After three refills and a detailed rundown of the weather she finally left, needing to get back to Meriden to meet Bonzado for dinner. She hadn't had the guts to introduce herself. Hadn't been able to come close, and yet as she got into her rental car she couldn't help feeling like she had found something, something she had lost a long time ago and didn't realize was missing until now. And she knew she would be back.

# CHAPTER 44

Luc stared at the pot on the stove. He couldn't have left it there. He had stopped cooking after he set fire to a skillet of sausages and hash browns, left on and forgotten until he smelled the smoke. From then on, he ate cold stuff, cereal and milk, sandwiches.

The pot's lid was still hot. He couldn't remember bringing out the huge roasting pot. He glanced around the kitchen. Nothing else seemed out of place. He checked the back door—closed. Kitchen windows were closed. Was it possible someone had been in here? Maybe he hadn't imagined someone following him. There had been someone hiding in between the trees. Someone watching. And the footsteps. He had heard footsteps. And the reflection in the old butcher shop window of a man across the street, watching one minute and gone the next. Had that not been his imagination playing tricks on him?

He stared at the pot again. He would never have used such a huge pot. He could fit a small pig in the thing. It overlapped onto two burners. He didn't even remember owning a pot that big. Why would he need one that large?

Someone had to have left it. Why would they leave it on the stove? Why would they do that? Unless someone wanted to confuse him. Freak him out. Unless… someone wanted to scare him.

Suddenly, Luc broke out in a cold sweat. His shirt stuck to his back. His heart began to pound against his rib cage. He glanced around the room again. Panic grabbed hold of him. His head jerked back and forth as he searched. His pace quickened. He moved into the living room, stumbling and rushing and searching.

And then the panic broke loose and he began to yell, "Scrapple. Scrapple, come here, buddy. Come, Scrapple. Where are you?"

Hot tears streaked down his face and he wiped at them with his shirtsleeve. He felt like he'd throw up. He could barely stand as he climbed the stairs, his knees going out halfway up. He fell and slid down several steps, smashing into the wall with a shoulder. He tried yelling again but his throat seemed clogged. A whine was all that came out, startling and panicking him even more because he didn't recognize the sound that came from within him. It sounded like a wounded animal.

He lay on the steps, unable to stand on knees that refused to hold him up. His cheek lay against the cold wooden step. His body shook. He couldn't control the convulsions. Was this part of the disease? He wrapped his arms around himself, hugging himself as best he could in the stairwell. He brought his knees up to his chest and buried his face, trying desperately to stop the nausea and chill. He could still hear the screech, the whine, that awful cry coming out of his mouth.

Then suddenly he felt a nudge. A cold nudge. Slowly he lifted his head. Slowly he forced his cheek off the step. Immediately, he was met by a wet tongue in his face.

"Scrapple. Scrapple, goddamn it, why don't you come when I call you?" He grabbed the dog around the neck and pulled him against him and held him so tight the dog began to wiggle and whine. But Luc only held on tighter.

# CHAPTER 45

Maggie watched Sheriff Watermeier stomp around Luc Racine's small kitchen, examining the calendar on the wall, the ratty towel hanging from the drawer handle, the dirty dishes in the sink. Watermeier seemed to be interested in anything and everything other than the human skull submerged in its own broth. The large pot on the stove still felt warm to the touch.

Adam Bonzado suggested Luc come with him outside for some fresh air, but not before Bonzado poured a glass of water and gulped it down. Then he poured another glassful, this time, Maggie knew, for Racine, and followed the old man out the back door.

"He's really shaken up by this," Maggie said.

"Of course he's shaken up," Watermeier answered with almost a snort. "I'd be shaken up, too, if I had a chunk of someone simmering on my stove and couldn't remember putting it there."

"You think he did this and just can't remember?"

"His damn dog has been digging up pieces for months now. Who knows what Racine has kept for souvenirs and what might be under the fucking front porch." He noticed Maggie's skepticism. "What other explanation is there?"

"Wasn't Racine one of the men who found the first body?"

"Sure was. And he didn't waste any time getting on TV to talk about it. This is probably another attention-getter for the sorry son of a bitch."

"He claims someone's been following him."

"Yeah, and next week he'll probably claim to be Abe Lincoln."

"Has he done this sort of thing before?" Maggie was growing impatient with Watermeier's sarcasm.

"What? Boiled up fucking skulls?"

"No. Has he done anything eccentric to get attention in the past?"

"Not that I know of. But you know the old man has Alzheimer's, right?"

"Yes, I'm well aware of that," she said calmly, but it was becoming more and more of an effort. "From what I know about Alzheimer's, it doesn't usually manifest paranoia."

"What exactly are you saying, O'Dell? You think someone's following him around, sneaking into his house and leaving him little presents like this to freak him out?" Watermeier crossed his arms over his chest and leaned against the counter as if challenging her. He made the small kitchen seem smaller. Even his size-twelve work boots took up too much room.

"What if the killer saw Mr. Racine on TV? What if he believes he's to blame for discovering his little hiding place?" She paused for Watermeier's response, but he was waiting for more, still unconvinced. "We talked about this killer being paranoid and delusional. Remember?"

"Yeah, I remember. You also said he might come after anyone he thought was out to get him, to destroy him. But why choose Racine to screw with? Why not Vargus? He's the one who really discovered the barrels."

"From what we can tell, this killer bashes in his victims' skulls from behind and then hides their bodies. We're not talking about a killer with a lot of arrogant false courage. If you were him, would you go after the strong, young burly construction worker or the old man with early-onset Alzheimer's disease?"

"You also said that he could panic. That he might kill again."

"Yes. And I think he may have taken the woman I'm looking for, Joan Begley. She may have driven to Hubbard Park to meet him Saturday night."

"Hubbard Park?"

"I found a note in her hotel room with Hubbard Park, West Peak and 11:30 written on it. The time fits with when she was last heard from. Could you check the park?"

"For her car?"

"Yes. Or her body."

Maggie could see Watermeier's eyes narrowing. He shifted his weight and leaned against the counter again, only this time he looked like he was seriously considering what she had said.

"You know I was with the NYPD for more than thirty years?"

The question startled Maggie. Watermeier was looking somewhere over her head, out the window, maybe watching Bonzado and Racine. Maybe. And although he hesitated, she knew he wasn't waiting for an answer.

"I've seen a lot of weird crap in my time, O'Dell." He glanced at her, then the eyes went back out the window. "It was my wife, Rosie's, idea for us to move out here. I didn't like it much at first. Her idea that I run for sheriff, too. I didn't like that at first, either. Too goddamn slow of a pace. Then 9/11 happened. I lost a lot of old buddies. In one day. Gone."

He scratched at his jaw, but this time he didn't look back at Maggie. "I could have been with them that day. And I would have been gone, too. Just like that. I ended up spending weeks there…there in that mess. Rosie hated it, but she knew it was something I had to do. I kept going back week after week. Had to. Had to help find my buddies. It was the least I could do.

"We kept searching every stinking day, as if we'd rescue them though all we'd find were scraps, bits and pieces. Thirty years on the force and I thought I'd seen it all. But there wasn't anything could prepare me for that mess. Faces melted off. A foot left in a laced-up boot. A severed hand still gripping the melted impression of a cell phone. I've seen a lot of crap, O'Dell. So this," he said, nodding at the roasting pot on the stove, "doesn't shock me. Neither does anything we've found in those barrels.

"But the difference here—" and now he looked at Maggie, making sure he had her attention "—this here I'm being asked to explain. Like there *is* some fucking explanation. I'm expected to figure this out. And then I'm expected to stop this asshole."

Maggie wasn't sure what he wanted her to say. Was she supposed to tell him it'd be okay? That, of course, they'd find the killer? That she already had a more detailed profile drawn up in her mind? That her profiles were always right? She wasn't even sure they could protect Luc Racine.

Adam Bonzado came in the back door, checking over his shoulder. Racine stayed seated on a bench on the stone terrace, his Jack Russell on his lap. The two of them stared out at the pond, the dog's head turning and following the geese as they flew overhead, but Racine continued to stare straight ahead.

Bonzado looked at Maggie and then Watermeier. "Mind if I take that back to the lab?"

"Help yourself. Stolz's not gonna be much help with this one. I need to get one of the techs to bag the roaster. O'Dell here thinks it might have the killer's fingerprints." There was no sarcasm in Watermeier's voice this time.

"What about the old man?" Bonzado asked the sheriff.

"What about him?"

"You have anyone to stay with him tonight?"

"My guys are pulling double duty as it is. I can't be asking—"

"I'll stay with him tonight," Maggie said, surprising herself with the offer almost as much as she surprised the two men.

## CHAPTER 46

Agents did it all the time—looked out for one another, covered one another's backs. Oftentimes that extended to one another's families. But Detective Julia Racine was with the District Police Department, not the FBI. And although she and Maggie had worked a couple of cases together, they were far from friends, tolerating each other as colleagues. Detective Racine had climbed the career ladder by breaking rules that stood in her way. She could be reckless at times, ruthless at others. But last year in a park rest room in Cleveland, Ohio, Julia Racine had stopped Maggie's mother from slitting her own wrists. Maggie didn't like owing favors. She owed Julia Racine. It seemed appropriate that she pay her back by protecting her father from a killer. Besides, Maggie sort of liked the old guy. He was nothing like his daughter.

She brought a tray out to him where he continued to sit and stare despite the fact that the landscape he seemed so interested in was disappearing into the night shadows. He had refused to go back into the house until the skull was removed and the smell of boiled human flesh could no longer be detected. Maggie had left the stove's ventilation fan on High and opened all the windows that weren't painted shut. She honestly couldn't smell it anymore, but Luc said he could.

"I made us sandwiches," she told him as she set the tray on the bench between them. Other than milk and juice, the cold cuts, mayonnaise and bread were all there had been in the refrigerator.

"I'm not hungry," he said with barely a glance at the food. Then he went back to what looked like a vigil, sitting straight-backed as if on alert and listening for something out of the ordinary. Instead there were only crickets chirping and nocturnal birds calling out to one another. Scrapple sat on Luc's lap, previously content but now interested in the tray of food, wiggling enough to get his owner's attention. Luc reached over and pulled off the edge of some ham for the dog, instructing him, "Chew it. Don't just swallow." But the dog gulped and waited for more.

"So I wasn't imagining things. He was in my house," he said without looking at Maggie.

"Yes."

It seemed a relief to him. Had he honestly believed he had imagined it? He even took a bite of the sandwich for himself and then pulled off another piece for Scrapple.

"But why? Why's he picking on me?"

"You and Calvin Vargus intruded on his private hiding place. He might simply be doing the same to you."

"Do you think he wants to hurt me? You know, like those others?"

Maggie looked for signs of fear, but now he seemed more interested in eating.

"He might just want to scare you," she told him, but she wasn't convinced. She wasn't convinced the killer wasn't still hiding in the shadows, watching despite Sheriff Watermeier's men having checked the premises.

"I think I saw him," Luc said matter-of-factly, but it made Maggie sit up.

"Where? When?"

"Yesterday. Maybe the day before. Just his reflection in a store window as I passed. I kept hearing footsteps…you know, following me, slowing when I slowed. Stopping when I stopped."

Maggie tried to contain her excitement, letting him tell at his own pace, but she was impatient. He had already put the half-eaten sandwich back down and was staring into the dark again.

"What did the reflection look like?" she asked.

Luc was quiet and she thought he might be trying to remember, to conjure up the image. After a while, she asked again, "Luc, what did the reflection look like?"

He turned to her, his eyes darting back and forth before meeting hers when he said, "I'm sorry, who did you say you were?"

# CHAPTER 47

Tully couldn't be sure what her reaction would be, but he knew Dr. Patterson might be easier on him than O'Dell would be. Or at least that was his excuse for calling her, asking if he could run something by her. He could have told her about it over the phone or shown her by forwarding it to her e-mail, yet when she suggested that he stop by her brownstone again, he didn't hesitate.

She opened the door to greet him with bare feet, but still wearing her skirt and silk blouse, her usual business attire, only without the jacket and with the blouse untucked, as if she had just gotten home.

"Come on in." She left him and headed back to the kitchen where a pot was on the stove, emitting wonderful aromas of garlic and tomato. "Have you eaten? Because I haven't and I'm starved for the first time in days."

"Smells great," he said, not wanting to admit that he had filled up on pizza with Emma and Aleesha.

"It's nothing fancy. Just some spaghetti and marinara sauce."

Tully checked her expression, wondering if perhaps this was some gesture, some reminder. Last year in Boston he had taken her to a small Italian restaurant, where she had shown him how to twirl his spaghetti correctly onto his fork in what he remembered to be an almost erotic experience. Or at least it had been for him.

While he looked for signs that she might also be remembering that evening, Gwen Patterson gave the sauce a quick stir, then starting slathering butter on a loaf of what looked like fresh bread. She wasn't even paying attention to him. No, he must be wrong about her wanting to remind him of Boston.

What an idiot he was. She had said she wanted to forget about it. She meant it. Why was he still thinking about it?

"Can I help?" he asked, taking off his jacket and putting the briefcase with his laptop computer on the kitchen counter.

"There're some romaine hearts in the colander." She pointed to the sink. "Would you mind pulling them apart for our salad?"

"Sure, I can do that," he said, rolling up his shirtsleeves. Pulling apart hearts for a salad? Sure, he could do that, feeling relieved to recognize romaine hearts as lettuce. Why didn't he pay more attention to these kinds of things and what they were called—romaine hearts and Picasso…Pablo Picasso? Maybe it was time that he did. If he could figure out who Britney was, what raves were and that the ingredients of wet included PCP and embalming fluid—which by the way, he had told Emma if he discovered her doing any drugs she would be grounded until she was thirty-five—then certainly he could figure out what made up the world of Gwen Patterson. Although Emma had already informed him that Britney was so like yesterday.

"Nice job, Agent Tully." She came up beside him with bottles of vinegar and oil. "I have the bread in the oven and the sauce on simmer."

She sprinkled the lettuce with the oil and vinegar, gently tossing it, then topping it with some freshly grated parmesan and black pepper. It smelled wonderful, and Tully felt proud for having had a bit part in its creation. How did she make this all look so effortless? Lately it seemed an effort for him to put his takeout on regular plates rather than eat it right out of its plastic containers.

"Let's put this in the fridge," she told him. "And while we wait for the spaghetti, you can show me what you've got."

Tully took out the laptop computer, opened it and turned it on.

"If the killer and this Sonny is one and the same person, then I'm almost certain he's the one who has Joan. He says some weird stuff in a couple of his e-mails to her."

He kept an eye on her, wondering if it was such a good idea to talk about her patient and what this killer may have in mind for her. She looked pale, maybe just tired.

"You sure you want to talk about this?" he asked.

"Of course. It's a case. I offered to help. And it might help us find Joan." She pointed to the wine rack at the end of the counter. "Would you mind opening a bottle?"

He checked for a red wine, pulled one out and showed her the label for approval, but she was handing him the corkscrew and reaching for wineglasses. What kind seemed of little consequence.

"Let's go back a step. Maggie said he's been taking parts from his victims," she said, looking as if she was trying very hard to be her normal professional self, though the color hadn't yet returned to her face. "But why? This doesn't seem like the regular sort of trophies that serial killers take."

"Yes," he said, "this is different."

"Is he on a mission to rid the world of those with deformities or imperfections?"

"I thought of that, but then why not show off his handiwork? Usually killers on a mission want to show off what they've done. This guy hides what he's done. Not just hides the victims but goes through a lot of trouble to stuff them in barrels and then bury them under tons of rock never to be found."

"Sort of overkill?" she said, then smiled. "Bad pun, sorry."

Maybe the wine was working. The color was returning to her cheeks. He filled her glass again.

"But it's exactly what I'm thinking. Why the overkill? I think he's embarrassed of what he's doing." He waited for her reaction. He wanted to know what Gwen Patterson, the psychologist, thought.

"Hmm…interesting."

"In fact, I don't think he gets much enjoyment or gratification from the killings. Don't get me wrong, I still think he gains something from killing besides just getting the pieces he wants. He might feel some sort of control, but again, I'm not sure it's from the actual killing as much as it is from simply possessing those pieces. Does that make sense?"

"What does Maggie think?"

He picked up his own glass of wine for the first time and took a drink. "I haven't talked to her about this yet."

"Really? Why not?"

"I wanted to run it by you first." He could tell from the look she gave him that she didn't buy that. "Okay, I haven't talked to her about it yet because I did something. And I'm not sure she's going to be very happy with me."

Now Dr. Patterson planted her elbows on the counter, leaning into him as if ready to share in his secret. "And just what did you do, Agent Tully?"

"I sort of pulled a Maggie O'Dell."

She smiled. "Oh, heavens, she's already a bad influence on you." She sipped more wine. "What did you do?"

He pulled the laptop closer and clicked on the AOL icon. "I sent him an e-mail."

"You sent Sonny an e-mail? That doesn't sound so unforgivable. Actually it sounds very much like something Maggie would do."

"I'm not so sure about that. Because I sent him an e-mail from Joan Begley."

He waited for her reaction. She sipped her wine, watching him over the rim of the glass. Finally she said, "You think she's dead, don't you?"

He could almost feel the blood drain from his face, replaced by embarrassment, embarrassed that, yes, he had given up on Joan Begley. Especially if Sonny was the rock quarry killer. And the e-mails that Sonny and Joan exchanged in the days preceding her disappearance had convinced Tully that Sonny had taken her and most likely had killed her.

"Let me show you some of their e-mail correspondence," he said in answer to her question. "And then you can tell me what you think."

He brought up the file on the laptop's screen and she came in behind him to look over his shoulder. Maybe it was the effect of the wine, because suddenly Tully found it difficult to concentrate on the computer screen. As Dr. Patterson read over his shoulder all he could think about was how good she smelled, a subtle soft scent like fresh flowers after a spring rain shower.

"It sounds almost like he's jealous of Joan's struggle with her weight," he said.

"Jealous?"

"He sees it as a reason for her to get sympathy, to draw attention."

"And you think that he's jealous of his victims' imperfections, their deformities?"

"Exactly. Here he tells her that he wishes he had a reason for people to feel sorry for him. In this one—" he scrolled down to find it "—he confides that as a child he had awful, terrible stomachaches and his mother never believed him. He says, 'She gave me medicine but it only made me sicker.' He tells her that's when he gave up on telling people about his own aches and pains because nobody believed him. He reminds me of a hypochondriac."

Tully felt her hair brush against his temple as she batted it out of her face in order to read the computer screen. He tried to focus. What was it he was saying? "So, anyway, I got to thinking, what if he had all these stomachaches, maybe he still gets them but the doctors have never found anything. Maybe the doctors even start telling him all his aches and pains are simply in his head, in his mind. But he sees people around him—a guy who has an inoperable brain tumor, a woman who's survived breast cancer—and he sees them getting sympathy or at least having justification for their aches and pains. He wants justification for his ailments, too. Maybe he wants it so much he decides to take it from others, cuts it out of them. By keeping these things for himself, these deformed pieces that have drawn sympathy for others, by possessing them he gains strength, control."

She came around to the other side of the table and sat down to look at him. He worried she was about to say he was way off base. But instead she said, "So he has no reason to keep Joan alive?"

She didn't wait for his answer. She didn't need it, having

come to the same conclusion. She got up and went to the stove, busying herself with the sauce they had allowed to simmer for too long. "I can't help but feel partly responsible," she said, surprising him with what sounded like a confession.

"Responsible? Why in the world would you feel responsible?"

"Sounds silly, doesn't it?" And she laughed, running a hand through her hair, a nervous trait he had noticed long ago. She seemed to do it whenever she was feeling a bit vulnerable, as if she had revealed too much and needed to remind herself to *not* let her hair down so much.

"No, it doesn't sound silly. I'm just not sure why you would feel responsible. You had no way of knowing Joan Begley would come across this killer when she went to Connecticut."

"But I should have been available that night when she called. If only I had called her back… She needed me and I wasn't available."

"And if you had been available?" He came into the kitchen, leaning against the counter. "It may not have changed things. It was still her choice."

She turned to meet his eyes, and he was surprised to find them moist with emotion. "She was asking for my help, asking me to talk her out of it." She wiped at her eyes and looked away, now trying to hide a flush of embarrassment.

"You're forgetting something, Doc."

"What's that?"

"It was still her choice to be there. A choice she was responsible for, not you. Didn't they teach you that in counseling school?"

She met his eyes again and tried to smile, but it looked like an effort to do so.

"Sometimes," he continued, putting aside every fiber in his brain that was yelling at him to stop while he was ahead, "it's not such a bad thing to give yourself a break. You can't be responsible for every patient." And without listening to his head, he stepped closer until he was wrapping his arms around her and pulling her gently against his chest.

He leaned down and kissed her hair. When she seemed to respond, moving closer into him, he kissed her neck. She pulled away just enough to offer him her face, and he didn't hesitate. He kissed her like he had been wanting to kiss her ever since Boston.

Again, she pulled away just enough to whisper in his ear, "Stay with me tonight, Tully."

His body had already begun to say "yes" when common sense struck him like a hammer. He held her tight, nuzzling her neck as he told her, "I can't. God, I wish I could, but I can't."

She pushed away from him and he could see not only embarrassment but hurt. "Of course," she said in that professional tone that she retreated to in order to distance herself from the embarrassment. "I'm sorry. I should have never—"

"No, you don't understand."

"Of course I understand." She was at the stove, whipping the marinara sauce. "I didn't mean to step over the line."

"I think I'm the one who stepped over the line first."

"It doesn't matter, I shouldn't have suggested—"

"Gwen, stop. I can't stay because of Emma."

Now she looked back up at him and he watched the realization sweep over her face, the sting of rejection slip away.

"Otherwise…well, otherwise we certainly wouldn't even be standing here discussing it."

"But maybe we should discuss it."

"No, absolutely not," he said, holding up a hand to stop her. "And that's why I better leave right now. Because I don't want to give us a chance to discuss it to death, to talk ourselves out of it before there's anything to talk ourselves out of." He started packing up his case without looking at her.

Finally ready, he grabbed his jacket off the back of a chair, pulled it on and then returned to where he had left her, at the kitchen counter. "I like psychoanalyzing killers with you, but I don't want to psychoanalyze this. Whatever this is right now, can we just go with it for a while, first?" But before she could answer he kissed her again, a long deep kiss that, when he was finished, left her without an answer.

# CHAPTER 48

He liked shopping at this time of night. The aisles of Stop & Shop were practically empty. The rage was still brewing inside him, threatening to dislodge the nausea, but there was no one to notice if he had to dart to the rest rooms or abandon his cart and leave the store suddenly. Which reminded him, he needed to stock up on more of the chalky crap.

Ever since leaving the library he'd felt a tingling in his hands and a weakness in his knees. He turned around to see if anyone was watching, if he was being followed. There was someone out to destroy him. But how did they know? How did they get his e-mail address?

At first he thought it might be the old man. But now he was convinced it had to be that nosy reporter. That bitch! He should have known she would be a problem. She was following him. He had seen her several places, snooping around. He had almost bumped into her yesterday, and she looked through him as if he didn't exist. Had she been pretending that she didn't know anything? No, she knew something. Why else was she everywhere he went?

And now was she playing games with him, sending him e-mails and pretending to be Joan. It had to be that reporter. *It had to be. Had to be.* But how did she know? How did she know he had Joan? Had the old man told her something? Had he seen him taking Joan that night in Hubbard Park?

He had to keep calm. He had to breathe. He would take care of his enemies, all in good time. He just needed to stay calm. He tapped his pocket, making sure the folded piece of paper was there. While at the library reading his e-mail he looked up the TV station's address and phone number. Some receptionist told him Jennifer Carpenter wouldn't be in until ten-thirty. That he could call back after the eleven o'clock news if he wished to speak with her. Speak to her? Well, yes, maybe he did wish to speak to her. Maybe he would ask her why she was following him. Why she was harassing him.

He searched the shelves, trying to relax, trying to concentrate on his shopping. He chose several jars of jelly. The twelve ounce would work fine. Then he noticed a large jar with olives. He hadn't seen these before. He picked it up to examine it, thirty-two ounces and a nice wide mouth with a screw-on lid. He put it into his cart next to the cans of soup and loaf of white bread. Mayonnaise. He remembered he was out of mayonnaise. If only it came in a larger jar, and now they were selling it in sixty-four-ounce plastic containers. Plastic just wasn't sufficient.

He tried to get his mind off the e-mail, off the rage it had made him feel. It was *stupid, stupid, stupid* to play games with him, to pretend to be Joan Begley. She was out to destroy him. They were all out to destroy him. That old man. Even that FBI agent. He didn't trust any of them. They were all out to get him. But they couldn't. No, they couldn't destroy him. Not if he took care of them first.

That made him smile. Yes, one by one he would take care of his enemies. They had discovered his dumping ground, but he could find other places. That made him feel back in control.

He started down a new aisle. Someone said the old man had Alzheimer's disease. He hated the way they had said it, like it was something that they were supposed to feel bad about. Like they felt sorry for the poor old guy.

He wondered what it looked like. What would something like Alzheimer's disease look like? Did it make parts of the brain shrivel up? Did it discolor it in any way? He wouldn't mind seeing that, taking a look.

Last time a large pickle jar had worked just fine, and he started to look for a similar one. Yes, Steve Earlman's brain fit perfectly in a large pickle jar and so would Luc Racine's.

# CHAPTER 49

Luc heard something. A noise had awakened him. He propped himself up on one elbow, glancing at Scrapple sprawled on his back, feet in the air at the end of the bed. Either he was imagining things again or his dog was totally useless as a watchdog.

He listened, trying to hear over the thumping of his own heart. Maybe it was only the FBI woman downstairs, Julia's friend. He wasn't used to having anyone else in his house. Maybe he just wasn't used to the normal noises that came along with having someone else in his house. She had promised not to call Julia. He hoped she kept her promises. He didn't want Julia worrying about him. He didn't want her running home just because she felt sorry for him. He didn't want her—

Holy crap! Something moved inside his closet. The night-light in the wall socket made it difficult to see. He squinted. The closet door was open about a foot. He never left his closet door open, always made certain it was closed. And now he could see a shadow inside. Yes, someone was inside his closet. Oh, Jesus! The guy had never left. He was standing inside Luc's closet. Standing there, waiting. Probably waiting for Luc to fall fast asleep.

He eased himself back down into the pillows, pretending he was going back to sleep but positioning himself so he could see the closet door. He listened again, only this time it was impossible to hear anything. His heart thundered in his ears and his breathing seemed hard to control. He had to think. What did he have close by that he could use as a weapon? The lamp? It was plugged into the wall and too small. His eyes darted around the room—looking, searching for something, anything—always returning to the shadow. Did it move again?

What the hell was wrong with Scrapple? The dog stayed on his back with not so much as a snort, let alone a growl. How could that dog have not sensed this guy?

Maybe a baseball bat. Yes, he used to have one around. A ball, a bat and a glove. He and Julia still hit it around sometimes. Who was he kidding? That was ages ago. No telling where the damn bat was now.

The FBI agent was downstairs. How could he get her attention? Could he sneak out of the room? But not without Scrapple. The dog might be worthless, but no way would he leave him here.

Then he saw the top knob of the baseball bat sticking out from under the bed. Yes, he had kept it here. He let his hand dangle over the edge of the bed. Shoot! He couldn't reach it. He glanced back at the closet door. Was it opened a little more? Oh, Christ, was he coming out now? This was no time to hesitate.

Luc jumped out of bed. He slammed his knee into the dresser with a bang that woke up Scrapple. But he grabbed the baseball bat and ran to the closet door, not stopping, not waiting, snatching at the doorknob and pulling it open as he raised the bat. He delivered several strong death blows, smashing the shadow to the floor. It took him a second or two before he realized he had just bludgeoned the only suit he owned, the one he had recently picked up from the dry cleaners and hung in his closet, left in the plastic wrap. He had wanted to be sure the suit was clean and pressed and ready one day for his own funeral. And now it was a crumpled mess on the floor of his closet, after threatening his life.

Luc sat on the edge of his bed, petting the now alert and confused Scrapple, waiting for the shaking in his hands to stop. How ridiculous had he become? What the hell was wrong with him? He wasn't only losing his memory but perhaps his mind, as well.

Then he heard a noise from outside. A muffled thump that sounded like it came from the back of the house. And this time Scrapple heard it, too.

# CHAPTER 50

It had been a long time since Maggie had slept anywhere and heard the howls of coyotes in the distance. But as she tried to get comfortable on the lumpy old sofa, she thought she heard Luc upstairs. It almost sounded like he was moving furniture around. After his blank episode earlier, Maggie wasn't sure she wanted to go up and find him, indeed, stacking pieces of furniture on top of one another like a sleepwalker unaware of his actions.

No, that was ridiculous and she immediately admonished herself. Alzheimer's didn't manifest itself in totally absurd behavior. At least not that she knew of, but then what did she really know about it? She wished she hadn't promised him that she wouldn't call Julia. Racine needed to know if her father's life might be threatened. Maybe the old man simply wouldn't remember her promise. Or perhaps she could get him to call his daughter himself.

She watched the shadows of branches outside the window dancing on the ceiling. Luc had night-lights plugged into the sockets all over the house. In a weak moment, he had mentioned being afraid that one day he might forget how to switch on a lamp and be forced to sit in the dark. What an awful feeling it must be to know that could happen. She couldn't imagine what it must feel like to realize that pieces of your memory, even the basic pieces, had begun to crumble. Or to not have any memories at all. She thought about Patrick again, wondering what, if anything, he knew about their father.

Her own memories, especially of her childhood, of losing her father and growing up with an alcoholic, suicidal mother, those awful memories were burdens she thought she could live without. But earlier today, remembering some of the good ones made her realize that she was cheating herself. What if she were like Luc, not able to sift and select, not having control over what went and what stayed… What an awful feeling that must be. And yet, she had been allowing herself to remember only the awful things when she, in fact, had a choice.

Maggie decided she would go out tomorrow and buy some timers for Luc's lamps. Also some of the longerlasting light bulbs. Maybe another lamp or two. She couldn't keep him from forgetting how to turn on a light, but she could be damn sure he wouldn't be left in the dark.

She heard him coming down the steps and she sat up. Before he got to the foot of the stairs she could see his elongated shadow carrying something over his shoulder and the little terrier following close behind.

Oh, Jesus! Was he, indeed, sleepwalking? And she tried to remember, were you supposed to wake a sleepwalker or leave him alone?

He rounded the corner and she recognized a bat hoisted on his shoulder in ready-to-swing mode. Instinctively, she bolted for her Smith & Wesson. As she whipped it out of its holster, she saw him putting his finger to his lips and whispering, "Someone's outside."

Maggie decided the old man must be sleepwalking or perhaps imagining things, the result of stress from an outrageous day. That was until she saw the shadow of a man pass by the front window.

She put up a cautionary hand to Luc and waved him away from the windows. The terrier growled but was sticking close by his owner. Maggie made her way to the front door, keeping her revolver nose down and close to her body. She worked the locks open, slowly, quietly. She looked back at Luc, making sure he was out of the line of fire. Then without hesitation, she flung the door open and stuck the Smith & Wesson's nose in the face of the shadow just as it stepped into the porch light.

"Jesus, Bonzado. What the hell are you doing here?"

# CHAPTER 51

She startled him so badly he dropped one of the bags, scattering groceries across the wooden porch floor.

"I didn't think you'd both be down for the night. I guess I didn't think it was that late. Did I wake you?"

"You scared the living daylights out of us. What the hell are you doing?"

Maggie watched him pick up cartons and cans. She looked back at Luc and worried that he had blanked out on her again. He stood there, bat in his hands, staring at Bonzado, as if deciding whether he needed to use the bat.

"It's okay, Luc," she told him. "It's just Professor Bonzado. Do you remember him from this afternoon?"

"Why is he back?" Luc wanted to know. "Why is he out wandering around in the dark?"

"Good question," she said, now turning back to the professor.

He looked up at her, still down on his hands and knees retrieving several cans that had rolled underneath the porch swing. "I wasn't out wandering around in the dark. I was just coming up to the door, and before I could knock you jammed a gun in my face."

"What are you doing here, Adam?" she asked again.

"I noticed Mr. Racine didn't have much in his refrigerator. I thought I'd bring out some staples. I really didn't think you'd be asleep already. It's not even ten. And—" he got to his feet and opened one of the other bags, pulling out a small white box "—I wanted to bring you some dessert, since our dinner sort of got canceled."

"You should have called first." It was difficult to stay angry with him when he seemed genuinely determined to please them.

"I tried calling you. Your cell phone must be off. And I didn't know Mr. Racine's phone number."

"I'm sure directory assistance could have given it to you." Maggie wouldn't let him off the hook. She didn't like how quiet Luc continued to be. Finally, he came out on the porch to help Bonzado, taking one of the bags and looking inside.

"I don't cook much anymore."

"I figured as much. So I bought some deli meats and cheeses, some bread, and several different kinds of cereals and milk. Oh, and some Pop-Tarts. They're pretty good cold. You don't even have to put them in a toaster. Really. You'll have to try 'em."

The two men came in past Maggie, and Bonzado glanced at the revolver she hadn't holstered yet, then looked up at her and smiled. "Jeez, you're tough on a guy for just wanting to bring you a little cheesecake."

"Did you say cheesecake?" Now he had Luc's full attention and enthusiasm.

"That's right. None other than chocolate almond from the Stone House." Bonzado followed Luc into the kitchen.

Maggie shook her head. But before she closed the door she stepped out onto the porch. Why hadn't she heard Bonzado's El Camino or, at least, seen his headlights? She saw the vehicle parked up the driveway, away from the house. Odd that he didn't pull in behind her rented Escort.

As she turned to go back inside, she heard another vehicle's engine, beyond the trees, back on Whippoorwill Drive. She could hear it but couldn't see it. She stepped off the porch into the dark, straining to see through the branches, trying to follow the low, soft rumble of an engine.

The reason she couldn't see the vehicle was because it had waited until it was almost out of sight before it turned on its headlights. And then it was quickly gone, the taillights disappearing around the first curve.

# CHAPTER 52

Joan couldn't look at the tray of food he left on the bedside stand. She couldn't eat it. She wouldn't eat it. Whatever he was putting in her food made her insides feel as if they were being slit open. He didn't even need to use the leather restraints anymore. She couldn't leave the bed if she wanted to. Instead she spent what felt like hour after hour curled up in a fetal position trying to ward off the pain.

She no longer thought about talking him into releasing her. She no longer dreamed about escaping the cabin. She only wanted to escape the pain. Maybe he would finally kill her. Yes, why didn't he just kill her and get it over with? Instead, he kept bringing her food. The smell of the soup alone reminded her of her body's reaction to it. And already her insides burned. The nausea had never left. For hours it continued, like being seasick on a cruise and not being anywhere near land. She couldn't think about it, nor could she feel anything else. So when he sat down next to her and started showing her his collection, she could only stare right through him and pretend to be interested.

He was the little boy again, excited and anxious, as if bringing his show-and-tell projects to share with her. Each one more hideous than the next and threatening to make her vomit, though there couldn't possibly be anything left inside her stomach. She tried not to think about the blobs as pieces of human beings. She tried not to think about the fact that he had taken them from their owners.

He was showing her something in a large jar with a white lid. She refused to look closely, not allowing her eyes to focus on what appeared to be a dirty yellow glob of fatty tissue.

"This one was a surprise," he told her, holding it up at her eye level. "I knew an alcoholic's liver would look abnormal but this..." He was smiling and explaining it as if it were a prize he had won in some competition. "They say a normal liver has the same texture and color as calf's liver. You know, like you can buy at the supermarket. Actually, I can't imagine anyone wanting to eat calf's liver. That's just gross." He turned the jar slowly around as if giving her a full view. "See, the alcohol causes that discoloration."

He got up to put the jar on one of the top shelves, and Joan hoped the presentation was over. He came back, stopping at the food tray. Oh, dear God, she couldn't handle him force-feeding her again. She simply couldn't survive another spoonful. But he left the bowl and picked up the brown paper bag that he had brought in with him on the tray. He sat down beside her and took another jar out of the bag. It looked like an ordinary twelve-ounce jelly jar. But it didn't look like jelly. The liquid was clear, like in the other jars. And like the other jars, something was floating inside.

"This is my newest acquisition," he told her, twirling it in front of her. Then he finally held it still and so close to her face that she couldn't avoid recognizing the two floating, bright blue eyeballs. "Amazing, isn't it, that these couldn't see except with really thick glasses."

# CHAPTER 53

It was after midnight.

He threw the mop in the corner, only getting angrier when it started an avalanche of gardening tools. He emptied the bucket down the floor drain, holding his breath while he sprayed at the vomit, yellow mucuslike chunks that looked all too familiar from a childhood of buckets kept by his bedside. He was tired of her being sick all the time.

Yes, he had planned it. Yes, he had wanted her to be sick. He wanted her to see how much control he had over her. He wanted it and yet it still repulsed him. He should have made her clean up her own mess. Clean it up like his mother had made him clean up his messes.

He should have been feeling strong and in control, especially with his newest acquisition. Instead, his own stomach ached despite gagging down half a bottle of the chalky crap. That stupid so-called medicine promised to prevent his nausea. He could no longer count on it. Why didn't it work? Why was everything and everyone working against him?

He wanted Joan Begley to see, to understand what control he had. He wanted her weak and helpless. It had worked all those years for his mother. She had maintained control, first over his father and then over him. Why couldn't it work for him? But he hated the mess. *Hated, hated, hated it!*

He grabbed a meat cleaver from the workbench and slammed it into the wooden surface. Raised it and sent it into the wood again. Another chop. Another and another.

He shoved the meat cleaver aside. The wooden bench had plenty of cuts and slits, splinters and raw wounds from other angry bouts. It had been his father's workbench and had been pristine until the day he died. Yet he had taken his father's precious workbench, his workshop, his escape, and turned it into his own escape. And it had been an excellent escape. The only place he allowed his true emotions to come out. It had become his secret vault, protecting and absorbing and withstanding all the hurt, the pain, the anger, as well as the feeling of victory and sometimes even providing him with a sense of control.

He turned and leaned his back against the bench, allowing himself to take in the sights and smells of the magic workshop. The smells he loved: fresh sawdust, gasoline and WD-40—remnants of his father's hideaway and smells that reminded him of his father—were, unfortunately, long ago replaced by the smells of his own escape: caked blood, rotting bits of flesh, formaldehyde, ammonia and now vomit. The only one of that list that bothered him, that repulsed him, was the smell of vomit.

He admired his father's collection of tools, a strange and dazzling assortment hanging on the wall by pegs and hooks in organized rows. He had added the old meat hooks, boning knives and meat cleavers that now hung next to crescent wrenches, pry bars and hacksaws. Otherwise, he kept the wall of tools exactly the way his father had left it, paying tribute to the painstaking organization by cleaning and replacing the items after each use. So, too, had he kept the handy vises attached to the workbench in the same spots, along with the bone saw and the huge roll of white butcher-block paper resting in its own contraption with a sleek metal blade, sharp enough to slide through the paper with only the slightest touch of the fingertips.

In the corner was an old, battered chest-size freezer, gray scratches in the enamel like wounds and a low, constant hum that sounded like a cat purring. It had also been his father's, used back then for premium cuts of meat and trout or bass from infrequent fishing trips. After his father's death, he began using it as his first container, before he knew how to preserve his treasures. Quickly it filled up. Now it was one of several, with one next door and another at the house.

The shelves on the back wall were his addition, too, as were the vials, mason and jelly jars, crocks, glass tubes, plastic containers, fish tanks and wide-mouth bottles. All were immaculately clean, waiting to store his prizes. Even the cheap, store-bought pickle jars sparkled, not a trace of their brand labels left to block the view.

The top shelf held his own proud assortment of tools, shiny scalpels, X-Acto knives and blades, forceps, stainless steel probes and basins in different sizes and shapes. Most he had stolen one by one from work so that they wouldn't be missed.

Yes, he was proud of his workshop. Here, he felt in control. Despite the smell of her vomit turning his stomach, here, he never got sick. This was where he cut out other people's pain, their abnormalities, their deformities, their bragging rights, and kept them for himself.

All through his childhood his sickness had been so obscure. He could never point to a bum leg or heart defect or a precious tumor and say, "See, this is what makes me sick to my stomach." Had he been able to do so, they wouldn't have dared to doubt him, to whisper about him in hospital corners, to suggest he "get counseling."

They wouldn't have dared to laugh at him and point and snicker when he asked to be dismissed from class. They wouldn't have dared to call him weak and silly. If only he had had one cancerous tumor, one deformed limb to point to, they wouldn't have dared call him anything but brave and strong, a little soldier instead of a whiny brat.

These people with their claims to pain made him angry, made him jealous, made him crazy with envy. They could complain all they wanted and no one told them to buck up and shut up. And they didn't even realize the priceless treasures they possessed. Fools. All of them fools.

And so he cut them, slicing out that which made them different, made them special, that which gave them the right to complain and brag. He cut out their prizes and made them his own. It gave him power. It gave him control.

That's what he needed to do with Joan Begley. He needed to

do exactly as he set out to do in the beginning. That was the only way he could gain control over her. But what would he use?

He examined the tools and scratched at his jaw. He wasn't even sure what it was that Joan possessed. Where would a hormone deficiency be located? Was it in the pituitary gland? That would be on the underside of the brain. He might need a drill and the bone saw. Or perhaps it was the thyroid gland, which would be a simple slit of the throat. Although, it could be one of the adrenal glands. Where the hell were they located? Somewhere over the kidneys, perhaps? He grabbed the illustrated medical dictionary off the top shelf and began flipping pages.

As he browsed the index, his fidgeting fingers found a boning knife, the curved blade razor sharp. And suddenly, he found himself hoping it was the thyroid. In fact, he thought he remembered her mentioning the thyroid. Yes, that would be good. After cleaning up her vomit over and over again, he wouldn't mind slitting Joan Begley's throat.

# CHAPTER 54

*Thursday, September 18*

"You don't have to fix breakfast for me, Mr. Racine," Maggie said, but her mouth was already watering from the aroma of hash browns and sausage sizzling in one skillet while Luc prepared another with scrambled eggs.

"No, no, I want to. God! I miss this." He splashed some milk and fresh ground pepper into the scrambled eggs, stirring and flipping with the expertise of a short-order cook. "I don't get to do this anymore. I don't trust myself to shut off the stove." He glanced back at her. "I'm only telling you so you'll keep an eye on things and make sure that I don't leave something on. Would you do that, please?"

He kept his back to her. Maggie knew it was not an easy thing for him to ask. She wondered if that was the real reason he wouldn't let her call Julia. Did his daughter know that he was deteriorating?

"Sure. Is there anything I can do to help?"

"Nope. Got the table all set." He looked around. "Maybe some orange juice. I noticed your friend brought some last night." He opened one cupboard door, then another and one more before grabbing two glasses to hand to her. This time he couldn't hide the slight flush of embarrassment. "I think he likes you."

"What?"

"The professor, he likes you."

This time she felt a slight flush. She found the juice and poured. "We're working on a case together. That's all."

"What? You don't like him?" He glanced at her over his shoulder.

"No, I didn't say that. It's just that I guess I haven't thought about him that way."

"Why not? He's a handsome young man. I noticed you're unattached."

"I don't know why not. I'm just…I'm not…" She realized that she sounded like some tongue-tied teenager. She wasn't sure why she thought she needed to explain it to him. "I'm not looking right now. My divorce was just finalized. I'm not ready to start another relationship."

"Oh, okay." He glanced back at her. "Sorry, I didn't mean to stick my nose in your business." He started cleaning the counter. "I like you. You remind me of Julia. I guess I miss her."

"I was thinking about that, Mr. Racine. I think—"

"I wish you'd call me Luc."

"Okay, but I was thinking maybe you should call Julia. I think she would like to know. Actually, I'd feel better if she knew."

He was putting away what he didn't use, sliding the egg carton back into the refrigerator and wrapping up the leftover sausage.

Maggie stopped him. "Where did you get this?" She pointed to the sausage he rolled tight into the white butcher-block paper.

"This? It's scrapple. I think they call it that because it's made from pork scraps," he said, misunderstanding what she meant and unwrapping the sausage to show her. "My wife was from Philadelphia. That's where they have the best. This stuff always reminds me of her. Partly why I named my best buddy Scrapple." He glanced down at the dog who, as if on cue, sat up to beg for a piece of his namesake. "Can't find it around here, though." Luc continued wrapping the sausage. "Last winter I had Steve Earlman make it for me out of some pork shoulder. He did a pretty good job, too. I think you'll like it."

Maggie wondered if Luc knew they had found Steve at the quarry. He had been to the site enough times he may have heard the rumors. Maybe he couldn't remember. Once again, she was reminded of that white paper that kept showing up. What was she missing?

"Luc, what did they do with the butcher shop when Steve passed away? Didn't he have any sons or daughters to keep the shop open?"

He scooped up hash browns, sausage and scrambled eggs, dividing the bounty between their two plates. It looked wonderful and she followed him to the table, bringing their juice.

"No, Steve never married. A nice guy, too." He pulled out a chair for her, waiting for her to get comfortable before he took his place. "It was sad to see the shop close. I remember hearing that someone bought all the equipment at the estate sale. I thought maybe whoever it was would keep the shop open or start a new one, but I guess not."

"Do you remember who bought all the equipment?"

Luc stared at her, his forehead furrowed in thought, the frustration playing in his eyes. "I should know that."

"It's okay if you can't remember. I was just curious."

"No, I should know. It was somebody I know."

Maggie's cell phone started ringing from the other room and Scrapple, who had taken his begging place under the table, now began to bark.

"Scrapple, that's enough. Hush."

"Excuse me. I need to get that," Maggie said as she hunted for her jacket, following the sound of the ringing. Finally. "Maggie O'Dell."

"O'Dell, it's Watermeier. I'm at Hubbard Park, the West Peak. We found something. I think you'll want to see this."

# CHAPTER 55

Adam Bonzado pulled the Polaroids from his shirt pocket. He took another long, studied look, then slipped them back into the pocket. It probably wasn't a good idea to have the photos out while he rummaged the shelves of the local hardware store.

He was trying to get Maggie O'Dell off his mind. It didn't help matters that he still felt like a complete bonehead. First the soup incident and then waking her and Racine up last night. Not only waking them up but scaring them. Although Maggie didn't look that scared behind the barrel of her Smith & Wesson. He smiled at the memory. He liked that she could take care of herself. He didn't like having her almost blow off his head, though.

Sometimes he worried that his mother was right. That he spent too much time with skeletons and not enough time with real people. His students, according to his mother, didn't count.

"Why can't you go out like normal boys," his mother usually began her lecture that included something about dating nice girls. "You don't even go to a ball game with your brothers anymore."

But he liked his work. Why should he have to make excuses about that? And besides, most women were immediately turned off when they learned what he did for a living. No, the truth was he hadn't wanted anyone else after Kate. He buried himself in his work instead. It took his mind off that empty void.

So here he was again, burying himself in work to get his mind off Maggie O'Dell. What better way to do that than at a hardware store armed with a handful of Polaroids and a mission to add to his tools-of-death list.

Dr. Stolz had given him Polaroids of the victims' head

wounds, all administered to the back top of the skull. Even the young man's skull Adam had in the lab, as well as the one he had plucked from the boiling pot at Luc Racine's, seemed to have been dealt similar deathblows.

He went down the aisle of hand tools, searching, paying close attention to the end of each tool. Ball-peen hammer, no. Bolt cutter, no. Then there were pliers. Adam scratched his jaw, always amazed at the assortment. You had your long-nose locking pliers, jaw, diagonal, duckbill, slip joint, Arc joint, groove joint.

Jesus! Forget pliers.

Drive sockets: metric or standard. Screwdrivers: Phillips, slotted or torx. Wrenches: crescent, adjustable or pipe. The bolt clamp looked promising or maybe even the steel bar clamp. Woodworker's vise, no. Level, no.

"Hey, a mini hacksaw," he said, picking up the contraption. "For all those hard-to-reach joints when you're in the middle of dismembering a body."

"Can I help you, sir?" A clerk appeared at the end of the aisle.

Adam immediately put the mini hacksaw back as if he had been caught. He wondered if the clerk had heard him. The kid looked like he spent more time down in his family's basement rec room than in his dad's garage. In fact, he looked like he belonged in an electronics department, selling Game Boys and DVD players, not drills or circular saws, let alone hand tools.

"Is there something in particular you're looking for, sir?"

"Yeah, but it's one of those things that I'll know when I see it. You know what I mean?"

The clerk stared at him. No, he didn't know what he meant. "Like for a special project or something?"

Adam smiled. He wondered what the kid would do if he told him about his tools-of-death list. Or better yet, if he showed him the Polaroids and asked him to help find the tool that cracked open the skull and left that triangle mark. Instead, he said, "Yeah, I guess you could say that."

"Okay, then. Let me know if you change your mind."

"Thanks, I will."

Adam started down the next aisle. This one was full of bars. Yes, this was more like it. There were pry bars of every shape and size. Some of forged steel construction, others with black oxide coating to prevent rust. He read the labels below each: "easy, comfortable rubber grip" and "lowprofile claw for more leverage." There was one called a "gorilla bar." Another, the "wonder bar." An I-beam, a double-end nail puller, a gooseneck and a wrecking bar. This was crazy.

Then he saw it. The angle looked right. The size looked right. He slipped out the Polaroids again for a quick glance. Yes, this was it. The end of the double-end nail-pulling pry bar looked like the impressions left in the skulls.

Adam picked up the pry bar and turned it in his hands, examining it at every angle and getting the feel of it. It weighed more than it looked. He tried to hold it the way he imagined the killer had held it up over his head. He tried to imagine how he would swing it. It wouldn't require much force. A bit of a twist and the heavy, hooked end could crack a skull quite nicely.

He lifted it higher, getting ready to reenact a deathblow swing when he noticed the clerk at the end of the aisle. And he was watching. This time he looked…oh, perhaps *concerned* was an understatement.

"I think I found what I was looking for," Adam said, bringing the tool back down without any more fanfare. "And it's even on sale." He pointed to the tag, smiled and retreated down the other end of the aisle.

He waited in the checkout line, tapping the pry bar into the palm of his hand. Suddenly, it occurred to him that this pry bar was exactly like the one he kept in his El Camino.

# CHAPTER 56

Henry watched from the top of the ridge. They almost had the car out of the trees, enough of a hood showing that he could tell it was a late model sedan. Jesus! What a mess. Why was it that when it rained it had to fucking pour?

He found himself wishing it was some poor drunk bastard who drove all the way up and simply lost control and went over the ledge. He wished it could be that simple. He had driven up here only to prove O'Dell wrong. But now he couldn't help wondering if they had just found Joan Begley.

He saw O'Dell leave her rented Ford Escort back behind the Meriden police blockade. They had the chain-link gate closed, padlocked and guarded down below at the entrance, but still it was a bit crowded up here along the winding road to the top of the peak. He waved to Deputy Truman to let O'Dell by.

"You found her?" she asked before he could say anything.

"I was standing here hoping that it was some drunk who took a wrong turn," Henry confessed, leaning on the wooden guard rail.

They stood quietly side by side, watching the tow truck cable pull the car up over the rocks and brush, listening to the scrape of metal against tree bark.

Finally, when it was on level ground, Deputy Charlie Newhouse yelled at him from the tilted smashed-in front of the car, "No one's inside, Sheriff."

"Jesus! I don't need this crap. Run the license plates." But even as Henry said it he could see the rear one was missing.

"Front plate's missing," Arliss said.

"So is the rear," Watermeier told him.

"You suppose it's stolen?" Charlie asked.

"Better give the boys a call to bring out a mobile unit." Henry walked around to the front, trying to get a look inside through the demolished windshield.

"Sheriff."

O'Dell was still at the back of the car, waiting for him. When he walked around she pointed to the trunk, where a small piece of fabric had gotten caught and was sticking out.

"Shit!" he mumbled, and felt the tightening in his chest. "Charlie, reach in there and pop the trunk, and try not to touch too much."

When no one moved, Henry looked up to find his two deputies and the tow truck operator staring at the trunk of the car.

"Charlie," Henry said again.

This time the deputy obeyed, but when the trunk snapped open Henry found himself wondering, once again, why the hell he hadn't retired six months ago.

He pushed the trunk wide-open and everyone remained motionless, wordless as they stared at the small body of a woman curled up inside. Henry noticed immediately that her wrists weren't bound. Neither were her ankles. But then there was no need. The back of the head faced them, a mess of blood and tangled hair where she had suffered what had to be a deathblow. It had cracked her skull open, an impact of force that seemed overkill for such a small woman.

"You suppose it's her?" he asked O'Dell.

"Hard to tell. All I have is a photo. The head wound definitely looks familiar."

"Yeah, that's what I was thinking." Henry swiped at his eyes. Jesus! They hadn't fished all his victims out of the barrels yet and here was another one. "Arliss, call Carl and have him bring the mobile crime lab. And Dr. Stolz, too."

"I think they're probably out at the rock quarry, sir."

"I know where they probably are. Call them and tell them to get their asses over here."

"Sir? You want me to tell them that exactly?"

Henry wanted to throttle the kid. Instead he said, "Charlie, would you—"

"I've got it taken care of, Sheriff."

Henry noticed O'Dell just standing there, staring as if she couldn't believe it, yet she was the one who suggested he search the area. He moved in for a closer look, leaning into the trunk and under the lid without touching anything. He examined the area around the woman for signs of anything that may have been left. Anything to tell them whether or not this was the missing Joan Begley. Maybe he even hoped the weapon accidently got tossed in or dropped inside. But there was nothing. From this angle he could see the side of her face and there was something familiar about her. Yeah, she looked familiar but he hadn't seen O'Dell's photo of Begley.

He gently touched the woman's shoulder, moving her only slightly to get a better view. But what he saw made him jerk away.

"Holy crap!" He bashed his head on the lid of the trunk. He stumbled backward, slipping and almost losing his balance. Almost falling down.

The others stared at the back of the woman again, trying to see what had spooked him.

"It's that TV reporter," he said, out of breath and hating that his chest felt like it would explode. "That one who's been following me around everywhere."

"What are you talking about?" O'Dell said, stepping in closer to the trunk but waiting for him.

He rolled his shoulders and brushed his hands on the sides of his trousers as if to prepare himself. Then he leaned into the trunk as little as was necessary. He hesitated for only a second before he laid his hand on her shoulder again.

"He took her fucking eyes," he said, moving her enough for them to see her face. Just enough for them to see the hollow sockets where her blue eyes had once been.

# CHAPTER 57

Maggie could hear her cell phone beep, warning her that the battery was low and reminding her that she had forgotten to charge it last night.

"Tully, I'm probably going to lose you pretty soon, so give me the bottom line. Were you able to find out anything by going through Sonny's e-mails?"

"He talks about getting sick a lot as a kid and his mother giving him medicine that only made it worse. Dr. Patterson suggested—okay now, this could be a long shot, but I think I agree with her—that he may have been the victim of Munchausen's syndrome by proxy. Are you familiar with that?"

"You think his mother purposely made him sick so that she could get attention?"

"Yes, exactly. Dr. Patterson is talking with the local hospital. She's hoping her credentials might get someone to check hospital records for maybe five to ten years ago."

"Could you check another name for me? Jacob Marley. See what you can find on him."

"Jacob Marley?"

"Yes, he's the funeral director. I think Joan Begley had pizza with him the night she was taken. It may have been exactly like he told me, a business dinner to wrap up funeral details, but when I visited him yesterday he seemed nervous and guilty about something. And he's a Junior who hates to be called Junior."

"If he's the funeral director he would have had access to Steve Earlman's embalmed body."

"Yes, he seemed too prepared to talk about that. But he doesn't fit the killer's profile. And now you're telling me I need to be looking for a hypochondriac who's also a paranoid delusional maniac because his mother made him sick on purpose? That should be easy to spot."

"Very funny, O'Dell. I'm trying to help you."

"I know you are. Sorry. It's just frustrating." She slowed the car, taking on more winding curves. "We just found another body."

"Oh, jeez. Do you know if it's Begley?"

"No, it isn't her. It may have been her rent-a-car. They're still checking it out. It was a local reporter with bad eyes."

"Let me guess, he took the eyes?"

"Yes. And he stuffed her in the trunk of a car. I worried that he might do this. He probably got paranoid that she was following him, but according to Watermeier she's been at the rock quarry every day and hounding *him.*"

Her cell phone beeped again.

"I'm going to lose you, Tully."

"I'll call if I find anything on Marley. Oh, and I'll have Dr. Patterson call you if she finds anything out from the hospital."

"The thing is it could take too long. If Joan Begley is still alive I have a feeling she won't be much longer. This last kill means he's getting panicky. And all we seem to have right now are too many missing imperfections, a whole lot of coincidences and some white, waxy paper from a butcher shop."

"Butcher-block paper?"

"Yeah, I guess that's what it's called. I'm guessing he has tons of it and uses it to wrap and temporarily store the body pieces. I keep thinking it's got to mean something, but what? Any ideas?"

"I'm just wondering where you buy that stuff."

"Well, not at the local Stop & Shop. We already checked."

"Didn't you say Earlman was a butcher?"

"That's right."

"Any sons?"

"No, I already thought of that. His shop closed when he died. Someone bought all the equipment but didn't continue the business." She almost drove through a red light, braking hard and drawing a honk from the driver behind her. Why hadn't she thought about it before? Luc had said that someone bought all the equipment. "Why would you buy all the equipment if you weren't going to have a butcher shop? Doesn't that seem a bit odd?"

"I don't know. You should see the crazy stuff people buy and sell on eBay all the time."

"And how do you know what people buy and sell on eBay?" Another beep from her phone. "My battery really is running low, Tully. Before I go, two things—how's Harvey? He's not driving you crazy, is he?"

"Not at all. In fact, I think you may have to bribe Emma in order to get him back."

"Don't you dare let her get attached to my dog, Tully."

"Might be too late."

"Second, how's Gwen doing?"

There was silence and she thought she had already lost him when he finally said, "I think she's doing okay."

"Will you do a favor for me and please check on her?"

"Sure, I can do that."

"Thanks, Tully, and tell Emma she does not get my dog."

"O'Dell, one other thing." This time she could hear his tone change. "Cunningham asked me about you."

Maggie felt her muscles tighten.

"He wanted to know if you mentioned anything to me about your vacation," he continued, sounding serious, almost apologetic.

She knew Tully was a straight-shooter. He'd never lie, especially to Cunningham, and now, she had probably gotten both of them in trouble.

"What did you tell him?" she asked, gripping the steering wheel in preparation for his answer.

"I told him the truth, that you said something about daffodils." Then he hung up before she had a chance to respond.

She smiled and pulled the car into a parking lot, trying to get her mind back on track and off a possible reprimand. Somewhere she had a city map, besides the one Tully had drawn for her. It was just a hunch, but then what else did she have to go on? She needed to find the county courthouse. She needed to find out who had bought all that butcher shop equipment, including what might have been rolls and rolls of butcher-block paper.

# CHAPTER 58

Henry started to head out to the rock quarry, had almost gotten there when he decided to go back to downtown Wallingford. He needed a strong cup of coffee, but mostly he just wanted to stop in at the bookstore and see his wife. After the media got hold of this latest development there was bound to be a frenzy, especially with the latest victim being one of their own. He was beginning to believe he and Rosie could kiss goodbye the idea of retiring in this community.

He took the back roads, winding around the edge of the city with the car window rolled down. He drove slowly, trying to suck in the fresh air, trying to relax enough so that the tight fist, that nagging ache in the middle of his chest, would let up. It'd serve him right for being so lax about taking—or rather not taking—his blood pressure medicine. Here he had escaped being with his buddies on 9/11 only to get a fucking heart attack while driving through the Connecticut countryside.

He drove by St. Francis Cemetery, curving around the hill, when he noticed a man hurry behind one of the tall headstones. At first he thought he had imagined it. Maybe he *was* having a heart attack. But that didn't make you see things, did it?

Henry pulled into the cemetery's entrance and stopped the car. From this angle he couldn't see the headstone without getting out. He sat there, wondering again if he had imagined it. If someone was in the cemetery there wasn't anything wrong with that. People were free to come in and often did to place wreaths and flowers on the graves. So there was no reason to hide.

He backed out and pulled onto the road. Rosie would laugh at him, not about forgetting his blood pressure medicine, but about seeing ghosts. He glanced up in the rearview mirror as he started around another curve. Just as the cemetery started to disappear out of view he saw the man again. This time Henry pulled the car off to the side of the road, out of view of the cemetery.

He left the car and backtracked down through the ditch, keeping himself out of sight while he took the long way around. The cemetery backed onto a forest, and Henry could see a pickup parked deep between the trees where he knew there wasn't a road.

Henry climbed up a steep incline, hoping it would hide him until he got to the trees. The mud and rock kept crumbling beneath his boots and he thought for sure the guy would hear him. Finally a windbreak of spindly evergreens allowed him his first look.

The man had his back to Henry, but he could see the guy had a shovel and was digging. Okay, so he was a grave digger. But then why did he hide when a car came by? And did they use shovels anymore to dig graves? Hadn't he seen earth-digging equipment out here before? One of those miniature things with the claw? Yeah, he was sure that's how they did it. In fact, he thought Vargus and Hobbs had a contract with several of the funeral homes.

Henry moved closer to get a better look. That's when he realized the guy wasn't digging a new grave, he was digging one up. Just then the man turned enough that Henry recognized him. It was Wally Hobbs, and he was hurrying away to crouch down behind a tall headstone as another car drove by.

# CHAPTER 59

Luc hadn't left the house all morning. Not even to get the newspaper. Ever since Agent O'Dell had left he had been pacing, trying to watch TV while he walked back and forth from one window to another with the baseball bat never leaving his hand. Scrapple had given up on him hours ago, finally settling down on his favorite rug. Except for a few ear perks now and then, the terrier was fast asleep.

Luc kept hearing vehicles up on Whippoorwill Drive. Maybe there was more commotion happening down at the rock quarry. He thought he had heard sirens earlier. On the midday local news there was mention of a car being found in Hubbard Park, but that was in Meriden, not down the lane. He wasn't about to leave the house to go see. Ordinarily they wouldn't be able to keep him away. But today…today he couldn't seem to set foot on his porch without getting the shakes. Is this what he was turning into? An old man who couldn't leave his house and then couldn't even remember whether or not he had?

Agent O'Dell had asked him this morning if he would please consider calling Julia to let her know that he was okay. But if his daughter didn't know about this mess, she wouldn't need to know that he was okay. Or so went his reasoning. He knew he needed to call her. He wanted to call her. Ever since he had talked to her…jeez, what day was that? Was it a few days ago or had it been weeks?

He heard another car, only this one sounded like it was in his driveway. By the time he got to the door, Agent O'Dell was coming up the front porch. He opened the door for her and felt a flush of embarrassment when she saw the bat still in his hands.

"What's the excitement down the lane?"

"I'm not sure," she said, sounding a little out of breath. "I couldn't get hold of Sheriff Watermeier. You think you might be able to help with something, Luc?"

"Sure. I mean, I can try."

She had a map in her hands and started spreading it out on his crowded coffee table. "You've lived around here for a long time, right?"

"Almost all my life. My wife, Elizabeth, was from Philadelphia, but she loved it here, too, so we stayed. Wish Julia would have loved it enough to stay, but…well, what can a father do, huh?"

"I wonder if you can tell me where Ralph Shelby's property is."

"Ralph the butcher? Ralph's been gone a long time. What's it been, maybe ten years. Jeez, I can't remember. Didn't I tell you this morning that Steve Earlman bought the butcher shop from Ralph? But now Steve's gone, too. I told you that, didn't I? Didn't we talk about that this morning?"

"Yes, you did tell me. But Mr. Shelby's property, the acreage where he lived, can you tell me where it is? It's close by, right?"

"Sure, it's up the road, past the Millers' old sawmill. Mrs. Shelby died just a few years ago, but I think her son still lives out there."

"Can you show me on the map?"

He stared at the lines and blue spots and nothing looked familiar.

"We're right here." She pointed to an area, but it didn't look like anything to him except some red intersecting lines. She was looking up at him with a frown. Or was it worry? He didn't know her well enough to know if she was upset with him or feeling sorry for him. He'd rather have her upset with him.

"Luc, can you show me?"

"I can show you, but I can't show you on the map." He went to the door and grabbed his black beret and a jacket.

"No, you can't come with me, Luc."

"That's the only way I know how to show you."

"Can't you just give me directions? How far up the road? Is it on Whippoorwill Drive?"

"I'm really not being stubborn," he said, and tried not to get embarrassed again. "But I can't tell you. I can't put it into words." His hands were already flying, trying to help him explain. "I have to show you by...well, by showing you."

She hesitated, standing with arms crossed, looking like she was trying to decide. "Okay, but you promise you'll stay in the car."

"Sure, I can do that. Why are you interested in the old Shelby place?"

"I need to check something out. Remember you told me that when the butcher shop closed someone bought all the equipment?"

"Oh, yeah. But I don't remember who it was. Seems like I should know."

"I found out. It was Ralph Shelby's son. He bought everything, every last piece."

"Really? Hmm...I wonder what he wanted with all that old stuff."

"That's what I want to find out."

# CHAPTER 60

Henry knew he had the rock quarry killer. The entire trip back to the station Wally Hobbs kept complaining about his stomach hurting. In that tinny voice he begged Henry to stop the car so he could throw up. Well, at least the bastard waited until they got to the County Sheriff's Office. He thought about making Hobbs clean up the mess, but he knew he shouldn't push his good fortune.

Now he had Hobbs handcuffed to a metal folding chair in their interrogation room. Actually, it wasn't really an interrogation room but a break room with a coffeemaker and an empty plate of crumbs.

He had already read him his rights, or his version of them. Sometimes he knew he left out a word or two.

"What do you think you were doing, Walter?" He wondered if he could bully the little man into confessing. Then he remembered that Hobbs's partner was the biggest bully in town. He had probably built up some kind of immunity. "You want me to call your sister?"

"No. Don't call Lillian."

"What's wrong? You don't want your sister knowing you dig up bodies and slice them up?"

"What are you talking about?"

"I've seen your handiwork, Hobbs. What is it with you? You kill some and when you get bored you dig some up?"

"I haven't killed anyone."

"How could you dig up someone like Steve Earlman? Don't you have any respect for the dead?"

"I didn't dig him up."

Wally Hobbs's eyes were the size of quarters and sweat poured down his forehead. Henry could smell him.

"How many have you killed and how many have you dug up?"

"Wait. You've got to listen to me. I didn't kill anyone."

"Right."

"Marley and Calvin and me, we just wanted to make some extra money."

"Marley? Jake Marley?" Henry sat down on the edge of the table. "Marley's in this with you?"

"We didn't think it would hurt anybody. Life insurance policies usually pay for everything, so it's not like we were taking it out of the families' pockets."

"What the hell are you talking about?"

"I was just trying to fix it so that if anyone checked they wouldn't know."

"Check what?" Suddenly it was hot in the room and Henry needed to open a window.

"If anyone checked…you know, Steve Earlman's grave. Marley sells them the vault, but we don't actually use a vault. We divide the money three ways." Hobbs looked scared. "It was Marley's idea."

Henry rubbed a hand over his face and he couldn't help but feel disappointed. Wally Hobbs was a weasel and a thief, but he was no killer.

# CHAPTER 61

Adam Bonzado didn't like what he was thinking. It couldn't be possible and yet it made sense.

He had driven back to West Haven, all the way to his lab at the university to retrieve the rest of the Polaroids Dr. Stolz had given him. It was bad enough that the victims' head wounds matched the exact angle of the pry bar he kept in the El Camino, but now he needed to check something else.

He grabbed the photos and rushed out of the lab, bumping into several of his students, barely mumbling a greeting. Now in the parking lot once again, he stood at the tailgate of his pickup. He stood there, hesitating with the Polaroid in his hand. It was a photo of the victim with the pronounced livor mortis on her back.

Adam knew that livor mortis was the result of gravity pulling and settling all the blood to the lowest area of the body. This victim had been laid on her back for several hours after her death. That's why the skin on her back was so red. Called the bruising of death, livor mortis also had the tendency of transforming the skin's texture. The skin often took up the pattern of the surface it was laid out on. So a body laid out on a brick sidewalk might have indentations resembling brick and mortar. A body found dead on a gravel road might have a pebbled texture. And in this case, a body laid out in a pickup with a waffle-pattern bed lining might have a waffle-pattern imprint.

Adam pulled down the tailgate and held up the Polaroid. The pattern matched the dead woman's back. And as much as he didn't want to believe it, he knew that Simon Shelby was the only person who had borrowed his pickup.

# CHAPTER 62

Maggie knew she couldn't wait for Watermeier. Wherever he was he wasn't responding to any of her phone calls and her cell phone was on the verge of completely dying.

Jennifer Carpenter had to have been killed within the last twelve hours, which meant that the killer was becoming more and more paranoid. If he still had Joan Begley and was keeping her alive, Maggie knew it wouldn't be for much longer.

She drove slowly on Whippoorwill Drive, in the opposite direction of the rock quarry. Luc sat quietly beside her. She hoped he hadn't blanked out on her again. At least not until he showed her where Simon Shelby lived.

"Turn up here. In that direction," he said, pointing with an animated wave of his whole arm. "You can't see the buildings from the road. The mailbox is one of those big galvanized steel ones that sits on a barrel. You know, one of those big wooden barrels."

Maggie glanced at him. He had to be kidding. A barrel? But Luc didn't see the irony.

At the courthouse, the clerk who helped Maggie look up the estate sale records of Steve Earlman told Maggie that Simon Shelby was a very nice young man. "Poor fellow," she told Maggie without any prompting, "he lost his father when he was just a boy. Loved his daddy. I remember going to the butcher shop and seeing him there on Saturdays, helping Ralph. He had a cute nickname for Simon. I can't remember what it was, though.

"Simon really was crushed, just crushed when Ralph died. I don't think Sophie knew what to do with the boy. I think that's when he started getting sick a lot. We all felt so bad for Sophie. All that worry probably sent her to an early grave. But he's such a nice young man now." The woman rambled on and Maggie, who usually hated small talk, simply nodded and listened, noting all the coincidences.

But it was more than coincidence when the clerk said, "He's working his way through college now, the University of New Haven."

"Really?" Maggie had said, still more interested in the individual auction items.

"Something to do with bones, of all things," the clerk told her, and Maggie almost dropped the book of records. "I suppose that makes sense in some way, huh? I mean being the son of a butcher." The woman had laughed. "Frankly, I think it's a little morbid myself. But he must enjoy that sort of stuff. He works part-time at Marley and Marley Funeral Home, too. Such a hard worker."

"That nickname his father used?" Maggie asked the woman, although by this time she had felt certain she already knew the answer. "Was it Sonny?"

"Yes, that's it. How did you know? Ralph called him Sonny, Sonny Boy."

Now Maggie saw the mailbox on the wooden barrel before Luc's arm started waving at it, but she drove past the driveway.

"No, it's right there," he said. "You missed it."

"I'm going to park the car over here." And she pulled into what looked like a dirt path to a field. "I want you to stay here."

"Okay."

"I'm serious, Luc. You stay here." As an afterthought, she pulled out her cell phone and handed it to him. "If I don't come back in fifteen minutes, call 911."

He took the phone and stared at it, but seemed satisfied that she was letting him do something to help. Which made Maggie feel more confident that he would stay put, never mind that the cell phone's battery was dead.

# CHAPTER 63

Simon stared at the tools on the wall, trying to decide which one to use on Joan. He had gotten used to her company. Despite hating to clean up her messes, he did like having her as his guest. He liked that she didn't even ask to be let go anymore. He had control over her and he liked that, too. But that reporter had ruined everything. And now he had to get rid of Joan.

He had called in sick, telling the receptionist at the funeral home that he might have the flu. It was something he had never done before. And he wasn't going to class this afternoon, either. Another first. Not since childhood had he missed a day of work or college classes. After all those missed school days growing up, he had always felt like he needed to catch up. Maybe he felt like he needed to prove something.

He hated missing. Hated ruining his regular routine. It didn't feel right. But this was important. Already he had cleaned out two of the chest freezers, one here in the toolshed and one back at the house. He had tossed all the parts he had saved, all those pieces he had saved and wrapped in butcher-block white paper. He had tossed it all in the woods, where the coyotes would take care of it once it thawed. He hated parting with the pieces, but none of them proved interesting enough to showcase. He really didn't need them. Besides, he needed some place to put Joan. At least until he found a new dumping ground.

He continued to stare at the tools. He had ruled out the chain saw, though it was tempting, especially since he still wasn't sure which gland caused her hormone deficiency. She tried to tell him she was fine. That she had only made it up to excuse her overeating. Poor girl. Like the rest of them, she didn't recognize what a valuable commodity she was in possession of. But it didn't matter. He'd just cut all of the glands out. Surely he would be able to tell which one looked diseased. And if he couldn't, he'd decided to keep all of them.

A knife would work. But which one? He had the entire collection now from his father's shop. Anything from the huge cleaver to the small, delicate filet knife. Maybe something in between. He really didn't want to do this. It was almost as if he had become attached to her. He liked coming home and having her there to talk to and share his collection with. He hadn't ever had a pet before. No, no, not a pet. He didn't mean that she was like a pet. No, no, no. It was like…actually he had never really had a friend before. That was probably what it was like. But he still reached for one of the boning knives. That was when he heard something outside.

Had the coyotes dared to come already?

He glanced out the small window of the toolshed. Nothing back in the woods. Then he saw her, walking around to the back of the house. He could see her, walking slowly, cautiously, sneaking toward the back door. And from this angle he could tell that Special Agent O'Dell had her gun drawn.

# CHAPTER 64

Maggie couldn't see a vehicle, but there were enough outbuildings to store several. Had he gone to work already? Or if not work, perhaps he had a class. Maybe he was even back at the rock quarry, helping Watermeier and Bonzado. What a pathetic twist. The killer not only returning to the crime scene but helping to process it. Simon Shelby had stood by and watched, actually even helped at times, while they sorted through his mutilations, his butchery.

The acreage was well maintained. All the buildings were whitewashed, the grass and meadow cut short, no discarded old equipment. One of the buildings looked like it had huge solar panels on its sides, renovated for perhaps a workshop.

She made her way to the back door but hadn't peeked inside any of the windows yet. She decided to knock. Make sure he was gone, despite her certainty. And she slid her Smith & Wesson under her jacket, in case someone answered the door. When no one did, she tried to the knob, surprised to find the door unlocked.

She brought out her revolver again and swung the door open. She stopped to listen. Other than an electrical hum of an appliance, she couldn't hear anything. She entered slowly, watching, looking, searching as she eased down the hallway. She came to the kitchen first on the left. She glanced in. Nothing out of the ordinary. The electrical hum was coming from the old chest freezer in the corner. She continued down the hallway. An open stairwell was to her right and she looked up. Nothing.

She could see the living room beyond the stairwell, or perhaps a parlor, furnished like a showroom with what looked like antiques, lace doilies and curtains. She got to the entrance and was paying such close attention to what was in front of her that she didn't hear him come up from behind. She didn't hear him until it was too late.

Maggie turned just as something came crashing down on the side of her head.

# CHAPTER 65

Luc didn't like waiting.

He wished Agent O'Dell had allowed him to bring Scrapple along. He didn't like being without the dog. They went everywhere together. And he really didn't like hearing Scrapple's howl of abandonment coming from the living room window as they drove away.

He tried to see beyond the trees. He tried to look down the path where Agent O'Dell had disappeared. He didn't understand why she hadn't driven up, or at least, walked up the driveway. She was being very secretive for someone who kept telling him not to worry. She reminded him of Julia. Before she moved to D.C. his daughter had always been going off checking stuff, stuff she probably shouldn't have been poking her nose into. Maybe that was just what law enforcement people did. Maybe it was in their blood. Although he and Julia did share some of the same blood.

He scratched his head, pushing back the beret and looking again to see if he could make out where in the world Agent O'Dell was now. He held up the cell phone. She said fifteen minutes. Well, it was close to that now, wasn't it? He glanced at his wrist, only to remember that he had stopped wearing watches long ago when he could no longer understand them. Numbers had become useless to him. He couldn't even write out a check anymore. They probably would have shut off his electricity months ago if he hadn't had the foresight to set up all the automatic withdrawals for his bills. Hopefully the money wouldn't run out before his time ran out.

He looked out the car window again and this time felt a slight panic as he tried to remember why he couldn't recognize anything. Oh, jeez! Where the hell was he? He twisted around in the car, trying to find something he recognized. Then he held up the black object in his hand. He was holding it so tight it had to be something important, but damn it, he couldn't remember what the hell it was.

# CHAPTER 66

Maggie woke slowly. Her head throbbed. Her legs felt numb, tangled, somewhere underneath her. It was pitch-dark despite her attempt to open her eyes. No use. It was too dark. She couldn't move her arms. Couldn't begin to untangle her legs. She could barely move her hands and tried to feel around the small, smooth space above her. Whatever he had shoved her into, it was too tight to move.

Too tight and cold. So very cold.

That was when she heard the motor kick on. That was when she recognized the electrical hum. That same hum she had heard when she first entered the house.

Oh, God! He had put her in the freezer.

She couldn't panic. It wouldn't help to panic. She couldn't have been in here long or she wouldn't have woken up. She had to remain calm. She tried to twist her legs out from under her. It was useless. They were shoved in tight. Even her arms couldn't move more than a few inches to the side. It felt like she was squeezing herself down into the chest tighter and tighter. That couldn't be possible.

She needed to stay calm. She needed to breathe. It was already difficult to breathe. How much air could she possibly have inside here? And the cold. God, it was unbearable.

Her fingers hurt, but she balled them up into fists and pushed on the lid. There wasn't even enough room to pound. She remembered her weapon. Yes, she could shoot some holes in the lid. Of course, why hadn't she thought of that? She patted down her jacket. She tried to feel her pockets. And despair came quickly with the realization that, of course, he wouldn't have tossed her revolver in with her.

It was useless. She started to scream "help" as loud as she could. Over and over again until her throat felt raw. She shoved at the lid. She slammed her fists, now numb from the cold. She kept slamming them into the lid until she could feel what must have been blood dripping down into her face. And all she could think about was that the only person who might know where to look for her was back in her car with a cell phone that had a dead battery.

# CHAPTER 67

Adam found Maggie's rental parked off the road but no one was inside. Did she know about Simon? How could she? He pulled his El Camino in behind the Ford Escort and jumped out, heading through the ditch until he thought of something. He ran back to the pickup and grabbed the pry bar from the back.

He barely got to the trees before he saw Luc Racine, wandering behind one of the buildings. The old man looked lost. Adam started to call out to him, then stopped, looking around for Simon. He had called the funeral home before he drove out here, hoping he'd catch Simon and be able to confront him in public. But they told him Simon had called in sick, and that alone sent a wave of panic through Adam. Simon never called in sick.

Now he wished he had tried to get ahold of Henry again, but each time he had tried, Beverly told him Sheriff Watermeier was in a very important meeting and could not be disturbed. That his deputy had been instructed to handle any emergencies.

Adam made his way to Luc, staying in the trees and watching for signs of Maggie or Simon. When he was close enough, he called to Luc in a low voice, "Mr. Racine. Hey, Luc."

The old man turned around so suddenly he almost tripped. His eyes darted everywhere and Adam worried he might be having one of his blank moments.

"Over here, Mr. Racine." He came out from the trees and walked to Luc, his eyes watching in all directions.

"Oh, Professor, it's you. You scared me."

"Sorry. Where's Maggie?"

"I don't know. But I think I heard someone in this cabin over here."

"Have you seen Simon?"

"No, no, not at all. We need to find Maggie. I just don't have a good feeling. I think she's been gone too long." He was shifting from one foot to the other, back and forth in almost a nervous dance.

"Okay, calm down. We'll find her. Let's check in here."

They couldn't see in through the windows and the door was locked with a chain and padlock. Adam used the pry bar, twisting and pounding at it until finally it broke open. The light in the room was dim. Adam thought it looked like a cozy cabin, except for the shelves that lined the walls. Shelves with rows and rows of jars and crocks that reminded him of his own lab back at the university. Then he noticed the bed in the far corner. Someone moved under the covers.

The woman curled up and strapped in the bed jerked awake. She cried out when she saw them, smiling and laughing. Then suddenly she winced and cried out with pain.

# CHAPTER 68

Maggie felt the exhaustion. She needed to think. She needed to stay calm. No good would come from panic. Her hands throbbed with pain. That was good, good that she could still feel something even if it was pain. Yes, it was good that the cold bit into her skin, that it hadn't gone totally numb. Good that she could still hear her teeth chattering and feel her body shivering.

Shivering was the body's way of warming itself. Soon she'd be too tired to shiver, her blood too thick, her heart and lungs too slow to respond. Even her brain would become less efficient as she crossed the boundary into hypothermia.

She tried to remember what she could expect. She tried to remember what happens during hypothermia. If she could remember maybe she could look out for the signs and fight them.

She knew it was possible to survive several hours in extreme cold, but how many? Two? Three? She couldn't remember. What else was there? She needed to remember.

Soon the cold would shut down her metabolism. Her lungs would take in less oxygen and her breaths would become fewer so that it would look like she wasn't even breathing. That was good, because there couldn't be much air in this freezer. Oh, God! Would she suffocate before she froze to death?

She knew the same was true for her heart rate. It would slow down, too, which seemed impossible at the moment. It seemed so loud, hammering in her ears. But it would slow to a faint, almost inaudible rate, so that if someone were to feel her pulse, he might not feel one at all.

She kept telling herself that she had plenty of time until they found her. But who would come looking for her? Other than

Simon the only person who knew she was here was Luc Racine. Would he come looking for her when she didn't come back to the car? Would he call for help? Oh, damn! How could he call for help? And again, she remembered that she had left him with a dead cell phone. What did it matter? He might not even remember where he was or who she was.

The panic clawed at her. She resisted the urge to beat her fists against the walls of the freezer again. She told herself that panic was also good. It was when the panic subsided that she'd need to start worrying. Although by that time she might not care.

She tried to concentrate again. She wanted to go through the list of things to expect. It would keep her mind working.

What other things were there? Oh, yes, the lack of oxygen would trigger hallucinations. They could be visual or auditory or both. She might see people when there was no one there at all. Or she might hear someone talking or calling to her, but it would only be her mind playing tricks on her.

There was also the sudden and extreme heat. Yes, heat after the cold. It was one of the cruel paradoxes of severe hypothermia. There was supposedly a burning sensation that made victims want to tear off their clothing and rip at their skin. No problem there. She couldn't move enough to do either. Ironically, the heat was one of the last things they remembered before losing consciousness. That's if they could remember.

Amnesia would eventually chip away at the brain. Maybe it was the body's last defense, a sort of odd blessing to replace the memory of pain and cold with a simple void.

She could feel her muscles already getting stiff. They throbbed and ached from the shivering. She tried to think of warm things. Maybe Gwen was right. Maybe she did need a vacation. And she tried to imagine a beach, hot sand between her toes, the sun beating down on her skin, warm, refreshing waves washing up against her. If not a beach then maybe her hands wrapped around a steaming mug of hot chocolate while her body cuddled into a thick down comforter while she sat in front of a roaring fire. So warm she could curl up, curl up and…sleep.

She was so exhausted. Sleep sounded good. She closed her eyes. She could feel her breaths coming slower, more and more shallow. The pain in her hands had gone away. Or maybe she simply couldn't feel the pain anymore. The panic had subsided. She felt it slipping away. She was so very tired, so sleepy. Yes, she'd close her eyes. Just for a moment or two. It was so dark, so quiet.

She'd allow herself to sleep. Just for a little while. She'd sleep under the warm sunshine. She could hear the waves splashing, a seagull up above. From somewhere in the back of her mind, someplace where her brain had slowed down but hadn't stopped working, from somewhere there came a faint whine, a soft, almost inaudible alarm insisting she open her eyes, pleading with her to not give in to the darkness.

At the same time came the realization that she had already stopped shivering. And she knew it was too late.

# CHAPTER 69

Luc searched every room of the house and still hadn't found Maggie. Where in the world was she? Sheriff Watermeier seemed convinced Simon Shelby had taken her with him. His deputies searched the surrounding woods while the State Patrol were said to be setting up roadblocks.

Luc could still hear the ambulance's siren as it whined up Whippoorwill Drive. One of the paramedics said it looked like the woman named Joan had been poisoned. What if Simon had poisoned Maggie?

He fidgeted, wringing his hands, then raced back up the stairs to check closets and corners he knew he had already checked. The whole time he kept thinking that she had saved him once. He couldn't possibly let her down. He didn't even know how long it had been since she left him in the car. Simon could have taken her hours ago.

"Luc?" Adam was in the hall between the kitchen and the stairwell. "Any sign of her?"

"No. I've looked everywhere."

"Henry's put out an APB on Simon. If he has her with him, they'll find and stop him."

"I just don't have a good feeling about this."

"She's a tough woman. She can take care of herself."

But as he said it Luc could tell Adam hadn't convinced himself.

"What kind of madman does this?" Luc hated that the panic was still caught like a lump in his throat, making his voice crack. "Out back in the trees there's a bunch of white packages of frozen meat or something. He just threw it all out there to rot. What kind of a crazy man does something like that?"

"Wait a minute." Adam started searching again. "You say he threw out stuff from a freezer?"

"Yeah, piles of it. It was back—" But he saw it at the same time Adam did. They raced to the chest freezer in the kitchen corner, both of them hesitating and looking at each other almost as if they were as afraid to open it as they were hopeful.

# CHAPTER 70

Out of the darkness Maggie thought she heard a hum, a faint whine that wouldn't go away. That kept getting louder, though was still in the distance. An annoying whine. Was it a voice? Was she only imagining it? Hallucinating?

She was too tired to care.

Her eyelids burned as a flash of light came at her, then was gone. Laser beams, another flash and then darkness.

"Gone."

Yes, they were gone as quickly as they came at her.

"She's gone."

No, wait. It was a voice. She could barely make it out. Quiet and muffled, the words didn't make sense as they came through a wind tunnel.

"She's gone."

Her muscles were stiff. Her arms frozen at her sides. There was no willing them to move. Another flash of light and this time it came with a flash of color, blue and a blur of orange.

"No pulse."

She was too tired to ask what the voices meant. She couldn't ask if she wanted to. She had no control of her body. It seemed gone, stolen out from under her. She couldn't feel it or see it.

"She's gone" came the words again, and this time that alarm in the back of her brain said, "They mean you! They're talking about you."

But no. She wasn't gone. She needed to tell them.

"No pulse."

No, wait, she wanted to yell but couldn't because she was floating off in the distance and had no command of her body.

They needed to listen to her chest. They wouldn't be able to get a pulse at her wrist. Her heartbeat had slowed down. It was a faint murmur, but it was beating. She could feel it.

"No dilation."

Please, wait. Why couldn't she see them? If they were looking into her eyes, why couldn't she see? The flashes of light. That had to be what it was. Her eyes wouldn't respond. But she was still here. How could she let them know she was still alive?

"She's gone."

*No, no, no.* Her brain seemed to be screaming it, but it was no use. They believed she was dead. She couldn't see beyond the black. She couldn't make her muscles respond.

No, wait. Maybe she was dead.

Wasn't this what dead felt like? A faint consciousness with no control over her body. No body to control.

Oh, God! Maybe they were right. Maybe she was gone. Gone forever. She felt herself slipping again. She'd close her eyes and sleep some more. Or were they already closed? She slept and woke again when she heard something. Nothing. More sleep. What felt like hours. A warm darkness slipped in tight around her. Liquid warmth ran through her veins. And she felt herself leaving again. Yes, maybe this was what it felt like. No second chances. No warnings. Gone.

Then suddenly she thought she saw…no, it couldn't be. Through a blur of gray haze she saw her father and then she knew it was true. She really was dead.

# CHAPTER 71

"Maggie?"

It hurt to open her eyes. The light blinded her. The images swirled above her head. The humming of equipment filled her ears. And her mouth tasted like rubber and cotton. She tried to focus on the voice and where it was coming from. If it was real. Then she felt someone squeeze her hand.

"Maggie? You have to come back or I'll never forgive you."

"Gwen?" It hurt to talk, but at least she could. She tried again. "Where am I?"

"You scared us, O'Dell."

She turned her head to look up at Tully standing on the other side of the bed. Just the slight turn made her dizzy.

"What happened? Where am I?"

"You're at Yale-New Haven Medical Center," Gwen told her. "You suffered a severe case of hypothermia."

"They had to drain all your blood out of you, O'Dell, warm it up and pump it back in. So you can't complain about being cold-blooded, okay?"

"Very funny." Gwen shot him a look.

"What, we're not allowed to make jokes?"

"You really did have us scared, Maggie," Gwen said, caressing her forehead with the warm palm of her hand.

"What happened?"

"Look, Maggie, you're going to have amnesia and probably not remember everything that happened. We can go through it later when you're stronger, okay?"

"But how long have I been gone?"

"You've been out of it since Thursday."

"What day is it?"

"It's Saturday evening, sweetie." Gwen was still holding her hand and smoothing back her hair.

"What about Simon Shelby?"

"That she remembers. Always on duty, aren't you, O'Dell?" Tully smiled. "Maryland State Patrol caught him last night. We're not sure where he was headed. He actually had taken some of his specimens with him in the trunk."

"Specimens?" Maggie asked, trying to fight through the annoying haze.

"We were right," Tully said. "He was cutting out deformed livers, tumored brains, diseased hearts, crippled bones. Meriden's police lab thinks they may have already matched a pair of eyes to that reporter. They're running DNA tests on some of the other pieces. They'll probably be able to match some of them to the bodies in the rock quarry. You should have seen his work shed, O'Dell. Shelves and shelves of jars and containers. It's hard to tell how many victims or how long he's been doing this. And he's not talking. In fact, it looks like he might end up in a padded cell somewhere."

"My guess is it started five years ago," Gwen said, "when his mother died. I talked to a nurse at the local hospital. She remembered Simon Shelby and his mother, Sophie. This nurse told me she even felt sorry for him. The mother was constantly bringing him into the emergency room in the middle of the night. He always complained of terrible stomach cramps, but tests never showed anything out of the ordinary. His mother may have been poisoning him, just like he was poisoning Joan Begley."

"Is she okay?" Maggie asked. "Is she alive?"

"She's alive and she's going to be okay," Gwen said. "She's up at MidState Medical Center in Meriden. It looks like Shelby was giving her low doses of arsenic. She has a long recovery ahead of her, but they think she'll be okay."

"I thought I died," Maggie confessed. That much she could remember.

"So did the two men who found you," Gwen told her, moving in closer against the bed railing. "Luc Racine told me that he was sure you were dead. They couldn't get a pulse. Your eyes wouldn't respond to light. But he said Professor Bonzado wouldn't give up on you. You're really lucky he didn't, Maggie. Hypothermia can easily disguise itself."

"You're probably going to wish you died when Cunningham gets ahold of you," Tully said, but he was smiling.

"So I guess he knows."

"Let's just say he sent that white flower plant." Tully pointed to the potted plant on one side of the table. "The card says it's a false dragonhead, commonly known as an obedient plant."

"Are Luc and Adam here?" Maggie asked, hoping to change the subject.

"They'll be by later. In fact, Tully, why don't you go call them."

Maggie thought she saw Gwen and Tully exchange a look, some secret between them.

"I'll be right back," Tully said, and squeezed Maggie's shoulder. "Emma wanted you to know that she's taking good care of Harvey."

"Just don't let her think she gets to keep him, Tully."

"Yes, I know." And he left.

"Maggie, there's something I need to tell you."

She braced herself and suddenly tried to move her legs. Yes, legs worked. Arms worked.

"What are you doing?" Gwen laughed. "No, you're fine. Really. But I just thought I should warn you. Your mother is here. She's down in the cafeteria taking a break. She's been here since Thursday night."

"Oh. Okay. Wow! You really were worried about me, huh?"

"The procedure for bringing someone back from severe hypothermia can kill the patient," Gwen said, the pent-up emotion of two days revealing itself. "I'm sorry. But I was really worried. Your mother's not the only one I called. Now, you can be upset with me all you want, but there's someone else I called." Gwen squeezed her hand then went to the door. "You can come in now."

Patrick walked in, not hesitating, and came directly to the bed. But then he stood there, staring down at her.

"They've told you?" she asked.

"And it's a good thing. I wonder how many more trips and how many more Diet Pepsis it would have taken you." He smiled their father's smile.

"It was you," she said.

"What?"

"I thought I was dead. I thought I saw my dad…our dad. But it must have been you I saw."

"So you'll tell me about him sometime?"

"How much time do you have?" She smiled at him.

He sat down, taking Gwen's chair at the bedside. "My shift doesn't start for a couple more hours."

# EPILOGUE

*Three months later*
*Connecticut Mental Facility*

Simon hated this room. It smelled of disinfectant, but it wasn't clean. He could see cobwebs on the ceiling in the far right corner. And the nurses or wardens or whatever they called them weren't very clean, either. The one with the tattoo had greasy long hair and bad breath. But at least they treated him okay. And Dr. Kramer had even given him something for his stomach that seemed to make it better…sometimes. It still hurt once in a while. Once in a while around midnight.

They had brought in two trays of food, which meant he was getting a new roommate. Already he had drunk his juice and hidden the plastic cup under the bed, under a floorboard he had worked on and pulled up. That's where he kept his new specimens. He had to pace himself, but it was getting easier and easier to steal jars from the supply closet. The night clerk, better known as Broom Hilda, forgot to lock it sometimes.

He heard the door locks click open. They still made him jump.

"Simon." And here she was now. "Here's your new roommate. I want you to meet Daniel Bender."

He looked like a kid, skinny and pale with shaggy brown hair and empty brown eyes.

"Hi, Daniel," he said, standing up to shake his hand and disgusted to find it sweaty and cold. Simon wiped his hand off on Daniel's bedspread while Broom Hilda showed the kid where to put his few things.

After she left, Daniel sat on the edge of his bed, staring at the tray of food.

"The soup is usually good," Simon told him. "It's hard to screw up soup." He picked at his salad, poking the wilted leaves with his fork and pushing them off to the side of the tray.

"I can't eat just anything," Daniel said in a little bitty voice. "I have a bleeding ulcer."

Suddenly, Simon was interested, and he shoved his salad to the side.

"Tell me about your ulcer," he said, while he slipped his fork under the mattress until he could put it in his secret place.

## ACKNOWLEDGEMENTS FOR *SPLIT SECOND*

Patricia Sierra, fellow author and friend—I'm not sure this one would have been completed without your tender, gentle nagging. Thanks for seeing me through all the anxiety attacks.

The amazing crew at MIRA® Books for their enthusiasm, hard work and dedication, especially Valerie Gray, Craig Swinwood, Krystyna de Duleba, Alex Osuszek and the best sales force in the business. Perhaps there is a reason we call them publishing houses—you've certainly made me feel as if I've found a home.

Megan Underwood and the gang at Goldberg McDuffie Communications, Inc for their expertise and hard work.

Annie Belatti, the only person I know who gets excited about describing gunshot wounds over dinner. Thanks for your patience, medical expertise and friendship. Sharon Car, fellow writer and friend, who listens and encourages through the good and the bad.

Marilyn and John Cooney and Mary Means for taking such loving care of my kids when I need to be on the road. Patti El-Kachouti for your unconditional friendship and encouragement.

Nicole Friend, who has often been my sounding board and voice of reason.

Tony Friend for sharing information, images and ideas that only you can provide.

Ellen Jacobs for telling the truth, first as a reader, then as a friend.

LaDonna Tworek for reminding me that some friendships are forever.

For their inspiration, enthusiasm and loving support, many thanks to Kenny and Connie Kava, Jeanie Shoemaker Mezger and John Mezger, Natalie and Rich Cummings, Marlene Haney, Sandy Rockwood, my mom and dad—Patricia and Edward Kava—Mac Payne and the Movie Club group: Lyn Belitz, Mary Michaelsen, Jo Ellen Shoemaker and Becky Thomson.

Also, I want to thank the many book buyers and booksellers for making room on your lists and on your shelves for a new voice.

And to the readers. With all the wonderful fiction available, thank you for choosing mine to be a part of your escape and entertainment.

Finally, thanks to Philip Spitzer, Amy Moore-Benson and Dianne Moggy. None of this would be possible without Philip taking a chance on me, without Amy being my personal crusader and without Dianne's patient, steady guidance and support. Together the three of you are truly a writer's dream team.

## ACKNOWLEDGEMENTS FOR *THE SOUL CATCHER*

I'm a firm believer in sharing credit and giving thanks, so please be patient, as the list seems to grow with each book. Many thanks to all the professionals who so generously gave of their time and expertise. If I've gotten any of the facts wrong or have creatively manipulated a fact or two, blame me, not them. My appreciation and respect go to the following experts:

Amy Moore-Benson, my editor, my crusader, my creative partner and my common sense—you are truly the best.

Dianne Moggy for your patience, your focus and your wise counsel—you are a class act.

The entire crew at MIRA® Books for their enthusiasm and dedication, especially Tania Charzewski, Krystyna de Duleba and Craig Swinwood. Special thanks to Alex Osuszek and an incredible sales force that continues to surpass goals and records I never dreamed to be reaching, let alone surpassing. Thanks to all of you for allowing me to be part of the team and not just the product.

Megan Underwood and the experts at Goldberg McDuffie Communications, Inc, once again, for your unflinching dedication and unquestionable expertise.

Philip Spitzer, my agent—I will forever be grateful for you taking a chance on me.

Darcy Lindner, funeral director, for answering all my morbid questions with professional grace, charm, directness and enough details to give me a tremendous respect for your profession.

Omaha police officer Tony Friend for an image of cockroaches that I'm not likely to forget.

Special Agents Jeffrey John, Art Westveer and Harry Kern for taking time out of your busy schedules at Quantico's FBI Academy to show me around and give me some idea of what it's like to be a "real" FBI agent and profiler. And also, thanks to Special Agent Steve Frank.

Dr Gene Egnoski, psychologist and cousin extraordinaire, for ing time to help me psychoanalyse my killers and not thinking it strange to do so. And special thanks to Mary Egnoski for listening patiently and encouraging us.

John Philpin, author and retired forensic psychologist, for generously answering without hesitation every question I've ever thrown at you.

Beth Black and your wonderful staff for your energy, your unwavering support and your friendship.

Sandy Montang and the Omaha Chapter of Sisters in Crime for your inspiration.

And once again, to all the book buyers, booksellers and book readers for making room on your lists, your shelves and in your homes for a new voice.

Special thanks to all my friends and family for their love and support, especially the following: Patti El-Kachouti, Jeanie Shoemaker Mezger and John Mezger, LaDonna Tworek, Kenny and Connie Kava, Nicole Friend, Annie Belatti, Ellen Jacobs, Natalie Cummings and Lilyan Wilder for sticking by me during the dark days of this past year as well as celebrating the bright ones.

Marlene Haney for helping me keep things in perspective and then, of course, helping me "deal with it."

Sandy Rockwood for insisting you can't wait for the finished product, which in itself is always a much-appreciated pat on the back.

Mary Means for taking such loving care of my kids while I'm on the road. I couldn't do what I do without the peace of mind you provide.

Rich Kava, retired firefighter and paramedic as well as cousin and friend, for listening, encouraging, sharing your stories and always making me laugh.

Sharon Car, fellow writer and friend, for letting me vent despite my good fortune.

Richard Evnen for witty repartee, kind and genuine words of encouragement and a friendship that includes pretending I know what I'm doing, even though we both know otherwise.

Father Dave Korth for making me realise what a rare gift it is to be a "co-creator."

Patricia Kava, my mother, whose undeniable strength is a true inspiration.

Edward Kava, my father, who passed away 17th October, 2001, and who was surely a co-creator in his own right.

And last but certainly never least, a "from the heart" thank-you to Debbie Carlin. Your spirit and energy, your generosity, your friendship and love have made an amazing difference in my life. I will always feel blessed that our paths have crossed.

## ACKNOWLEDGEMENTS FOR *AT THE STROKE OF MADNESS*

My sincerest appreciation goes to all the professionals whose expertise has, once again, proven invaluable. And to my family and friends who put up with my long absences while I'm in writing marathon mode. Special thanks to:

Patricia Sierra for the occasional swift kick in the pants, the numerous pats on the back and always, always being there.

Leigh Ann Retelsdorf, Deputy County Attorney, who over lunch one afternoon helped me create an intriguing MO for a killer.

Laura Van Wormer, fellow author and friend, for taking time out of your crazy schedule to show me around Connecticut and for sharing your enthusiasm for your adopted home town of Meriden.

Leonardo Suzio of York Hill Trap Rock Quarry Company for an interesting tour despite it being in the middle of a blizzard.

Lori O'Brien for being my go-to person whenever I had a question about the area.

Dianne Moggy and the rest of the team at MIRA® Books, including Tania Charzewski, Craig Swinwood, Krystyna de Duleba, Stacy Widdrington, Kate Monk, Maureen Stead and Alex Osuszek.

Megan Underwood and the crew at Goldberg McDuffie Communications, Inc.

Mary Means for a friendship that includes loving and caring for my kids while I'm on the road.

Tammy Hall for filling in the gaps and always being available at a moment's notice.

Sharon Car, fellow writer and friend, for once again helping me weather the good and the bad.

Marlene Haney, Sandy Rockwood and Patti El-Kachouti for unconditional friendship that withstands absences, that knows no guilt and that celebrates strengths while allowing and unmasking vulnerabilities.

Kenny and Connie Kava for listening and encouraging.

And to the rest of my family and friends whose continued support is greatly appreciated: Jeanie Shoemaker Mezger and John Mezger, Patricia Kava, Nicole and Tony Friend, LaDonna Tworek, Mac Payne, Gene and Mary Egnoski, Rich Kava, Annie Belatti, Natalie and Rich Cummings, Jo Ellen Shoemaker, and Lyn and David Belitz.

Also a sincere and humble thank-you to:

The many book buyers, booksellers and librarians for recommending my books.

The readers, who are truly the ones responsible for keeping Maggie O'Dell alive.

The residents of Meriden and Wallingford, Connecticut, for welcoming me into your community. Please forgive me for any liberties I may have taken with the geography and for dumping dead bodies in your backyard.

Last, to Mike Vallier. MIRA® Books lost one of its brightest stars on 26th October, 2002. I always thought it was appropriate that Mike was the very first person I met from MIRA, because he genuinely exemplified its generosity, enthusiasm and dedication. We're going to miss you, Mike, but your spirit will always be a part of this team.